The men in Clare Barrow's life....

LAWRENCE SAYLES. A powerful and revered New England blueblood thirty-five years Clare's senior, he is her mentor, her friend, her lover, and eventually her husband. He tries to heal her with his love, but can she ever be truly his?

TARIK. The American-educated son of a Middle Eastern revolutionary hero, he is groomed by the United States to rule his Arab country. A prince among men, he vows to yank his backward kingdom into the modern world by sheer will—and the knowledge that he and Clare are two of a kind.

ARTHUR OLSON. A State Department careerist, he orchestrates the coup that was planned from the moment two-year-old Tarik arrived in the United States. His life's goal: make the obscure but strategically placed Middle Eastern kingdom Washington's most reliable ally in the Persian Gulf.

WALTER WHITE-LYONS. The former top level British officer is now the kingdom's chief administrator; it is he, not the U.S. government, who brings Tarik to his destiny. The only thing that stands in the way is Clare. And the shattering secret he has spent thirty years hiding.

KINGDOMS

Mary Jane Salk

BALLANTINE BOOKS • NEW YORK

Copyright © 1993 by Mary Jane Salk

All rights reserved under International and Pan-American Copyright Conventions. Published in the United States of America by Ballantine Books, a division of Random House, Inc., New York, and simultaneously in Canada by Random House of Canada Limited, Toronto.

Library of Congress Catalog Card Number: 91-92157

ISBN 0-345-38873-9

Manufactured in the United States of America

First Hardcover Edition: April 1993
First Mass Market Edition: June 1994

10 9 8 7 6 5 4 3 2 1

To Evelyn Brodkin

For their guidance and support, I would like especially to thank Jane Rotrosen, Meg Ruley, Patricia J. MacDonald Bourgeau, John Robinson, and my husband, Lee Salk.

Prologue

Waking, Clare still had the taste of his blood in her mouth.

She would have given anything for a cold, clear drink of water, but water was rare as rain clouds in this part of the world. She had dreamed of meadow grass, velvet green, with buttery light shining through it, and now the dream hung pleasantly in fragments in her memory. She didn't have a watch and supposed it was much earlier, but the heat lay on her body like a panting weight and told her they had slept through the dawn. She heard mechanical sounds, Land-Rovers and command cars and what had to be soldiers pulling back to Brater.

Watching that she didn't wake him, she kicked away the winding sheet that covered them and pulled on her yellow dress, torn and streaked with dirt and blood after her five days in captivity. She wiped her hand over her sunburned face. Her bottom lip was split, and she winced when she touched it and wondered if she would have a scar. Scars were battle ribbons, medals for brave acts, and she had many. She had not been particularly brave this time, but a scar would memorialize Duru and offer empirical evidence these events actually had happened. Otherwise she worried she might be hallucinating.

She smoothed her hair, reaching for a modest restoration of her looks, then thought better of it. There was no need for her to try to be attractive; they would have to take her as she was. She padded barefoot across the dirt floor, opened the door, and stepped into the molten sunlight.

Duru had the look of a siege camp turned toppled house of cards. The place Clare had slept in was sandbagged up to its roof and men in combat fatigues, grenades laced around their waists,

1

kept guard by the windows and door. Hundreds of townspeople
and soldiers rushed back and forth, sending up clouds of rufous
dust in their panicked hurry to get out. The Marib, who had come
with Hadi to claim Azarak's body, held tight to their Enfield rifles
as they threaded their way through the crowds, making for their
encampment outside the town wall. Aloof and dangerous, their
faces fiercely shrewd, the Marib quieted the throng like a sword
thrown down in its midst. Even the soldiers stiffened and held
their breath until they passed, checked nervously to be sure they
were gone, then relaxed and resumed their boisterous evacuation.
At the east end of the narrow, unpaved track that passed for the
main street, upward of ten trucks were lined up and soldiers clam-
bered aboard them. Deep-throated officers shouted out orders, and
one stood in the road, trying to direct traffic.

A throng of women had gathered around the trucks, begging
with strained faces for rides. They lugged packages and sacks and
a bizarre array of household goods—an old treadle-operated
Singer sewing machine that must have weighed a ton, boxes of
Rinso-Blue, bundles of cheap household goods. A bag of flour
had broken and was blizzarding around their feet. Gently, the officers pushed them back.

Clare shaded her eyes with her hand and watched the scene.
Her heart cramped for the ferociousness with which the women
clutched their pathetic treasures. When one of them obdurately sat
down in front of the truck wheels, a soldier prodded her out with
the butt end of his rifle. Clare was about to protest but held her
tongue. The heat was beginning to make her head pound—that
and the supreme regret she was feeling for being the cause of it
all. A sergeant jogged across the road, briefly caught her eye, then
looked the other way. She shrank back into the doorway and was
about to shut the door behind her when she felt the hating eyes of
White-Lyons pulling her around.

He sat upright in his Land-Rover as if bolted into the seat,
khaki uniform prim as a wimple, gray mustaches raked to the
right and to the left, dry as gin while marinating under the white
sun. His face was set so stonily against her and he was giving her
such a long, measuring stare that Clare reflexively crossed her
arms over her chest and spread her legs for balance. She thought
she could hear his brain whirring, like a squirrel running in a
cage.

They stood there in charged silence until a truck horn sounded
abruptly and reality was restored. White-Lyons touched his hand
to his military cap in a weak salute and Clare mistook this empty,

automatic gesture for some sort of tribute and made a step toward him. But the minute she did, he turned away his eyes, tapped the steering wheel with one bony finger in a signal that carried as much disdain as instruction, Nal shifted gears, and they drove off, taking her hope with him.

Once inside with the door closed, she took several deep breaths. She turned and looked at Tarik, his black hair spilled across the white sheet like ink on snow. His heartbeat pulsed out to hers in the suddenly silent room. The night before he had brought her into the little basalt stone house and laid her down on the dirt floor. She had run her tongue down his chest until it found the knife cut Azarak had made. She had thought it might be possible to heal him, kiss away the blood, then press her finger to the wound and the flesh would mend without a mark. She moved her mouth between his legs. She would heal the other wound this way. He had sighed and turned her over on her knees and made love to her, the wind in her face hot as a furnace and the taste of his blood in her mouth.

After they had rested for a while, he put her on her back. She noticed again the obvious things: the broadness of his shoulders, the texture of his hair, the pleasurable grate of his beard stubble on her face. He pulled his mouth down to the little hollow at her throat and then dragged it down to her nipple. He grasped it with his lips, it slipped away, he caught it again and then began to suck hard. His hand glided back and forth between her legs in the preparatory motions, but she was already aroused from their earlier lovemaking and ready for him. After he had been inside her for a moment she broke free, turned him on his back and began to stroke his penis. She got to her knees and bent over him, taking him in her mouth. With one hand she pumped the shaft, the other had cupped his balls. After a minute of stroking, she parted his thighs farther and gently found his anus with her finger.

He fought her for a moment, but the action of her mouth on the knob of his penis and her finger working his testicles and anus, probing, pinching, was too much for him and he began to buck and thrash as she took him with her mouth.

Just before dawn she awoke to discover he was inside her again. They had moved together slowly, then fell asleep again.

Now Clare had a pleasurable ache between her legs. She closed the door and crossed the room. She lay down next to him. In a moment he would wake and they would leave with the soldiers. She tried to order her thoughts, but her mind moved slowly from fatigue. White-Lyons had always veiled his antagonism in supercilious concern close to maddening in its fakeness. Now he was nakedly hostile and his contempt flared and scorched like a gas flame, so strong it shocked Clare and left her feeling frightened and uncertain. She tucked Tarik's head into the crook of her arm and pulled herself closer to his sleeping body. Lying there in the stifling heat, breathing in the clove-laden air, she closed her eyes and on the brink of sleep her mind left her body and floated to where there was neither exhaustion nor hostility. And the higher it rose, the more she comprehended. Let them do their worst, she decided—and even though she was young she was not naive and she knew their worst could be past terrifying; Azarak had offered evidence of that. The future would spread out before them like a boundless, motionless sea, to be glided over, sails untrimmed, full speed ahead. Nothing would turn them around. Picturing it in her mind comforted and strengthened her and made the memory of White-Lyons and Azarak with his poison eyes begin to fade.

What she arranged to forget—or was too young to know—was that because they were so guileless they were a provocation to the likes of those arrayed against them. The impulse of the world was to break them down and destroy them, but she was full of plans and her expectations were limitless. She believed the world could be mastered and that living with Tarik, and staying alive in the bargain, would be just one more in her lifelong succession of goals, another car hitched to a train engined by her sheer will and youthful exuberance. She was shameless in her faith in love.

She turned and studied his profile. He was her husband, and her loyalty was all to him. Everything began and ended with him. She believed they had bartered some secret compact with the world that invested them with a magical proof against disaster, and like a mirror to a vampire it was the antidote to evil. With three fingers she began stroking his back and buttocks. As soon as she touched him he was awake and his hand reached out for hers as if it couldn't stop itself. In his eyes she saw reciprocated all her own love and admiration, and with her inward ear heard his heart beating, and thinking it the bravest sound in all the world, she had just opened her mouth to tell him that they would never be parted, when she was brought up short by two sharp bursts of machine-gun fire coming from outside the house. There was a dreadful stillness and then both saw the grenade arc through the open window and skitter across the dirt floor. She gasped a deep breath but could not move because he had covered her body with his. She met his eyes squarely and in them saw the sad dissipation of all their illusions. She gave him a defiant smile, then cast her mind as high and as wide as she could. But before it could take flight, every color in the room stood out with incredible vividness, Clare was inside, outside, all around, the air caught fire and there was nothing. Only the quick decomposition of a dream.

1952

1

Just as she was reading how Anna Karenina peered over the platform of the Obiralovka station to assess the distance between the first set of train wheels and the last before consigning her ruined life to the final judgment of the rails, Clare heard a soft rustle in the thicket of holly bushes.

She jerked her head off the rolled-up coat that was her pillow. There it was again. A crackle in the thick underbrush. She popped up on her elbows, pine needles embedded in her arms, every hair on the back of her neck on alert. She squinted deep into the dark recesses of the holly bush roots at the same time her finger moved to save her place in her book. To stay a step ahead of a rattlesnake you had to turn into human radar. She made her ears pointy. She held her breath. She peered harder at the bush. Time stopped. Not a sound. Maybe that meant the snake was gone. Or maybe he'd never been there in the first place. *I'll give him ten seconds to come out.* Five. Four. But she'd already been holding her breath for so long that by the time she got to three she exhaled with a loud whoosh and her head fell back to the ground.

Rattlers were everywhere in this country, and while they preferred dark, cool places, they weren't known to be fussy. Last fall an especially bold one had squeezed through the floorboards of the living room to find them in pulled-up chairs around the radio listening to Earl Scruggs. Clare didn't know who was more surprised—her family or the snake. Its rattles had commenced singing right along with old Earl until Grandpa got his pick from the corner and cleaved its head from its body just as quickly as he had separated coal from its mountain seam for thirty years.

That was then, however. Now Clare was on the ridge all alone, with no pick, no Earl, and worst of all, no Grandpa.

Of course it wasn't smart to be stretched supine on the chill

9

ground in a part of the country crawling with every manner of varmint on two feet, four feet, or its belly, but this was the perfect pine tree, its sagging outstretched boughs a canopy that when she was younger swayed and shimmered like Scheherazade's desert tent. Now it had become that grimy station on the Nizhny railway line, the end of the line for the tormented, adulterous Karenina, with her heavy plaited hair, brilliant eyes, full red mouth half open in a final rebuke to the faithless Vronsky. Well! What was likely a twenty-foot snake with a hundred rattles compared to all that?

So after a few more minutes of hard, tense listening, Clare returned to her Russians and, slowly becoming transfixed, forgot about the rattler that was or perhaps was not in the holly thicket.

It was a long pull from her house to the hiding place on the ridge, but Clare made it every day weather allowed, breathing hard, legs crashing through tough saw-brier vines, spring slush, and flowering dogwood, walking a determined path to her familiar place of dreams, till the topmost plume of the pine tree showed above a heavy outcropping of rock. Then it was down, down past the creek trickling poisons leached from mining wastes, until she collapsed, panting, under the tree. Then for as long as the light lasted she read.

At thirteen, Clare was tall and not much more than a lanky collection of bones, with eyes close to lime green and glazed blond hair. But it was her mania for the written word, not her remarkable physicality, that set her apart from the other girls her age. Every book was a small miracle. "Oh, thank you," she whispered at Christmas or birthdays when her father pressed another one into her hands.

Then she would pump up to her secret hiding place, smooth open the crisp new pages, and be carried up over the mines that were like small black mouths in the hillside, over the smokestacks and the great parkways threading the Appalachian mountain ridges, to the musical, unpronounceable places named Bandar Abbas, Ahmadabad, and Kaunakakai on the broad shoulders of Robert Louis Stevenson or Rudyard Kipling when she was young, and these days to Tolstoy's wretched Anna, or the wrecked lives in Fitzgerald—any book she could get her hands on that her mother did not censor.

Now, all of this would have gone down all right in some other state, but the mining town of Mills Bend, Kentucky, is in the business of coal, not dreams. And certainly not hope. In fact, next to coal—or because of it—Appalachia's chief product is despair, which is why a lively, bright, dreamy girl like Clare was as singularly odd there as a glittering clear diamond wedged into a coal seam.

Clare's mother, Kath Barrow, knew this and knew the danger of it. Had she been able to articulate any emotion, perhaps she would have warned her daughter of what was ahead, of a life gouged of dreams and hopes the way the mining companies strip the hillsides.

Kath's current misery had not dispossessed her of her memories, however, and she could remember her own eager girlhood spent studying the windows of Pikeville dress shops, thinking, ah yes, one day this will be mine, and those shoes, and those darling little gloves. Or she would stand in her dirt yard, chickens pecking at her shoelaces, and search the velvet contours of the mountains for a path out and think soon, soon. But of course when you are a mountain woman it is already too late, although for a year or two after she married Hillard Barrow she thought there might still be a chance. But then he had become a work beast like his father, Kath's dreams were extinguished like the daylight in a shaft, Clare had been born, and that was that.

Kath wrung out the dishcloth into the sink, then wiped it over the drainboard, sweeping the corn-bread crumbs into her cupped hand. She tossed them into the sink at the same time Clare stumbled into the kitchen, having made it off the ridge just as darkness fell.

"Sorry, Mother. Late." Her words came in breathless bursts.

"Missed your supper," Kath said, slapping the cloth around the stove. It was the second time this week Clare had not shown up at the dinner table. Without having to be told, she picked up a towel and began drying supper dishes, hoping this small act of volunteerism would be enough to distract her mother. No such luck.

"I'm not here to waitress you, missy. This ain't a restaurant. You think Daddy breaks his back so I can toss good food in the garbage pail?"

"There was a snake."

Kath swiped at the table with the cloth. "Last time it was a skunk." Whack on the icebox with the cloth. "There weren't no snake. You were just too lazy to hustle your skinny little backside down here." Slap at the countertops. "See what your grandpa's done to you, making you think you deserve special treatment. You two making moonbeams all day."

Clare's eyes skipped around the kitchen, searching for a leftover. Nothing, and she was starving.

Kath's eyes intercepted Clare's hungry glances. "And there's nothing been saved, miss. You sit down with your daddy and your grandpa to get fed, and that's it. Five-thirty every night, if you can spare the time."

Kath was in the rhythm of her anger now, her hands washing down the kitchen and her mouth working all to the same beat.

"You ain't nothing special, Clary. Readin' those books. Thinkin' you're going somewhere. Poor like you don't go anywhere—you better face it, girl, the sooner the better. See that down there?" Clare followed Kath's finger down to the lights of the coal camp below. "That's what you ought to study 'cause that's what you'll get. Get used to it."

Clare clenched her teeth. Nothing got her hackles up faster than to hear her mother tell those grim beads of a hopeless future. The very mystery of what she would become excited her imagination so much that she could sit statue-still for hours dreaming daydreams of such intensity that her mouth went dry. She had all the earmarks of success—beauty, brains, ambition. But she had not a penny. There was no telephone in her home, no toilet, no running water. Like Kath said, she was poor, and the poor do not go to great northern universities where young men and women drive convertibles and wear different clothes every day and do not care to know a pick handle from a pump handle.

Miss Hanson, who had taught her eight grades in the one-room schoolhouse before Clare went on to the high school in the junction, saw it otherwise and filled her head with the notion that anything was possible. Miss Hanson had gone to Berea College, in West Virginia, which she declared the best college in its category in the country. She had ambitions that Clare would follow her to Berea, a college for the children of the mountains, but the possibility of even that success was too much for Kath to countenance.

Homer and Hillard were convinced, however, and already the notion that Clare would leave the holler and go up to Berea College had sunk its roots into the imagination of the men of her house. Hillard had been working an extra shift every week for more than a year to put aside money for her education. Grandpa Homer, lame as he was, had a business scheme of his own. He had carved a rocker from walnut and sold it to a collector in Wheeling. With his profits he had bought hogs. When the hogs were fat enough, he would sell them, too, and bank the money in Clare's name. Whatever the world afforded her, Homer and Hillard wanted for Clare. But the fear that they would not be able to deliver on her promise became a bitter, regretful thing. Their own dreams long since entombed in coal, they had found that the empty places of life could accommodate them very well, and they interpreted this as portending the same for Clare. Now, in late October, the air in the house was three parts despair, and Hillard and Homer drew it in with short, frightened breaths, both of them clinging to the notion that they still might somehow pull it off.

Kath continued her rant. Clare held her breath. Best to be still, best to find the eye of the hurricane in the center of her chest and wait it out. She wiped a hand over her cheek, wine-red from the cold. Her mother confused her. She was still a very pretty woman, despite a permanently sour expression and a sharp tongue, and down deep Clare sensed they shared something. But as Kath never spoke what was on her mind, Clare had no way of knowing what it was, just felt a long, thin, invisible thread pulling them together. What she would have given if just once Mother had put the kettle on the stove, pulled out a chair for her, and sat with her at the kitchen table, sipping coffee and talking things over. But it never happened. And yet . . . the slender hands that could cut biscuits lightning-fast could also reach out and give her cheek a floury pinch, or be sunk deep in viscous Niagara Starch stiffening her summer dresses past dark. Kath ran hot and cold, and Clare was never certain whether she would be bathed in warmth or frozen out. With her natural generosity, however, she gave her mother the benefit of the doubt. Clare had a forgiving nature. Besides, what Kath could not say with words she signaled in gestures. Clare began looking around the kitchen for one of them.

"I've got a good mind to keep you from going onto the ridge at all," Kath said. "It was bad enough when you was little, but now—time you acted like the woman you are. Wandering all over the countryside. Shouldn't be anywhere but home. No more. No more." And she threw the dishcloth at the faucet, tore off her apron, and ran out.

Poor Mother. Clare stepped to the sink and refolded the dishcloth into deliberate squares and replaced it on the faucet. She smoothed the apron and hung it in the broom closet, and just as she was about to resign herself to a long night of lengthening hunger, her eyes fell on a hunk of corn bread puddled in milk in a shallow dish on top of the icebox. *Aw, Mom.* Kath may not have understood herself, but Clare certainly understood her mother.

After a man has worked it long enough, coal imprints his skin. He can take a handful of Boraxo and a hunk of pumice and grate it over his body until his flesh is a million pinpricks of blood, but the coal mark is still there, embedded even deeper into his skin, as if it had the instinct to bury itself all over again. It black-flecks his body, turning him into a man-sized tattoo. It can do the same to the delicate tissues of his lungs.

Homer Barrow had all the symptoms of simple coal workers' pneumoconiosis, category two—wheezing, coughing, nasty-looking sputum. He never called it that, of course, or bothered getting a certified medical diagnosis. He would just sit in the living room, the creak and rock of his rocking chair accompanied by the wheeze and gasp of his aching lungs, his chest rising and falling in a shallow way, a cacophonous symphony, a man not much improved over a Waring blender. That is the sound Clare remembered from her childhood, that and the shudder of the coal trains rolling every day out of the narrow, gray, coal-dust-coated valleys to the world beyond the Appalachian Mountains.

Clare's grandpa Homer was the center of her life. He was a tall man and flinty as the slate he mined. He had worked every mine in Kentucky—Ferguson, Cork, Corina, Willewaite, Battle, Treen—names that when she was little sounded tinny as thumb cymbals to Clare, and as far away and romantic as Katmandu.

Although most miners considered it the worst kind of bad luck to have a woman enter the mines, Homer's ambitions for Clare had outdistanced his superstitions. He had taken her down into abandoned shafts almost since she could walk. "I've done just about everything there is to do down here, girl," he would say with satisfaction as he led her gingerly down the thirty-degree incline of a blowed-out shaft. "Got my legs smashed, my ribs stove in, my back broke. Half a ton of slate fell on me once. They folded me in two, slung me over a mule, gave him a whack, and I saw daylight in ten seconds. Split my collarbone. Darn near split my skull." And he was proud about it. Bone by bone, a litany of dumped loads, gunpowder misfires, kicking mules, and heaving earth took them down the throat of the mountain. Coal dust mingled with apprehension in Clare's mouth, and her ears pricked at every drip-drop of the earth, waiting for the mountain to fall in on her.

Homer was a wreck of a man, with string-bean legs and buttocks flat as dinner plates that scraped together underneath his denim overalls as he walked along. There was nothing tricky or devious about him. He was as no-nonsense as the pick he had swung for thirty years. Whatever he thought he kept to himself. His wife, Betsy, had packed him the same lunch every day of their marriage: a sandwich wrapped in waxed paper, cake or corn bread, fruit if she could find it, and a Thermos of coffee so thick he could practically stand a roof bolt in it. He had eaten all of it slowly, sitting apart from the other men, treating himself to a wad of Red Man tobacco when he finished. His father had been a hardscrabble farmer until the huge northern coal companies figured out how to dig coal out of Kentucky in the 1880s and the sad story of Appalachia had begun. His father and his uncles had walked away from their farms and gone to live in the coal towns, and since then every man in his family had been pulled deep deep into the bowels of the earth as if tethered to the devil.

In 1940, just a few days after they buried Betsy, he had arisen at dawn as usual, but instead of heading down the hollow to the camp to begin his shift, he had dragged his wife's rocking chair onto the porch and commenced to rock. Rocked right through the shrill blast of the whistle signaling the start of his shift, and for every shift thereafter. The mine manager had sent a man up but Homer had kept his mouth screwed shut, just went on staring down at the coal camp with flat eyes. Hillard had squalled around the porch but Homer stayed mute.

For a week he had neither eaten nor slept nor taken any water, and Kath was frantic, rubbing her red hands together and alternately threatening and pleading. Homer hadn't even coughed— and this was a man who could be bent over double gasping for air. He had not disturbed a muscle in his body as he performed his silent exorcism, purging his body of the man-trip, the pick, the shovel, the mules, the machinery, the dust that billowed around his nose and the gut-wrenching terror.

And then one day, when there had been nothing in his ears but the dull roar that comes from putting all concentration into keeping out sound, Clare's rubber teething ring landed at his feet with a thud. It took him a long moment to identify the strange object covered with teeth marks and drool, but slowly his eyes focused and he awakened as if coming out of anesthesia. He looked at Clare, teetering on fat legs recently come to walking. She returned his stare, her eyes big with shock that he had not moved to pick it up. She looked at Homer, then at the ring, then back at Homer, as if to say, *Well, what are you waiting for? I can't stand here all day. Pick it up!* And Homer laughed out loud at her arrogance and pulled her onto his knee. That was the end of the rebellion, along with his mining life. Now he earned his living carving wooden folk objects for sale in northern stores and raising and selling the hogs that would help Clare go to college.

From that day until her first day of school, they were never apart. It was from Homer that Clare got her white-blond hair and the long body without a surplus ounce of flesh, and for the first few years of her life, until she started school, all the knowledge she possessed. He never spoiled her, never after that first day let her boss him around. He never treated her like a child or beat her. If she misbehaved, he fixed her with a steady knowing look that cut deeper than a razor strop. It was hard to describe what went on between them, so much of it consisted of simply reading each other's minds. They constantly sent messages back and forth with their eyes, glances performing the service of words. She might be sitting playing with some toy, he would limp into the room, shoot her a summoning look, and wordlessly they would go off.

He let her roam anywhere she wanted, even onto the slag heaps and the hillside strip mines, crawl all over the heavy earthmovers, let her touch anything until she learned herself what could hurt her and what could not. He taught her that life was unpredictable and could be dangerous; he never tried to blunt its painful edges. He explained what to watch out for in people and what to value. He let her romp and laugh and shout. He taught her how to build a chimney, how to fry an egg in a paper bag over a campfire, how to press wrinkles out of clothes with the hot chimney of a kerosene lamp. How to hunt rattlers and how to skin a squirrel she had shot herself. When she got older, he showed her how to roll cigarettes. He gave her doughnuts. He never told her a lie, and when she became an uncannily realistic child and developed a nature of her own, he felt inspired to self-congratulation. At the end of every summer day he let her drink a whole bottle of RC Cola on the steep porch steps while he whittled kitchen spoons for Kath from pieces of discarded mine lumber, his desiccated hands, every other finger missing a tip or joint, making the chips fly. When she became drowsy, he carried her to bed in his skinny arms, wheezing and struggling from the effort.

And he did all this not so much because he loved her (which, of course, he did), or because she was beautiful or his own blood, but because she was—*hallelujah!*—a girl and would not become a work beast. He had barely given her a second glance when she was born; Betsy was well advanced in her illness at the time. But on the day of the rocking and the rebellion it was as if a flashbulb had gone off in his eyes and momentarily blinded him. And then his vision had cleared and he had gotten the picture—a girl! End of the line. This is it. Not one more mining man from the Barrow family. And it made him happier than when he had married Betsy, or Hillard was born, or the day Vance Lawler shot the mine operator dead. The end.

"I started down here as a chalk-eye for my uncle Matt in 1910," he had told her once when she was little and they were inching their way down an abandoned shaft, hunting for coal hunks for Kath's cook stove. "Dollar and a half a day and a cot to sleep on in camp. I was ten. The first time I came down here I thought I was in hell, so much clanging and banging and smoke, and I said to myself, 'Boy, you are in for it now.' "

He stooped to pick up a discarded pick handle, an everyday gesture—but it felt unfamiliar in his hands suddenly, as if it were some other man's amputated body part, and he stood there, studying it dumbly. You go along for years, he thought, feeling blank and vague, and then from out of nowhere there is such a shocking soreness of the heart that there is nothing to do but stand there and take it. His heart fluttered. Oh, he had been such a little boy when life began failing him so relentlessly, when he had had to face that he would never leave the mines. It was a self-confrontation that years later he recognized as oppression but others believed was patience and composure. What a worn-out, lousy life, most of it spent clammy with terror. For a moment he felt ill, and his body was running with sweat. Clare saw the expression of despair in his milky blue eyes and pressed her hand against his damp shirt.

"Grandpa? You okay?"

He threw away the pick handle. Chances are Hillard would get the black lung too. Or lose his mind. He seemed a little rheumy already. He would rest easier if he was really sure Clare would get out of the mountains, that everything he had said to her had had some impact. He had shaped her into an independent girl, the kind, he hoped, who would not think that marriage to a miner, four kids, and indenture to Beneficial Finance was the best life had to offer. But he couldn't force her to see his vision; she had to discover it for herself.

He resumed his speech. "Young as I was, I thought the First War would save me, but they ordered me to stay put. Well, I wound up soldiering anyway, for the companies." He spat. "Boys died down here just like at Château-Thierry, only we did our dying on the Dimity coal field. We was in a war and we didn't even know it."

He was walking uncharacteristically fast, stumbling over huge hunks of coal. The airless ambience of the shaft made Clare feel as if she were a bug in a mason jar. She had never seen her grandfather anything but utterly self-possessed, and she picked at his flannel shirt to reassure herself that this wild man was still Homer.

"I should have planted myself right in the mine mouth and refused to let your daddy go down. All he thought about was the money, like every other fool mining man. And now look at him. Half the time laid off, t'other half sick. Being a miner is hell on earth, Clary, and you got to thank God every night that you're a girl. No matter what terrible thing God sends your way, I want you to promise me"—he grabbed her by the shoulders and squeezed—"swear it!"

"I swear, Grandpa," she cried.

"Promise me you'll taste that coal dust and thank God He didn't make you a man and put you in hell in Kentucky!"

Hillard Barrow had seen the world, or the view allowed through the periscope of a Sherman M1A3 tank anyway, and had handed along his broadened horizons to Clare.

He had walked down Barrow's Hollow, over Martin's Creek, all the way to the U.S. Armed Forces Induction Center at Wheeling on February 7, 1944. He'd been exempted from the draft during the early years of the war because coal was critical to the wartime economy, but the government ultimately decided Hillard was a better man for them in Europe than Kentucky, working for the Aylesworth Coal Company.

He shipped out to basic training at Fort Knox for instruction in the methods of armored warfare and how to turn himself into an infantryman if his tank was shot out from under him, which it was.

He was assigned to George Patton's Third Army, Fourth Armored Division, as a replacement, and in December 1944, when Patton swung north to rescue the eighteen thousand men of the 101st Airborne pinned down by the Germans in Bastogne, France, fought the Battle of the Bulge. The snow, the cold, the massacre of American GIs at Malmédy—Hillard had witnessed history and memorized every foreign blade of grass, mud hole, roadside flower, sunset, wrecked village, and starving villager. Years later he cloaked the tedium of his everyday life with the memory of his days in battle, like millions of other warriors since time began. Kath had no patience for his war stories, but Homer and Clare were captives, although by now they knew the details as well as they knew the contents of the company store.

On this chill October evening Hillard fired up a hand-rolled cigarette, whistled blue tobacco smoke from between his teeth, and shook his head at the wonder of the queer folk who dwelled beyond the limits of his geography and imagination.

After Clare had settled herself beside him on the porch swing, Homer had taken his usual position on the top step, and the ceremony of the cigarette rolling having been dispensed with, Hillard began, "Jew named Franks bought that property over by Turkey Meadow."

"What's that?" Homer, who was using a buck knife to work out a pebble lodged in the sole of his boot, lifted his head.

"Jew bought land next to Lundy Mite's place," Hillard repeated. "Least they say he's a Jew. Name of Barton Franks."

"A Jew?"

"They *say*, Dad."

"What's he a-fixin' to do with it?"

"Don't know."

"Lundy had the idea of spreadin' out his own place."

"Too late now."

"Too late, yup."

" 'Course now, I had that Jew-boy sergeant down there at the Fort Knox army base," Hillard said after a long pause to smoke. Clare and Homer shifted around on their perches, fitting themselves into the routine of this familiar story as if it were a deep, eiderdown-filled cushion.

"Now, he weren't half bad—I said it before. It didn't bother me all that much, takin' orders from a Jew, but some of the other boys thought it were pretty bad. He was a skinny little thing, with black hair curly as your dolly's, Clary. From New York, where all the Jews are. One of the other soldiers, a feller from Harlan County, told this boy that he'd rather be in a tank with a nigger than a Jew. Some of the boys didn't like the sound of that, 'cause the boy was fair, in his basics. Second time he said it, one of those ol' boys pitched him out a second-story window. They was always a-fightin', those Harlan County boys. Figures, don't it, Dad?"

Homer wagged his head.

"Night like this," Hillard went on, taking the measure of the cold, damp air, the smell of a dozen wood fires, their smoke pinwheeling up the holler, "puts me in mind of the Ardennes. Only the hills weren't near as tall." He measured the mountains between his thumb and forefinger, squinting as he sightlined. "They was kinda low slung and purplish this time of night. I was sitting in the turret, trying to get some sleep. My Lord, but it was cold. Snow blowing right through the hatches into the tank. Dumbest

thing they ever did, those Germans. Throwing everything they had
into the Ardennes. We caught 'em and turned 'em around and finished 'em, right there in the snow."

These were the parts that Homer loved, Hillard imitating the
whiz of a 75 millimeter cannon shell, *kaboom!* Thirty-caliber machine guns blasting away, engines screaming.

"Flanked 'em all on the left, weren't that how it went, son?"

"That's right, Dad. You got it right. We surprised 'em. 'Course
now, they *was* out of fuel."

Homer bobbed his head at the stupidity of the German commanders. "Got what they deserved, but Lord help them, they
burned in them tanks like gas in a lamp."

Ugh. Clare pulled a face. It was the romance of the foreign
place that captured her, not all this business of dead tank drivers.
In her dreams, that cohort of Panzer soldiers skidded up to her
bedside in their charred tank suits, with claw hands, gaping
mouths, all burnt black as trees killed by lightning strikes. Every
detail of the human anatomy fried to a hideous crisp staring down
at her in her little narrow bed. She put her fingers in her ears.

Eventually, Homer and Hillard would have their fill of gore and
Hillard would devote himself to answering all her questions, about
the people of Belgium, their odd wooden shoes, the way they
walked and spoke, the way they kept their animals. About the
family who shared their thin goose with Hillard and his tank crew.
The old woman in the starched linen hat whom Hillard could
never quite describe. The hungry little children. Clare would remember it all, then later in bed, or the following afternoon under
the outstretched arms of her pine, embroider herself into her dad's
adventures.

Flattered that his girl embraced the one moment in his life
when he had felt brave, useful, set apart, Hillard never lost a
chance to fill her head with more. And she had a thousand questions.

Hillard capitalized on this by giving to her whatever he took to
be European, especially French—a bit of lace wrapped around a
card from the notions counter of the company store, a black beret
ordered from the Sears, Roebuck catalogue, little pieces of extravagance he could not always afford. Other children mocked her
pretensions but she didn't care. Her dad had made her part of his
history and it was his approbation, not theirs, that she craved.

Through the mails Hillard bought her the adventure stories by
the Dumas father and son, a dictionary of French vocabulary,
gruesome mystery tales of murders on rue Morgue or rue

Michelle Demas. One Christmas he gave her a copy of *Madame Bovary*, having no understanding of the illicit nature of the love Flaubert portrayed, and Clare sat up for two straight nights reading it by candlelight. Later she asked so many pointed questions about the male-female nature of things that Kath, suspicious, took the book to Reverend Nute, who lectured a horrified Hillard on the degeneracy of French writers, and the entire French nation, as a matter of fact.

When her classmate Vernon Tile told her about his uncle Brad Tile's service at the battle of El Alamein, she became obsessed with Morocco and harems and tried to get her father to tell her what a eunuch was, but he didn't know exactly, except that it wasn't fit for a young girl to find out.

"So this Barton Franks," Homer said as the light began to go out of the day, "he bought that Turkey Meadow land, you say?"

"That's right, Dad."

"Too bad for Lundy Mite."

"That's right, too bad for old Lundy."

When he had smoked the last of his tobacco, and Homer had gone off to tend his hogs and Clare to wander down the holler, Hillard went to his easy chair in the living room.

"Coulda used Clary to weed the garden," Kath complained, a dishrag in her fist.

Hillard kept his eyes on his newspaper. "She'll be back soon enough. Reckon she's gone to see what Toby's doin'."

"Saw Toby this morning. Those two are up to no good."

"Keep a chaste mind now, Kath."

"T'aint decent, all that time with that boy. He's as big as a man."

"Kath!"

Hillard's wife crossed the room and stared off through the screen door at her garden. "The squash is gonna be tough if it's left much longer."

"I'll help you pick." He made an attempt to fold his paper, but Kath was already down the front stairs, the door slamming shut behind her.

She fussed with the garden for a minute, then straightened and stretched her back. She had seen moonshiners hanging around the mouth of the hollow earlier in the day, a tough bunch. They might pester Clare, maybe try to touch her. She was only thirteen, but already all the boys were looking at her, and some of the men too.

Kath bent, felt around under the beet greens, and found the garden hoe. If she had to face down 'shiners troubling her girl, she'd need something to swing at them.

Through the scrim of the screen on the door Hillard watched her go, saw the business end of the hoe straight out before her like the point of a lance. She'd use it too, he knew, lay it into some critter's skull and never give it a second thought. He sighed, closed his paper, and tossed it on the table as he walked out the door. Kath turned to glare at him when she realized he was following her, but she didn't tell him to go back. He walked behind her down the holler wondering why, short of death itself, the woman most feared the revelation that she had anything of a caring heart.

2

Where the rutted trail that descended sharply from her house met the dirt lane that led eventually to the paved road to the coal camp, Clare waited for Toby Stivers to walk her to school as he had every day since they were first graders.

At seven in the morning, long fingers of mist still probed the ridges and hollows, chilling any hope Clare had to feel the sun on her face. She gathered her coat collar around her neck. It would rain some more before they got there, she decided, and while she had forgotten her umbrella, she was certain that Toby would divine this and remember his. From her first day at school, after Kath had torn her from Homer's lap and dragged her, wailing, the entire mile and a half to the one-room Double Creek schoolhouse, Toby had shown a preternatural instinct for knowing exactly what Clare needed before she knew herself. On that day of black memory she had flung herself into an empty desk chair and sobbed for ten whole minutes while Miss Hanson tried without success to calm her. With the child compassion that most human beings have bred out of them by adulthood, Toby had pulled from his lunch pail and passed to her a slice of American cheese, the sight of which in all its pumpkin-colored blandness had stunned her into silence. He had surprised her, and in doing so forged a friendship that would last long past the day when he no longer did so, when she understood that their lives would take separate paths.

Clare took a long, deep breath. A coal speculator from Georgia had burned a big section of wood near the Cowens place to clear land for his strip-mining machinery and the smoke had hung in the atmosphere for days. This breath was full of it.

"Smell that smoke! It stinks," Toby shouted as he came upon her. "I hate that smell. It's a sign of everythin' that's wrong here." He put his umbrella in his other hand and took her books from her arms. "Pretty soon this'll just be a sad old place, everything destroyed. All the big trees gone, and the crows and hawks with no place to nest. We may's well be living in the city, with no normal people round us."

"I guess," Clare said. Long ago she had stopped telling Toby it was her ambition to live in cities.

"I hate to see living things destroyed," he went on. "What will I look at when I get older? Already there's no deer till Scarbro. Daddy searched for days last week for one little ol' four-point buck."

Clare bit her tongue. Toby's father would have put his time to better use as family breadwinner, instead of hunting for the deer that every man in three counties knew had been driven out of the territory by the strip-mining operations. Robbie Stivers, like many miners, cherished his liberty, but unlike most of them he exercised his by working only when he felt inclined, never mind that his wife and kids led a corn-bread existence. Clare's father, on the other hand, had had his skull busted by a rock and his foot mashed in a slate fall, yet he worked every day he wasn't doubled over in pain. Last night, however, Robbie's wife had shamed Robbie into going down to the work muster, and now he and Hillard were breaking their backs together in Number 9, eight miles long, six hundred feet deep, on the midnight to eight A.M. shift.

When Toby and Clare were little, they dreamed of traveling the world together. They would blow here and there like the breeze, seeing for themselves the strange places captured in photographs in Clare's many books. Toby had drawn a map of the world in pencil and pinned it to the wall of the bedroom he shared with his brothers; red x's marked the spots he and Clare would see together. But when he was eleven or twelve, paddling up the Amazon or hiking Nepal began to strike him as childish, and he succumbed to the ambition that had always been more likely anyway: mining coal alongside his father, brothers, and uncles. The moment Clare realized this, she silently cut the dream-membrane that connected their hearts. In another incarnation she would have married Toby, but not now—Homer had long ago shaped her into a woman who could never love a miner. Toby had not stopped loving her, however, nor did he grasp very expertly why he could never have her. There wasn't an unprincipled bone in his body. He loved the mountains. He said that when he was in them they made him feel just like himself. He talked to animals, and when they saw that his heart was clear, they sometimes talked back. Tall, dark-haired, and handsome, a catch in their tiny community, Toby followed Clare around with big eyes. She had long since stopped him from kissing or touching her, thereby quashing the plan suggested to Toby by his father, of getting her pregnant and forcing a marriage, even though she wasn't much past babyhood herself. Which was just as well, because Toby had no wish to have Clare on anything other than equal terms. He sought instead to win her with romantic skills as artless as his home-made clothes: an unpretending tongue, genuineness of character, and an accurate if bittersweet view of himself in the world. Toby exuded the dignity that comes when a human being chooses his own fate and accepts the implications of that choice. He understood just how he fit into the scheme of things and had decided that it was not half bad.

"Times aren't like they was." He gave a weary sigh.

"You sound like an old man."

"I am old."

"You are not!"

"I'm two years older than you. Anyway, my soul is old." He put his hand over his heart and rolled his eyes up.

Clare giggled and gave him a playful shove. He was pleased to make her laugh. It made him feel he was making progress. He no longer enjoyed it when she talked about seeing the places where her father had been at war. So he resorted instead to his not-so-subtle campaign to convince her that outside the security of the hollow, the world waited with sharpened teeth.

"Anyway, some businessman comes up here from Atlanta, in a pair of alligator shoes, I'll bet, takes the coal out, scatters all the birds and critters, puts back nothin', then turns his back on us and goes back to the city—and calls it hard work.

"See, Clary, the thing about this place is the community feeling," he went on. "Everybody pullin' in the same direction, believing in the same things, countin' on each other. In the cities, the people are pulled all apart: keepin' all day in offices, worryin' about this piece a paper or that. And then they get outside, ha! They's like chickens in the chicken coop, just waitin' for the fox to come up and bite their heads off. Crime, murder, stealing, and what-not! Coal mining may be a fearsome business, but nobody sticks a gun in your face. Something to be said for that. Damn that smoke." He rubbed the back of his hand across his eyes, then stopped abruptly and sucked in his breath, once, twice.

"Do you hear that, Clary?"

Clare halted. "Hear what? I don't hear anythin'."

Toby cocked his ear in the direction of town. After a moment of listening, he looked Clare hard in the eyes, hoping to find reassurance there, but saw instead that she too heard the siren.

Without a word they broke into a trot, then a wild run, their books dropping one by one out of their hands into the mud. Panting for breath, they reached the outcropping of ridge where the lane meets the paved road. Below them, a wisp of black soot rolled up in a thin column from the portal of Number 9, a telltale mark that Clare and Toby understood exactly.

They charged through the underbrush down the hillside, heads back, running for all they were worth, across Main Street to the coal company lamp house, where frantic men and women were pounding on the locked door. Inside, a boss was running his finger down the list of names on the work roster, shouting out telephone numbers to another man, who was dialing other coal operations around the county. Another dozen or so people surrounded the eight miners who had been hoisted out of the mine, badgering the exhausted men for news of their loved ones. More people were racing up, banging on the door, demanding news. Miners who had been getting ready for the next shift called out to each other for lifesaving equipment. The mine boss came out of the lamp house to calm the crowd and to say that A. W. Aylesworth, Jr., who owned the mine, was on his way over from his operation near Pats Creek.

Clare was torn between dashing back to her house to tell Kath and Homer that Hillard was still in the mine and staying put and seeing what would surely be the sight of her dad, and Toby's, being hoisted to the surface like the eight saved miners. She was making up her mind when she caught sight of Kath, still in her apron, running up Main Street. Behind her Homer hobbled along, his hat forgotten for once. Even from hundreds of yards away Clare could see he had the look of a man whose mind had slipped out of focus. He looked pathetic, with his composure gone, and Clare, for whom he was the centerboard of life, received the sight as a stunning blow. She shrank closer to Toby and took his trembling hand in hers. It was good to have her best friend with her, even if his face was set and his jaw clenched so hard she could not imagine what he was thinking. She would have welcomed words, but he refused to speak.

Quickly they knew the whole story: that one of the timbers that held up the mine roof had collapsed and that Hillard and Robbie Stivers and two other miners had been trapped by tons of rock. That the other men believed they had heard them crying for help on the other side of the fall but could not be sure. Parties of miners were already on their way down to try to dig them out.

It was while the men were strapping on their safety equipment that Aylesworth and two of his men pulled up in his four-door two-tone Lincoln automobile and a horrible silent rage overtook the crowd.

They watched as the car door opened and the man who held in his hand the fate of the trapped men—in fact, the fate of every miner and his family in Mills Bend—pointed first one, then the other of his Thom McAn black loafers over a puddle of rainwater and stepped out among them.

His proper name was Arthur Wales Aylesworth, Jr., but behind his back the whole town called him Muddy. When he was ten years old he had stolen a bunch of green bananas left to ripen on Violetta Piccione's porch rail and eaten all of them on his way to the Double Creek school. Around the time that Miss Hanson commenced the geography lesson, Arthur's bowels churned to an uproar. With no time to race to the toilet outside, he had dirtied his pants. How he carried on about the "mud" that had appeared mysteriously on his chair seat! "Where'd this mud come from?" On and on, looking around melodramatically for a leak in the roof or a hole in the floor. But none of his classmates was deceived, and even though his dad owned the mines where their fathers worked, they hooted him out of school and chased him home. After that he was always Muddy Aylesworth to the whole town. But not to his face, never to his face.

When his father, A. W. Aylesworth, Sr., died from a heart attack while trying to land a forty-pound kingfish in the Tasman Sea, Muddy inherited the family shop—nine drift mines and the souls of every miner within. He cheated them out of their wages, put their lives at risk with inferior timbers and bolts, ransomed their families to the company store, and tossed them out of their company homes when he felt the whim. But he'd dirtied his pants in front of them, and whenever they dared, they never let him forget it.

Now he herded the families of the four cut-off miners into the cinderblock company store, across a potholed road from the coal cleaning and loading plant at the east end of the mine, miles from the spot where the timber gave way. He claimed it was for the safety of the families, but one of the men had shouted that it was to keep away prying eyes.

The families kept vigil in tight, stoic circles, their initial hysteria supplanted by grim forbearance of tragedy. Miners and their loved ones are companioned all their lives with the prospect of death and disaster. What was the horror in Number 9 but the drama they had been playing out in their minds forever at last set onstage for real? Although they wept, most of them seemed resigned to the inevitable. Kath, who had been wild-eyed at first, had now fixed her face in such a posture of resignation that Clare could not bear to be anywhere near her. The girl who believed in the miracle of her own future refused to accept the inevitable. Clare owed it to her father to maintain hope, to picture in her mind's eye him striding toward her, his coal-blackened face breaking into a broad white smile the moment he saw her—if she let go of hope, then somewhere in the subterranean misery of Number 9, Hillard would let go of life.

After a few more minutes of vigilant watching, however, Clare decided she'd better remind the mine boss how they'd dug a borehole at the Red Hat mine two years ago and Richie Tyler's uncle, Tole Tyler, had been saved. She got up to look for Toby.

It was raining again when Norton Tile barred them from entering the lamp house, where the rescue plans were under discussion. She made such a nuisance of herself that he finally got tired of seeming nice and demanded that she leave and take Toby with her.

For a while they hung around the area of the mine's aboveground facility, a complex of towering coal graders and cleaning buildings, then went back to the company store. They'd just arrived when one of Muddy's lackeys came in and announced that everybody knew mining was a risky business, and that as long as there were men trying to get coal out of the earth, there were going to be disasters. Homer spat when he heard that one.

At midnight Clare and Toby crept off to hide in the underbrush while the rescue teams tore boreholes eight hundred feet down to see if they could make contact with the trapped men. Teeth chattering in the cold, they somehow fell into a fitful sleep in each other's arms until they woke close to dawn. For a moment, stiff-legged from sleeping outdoors, Clare could not remember where she was, until the sound of the drilling equipment shocked her into wakefulness. Then she remembered everything. Was it only yesterday that she felt safe and secure? Every well-remembered tree and creek and rock, every home and shed and gaunt coal grader had taken on unearthly tones and told her life would never be the same again. She felt strange and out of place in her own familiar country.

She walked alone back to the company store. The families had taken coats off a clothing rack and made rough beds from them, but Homer and Kath were sitting up straight on their metal folding chairs, saying little, picking at their food. Clare had never been afraid in her life, but at that moment a fear of the unknown had seized her. Questions dammed up at her lips, but she wisely chose not to pose them. Instead, she caught Homer's eye, and emptied her eyes into his. Reading her thoughts, in a sure-handed motion he wrapped his arm around her shoulder and tugged her against him, and through that simple gesture said to her, *We can imagine peace again, can't we?* But Clare could not be sure. Now there was an inconsistency in her self-belief, the first of her lifetime, and while Homer's rearing had prepared her for it, it had in no way steadied her for the dawn of grief that was breaking over her heart. She felt spent, in shock, as he rocked her in his arms, her face buried in his damp wool jacket until she finally drifted off.

She awakened when Doc Noor came through the door in a blast of frigid rain, the dim light behind him throwing the thin displays of cheap clothing and housewares into sad relief. Noor, a Palestinian, doctored four counties of miners and their families from the backseat of his Hudson Hornet, the only physician the counties could find who would practice medicine for eighteen hundred dollars a year.

Noor circled the store, shaking everyone's hand and lingering over the women and children. "Have faith," he kept saying in heavily accented English. "God is good."

He handed out white tablets ("for the nerves"). Rebecca Stivers took one with a glass of water, but Kath told him she didn't want anything to dull the truth of these events and Homer shook him off with a grunt.

"Clare, you get some sleep?" he asked.

"Uh-huh."

"You don't need a pill?"

"No."

"You're too young anyway." He sat down alongside her in a metal chair, which she wished he hadn't; she was in no mood for conversation. He told her that he'd telephoned a colleague, a Hindu doctor who worked over near Pikeville. Few American physicians cared to work for a pittance in the mountain communities, and so Appalachia was full of doctors recruited from Pakistan and Palestine and India and other underdeveloped nations, who were willing to take low pay in exchange for a chance to immigrate to America.

Dr. Noor's Hindu friend had told him a fantastic story of a rescue in Mingo County, West Virginia, just last month. Three men buried behind a slate fall and all of them saved.

Clare made him promise to go up and tell the mine operator in the lamp house, and after tending to Toby's mother, who was hysterical, he went out to find Norton Tile.

At eleven that evening Muddy came into the store, and loading his voice with emotion he did not feel, declared that efforts to free the miners had come to nothing. That the boreholes had yielded nothing. That the fans set over the holes to blow air down to the men had burned out and no more could be found. That they could never move the rock without blasting. That he planned to commence this blasting around one in the morning. He did not have to explain that blowing the rock signaled the loss of all hope for the trapped men.

His words touched off wild screams and hysteria among the four families. They overturned the metal chairs they had been sitting on as they fell about weeping into each other's arms. The world became a hell of grief and rage so overpowering that it swept away all their trademark stoicism. "No, no!" they cried out. "Keep digging!" Muddy, seeing they were out of control, tried to quiet them, and failing, began to edge off toward the door.

"Muddy, you know those timbers weren't solid. You put 'em twelve feet apart and they should have been eight, at least," Millard Jenkins shouted out. "And they weren't good timber. They was poor quality, all the timbers was poor quality, and there's not even enough of that!"

Muddy had frail white hands unspotted by coal grime, and when he held them up to try to halt the knot of enraged miners and families, they appeared to tremble. "Millard Jenkins, you know as well as I that I wouldn't do a thing to endanger you men. If the timbers was set too far, why didn't you tell me? Huh? If the lumber was poor quality, how come you didn't march right up to my front porch and tell me right then? I would have fixed everything. You should have told me. I got nine drift mines to take care of. I don't know every single detail. If you had called my attention to any unsafe thing, I would have changed it like that!"

He patted his bird-fingers around his reddish hair, the steady disappearance of which he attempted to conceal with an elaborate comb-over. He was becoming more haughty by the minute, pretending to be indignant that anyone would think him guilty of setting bad timbers. But the whole town had heard these excuses before. They pushed in on him, sending their furious eyes right into his heart and scaring him a little. He backed out the door, shouting for his car.

But the car was now nowhere in sight. The rain was falling heavily again and he began to pace back and forth anxiously, all of the families out of the store and hot on his heels, pressing up against him in the soggy coal yard, demanding answers to their questions. He had neither the physical strength nor the moral authority to save himself. He was in deep trouble without the faintest idea of what he was supposed to do next. It was bad, very bad. And he was a little hurt and surprised at how much they hated him. Well (he squared his fleshless shoulders), he hated them right back! Disdained them, pitied their pathetic hillbilly dinner buckets and outdoor shitters and falling-down houses in the hollow. Most of all their puny dreams—for land they might own outright, a car they could meet the payments on, a trip to Daytona at the height of winter. He was the boss, the liege lord, and he had big liege-lord dreams. He wasn't going to live out his life down here in Kentucky with a bunch of jerk miners and their bony wives. Sure, he had a bony wife of his own, but he wouldn't keep her forever. He was going to make something of himself. He was going to use these grime-blackened hard-hearted miners to launch himself into the future. He wasn't going to waste his hard-won dough on quality lumber to shore up mine roofs that might come down anyway. Goddamn Hillard Barrow probably knocked a roof bolt out. These guys did it all the time, just to make their point. Well, they weren't going to stop him now. He wasn't one of them. He was going to get out. Go north where nobody called him Muddy (goddammit, there had been a roof leak!). Live in a big white house, a big blonde in his bed. Roll in dough with the blonde.

His imagination had become so pleasantly overheated that he was almost sorry to see through rain-streaked eyeglasses his Lincoln sedan looming up Main Street. He had nearly launched himself into its backseat when thin-nosed Homer Barrow threw himself in his path.

"Why ain't there more crews diggin'?" Homer demanded. "Why're you givin' up on those men who served you so well, and for no money? Is it drills you need? We can get some. There are hundreds of drills in this state. It seems to me there ought to be a drill crew working over every spot where you think the men might be. I know this mine like the back of my hand. I can show you right now where to drill. They's places down there a man can hole up for days. It can't cost that much money. What's the price of a life?" He had not spent a whole year frantic over Hillard in a tank, besieged by Nazis, to surrender him to a ton of bituminous coal. By God, if the army could send him home in one piece from the hell of war, Muddy Aylesworth ought to be able to deliver him from a Kentucky deep mine. He could not imagine how he could go on without his boy. He could not imagine what life would be worth without the one he loved best, and so he took another step closer to Muddy and again demanded, "What's the price of a life?"

Muddy cast a loving glance into the dry shelter of the backseat—so near and yet so far—angry suddenly that old man Barrow stood between him and its enveloping security. He stuck a finger in Homer's chest. "Money isn't the issue, Homer," he said. "You Barrows, always causing trouble. How do I know Hillard didn't knock out a roof bolt just to make his point? Yeah, maybe he knocked out a roof bolt just to try and make me look bad. He was always thinkin' he was some damned hero. He shoulda stayed in the army. Shoulda stayed where he was good for somethin'."

Through sheer equability of presentation, Homer had thought he might convince Muddy that only a little elbow grease stood between the men and their salvation. With his inward eye he saw hundreds of miners from all over the region streaming into town to put their muscles to the rescue. And they would come! Would walk through this god-awful weather to save their brothers! The only thing he had needed to do was to make Muddy get the picture. Muddy was one of them, a man of the hills, no matter how big the cars he steered or strange his footwear.

But after two days of deathwatch, Homer had only the weakest grip on his emotions, and so when Muddy, with unguessed-of depths of vindictiveness beneath his owlish facade, began poking him in the chest with his finger, Homer lost it.

"If it's not money, then what is it? Tell me, please," he shouted. The rain poured down on his face and pounded on the corrugated metal buildings in the yard. Pain and fear distorted his features, and Clare, who had pushed through the crowd to stand next to him, made pressure with her hand on the small of his back to support his shivering body. Her own heart was thumping so hard she thought it might burst her chest. Toby stood behind her with a hand on her shoulder, prescient of coming trouble.

"There's a limit to what I can do," Muddy said, screaming to be heard. Rainwater filled his mouth when he spoke and he despised Homer for making him spit it out again as his words flowed. Nothing disturbed him more than to appear unseemly or in any way discomposed. "This mine is eight miles long. I can't cover every piece of ground. I'm doing everything I can. I don't know what else to tell you." He put his shoulder against Homer's to try to drive him out of his way.

"You think I'm stupid?" Homer kept up. "Some stupid old hillbilly you can fool? Answer my question! Why can't we put a drill everywhere there might be men? I can show you how. We'll go all around this state and get the drills. We can leave now. Sink a borehole here, and here"—Homer's arm beat the air and accidentally grazed Muddy's cheek. The younger man grabbed him by the lapels and began to shake. As weak a creature as Muddy was, Homer was weaker, and his knees collapsed at the thumping.

At that Clare, her hair and clothes drenched, lost reason herself. Tall and strong on any day, rage and hatred now surged through her arms and legs and she broke free of Toby and leapt at Muddy, slapping his face and shoving him off Homer. "You get your hands off him, you hear? Don't you dare touch him, you"—her mind jumped around, trying to think of names to call him—"you son of a bitch!" She had cursed for the first time in her life, and Homer registered his shock with an open mouth and a surprised expression.

Muddy used the opportunity to dive into the backseat of his car and slam the door shut.

"You're gonna leave 'em in the dirt, ain't you?" Homer shouted at him through the glass of the window. "When nobody's lookin', you're gonna do it. You don't give a damn about the men." Muddy pounded on his driver's shoulder to get going. "I'm beggin' you . . . Arthur. I knew your dad." Homer slammed his open palms on the window glass. The tires spun in the mud and the car fishtailed wildly. The people in the crowd screamed and jumped back, but Homer stood his ground. Although he could not see Muddy behind the car's tinted windows, he went on yelling at the glass, mud now covering most of his face and the rain muffling his words so that all Muddy could see was this great choking mouth and huge ghostly, glaring eyes. He wished he had a knife so he might spring out the door and drive its blade up against the bone of Homer's throat, twist it until the tip went in all the way just to shut him up. "Even if one man gets out alive it will be worth it," Homer yelled. He grabbed at the door handle. Muddy threw himself across the seat and jammed the lock down. "That's my boy down there in that mine. Don't you have a boy of your own?" The car steadied itself. The driver gunned the engine, and another wave of mud splattered Homer and Clare. "That's my only child! Don't you understand?" Homer shrieked. But already the car had driven off into the dark of the night.

Two days later, when the bodies of the miners were recovered and placed in the arms of their families at the mine mouth, Homer had already decided what he was going to do.

"I'm going to bury him in the Arlington National Cemetery in Washington, D.C.," he said in a voice that brooked no opposition.

Reverend Nute had come up to tell Homer and Kath the ideas he had for the service, which was to be for the four miners together, and how he had better get on over to the cemetery as he had heard that the backhoe that would dig the graves had a broken starter motor and he himself might have to drive to Pikeville for the part.

"Arlington Cemetery?" Reverend Nute sat down slowly in the only armchair in the living room. Homer watched as he fitted himself into what had always been Hillard's chair, allowing his brain time to register the shock of the sight, and resumed staring blankly out the window.

"Homer, you don't want your boy here in the hills with you?"

"Nope."

Kath, who was feeding pine kindling into the wood stove, sighed loudly. "T'ain't no use in talkin' to him. He's a stubborn old mule and he's made up his mind. He's takin' Hillard to that cemetery and that's that."

"Served his country in war, he has a right to be buried in the national cemetery," Homer said, vexed that anyone would be less than one hundred percent behind his plan. "It's the only fit place for a soldier to be buried. He served his country, and now his country's going to do right by him." He folded his arms over his chest.

"But, Homer, how you gonna do it? How you gonna get Hil"— Reverend Nute hesitated and lowered his voice—"his *remains* all the way up to Virginia?"

"Clary's working on it."

Clare, who had been listening from her bedroom, stepped into the room. "I called the interment office at Arlington and they told me how to do it. An undertaker in Pikeville will drive Daddy to Virginia, and then the army meets him with horses and a caisson and then we all walk behind the caisson and then they bury him. With a bugler. We can ride up to Washington in the hearse with the undertaker and they've given us the name of a cheap hotel."

"Maybe the YMCA would be better," Homer offered in a businesslike fashion and Clare nodded in agreement. Seeing how in league they were in the business of burying her husband, Kath closed the door on the wood stove, stood, and walked into the kitchen.

Now a man without a mission, the Reverend Nute sat quietly for a moment in Hillard's chair. He had planned the funeral in detail in his mind and this change from four coffins to three meant he would have to start all over again. Just like Homer Barrow to go against the flow.

Ah, well. He clamped his hand on Homer's shoulder and said, "Well, I do believe you're a-doin' the right thing, Homer. Your boy belongs up there with the other heroes. Served his country all the way, and now his country's getting him back. Right there with generals. It's the right thing, Homer. It's right."

In the dull twilight Clare marched up the steep trail to her ramshackle house. She reached the front door, walked through the darkened parlor and into her bedroom in the back. Out of the corner of her eye she had seen her mother sitting alone at the kitchen table, but she did not cross the room to keep her company. With only hours to go before they were to leave for Washington, Kath, Homer, and Clare had staked out their own solitary corners of the house and settled into them.

Clare stepped up to her mirror and studied her reflection. She tilted her head so that the thin sunlight fell on her face. Toby was right; she did look different. The soft edge of girlhood was gone out of her features. She stepped away from the mirror and sat on the bed. Not now, but soon, she would think to examine everything that she felt about her father's death. At some later date, when the consuming soreness of her heart abated and let her see clearly the core of things. It was enough now to just take things as they were, she said to herself, and the minute she had resolved to do that, she began to cry in that silent way of hers, tears running down her cheeks, silent shock.

She was not aware that her mother was standing in the doorway, nor did she hear her footsteps as she crossed the floor. She knew only that there was a breast to lay her head upon, a small waist to curl her arms around. It was long minutes before she realized that her mother's arms jutted out stiffly from the elbows and that her hands made awkward fluttering motions to stroke and hold her but could not settle into the rhythm of comfort-giving. The breast that had at first seemed a pillow now felt stony. It seemed to thrust her away, the signal that intolerable uneasiness with such intimacy had arrived, the usual business with her mother. Clare was embarrassed for both of them and sat up.

"Your daddy loved you very much, Clare," Kath began.

"I know he did, Mama."

"He was probably a better dad to you than I ever was a mother." Kath pulled the sleeves of her sweater down over her wrists in a matter-of-fact way when she said it.

"That's not true!"

"You don't have to spare my feelings, girl." She pushed Clare's hand away. "I told Hillard 'fore I married him I wouldn't be any good at this baby thing. That's why we only ever had one a-you.

"You're not much like Hillard." Kath took Clare's chin in her hand and turned her face to see all its angles. "His life wasn't worth a whole lot to him. He wouldn't let his dad make him into somethin' else, but that man, he was the tough kind that wouldn't quit. Once he put his eye on you he wasn't 'bout to let go. You are his life's work. And you don't quit neither, do you? You an' Homer, you're like twins. One always knowin' what t'other one is thinkin'—making moonbeams all day."

Kath sighed and dropped her shoulders. What was the use? Clare had never been hers, had never belonged to her or anything that she could understand. The more her daughter pined to leave the holler, the more Kath perceived it as a rebuke to herself, a further insult to an already overpunished life.

"There's only room for two, Clary."

"Huh?"

."In the undertaker's hearse, there's only room for two people, plus the driver, to ride to Washington."

"I'll stay home, Mama. I'll be all right. It's your place to go and take the flag for Daddy."

"No, Clary. You and the old man should go on up, not me. You're the ones belong with him there. You'll be better at it'n me. I couldn't stand anybody seein' me that way, especially not the old man. You take the flag, Clary. It's more rightly yours than mine anyway."

"Mama! That's not true."

Kath stuck out her lip, seeming to ponder information that made no impression on her one way or another.

"Well, anyway, maybe you were easier to take, softer. I was always gittin' on Hillard's nerves."

When Clare began to cry again, Kath released an exasperated sigh.

"You stop that cryin', Clary. Stop it right now." She shook her daughter's shoulders. "Don't you dare cry. You dishonor your father with those tears. Your eyes have got to be clear from here on in. You have to see the way for yourself from now on. You won't have your dad to look out for you. You gonna have to start takin' care of yourself. I don't know what's gonna happen next. I 'spect Muddy's gonna be dragging his sorry self up here to toss us out of this house as soon as your dad's buried. So you gotta stop that weepin'."

She gave Clare's shoulders one last emphatic shake.

"Yes, Mother."

"Good." Kath stood up, pleased. "Daughter oughtta listen to her mother. Once in a while. Hope you have a daughter hears you better than you ever heard me." She had said it in an angry tone, but when Clare looked up, her expression was mild, almost warm. "Don't know what I'm goin' do with you. And you watch yourself up north there." She turned and walked across the parlor to the kitchen, shutting Clare's bedroom door as she left.

Clare sat on the bed and stared at the closed door. Did her mother love her? Not by any normal definition—not by the one with which Toby could measure his mother's love, which flowed warm and soothing as honey to her children, and other people's children. Yet having Kath for a mother had given Clare the skill of discerning the thin, faint emotional faults that cut through the nature of certain people, those who otherwise seem aloof and cold. It was a hard gift now, but it would stand her in good stead later in her life.

Clare looked around at the familiar objects in her bedroom. The books her father had bought for her filled the brick and lumber shelves lined against one wall. Colored pages ripped from magazines were tacked up on one another, each one illustrating some dream or future plan. Standing in a corner was her great-grandfather's .22 Winchester rifle that Homer had given her on her tenth birthday. Treasured objects, gifts from Toby and her friends, littered the top of her bureau. Her few dresses hung in the armoire that had belonged to her grandmother Betsy. On her chair was her father's tin mining hat, rescued from Number 9 with his body. She walked over, picked it up, and examined it with glazed eyes. Inside, Homer had scratched his son's name with a knife: *Hillard Barrow*. She ran her fingers over its every dink and gouge and rubbed away the coal marks. She set it on the bed, and with a corner of the bedspread began to wipe hard over every inch of the beat-up hat. She could feel the tears behind her eyes, felt their urgent longing to fall, but she refused to cry. She kept on with her task until it was clean and close to bright, then returned the hat to the chair, walked to her bureau, and pulled out the few clothes she would take with her to bury her father.

3

"Clary, you got to eat."

They were at the lunch counter at a Woolworth's not far from the White House.

"The bus don't leave till six," Homer pressed her, "and you got to keep up your strength."

They had checked out of the YMCA before the burial because they would be charged for an additional day's lodging, which they couldn't afford. Now they were adrift in the capital with hours to go until their bus left.

A hamburger and a grape soda sat untouched before Clare. She glanced at Homer's plate. One bite was gone from his grilled cheese sandwich. "You didn't eat anything, Grandpa."

"But I drank my milk."

She sighed and sucked on her soda straw, but the grape drink had the flavor of iron filings in her mouth and she pushed the liquid back down the straw into the glass.

"I can't."

Three Amish women took stools across from her and examined the menu silently. Clare studied them blankly, took in their plain dresses and bonnets but was too numb to react or register surprise. Absently, she kneaded the wrinkled brown paper bag that held her change of clothes and, now, the American flag that had covered Hillard's coffin.

She stared so hard at her own hands that finally her vision blurred, which is what she had hoped for. She did not like to imagine that flag degraded by that shabby paper. She had started in astonishment when soldiers snapped it over the coffin so sharply it had cut a wedge from her heart. And then the monster recognition had taken shape: that her dad had survived in the gut of a roaring hot tank, thundering shells seeking him out at every turn, only to die like a bug under a rock in Number 9. Realizing this, she had gone into something like a trance, following the six white horses, the flag-covered caisson, the robotlike escort of soldiers of the Third Infantry, Old Guard, willing herself to remember every word he had ever said to her, every cast of eye, every set of his mouth.

At the grave's lip she had made the effort to raise her eyes and take sightings, putting to memory the precise detail of the rolling hills of Arlington, the stubby columns of the Custis-Lee Mansion, the Tomb of the Unknown, and oh the graves, the hundreds and thousands of graves, flowing away neatly down the hillsides. She burned the scene into her brain and decided it was a worthy plot of land to which her father had been consigned. Noble, honorable, dignified, and on this first day of November, even beautiful. For a moment she had nearly convinced herself that this setting might somehow bring her peace, but young though she was, she was not deceived. They folded the flag ritually and presented it to her and told her the President was grateful of her loved one's faithful service. The instant that rigid package touched her fingers, she was full of resentment. Over time that resentment would take the shape of resolve—to make herself worthy of her father, to give a philosophy to her life and her actions that would make sense of all he had given to her—but for the moment, the machinery that pulled him into his grave whirring easily from frequent practice, she could only wail her grief.

"Clary . . . Clary." Homer's voice shook her back to the Woolworth's counter. "Missy, we better go. They're piling up behind us." With his thumb he indicated the clot of office workers jockeying for stools at the counter.

He paid the waitress, buttoned Clare's woolen jacket and then his own, attempted to take the brown bag out of her hands because he believed it was having a malignant effect on her but she would not turn it loose, and then pulled her off her stool.

They left Woolworth's, and the counters of combs and lipsticks and brassieres and candies and nuts by the pound that on any other day would have riveted her in her shoes with longing, and came out onto the street without any thought of where they would go next. They walked in a dream, Homer eyeing her all the time, more and more disturbed by the collapse of her spirit and the total devastation of her grief. Close to the White House, he came upon a man selling tickets for a bus tour of the District and on an impulse bought two tickets, deciding that he had a responsibility not to let Clare fall so utterly into misery that she would be altered forever.

Ten minutes later they were in their seats, rolling slowly past the federal monuments, Homer working overtime to try to interest her in the words of the guide and the wonders through the window. No reaction.

They piled out at the Lincoln Memorial. Homer moved his lips soundlessly as he approached the massive seated statue. Here was a man to whom he could bring his heavy heart, to whom he could pour out his troubles! He wished it were nighttime. He wished that he might come to the Lincoln Memorial in the darkness. He wished that he were alone. He stood there for a very long time, willing his heart into the hands of that man, Clare beside him with an empty face.

The bus resumed its touring, past the Washington Monument, to the Jefferson Memorial, the Smithsonian Institution, on and on until all the monuments had been accounted for.

Then they turned west onto M Street, to Georgetown. The sidewalks narrowed. The light played over private gardens and ancient trees. They were suddenly in another world. No, not another world, in Europe—London or Paris. The historically preserved community inside Washington existed within the capital's modern roar. At the Chesapeake & Ohio Canal, clapboard houses crowded the water's edge. On the residential streets, Federal mansions directly influenced by the Georgian architecture of England in the eighteenth century stood aloof in stately dignity.

As in France and England, identical ivy-covered row houses were attached side by side, set on four lots. Flat-fronted red-brick Federal-style residences shielded furniture once admired by Thomas Jefferson and George Washington. Georgetown was gardens, lights, trees, and elegant affluence. Here and there Clare watched a man or woman, muffled against the cold, step into the warm embrace of a dark limousine and pull away over bricked streets. Separated from her by a mere pane of glass was every romantic fantasy she had ever conjured, every cobbled street of Paris, every London mews house.

Up on her knees, she pressed two flat palms against the window. Hillard would have recognized this place. Oh, perhaps not such grandeur. But these narrow bricked streets, the overhanging elms, the wrought iron gates and air of both mystery and composure that was not American would have seemed to Hillard, aging veteran of the European campaign, like an old familiar place. As she stared at Georgetown through the bus window, Clare's life was changed forever.

Homer watched her proprietarily, trying to read her mind but not quite comprehending what she saw. When she turned to grin at him, he wiggled his eyebrows and gave her a smile.

When the bus stopped to let the tourists lunch and wander for an hour, she bounded over him and out the door. He followed her down O Street, hurrying to keep up, and nearly ran up her heels at 37th Street when she came to a dead halt at the gate to Georgetown University.

"What's the matter, Clary?"

"It looks medieval, Grandpa," she said, bending back her head to see the gray stone Gothic spires. "Like those pictures of Chartres. Like something you'd see in a book."

"Did your daddy see something like this, do you think?"

"Not like this, I don't think, Grandpa. He would have said. But he could have if he'd had time. He could have."

They stared at the statue of Archbishop John Carroll, founder of the university, wondering who he was, until Clare became absorbed with the passing students, all of them to her way of thinking bright, lively, rich, beyond her. They laughed with confidence. They hugged their books to their chests. They had never eaten squirrel meat—there was no doubt in her mind about that; their dads did not mine coal.

After more awed wandering, she came finally to the Potomac River and looked over to the Virginia shore with such an expression of pleasure that Homer received an inspiration. All day he had been turning over in his mind ideas of how he might do justice to his poor lost boy. And then it came to him on the riverbank, the November wind seeking out the thin spots in his jacket: Clare must come to this university. Clare must live in the town where she feels so connected to her dad. It made perfect sense.

"You're going to come to school here!"

"What?"

"I've made up my mind. This is where you'll go to college."

"Grandpa"—she rolled her eyes—"you can't just *go* to school here. You got to have money."

"We'll get some."

"Not this much, you won't. Nobody in Mills Bend has this much money. Not even Muddy. Can't you just tell by lookin' at the place how much money it would cost?"

"Let's find out. Maybe they give special privileges."

After collaring two students, he found one who could direct

him to the admissions office. They tramped down hallways and cooled their heels for ten minutes before a man named Wilson ushered them to a quiet corner, heard their story, and gave them the bad news.

"Georgetown University," he began, sensible of their inexpensive clothing and open mountain faces, "is a private institution. It doesn't really provide the kind of financial aid you might be needing. And, I must tell you, the academic requirements are very high."

"Clary here's a good student. All one hundreds," Homer boasted.

"I don't doubt it, but"—again Wilson hesitated—"from what you've described, all your schooling was in the mountains."

"She's at the high school in the junction now."

"Ah, that's fine ... but ... I'm not sure that your academics are on the level of this university." He leaned forward in his chair, struggling to keep any deferential tone out of his voice. "Berea College in Kentucky is a wonderful place. Have you heard of it?"

" 'Course we have." Homer was getting impatient. The man didn't seem to get the point. "But now we been here, we want Clary to go here."

Wilson made a steeple of his fingers and pressed it against his mouth. "I guess what I'm trying to say is that I don't think Clare will have studied at the level necessary to be accepted at Georgetown. No matter how many hundreds she gets. I wish I could be more encouraging. But yours is a mountain school after all, and most of the students who come here are from schools in the East, prep school, private schools, Catholic schools."

"Catholic?"

Whoa! That stopped Homer cold. He jumped back in his chair and clamped his lips over his teeth. *Catholic* put a whole other spin on his thinking. Catholics were idol worshipers, Italian, close to Antichrists. He had no intention of turning his baby over to the soul-twisting philosophies of priests and foreigners. Hillard would roll over in his grave. Clare would burn in hell. And the Reverend Nute would personally drive him out of his religion.

"Didn't you know Georgetown is a Catholic University, Mr. Barrow? It's a Jesuit college, with all the requirements of a Catholic education: philosophy, theology, and the other core subjects of Jesuit study—history, English. The course requirements are extremely stiff. I just don't think Clare is prepared to work at this level."

"Well ... I don't know ..."

Clare rolled her eyes at him and glared. "Grandpa! You don't have to become a Catholic to come to Georgetown. That's right, isn't it, Mr. Wilson?"

"Not being Catholic is the least of your problems, Clare."

"What if I get all hundreds from now till graduation? What if I do really well on my college board scores?"

"Well . . . that would be wonderful. You could probably qualify for any state school in Kentucky or West Virginia. I'm sure you would be a complement to any academic community. But the competition is so stiff here. You're up against kids with straight-A averages from excellent prep and Catholic schools. Some of them have parents who are Georgetown alumni, or alumni of other Jesuit colleges, and they have first preference. Most of these freshmen have skills in a second language. Do you?"

"No."

"Do you have any outstanding achievement that might make the admissions people sit up and take notice? Any special awards? Any kind of work experience in an area of interest you want to follow? Membership in a national honor society? You see what I mean? Why not take what you can get and be happy? Anyway, it doesn't matter all that much where you go to school. It's what happens after you graduate that counts. It doesn't have to be Georgetown."

"Yes it does." She stared him in the eye.

"Can I ask you why you are so determined?"

"It has to do with my dad, and that's all I'm going to say." She stiffened up.

Wilson sighed and slapped his hands on his knees wearily. "Well, if I can't talk you out of it, at least I can tell you that you've got four years to get to work. You have to find some way to distinguish yourself, learn another language, win a science prize."

"She's no good at the arithmetic." Homer had regained his senses.

"Well, there you go, Clare." Wilson sighed. "Your chances are really limited. I wish you all the luck. You can't lose anything by trying, I guess, except the application fee."

They shook hands all around and he passed her his business card and said that when she did apply she could send her application in care of his attention and he would help all he could. "But I still think you ought to think about Berea. I think you ought to reach for what you can touch," he told her. But she only smiled at him.

* * *

By six-thirty they were on the bus, speeding south, Homer smoking hand-rolled cigarettes and Clare saying nothing for a hundred miles before she asked, "How long will it be before the grass grows on Daddy's grave, Grandpa?"

"April. There'll be grass by April."

"Will the grave fall in during the winter? I wouldn't want the grave to fall in."

"I reckon they have people who go around and prevent that sort of thing. That's one reason why I wanted your daddy to rest in Arlington. Long after you and I are gone, there'll be Americans caring about the dead who served them."

At Huntington, West Virginia, they changed for Ashland, Kentucky. It was very late and Homer had to steer Clare through the Greyhound station and onto the bus. He smoked some more and sipped at the RC Colas they had carried aboard. He was making a blanket of his jacket when she said to him in a matter-of-fact voice, "I've got to be different, Grandpa. I've got to do something that will make them pay attention to me."

"Who pay attention?"

"The people at Georgetown University. I'm going to learn to speak another language and it's going to make them change their minds about me. I'm going to ask Doc Noor to teach me Arabic."

"Oh, my goodness! Arabic."

Homer mulled that over for a moment in the blackness inside the bus. Then he found her hand in her jacket pocket and squeezed it. "Well," he said, "I must say, I thought that's what you might do."

She squeezed his hand hard. "That's what I love about you, Grandpa. You always do know what I'm thinkin'."

1963

4

Arthur Olson settled back in his chair and pretended to listen as Davis presented the briefing paper, but his concentration was utterly focused on the faces of the men in the room. In addition to himself, three others were seated around a long, polished conference table in an eighth-floor suite of the Department of State on C Street, in Washington, D.C.

Davis had gone on already for twenty minutes and, as Olson noted from the number of pages yet to be turned, gave every indication of going on for another twenty. Olson himself felt tired, burned out from the long flight from Ankara and impatient for Francis Riston to arrive so they could get on with it. In deference to Riston, who would conduct the meeting, Olson had not placed himself at the head of the table, even though he was far and away the other man's senior. Instead, he sat across from Charles Hudson, a tall, thinnish anxious type whom Olson knew to be a brilliant strategist and a man of great ambition but who was unsuited to go the distance at State because of an angry impatience that bordered on volatility. Still, he was more than capable of holding his own intellectually and had proven to be a good conduit of information, with a knowledge of details and the problems they might present for American policy. Olson was glad Hudson was there, even if at the moment he was involved in the business of picking a speck of dried food from his necktie.

Opposite him, at the other side of the table, Elliott Tomlinson, the CIA liaison to the project, gazed out the curtained window at the sky with such an unwholesome expression on his face that Olson felt depressed just wondering what he might be thinking. They had not met before, but Olson understood him to be a go-getter and a rising star at the Agency. Unlike Hudson, Tomlinson did not consider the kingdom Siberia. He had moved up the lad-

49

der at the CIA on his own motion and had an encyclopedic knowledge of the region, where his father had operated various branches of the City Bank of New York.

Tomlinson had been born in Muscat and raised in Aden, and had worked briefly (under an assumed name) for army intelligence in the area. He understood the politics and culture of the whole region inside and out, spoke its languages idiomatically, and had maintained childhood contacts that kept him abreast of developments at the highest levels. He was a strong voice for accelerating American involvement in light of the French and British setbacks of the last decade. He was a fast talker, very animated, and interested in moving ahead, conscious of the career implications of every move he made. It was no secret that he wanted the station chief job in the kingdom when the time came. Olson knew Tomlinson coveted the assignment—the chance to get in at the bottom and take the ride to the top.

Davis, who had written the briefing paper on economic conditions (an area Olson had no use for whatsoever) and was now reading it aloud without enthusiasm, was unknown to him but a familiar species nonetheless—the burnt-out foreign service officer whose enthusiasm for his work had waned in direct proportion to the waxing of his career. Between Davis and Tomlinson sat the man Riston had brought Olson to Washington to meet.

In body, he was very tall—Olson guessed six-feet-three or -four—very broad-shouldered and heavily muscled. His hair was black, lank, and quite long. Most dramatic were his eyes. Rather than the coal black his coloring should have dictated, his were pale dove gray, nearly transparent, and so intense they made it seem he could see right through flesh to bone. He was twenty-six years old, with the rough, handsome face, Olson believed romantically, of a Barbary pirate or a darkly beautiful sorcerer. But to Olson's thinking the physical elements were his least striking feature. The man had *size,* an aura of total composure and collected strength. He was the most utterly assured young man Olson had ever seen. From the thin hawk nose to the cut of his black wool suit, there wasn't an ounce of self-doubt in any of it. In terms of what we're grooming him for, Olson decided, he looks almost too good to be true. He is exactly what he believes himself to be: a lord. They all realized it, but one look told him that Tarik realized it better than any of them, and always had. He was the anointed one, the great pretender. They had mulled it over for years and finally decided. In their eyes he was only marginally foreign. He would go to the kingdom and do the job and it would be almost as if he were one of them, with his perfect English, and his moderate politics and his Bay Area sensibilities. For all this, however, Olson sensed something disquieting about the man that he could not quite put his finger on. He put his mind to figuring out what it was.

Riston had asked Olson, a State Department careerist who knew the bizarre political machinations in the kingdom better than anyone, to give Tarik the once-over. And even though he had flown all night and was just as exhausted as he knew he would be, he had done the favor. And it had been worth it, because the boy did not disappoint and because while they would have to go a long way to create a surprise-free Gulf region, this was a pretty impressive first step. It occurred to Olson that it might be a good idea to steer Tarik toward a degree in economics, now that he had gotten his law degree. Oxford would have given him a certain international élan that might stand in him in good stead later, but they couldn't risk losing him to those damn Brits, who would throw a fit if they knew what was being cooked up for Turkit, the lunatic client-king they had supported in the kingdom for forty years and in whose basket they had once put all their eggs.

Olson recoiled from speculating on just how the coup was going to be pulled off. He had not been elected to a higher awareness of the details of the adventure, *thank God*, and he was about to ponder who the players might be, but he had thought of eggs, and that had started him thinking that he hadn't eaten since the night before, and so he wheeled his mind away from thoughts of Tarik and the kingdom and malignant plots to consideration of where he might get breakfast at three o'clock in the afternoon in Washington, D.C.

Tarik relaxed imperceptibly when he felt Olson's gaze shift. It had been a challenge to evidence no boredom while Davis droned on, but it had given him a chance to contemplate the scheme of things, to go over again in his mind what he wanted to say when Riston arrived. He permitted himself a quick glance at the faces in the room. He had known Tomlinson for five years, since he graduated from Stanford and the State Department had brought him east to study law at Georgetown University Law School. Tomlinson was a creep on the make, but he was one hundred percent behind the project, so he had to put up with him. Hudson was another story. He sensed correctly that he had no affection for the scheme, perhaps because, as Tomlinson had told him, he had seen himself in something rather more critical to the balance of power than ushering into history and onto the throne of an obscure kingdom an even more obscure young man whose father had been some kind of hero. Hudson caught his eye and rolled his eyes in the direction of Davis. Tarik nodded to convey comprehension, a conspiratorial exchange that he knew was meaningless, but he could never be too circumspect when the thinly veiled objective of any meeting was the never-ending, never-sated, all-consuming best interest of the United States government and the self-aggrandizement of its various players.

Long before he had even entered the room, yesterday morning when he had called Riston at home and demanded that they meet, Tarik had clicked his brain into that familiar guarded quarter that it now held where every word, gesture, and pause was processed, checked, and balanced before consigned to comment or decision. His mother had taught him how to accomplish this, how to appear superficially composed while his brain was roaring. In the kingdom it was a little trick of feminine culture, a mantra devised to punish men. *You are windbags and bluster. We are cool, sure-handed, and unbreakable.* It never failed him.

Riston came through the door, breathing hard. "Sorry I'm late—"

"Don't worry about it, Francis," Olson said, cutting off an apology. He rose and shook his hand.

"What's been going on?" Riston asked. He was a tall, portly man with sad, dark rings of fatigue under his eyes, an overworked undersecretary whose career had stalled. Tarik found him consistently courteous and deliberate but dull and deservedly deskbound. He had a stack of files in his arms that he set down and began to arrange in piles on the table.

Hudson yawned and cracked his knuckles. "Davis here has been fascinating us with news of basalt shipments to North Yemen."

Davis looked away and immediately Riston felt sorry for him. "So," he asked, sitting down and turning to Tarik, "what's up?"

Tarik experienced a sly excitement, the pleasurable jolt he always received when he prepared to burn one of his bridges. He reached into his vest pocket and pulled out a flimsy piece of paper. He had a rush, like a drug in the blood, as he pushed the paper across the table to Riston.

Riston picked it up and began to read to himself. The paper was the onion-skin type used for overseas air mail. There were no more than fifteen lines on it, densely black, made by a cloth-ribbon typewriter. After a moment Riston set the paper down.

"Where did you get this?"

"The usual place."

Riston went on reading for a moment, then said softly, "I guess we've got a problem."

"Oh?" said Tomlinson, interested suddenly.

Tarik saw Riston cut him a quick look, a let-me-handle-it glance that Tomlinson did not pick up on. He realized again that he could not trust them and reconfirmed his conviction never to tell them what he was thinking. They thought they knew everything about him, but they had missed the essential truth: that he was as at home in the world as they.

"Tarik's man in the kingdom is claiming that eleven Russian MIGs, with pilots and about thirty support personnel, have been moved onto the old British air base at Hirth near the kingdom's northeast border," Riston told Hudson as he handed the paper across the table to Olson.

Davis whistled softly through his teeth, but Tomlinson sneered. "That's ridiculous!"

"Why is that, Elliott?" Tarik turned in his chair to face him.

"Because I know about every arms shipment that comes into the place. If they'd escalated to fighter planes, don't you think I would know about it?"

Tarik stared at him mildly for a long moment, a small, sardonic smile at the corners of his mouth. "No, I don't," he said finally.

Tomlinson twisted toward Riston. "Francis, I don't believe you can move eleven MIGs, all the technicians, flight crews, mechanics, electronics, whatever, onto the Hirth base and I don't find out about it sooner or later. I mean, this is my job. The kingdom is a backwater sinkhole, let's face it, but this is a monumental alteration and I think—" He broke off and turned back to Tarik. "It's not like you to showboat." He tried to put a trace of irony in his voice, but already he was angry and it showed.

Riston cleared his throat. "Okay, Elliott, let's not get hung up on who found out what first, okay? You know as well as I do that a whole Soviet flight wing could show up over there and we probably wouldn't know a thing about it for a year. What can you expect from a country with no electricity and exactly six miles of paved road, for chrissakes? The place is barmy. It's those damned mountains, that's what's wrong."

Riston heard his voice rising and stopped himself. Sorting out the kingdom to him was like playing evil pinball. Bells clanged, horns sounded, lights blinked, and as soon as he got the little steel ball in the hole, it popped right back out again and went whizzing around on its own. The land of the cosmic tilt. "Or maybe it's the altitude," he added with a weak smile. "At that elevation their minds are all in the ozone.

"Anyway, if Tarik's man is correct—and he's been impeccably reliable to date—then there are elements of the Soviet air force in the kingdom, which means Turkit has cut a deal with the Russians, the terms of which will probably make us all choke when we find out the details, if we ever do. Anyway, let's not get bent out of shape over who brought it home, okay? What's important is that the Soviets have military hardware and personnel in Egypt and Yemen and Syria and now, possibly, the kingdom."

Riston returned to Tarik. "All right. Let me kick this upstairs to the Secretary the minute he gets back from Brussels and we'll decide how to respond. There doesn't seem to be much point in going on until we get his reaction. In the meantime, Tomlinson, see what you can get on it, okay? Let's get a second opinion." He pushed back from the table. "So, Tarik—" He stood up and began to gather up his papers. "Tomlinson will call you the minute we hear something."

"As soon as I get the word, I'll be in touch," Tomlinson said, and he stood, as did Davis and Hudson, and began to pack his briefcase with his papers. Talking among themselves, they moved toward the door. Only Olson remained seated. He rested his chin in his hand with a weary sigh. He was unsurprised that the Soviets had scammed a way to put fighter planes on an abandoned air base; it had been an inevitability since Turkit had kicked the British out seven years before.

What was more interesting to Olson, as he set his elbows on the arms of his chair and sat back to wait, was Tarik. It struck him again how utterly smooth he was. He did not move a muscle as the others hurried about in the business of getting on to the next meeting, caught up in their own conversations and ignoring him. It was impressive behavior and Olson found himself wondering where it came from. Nila, perhaps.

Back in the mid-thirties, when Olson was just at the start of his career, he had arranged the sale of arms to the kingdom in support of a revolution by the Sur general Malik. Malik had been the only authentic hero in the kingdom's history—and it was a history as long as your arm—wild and brave and in the end a loser because he didn't use his head and Turkit had cut it off for him as a consequence. Malik had been the real thing, bigger than life, contemptuous of everybody, like all the Sur.

He had given the people his vision and they had followed him, goggle-eyed, down the road to revolution. He had married Nila to cement an alliance between the Surs and the lowlanders. Tarik's birth sealed the bargain. Malik had failed, but Tarik would not. They had backed a winner for once, Olson could feel it in his bones. Look at him—he sits there and events flow over him just like water over glass. He radiates strength; they're missing it entirely and he knows it and doesn't give a damn. Thinking this made Olson smile to himself. When he looked up, Tarik was assessing him coolly, and at once Olson understood what had troubled him since they met—that mouth. It was full and red, the mouth of a sensualist, a sybarite even. There was a cynicism in its set that came close to impertinence.

All of a sudden Olson knew they had been playing him too naively and that it was extremely unlikely that the man was so innocent as they had presumed. He was about to give Riston some sort of signal to pay attention when Tarik spoke.

"Just one thing I think you ought to know, Francis," he said. Riston, half out the door, halted. "What's that?"

"Why don't you sit down?"

"Oh. Do you want them too?" With his thumb he indicated the other men as they disappeared out the door.

"No. Just you."

Riston shut the door and sat down. "What?"

"I think you ought to know that I'm changing the game plan, Francis," Tarik began.

"What game plan?"

"The game we've always played at, Francis. You, me, the powers that be. I'm changing the rules and you're going to have to adjust."

"I don't get it. What are you talking about?" Riston looked at Olson for explanation, and getting none, turned back to Tarik.

"This time I'm not waiting for everybody to kick it around. I won't be by my telephone hoping you'll call me down here for another meeting. That's finished, Francis. If you don't make a decision to move now, to get rid of Turkit, I'm going to the British with the whole proposition." All of it said in a flat, matter-of-fact voice.

Olson saw Riston's jaw drop. "What are you talking about?"

"Either you move to get me over there now, or I'm going to the British and let them do the job."

Shocked, Riston said, "That sounds like a threat."

"Of course it is, Francis."

"We can't just go in and kill the guy, Tarik."

"Since when?"

"Well, not us, I mean. Look," Riston said soothingly, leaning forward and adopting a pacifying attitude, "I can understand your impatience, but it's all in the timing, Tarik. We can't just go over there and shoot him in the head, even if he is a baby-murdering lunatic, because you're fed up with waiting. We're not in the business of contract murder. Do the Brits know about the MIGs?"

"Not yet."

"Have you spoken to them about any of this yet?"

"Not yet."

"What makes you think they'd be interested?" As soon as he said it, Riston felt embarrassed. It made him seem stupid and he wished he could coil the question back onto his tongue. But Tarik did not respond. He sat without speaking for a moment with his head bowed. When he looked up finally, he gave him such a contemptuous smile that Riston hurriedly added, "Okay, so you know what I mean. So the Brits will bite, of course, I know that. So let's just stay calm here."

"I don't think you're listening, Francis," Tarik said after a silence. "I'm saying that it is now or never. I'm not listening to another briefing paper on the oil deposits at Duru or the quarter-inch of mica deposits the UN discovered in the third quadrant near Im, or anything close to that. Do anything you want with Turkit. Set him up in a villa on the beach at Nice if that will make you happy. It doesn't make any difference to me, because I will settle with him on my own for the death of my father and you won't have to lose a single night's sleep over it. That's *my* problem. But it's your problem that I refuse to go on like this. Tomlinson tells you what great sources he has. Let him fill you in on recent events. Let him give you all the gory details. That's what ought to be keeping you awake at night, not what kind of a corpse Turkit will make. Let him fill you in on the bodies piling up on the roadsides, and the starvation, and the death squads, and the bodies stacked in the freezer and who exactly is being served up for supper. I'm not going to sit here while all of you equivocate and half the population is killed off by an addle-brained lunatic."

"Don't underestimate him!" Riston shot out.

"Don't underestimate me."

"I've never underestimated you. Never."

They stared at each other in electric silence, until the familiar smile broke over Tarik's features. "Really? Then I've made a good impression," he said. "That's nice to know. In any case—" He moved for the first time since the meeting began. He pushed away from the table and drew up to his full height in one quick, fluid motion. He walked to the door, then swung about to face them. "You can look good or you can look bad, gentlemen. It's all up to you."

He opened the door and stepped into the hallway. "You know where you can find me." Then he paused, clicked his heels together theatrically, and gave them a smile. Olson could see that he was not the least bit ashamed or worried about his ultimatum. He was confident, and watching their faces with keen interest. He bowed slightly and closed the door behind him.

Tarik was on the street in seconds and climbing into the passenger seat of the car waiting for him at the curb.

"So?" Stanley Cobb, his driver, inquired as he slammed the door.

"So, everything went just as I told you it would," Tarik said.

Stan checked the rearview mirror and pulled the car away from the curb. "And are we going?" he asked when he had eased the car into the traffic flowing up C Street.

Tarik loosened his tie and stretched his long arms across the seat back. "I believe we are, Stanley," he said. "I believe we are."

His mother's name had been Nila, and until she died no other human being had had a greater influence on Tarik's life.

Her roots had not transplanted easily from the kingdom to the United States. To her mind she lived in a nation of bottomless dancers and car thieves, where the women wore poodle haircuts and the poor ate dog food. It appalled her that the supermarket checker called her sweetheart as he bagged her groceries and pushed his big jokey face into her small dark round one. She longed for the time when just the flutter of a butterfly eyelash could signal elation or despair. What were mystery, nuance, subtlety in a nation of straight shooters? Here everything was barefaced, big ugly bare faces.

Tarik was just two years old when they came to America after Malik was murdered. They lived first in New York City because the State Department thought Nila would be happy in a polyglot city where dark skin and a heavy accent were part of the cultural landscape. There they were under the interested but often less than passionately supportive supervision of the State Department, which considered giving sanctuary to Malik's family more a tweak to the British than an investment in future reprisals against Turkit, who was so securely enthroned he seemed unassailable. In reality, young Tarik was little more than the son of a failed revolutionary and any potential he possessed derived from the romance of Malik's story and the guaranteed popular support he

would have as the son of the man considered the country's only
hero. So successive administrations paid the boy's bills, kept tabs
on his interests, channeled his political leanings, refined and polished him with excellent schooling and exposure to the arts and
culture. Just in case.

It was not until 1956, after the Suez crisis put an end to British
dominance of the region, that Tarik, then twenty years old, took
on more appeal. Turkit kicked out his British advisers and sought
an arms deal with the Soviet Union. The United States, fearful of
Soviet domination of the area, began entertaining the attractive
notion of eliminating Turkit and putting Tarik—raised in America
and virtually one of their own—in control.

All this was years in the future that icy night in 1938, when
twenty-four-year-old Nila, Tarik in her arms, made her first tentative, shivering step onto the tarmac of LaGuardia Airport in New
York. She who had never shopped for food, cooked a meal,
washed clothing, handled money, operated a household, or func-
tioned in any way proximate to the Western notion of women's responsibilities was overnight forced to become an American
housewife. Already exhibiting the chronic fatigue and fever that
are the prodromal signs of tuberculosis, she adjusted to her new
land painfully slowly. Like most immigrants, she had a story. But
hers, palpable with violence, could be told with such a melancholy force that it bore the unmistakable claim of a right to precedence above all others.

When she left her native land she went in a wash of blood, and
now the bodies of the ones she loved lay so heavily across the
path of her life that in the beginning she couldn't do much more
than wail. Every bulwark she had ever known had been
destroyed—father, brothers, husband, friends, the security of her
own culture and heritage. Every material and emotional safety she
had had since girlhood was gone. All she had was her son. And
he did not disappoint. He could read and write by the time he was
four. For his seventh birthday she gave him an English saddle and
a broadchested chestnut mare named Joan, which they kept at the
Claremont Stables near Central Park; in six months he could ride
well enough to jump two-foot fences. When he was fourteen, the
kingdom, at the urging of the Soviets, joined the United Nations
and Nila became so fearful of living in New York, where Turkit's
men might discover and harm her son, she insisted they be relocated. So in 1950 they sold the mare and moved to San Francisco.
By then Tarik was a tall, handsome teenager with a sharp nose,
curly black hair, and a sad face that seemed lit from within when

he smiled. He had a keen intelligence, a love of boxing and foot-ball, and an astonishing memory. Nila taught him as much of the Sur language and culture as she understood, but even in its pau-city this was still enough to foster in Tarik his lifelong arrogant conviction that while he may have been a mixture of both races, there was nothing of the lowlander in him. He considered himself to be Sur, and from the day he comprehended the cultural, reli-gious, political, lingual, and racial gulfs between the two, he for-swore any connection to his mother's lowlander tribe. The Sur were his father's people, and so his own. Through a tremulous vi-bration from ten thousand miles away, he believed he could dis-cern their mysterious rhythms, hear the cadences of their singsong speech, feel the pulsing of their blood. He was one of them, these imperiously brilliant, tall, warlike men and women.

Tarik considered moving to San Francisco the luckiest thing that had ever happened to him. There wasn't a gloomy scene any-where in the city. There were tourists with cameras in Union Square, and sailors on leave from the big carriers anchored in the Bay hanging around peep shows on Market Street. There was a bone-numbing fog that he could breathe in and out like cigarette smoke that gave the up and down parts of the town a creepy crawly feeling. There were rich old ladies with fur stoles around their shoulders on one corner, and weird guys with long, stringy hair shouting poetry that made no sense on another. Tarik would sit and mull over that poetry at one of his favorite hangouts, the Pam Pam Room of the Bellevue Hotel on Geary Street, where the young black cooks behind the counter wore tall chefs' toques as they flipped burgers and shook grease off fries with theatrical flourishes that customers sometimes applauded. He would chew his soda straw to mush, watching them, and think that if his own future had not been cut out so securely he might like to be a short-order cook at the Pam Pam Room.

From the Bellevue it was a short walk to the Simpson Hotel, where he discussed recent broadcasts of *True Detective Mysteries* with Bill, the afternoon desk clerk. Visiting Bill gave him a chance to check out the hookers on Ellis Street, and, if one of the big battleships was in, watch the sailors bargain for sex with them. During summer vacations he would get up early and go down to Bay Street to wait for the fishing fleet to return to port. He would lean over the railing and watch the fishermen as they eased their roughed-up wooden boats into the slips. He had been doing this for so long that he knew all the men's names. They would let him jump on board and peer into the holds at the wriggly fish. He loved the men and the way they bellyached about their jobs and the big commercial fisheries that were putting the little guy out of business and overfishing the shrimp beds. If he had money, he would step over to Fisherman's Wharf and buy a walkaway crab cocktail. He would stomp around the docks of the Embarcadero, daydreaming about his father and about the misty mountains where the Sur people had staked out their strongholds thousands of years before. Later he would take the cable car up Hyde Street to Geary and catch the Number 38 bus out to the Avenues, where he and Nila lived.

He had always been able to take care of himself. If he came up against something that scared him, he felt compelled to go back to it over and over again until the fear was erased.

That was how he had first met Stanley Cobb, the operator of the Tilt o'Wheel ride at Playland, across the Great Highway from Ocean Beach. The first time Tarik had ridden the Tilt o'Wheel he was filled with terror to the roots of his hair. His legs had gone to water and his stomach churned. But because he never wanted to go near the thing again was exactly the reason he went back again, so many times that Stan finally let him ride free until it was a piece of cake. The first time Stan had shown him pornographic magazines he had been shocked and afraid, but he made himself look and look until flipping through them was as easy as reading box scores.

Stan was a huge man, the strongest man Tarik had ever known. Besides running the gut-busting Tilt o'Wheel, Stan had endeared himself to Tarik with a job history composed of every kind of blue-collar employment known to man.

"Go on, Tarik. Name something," he would demand.

"Pearl diver!"

"Done it!" Stan would say as he put the Tilt o'Wheel in motion. "May 1938, Gosako Bay. Down fifteen feet with these half-naked Japanese girl divers. They could hold their breath for seven minutes, hunting for oysters. Had sticky-outy little titties. I'd swim up behind them real close and stare right up their little coozes when they frog-kicked. Dyin' jumped-up Jesus! They was somethin'. Think I got more pussy than pearls?"

"Bet you did."

"Bet I did! Name somethin' else."

"Locksmith!"

"Been that! Security specialist. Had my own little shop in Hollywood, California. September 1933 to February 1934. 'Stan and Dave—Locksmiths to the Stars.' I was Stan. Dave was my partner, so dumb he couldn't pour piss out of a boot if the instructions was written on the heel. Could have made a fortune too if it hadn't been for Dave. Ever hear of that actress Rhonda, Rhonda something? No? I installed her burglar alarm system. Eight-volt batteries with horns on fifteen-minute timers in every room. Knew exactly what she wanted. Smart cookie. And nice too. Most of them Hollywood broads are tougher than boiled owl."

Stan pushed the throttle forward, setting the centrifugal force machine spinning on its side and smearing the terrified riders' faces against the blue sky.

"Try again," he said.

They had been at this game for so long that Tarik was hard-pressed to come up with labor Stan had not put his hand to over the years. Wisely, he avoided guessing professions like doctor or lawyer, knowing this would stump and possibly irritate Stan and cause him to call the game before the second half, which was Whores Around the World. The more ridiculous the job, the better the chance Stan would have held it and the better the chance Tarik would get to hear more about the woman with three breasts and two vaginas and the other sexual novelties.

"Bird-watcher!"

"Done it! And made a living at it too," Stan shouted over the screams of his customers. "Found 'em half a dozen semipalmated sandpipers in Surinam. Their mouths dropped open like chicka-dees' assholes in a windstorm. Name a place!"

Bingo! Tarik thought as twenty dazed riders lurched down the exit ramp while Stan punched the ride books of twenty new victims.

"Burma!"

"Been there! Overland from Dacca to Rangoon. Hauling two hundred and thirty-five pounds of frozen shrimp—why, I don't know—in a 1934 Daimler truck. Found a little whore on Dieppe Street who'd do it for one penny. Homelier than a stump fence, but could she suck the tits off a brass monkey!"

Stan knew the longitude and latitude of every hooker hangout from Tacoma to Tangier, every glory hole, basket fuck, ben-wa ball on the planet. He had performed the legendary String of Pearls! He also kept the largest collection of girlie magazines in the Bay Area in a run-down one-room shack at the edge of the amusement park. Tarik would go there to flip through *Slash*, *Man*, *Shot*, *Beaver*, and the rest. Stan wet his thumb deliberately as he turned the pages.

"Ugh. This one," he would say, sticking out his bottom lip in disgust, "looks like she been rode hard and put away wet."

And Tarik would peer over his shoulder at Marilyn, showing every one of what had to be her fifty-five years in her drooping breasts and scrawny thighs.

" 'Milkmaid Marilyn is sure to get your juices flowing,' " Stan read from the caption. "Boy-o, she's got about as much chance of getting my juices flowing as I've got of drinking turkey-turd beer." He flicked the magazine across the room and drew another from one of the towering stacks.

"Now, this is more like it." He spread the May 1948 issue of *Slash* open on the couch so they could take in every crease and hairpin curve of Carmen. Blue shadow caked the lids of her brown eyes, which were rimmed all around with heavy black liner. Her mouth, out of which a wet tongue poked lugubriously, was a deep purple-red. The rest of her lay across the page like an unfitted bedsheet. Her massive breasts were so transparently white that broad blue veins showed through, tributaries of the deep river of lust that Stan declared flowed through her body. Her nipples were the size of a man's thumb—clam heads, Stan called them. Supported by an orange vinyl lounge chair, she had obligingly thrown open her legs and the rucked flesh of her private parts was florid and slightly pendulous. Stan heaved the disappointed sigh of a man in full possession of the knowledge that the only woman he ever truly wanted was the one woman he could never have.

"I coulda dumped one in her," he said softly.

Tarik sighed and said he could have too, although after an hour with Stan in a shack whose every square inch of wall space was covered with colored pinups of gaping vaginas, Tarik was as uncertain of what he could or could not do as a Tilt o'Wheel rider. He never had much to say after an outing with Stan. He was usually exhausted. While he walked home, he would dream up a story to tell his mother to explain his lateness. Usually he said he was at the Planetarium, but she had become suspicious after he could not find the North Star in the night sky.

Tarik and Nila could chart their fortunes by their progress through the neighborhoods of San Francisco. When they first arrived, the government had set them up in a three-story house on Jackson Street, near the Spreckels Mansion, with round-the-clock security and staff. When the State Department grew unconvinced of the importance of a boy and his widowed mother to the great scheme of things in world politics, they were relocated to a four-room apartment on Webster Street, where their eighty-year-old landlady picked through their garbage and fumed about the "black-African-Negroes" on Fillmore who had designs, she believed, on her Motorola console phonograph.

By the end of 1951, when all anybody in Washington cared about was Julius and Ethel and the Korean conflict, and the young man who would or perhaps would not one day rule an obscure kingdom did not have half the appeal of a two-bit Dominican dictator, their living allowance dropped to low double digits and they were placed in the working-class Avenues neighborhood, the last stop in San Francisco before a traveler falls into the Pacific Ocean. Here they had withstood together the tremble of their fortunes, put a brave face on their miseries, toughed it out, burned the midnight oil, set their noses to the grindstone, all in the service of making sense of their bewildering lives. Behind the garage, in a backyard the size of a playing card, they would sit on rare warm evenings on canvas lawn chairs, swat mosquitoes, and wait for the stars to come out.

Whatever Nila thought of her new homeland did not signify in the long run because her life's objective was not to fathom the ulcerated culture and moral sneakiness of the United States, but to fit her son out for the long, stony path to the inevitable. Let the Americans abandon him, lose faith, cut deals behind his back. Day by day, in exacting detail or simple parable, she shaped his character, molded his conscience, and got him ready to go back. Even when it seemed too outlandish to believe he would ever get any farther from San Francisco than Ling's Laundry on Balboa, she would sit him down in the backyard, the splendid throb of the Pacific behind them, and talk the talk of expectations, duty, birthright, and responsibility. Usually, all she needed to do was tell him the story of Malik.

His mother died of tuberculosis the June before he was to enter Stanford University. When the State Department sent him east to law school, he brought along Stanley Cobb as his driver/bodyguard, in order to maintain his connection with his San Francisco past and because there was a certain symmetry with his adolescence in providing Stan with one of his more bizarre employments.

Tarik was questioning the wisdom of that decision, however, on the evening of his showdown with Riston at the State Department as he sat in the living room of the small house he rented on Rhode Island Avenue. Stan was haranguing him once again on the virtues of the democratic man.

"I'm gonna say this one last time, Tarik—and I know it's probably too late—but personally, I think you're making a big mistake getting all mixed up with politicians. Men like that don't cut any ice in my pond. Can't trust 'em. And another thing, this kingdom we're going to. Now, boy-o, I'm going to talk to you straight, like the dad you never had. I've always told you the truth—told you what broads like, didn't I? How many other grown men share that information with a young kid?"

"None."

"Which goes to show you can trust me." He put his big hand on Tarik's shoulder and fixed on him such a look of concern that Tarik ceased his grinning. "Now, we all come from someplace. My mom and dad came from the state of Maine, but that doesn't mean I have to live in Maine and freeze my ass off logging trees for the Great Northern Paper Company—goddamn their eyes—now does it? Just because somebody says you're something doesn't mean you have to be that. A man can be anything he wants to be. I am the proof of that, boy-o. Remember the Tilt o'Wheel?"

"Of course."

"And the pee-wee golf course?"

"Was that before or after the fountain pen repair shop?"

"After. Before, I had the steam shovel dealership."

"How could I have forgotten?"

"Yeah, well." Stan cleared his throat. "Anyway, what I'm saying, Tarik, is that you can have a career of your own. Be a lawyer. That's what you're trained to be. And no one but the tax man can tell you what to do once you decide. That can be a kind of kingdom. Not there. Here! I know it's a little late in the game to say this, but this is where you belong. And I gotta say one more thing"—he thumped Tarik in the chest with his index finger—"no real freedom-loving American wants to be a king. You can drive a truck, you can punch cows, you can even kill people for a living—this is not un-American. But one man bossing a whole country, answering to nobody, telling the little man what to do and what to not do—dyin' jumped-up Jesus, this is not the American way, Tarik. No decent American wants to be king. Now, there is that tight-ass blonde actress from Hollywood—not my type—who married that jumped-up prince in, ah—"

"Monaco."

"Right. Now, she's kind of a king, but didn't I always say them Hollywood broads is tougher than boiled owl? If you don't want to do it, you don't have to, I guess is what I'm trying to say."

"I want to go, Stan."

Stan slumped back in his armchair for long seconds, then exhaled an expressive sigh through his front teeth.

"All right, boy-o," he said. "You're the boss. I've thrown in my lot with you and I'm not going to back out now. Thick or thin, that's you and me. Wherever you go, I go."

He sat thoughtfully for a moment before something else occurred to him. " 'Course, there might be a bright side," he said. "You being king, I'll be able to get all the pussy I want." Concentrating on his sexual fantasies, an insalubrious look on his face, Stan stared off into space. Tarik was about to disabuse him of this notion of a land of topless harem girls, when the doorbell rang.

Stan roused himself quickly and removed his revolver from the drawer of the end table near the couch. He released its safety and walked to the door.

"Never seen him before," he whispered to Tarik after checking the peephole.

Tarik put his eye to the tiny opening and recognized a familiar face. He opened the door to Arthur Olson.

"I hope you don't mind my stopping by without telephoning first," the older man said as he stepped over the threshold.

Tarik turned, and, catching Stanley's eye, gestured with his head toward the kitchen. Stan disappeared there without a word and closed the door behind him. Tarik waved Olson to an armchair while he took the one opposite.

"Well," said Olson, looking around, "this is nice. Kind of spare, but functional. You have everything you need?"

Tarik nodded.

"Yes, that's right," Olson corrected himself. "You've been living here for nearly five years."

"You keeping track?"

"Always." Olson gave him a smile Tarik could not read. "Anyway, five years is a long time. You're practically a native. So," he said, pulling a cigar from the breast pocket of his jacket, "you've thrived here in Washington."

"That sounds vaguely like an insult," Tarik said.

"Really?" Olson said, sounding genuinely surprised. "I would have thought this was just the place for you."

Suspecting a trap, Tarik did not respond, just continued to stare across to Olson, unfazed.

"I would have thought you'd love it here," the older man repeated.

"Actually, I prefer San Francisco. I have no patience with this kind of politics. It's a miserable business to my way of thinking—trading votes on trade tariffs for army bases in the home county of some second-term congressman, that kind of thing. It bores me. I'd never be able to do what has to be done to get ahead in this town."

"You just don't like being local. I have a feeling you like it fine when it's on a grand scale. Perhaps you're more of a big picture man."

"Perhaps."

Olson trimmed the cigar and set it aflame, bellowing smoke all about him. He drew on it appreciatively, removed it once or twice to look it over, and then sat back to smoke contentedly.

Tarik raised his eyebrows in the direction of the wrappers, which were Cuban and contraband.

Olson threw him a wink through wreaths of smoke, but went on blowing out forceful plumes. He watched Tarik, continuing his interesting game of trying to figure out just how good he really was. After his speech today to Riston, Olson suspected that under that studied worldliness thundered the heart of a raging idealist.

"I'm curious to know if you remember the kingdom. You were only two years old when you left," he said. "Do you remember anything, any faces?"

"You mean my father?"

Olson drew on his cigar. "Anybody."

"Not really. Some impressions, but I don't know if they're real or if I dreamed them."

"Yet you feel yourself to be one of them?"

"Totally."

"Interesting."

"Why is it interesting?"

Olson pulled a piece of tobacco from his lip but his eyes remained fastened on Tarik's. "Well, it's unlikely, isn't it? I mean, in a way you're just another immigrant, aren't you? Yet you elected not to assimilate, not to go with the flow into the melting pot. Not to put the miserable old world behind you, like all the others that came here. My parents came from Norway in 1897. I remember when my father finally understood that a foul tip on a third strike meant you were still alive at the plate. That was the first day he felt himself to be a real American. Oh, he still considered himself Norwegian and he still talked about the day when we would all go back to Norway, but in his heart of hearts he would no more have gone back to the old country than vote Republican. But not you."

Tarik stood and walked to the liquor cabinet in the dining room. Without asking, he poured Olson a tall scotch and one for himself.

"It's not quite the same," he said, handing Olson the drink and sitting down again. "I understand from Riston that you knew my father."

"I knew Malik, a little. When he was at war with Turkit in 1935 I arranged the shipment of arms to him through a middleman, but I met him once or twice. He was quite something. And it was quite a time over there. Scary, although I was too young to be scared."

Tarik ran his finger around the rim of his glass. "Did you know that after Turkit murdered him—he personally bashed his brains in with a two-foot length of rain gutter and then cut his head off—he had his air force make bombing runs over the Sur mountain strongholds and principal lowland villages? Thousands were killed. But it wasn't enough for him, because Turkit had this idea that twenty years later, Malik's son was going to come walking out of the mountains, like Jesus out of Nazareth, and pick up the rebellion where Malik left off. I mention the New Testament because that was exactly the source Turkit drew on for his revenge. He did what Herod did when he was scared witless by the notion of a Hebrew Messiah—he ordered the murder of all the babies. He wasn't quite sure how old I was, so he decided on all the male babies three years and under, just to be on the safe side. And they were murdered, these babies. Hundreds and hundreds of them."

"I know." Olson softened his voice when he said it, out of consideration to Tarik, but he stayed wary.

Tarik took a long drink. Repeating this business had reminded him of his mother. The real injustice was that she would not be going back with him. "So you see," he said, "unlike your father, I wasn't launched here through that quick cut-through of ties to the old country. Rocketed here with a breathtaking snap, and then all of a sudden you're drinking Coca-Cola and shopping at Sears and never want to go back. Not going back was never, ever an option for me. My mother forced this choice upon me when I was a little boy, but when I was old enough to understand the details, I made it again for myself.

"That country is knee-deep in corpses and half-dead people, waiting for Malik's son to come back and turn things around. I've never been an immigrant in the true sense, Arthur. I grew up here, I went to school here, my mother is buried here, and no one would ever mistake me for anything other than American, but in my mind, to this moment, I have only ever been a tourist."

Olson swallowed the last of his drink. Deep in his brain a faint bell of alarm was sounding, and a quiet voice nagged: How sure can we be of this one, our home-grown lord of the polished manners and the sly smile and the hidden agenda? What will become of our vaunted interests once he gets over to that godforsaken place and begins dealing on his own? Riston and Tomlinson and the rest of them on the eighth floor think he is in their pocket forever, but Olson, staring over at the slightly hooded eyes and that soft and sullen mouth, recalling the showdown earlier that day, knew at once that if Tarik was mastered, it was by Malik, the fundamental notion of Malik, that is, and by the conflicting elements of high adventure and gruesome responsibility Tarik believed he had bequeathed to him.

He set his drink on the table and got to his feet. "Well . . ." he said, his words trailing off. They walked together to the front door.

"You put on quite a show today," Olson said, turning back once he had stepped outside. "They very nearly, to use the disagreeable vernacular, shit their pants."

"Is that what you came to tell me?"

"No, but I thought you might like to know. What I came to tell you is that they have agreed to your terms. They're going to help you 'facilitate' the removal of Turkit—their word, not mine; I asked not to be privy to the details—as soon as they can set events in motion. You're going to get what you want."

"How long?"

"Soon. A month or two at the most."

Tarik took a deep breath.

Olson paused on the top step. "I'm going over with you, by the way. Help you with the lay of the land."

"I'm grateful. You know the place better than anybody else."

"I used to. I don't know about it anymore. One thing I do remember, it's a true hell. Hellish people, hellish things happen. Surprises you could never expect. Always be ready for the surprise, Tarik. Expect the surprise." He flicked away the cigar.

"Thank you, Arthur," Tarik said. "I know you had something to do with this."

Olson turned and gave him an appraising look. *You're going to do it your own way, aren't you?* he thought to himself. *Well, more's the pity, because one day, if you do, I'll have to deliver the surprise to you and then you won't believe how bad you are going to feel and what a mess you'll have on your hands.*

But he said none of this. Instead, he fixed his eyes on Tarik's and loaded his voice with meaning. "Well, I suppose you're welcome," he said. "But it did have a certain condition of inevitability, didn't it? Anyway, we can't deprive History of the romance. But if you will permit me—considering what awaits you, I wonder if in a few years you will still be thanking any of us."

5

Lawrence Hopkins Sayles carried the dress to the window, and in the bright sunlight studied its every aspect as earnestly as if it were a missive from the president of the United States.

The heir to one of the country's great fortunes, Sayles had never wavered in the single-minded purpose of his life: the continuing prosperity of America and American interests around the world. He had served as diplomatic troubleshooter for four presidents, advised Roosevelt at Yalta, acted as ambassador to the Soviet Union, negotiated Geneva accords on a civil war in northern Africa, was the current administration's ambassador-at-large, and a strong proponent of nuclear arms limitation. His résumé read like a time line of the twentieth century.

Nature had cast Sayles to his role. He was tall, reed-slim and silver-haired, with intent brown eyes that seemed lit from within by vitality. He had the handsome, bony countenance of a Founding Father, patrician features that, reproduced in oils on canvas, could have hung easily in the National Gallery alongside his famous ancestor, a signatory of the Declaration of Independence. He had a demeanor of seriousness that made his sudden broad smile all the more disarming. Those who knew him had never seen him anything less than austerely placid, and he was capable, by turns, of eloquence, wit, and bruising bluntness. He had a reputation for impeccable fairness and consistent courtesy, and he never raised his voice, preferring to command through sheer strength of personality and the heavy imperative of his vaunted ancestry and breathtaking wealth.

If there had been some quibble over status in his family, his forebears had thrashed it out coming over on the *Mayflower*. By the end of the nineteenth century, after they had built the largest privately owned railroad in North America, the Sayles family joined an immense fortune to an already famous family name. Generations of Sayles men had been statesmen, economists, ambassadors. Promoting American interests was the Sayles family business.

Lawrence Sayles was born on Beacon Hill, Boston, in 1905. After St. Paul's he went on from Harvard to a life of grace and social usefulness; when his grandfather died in 1919, he inherited a private trust worth eighty-eight million dollars. He had converted an early career in international investments on Wall Street into an expertise first in European business and, soon thereafter, into diplomacy in France, Germany, and the Soviet Union. His peripatetic international career was launched during the lend-lease phase that preceded American involvement in World War II; by the end of the war he was commuting nearly on a weekly basis between London, Paris, Moscow, and Washington.

He was briefly ambassador to Paris, before taking the same assignment in Moscow, and in the early 1950s held two successive cabinet posts; so apolitical was his ideology that whether a presidential administration was Democratic or Republican mattered little to him. In addition, he headed international committees on commerce, produced policy papers that had worldwide effect, helped rebuild postwar Europe, and assiduously rejected offers from both parties to run for political office.

By now, in his late fifties, he had reached plenipotentiary status on the international stage and had made it his life's mission to achieve world disarmament. He led the American team currently negotiating the test ban treaty in Moscow.

He had made the right marriage—his late wife, Connie, had been both a Chew and a Livingston—and like all those who occupy the heights, he dealt only with those at the top.

Yet despite his magisterial air, or maybe because of it, he was an immensely popular diplomat, concerned that the world be a better-ordered place for his having been here. Concerned that American stature remain undiminished. Concerned that his own place in history be assured. But concerned at the moment, as he stood in a showroom of Garfinckel's department store, that the color of the satin dress in his hands was not the correct shade of green. He would not settle for anything less than vivid green, near to lime green, more exactly: the precise green of Clare Barrow's eyes.

"It seems to me to be too deep," he said to the saleswoman. "It should be brighter. Less emerald. More of a lime. Let's try again."

The saleswoman was tempted to show her annoyance with a

loud sigh, but she stopped herself. It made her mind spin to think of the price she would have to pay for evidencing impatience with anything having to do with Lawrence Sayles. They would can her on the spot. Or even worse, snatch away her salesbook and cast her out of prestigious designer gowns and better dresses down to the main floor, near the front door, to some department like wallets and keycases. Lime green! It was the middle of January. Where in heaven was she going to find a spring shade like lime green in a fall/winter fabric like satin at this time of year? This would never have happened if Lawrence Sayles's wife, Connie, were still alive.

Now, there was a woman who could spot a handstitched hem at a hundred yards! Who understood that the construction of a dress was as time-consuming, backbreaking, and ultimately as enduring as that of the great pyramids. If an armhole was off by a millimeter, it cried out to Connie Sayles with all the force of a fire alarm. Toted up, she must have given at least ten years of her life to the quest for the perfect fit, standing for hours on end, day after day, in the dressing rooms of the great Paris design houses, setting the seamstresses straight about bias cuts and buttonhole stitching. There was the story told about the contained but nevertheless furious fit she threw at Chanel in the mid-fifties because the navy blue of the lining was not quite the same navy blue of her little luncheon suit.

Such compulsion for detail! Such an infallible fashion sense! Such expertise in the minutiae of dress construction, of fabric, fasteners, buttons, pleats, peplums, and more—immaculate grooming, flawless dressing, the unerring sense of elegance that rendered even the simplest scarf or jewel *perfection*. And always beauty, beauty in her table settings, flower arrangements, writing papers, bed linens, the decor of her many homes. Had she worn a hairnet or dress shields, they would have seemed perfection as well.

Never had such wealth, status, and prestige hove into society's view with greater wit or better taste than with Connie Sayles. Every newspaper article and magazine feature said so. Everyone adored her—only a philistine could not!—right up to the minute unstylish cancer brought her life to a slow close, age just forty-nine, in 1955.

And now, here was her widower demanding lime green, a color worn by Gypsies, by Puerto Ricans, by Negroes, but by Connie Sayles? Never. He must have a new woman, the saleswoman decided, someone with no style, with no breeding, from some underdeveloped country. She dearly longed to ask him about this, but wisely chose to say instead, "You couldn't be more right, Mr. Ambassador. This green really is so much darker than the color you described. I'll find something else."

She took the dress and disappeared through a curtained doorway to dig through the spring stock still boxed in the back.

Sayles watched her go with a kind of misery. Not because he had felt her reproach. He was hardly aware that she even existed beyond a mouth that spoke and hands that fluttered through racks of dresses. But because this was to be the first gift of a personal nature that he would offer Clare and he fretted that he would not be able to find exactly what he wanted. The dress must be exactly right because it was to symbolize the new direction in which he intended to take their relationship. After tonight, he would no longer be her mentor but . . .

He felt a little high as his brain poised to name that which he had so long denied and now longed to give swift indulgence to. The word was *lover*. And in his mind, already taking shape but too exciting to yet make concrete, was another word, *husband*.

He had made up his mind to have her on the day they met, at a reception in the dean's home following a policy panel discussion on the long-term effects of the Suez crisis. He was there, bending to catch something the dean's wife had said, when he noticed the tall blonde across the room as she was in the act of tucking her blouse into her skirt, a gesture that caused her to straighten up and reflexively push out her breasts.

For a man impervious to any eroticism, Clare's hand under her waistband as her persistent nipples appeared against her blouse became the sexual epiphany of a lifetime. His body received the sensation as the desert gratefully accepts the rain. But he was far too rigid to act on his desire, or even admit that it existed. Still, the memory of that electrifying moment lay on his brain like a lantern slide, sometimes flickering with excitement, sometimes difficult to discern, but never extinguished. It had given his soul the kind of weightlessness that he had never experienced before but had imagined all other men enjoyed.

For the first time he was aware of the sexual pull of a warm summer breeze, the feel of something soft and smooth in the palm of his hand, the odor of a woman. And now that he had it, he could not give it up. He did not believe he could continue without it.

A few years later, when she was a student intern on his staff, she had told him she would have to resign over some policy issue that he supported and she opposed. She had squared her shoulders and run up all her pennants, and without an iota of apparent self-doubt had stepped up and told him that she had to go on principle. And rather than be offended, he had concentrated on who she was and the nerve she had to tell him she was leaving after all he had done for her. He had sat back in his armchair, cosseted by his practiced civility, and felt coming from her such a slow burn of will and desire and something he could not quite put his finger on that her skin seemed to shimmer.

He did not want her to go, especially now, when she was so young and naive and her idealism could cover his desolation like a perfume. He did not want her to know that he was without hope, that he was drawing his strength from hers. She was smart and clever. He brought her along and tempered her idealism with his pragmatism. He turned her into a realist; she eased his despair. She wanted her life to count for something and he was helping her do that. He would never let her go.

He knew that she would grasp immediately the symbolism of the dress. It would be clear to her that only a man with deep emotions could have chosen something so completely suited to her eyes, her body, her sensibilities. She would miss none of this. It would be just as clear that if she refused to wear the dress, through her own symbolism she would indicate that she rejected him.

It was typical of Sayles to obscure real events with such devices rather than state what he wanted plainly. He was a shrewd man who held his cards to his chest. He had saved more than one day for his country this way, carefully narrowing options while withholding commitment, then zeroing in on his objective and nailing it down.

His campaign to win her had been a virtuoso performance, so subtle as to be virtually inscrutable. He was famous for his patience and persistence, which he accomplished with a low voice, a slight smile, and utter fearlessness. He understood that any overt action would drive her away. Not that he was a passionate man. All his years he had dealt only with the reflection of life, satisfied to live in emotional shadows. His marriage to Connie had not been unpleasant; it had not been anything at all that he could recall, except attention to form. With Clare he would have substance. Although he was too chaste to be comfortable with the notion, he was emboldened to think himself capable of satisfying her physical needs. Just thinking this made him light-headed.

He paced the showroom floor, his fingers interlocked behind

his back. After five years of working together, he could now discern a change in her feelings toward him. From much-senior mentor, she had allowed him to progress to—what? Friend? Suitor? Yes. Now she accepted all of his invitations to dinners, concerts, public and private events. Several times in the last two months she had acted as hostess of the little dinner parties he gave, as she would again tonight. His friends had begun to take it for granted that they were a couple, and that to curry favor with him they must pay attention to her. She was on the brink of arriving. He would carry her over the edge.

Sayles discerned no impediments in this scenario, although he was sanguine about the enormous disparity in their ages—his fifty-eight to Clare's twenty-three—and the wide gulf between their social and cultural experiences. She was the daughter of a coal miner. He was a famous New England blueblood, and she— she was the most exciting, fresh, and vibrant woman he had ever known, a complete alien to his world and thus deliciously forbidden. What problem could there be? Lawrence Sayles did not waste his time on problems, he concerned himself with solutions. A prince of the republic, he had been made to understand since birth that for men of his class, nothing was out of reach. He knew the drill. He never took no for an answer. He had been raised from the cradle to accept only yes, and so he knew in every bone in his body: She will wear my dress.

Hearing muffled footsteps, Sayles turned to see the saleswoman walking toward him. A bright smile split his stern features. Had he needed a sign from heaven that Clare would be his, then here it is, he thought. Over the saleswoman's arm was a lime-green satin dress.

After a hasty inspection to check the details, a thoroughly pleased Lawrence Sayles paid for the dress that had become his talisman, took the elevator to the street, and stepped into his waiting limousine. He was eager for action, eager for evening to come, and impatient to complete his strategy. He felt completely concentrated and focused toward the accomplishment of his goal.

In the hush of the backseat, he pulled a cream-colored card embossed with his initials from his wallet and inscribed a short message to Clare on its back. He tucked the card into a fold of the dress and settled back, clutching the box with both hands and feeling boyish. Soon he would tell her what was in his heart, that she was the joy of his life. I'll spoil her, he vowed to himself. I'll give her everything she never had. She will never have to worry again. He would rescue her grandfather back in Kentucky from the hard life. That last thought gave him a surge of pleasure and pride that he could stint on nothing. If she chose to continue with her career, he would not object. He was in a position to open every door to her and he would do that. Whatever she wanted he would help her get. What a time they would have together! He had never felt so energized.

Henry, his driver, pulled the car up to Clare's apartment house. Sayles got out and rang her bell, but when she did not answer, he left the dress box with the building manager to give to her when she came back.

He returned to the car and rode back to his N Street mansion to oversee the last-minute details of the dinner party. What a relief it would be when he no longer had to do these things alone.

Clare pulled her car to a stop against the curb on Potomac Street and turned off the engine. By the fading light she checked herself in the rearview mirror. More important, she needed to calm her nerves. If she had left her apartment earlier, she would have had the time to walk the towpath by the canal and found some palliative for her nerves there in the fern-covered cliffs, the dark wood, and spindly pines.

But it was close to dark and, in January, far too cold for soul-searching in the murky wash of the C & O Canal. And then, of course, there was the dress. It was sleeveless and tight and to her eye far too expensive to risk damage by the rough stones and splintered railings of that historic hike.

She switched on the overhead light so that she could read her watch. Seven-fifteen. In another few minutes she would be late and Lawrence would excuse himself from his guests and begin telephoning her apartment from his second-floor library. When she didn't answer, he would conjure up morbid scenarios of car crashes. It both thrilled and mortified her that one of the world's preeminent statesmen always thought the worst if she was even five minutes late.

Not so long ago his possessiveness had made her itchy and resentful. But in the last year she had softened her independence and now accepted his fussy ministrations as proof of how much he cared for her.

That she had been accepted into Georgetown University and its School of Foreign Service would have been miracle enough, but to have captured the attention of Lawrence Sayles seemed even beyond the great romantic novels she devoured as a girl.

She had been certain from the beginning that he wanted her,

and just as certain in the last year that he would ask her to marry him, and that she would say yes. She suspected, rightly, that her appeal to him was grounded in her very failure to comprehend it, because she was artless in her dealings with men and showed to Sayles the same open heart that had caused Toby to love her. Sayles was an amazing man, and while she was far from arrogant, Clare had enough vanity to congratulate herself for having won him.

She could not, of course, have conceived of any of this back in Mills Bend. For four years at the junction high school she had bent to her books. In her free time she baby-sat, cleaned house, and cooked for Doc Noor and his family. In exchange, they had taught her to speak, read, and write conversational Arabic. When she submitted her application to Georgetown, along with her high school transcript she'd enclosed a three-page essay in perfect Arabic (with English translation) explaining why she wanted to join the School of Foreign Service. The admissions committee had been so intrigued at the notion of an Appalachian mountain girl fluent in an obscure and difficult language that they invited her for an interview. Mr. Wilson, whom she had met with Homer on that grim day when Hillard was buried, had coached her for hours before the interview; she had sailed through with flying colors.

In her sophomore year she was named a Sayles Fellow, entering the most prestigious study program in the school. Established by Lawrence Sayles as a family philanthropy in the late thirties, the fellowship offered not just financial aid and special study, but internship in Sayles's busy office on K Street in the District. Over time and exposure to Sayles, Clare's area of interest shifted from the Middle East to the European arena in which he held such sway.

In the beginning she hadn't served a use to him except to type and file and run for coffee for his staff. But in her senior year he had asked her to prepare a paper on the precedents of limited warfare and he had deemed her effort brilliant. After that he had assigned her more and more important projects to manage. By the time her graduate work was completed, she was on his staff full-time. She had passed the Foreign Service exam the previous June, and could have joined the State Department diplomatic corps, but he had persuaded her to stay with him. He had mounted a well-thought-out argument, but in fact she had needed little convincing, because by that time she was aware that he was emotionally involved with her and she no longer wanted to play the waiting game. If Lawrence Sayles, one of the wealthiest men in the country and one of the great statesmen of the twentieth century, wanted her, she would give him what he wanted.

It was a thrilling prospect, marriage to this famous man, luxury beyond imagining, work on a world scale. She could conceive of their shared future through clear eyes. Sitting in her little car, the chill air seeking her out through a broken window vent, she believed that life had delivered all of her dreams. She felt overcome by a sense of duty and responsibility, certain that with Sayles she would play a useful, legitimate role in a career run on principles. She would be a good wife to him. He would have no reason to regret his choice. She wore his dress tonight as a sign to him that she agreed to their unspoken arrangement.

Her nerves restored by the image of the life that awaited her, she stepped onto the sidewalk and locked the car doors. She tugged the green dress, which really was too tight, over her hips, and with quick steps turned left onto N Street.

It was the classic Washington entertainment: the Little Georgetown Dinner. And Sylvia O'Dowd preened that once again she would mix, however briefly, with the most attractive and, more important, most influential people in town.

Concealing her curiosity none too well, she stared boldly around Lawrence Sayles's home. Even to a woman accustomed to the fine houses of the privileged, this mansion, three stories high and constructed along austerely Federal lines, was imposing. When she arrived, she had made a circular march through its first-floor rooms, twice passing the great curved staircase in the entry hall, eyeing everything expertly.

The house had been called The Heights since it was built in 1806 by the architect Robert Mills, a protégé of Thomas Jefferson, because it sat on a hillock of land in Georgetown that distinguished it from the flat-land property nearby. This small rise and its original landscaping had disappeared as other homes sprang up tight-by at the same elevation, but the name, foolish as it now seemed, had remained.

The mansion's chief attraction was its priceless museum-quality collection of Federal and Empire furniture, the last period of handmade furniture in America. Room upon room was filled with gold-pawed Duncan Phyfe sofa and chair suites. On the walls, which were painted variously red, cream-yellow, or dark green, were hung ornately gilded mirrors, with fleurs-de-lis and Winged Victorys atop the frames. The artwork, also in gilt frames, was eighteenth-century American portraiture, many of them Sayles's forebears. The chandeliers were Waterford, dripping lacy crystal beading; they burned beeswax candles in the formal rooms.

It was an elegant and lavish residence, relieved from its formality only by the homey bibelots collected by Connie Sayles in her world travels—lacquered boxes from Japan, sets of nesting dolls from the Soviet Union, lattice-work silver chests from India, and so on—scattered on tabletops, and by the heavy perfume of brass polish, silver polish, floor wax, and furniture polish used daily to keep it all burnished and glistening. Fresh flowers, cut from the greenhouses on Sayles's Middleburg, Virginia, estate and driven into the District every day, were set in tall Baccarat vases on pier tables in the hallways, on sideboards and end tables elsewhere.

When Sayles inherited the house from his father at the end of the second World War, it had been a hodgepodge of the best and worst of design styles over many generations. Victorian was mixed with Georgian. The carved paneling and ceiling medallions had been painted over. The many-paned windows were curtained in dingy brown velvet, the carpets threadbare.

Connie Sayles had taken the place in hand, and in the process added to her other talents an expertise in eighteenth- and early nineteenth-century furniture. She knew how to put a room together, and she made The Heights a showcase; it, and the perfect entertainments she created under the Waterford chandeliers, enshrined her permanently in the ranks of the stylish.

But the most striking feature of the house now, to Sylvia's way of thinking, was the uninterrupted fidelity to Connie's original design. She settled back in the Recamier sofa and lit a cigarette with the last match in her White House matchbook. He hasn't moved so much as an ashtray since she died! Sylvia could feel Connie's presence wafting through the rooms, grimly pesky and impossible to ignore, like the ghost of Hamlet's father. She haunted the Adam chairs, the Georgian silver, the Ming vases scattered wittily atop spindly-legged tables, even cast her hoary shadow over the Charles Peale Polk portrait of George Washington. Connie's hand was everywhere here, just as icy and unwelcoming as when she was alive.

Through the soles of her shoes Sylvia absorbed the pillowy comfort of the custom-made carpet. It recalled for her an unpleasant business of her childhood, of her mother pulling splinters gotten from their wooden floors from her bare feet. She winced at the memory and squeezed her thighs together. Nobody here ever got a splinter from a bare floor. Maybe the odd shard from a broken piece of Lalique crystal, but no one in this gang knows that some floors come without rugs, Sylvia thought bitterly as she drained her glass down to its ice cubes.

Preston, Sayles's vinegar-faced butler, materialized at her side, removed the empty glass from her hand, placed it on a silver tray, and wordlessly filled her hand with another Chivas on the rocks.

Without so much as a glance in his direction, Sylvia accepted the drink. "Thank you, toad," she murmured under her breath.

"Madam." Preston dipped from the waist and glided soundlessly away in his high-polish shoes.

Sylvia could have sworn that he had lingered on the first syllable of that *ma-dam*, making it sound as if she were not a bona fide lady but the proprietress of a whorehouse, which, of course, she was not. Not now, anyway. She shuddered a little to think that Preston might somehow have gotten the goods on her, that he had found out about the little house in Kansas City. But impossible! She dismissed the thought with a mental wave of her hand. That was a thousand years ago, when she was Sally Herskewictz, before she'd pulled herself up by her drawers all the way to her current status as the wife of Washington's most influential political newspaper columnist. Besides, with her own two eyes hadn't she seen the chief of police, standing in her bedroom in his underpants, tearing up her arrest record?

No, she consoled herself, it was not her ancient history that she imagined Preston was privy to, but more recent events.

Last year, in this same house, she had poured one too many scotches upon an empty stomach and had committed the unpardonable social gaffe in Washington: She had passed out at a Little Dinner. Preston had had to carry her to the powder room off the kitchen and hold her head over the toilet while she vomited. The toad had nearly drowned her, flushing over and over again while her mouth was still kissing the porcelain. Sayles had banned her after that stunt, but he was too humane to hold a grudge and had finally summoned her back. This evening marked her return to acceptable society and Sylvia was on her best behavior.

She narrowed her eyes at Preston as he floated effortlessly among the guests. It might behoove her to run a background check on him, just in case. She would fiddle with her husband's locked, confidential file drawers in the den at home and see what she turned up. She filed the plan in the back of her head for future action and returned to her scrutiny of the party.

The most critical element of any Little Dinner is not food (which in Washington is merely fuel and taken for granted to be only adequate) or drink, or the setting, although it is imperative to possess a huge, stately mansion such as Sayles's, but the Guest List, and in this Sayles succeeded beyond anyone short of the President.

Sylvia scanned the room and whirled her mental Rolodex, matching faces to money and status. There was one senior senator, one top-echelon White House aide, one congressman from a populous western state, one former Secretary of State (now the head of a billion-dollar law firm) and one very urbane foreign ambassador possessed of the hottest gossip in town, plus the women they married when they were very, very young. Best of all, there was one actual Kennedy and two Kennedy in-laws. A man may be richer than Croesus, but without a guest list of this caliber, he would never achieve true status in Washington. Sylvia knew this truth was probably lost on Lawrence Sayles, because he was so rich and so powerful and had so much status that he had no need to impress anyone, and never tried. For him this night was simply friends over for dinner, never mind that they were the most important people in Washington, read: The World.

The ringer in all this, to Sylvia's way of thinking, was the tall blonde in the corner in the tight lime-green dress that could have been a second skin, who had neither power, nor money, nor status, but upon whom all these were automatically conferred by virtue of her association with Sayles. She is young—oh God is she young! Sylvia despaired. He hadn't just robbed the cradle, he had invaded the womb.

She had heard all about her already. The scandal had been on the jungle drums less than twenty-four hours after the dinner party where Clare, nervous and tongue-tied, had first played hostess. And then there were the concerts, and the Blair House dinners, and the Smithsonian openings, and the State Department receptions, until everywhere Lawrence Sayles went, short of the Oval Office, it seemed that Clare was on his arm.

It had come like a blow to the chest to one incredibly wealthy and status-mad member of the ladies luncheon crowd, an old friend of Connie's, who had consoled Lawrence Sayles when she died and had hoped to take her place when he overcame his grief. He was the catch of a lifetime and he was lost to her because of some Kentucky hillbilly! Yesterday, when Sylvia had lunched with her at the Summit Club, she had cut through her house salad as if it were Clare's heart.

Sylvia did not find the emergence of Clare as appalling as she, although she would have ditched Charlie O'Dowd, her husband, in about the time it took to get out of her girdle if Sayles had given her even a glance—highly improbable, she knew, considering her recent dishabille in his kitchen toilet. So it was unproblematic for her to remain the disinterested observer of Lawrence Sayles's love life. Anyway, Charlie was currently in Rome, on assignment for his newspaper, he said. Actually, a friend had called last night to say she'd seen him on the Via Veneto slobbering over a movie starlet with breasts like the tail fins on a Caddy. Who would dump whom in the O'Dowd marriage had been a moot point almost since the honeymoon.

Wishing for a better look at what the whole town assumed would be the next Mrs. Lawrence Sayles, Sylvia raised herself from the couch, surprised to feel so heady after just two drinks, and made her unsteady way across the room, wondering with every step if the toad had slipped her a mickey.

Clare watched her approach with a mix of fascination and dread. Sayles had described in unpleasant but uproarious detail Sylvia's crime against society. He had added that she got away with murder because her husband's column was syndicated to more than two hundred newspapers. "Don't let Sylvia scare you, Clare," he told her. "Her bark's a lot worse than her bite. But if she starts to give you a hard time, you tell me. I'll let Preston give her the boot. He loves that kind of stuff, and he does it better than anybody." He chuckled so mischievously that Clare believed he was hoping for another chance to drop Sylvia down a peg.

And here she is, Clare saw with dismay, insinuating herself between the senator and the ambassador, and giving her a look of such rapacious scrutiny that Clare believed for a moment that twelve inches of dorsal fin had appeared between Sylvia's shoulder blades.

"Now, what kind of bullshit are you-all boring this little girl with?" Sylvia demanded.

"Ah, Sylvia! Just the person we need," said the ambassador as he slung his arm around her shoulder. "This is very top secret stuff. We were telling Clare here about the senator from a benighted southern state who was caught today in a toilet in the Senate Office Building doing very nasty bad things to a big Negro woman not his wife."

"You don't say!" said Sylvia.

"We do say!" said the ambassador. He squeezed Sylvia's shoulder and lowered his voice conspiratorially. "He got her up on the top of the john walls, one leg on either side, you know, and he had his head stuck up her dress when the cops came in."

Sylvia stared at him for one clock tick, debated whether to tell him that she knew for a fact that the Negro *she* was really a *he* in a neat blue luncheon suit, but thought better of it. If Lawrence found out she was telling tales about a member of the Senate Foreign Relations Committee whom he was courting on the disarmament vote, he would kick her out of The Heights forever.

But, God, this was juicy stuff and it took all Sylvia's self-control to bite her tongue, take Clare by the elbow, and say, "Come on, dear, let's us girls get to know each other."

She had tugged Clare almost to the solarium when Sayles intercepted her.

"Hold on now, Sylvia," he said. "You aren't stealing Clare, are you?"

"I am, Lawrence. I'm the only one here who hasn't met Clare, and I thought it only fair that we go hide ourselves in the solarium and sip champagne and sniff your gorgeous gardenia trees and get to know each other. I want to find out all the little details of her life."

"You might be disappointed, Mrs. O'Dowd," Clare said in a quiet voice.

"I don't believe that for a minute, my dear," she said, pulling her close. "And please don't call me Mrs. O'Dowd. Everybody calls me Sylvia, even the pizza delivery boy. Especially the delivery boy. I can feel in my bones that you are one of the more interesting people I will ever meet." Clare gave her such a cool look of disbelief that Sylvia turned back to Sayles.

"Besides, Lawrence, you are working this girl too hard. All day in the office, and now here at home, riding herd on all us big bores. She needs to get off her feet for a minute."

"Another time, Sylvia. I need Clare now to help me with the seating plan," Sayles said. He unpeeled Sylvia's fingers from around Clare's arm. "Why don't you go talk to Harold Pressler's wife over there. She's all alone in the corner."

Sylvia turned to look at the wife of the powerful senior senator who was plain, not young, and spending a rare weekend in Washington away from the family home in Grants Pass, Oregon. Sylvia wiggled her nose distastefully, as if she smelled something bad.

"Oh, Lawrence," she whined. "Do I have to?"

"Yes."

She shook her curls and made a sour face. "Well, I'm gonna have to have another drink to work up my courage, and you know what that'll do to me. You better ring the dinner bell pretty damn soon or I won't be responsible."

"I'll send Preston over with a drink."

"Well, check it, will you? The toad has it in for me."

"Thank you, Lawrence," Clare whispered when they were out of earshot. His arm was looped through hers so casually as they walked toward the dining room that she could imagine it remaining that way forever. With a bit of recklessness, considering the formality of their courtship, she allowed herself to sway a little into him. With pleasure, she realized he did not stiffen or pull away.

As they walked slowly down the hallway, drawn close together, her hips lightly touching his, conspiring against Sylvia, Clare felt an enormous sense of relief and gratitude. Sayles, sensing her mood change, stopped, and took both of her hands in his.

"You have to be careful of Sylvia, despite what I said earlier," he told her. "She thrives on gossip and can turn the most benign bit of information into a capital offense. Being alone with her is like being under arrest. She'll grill you like a cop until she gets you to admit to something. And you're damned if you tell her your secrets, and you're damned if you don't, because then she thinks you have something to hide and she'll never relent."

"I doubt she could have gotten me to tell her anything."

"Really? You think you can handle Sylvia? You would be the first." He raised his chin at her.

"I do."

"Tell me."

"Well, in the first place, I'm not hiding anything, so if secrets are Sylvia's bread and butter, she will certainly go hungry with me. From what you say, she gets only those who can be gotten. And in the second place, even if I did have secrets, I would still know how to handle her."

She resumed her slow walk down the gallery hallway with Sayles at her side, his head bent, listening.

"Knowing Sylvia is like hunting rattlesnakes. You can catch one if you know what you're dealing with. See, a rattler can strike only about half the distance of his body. If he's four feet, you stay back two feet. Five feet—two and a half feet, and so on. He can make his rattles buzz, he can hiss, spit, scare the living daylights out of you, but he cannot bite you if every time he comes toward you, you back up.

"Now, the only difficulty," she went on, "is that you have to be able to assess his true length. Sometimes it's obscured by the underbrush, or he's coiled so tight he can disguise his size. Snakes are very clever that way. They can make you see what they want you to see, like people. The secret of surviving is to keep your eyes open wide and to always gauge correctly his true size. When you've got him where you want him, you just snatch him up from where he's hiding with a hickory stick rigged up with a length of wire and he's yours."

Her eyes went over his shoulder to the sound of Sylvia's brittle laughter cackling out to them from the living room.

"And what do you do with your snake once you've got him?" Sayles asked.

She returned her attention to him. "What do I do with him?"

"Yes."

She leaned into him, opening her eyes wide. "I eat 'im."

Sayles drew back, surprised. He gave her an appraising look, trying to decide if she was telling him the truth. But of course she was, alien creature who knew of snake hunts and coal mines and handmade clothing. He put his head back and laughed out loud appreciatively.

"I've never met a woman who's eaten snake before," he said.

"That's because it's usually the other way around."

He did not quite understand her, her endless expectations, the innocence of her gratifications. But with as much insight as he could summon he decided he didn't need an explanation. It was enough to know that she was fantastic and that he loved her. She had spirit. To her, life was basic and direct. She took the measure of men and events with the hard, unforgiving inches of Homer Barrow's yardstick, and that being an accurate measure to Sayles's way of thinking, he believed that he and Clare shared a moral and emotional equivalency.

I should kiss her right now, he realized suddenly. I shouldn't wait another instant. I should take her in my arms and tell her that I love her and ask her to marry me. They were alone in the dining room, uninspected except for the staring eyes of his glum-looking ancestors in portraits on the walls. He took a step toward her. A look of expectation flickered over her face. He felt a click in his brain, a surge of awareness. It is here right now, that mysterious convergence of opportunity and geography and chemistry that signals the arrival of a moment past which life will never be the same. Tell her, ask her! It is time to give her a sign of what we have entered into.

"Clare . . ."

"Yes?" Her eyes searched his.

His awareness was so heightened he could actually believe time was suspended. He collected his thoughts. He wanted to be perfectly understood. He took another moment to coil onto his tongue the perfect sentence of love and desire. He knew at last exactly what he wanted to say.

"Clare, I—"

But before he could declare himself, a maid bustled through the kitchen door and set about lighting the candles. Startled, Clare shifted to watch her, pulling her hands out of his. Sayles's moment evaporated on the candle-scented air. He experienced an immediate sensation of loss, but contained it quickly with his usual optimism. Never mind, he said to himself, there will be many more opportunities. For a prince of the republic, there are nothing but opportunities.

"What do you think of my seating plan?" he asked, leading her to the table and bending to look at the place cards. He was feeling better than ever. "I think we should put Sylvia nearest the kitchen, don't you? So she'll be close to the bathroom, just in case."

In the afterglow of the meal, after the servants had cleared the table and Preston had placed the tray of liqueurs and dessert wine on the sideboard and withdrawn, Clare composed herself with a glass of port. For nearly two hours the room had swirled with the babble of politics, deals, and gossip of every coloration, sexual and political, although Sylvia had maintained loudly that there was little difference, as all politicians are whores anyway. Although she had hooted too loudly at the ambassador's asides and made her usual breaches of confidences, Sylvia had remained sober, her brown eyes darting over the faces of the guests, taking in everything.

Sayles sat at the table's head, erect in his chair, radiating quiet charm and unfailing hospitality, worrying over the comfort of each of his guests. Clare had matched his poise all evening, but at that moment, while her features were fixed in an interested expression, under her skin her heart was thumping.

She drew a deep breath to collect herself, taking in the riches of the evening, the lavish food, the quantities of wine, the mansion, the high and mighty of Washington on her right and left, and most of all, the soft-spoken, silver-haired man who through his confident reserve commanded them all. *Can it really be possible this is happening to me?*

She shifted in her seat, remembering the dress. Without drawing attention to herself, she slowly ran her hand down her bare arm until it reached one of the deep fabric tucks at the dress's waist. With two fingers she caressed the smooth satin, an extravagance of fabric beyond imagining not so long ago. It was possible that this dress cost more than her father had earned in a year.

That notion filled her with pleasure, and just as quickly with a deep sense of regret. Exactly as her mother had predicted, Muddy had come up the holler not two weeks after Hillard was in the ground. He walked into their unpainted company house and plopped himself down as if he were an old friend. He told them that the final report on the accident was in. The dead men were supposed to have set ten timbers that night, but they set only seven! He couldn't have been more surprised, and disappointed. What did they think was going to happen? He'd gone down to eyeball the shaft for himself when the rubble was cleared and there was their negligence, right there for any man to see. It had cost him a pretty penny to get the mine up and running again. Times were tough. Coal prices were down. And so . . .

He pressed a hundred-dollar bill into Kath's hand, then announced that he needed his house back for another miner, so he'd appreciate it if she'd take her family and leave. He didn't even give her time to gather in her little garden harvest. They had used their cousin Helmut Barrow's mule to lug their pathetic possessions down the holler to two rooms they rented in a ramshackle house in town.

Kath had gone to work at the snack stand off the highway, a miserable job that kept her over a hot, greasy grill ten hours a day—bad enough, but it was Clare's particular horror to watch Homer sell off his last hog and go back down into Number 9 mine. December 14, 1952—as long as she lived, she would never forget the desolation of that day. Reexposure to coal dust escalated Homer's lung disease to a more complex version; in years to come, large opaque patches of carbon and scar would form on his lungs where the dust had collected. Muddy had offered him a job on the tippler, but Homer said he'd only ever worked right up at the coal face and that settled that. Actually, he made Norton Tile deliver the message to Muddy; he never spoke to, or as much as looked in the direction of the man, ever again.

Like most servicemen, when Hillard went to war he'd enrolled in the National Service Life Insurance plan. While on active duty, six dollars and forty cents was deducted every month out of his military pay. He elected to maintain the policy when the war ended, and two months after he died, the government paid Kath the ten-thousand-dollar benefit. For a day or so she was on a cloud. She would get them a decent home. They would buy so many groceries the cupboards would bulge. Maybe they might have an inexpensive little car. Life would be good again. Life would be good for once.

But Homer had fixed her with a look of fierce refusal and told her that Hillard would never rest easy if that money wasn't put away for Clare's education. Kath became sheepish finally and agreed to bank the money in a savings account. Homer did allow her to keep the interest, however, and so she had some pleasure out of it. Actually, pleasure was a relative term, to Kath's way of thinking. Sometimes the best times she had were when she was the most unhappy. She died when Clare was nineteen; Doc Noor said it was from a cerebral hemorrhage, but Homer always maintained that her brain couldn't bear the strain of that much joylessness and just shut down.

How much had Clare's family sacrificed to bring her to this table, to sit among these rich and famous people, to have won the affection of this famous man? Through an act of will, she commanded herself to put aside that particular calculation, knowing that it always made her uncomfortable. What mattered now was that once she was married to Sayles, Homer would be rescued. Before she could stop herself, she wondered if that was reason enough to marry Lawrence Sayles. If he asked her, would she marry him to save Homer? The thought unsettled her and her brain began to rush around in such disorder that she had to press her palms flat on the table to try to center her emotions.

Anyway, she had a nagging fear that Homer would turn down anything that Sayles offered.

He had come to visit her several times since she'd moved north, and she had introduced him to Lawrence Sayles in the K Street office, meetings made memorable by Homer's rudeness. All of Sayles's possessions, to Homer's mind, came from generations of Sayles men who in their forms exactly duplicated other men but whose hollowed-out hearts hid stiletto teeth that peeled the flesh from the workingman and made money doing it. Railroad workers, mill workers, shipbuilders, men like her father and grandfather. The rich and the workingman, Homer liked to say, are natural-born enemies, like the miner and the mine boss, and if there is one sinful resource in this great country, it is the wide river of privilege that put the few in the swim of things and the many haunting the banks. To Homer, the ruling class was a fist in the entrails.

Clare reddened thinking what he might do when presented with all this luxury. She would never get him to live in The Heights.

He would stomp through the house like an old bull, snorting at treasures, railing and carrying on something awful.

Forty-five minutes later, the dinner guests clustered in the doorway. Sayles convinced Clare to let his driver, Henry, take her home; he would make arrangements to have her car delivered to her apartment before she left for work the next day. He was leaving in the morning for Geneva, at the President's request, to try to resolve the conflict in Laos.

Clare would have preferred a more private parting but Henry was waiting at the curb, the engine running, and Sylvia had made a fuss about catching a lift home with her. Fueled by wine, the guests enacted the good-bye ritual. They made kissing sounds around each other's cheeks, pressed elbows, and promised to do it all over again very soon.

Sayles walked her to his limousine, Sylvia hot on their heels. Henry popped open the door.

"I don't believe I'll be in Geneva more than three weeks," he told Clare as they walked along. "I've told them I can't stay any longer, in any case."

"To force their hand?"

"What do you mean?"

"A protective measure, to keep the negotiations under control?"

"I suppose they could take it that way, but I didn't say it for effect. I have other reasons for not staying away too long."

In the shadowy light he tried to hold her with a speculative look, but she turned away, uncomfortable because she appeared so old in the lamplight. "Thank you again for the dress, Lawrence," she said. "I've never—the color is perfect. How did you know?"

"Did you think I don't carry the color of your eyes in my mind?" he said.

She wished he would touch her, take her hand or loop his arm through hers, offer her some evidence of what he surely must be feeling. But he did not, and neither did she, and she experienced a return of the anxiety she felt earlier in the evening.

"I'll call you from Geneva," he told her.

He had said it in a low voice, his mouth almost at Clare's ear, but Sylvia, whose own ears were as unfailing as radar, able to detect cries and whispers from places only slightly less distant than the Big Dipper, had heard it, and in the backseat of the limousine she silently gloated.

In the sealed confines of the car, Clare struggled to calm herself. She was sorry that she had let him talk her into leaving her car behind. She wanted to drive fast down the empty city streets. She wanted to play the radio loud. She did not want to sit in silence where uncomfortable ideas took shape in the backseat of a rich man's limousine. He should have kissed her. He should have asked her to marry him. He should have made love to her and used his body to drive away her doubts. She had fallen in love with him as an act of will. She admired him. She may have even revered him, but if she felt love, it was an intellectual exercise: She had decided she should and so, after a time, she did.

Somewhere in this swamp of guilt and confusion was Homer, humbled by despair in Kentucky. Somewhere also was the conviction she had shaped so clearly years earlier that she must resist Lawrence Sayles, because she understood that he would always love her more than she loved him. When had that changed? Had it? A headache began shaping at the back of her skull.

None of this was articulated very acutely in her brain. Disheartening notions charged back and forth chaotically, and she could not make any order of her thinking. It was easier to resort to the practiced consolations: I am a lucky woman. A great man loves me. I have more than I could ever have dreamed of.

To her great relief, Henry brought the big car up to the curb in front of her house and she jumped out with a quick good-bye to Sylvia.

Through the lowered car window, the older woman watched her go. After Clare was safely inside the apartment house, Sylvia inhaled a deep breath. There was some reassuring element contained in the atmosphere of any expensive automobile chauffeured by a black man in a blue suit; it acted as a balm on her jangled nerves. Riding in a limousine always made Sylvia feel that she could do her trapeze act, throw triple somersaults blindfolded, and net or no, land on her feet light as a feather. She closed her eyes against the passing streetlights, forgetting about Clare and drifting into wine-soaked sleep. She would be working the jungle drums overtime tomorrow, and doing such hulas with the files and the hot news and the luncheon ladies. It was going to be a busy day and she needed her rest.

6

The afternoon of the following day, Clare pumped north on Nineteenth Street, documents she had picked up at the State Department tucked safely into her heavy, bulky briefcase. She hadn't slept well and felt weary and a little edgy. She turned her collar up against the chill wind, though the day was clear and the sun bright.

There had been long months when she first arrived in Washington that Clare worried that what Kath had said years before might be right, about trying to be something she wasn't. To Clare's country mind, every last Georgetown student was the epitome of the mysterious upper class. They understood good food, wine, fine clothes, and expensive cars. Yet while she lacked a knowledge of the world, she was full of knowledge of herself, and in the end she left the world of her girlhood in a swift and painless departure, the only evidence of its passage the silky lilt of a southern accent; over time, even that vestige faded.

The adjustment to big-city life had been difficult in the beginning. Washington had seemed as foreign to her as Addis Ababa, although she was surprised that the tall buildings had been more of a comfort than she could ever have imagined back in Kentucky. She had always lived in the shelter of the mountains, and now these buildings and monuments loomed over her like protective surrogates of the Appalachians, making her feel safe and nested.

Her deepening relationship with Lawrence Sayles had changed her more profoundly than any other event. It was she who now knew food, wine, cars, clothes. She had a modicum of local fame, just being associated with him. In the dining room of The Heights, she was privy to the intimate discourse of the world's most powerful men. Young as she was, she had a core of quiet confidence and common sense that drew these men to her.

She turned right at the corner of E Street. The lunchtime crowds were pouring onto the sidewalks from the Department of Interior and she was forced to slow her pace. She was not the only one with a plan to catch the first warm rays in weeks. Workers and tourists brushed past her, eating from their lunch bags or rushing away to restaurants. Clare checked her watch. She would have just enough time to wolf down a sandwich somewhere, retrieve her car, and get back to the office. Sayles was compiling a projection of the current Soviet outlook on a broad range of subjects for the President, and Clare had collected portions of the research and would categorize and distill them over the next several weeks. As she walked along, she made mental notes about the order of presentation. A red light stopped her at the crosswalk at Eighteenth Street. Men in business suits crowded her, pushing her forward to the curb. The light turned green. She shifted her briefcase to her other hand and was about to go with the flow of the crowds crossing the street, when a face coming toward her stopped her cold.

In the midst of a throng of perhaps twenty people was a face she knew somehow. She made eye contact with the man behind his round rimless glasses, and that exchange of looks bore into her memory and set off an alarm bell of recognition. Associations whirled around her brain—of stricken voices, shouts, a terrifying flurry of hands. She could hear the voices, but the words were muffled and she could not make them out.

Her face was twisted in a fury of concentration. A great deal seemed to depend on her remembering who the man was. She walked, one slow foot at a time, toward Seventeenth Street, and then all of a sudden the mists disappeared and she remembered. Muddy! Arthur W. Aylesworth, Jr., of the A. W. Aylesworth, Sr., Coal Company, who had caused her father to suffocate in Number 9. He had strolled past her, not a foot away, a toothpick between his teeth and not a care in the world, taking in the blue sky and yellow sun, with the clear-eyed stare of a man with an unstained soul. *His* heart still beat, *his* life progressed. Hillard Barrow lay dead and buried, but Muddy Aylesworth, who would feel the season's change on his face, walked free. Right down to the last cell in her body, she knew she had a moral responsibility to accuse him.

She whirled on her heel and began walking fast in the direction she had come from. Every time her shoes hit the pavement, his name came thundering up to her. Muddy—who had killed her father, and Toby's, who had broken Homer's spirit and sent him back down to the mines, who had cast her mother into impoverished widowhood and an early death—was up ahead somewhere. She began to trot, pushing roughly past pedestrians and ignoring their angry glances. She was into the intersection of Nineteenth and E streets against the light, jumping over car bumpers as drivers braked and blew their horns at her, but her eyes never stopped seeking him in the clot of pedestrians up ahead.

She threaded her way through lunchtime strollers until she spotted his disappearing back and saw him turn south on Nineteenth Street. What was that varmint doing out of the holler?

She was panting hard and felt so warm she unbuttoned her coat, awkwardly tearing it off with one hand, and threw it over her arm. The heavy briefcase was giving her gorilla arms, and she shifted it from hand to hand to relieve the misery.

Three blocks and she still hadn't caught up to him. Every inch of concrete increased her fury, gave her time to compose the sentences of rage and annihilation that she would hurl in his face. Tell him all that he had not given her a chance to scream as his car skidded away in the mud. Tell him that she held him criminally responsible for the death of her father. Tell him to his face in front of the world and watch him be destroyed.

She was almost there. Why was he walking so damned fast? Had he seen her? She panicked thinking he might have recognized her and, knowing what was coming, outrace her.

He turned right on C Street, familiar territory to Clare. The State Department was just a block away; she could see the big red brick building she had left less than fifteen minutes earlier up ahead. Where was he going? What business did a hillbilly like Muddy have in Washington, D.C.? All of a sudden he slowed down, tiring perhaps. She was getting closer to him with every step. She could make out the chalk stripe in his suit. His suit! Muddy Aylesworth owned a suit?

Oh, God, what if he turned into some building before she reached him. She redoubled her efforts, but the briefcase was slowing her down; she pulled it up and clutched it hard to her chest, popping its clasp as she did.

She was close enough to call out his name several times, but the traffic noise covered her voice. She began running again, dodging a fresh swarm of pedestrians out of the Federal Reserve Board. She shouted his name again, louder now.

Startled, Muddy turned at the sound of his name to see a madwoman running toward him. He didn't recognize Clare Barrow of

Mills Bend, Kentucky. All he saw was long hair flying and per-spiration wetting a reddened face. Wild, madwoman eyes.

Her coat was half dragging on the sidewalk, filthy, and she was clutching a huge, bulky briefcase spilling over with papers. He had no idea who she was, but from the look on her face he knew she meant him no good at all. He started to run.

Exiting the State Department after a meeting with Arthur Olson, Tarik saw her racing toward him, chasing a thinnish sandy-haired man with glasses. She had such a look on her face that it brought him up short. He made himself look away from her eyes. Eyes that masked nothing, angry and uncompromising. The most beautiful eyes he had ever seen. She had a common-sense beauty and dead-white skin that glowed with a quality of flushed trans-parency.

But it was her expression that made his blood rush. A hungry look that said she wanted it all. Deserved it all. And it cast a kind of nimbus around her, so that against the backdrop of bland gray faces behind her, Clare stood out as bright and surprising as phos-phorus on a darkened sea.

She was directly in front of the State Department when Muddy made a quick cut across C Street and dashed between the speed-ing cars. She would have done the same, but at the instant her foot touched the pavement, a bus loomed up before her. She heard its roar and felt the cold rush of wind it pushed along, and she would have collapsed under its wheels had not Tarik at the last moment grabbed her arm and jerked her out of its way. The sud-den motion caused her to lose her balance and fall to the street. He pulled her to her feet.

"Get away from me," she snarled. "Get your hands off me." She watched Muddy make it through the traffic to the south side of C Street. "Turn me loose. He's getting away!" But the man wouldn't let her go.

"Hold it, hold it," he said. "Calm down. You're going to get yourself killed."

Clare strained against his arms. She wiggled and fought but he pulled her against him. With a violent jerk of her head, she saw Muddy jog down Twenty-second Street and disappear behind the National Academies of Science.

"Damn!" She twisted back to Tarik and with all the anger she could summon glared at him. "I could have caught him. I was right there."

"You could have gotten killed too. Whatever it was, it can't have been worth that."

"What do you know about it?" she shouted. "Who asked you? I might have been able to make it. My one chance and you ruined it for me. Let me go."

"You won't run into the traffic after him?"

When she refused to answer, he squeezed her tighter in his arms. She could feel the heavy muscles of his thighs and his suit buttons pressed into her chest. His breath was on her face, warm and sweet, and the slight stubble on his cheek scratched her when she struggled against him. Pedestrians walked by, slowed to stare, shook their heads at the scene she was making, walked on.

She was angry and confused, realizing suddenly that if she could feel his buttons, he must be able to feel her breasts. A disturbing sensation crawled along her legs, awful in its pleasantness. When she looked up, he was smiling, reading her mind. Insulted, she stiffened her body.

"All right, I won't run into the traffic. Now let me go." She lowered her eyes. Her face flushed because she could feel acutely every inch of his muscular body.

"You're sure?"

"Yes," she said quietly, turning her face away.

He released her and immediately she got down on her knees and gathered up the papers that were blowing about in the gutter. She let her hair fall over her face. She wanted to cry. She had failed her father, and to compound her sin, her body had betrayed her with this total stranger. It was misery of the worst sort, but she could still salvage some self-respect if only she could get away.

She stuffed the papers into the briefcase. Tarik gathered up a few and offered them to her. She snatched them out of his hand and struggled to her feet. When she wobbled a little, he reached out to steady her.

"Maybe you should sit down for a minute."

"No, I just want to get out of here." She retrieved her dirty coat from the sidewalk. Her hands fluttered up and down, searching for buttons. She patted her hair a little, trying for a restoration of decorum. "Look," she said, "I'm sorry I was rude, but I had a good reason. I appreciate that you probably saved my life and I'm sorry I gave you such a hard time. So thank you." She stuck out her hand and he shook it.

"You're sure you can walk?"

"Yes, thank you." She walked west for a moment before she realized she was going in the wrong direction, turned, walked past him, said thank you again, and limped on.

He ran and caught up with her. "You know, I think you should stop for a moment."

"Leave me alone." She refused to look at him and walked faster.

He took her by the arm and brought her up short. "Look!" he said. She followed the direction of his eyes. "You're bleeding."

She stopped and looked down, aghast that the entire lower portion of her left leg was covered in blood.

"Oh," she said in a quiet, surprised voice. She gave him a bewildered look, clearly not knowing what to do next.

He put his arm around her waist and turned her around, motioning for Stan, who was in the car on the other side of the street, to pick them up.

They headed toward George Washington University Hospital a few blocks away, Clare in the backseat with him, a little dazed, giving him sidelong glances as he held his handkerchief to the gash in her knee. She told him her name. He shook the hand she offered and awkwardly introduced himself. They rode the rest of the way in silence.

He stayed behind in the waiting area while an emergency room doctor took eleven stitches in the two-inch-long cut. He was still sitting there, his long legs stretched out in front of him and his hands interlocked behind his head, when she came out an hour later.

She greeted him shyly, a little embarrassed now by her scene on the sidewalk, but relieved that she would not have to make it home on her own.

Stan waited below, while Tarik took her into the apartment building. He followed her down the hallway, his eyes concentrating on her lanky figure. She was not quite beautiful, but all her features taken together, especially those incredible eyes, and the drumbeat of nervous excitement carried in her bones that conveyed an air of unpredictability, made her seem strikingly attractive and unlike any woman he had ever seen. She had the soft, puffy lips of a child, which parted provocatively with a quick intake of breath when she turned on the first-floor landing and caught his eye. He watched as a look of cool shock came over her face and she quickly turned away. He knew it when he saw it. He could recognize the beauty of inner surety.

With the door unlocked, she invited him in. He hesitated, debating. Finally, he said, "No, I think it would be best if you rested."

Something about his drawling voice made her feel pleasantly at ease. It was calm and soothing and at odds with his looks, which were dark and dramatic. She remembered the sure-handed motion with which he had pulled her up from the pavement. There had been tremendous strength behind it, and yet he had lifted her to her feet and held her there as lightly as if she were a bit of cotton wool. Her rage at him was gone, and in its place a curious excitement. He came too close to her when he spoke, lounged too languidly against her doorway as he said good-bye. Electricity snapped between them and drew her eyes to his mouth. In her bones, without her even knowing it, he had begun to stir some rhythm, and while her conscious mind cried out of the danger, her secret self began to order the cadence of the warm, unspoken implications of his body, taking the measure of his heart. When he asked if he could call her the next day to be certain that she was all right, she said yes. And when he asked her if he might see her again, between the time he posed the question and the time she closed the door, she again said yes.

She met him four times, for dinner or drinks or long walks around the city, before the night in her apartment when she had passed by him on some errand to the kitchen and he had reached out and grabbed her hand, turned it over, and pressed his lips to her palm. She struggled to pull back, because the action of his mouth on her hand had become a slow, thrilling caress of her whole body. A warm tide of feeling sapped her strength and made her knees weak, washing away in its run every well-thought-out plan of her life.

She forced her mind away to Lawrence Sayles and fought to hold on to the image of his face and the grand design she had made for their shared future. But then the pressure of Tarik's mouth, the way he held hers open and worked her tongue with his, made the image of Sayles blur and disappear. Just his tongue evoked sensations she had never felt before. She had not bargained on some other man coming along to rock her senses and her convictions. So for a long, confused moment, she resisted. But finally she began to kiss him back. Her hands came up around his neck and clutched at his hair. For the longest time it was just their mouths, kissing each other into a frenzy.

He walked her into the bedroom and sat her down. He unbuttoned her sweater and ran his tongue down her breast in the blind, instinctive search of ages. He took her taut nipple point into his mouth and began a frantic, insistent suckling that stopped her breath. His hand pushed down between her legs and eased them open. She gritted her teeth and commanded her body to stop, but she was powerless to call a halt. With quick shocks the sensations built, until with a little cry she gave up a part of her she scarcely knew existed. She sat there, dazed and stricken, while he continued working her nipple with his tongue until a deep, agonized shudder signaled his own orgasm.

His head fell into her lap, his face between her thighs, which were smooth and fresh. When he stopped panting, he collected himself and got to his feet. He undressed her with deft motions and laid her on the bed. He undressed himself and got on top of her. With a quick painful thrust he forced her to give up everything—weakness, fear, inhibition, all her schemes. She drew back her legs and made herself a perfect vessel for his pleasure, driving him on with a will to drain him dry. Later, he showed her how he liked to be sucked, gliding her lips back and forth over the smooth, extended flesh. He turned her this way and that, overcome with a fear of finishing it. But he was so aroused he couldn't make it last. He coaxed her over on her side and took her from behind. When it was over, he made himself believe that it had been a metaphor for the rest of their lives. In that moment he knew, beyond reason, beyond logic, she was the one.

It was on a wild, wet night two weeks later that Sylvia O'Dowd, drenched to the bone and weary from chasing cabs, saw them walking together on Fourteenth Street. Discouraged and close to tears, her hairdo and her spirit both wrecked, Sylvia had abandoned any hope of ever making it home and instead had stopped at the bar of the Willard Hotel. Indifferent to the appalled stare of the major domo, she'd thrown herself into a padded chair and ordered a Chivas on the rocks. She'd drunk it down, and although the rain had stopped, was waving for another when she saw them through the window.

Even from a hundred feet away it was clear that the tall, graceful figures moving against the winter wind were lovers. And just as apparent to Sylvia that for Clare, and thus for Lawrence Sayles, everything had been decided.

As they came closer, Sylvia could see their faces very clearly. This time Clare seemed different from when she had met her only weeks before. The eyes that assessed her coolly at the dinner party now burned when they turned on the broad-shouldered young man to whose arm she clung.

Sylvia could feel on the air the sense of elated happiness that came from them; they were both a little drunk on it. She knew the signs, although she could restore those memories only by an act of will; it had been so many years, a thousand, since she had been in love. The involuntary smiles of happiness that curved their lips, the excitement that flashed all around them. The way he bent his head to hers, submissive.

She saw their faces glowing in animation. It could have been the most trivial conversation, but to the one who witnessed them, their fates seemed suspended on every word.

They passed directly by the window. Sylvia saw Clare's brilliant eyes rest on his face a moment. She seemed to be brimming over with vitality and happiness. When he bent to whisper something in her ear, she saw plainly the mirror of Clare's face in his. He held her arm with an air of ownership.

Sylvia sat there with a beating heart, waiting for them to pass, going over things in her mind. Clearly she had been mistaken in her assessment of Clare's relationship with Sayles, or something had gone badly wrong in a very short span of time. She was surprised that she felt a little ashamed that she had seen them, but the moment passed quickly as she turned her thoughts to Sayles. He should have married Clare when he had the chance, Sylvia decided. For the first time in his life, the prince of the republic had turned up a day late and a dollar short.

7

They were in a restaurant near Dupont Circle. "What does he mean to you?" Tarik asked her when they had finished their meal. Clare had spoken of Sayles only in passing, but he inferred from her evasiveness that more than work connected them. He'd never met the man, but he knew him by reputation and because, of course, he was in the headlines. The prospect of so powerful a rival made Tarik uneasy, impatient.

Clare averted her eyes. "He's been a wonderful friend to me, and mentor, since I came to Washington. It's possible I wouldn't have done so well at Georgetown without his help."

"You haven't answered my question." He held her with his eyes and refused to let her look away.

"At one time I had thought that Lawrence Sayles and I would be married." She gazed back steadily at him and let this news sink in.

She couldn't deny what she'd once felt for Sayles and thus betray an honorable man. But she knew that whatever had passed between them, so full of meaning at the time, now seemed as insubstantial as a shadow play. With utter clarity she knew now that Sayles might make her content, but in a lifetime he could never have rocked her in body and soul as Tarik had. He could never have filled her with both dread and longing, the need to go and to stay at the same time, until her mind was so unloosened she was uncertain even of her name.

And more. He was young and, like her, on a mission. He had been steered by Nila, as she had been steered by Homer and Hillard, onto the mission road almost from the day he was born. They imagined they could order the world—or a small part of it, anyway—to their moral requirements. They were instruments of justice, and the context of that responsibility never changed. They intended to measure their self-worth in rights wronged, fathers' fates to be compensated for. They burned with the need for it and made it the rocket fuel of their lovemaking. It made them a little frantic, although Tarik was more successful at disguising this with self-composure than was Clare, who was excitable. They were positive thinkers. Who would not be, when convinced since childhood that each held a reputable place in the larger scheme of things that required neither justification nor apology?

She had planned to marry Lawrence Sayles. "And what about now? What do you feel for him now?" he demanded.

She sat there for the longest time, and then slowly, rhythmically, he felt her answer pulsing up to him through her fingertips, the warm, ever-widening rings of desire that he had felt in the arch of her back and the thrust of her hips when he was inside her. Slow, hurting almost. They melted through the nerves in his fingers, down his chest, until the soft ridge of his body became hard as a rock, making him want it for the rest of his life.

He threw his napkin on the table and got up, tugging at her arm as he stood. He felt as if he were standing at the edge of a precipice. Below him spread an ocean of infinite size, with tides and currents that throbbed in tempo with the beating of his heart. He closed his eyes and consigned himself to it, tumbling, uncertain that he would survive but unable to resist its pull.

She consumed him. He could not finish a thought without thinking of her. Or drive down a street, or knot his tie, or open a book before his obsession would wheel his mind away to some lurid fantasy or imaginary conversation. He couldn't concentrate anymore. She had taken over his life—the way she looked, the manner with which she dealt with her own life. And he had to make it stop, because he had become useless and there was too much to do and almost no time left. They had to settle it between them, and then the reeling and the giddiness and the fever would stop. He had to drive from her the notion that she might belong to Lawrence Sayles, or any man other than himself, for the rest of her life.

He was on his feet, looking down at her. He believed he understood her better than she understood herself. It had all been in her eyes the day she chased Muddy Aylesworth down the street, the day he discovered that he could not go on without passion. That he had to love in some way that made no sense whatsoever.

He pulled her up out of her chair, taking money from his pocket and without counting tossing it onto the table. He steered her out of the restaurant.

He was driving himself tonight; over protest, he had ordered Stanley to stay at home. He took her to Georgetown and parked the car. They were in her apartment. She turned to face him, panting as if she were out of breath.

Her eyes remained fastened to his as she undid her blouse and removed her bra. She dropped her skirt around her ankles, peeled off her stockings and panties, and kicked them away. Then she just stood there. Her breasts were high and large, her legs long, athletic. There were surgical stitches and a crimson bruise at her knee where she had fallen on C Street, and old scars on her other knee and at her forearm.

His eyes lingered on the details—the hair that had fallen away from her shoulders, nipples thick as the ends of his thumbs, the slightly swollen belly. *It is very possible that I am losing my mind, that it's already gone.* He took a step toward her. The anticipation was painful. "You are so white," he said.

He took her into the bedroom and sat her down in the small armchair alongside the bed. Naked, she opened her legs and slung them over the arms of the chair, knowing instinctively that he would want her to do this. He turned on the bedside table lamp so that he could see better. Still dressed, he knelt prayerfully before her and kissed her lightly on the lips. *Rest your head back a little bit. Relax your shoulders,* he said. He began an inspection of her body with his right hand until he reached the exposed area between her legs. He massaged the damp rose-colored flesh, all the while staring intently at it, slack-mouthed. He began speaking to her there, as if her sex had a life of its own. *Is it too fast? No, no. Just like that.* He parted the soft flesh and worked one finger up into her. *You're so swollen.* He moved the finger up and down, feeling her reflexively tighten and surround it. Her body stirred against the palm of his hand. It was difficult for her to keep still, but he was taking his time, all the time talking. *You're so soft. You're so wet. You knew, didn't you? You knew I wanted you to let me do this. I knew, I knew. I just wanted to see it.*

His voice was husky. She could hardly hear what he was saying. *Okay, Okay,* he said, *okay,* unable to resist any longer the sight of her open before him. He lowered his mouth to her and in one soft gulp took her in, his tongue searching until he found the small tight bud hidden there. Instantaneously, she cried out.

His fingers found her nipples, then her mouth. He ran a finger around her teeth until she caught it up and began to suck. Throughout it all it was her heart, beating up to him, partnering his own. He felt full of love for her. He had wanted her completely open to him and she had done that. They had experienced it together.

It was no longer possible to make it last. He got to his feet and bent at the knees so that he was level with her. With her eyes on his swollen penis, she slid her backside down into the cushion of the chair, her knees in the air, her feet against the backs of her thighs, exposing herself to him completely. She was without shame, she showed him. His penis leapt and grew harder.

The instant he was in her he was liberated. They both watched as he pumped hard, groaning loudly in the anguished strain of finishing it. In the moment when he emptied himself into her, with his inward eye he saw his universe with stunning clarity. He felt the blood and pulse of his life gather forever around the clear and consistent core that was Clare. He had plumbed some place within himself where passion could companion his natural composure. Once discovered, he would never give it up again.

It was hardly Clare's fondest dream to have Stan Cobb accompany them on any night. But on this night she found it particularly unpleasant to have him along. Tarik had pressured her gently, saying that he could not leave the big man behind.

Clare approached Stanley the way one befriends a very large animal, downwind and with a great deal of caution. She had seen the Colt revolver that he carried everywhere in a shoulder holster, although the notion that he might have to use it remained unreal to her.

When Tarik had formally introduced her to him the day after the incident in front of the State Department, Stanley hadn't tried for a minute to hide his dislike. He had looked at her as if she were something bad he'd found in his soup, rolled his eyes, and mumbled, "Okay, if that's what you want, boy-o."

Startled and a little abashed, Clare had stayed out of his way ever since. Tarik had a curious, and to her mind misplaced, attachment to him, but she had no choice except to put up with it.

"Another five, ten miles," Stanley said, aiming his mouth over the front seat. He got into a fight with the roadmap, trying to refold it, and after much cursing wadded it up in a ball. "Can't nobody make nothin' right anymore." He threw it on the floor of the front seat. "Well, we'll get there, boy-o." He looked at Tarik in the rearview mirror and gave him a sprightly wink.

"Well, it's the end of an era, I guess. 'Course, I never wanted to get married myself," he volunteered. "Not that I didn't have the chances. Believe me, I can tell you some stories. Had a broad once—" He glanced quickly at Clare in the mirror, saw her give him a stony look, but decided he would not let that stop him. Ever.

"She was something. Short, dark, tiny little bit of a thing, perfect to my mind. And, get this, a professional house painter! Ever hear of such a thing? Me neither. First lady house painter I ever met, before or since." He shook his head in appreciative wonder. "And was she strong! She'd slam a fourteen-foot extension ladder up the side of a two-story house and bang up there with a gallon of paint in each hand and a horsehair brush in her teeth. Get after those eaves and gutters in no time. And she'd scrape the damn place first too. That was some woman." He paused to savor the memory.

"How much farther do you think, Stanley?" Clare thought he had finished.

But he hadn't. "There was a catch, naturally. 'Bout four, five months later, she starts the usual thing—like every other woman on God's green earth. Marry me, give me some babies. I liked that gal better than I liked any gal before or since, but Jesus Christ, the old ball and chain! Oops—almost got by the exit." He pumped the brakes and slowed enough to take them off at the Viers Mill Village exit.

Turning right, they drove another two miles, down a two-lane road shaded by overreaching oaks, until they arrived at a low-slung nondescript municipal building with a sign on the front that read TRAFFIC COURT/VIOLATIONS/JUSTICE OF THE PEACE. Once inside, with the license applications completed, the fees paid, and all the necessities required by the State of Maryland for a legal marriage attended to, Tarik and Clare stood, Stan behind them, before a judge named O'Toole, who would marry them.

It was her bad luck to think then of Lawrence Sayles. The day he'd returned from Geneva she had gone to his office. He had led her around to the chair beside his desk, nervous and wary.

"I tried to get you at home on the phone a number of times, Clare," he began. "I know how hard it is to talk in the office. Everybody around everywhere. I thought maybe we might give a dinner party later this week. I thought maybe you could work out some things with Preston in advance."

He had never used *we* before.

"Lawrence," she started, and then quickly stopped. She assumed that she was about to break his heart and was tongue-tied with guilt. She began again. She told him about Muddy Aylesworth, her gashed leg, Tarik. That their relationship had taken hold almost overnight. That she hadn't planned any of it. Finally, she told him she was going to be married. At that he visibly started, then just as quickly the old familiar mask came down over his face and his features resumed their normal composure.

He said nothing for a long time. Then he said, "Well, congratulations are in order, then." He got up quickly and moved back to his desk chair. He sorted through papers and began discussing the Geneva talks. But shortly his voice trailed off and the silence between them became so oppressive that Clare finally stood and said a weak good-bye. In the office he was cordial; they discussed only work. A few days later he announced that the talks were resuming and he returned to Europe. He was so diffident, so unmoved, that Clare decided finally, with a regret that surprised her, that she had misinterpreted his intentions all along. Perhaps he had never meant to marry her.

Tarik took her hand in his and pushed the gold band onto her finger. Later that night, after they had made love and fallen asleep, Clare dreamed that she and Homer were riding Isaac, his old mule. She dreamed she reached up her hand to touch an extravagantly flowering dogwood tree and the blooms showered down on them. And then the moon was out, and they were picking corn. They pulled the tall, heavy stalks toward them to snatch the golden cobs, when the stalks began to wail, softly at first, then louder and louder. She woke up, screaming, to the sound of a police siren going by.

Tarik pulled her up next to him, stroking her hair until they fell asleep under the weight of their infinite expectations, young and convinced they could take things as they came.

8

Brevet Colonel Walter White-Lyons had made the bomb himself, so there were no second thoughts about its getting the job done. And he was gratified in retrospect that he'd gone with the basic works—plastique, detonating cap, radio transmitter. Nothing too elaborate or unstable. Just the sine qua non of the coal miner. And the terrorist.

That last made him uncomfortable. He touched the insignia of his rank, then absently stroked his battle ribbons, reassuring evidence of his own legitimacy. He pulled his sidearm from its holster and checked the clip. From start to finish, the whole operation had a pleasing simplicity. It was Dinh-Hoa who was proving rather more problematic. The pastry chef's tall white toque had become an exclamation point to his hysteria, and White-Lyons's impatience was keeping pace with Dinh-Hoa's rising panic. He lofted noisy imprecations to some Vietnamese deity, quaked violently, inhaled loudly to connote renewed courage, collapsed anew. The ebb and flow of soul-shattering terror.

"Calm now, Dinh-Hoa. Nothing to fret about." After thirty-three years in the kingdom, White-Lyons still carried in his voice the evidence of his English birth and breeding. "There's the good fellow." White-Lyons poured him another rum and the tiny cook drank it down gratefully. "Petals, remember how His Majesty loves your little petals."

Dinh-Hoa tried again, but his hands clenched the pastry bag so tight that the rosettes that in previous times had seemed actually redolent of perfume were tonight blistered smears of whipped cream trailing off into a procession of squirts and blobs. He was pale and sweaty and his eyes were pathetically red-rimmed from weeping.

Five years earlier, addicted to his *vacherin glacé* and vanilla

soufflé, Turkit had had Dinh-Hoa kidnapped from the kitchen of
the George V in Paris. Had him torn away from his copper bowl
while he was stiffening egg whites, his wire whisk still in his
hand. He'd been turning out his exquisite tear-stained pastries
ever since, a prisoner.

Now all Dinh-Hoa had to do to get back to Paris and his family
was to roll the pastry cart into the dining room, push it up to His
Most Inestimable Majesty, and one gets his ticket out and the
other gets his ticket punched. White-Lyons rocked back and forth
on his heels. It had a Zen quality of wholeness to it that he appreciated agreeably.

With a final entreaty White-Lyons left off with Dinh-Hoa,
pushed open the pantry door, and walked to a narrow hallway
lined with cupboards. At one of them he crouched down and, removing a small key from his breast pocket, unlocked the cupboard. He moved his fingers around the pots and pans until he
found the transmitter. Just checking.

He relocked the cupboard and walked the twenty or so steps to
the kitchen. The cavernous room was a hot and steamy tempest of
cooks, sauciers, scullions, feather pluckers, and slaves staggering
under the weight of solid silver trays mountained with food.
White-Lyons stood there amid the tumult and selectively dismissed all but the most irrelevant sounds. The quiet rustle of the
date trees, the steady hum of the generators, the flipping of his
heart. The shutters were open to receive the evening breeze and
he discerned the rich scent of the coffee beans ripening in the terraced garden outside. It seemed to him that the wind had driven
the fresh smell of the sea across the five hundred miles of desert
from the Gulf of Aden. Absurd, he knew; much too far. Yet on
this night of nights, he had the notion he was aware of wind
change and bird cry, in rhythm with the oceans.

He swung the kitchen door open softly and with a quick step
was in the dining hall. Four dozen men sat the length of a long,
narrow table, all in various stages of stupor, their fat behinds
weighted to their cushions from five hours of eating and drinking
and getting their piece of the pie. Through an eye-stinging haze of
frankincense, White-Lyons could see Turkit, His Most Matchless
and Law-Loving Majesty, at the table's head, and arranged hier-
archically around him the royal relations, the Crown Council,
tribal chieftains, two foreign diplomats, a contingent of British
businessmen, fortune tellers, and the local Rolls-Royce importer.

White-Lyons could hardly believe his eyes, although he had
witnessed a hundred such debauches in the past three decades.

The glint from dozens of silver candelabra illuminated a table heaped so high with food that it had buckled here and there from the sheer weight of the delicacies. The floor of the dining hall was laid end to end with precious carpets, and across these were strewn another carpet of flowers, so that everywhere a guest's foot rested it crushed some fragile orchid or lily. And throughout the hall there were men unconscious from drink, or fornicating with slave girls, or relieving themselves in buckets held by servants, or vomiting so they could go on eating. It was a spectacle of such violent and lavish corruption that White-Lyons could hardly bear it.

The food had been bought in Bahrain and ferried to the kingdom in a McDonnell Douglas DC10. Its arrival had been so exciting to the populace that thousands of the ragtag and starving had appeared ghostlike at the airport to press their faces against the chain-link fence and gape at the crates stenciled LOUIS ROEDERER and US GRADE A PRIME BEEF— GOVERNMENT INSPECTED. Once or twice they tried to rush forward onto the tarmac and White-Lyons had been forced to order the household guard to drive them back with tear gas, but Turkit had countermanded the order and demanded live ammo. White-Lyons could hear them outside the kitchen now, utterly famished, their bones poking through their skin like carpenters' angles, sucking and slurping on every feather and fish head wiped from the plates of the guests of the Royal Plate Scrapers.

White-Lyons closed his eyes and conjured an image of the coming slaughter. He shivered. Had he been less ardently anti-Marxist, he might have admitted that his understanding of History had made him fearless, even endorsed the bloodletting; he supposed that every assassin took this as his blessing. He would kill Turkit himself, as he should have years ago, and then the long, imprisoned night would be over and none of them would fear the sunrise.

In his mind's eye he could see coming dimly toward him all his dreams, like a ship cutting through the fog, and on its prow, glistening and white, a bowsprit prince to remind the people of that which was good and decent and all that they could be. Later, when everything had settled down, he would tell Tarik of the deal he had been forced to strike with Hadi. All along he had known he would have to come to terms with the old murderer. White-Lyons had dickered with him throughout the night, threatening, cajoling, in the end even offering cash. He had been at his wit's end until Hadi finally had made plain what he really wanted and they had struck a deal. A deal so simple they had both laughed at its childishness.

White-Lyons was brought up short when he opened his eyes to find those of Turkit, opaque and hooded, staring into his own with a ghastly intensity from across the room. The muscles in the king's face danced as he twisted a lank, dirty strand of hair around his fingers and threaded it between his rouged lips, his eyes fastened all the time on those of White-Lyons. *God help me, he knows. Surely that is an accusation forming in those feral eyes.* Turkit held a fat fig in his left hand and filled his right with the lush breast of a mahogany-colored young girl sent along by some sub-Saharan president-for-life as an anniversary gift. When his fingers began plucking at her nipple and his lips rolled back over his gums in a smile, White-Lyons exhaled and relaxed.

"How much, my friends, like the humid secretions of a sexually aroused woman is the juice of the fig," Turkit declared. "How much like a good juicy woman, and I mean this very, very sincerely—and I certainly ought to know, hadn't I?—is this juicy piece of flesh. Ripe for the eating." He squeezed the girl between her legs so hard she yelped, and all the men laughed.

White-Lyons pushed open the kitchen door to look for Dinh-Hoa. "Here we go," he said when he found him, still clenching his pastry bag.

"Tieu-ta, toi so!" the little cook wept.

"Dung so. You have nothing to fear. Get a grip on."

"Cai nay that xau!" the chef cried.

"Khong sao dau! Understand?" White-Lyons roared. "You can't get hurt. Move your arse."

He yanked Dinh-Hoa to the pastry cart, clamped his hands around its brass rail, and with a hard shove sent him flying down the corridor and out into the dining hall, where he was quickly swallowed up in the turmoil of the room. White-Lyons tracked him by his bobbing white toque, rising on his tiptoes once or twice when, like foam on the sea, it disappeared in the crowd, all the while listening as Turkit went on in his same bemused vein:

"And, loyal understrappers, who could fault me on this day of days, when we celebrate that moment forty-four years ago when fate blessed me and this some-parts-green and some-parts-gritty kingdom—"

Dinh-Hoa laid into the cart, head down, heels digging in, picking up speed as he careened around scurrying servants, upset the orchestra, dodged the shambling dogs, overturned piss pots—"by escorting my venerable father into paradise, albeit a year or two before his time—"

Turkit halted in mid-speech as the cart, sailing from a hearty shove from the long-gone Dinh-Hoa rolled solidly into his backside. The humor that had been playing on his features flew away and his face became dark and miserable. His guests gasped and each man pulled his shoulders up around his ears lest his Most Fair-Minded Majesty find fresh inspiration to savagery in their long, inviting necks. But after taking in the mess of pastries, particularly his beloved charlotte russe, Turkit released a squeak of joy and produced a smile. The girl's breast was discarded as he rushed to fill his hand with an even creamier goody. He shifted his three hundred pounds and struggled to reach the cart, and as he did, dozens of the tiny diamonds sewn onto his garment tore their threads and spilled onto the floor. One of the royal nephews furtively pocketed a few.

Turkit wrestled the pastry onto the table. He stuck out his bottom lip in disappointment over the disreputable rosettes, then ran his finger through them and licked it extravagantly.

"I was speaking of a concern of great interest to the general public . . ." He searched his memory. He knitted together his plucked brows. The light dawned. "Ah, yes! For taking my esteemed father to paradise and making me king, for speaking of recreation and procreation in the same breath—"

White-Lyons retreated to the pantry, unlocked the cupboard, and removed the transmitter. He inserted the tiny key into the unlocking device and activated the transmitter. He walked in the direction of the dining hall until he approached the swinging door. He spread his legs and braced himself, then set his finger lightly on the flashing red button.

"—for the seed planted in amusement now," Turkit went on, "can in years to come sprout into a warrior ready to give one's enemies a good trouncing. For even with a just and right-thinking monarch such as myself, and I mean this very, very sincerely, enemies proliferate with the speed and profusion of beans on our beloved coffee bushes—"

And with that, the charlotte russe exploded, the room filled with light, and the head of His Most Unbeatable Majesty was blasted from its shoulders and streaked across the room like a cream-dappled comet with a bloody tail.

9

Clare began, "I found this road yesterday—"

"Road?"

"Well, actually it's more of a path."

"That sounds more like it." Tarik lay back on the bed, mellow after their lovemaking. Sunrise was only minutes away but their bedroom was dark, shuttered against the heat and lit by a single kerosene lamp.

"Anyway, all it needs is a blade taken over it for about three-quarters of a mile to make it accessible. Just some grading with a bulldozer in that one spot and then the truck can get through."

"What about the wives, Clare?"

"I was talking about the road to the health clinic."

"I know, but what about the wives?"

"Can I talk to you about the clinic first?"

"Yes, but you have this slippery way of getting out of telling me what you're going to do about Turkit's wives."

"His widows, you mean."

"All right, his widows. And his children, and grandchildren. There must be dozens of Turkit's relatives still living here. Yesterday, outside my office, six of the wives showed up with lunch for me—quail eggs. And *boudins noir*. Where do they get this stuff? I walk from one office to the next and there are nieces and cousins and aunts trailing behind me, picking lint off my suit, trying to straighten my collar. Asking a million questions. What are you doing to get rid of the wives?"

"In a minute."

He rolled his eyes, pulled a pillow behind his head, and made a big show of settling down into the mattress. "Okay, the clinic."

"It's the prototype for all the others that will follow. Really simple construction—cinderblocks all around, three windows, tin

110

roof, one entryway. The blocks are already made. Everything is warehoused and can be ready to go overnight."

He gave her a look.

"Well, in a couple of days, anyhow. It's not much more than a shack, but it's a start. It's easy."

In the lamplight she appeared nunlike to him, the white sheet tucked up around her chin and the ever-present three-ring notebook open in her hands.

"Nothing's easy here."

"I know, but I'm thinking positively, that's all."

"How are you going to equip the clinic?" He pulled the notebook toward him so he could read her notes in the dim light.

"I've asked the World Health Organization for a definite date for the arrival of the representatives, and they've sent me a bill of lading for the stuff that's already on the way—examination tables, equipment, instruments, medicine, supplies, just the basics to get up and running. And of course I'm begging for doctors and nurses."

"How did you get out there?"

"Nal took me in the Land-Rover."

"You mean that heap that I saw steaming in the courtyard yesterday?"

"It's all we've got."

"I bet it has a hole in the radiator the size of a fist."

"We took water with us."

"Did you use it all?"

"Uh-huh . . ."

"So there was none left for you to drink if you'd broken down."

"We didn't break down, did we? Anyway, what do you know about radiators? Homer taught me more about car engines when I was five than you'd figure out in a lifetime."

"Did he teach you how to survive in one-hundred-twenty-degree heat with no water?"

"Of course. He taught me everything. I'll teach you one day, if you let me finish. Anyway, I'm not going to rely just on the UN for all this stuff. Arthur Olson has promised me that more medical supplies for the clinics will be shipped over along with the road-building machinery he has scheduled to fly in next week. That's where I'm hoping to get that bulldozer, by the way. He also promised me that he'd get the State Department to make up some sort of announcement that could be sent out to American medical schools to solicit fourth-year students for service here. Actually, I have my own contacts at State. I might try on my own, and I think we ought to seriously consider asking the Peace Corps."

"We have three doctors in the country. One is Howard Van Damm, whom you know. The other two graduated from the universities in Ankara and Damascus, so I can't make any promises."

She took the notebook out of his hands and snapped it shut. "Olson's priorities are lawyers and bankers and military advisers. Doctors and medical personnel do not take precedence on his list."

"Only for the time being," Tarik interjected, but Clare wasn't listening.

"Actually, I think I'll intercept him when he shows up for your seven o'clock meeting, if you don't mind."

"I don't mind."

"Or maybe I ought to talk to Elliott Tomlinson. That would get on Olson's nerves."

"And mine."

"Yeah, but it might get Olson moving for me."

"The last thing on Tomlinson's mind is the health and welfare of the people. He's busy doing spook stuff and trying to outfox me."

"Anyway"—she turned back to her notebook—"I've got to figure this out." Her eyes glazed over as her mind calculated the benefit-loss of Olson versus Tomlinson. "Yeah, Olson is my best bet. And I really need that 'dozer."

She had spent her first weeks in the kingdom in a near panic. Happy to be married and in love, yes, but what exactly would she do with herself in this god-forsaken place for the rest of her life? Clearly, there was no call for the civilized diplomatic and negotiating skills she had learned from Lawrence Sayles.

Then, on a day when the heat was so stifling she could not bear to be outside, she came upon one of Turkit's granddaughters in the throes of a tubercular fit. That brassy cough had evoked memories of the old miners of Mills Bend, their lungs wrecked by black lung; Homer had hacked like that when he called her from the company store, just before she left for the kingdom.

She put her arms around the little girl until she calmed her lungs. She helped her sip from a bottle of water. The cough was dry now, unproductive, but in a few years she would be bringing up pussy, purulent phlegm. Clare had seen so many people coughing bloody sputum since she arrived in the kingdom that she was almost used to it. She checked the patch on her forearm where Dr. Van Damm had administered the tuberculosis test and felt grateful to see there was no discoloration on her own skin. She was surrounded by ill and dying children and adults. Hunkered down on a Persian Mulberry rug that ran the entire four thousand feet of the hall, a sudden realization rocketed her out of the honeymoon reverie that had enthralled her for two months. Her mission was swiftly defined. Turkit had cared nothing that the people were starved and debilitated by disease; he preferred it, in fact. A population too ill to walk could hardly rise up and cut his throat.

Dr. Van Damm, whom the State Department had appointed to oversee the health of Tarik and the American delegation, agreed to administer the medical aspects of the vaccination program, but the overall responsibility was Clare's. No easy task, since there were no roads, no telephones, no nurses, no medical supplies, no medicines to speak of, and no understanding of basic disease prevention. But she had made up her mind.

Tarik was out of bed and dressing. "Promise me you'll be careful, okay?" he asked her. "I don't want anything to happen to you on these little adventures with Nal."

"All right, but ask Olson to help me, will you?"

"On one condition."

"What condition?"

"That you do something about the wives."

By six forty-five she had already pressed her case with Arthur Olson. She liked to get an early start, before the sun reflected heat off the buildings like a grill.

On days when she wasn't roaming the countryside, she explored the capital. Her escort and chauffeur was Nal, who was White-Lyons's batman and who spoke perfect English, and a bodyguard named Het, who wore his hair long and curly, and crisscrossed ammunition belts over his shoulders. His left hand was wrapped around his knife hilt; he filled his right with an old-fashioned, gas-fueled Bren machine gun. Het never spoke and Clare at first supposed this was because he was as big as the biblical Goliath and his size rendered words superfluous. Later she came to understand that the people of this country had so long ago surrendered their will that they had forfeited their tongues in the bargain.

Het opened the towering cedar doors of the seventeenth-century limestone palace and cleared a path as Clare and Nal plunged into the suffocating heat, into the purgatory that was the country's only city.

The capital carried the kingdom's history on its torporous

breath. Around dusty alleys and sun-baked squares, it was there to be found—a fifteen century spectacle of depravity, double crosses, vengeance, mind-boggling violence, and every imaginable excess of food, sex, and money-spending undiluted by any sense of personal restraint. If the lowland people longed for anything of beauty or poetry, they had to find it within themselves, for except for the mountainous Sur region, the place was one continuous rock without a blade of grass. Nothing but unremitting, detestable barrenness.

Four crumbling mud walls enclosed the town in all its appalling swirl. People and their pathetic animals struggled down airless, catacomblike streets. Dogs snarling over food scraps; the aromas of cinnamon and burnt sugar mingling with that of raw sewage; cannon fire thundering the arrival of dawn, midday, and sunset; women balancing piles of rags and cheap household goods on their heads; stick-thin boys driving sheep along in ragged formation; hundreds of people and animals somehow squeezing through labyrinthine streets, shuffling on in the ongoing drama of close-quartered living—and all of it fermenting under a sun that was colorless with heat by seven in the morning.

Five- and six-story buildings made of stone and mud loomed over dirt paths. The less well-made houses were subject to the erosion of time and nature. Masonry, some of it a thousand years old, periodically fractured from its mortar and crashed down on the heads of pedestrians. Better homes were constructed of limestone blocks fitted together without mortar, whitewashed, with lacy bas-reliefs and hand-carved wooden balconies where old men gathered in the early evening to play dominoes.

Well, at least they aren't starving anymore, Clare consoled herself as she walked along. Food distribution centers were up and running in neighborhoods around the city, sometimes from the tailgates of army trucks. The countryside was another story. Without a trained civil service to manage government services, progress came slowly.

The deeper the human current carried Clare and her escort into the city, the narrower the streets and the more surreal the action. The taste of the sesame and honey simmering together on braziers to make a sticky candy, floated on the air to the tip of her tongue. A glassy-eyed lunatic, waving a length of leather like a whip, scattered the crowd, until Het subdued him and handed him over to a passing policeman. Iron clanged on iron; behind a heavy door a blacksmith worked a glob of molten iron. Clare felt a tug at her sleeve: a hideously scarred man pleading for pennies. Nal tried to shoo him away but Clare dug into her pockets for a few coins and pushed them into his hand. They wandered into the bazaars but there was nothing to buy.

The entire population seemed afflicted. Many were missing limbs, or were wasted by disease, had cataract-beclouded eyes, or faces disfigured by bulbous birthmarks. They were ragged and none seemed all of a piece or looked healthy, the walking dead of centuries of abuse and neglect. They scutted by, cautious not to look her in the face, or let her see theirs.

At first she had tried to catch the eye of the most pathetic cases and show them a reassuring smile.

"It might be a good idea if you didn't smile so much, or so openly, madam," Nal chided her, provoking another of his longwinded lectures—Nal's book of etiquette for underdeveloped nations.

"Smiling won't convince them that you like them. In this place, genuine affection and a warm smile aren't necessarily synonymous. As a matter of fact, my brother Arn once cut the throat of a man he professed to admire—and at the time he was grinning ear to ear."

"The man who was murdered?"

"Arn."

Clare was having trouble adjusting to a society where disputes were regularly settled with a bullet to the brain or a blade in the heart, while Nal could appreciate a good murder as smoothly as he did a well-cut pair of worsted trousers on an English gentleman.

"Anyway"—he looked around—"there's absolutely nothing to smile about in this place. Everyone's starving or sick. Or half dead. Only a lunatic would smile in a place like this. That's what they think you are when they see you grinning.

"Of course," he went on, "I don't want to tell you what to do, but it might be a good idea to behave with more reserve. You have a certain status now. You've been elevated to a very rarefied position. You can't go around showing your teeth. Shopkeepers smile. Salesmen smile. Whores smile—or they do until they get your money. But the wife of the king definitely doesn't. She possesses a certain . . . *aura*. Serenity. A reassuring wisdom. A sense of quietude within and without. She is"—he let the word spill softly from his tongue—"*still*.

"But—" and he put up his hand to silence her protest. "Not that I don't know that this kind of composure comes with age, but the people will be more inclined to treat you with genuine affection when you deliver on your promises, not when you're showing them your teeth."

Clare had quit defending herself to Nal; it wore her out. Anyway, she had come to believe that relentless in his criticism, pompous and thoroughly self-satisfied though he might be, Nal was almost always right.

"You should take my word on this, you know," he added. "I'm very good at these things."

He began eating the fig he was carrying. "I'm not advising you to be false, you understand. I just think it might be a good idea to make an adjustment. I'm thinking that it might be wise to try to seem a little less emotional. A little more reserved. A little less American. A little more . . . *Canadian*."

So she stopped smiling quite so broadly.

In a place where it was impossible to lay hands on so much as a penny nail, Nal could find anything. Somehow he had procured for Clare a typewriter, writing paper from Harrods, an ancient but still functioning Land-Rover that he used to chauffeur her around, hair rollers, jars of Vaseline for her sunburned skin, Pears soap. Where he got these goodies Clare could not guess, nor did she want to know the details. Suffice that if Clare wanted it, Nal found it.

He knew the city, the whole country, in fact, like the back of his hand. He could recite its history as if it were the intimate story of his own family.

Understanding the kingdom, he liked to tell her, was equivalent to how much one's imagination could encompass. At times it was epic—warrior kings with unpronounceable names riding at the head of thundering armies, back and forth across the plains to spiking mountaintops. Just as easily, it could swing wide to the most petty and depraved forms of human behavior. This may have had as much to do with the unfortunate geography of the place as with the nature of its population, for by and large the people of the kingdom were ambitious, freedom-loving, and agreeable. But with the country closed off almost entirely by mountains, and only a slender portion of the rubbly plain jutting tonguelike to the sea, they were completely isolated and lived happily out of harmony with the rest of the world.

Hidden away, they invented an inverted culture that reflected the ruthless changeability of their desert and the implacability of their great dolomitic mountains. The soft, humanized side of their nature must have come from the veldt at the mountain foothills of the Sur territory, which resembled East Africa and was covered with lacy maidenhair ferns and oleanders wherever the coffee trees weren't blooming.

In its entire history, the place had never been conquered by an outside force. A dozen different generals at the head of enormous armies had struggled Hannibal-like up over the mountains and down to the plain, only to be turned around, their arms and legs gone, the bodies of their dead left to melt in the sun. Persians, Greeks, Romans, Turks—all had at one time stood on the mountaintops beating their chests and then had their brains knocked out for their hubris. The Portuguese in the seventeenth century, and the French in the early eighteenth, had pushed in from Yemen and Muscat and been routed.

The internal politics of the kingdom were especially unpleasant. Century after century, king after king had employed only the most direct methods of assuming power, and only in aberrant instances had that method not included making some other power seeker pay for his ambition with his life. Turkit came to power in 1919 by stalking up to his father the king as he was about to eat one of the thin crepelike pancakes smeared with burnt sugar that is the national addiction, and bashing in his brains with a teapot that was part of a silver service sent along by George V.

Greedy and ambitious, Turkit invited the British into the kingdom in the same year. Within months they had turned the country into a virtual English preserve, subsidizing him to the tune of millions of pounds every year. British officers trained and led the nation's small but top-rated army; British mercenaries made up two-thirds of the fighting force. A Royal Air Force base was built at Hirth and British advisers administered every government agency. British oil exploration at Duru and commercial interests were given favored status.

Appalled by the state of things in the kingdom, in the 1930s and '40s the British had begun halfhearted attempts to change some of the worst aspects of Turkit's rule and correct the deplorable conditions of the people. A development department was established, but by and large Turkit did exactly as he pleased and the British looked the other way. Even after he kicked them out in a fit of nationalism following the Suez crisis and allowed himself to be courted by the Soviets, many top-level officers and administrators, like White-Lyons, stayed behind to run the country.

But current events did not capture Clare's imagination the way the ancient history did. When Nal would go misty-eyed with tales of perfume caravans rolling from Sheba across the kingdom's arid plain to Muscat, chin in hand, eyes closed, Clare would dream along.

She rested in the heat of the day. She stripped and stretched out on the George III mahogany settee in their bedroom because the silk upholstery was cool on her skin. Turkit had had a positive passion for English antique furniture, silver, objects of vertu, porcelain, decorations, watches, scientific instruments. He had kept an agent on retainer in London whose sole job it was to cull from British auction houses, estate sales, and private collections the finest examples of Georgian decorative art that money could buy. In the 1920s and early 1930s, these objects were shipped to the kingdom by the carload.

Clare slept for an hour, not dreaming. When she awakened, she meditated on her dilemma for another twenty minutes. But by the time she was up and dressed and Nal was tapping lightly at her door, she was no closer to constructing the perfect sentence with which to tell the wives that after a lifetime in the palace, they would have to move on.

At one time there were more than three hundred wives in the west wing of the palace or squirreled away in houses just inside the city walls. But toward the end of his life, Turkit had become so obese that his penis could be liberated from under the mountain that was his abdomen only by the most slippery and time-consuming methods and actual intercourse with the wives became extraordinarily difficult. He would be carried into the west wing, deposited on a priceless settee reinforced with eight-by-eight pieces of lumber, and select the one, two, or three wives he wanted to amuse himself with. In the end, however, the actual act had more to do with engineering than Eros and the wives were invariably left underused and unsatisfied.

Some of the wives were elderly, women who had wisely melted to the background when Turkit was on the scene and saved themselves from banishment. Some were middle-aged mothers. But most were young, gifts from clan chiefs currying favor or tokens marking anniversaries or birthdays from fellow despots of the sub-Sahara. A few had been able to hang on to their virginity in the face of Turkit's avoirdupois. By the time he was assassinated, the wives had been reduced to a mere thirty-two.

The west wing was enormous, room after insanely lavish room. Once a thousand servants polished its acres of marble, arabesqued ceilings, precious woods inlaid with gold and silver. Thousands of workmen encrusted every available surface with rubies, emeralds, pearls, diamonds. Colossal crystal vases held stalks of imported lilies and gladiola. Chandeliers dripped teardrop crystals. The furniture was a mix of English Regency and Oriental—Syrian and Turkish—upholstered with fabric shot with real gold and silver threads or covered in buttery Hermès leather. It was sumptuous, suffocating, and should have been ridiculous. But taken all together, the gold, silver, ivory, mahogany, and jewels were homogenous somehow, startling. Clare was mesmerized whenever she went there. While Turkit appalled the world with his massacres, terrified his people with murder and lunatic thinking, he had created within the palace an oasis so precious, so sensible of beauty and unremitting luxe that it wobbled even the most ordered mind.

But after he grew old and fat, Turkit didn't care to be reminded that he'd lost his sex drive and turned his back on the wives. The place began to look like an out-of-season hotel, the wives standing around waiting for that all-important guest to come back.

Some of them fit the stereotype—languid, sultry-eyed, gowned in gauze and draped over priceless furniture in postures of ennui. Most of the wives had lived away from the world for so long that their minds had gone to gauze as well. When Turkit was killed, they had no purpose. They were irritable most of the time. None knew how to take care of herself outside the palace. None cared to try. All fretted because Tarik, who should have become their master, had no use for them. They devoted themselves to needlepoint, grew pudgy, got sloppy. They talked about sex incessantly. With that many women locked up together, premenstrual tension ran high.

They had voted Jule, who was younger than Clare, their spokeswoman in all discussions.

"Why can't you share?" Jule demanded when Clare arrived with Nal.

"Share what?"

"Your husband."

"I'm not going to share my husband!"

Jule narrowed her eyes at her. "That's a limited kind of thinking. You're not going to be a wife for very long if you keep that up. Oh, everything is working out for you now because you've been married only a few months. Wait and see. In a year or two he'll be bored with you in bed and he'll come snooping around down here on some pretext or other. Is everybody getting enough to eat? How is the furniture holding out? That kind of thing. They all start out the same way—wondering if those are really goosedown feathers in the bed. Poking around with his finger. Then he'll finally succumb. Why don't you just let it happen now? It will make things easier in the long run."

"No."

"Or the reverse: five years go by. You have a few children. You've put on a little weight. You're worn out, and to tell the truth, this life is not as much fun as it used to be. He's not a happy man. The weight of the world is on his shoulders. You are tired of hearing his complaints and you coax him down to us. You are free to go to Geneva to shop."

"That will never happen."

Jule sighed melodramatically, took a moment to confer with the other wives, then tried another tack.

"We have children," she said. "Only a few, although that blame can be laid on Turkit's doorstep, as you know, but still, there are a few children."

"I promise you the children will be cared for as well. I will make arrangements to have each of you and your children be given enough money to survive until you find someone to support you."

"What's that mean, 'someone to support you'?"

"Well, don't you want to get married?"

"Not particularly."

"Don't you want to have a man to look after you and your children?"

"Look at how we live." Jule made a wide sweep with her arm so that Clare could take in the Bohemian glass chandeliers, the beds inlaid with mother-of-pearl, the immaculate marble floors. "Everyone is hungry out there. Or sick. Why would we want to go out there?"

"That's changing, Jule. You would see that if you would step outside once in a while. Anyway, my husband doesn't want to have a harem on the premises. It's from another era. Times change. I know you can understand that. Keeping wives is a thing of the past and the country is changing. It's time to do something else with your lives."

"Like what? Would we have to work? We aren't prostitutes."

"Of course you're not prostitutes. I don't have all the answers yet."

"Well, we won't go until you have all the answers. I can tell you that's the opinion of all the wives. We won't go until there's an actual plan. Otherwise, we're staying put."

Jule squared her shoulders and sat down with authority on a Queen Anne chair.

Clare stood alone in the middle of the room. Nal walked over to her.

"It's not going very well, is it?" he said, turning to glare at Jule, who glared back.

"That's an understatement."

"You know, your husband isn't going to be very happy if you don't solve this problem. He told Mr. Olson you were going to get the women out by the end of the week. Can't you just give them the boot?"

"I want to be fair. I can't throw them to the wolves. They seem quite nice. It would be simpler if they would just take money, an allowance, to help them get settled."

"Let's ask them."

Nal gestured to Jule to come over. When she stood, all the wives stood; when she walked over, they walked with her.

Clare attempted to say something in Arabic, thinking this might placate her, but Jule stopped her.

"I have perfect English, as you can see," she said. "The British were here for forty years, you know. We all have perfect English."

"Would you accept money to leave?"

"Yes."

"How much?"

"One gold piece for every month of service."

"That's a fortune!"

"I know! That's why it would be so much easier if you let us stay here. Cheaper, more convenient, none of the risk. We'll stay very quiet. We'll be like little mice."

"Jule . . ."

"Think about it."

"You're giving me such a headache."

"Mr. Cobb says you have lots of headaches."

"That's not true! I never have. How do you know Stanley Cobb?"

"We all know Mr. Cobb." The wives grinned and nodded their heads in unison.

"Has he been down here?"

Jule rolled her eyes and stuck out her lip provocatively.

"Has Stanley Cobb been . . ."

"Been what?"

"You know."

Jule smiled brightly. "No, but I think he might want to."

"Oh God."

"But he is the best friend of your husband. Maybe it would be acceptable. He said that thirty would be no problem for him."

"Listen, Jule. If Stanley Cobb comes down here, I want to know about it. He has no right to be in here. No right at all. You know there aren't supposed to be any men here. I thought that's how it worked. I thought only eunuchs could be around a harem—"

Nal made a *pffft* sound of indignation through his front teeth and opened his mouth, but Clare shut him off. "I don't mean you, Nal. I'm sure you're . . . *intact*." She rubbed her head with her hand. *How had she gotten into this?*

"Men are not supposed to be down here, Jule. No men!"

She realized all of a sudden that her voice was a little too high-pitched. That her cheeks were hot and probably red. Jule had a face full of pity, at least that's what Clare believed she saw. She laid her hand on Clare's arm and patted it the way a mother might pet a frantic child. All the wives were staring at Clare as if she were some pathetic specimen of bad Western thinking who needed their enlightened ministrations to find the true path.

"You need to relax a little," Jule said in a soothing voice. All the wives pressed in closer, nodding their heads in agreement. "You need not take this all so seriously. We'll work out our problems. Come back next week. We'll talk some more. Tell your husband it's only a matter of time. That will make him happy."

Tarik had Cobb meet him at the stables the next morning. He told him he'd heard he'd been down to see the wives.

Stan didn't deny it.

"Now, boy-o," he began after Tarik had dismounted, "tempted as I was, I didn't lay a finger on them. Most of them don't have any teeth anyway, so there was no real danger."

"I want you to promise me that you won't go over there again. It's bad enough having them here, but if there were any kind of scandal about Americans keeping a seraglio, I would be very embarrassed."

"Have you seen that place? I've seen cat houses in my day, but that place is unbelievable, boy-o. Gold and silver and candles and red velvet everywhere. One day I'm going to have a spread like that. A man could lay down there and die, except, as I said, most of them don't have teeth."

"Keep that in mind, Stanley. No teeth."

" 'Course . . ." Stanley stroked the stubble on his chin. "A woman without teeth has advantages . . . I remember a little tooth-less gal in Juarez, Mexico, 1932. She could—"

"Promise me."

"I promise."

"Good."

"Tell the truth, boy-o"—he cleared his throat—"I wanted to see you anyway. To discuss some business. Um . . . dyin' jumped-up Jesus, it's hot!" He began fanning himself in an exaggerated manner with his open hand. "I don't know how you can ride around on a horse in this weather anyway."

"It helps me clear my mind," Tarik told him. "And it's a lot more pleasant than those old Land-Rovers. None of them has shocks. It's going to take forever to get anything going here—and I don't think I'm going to live that long."

Talk like that worried Stan and made him doubt the heavy decision he had made just that morning. Was he betraying Tarik, the man he considered his best friend, his brother, and, when he could tolerate such purple reflection, the son he never had? "Aw, don't take it so personally," he said. "There's only so much one man can do. You can't remake this hellhole into paradise overnight."

Silence.

The longer Stanley postponed telling him of his decision, the greater his misery became. After a bit, it filled the air. He stopped in his tracks, started up again, stopped, started. He wrestled with his conscience, busied himself with some imaginary insect bite on his arm, then let his hands fall limply open at his sides in an uncharacteristically helpless posture.

"What's up, Stan? What's on your mind?"

Stan would put his hand in the fire for Tarik. He would take a bullet in the heart for him if anybody asked, which was the problem. He wiped his hand over his face several more times. He had the look of a man who had just backed his truck over his favorite hound.

"It's just that—Aw, let's leave it to another time. You've got work to do." He started to walk away.

Tarik halted. "If it takes all day, Stan."

The big man balled up his hands and resumed his pacing. Tarik prepared for the long haul.

After a few more expressive sighs, Stan spoke. "We've been here for three months now. And it's been something, I'll tell you. Everything we ever talked about—adventure, doing good, helping people. But the truth is"—his face was twisted with concern—"the truth is I'm about as useful to you now as tits on a bull."

"Good Lord, Stanley."

"Back home it was different. Just me and you. Me watching

out for you, that is. Always on the alert that somebody might take a crack at you. But now, I mean, look around. This place is crawling with soldiers."

"So?"

"So, you don't need me."

"Yes, I need you."

"As a friend, not a bodyguard."

"As a friend. You're very important to me."

"But you don't need a bodyguard."

"No, but I need a friend."

"We'll always be friends, but"—he drew closer and whispered next to Tarik's ear—"I've got a whole other plan. I've got a line on something big-time. In Duru."

Duru was the magic word. "In the oil fields?"

"I met a guy, a straight sort named Hawkins. I won't bore you with the details, cut to the chase: He offered me a half share in his well, which he owns outright."

"How much?"

"Ten thousand."

"That's very little."

"He needs the cash."

"Have you got it?"

"Uh-huh."

"This Hawkins, what do you know about him?"

"Enough to know that I can trust him. I've seen the documentation on the drilling rights. I've gone over his equipment expenses, output projections, that stuff. He's straight. The problem is, he's physically weak, with a sick cough down deep in the chest. TB. Everybody's got it here. So it's just like always—I supply the brawn, somebody else supplies the brains." He smiled brightly. He could appreciate simple equations.

Stan's forty-eight-year-old face was soft and unlined and his blue eyes youthfully clear and unworried. Worry, in fact, did not tax his brain. And why would it? Unbound by conventional responsibilities of wife and children, his life was not much more than a string of interesting jobs, occupations that marked passage from one location to the next like beer-can litter. Chiefly, boredom was the culprit. Stan's attention span had a short shelf life.

Had he ever been in love? After all these years of friendship, Tarik did not have the temerity to probe around his unsavory personal life. Beyond the oft-recalled female housepainter of years ago, the need of love and family seemed never to have touched him, except in the shape of hookers or porn stars, and on that subject Stanley could rhapsodize to the level of ecstasy usually reserved to those who have climbed Everest.

Behind that roaring bluster, however, was a tender heart, although his vanity would have suffered fatally had he known anyone guessed this about him. Stan believed the world viewed him as a man of action, a man to be feared and obeyed.

"You can go bust, you know, Stanley," Tarik warned him. "Despite the geologists' reports, no one has been able to get at that oil. There's a tremendous risk that you could lose everything, come up dry. You know how many guys have gone belly-up in Duru? We may never be able to get at that oil."

"Yeah, but if I strike it rich—look out, mama!" He did a little stylized bump and grind.

"Of course, if you do get lucky and strike, Stanley," Tarik added, "you know you have to lease the well back to the government and take a percentage. I can't make any exceptions or show any favoritism."

Stan held up his hand like a traffic cop. "Wouldn't dream of asking for any."

"When will you leave?"

"Tonight. Today. Now that I've settled things with you." He heaved the sigh of a man released from a dreadful burden. "I can't tell you how much it means to me, your understanding what I'm trying to do."

"I want you to get rich, Stanley. I want you to buy a million Tilt o'Wheels. And I want you to keep me up-to-date on the independents and the big drilling companies. The Brits would love to have the first strike and then lock up all the fields. And keep an eye on the Yemenis especially."

"How will I know them?"

"They're the ones with blood in their eyes. Turkit stole Duru from the Yemenis forty years ago and they've never gotten over it. They would kill me if they thought they could get away with it, but they'll settle for Duru back. It's a nasty place, Stanley. Not even Turkit had the guts to go there, so you'd better watch your backside." Tarik clamped his hand on Stanley's shoulder. "So, I hope you make a million."

"I make a million, you make ten. That's how it works. What's good for me is good for you, just like always. Hell, this isn't good-bye. It's aloha. It's palm trees, coconuts, grass skirts, and what's under 'em. So long, boy-o," Stan called out, backing down the gravel path and disappearing around the corner.

10

That same afternoon, Tarik met with Elliott Tomlinson.

He did not raise his eyes when he said, "This business of Rahal, Tomlinson," just went on examining the briefing paper in his hand.

Tomlinson's pencil stopped moving. "What about Rahal?" With his middle finger he pushed his glasses back up on his nose. He glanced at White-Lyons and then at Arthur Olson, but their faces registered nothing. "What about Rahal?" he asked again.

"Well, I see you targeted another twenty thousand acres."

"The strategy's been remapped," Tomlinson said, wary. "The engineers gave me a new breakdown. You should have it in your file there. We're adding another radar installation to the one already in place."

"I saw it, but I'm curious to know when construction at Rahal, or any sort of emplacements for that matter, came under your jurisdiction. I thought you were strictly cloak and dagger stuff." Tarik made it sound like an insult.

"I asked for the breakdown and I got it. It falls under the intelligence aspect." Tomlinson looked at Olson for help but the older man only gazed back at him mildly. "Anyway"—he turned back to Tarik—"Arthur okayed my writing the report, mostly as a way of acquainting myself."

Tarik made a soft sound of comprehension. He sat back languidly in his chair, seeming sleepy and relaxed.

Tomlinson stared at him for a moment, then suddenly understood. Olson had set him up. He had encouraged him to write the report, knowing it would irritate Tarik. Not the first time he'd double-dealt him since he got here. But then, they all disliked him, didn't they?

Realizing this made him feel off balance, a little fucked up.

Made him wonder again if he'd made a mistake coming here. Maybe he should have gone to Saigon when they gave him the chance. Then again, maybe not. Probably he'd be behind a metal desk in the cellar of the U.S. embassy there, just one more ant grinding away. At least here, in the kingdom, he was top dog, station chief. Besides, he couldn't speak French.

He took a deep breath and tried to shrug off their contempt. Screw it. Their hatred made him strong, made it easier for him to do his job and not worry about whose balls he busted along the way.

After a bit, Tarik spoke again. "Of course, Rahal has potentially some of the finest farmland in the kingdom, once the irrigation systems are in place."

"Farmland? You want to put farms into Rahal?" Tomlinson was incredulous.

"It was only a thought."

"It would take years to turn Rahal into a farming province."

"You think so?"

"Of course," Tomlinson answered, exasperated. "This is a ridiculous discussion. We chose Rahal because of its inaccessibility, its strategic proximity to the border. I don't understand. Why are we talking about this now? It's all been settled."

"I was just thinking that I hate turning a whole province into an armed camp," Tarik said mildly. "Rahal is beginning to seem to me to be a little bit like the Fuehrer bunker."

"What?"

"You know, everybody hunkered down, reading war maps, leading lives of quiet desperation. Pictures of Frederick the Great around everywhere." Tarik swung back and forth in his swivel chair, clearly enjoying himself.

"There's no comparison."

"No? Well, I guess you're right." Tarik shrugged his shoulders. "Forgive me, Tomlinson. I got a little carried away. On the other hand, it's unpleasant, isn't it, to think of hundreds of square miles surrounded by barbed wire, bristling with weapons and intelligence equipment? You know, I wouldn't object to some arrangement like your CIA headquarters in Langley out there in Rahal. An oasis maybe. Overhanging palm trees, gardens, picnic tables. Makes it seem a little less Wernher Von Braun. A little more Heidi." He looked across his desk at Tomlinson, who glared back.

Olson cleared his throat. "Shall we move on, gentlemen?"

Tomlinson could not hold his tongue, a defect of character that Tarik played on constantly. No matter how many times Tarik

baited the hook, Tomlinson rose to take it. Tarik always got the
best of him, which gave Olson enormous pleasure. He despised
Tomlinson but was too clever to put the screws to him himself.
Let Tarik do the dirty work. Keep his own hands clean. He had
other fish to fry.

Finally, Tomlinson spoke again. "So, are we staying with
Rahal, guys, or are we going to move on to something else?"

Except for Stanley Cobb, none of them had continued to address Tarik so informally. For Tomlinson to do so was a deliberate
slight.

Tarik allowed him to realize this and smiled without humor.
"No, let's move on. I want to hear more from Olson."

"I don't care what you say, he's an ass." After the meeting, Tarik
walked with White-Lyons back to the living quarters. Courtiers
skittered past, averting their eyes when they saw him, a sign of respect.

"Tomlinson may be an ass," White-Lyons countered, "but it
serves no purpose to alienate him so early in the game. Besides,
we have no idea for sure whether he's friend or foe."

"He's the Agency's guy."

"Which by definition does not make him a foe. And in any
case, you're not being wholly honest, are you?" White-Lyons kept
his eyes straight ahead as they walked along. "It's pure self-
indulgence that makes you bait Tomlinson. You don't care for him
personally and you've given yourself permission to treat him any
way you like."

"It was Olson who set him up. He believes Tomlinson will
screw up. He wants to dump him."

"He told you this?"

"Not in so many words."

"But you can read his mind."

Tarik seethed but said nothing.

"Why are you so confident about Olson's motives anyway?"
White-Lyons pressed him. "He was a slick fellow when he was
selling arms to Malik in the thirties, and he's twice as slick now,
I'll bet. It's just as likely it's you he's playing off against
Tomlinson. Did you ever think of that?"

Tarik hadn't, but he had no intention of admitting this to White-
Lyons. "I won't have you impugn Olson," he said defensively. "If
it weren't for him, I wouldn't be here."

White-Lyons said nothing, but Tarik immediately realized his
gaffe and felt ashamed. It was White-Lyons who had assassinated

Turkit for his sake, who had delivered to him Malik's legacy, who had put an end to the misery of the people, who had launched all of them on the adventure—not Olson, and certainly not the others in Washington who had equivocated for so many years. It was White-Lyons who had brought Tarik to his destiny and who deserved all of his appreciation and respect.

Yet he could not stand the man. Could not abide this humorless, relentless, formal, unforgiving, pedantic, and altogether insufferable martinet.

So he did not bother to apologize, just added, "Olson is our man. I have no doubt in my mind about that. He is as loyal as anyone I have ever met. More so. His reputation is impeccable, unlike Tomlinson's."

But White-Lyons was no longer concentrating on Tarik. Instead, he was listening to his own footsteps reverberate on the stone floor, his mind drifting.

How many times had he walked this passageway? How many nights had the screams of the tortured ones below floated up to him through the stones? But was it a real memory? Had such things really happened? He could no longer be sure. He was grateful events had become blended after all these years.

He checked himself. He must never forget. He bore down and made himself remember in exact detail. One man in particular came to mind, a petty thief. Turkit had threaded his splayed anus with red-hot piano wires and the man's screams could have skinned a horse. White-Lyons blamed himself for that one. He had once told Turkit how Edward II had been assassinated in similarly volcanic fashion in the fourteenth century and of course Turkit had been inspired to imitation.

Had that been the moment when he'd made up his mind finally to kill him and bring the boy over? No, he'd decided that years before. For decades, the only real question had been timing.

Thinking about those days made him light-headed, as if the poison of his life were expelled just at the instant when he knew he could no longer endure another ounce of it. At his high-minded best, he would think the boy would save all of them. He could not bear to admit that it was he who needed saving.

He shook off his fatigue with a soundless sigh. He was fifty-five years old, a time in his life when he should have been taking things as they came. Instead, he was in anguish night and day—but it was no burden, never a burden, because Tarik was everything he had dreamed of and more. White-Lyons permitted himself the luxury of hyperbole: Tarik was nothing less than Alexander. He blushed to himself to think of it, but he didn't cringe. Hyperbole had long ago been reconstituted as moral imperative when it came to Tarik and all they might accomplish together. With his bare hands that young man would yank this backward country into the modern world.

And then what? With his inward eye White-Lyons conjured a diorama of unfurled banners and reclaimed missions. This made him feel as if he were twenty-eight again. So many memories, so many. For once his machine brain became blissfully inarticulate. His mind swam at the spectacle of what had been and what might yet be. Perfection.

The instant he thought this, he brought himself up short. Not yet perfection. He would not make the same mistake again. He had been soft-hearted then. It had taken him almost thirty years, but he had made a stone heart for himself. *So the truth then, old man. There is one glaring impediment to perfection. A misery named Clare.*

Saying her name in his brain made White-Lyons slow his step for a heartbeat. He would have to tell Tarik now. He could not postpone it for another moment.

What a lurid business, he thought, not for the first time. He resented Clare all over again for involving him in emotions he had spent a lifetime avoiding.

The airplane had rolled to a halt almost at his feet. The steps pushed up, the door swung open, and the longed-for one materialized in the doorway—tall, beyond handsome, with that irresistible air of complete assurance.

It had been a stunning moment and the machine man had been thrilled to his soul.

He had stepped out into the sunlight; all their dreams were about to become material. But what—he turned to the tall blonde suddenly in the airplane doorway, her face registering shock at the blast of midday heat. He put out his hand to steady her, and then together they descended the plane steps. White-Lyons's thrilled soul spasmed.

In that instant he knew they were lost.

He had taken the front seat in the car that drove them from the airport to the capital, his heart turning over wretchedly. Through an act of will he forced his mind to work. How could they not have told him the boy had a wife? He would never have killed Turkit had he known.

He steadied his emotions. Despair was demeaning. Peevishness served no purpose. He glared into the hot eye of the sun. Slowly, clouded vision cleared. She would go. There! In his mind she was gone already. Instantly White-Lyons felt the release of helplessness. Then just as suddenly an appalling fear broke over him. Tarik would hate him for this; it was hardly his fault, but still, Tarik would hate him forever, and that hatred would be a knife up under his ribs. Then, a reassuring realization. This is what I understand best, he thought. This is war. The mind-machinery began to click and hum its familiar rhythm.

That day, driving in from the airport with them for the first time, he had glanced over his shoulder to assess his enemy, and he was surprised to find Clare staring back at him, her eyes narrowed in a frown. He saw nothing of her hair, her body, the uncompromising intelligence that showed in her face. What he saw, he believed, was his nemesis. What he saw, he believed, was a woman in big trouble.

Because Tarik was meant to have a wife—there was no question about that—but the wife was definitely not meant to be Clare.

White-Lyons took another calming breath. Desperation had cut a little wedge into his confidence; Hadi could not be put off any longer.

He snapped back to reality when he heard Tarik say something further about Arthur Olson.

"I can't tell you what to do," he said when Tarik finished speaking. "I defer to you. But let me warn you that it's a mistake to take Tomlinson for a fool. You won't be the first man to mistake a man for an ass and get his brains kicked in for his bad judgment."

Damn the boy's arrogance. He could forgive him anything, even his marriage to Clare. But he could not tolerate his arrogance.

But this was a mistake. He should be soothing the boy, preparing him for what was coming. Tarik needed to be calm so he could receive the news with logic and without emotion.

"One more thing," White-Lyons said. "I need a personal word with you."

"Now? It's late."

"It can't be put off."

They found the small, enclosed garden alongside an old potting shed. Tarik sat down heavily, annoyed at the delay.

White-Lyons paced for a moment, his head down, and then began. "You recall my letter to you just before Turkit's death?"

"Yes."

"It was very difficult to send that message. I had to get Nal to Yemen. There was no postal service here at the time. It took nearly three days to get him out safely."

"Yes."

"It wasn't easy."

"I'm sure. Killing Turkit was an act of courage. You were in grave danger."

"From Turkit, yes. From both of them."

Tarik gave him a baffled look. "Both of whom?"

"From Turkit, naturally. He would have loved to have pinned something on me and let them haul me away. But the real risk was from Hadi."

"We'll take care of Hadi in time."

"No. You must take care of Hadi now."

"I'm not in a position to move against him now. In another year, when I'm certain I can rely on the army."

"He has to be taken care of now. The real risk in killing Turkit was—*remains*—Hadi. It was Hadi who enabled me to kill Turkit. The means with which to take care of Hadi is within your grasp."

"In time."

"Now. Easily. Without violence."

"What are you talking about?"

"I was forced to come to an understanding with Hadi before I could bring you over here."

Alert, Tarik straightened his back. "What kind of an understanding?"

"Something personal. At the time, it seemed a meaningless concession."

"What concession?"

White-Lyons steadied himself. "An alliance of marriage."

"Whose marriage?"

"Yours, to Hadi's daughter Topaz."

Tarik stared at him for a long, surprised moment and then began to laugh. He laughed and then shook his head. "Well, I certainly ruined that, didn't I?"

"That's the problem. You see, the arrangement is still in force."

Tarik looked at him to see if he was joking. But White-Lyons never joked. "You can't be serious."

"I'm completely serious."

"Then I'm sorry for you, old man. I'm not giving up my wife for some two-bit clan chief with delusions of dynasty."

"Well, I'm sorry for you, but you are going to have to make this marriage."

Tarik stood and prepared to leave. "I think you've been living here too long, White-Lyons. I think all those years with Turkit got to your mind. This notion of political marriage is from another century—"

"No, it's not. It goes on all the time, at every level, all around the world."

"You really believe that?"

"Of course. You know it's true. You're being deliberately disingenuous."

"Well, it's not going to happen here. This is the new order, White-Lyons. Political marriages went out here with, I don't know . . . Times change. Tell Hadi the news."

"You cannot hold on to power here without Hadi's cooperation—not now anyway. Not for years and years, and you know that. That's why you've left him alone. There are two hundred fifty thousand men out there who would have no problem riding in here and cutting your throat if Hadi told them to do it. They have no sentiment for you. They don't subscribe to the Malik legend when it comes to money and the disposal of power. They follow Hadi. Turkit had no control over him, and neither will you."

Tarik made a move, impatiently waving his hand at White-Lyons, but the older man blocked his way.

"Have you never wondered why it was so easy for you to just walk in here after all these years? Maybe I should have waited to get rid of Turkit until you got here. Then you could have seen for yourself what you would have faced without a deal to keep Hadi off your back. What would you have done if you'd arrived and found the Marib camped out in your palace? You would have had such a fight on your hands that you would have turned right around and gone back to the airport with your blond wife. You wouldn't be here now if Hadi hadn't agreed to go along with this. And he went along with it because I promised him you would take Topaz. Because he's willing to settle. He doesn't want a fight. But if you don't take Topaz, he'll set Azarak and the Marib against you."

"Azarak? That lunatic son of his? Is that the alternative to my marrying Topaz?"

"Yes. It still is the alternative if this marriage doesn't come off."

"This is ridiculous. Nobody will stand for Azarak."

"No, but you're going to get bloodied stopping him. Who's going to help you? An army that you've commanded for exactly

three months? How do you think the officers are going to feel
about you when they find out that your plan is eventually to replace them with men you've trained? You think they won't go to
Hadi if he makes the deal sweet enough? You think the Americans will send troops in here to support you? You know better
than that. They'll tell you to do the right thing, marry Topaz, relax. You think the people will rise up and declare you their sav-
ior?"

"Yes."

"Maybe so, but they're sick and degraded and they have no
political or military influence. Do you want to be responsible for
the Marib slaughtering them? You are on your own here. Hadi
will rain down hell on you if you don't comply."

"Really, I think you've been here too long, White-Lyons. I
think you ought to take a good hard look around you. Take a look
at what Tomlinson's doing up at Rahal. I have the hardware to
take care of Hadi, with or without the army."

White-Lyons sat down heavily on the stone bench. With unfocused eyes he looked up at the ficus tree that overhung the palace
wall, searching for some unnamed thing in its bony branches. In
a low voice he said, "I don't know. Maybe you should have come
over when you were younger. When you could still be shaped by
what goes on here. You've spent too much time riding around in
convertibles, or whatever it is young people do in the States. You
miss the central aspect of thinking over here: that nothing is as it
appears to be. I thought Francis Riston had had some influence
with you in all this. Arthur Olson should have known.

"Hadi has left you alone because I've kept him away, and because he has a warped sense of time. He has a warped sense of
everything. But I can't keep him at bay forever. If you don't
marry Topaz, he will know that you are soft. That you don't have
the commitment. That the country will go to hell while you moon
around after love and sex. He's not going to let that happen, especially if there's an oil strike at Duru and there are billions of
dollars to be had. If you're not strong enough to hold him off,
he'll take you and he'll take the oil and then we'll all be dead."

"Let me talk to him. We'll work out another deal."

"Another deal? You're not listening. The deal he wants is the
one having to do with his spirit tossed into the future, genes carried forward, no other deal. He hears voices, sees visions. In his
heart of hearts he knows it can't be Azarak, but that wouldn't stop
him from inflicting Azarak on us just for the fun of it. Turkit was
a walk in the park compared to what Azarak could do."

White-Lyons made his voice soft. "You must understand that your notion of marriage is a meaningless concept to Hadi. If you don't marry Topaz, he will believe it has nothing to do with sentiment but everything to do with enmity for him. Something evil up your sleeve for him. You have to have the clans behind you not just to survive, but to make something of this place. Isn't that what you want? How can you let anything stand in the way of that? You must give up Clare. You can send her away quietly. There'll be a very quiet divorce. After a time, after Hadi has this marriage, perhaps a child is born, you can fly to Europe to see her. She may even be able to live here on a limited basis. I'll help you work it out."

The garden felt hot and cramped, too small to contain both of them. Tarik watched him for a long, silent moment, then said with a tone of great resignation in his voice, "You should know that I'm grateful for all you've done for me over the years, White-Lyons. For my mother as well. But we're very different, you and I. I've felt that from the moment I got here. You must feel it too. I don't want to be unkind, but I think you ought to stop playing at politics. I think you ought to have a talk with Elliott Tomlinson, or Arthur Olson. I think you'd understand then that we're in a much better position here than you seem to think. I think you would understand that tough as things are now, times have changed. The day of the assassin is over."

"Not for Hadi."

"For everyone."

"You're making a mistake. He will have no trouble killing you, and he'll do it. You make a much easier target than Turkit."

Offended, Tarik stared at him. "You're the expert on assassination, White-Lyons. I bow to you in this regard. But you're wrong. And one more thing—I don't want Clare to know anything about this business. She would leave tomorrow if she believed I was in danger because of her. If she finds out, I'll know it could have come only from you. And I'll make you very sorry for that. It might be a good idea for you to get away for a while. Maybe go up to the Sur."

"Hadi will kill you," White-Lyons said in a flat voice. "You don't understand how things work."

But Tarik kept walking, the silence in his wake the loneliest sound White-Lyons had ever heard. He sat for a very long time on the bench, all the strength out of his body.

* * *

When the moon was up, when a rare breeze stirred the ficus tree, White-Lyons left the garden and marched down the darkened hallway to the apartments that had been his home for decades, turning things over in his mind.

The compulsion to love and be loved in return is universal, and in that White-Lyons was an ordinary man. He had seen too much of torture and cruelty not to be a cynic—and enough of love not to be a true believer, although no one would have suspected that of him. He was strong and tough. Sometimes, one had to hang it out there and risk the crushed skull and the corroded spirit. He would overcome these things; consistency would see him through. Tarik could say anything, do anything, and it would make no difference. White-Lyons would never let the standard fall.

Philosophies, even principles, changed; the natures of men and women did not. White-Lyons knew this as surely as he understood the mechanics of the Browning High-Power pistol he had carried on his hip for thirty years. He had broken down, cleaned, oiled and reassembled the pistol every night for three decades. He knew its parts through blind touch, every little chink, groove, slot. Similarly, the natures of men and women could be revealed and, this accomplished, he could then manipulate the parts into any configuration that he chose.

But White-Lyons could not begin to guess the depths of ambition, jealousy, and sheer murderous rage that lay beneath the complex layers of Hadi's personality. Hadi was a brilliant observer of man's nature, and wholly evil. White-Lyons would not be able to spin traps for Hadi and get away with it.

He turned right at an intersection of hallways, swung open the door, and entered his darkened parlor. He tripped over the edge of a rug and cursed Nal for not having lit the kerosene lamps. In pitch dark he felt his way to the bedroom. He fumbled for a match and struck it on his bedstead. The thin light caught in its halo a pair of yellow eyes. White-Lyons drew in his breath as Hadi, master of the four hundred thousand Marib, hound of hell, stepped into the little ribbon of light.

"You are going to burn your fingers, White-Lyons," Hadi said mildly.

White-Lyons shook out the match, struck another on the edge of the table, and lit the kerosene lamp. He turned the wick up all the way. He wanted to be able to see Hadi clearly. He needed the advantage of light. "It's good to see you, Hadi," he said without enthusiasm.

"Oh, I doubt that very much, White-Lyons."

Hadi moved out of the shadows. Although his demeanor was utterly formal, that slight advance caused White-Lyons to stiffen. Hadi carried about him the aura of some terrifying, unspoken threat. His voice was impassive, but then even the mildest salutation on Hadi's lips sounded like a sword being drawn from its scabbard.

He looked around the room for a moment, assessing it. "Very plain, White-Lyons. Very much the rooms of a military man. I like to keep things simple too. Goodness, but I hate knickknacks, clutter. All that bourgeois nostalgia, like photographs."

His eye fell on a sepia-toned photo of White-Lyons's mother in a silver frame.

"Oh," he said, and pulled a face.

White-Lyons kept his eyes on Hadi's face but focused his fingertips so he could sense the pistol on the bedside table, just out of his reach. "You didn't come here to see how I live."

Hadi gave him a lupine smile. His eyes were flat and his bland, expressionless face was a mask, a hedge against the peculiar edginess of his pillar-straight body.

"No—no, of course not," he said. "On the other hand, I've always wondered how you managed to hang on here, what with Turkit and those nephews of his. I thought maybe you lived in a cell, with iron bars to keep them out. He killed everybody else; I was always impressed that he never got you. You must have been very clever all those years."

"That's right."

"And in the end it turned out to be the other way around, eh?"

"Also correct."

Hadi bobbed his head appreciatively, pondering the knowledge as if he were turning over on his tongue a very sweet fig.

White-Lyons glared at him. "You didn't come here to go over my history."

Hadi came back to life. "No, no. As a matter of fact, I came here to fill you in on my plan."

"What plan?"

"My plan to kill Tarik."

"I've just left Tarik."

"Really? How is he looking? He's very handsome. Those broad shoulders, and so tall. And all that black hair! If I were a woman—and I certainly am not—I would go for him. Did you tell him that I'm going to kill him?"

"Why would you kill him, Hadi?" White-Lyons made himself

sound unconcerned. "He's going to send the blond wife away. But these things take time."

The yellow light in Hadi's eyes flashed in menace, the most hating eyes White-Lyons had ever seen. "But it's been three months," he whined. "How long does it take for a woman to pack her bags?"

White-Lyons gave him his best smile. "Tarik isn't stupid. He knows what he has to do. But she's an American, after all, and the Americans will not be happy to see her go. They view it as political influence of the most intimate kind. They are taking it personally. He's up against a terrific amount of opposition."

Hadi gave him a fake smile. "Oh? How odd. I know everything that's going on and I've heard nothing of this. I hear only of the current wife riding around the countryside with that fool of a batman you gave her. She ought to be more careful out there, White-Lyons. All kinds of things could bite her head off."

"She's going, Hadi. Just give the boy a little more time to get rid of her in a way that doesn't so directly offend the Americans."

"Clearly, you've forgotten this delay was a gesture of great faith and magnanimity on my part."

"I appreciate it, Hadi. I haven't forgotten."

Hadi let go a deep theatrical sigh, as if he alone carried the burden of the kingdom's future, as if he alone comprehended the tragedy of the country in a rudderless state. Such a weight. He positioned himself slightly closer to White-Lyons and gave him a sincere look. "You and I, White-Lyons, we're men of the world. I don't have to tell you how things work. We disdain the smarminess of politics, you and me. We're men of action, not deals. We cut off heads, we grab for what we want. We don't debase our souls for public housing or trade restrictions. Myself, I count my wealth in the number of men who press their faces against the floor in terror when they see me coming. That's the prize, that's the power. Glory is merely further evidence of man's inabstinence. Who would want such a life? More than two hundred and fifty thousand men, White-Lyons, more than your puny army. That's what I could have outside these gates in one day. Pretty impressive."

He stopped abruptly to admire an old revolver on White-Lyons's desk.

"What is that? A Webley?"

"Yes."

"Is it very old?"

"My father's."

Hadi broke the barrel and spun the chamber. He sighted down the barrel. "It's off by a hair, White-Lyons." He made a *tsk* sound. "You should have it fixed."

At fifty, Hadi gave the appearance of a much older man. His complexion was pitted from smallpox and White-Lyons suspected he was in the prodromal stages of tuberculosis. Which is what made him all the more dangerous. A man with a limited amount of time to make his mark on the future is a man capable of anything.

Gently, Hadi returned the revolver to its place on the table. "I never sit still for a wholesale slaughter," he said. "But I think a man should reach his goal any way he knows how. So it's true that when a man kills a king he takes on an awesome responsibility. Not just his peers, but History itself sits in judgment upon him. But then, if the man has a political conviction and, more important, two hundred fifty thousand men to back him up, why should he care if History or his peers refuse to absolve him?"

"Your point is what, Hadi?"

"You Brits, so to the point. All right. If Tarik does not marry my Topaz as we agreed the night before you killed that old fucker Turkit, then I will set all the clans against him, not just my Marib. Oh, and I personally will kill him. Then, as I said, Azarak would have the throne."

"Azarak is a lunatic."

Hadi shrugged. "Turkit was a lunatic, Turkit's father was a lunatic, and his father's father. We all come from a long line of lunatics. What can we do, White-Lyons? It's the same old story. I don't have to tell you how the world goes. You understand this perfectly, the politics of dread. You practiced it for years, with Turkit."

"The Americans will not tolerate Azarak on the throne."

"Then I will go to the Russians." Hadi chuckled a little, showing his dark teeth.

White-Lyons also smiled and did a business with his hand, as if he were swatting away a bug. "The Russians will have nothing to do with Azarak, and you know it. Azarak is a monster," he asserted. "And if you kill Tarik, then you and the monster will have to answer to the Americans, who will murder you in turn, and then where will your dreams of dynasty be?

"No, Tarik will marry Topaz. I guarantee it. Their children will carry your seed unto the generations, that's how you see it, eh, Hadi? That is precisely what will happen. Your blood, your genes, your vision of the world. Tarik will come to see the wisdom of divorce. He's a man of character. You have my word on it: She will go."

Feeling victorious, White-Lyons slumped into a chair and reached for his pipe. Hadi watched him fill it, his eyes smoldering in the dim light. He moved toward the door and was halfway gone when he thought better of it.

"Tell me something, White-Lyons."

"Perhaps."

"Tell me what it is about Malik's son that fascinates you so. Do you have some old debt to the father that you pay back through the boy? I'm really curious."

"He's Malik's son. That's reason enough. He is the only one who can unite the clans, who can save the kingdom."

Hadi nodded to indicate comprehension but he remained skeptical. A thousand legends flew through his mind but he could make sense of none of them. There was some old detail, an ancient piece of business between Malik and White-Lyons that must have been left undone, that would explain the old man's obsession with the boy. He wished his own father, Agesh, were still alive. Agesh might remember. But then if Agesh were still alive, Hadi realized wearily, he would have to kill him all over again, so that was no good.

He considered pressing White-Lyons further but changed his mind. He had to come up with a great exit and wanted to get on with it.

"By the way, White-Lyons, I have his head, you know," he said slyly.

"Eh, what's that?" White-Lyons exhaled a perfumed stream of pipe smoke.

"I have the old fucker's head. Here." Hadi opened his cloak and there on his belt was a dried and shrunken head. White-Lyons had to stare at it for a long time before he recognized it as Turkit's. The eyes rolled up and the whites were black. The tongue was black and had swelled to fill the whole gaping mouth.

Against his will, White-Lyons gagged. "How did you get it?"

"It flew to me, I swear." Hadi put his hand over his heart. "It came to me on its own, on wings. I woke up the morning after you killed him and the head was on my pillow. I thought you had put him there to show me what can happen to a man who resists his fate." Hadi threw him an exaggerated wink and did a quick shuffle with his feet. Always more effective to illustrate a threat than rely on the weight of words, he thought to himself. Cuts to the heart of the matter.

"I have his head, old man," Hadi said.

White-Lyons took a calming draw on his pipe and blew out more smoke. His customary composure resumed. "And don't you forget who took off his head in the first place, you bastard," he said with a bland smile. "Don't you dare forget."

But Hadi only shook the head at him and backed away, closing the door with his foot as he left.

White-Lyons turned down his lamp and went on smoking in the darkness, alone. After a while he reached over and picked up the Webley, and set it on his lap.

Everything's going to be fine. Everything's going to be just fine. Tarik will come to understand what he must do. Clare will go. It will all work out. So silly, this business about marriage.

But that night, the hum of the generators moving him deeper into sleep, he dreamed it was Tarik's head that decorated Hadi's gory belt.

11

If White-Lyons slept uneasily, Tarik did not sleep at all. In the dead of night, the heat gentled to mere furnace strength, he battled malignant dreaming. The bedroom smelled of lamp smoke and, vaguely, of the hair oil sloughed off onto the mattress by some old courtier of Turkit's who had slept there for a dozen years.

Tarik twisted in the linen bedsheets, reconstructing what White-Lyons had said, denying to himself that the words had any relevance. Then, with dread, accepted that there was more than a little truth in it, and a quick rush of despair. Finally, first light breaking through the louvered shutters, the resurrection of hope—he could handle everything. He was strong, he had powerful allies, he had a legitimacy based on moral authority. He would not have to give her up.

In the morning he was exhausted. Clare followed his movements around the bedroom with calculating eyes, probing him for explanations. But he only made excuses.

The nights that followed were the same. He would toss and turn, then slip out to sleep on the little balcony attached to their room so he wouldn't wake her. But the fruit bats would swoop and dive, the moon would be too bright, or not bright enough, and back he would come inside. Nal mentioned that the Marib believed that Hadi could transform himself into animal shapes. That he had been seen once, under direct moonlight, conferring with the devil. Tarik was a clear thinker, but Nal had given him a whole new perspective on fruit bats. He never went back to sleep on the balcony.

He was sorry now that he had let Stanley go off to Duru. He could have used him to keep watch over Clare, reinforcing Het and his Bren gun. He could trust Stanley. Others he might trust made for a short list. He told Het that he wanted Clare's guard increased to five men at least and the giant had taken it as a personal affront, giving him an I-can-handle-anything look. But Tarik had insisted and so now wherever she went outside the palace there were six bodyguards, including Het, plus Nal, who was useless with any weapon but words.

With the arrival of medical supplies and medicines, Clare had been able to put her immunization program to work on a limited basis. Already she and Dr. Van Damm had been to four villages (each, in reality, never more than a murky water well and a few shacks) in the eastern portion of the country. They would pull up in Nal's ancient Land-Rover, the squad of bodyguards in a similarly decrepit vehicle. Nal would honk the horn to get the villagers' attention, climb onto the car hood, and begin a spiel about the miracle of vaccination. He had thrown himself so much into his role as barker for science that Clare sometimes had trouble getting him down from the Land-Rover.

Van Damm taught her how to give intramuscular injections, which were easy and not at all risky. It was her job, as well, to take medical histories from each patient and set up a timetable for inoculations for basic diseases—measles, poliomyelitis, mumps, diphtheria, rubella, and so on. But there were so many people in advanced stages of tuberculosis, so many malnourished, half blind, ulcerated, nearly dead, that it was impossible at times to believe they were doing any good at all. But they kept it up, Nal wincing every time the needle went in, Het itchy when even the most harmless-looking villager came too close to Clare.

On the day of the dust storm near the air base at Hirth, poor visibility had separated them from their army escort when the Land-Rover broke down. While Het marched the three miles to the base for help, Clare shielded herself as best she could with Nal's umbrella against the blistering heat. Although the Land-Rover had a canvas top, the sun sought her out through every space.

It was the heat that got to her most. There was no decent shade in the whole country, outside of the Sur. Kentucky had some boiling summers, heat that could peel the vinyl off car upholstery, but nothing even close to this mind-clouding, strength-sapping, dizzying sun.

Het was gone for hours and Clare had begun to worry. She could feel her head swelling. Her eyes flooded with sweat. A little demon of panic formed in her chest. If Het did not return, if no help came, they still might survive a day or two. She looked over at the Land-Rover's radiator; they could funnel off its water—if it even had any water. Or drink their own urine. Van Damm had given her a basic survival lecture on the trip out.

She wiped the perspiration from her face with her hand and closed her eyes. What she wouldn't give to feel one of those bone-chilling fogs rolling up the holler, sending its icy fingers through the boards of her bedroom walls.

"I remember when I could never get warm enough," she said to no one in particular. Nal and Van Damm each had their own sunstroke stories and they passed another hour trying to impress each other.

"We could be more useful administratively, believe it or not," Van Damm said. He was beet-red and a blister was taking shape on his bottom lip. Clare made no comment. He had been an active-duty navy officer, stationed at Bethesda Naval Hospital, when he was recruited for the job in the kingdom. Probably he has a house with a pool, and a lawn sprinkler, and two kids, she thought to herself. He'd rather be in some suburban Sears, shopping for a new toolshed, than out here on the plain with a cooler full of tetanus-diphtheria toxoid and an empty radiator. But then, who wouldn't? She was the only one crazy enough to be on a mission.

She didn't say any of that, of course. Instead, with a dry mouth she told Van Damm she thought that what they really needed was a cohort of physician assistants. Or at least women trained to vaccinate and take medical histories, to take the burden off the doctors she was convinced would be coming any day now.

"We need to blanket the country with physician assistants."

"Yeah, but where you gonna get 'em?" Van Damm unlaced his boots and shook out loose gravel. "Nobody around here understands the simplest principles of hygiene. They drink out of the same cup. Eat out of the same pot. Set their privies next to their drinking water. You're gonna have a helluva of a job raising a cohort of physician assistants. God help us—Jesus, but it's hot. Where the hell is Het? Nal, which way did he go off, do you remember? God, what I wouldn't give for a cold beer. A cold Coke. Anything cold."

But Clare had quit listening. Her imagination flamed. She felt invigorated, as if a great weight had been taken away. The old strength returned to her body. She forgot about the sun and her thirst. By the time Het came back with a skinful of water, she knew what she was going to do with the wives.

* * *

That evening, in the bedroom, she began to explain it all to Tarik but, when she mentioned the wives, he interrupted to say that, by the way, he had met Tern.

"Tern?" she said, stepping out of her dress.

"Yeah, the one with the kind of blond hair. The one from Bahrain."

"The little one?"

"I guess she's little."

Clare sat down on the edge of the bed. Tern was the prettiest and youngest of the wives. Clare tried to put a disinterested tone into her voice. "How did you meet her?"

"She came in with one of those huge silver trays a few days ago," he told her. "The tray was bigger than she was."

"So you probably had to help her with the tray."

"Sort of. It was too heavy for her."

"What was on the tray? The head of John the Baptist?"

"Coffee. Very good Sur coffee."

"Have you seen her since?"

"No. You jealous?"

"What was she bringing you coffee for? What happened to that little guy with the bad teeth?"

"He was ugly. Tern is cute."

"I can't believe you! One minute you want the wives out of your sight, the next minute you think they're cute."

"I think they might make good waitresses."

"Where? Here?"

"Somewhere. Maybe here. I got rid of that little guy with bad teeth. Tern is better. And she makes a good cup of coffee."

She stared at him for a long time, trying to decide whether to take him seriously.

"Tern, huh?" she said out loud.

"Tern," he said, and gave her the smile.

The next morning Clare marched down to the west wing. She walked through the reception area, under the arabesqued ceiling, past the smoking *torchères*. After a search she found Jule in a marble bathroom a good city block long. Except for two serving women, Jule was alone.

She was also naked and lying at total ease on a slab of unblemished Carrera marble. It was a tableau of such sybaritic self-indulgence that Clare stared open-mouthed.

"What are you looking at?" Jule demanded.

"I'm—It's just so much like what a harem should look like!"

"Well, what else would it be?"

"I don't know. In books, it's just like this."

Jule had the short, squat body of a peasant, with unremarkable legs and breasts. Watching her, Clare thought she hardly fit the stereotype of exotic seducer. But then Jule opened her eyes and smiled, her face luminous from the genuineness of her smile, and Clare decided she was lovely.

One of the women was massaging Jule's feet; the other was working some kind of aromatic oil into her long black hair. The room was hot and steamy. The marble gleamed. No clock ticked—no need to rush utter self-indulgence. Time allowed the languid gesture, the hazed, unhurried motion. Somewhere, water was doused onto hot coals and a fresh cloud of steam billowed around the marble slabs and the gold-footed bath fixtures.

Jule stirred and pulled herself up on one elbow as if to say something, then lay down again, the women doing their jobs and Jule so eased that Clare suspected she had fallen asleep.

"It's about Tern," Clare said in a voice more strident than she intended.

Jule's lips curved in a smile.

"You sent Tern to my husband."

Jule smiled broadly. "I did. I'm sorry. You probably hate me."

"No, but I'm happy to say that your little ploy didn't work."

"Because he told you?"

"No, because he's not going to go with Tern. He's *my* husband."

Jule seemed to ponder this. Then she said, "Yes . . . well, maybe Tern was a little too cute. Maybe I should have sent someone like Cilla here"—she tugged at the woman rubbing oil into her hair, who giggled—"she looks more like a housewife. That Tern. She sends signals with her body that make men think they would be nothing but a soft peach in her mouth. Ah, well, it was a good try, eh? I knew it would either get us in or get us out."

"I could have told you it wouldn't work," Clare said with self-satisfaction. Perspiration from the steam was running down her back. Her blouse was glued to her skin.

"You're pretty sure of yourself." Jule gave her a long, slow smile. "But then, brides always are. You'd be surprised how fast you run out of ideas for the bed."

"How do you know so much about brides, Jule? You only ever had Turkit, and from what I hear, he wasn't good for much of anything."

"That's true."

"So?"

Jule gave a loud sigh. "I have an imagination. And, you know, there's nothing but women down here. All we do is talk, and all we talk about is men. After a while you become an expert, whether you have a man or not. The same things happen over and over again, and the only differences are of shading. Hearts ache, men love or don't love, stay or go, cause pain or give pleasure, it's all the same. It's just the techniques and degrees that vary."

She lay back down on the marble and closed her eyes again. "But you're right, I don't know from personal experience. Although I do believe that you don't have to be a chicken to recognize an egg."

Having no good answer for this, Clare fiddled with the top button of her blouse, finally undid it, and sat down on the slab. She was two years older than Jule, married, and a woman of the world, but it was Jule who seemed worldly, world-weary, and a fountain of experience.

"It's nice and steamy in here, isn't it?" Jule said. "You couldn't imagine that you would ever want more heat in this country, but there's something about the steam on your skin and the cool marble on your back that's very nice. If you wanted to, you could take off that skirt and blouse. We're all women here. Cilla gives a wonderful massage. I'll bet you need one. You'd give a massage, wouldn't you, Cilla?"

Cilla nodded vigorously.

"I don't have time," Clare said. In her life she had never taken off her clothes in front of anyone but her husband. She certainly hadn't sat naked in a marble bathroom, enveloped in steam, massaged by a servant. Jule was gazing at her through a fringe of black eyelashes, looking too much like Bathsheba at her bath, and that made Clare edgy.

She stood up. "I have to get going."

"But we could talk some more."

"I've got a lot to do."

"But you'll come back? I promise I won't send Tern around again."

"Good."

"You didn't come down to steam?"

"No . . . I was going to ask you something."

"You don't want to ask me anymore?"

"Yes. No. I mean yes, I still want to ask you."

Jule looked at her expectantly. The women halted their ministrations to her hair and feet and turned their eyes on Clare. Feeling stupid, Clare sat back down. "What I wanted to ask you is—"

Jule interrupted her. "Have you ever tried *kat*?" She reached into a willow basket heaped with green leaves. She gathered up a handful of the leaves and with surprising delicacy pushed them all into her mouth. "It's from Yemen," she said. "And it's very nice. It's a good way to begin a chat. We all chew *kat* down here. You'll feel wonderful. It's really bad form not to chew. You must observe the form."

"But what is it?"

"It's an herb. Or a shrub. I don't really know. We're not supposed to have it, so don't tell anybody, please? Cilla has a cousin who brings it to us from Sana. All the wives chew *kat*. You don't want to try?"

Clare leaned in to see the leaves through the haze of steam. They looked like mulberry leaves. She took some and held them under her nose. She crushed one between her fingers. She had her doubts. All the while, Jule was staring at her, challenging with that smile to try. Not wishing to lose face in front of Jule and feeling sufficiently intrigued to attempt something new, she pushed the leaves into her mouth. They were awful-tasting things. She chewed them into mush, then shifted the *kat* from one side of her mouth to the other. Jule watched for a long, skeptical moment, then stretched out on the marble like a lazy cat, her legs wide open. Not for the first time in the last five minutes did it occur to Clare that the woman with no clothes seemed more at ease than the one fully dressed.

"Is this *kat* supposed to do something?"

Jule plucked more leaves from the twigs. "Oh, yes. It makes you feel like you're floating on cotton wool. Like you don't have a care in the world."

"I don't feel anything."

"It takes a little time."

They chewed in silence. Clare accepted more leaves. Her clothes were soaked with steam and perspiration and stuck to her body.

"I still don't feel anything."

"Maybe it doesn't work for you."

Cilla and the other woman reached into the basket for a handful. Clare checked her watch. Water hissed on hot rocks. Fresh steam rolled into the room. Clare hiked her skirt up over her knees and rubbed her legs. She did not get this *kat*-chewing business at all. Some weird salivary craving incomprehensible to the

American tongue. She felt nothing at all. She felt proud that she felt nothing. She was too strong for the *kat*; it would not get the better of her.

And then she realized that she'd been staring at the same gold faucet fixture for probably fifteen minutes. She checked her watch. Had it really been fifteen minutes since she last checked the time? That faucet was the most interesting piece of bathroom plumbing she'd ever seen in her life. She would have walked over to get a better look at it if she felt any sensation in her legs at all. But her legs were numb. More surprising, this was not an unpleasant sensation. It was pretty good, as a matter of fact. But her clothes were a problem. They felt like a hide. She could not imagine why anyone ever wore clothes.

"I think I'll take my clothes off," she said.

Jule didn't bother to open her eyes. She seemed blissed out, her mind numbed.

Clare sat in her bra and panties.

"You could take them off too, you know," Jule said finally. "We're all women here."

"It's very warm."

"But not unpleasant, do you think?"

"No, I rather like it. But I think I'll leave my underthings on."

"Whatever you want—that's the whole idea."

After a few more minutes—or maybe it was an hour—Cilla stood up and came over to Clare with the little jade pot of oil and began to massage it into her scalp. After a few minutes, or maybe it was only a clock tick, Cilla began to rub the base of Clare's skull, then her shoulders. Time dissolved, disappeared. Cilla's strong hands were the only thing in the world. Clare slipped out of her bra and stretched out on her stomach. Cilla worked the muscles in her shoulders and neck. Clare had never noticed how tight those muscles were until Cilla freed them from their knots. The room was enveloped in steam; she could barely make out their faces. Jule's hand, full of *kat* leaves, appeared through the haze. Clare added fresh leaves to the wet wad in her mouth.

Jule opened her eyes. "How do you feel?"

"Relaxed."

"I told you."

"Really relaxed. Do you do this all the time?"

"Now I do. In the old days, when Turkit was alive, I was too busy trying to stay on his good side. But now ... well, as you know, there's nothing much for us to do down here. So I may as well lie around and chew *kat*. Now that you know how nice it is, you can come down every day. We can talk. Cilla will give you a massage. We'll chew *kat* and be friends. All of the wives are really curious about you. They want to hear about America. They want to go through your closets and ask you every kind of question. Is that your real color of hair?"

"Yes."

"Tell the truth."

"That *is* the truth."

"That's what Tern says. She bleaches her hair, but no one is supposed to know. I think most blond women lighten their hair. Turkit even lightened his hair at one time. He liked blond hair. He didn't care if it was natural."

"Mine is natural."

Jule raised her eyebrows.

"This is my natural color of hair," Clare insisted. "I can prove it." Abruptly, she stood up and kicked out of her panties. "See!" She gave Jule a smug smile and sat down again. "Tell Tern."

"Tern will be disappointed."

"Good."

Cilla giggled and moved down to work on Clare's feet. How had she made it through her life so far without Cilla?

Jule dispensed more *kat*. More steam rolled from the secret source.

"Do you find living here difficult?" Jule asked.

"I was brought up in a very hard place, almost as hard as this. At least you have indoor toilets. Besides, I have my husband, and he makes things easy."

"He's very handsome."

"He is."

"Are you going to have a baby soon?"

"I hope so."

"I don't have any children. Turkit was almost out of steam by the time my father sent me here. Did you have many men before you were married?"

"None."

"I only ever went with Turkit."

Cilla, flexing Clare's toes, snorted.

Jule took a cotton towel and rubbed the perspiration off her arms. "Cilla thinks she knows everything."

Clare turned to look at Cilla, who gave her a broad wink. "Maybe she does."

"To tell the truth," Jule said, "Turkit had a nephew I thought was rather nice looking. He had good eyes."

Cilla snickered.

"Actually," Jule added, "he had a good body. Long, long legs and a very nice chest. Not scrawny, you know. I hate a scrawny chest. He used to sneak down here every once in a while. Turkit would have killed him if he'd found out, but he never did."

A woman Clare had never seen before padded into the bathroom and handed each of them cold tea in Wedgwood cups. The tea tasted like elderberries. But then, she couldn't be sure. Everything seemed slightly off kilter, slowed down, easy to take.

"The nephew taught me everything I know about men."

"Like what? I thought you said you didn't know any men."

"Just this one."

"So what did he teach you?"

"Well, have you ever noticed—"Jule slid across the marble to her—"that just behind a man's testicles there is a muscle, or vein, I don't know what it is exactly except that when you touch it it feels like a thick cord? And that when a man has an erection if you stroke your finger up and down this cord very gently his penis will jump up by an inch?"

Cilla giggled.

"It's true."

"Really?"

"Next time, try it. You'll see. It grows a whole inch."

"What other tricks do you know?"

"Ah, so you admit I do know something? You want to learn all my tricks. I can't tell you them all at once. You come down here and chew *kat* and maybe I'll tell you another secret about men. One at a time. What good will I be to you if I tell you everything all at once? You won't have any use for me at all."

"I almost forgot—that that's why I came down here, before you got me sidetracked with *kat*. Jule, you don't want to lie around and do this all day, every day."

"Yes, I do."

Clare rolled onto her back so Cilla could go to work on her arm muscles. "No, you can't spend your life doing this. Besides, my husband isn't going to change his mind. He doesn't want the wives in the palace. You know all this. I've been stalling, trying to help you. But now I think I have a solution. I want you to join my inoculation program. I want you to learn how to give the vaccinations that will keep people from contracting the diseases that are killing them. And learn how to take medical histories and do all those things that the women who assist physicians in the U.S.

do. You'll travel all around the country. You'll play an important role. You'll help my husband rebuild the country."

"I don't know . . ."

Clare sat up. "You really don't have a choice. You have to leave, and this way you have something to go to. We'll work together. It's going to be exciting."

Jule stirred and yawned. The effect of the *kat* was wearing off. She looked around the gorgeous bathroom, at Cilla, who was rubbing musk oil into Clare's hands.

"We have to go out on the plain?" She winced. "It's so hot. Everybody's starving. And there's no *kat*."

Clare's plan didn't seem quite so inspired to Tarik. The image of Turkit's wives playing nurse when their former assignment was to drive His Most Stainless Majesty to paroxysms of sexual pleasure was hilarious to him.

But Clare was convinced and went down to the west wing again to chew *kat* and steam and press into Jule's brain the notion that this was the thing to do. Finally, Jule was persuaded they didn't have any choice.

Not all of the wives agreed. Most of them drifted out of the palace to take their chances on the outside. But Jule and eight others took the hygiene classes with Dr. Van Damm and learned how to give the intramuscular injections.

Clare divided the wives up into teams, rotating them so that after a few weeks each had gone to the countryside with Van Damm to help with inoculations and take medical histories.

The night before she was to take one of the teams to Turma to teach hygiene and wait for Van Damm to come from Nizra to begin inoculating, Clare trimmed her hair in front of the bedroom mirror.

Tarik watched her from the bed. "Now, if something happens—" He couldn't get the vision of Hadi, coming after her, out of his mind. But he couldn't share this with her, of course; he intended that she would never know.

"Nothing is going to happen." She looked at him in the mirror. "Why are you always so worried about me? I have Het. I have the bodyguards."

"I'm worried because it's rough out there. Turma's very near the Yemeni border. And Duru. I want you to promise me that you won't let yourself get separated from Het, no matter what. Het can handle anything. Promise me."

"I promise I won't let Het out of my sight."

"If something goes wrong, get to Stan Cobb in Duru."

"Okay. Nothing will happen. I have so much protection, I can hardly move."

She looked at her hair in the mirror. The ends were ragged. "Want me to trim your hair? It's awfully long."

"I don't know . . . Look, one side of yours is longer than the other, isn't it?" he said.

She snipped off more hair, frowned, but said, "It'll be okay. I'll do yours now."

Reluctantly, he came over and sat down on a chair in front of the mirror and took off his shirt. She spent some time brushing his hair, which hung nearly to his shoulders, trying to get it smooth enough so she could cut straight across. Then she began to cut.

"It's not even," he complained right away.

"I'll fix it." She pulled up a straightback chair and sat down behind him, nearly surrounding him with her legs. "Stay still. I can't see what I'm doing."

"You know," she said, concentrating on her job, "it's over thirty miles from Turma to Duru, all terrible road. I've never wanted to walk across the room to see Stan Cobb."

"He's not so bad."

"He *is* so bad. That's why you like him."

"He's harmless."

"In a disgusting sort of way. But if I need him, I'll find him, I guess."

She came around to cut the sides of his hair.

"You've been down to the bath again."

"You have spies."

"No." He pushed his face against her arm. "I can smell the musk."

"Jule gave a farewell *kat* chew and steam. Her last hurrah to the good life."

"Who went?"

"Well, I'm not going to tell you Tern was there because you'll ask me what she looks like with her clothes off."

He examined his hair in the mirror; it was getting more uneven with every slice of the scissors. He kept his eye on her every snip, saying, "There's no law says you and I can't go down to use the bath ourselves," he said. "You could show me what you girls do down there. What do you do, by the way?"

She caught his eye in the mirror. "Completely innocent stuff. Girl talk."

Her breasts brushed against his face when she moved in to try to even up one side of his hair. Reflexively, his hand began stroking her thigh.

"Are you wearing panties, by the way?"

"No."

"So tell me, what do you talk about down there?"

"We talk about men."

"I bet the girls have plenty to say."

"Actually, most of them haven't been with a man in years."

"Oh, that's disappointing. So you supply all the information."

"Sometimes."

"Like what?"

"What do you want to know?"

"Do you tell them about me?"

"Of course not!"

"Why not?"

"Because they want to jump on you already. I'm not giving them any details."

"What do they do all day besides chew *kat* and get massaged? All those women. No men. All that nude bathing. Do you take your clothes off?"

"Uh-huh."

"And Cilla rubs you down?"

"Yes."

He put his hands on her waist and pulled her a little closer.

"You better watch out. I've got the scissors."

"Is it nice?"

"The massage? Yes, very nice."

"And the *kat* gets you stoned?"

"A little bit. It's nice. You're kind of half asleep and time gets all weird and floaty. We drink elderberry tea—I think it's elderberry. Actually, I have no idea what it is."

"It could be ox blood, for all you know."

"Are there oxen here? I thought the women pulled the plows."

"There aren't even any plows to pull. Does Cilla rub you here?" He massaged her hips.

"You're really into this bath business."

"Come on, Clare, it's the only pleasant thing that goes on around here. So what about it? Does Cilla rub you here?"

"Yes."

His hand to her belly. "Here?"

"Yes."

"Really?"

"No."

"Here?" His hand between her legs.

"Definitely not."

"What about Jule?"

"I can't cut your hair if you keep that up. I don't know what Jule and Cilla do together. I don't ask them."

"But they could."

"You want me to say they do? I don't know if they do."

"Make it up."

"I think they do. They're always naked. They rub each other down with oil and then they do it on the marble slab for hours and hours. Dozens of them, writhing, moaning, women on top of women—God, it's such a male fantasy!"

"And such a good one. It's a harem, dammit! They're supposed to do sexy things."

"Mostly they sit around and do needlepoint all day."

"Clare!"

"They do. They all need glasses because they've gone blind from needlepoint."

He took his hand away. "I thought we could have some fun."

"We can. We can have fun right now."

She put the scissors away and knelt down in front of him. She unbuttoned his trousers and buried her face between his legs. In the mirror, he watched her working at him. He also saw with regret that his hair was a mess; he'd have to have Nal cut it again in the morning.

She ran her hands between his legs, hunting for the little muscle that Jule had described.

"What are you doing down there?"

"Looking for something."

"Something I don't know about?"

She dug deeper. "I think so."

"Tell me if you find it—ah, I think you just did." She stroked the little muscle behind his testicles. With her other hand she tugged his trousers down.

He closed his eyes. His head fell back. His breath came faster. He panted quietly for a time. He felt as if he were nothing more than a tender peach in her mouth. He sent up a silent prayer that she would never stop. He opened his eyes and watched her in the mirror.

"So what *does* she look like with her clothes off?" he said.

She raised her head and gave him a look. "Who?"

"Tern."

12

There were problems at Turma. Van Damm and the medicines never showed up. Yemeni guerrillas had crossed the border the day before and driven off the villagers' cattle; rounding up the animals took priority over immunization. The wives were terrified that the guerrillas might come back. They refused to wait for Van Damm unless the bodyguard stayed behind to protect them. The battery in the bodyguards' Land-Rover died; nobody had jumper cables. Clare decided the only thing to do was to drive to Duru in her vehicle to borrow cables and a battery charger from Stanley Cobb. Nal wouldn't go without the wives. Het said Clare couldn't go to Duru without him.

In the end, she and Het set out to find Stan Cobb, leaving Nal behind in charge of the others.

As far as she could see, there was nothing but stone—a vast carpet of bleached stone of every shape and size stretching out to the horizon. Then, every five miles or so, a group of hovels materialized out of baked earth, no more than five or six of them, huddled around a well. They had no dignity at all. They merely served as further evidence, if it were needed, of the country's miserable condition.

Once in a while a few young boys would appear, urging goats over the rocks to meager grazing. The rest of the time there was nothing in either direction but rubble. And the sun, of course. Always the sun.

The road, such as it was, was an old caravan trail beaten into gravel from centuries of use. It ran exactly parallel to the rocky cliffs on the west, the unneighborly snake-and-rider fence that marked the kingdom's uneasy border with Yemen. Het checked his compass more than once. The road was hard to follow and drifted off every few miles into scrubby patches and trails. They had followed one of these for a quarter of a mile before realizing they had left the main road. Het was afraid of wandering into some gully that the Yemenis counted as their own.

They would pass through a shantytown village, Het would roll his eyes at the sad-eyed children, and Clare would nod her head up and down to convey comprehension. But when the village washed away in their dust, she didn't have the courage to turn to look behind her. Het watched her out of the corner of his eye when he thought she wasn't looking.

Het took his job beyond devotion. Whenever they were in the countryside, he checked her like a hen, cooking her food and clucking when she was too hot or tired to eat. He sat vigil outside her tent at night, lifting the flap every once in a while to see if she was asleep. Most of the time he stared at her with such a profound expression of worry that once she finally went over to him and said, "I'm okay, Het. I'm okay."

"Good," he responded in perfect English, which took her aback.

He never once troubled her or was anything other than utterly constant. Never a look or a gesture that wasn't at all times completely supportive and sympathetic.

After a thirty-mile trip through hell, they pulled off the main road and turned west, to where Cobb had made his camp.

There was suspense in the approach. They drove upward from the main road for nearly a mile, the road disappearing at times as the earth changed color from pink to brown to tan to mauve. And then Stan Cobb's drilling site appeared. Squalid and tumble-down, it was a collection of shacks surrounding huge pieces of drilling equipment. A tin-roofed house trailer shimmered in the sun, blinding them. As they pulled up in a cloud of grit, Stanley came out to greet them.

Quickly Clare explained their problem and just as quickly Stan found jumper cables, a fifty-watt electric generator, and a five-gallon can of gasoline. He sent one of the workmen to find the battery charger, and settled down in the shade of a tattered awning to talk.

"You look good, Clare," he said, not knowing any other way to begin a conversation with a woman.

She told him she was sorry to hear that Hawkins, his partner in the enterprise, had died.

Stan pointed to a scrub patch of shrub. "He was right over there. Weaving all over. His tongue hanging out of his mouth like this"—he paused for a gruesome imitation—"junk dripping out.

Ugh, it was disgusting. Then he just kind of twisted around and keeled over and that was that." He shuddered theatrically. "Never want to see anything like that again. Had to bury him that very instant, so the sun wouldn't rot him out."

Clare smiled sympathetically and changed the subject. "I'm setting up a medical dispensary over in Turma. And we're coming to Duru next. Always some problem or other."

"Who's we?"

"Well, I've gotten some of Turkit's wives to help out."

"What a waste of good"—he made a quick mental substitution of a female body part—"women." He exhaled. Biting his tongue didn't come easy. And Clare was giving him one of those icy-blond looks, which made him twice as nervous.

"Not really," she said, fanning herself with a piece of corrugated cardboard she found at her feet. "I don't know what you think I should do with them."

Stan was about to tell her that she ought to turn them loose in Duru for fun and games but was too wise to open his mouth. Best not to offend the bride. Tarik put an awful big stock in everything she said and did. And he didn't like the looks of that big giant with the Bren gun who was looking over at him as if he were something stuck to his shoe.

To Stan's relief, the workman finally came back with the battery charger. Clare stood up. Neither of them could think of another thing they might have to say to each other.

He walked her over to the Land-Rover. Out of the corner of her eye she saw him wiping his filthy hand against his trousers. He was trying to clean himself up in preparation for a handshake and kiss. She felt a rare moment of compassion for him. He was Tarik's friend, after all, even if what constituted that friendship was lost on her. Some sort of male attraction that eluded her understanding. She didn't want to know the details.

So he was mildly surprised when she embraced him, looking him in the eye in a sincere way, and told him to take care of himself. His heart began to thump pleasantly to think that this cool, beautiful blonde had softened. But then, in the last few weeks he had grown accustomed to the warmth of a woman and her many moods.

"Want a sip of 'shine before you leave?" he asked her, making the ultimate gesture of the host.

She shook her head and pointed to the sun. "Hot. Can't do it. Wish it were cool."

He nodded in comprehension.

When she was in the vehicle and he had shut the door, he asked her if she had a gun. She told him that Het was fully armed but he held up his hand for them to wait and ran inside. He came back with a .22 Magnum pistol.

Het began to protest, but Stan silenced him with a look.

"Know how to use it?" he asked her.

Clare took the heavy gun and cocked and uncocked it. "I can use it," she said.

He pressed a handful of bullets into her palm. "Load it before you get to the main road."

"Okay."

He looked out to the western horizon and rubbed his stubbly chin. "I don't know. I don't like this. I shouldn't let you go. If anything happened to you, Tarik would never forgive me. Promise me you'll go straight to Turma like a bat out of hell and then radio for an army escort. These Yemeni bastards aren't joking. Last week they ambushed a military convoy and killed six men. It was over east"—he looked in that direction—"but . . ."

He threw up his hands resignedly. "I guess it's okay."

"It's okay, Stan. I have Het. And I have the pistol. And I have you. Thank you for everything."

He pulled a face.

"You know," she said, rearing back in her seat and looking him up and down, "I can't quite put my finger on it, but something's come over you, Stan. You've changed."

She noticed, he thought as they pulled away. *I hope to Christ nobody else does.*

Stan watched the Land-Rover until it was out of sight and the last cloud of dust drifted off on the air. Then he returned to the metal trailer, checked the various dials and regulators, and saw that everything was running smoothly. That accomplished, he crossed the dusty footpath to the shack he called home.

From beneath a large square of tin he drew out a basin, filled it with precious fresh water, and unwrapped a worn-smooth bar of soap from a pair of clean cotton underpants.

He stripped naked, lathered the soap, and methodically began washing himself. The soap clotted in the acres of coarse black hair that carpeted his body, and he had to waste water rinsing off. After he had washed all the way down to his toes, taking extra care with his private parts, he lathered his face again, found his razor, and shaved himself, using his fingers to direct the blade around his nose and mouth. In the warm air he dried quickly.

Then he removed a clean shirt, pants, and socks from his foot-locker and slipped them on. He wished he had something other than his filthy work boots to wear, but no such luck. He refused to look at them as he laced them up. No need to spoil a pretty picture.

Only after he had slicked down his hair, checked his fingernails (which were dispiritingly black no matter how hard he scrubbed), made sure his shirttails were in and his fly zipped tight, inventoried, in fact, every thread, button, and body hair, did he feel he was ready to go to town.

Twenty minutes later he was steadying his pickup through the narrow streets of Duru.

The place could have been any boom town anywhere in the world. But for sheer heat of day and pollution of character, there was only one Duru. Even though he sweltered, Stan kept his car windows rolled up. The stink of sewage, garbage, and animal dung in the streets made for a mix he wanted no part of, not when he was smelling of hand soap and good intentions.

Already the streets were clogged with the pickups of prospectors from drilling sites for twenty miles around. Stores shuttered against the midday sun had reopened, and hawkers shouted out the value and dubious beauty of their wares. Many of the goods were English—Twinings tea, Pears soaps; tastes developed during colonial times. But most were oddments from the underdeveloped economies—Fang Fang baby powder from China and Cuba Cola from Havana—third-rate consumer goods.

Other, more ancient enterprises thrived out in the open. A boy no more than eight, with antimony-rimmed eyes and a lipsticked little mouth, was being pimped by his mother. She pushed him forward and made lewd sucking motions with her mouth when Stan drove close. He slowed the truck a little, then gunned it hard and swerved the wheels as he went by, hoping to kick a little gravel in her teeth. God how he hated dames like that.

For four years, ever since geologists' first reports of an ocean of oil sunk deep in the sand, engineers from the big American and British oil companies had hustled to Duru to set up operations. A second wave brought the independents and the entrepreneurs, speculators who might get lucky and never have to work again, men like Stan and his late partner, Hawkins.

On the third wave arrived the flotsam of the world, scum who fastened themselves to those on the upper rungs and, like culi, sucked blood for all they were worth. They provided the drugs, the drink, the orifices, and whatever else it took for their betters

to take the slippery chute to depravity. One of these was the Brit
Jack Brewster. It was into the back parking lot of Jack's Place, a
dive, that Stan pulled his pickup and parked it alongside the dozen
or so others haphazardly left there. It was Saturday night in Duru
and everybody was in town for their quota of flesh.

Stan checked his look in the rearview mirror for any esthetic
flaws. Finding none, he slid off the seat and slammed the truck
door shut. His pulse began to jump pleasantly when he heard the
bass thump of the jukebox pounding through the bar's thin walls.
He pushed open the door and took a deep breath.

He believed he could smell her before he saw her.

Through a mist of cigarette smoke, kerosene fumes, and body
sweat, his eyes narrowed, focused, and then rebounded with light.
On a dance floor the size of a card table, buck naked, body
agleam with perspiration and oil of frankincense, dappled with the
light of Coleman lamps, she was in the act of taking the forty or
so oil prospectors packed into Jack's on a trip through the gates
of heaven.

Sirah. Sirah. Saying her name under his breath brought pinpricks of heat to Stan's flesh.

He pushed his way through the tight mob of men to a tiny spot
of floor space. He wedged his broad shoulders between two Germans whom he knew were working a claim at Brater, about half
a mile from his own. One of the men was so drunk he had uri-
nated down his pants leg. Stan turned his head from the stink. The
other man had such an unholy look on his face that Stan couldn't
imagine what he was thinking, until he glanced down and saw
that he had taken his penis out of his pants and was slowly mas-
turbating.

Stan inhaled deeply to calm himself. In another lifetime he
would have taken the man's pecker and snapped it in half like a
Popsicle stick. But that was the old days. Love had steadied the
new Stan. The bad-tempered beast had received the balm of sure
and certain knowledge and he had changed, as Clare suspected.
Let them jack off from here to Timbuktu, he thought. She is mine.

Still, he resented the intrusion of the hard-pumping German and
worried for a moment that he would not be able to resume his
reverie.

But of course she did not fail him.

Her body was the color of milky tea, her eyes black as a star-
less night. High, firm haunches and buttocks tapered down tanned
legs to the tiniest, most cunning feet Stan had ever seen. Her

stomach was taut but swelled to a sweetly swollen mons. She had very little pubic hair.

But it was her breasts that slackened Stan's legs and stiffened his penis. Although Sirah claimed to be twenty (really she was twenty-four), she had the undeveloped breasts of a very young girl. Only slightly rounded, with babyish nipples that barely showed through the areolas.

How many nights had Stan pumped away like this snorting German beside him, pretending he could free those nipples from their flesh cocoon. He would suck them until they were hard and raised and eager. If he pulled away his mouth, they would quickly soften and retract and he would have to resume his work all over again. Pump, pump into the night for two whole months, dreaming of Sirah's inverted nipples.

She had raised her rump to the men and was expertly fingering her anus and vagina at the same time. Her long black hair had parted over her back and gathered beside her on the floor like pools of oil. Some Texans shouted obscenities at her, but most of the men were too numbed by lust to say much of anything.

She was coming to the end of her performance. Not for Sirah the dildo or the long-necked beer bottle, or anything other than her own expert fingers. It had never occurred to her to use any device to bring herself to orgasm. If these red-eyed men didn't like it, she couldn't care less. A hundred of them could watch her, but she was still doing it only for herself.

Squatted on her haunches, she opened her bent legs as wide as they would go. She closed her eyes and began a relaxed inventory through the familiar folds and creases. She winced a little when she touched her tiny clitoris. She believed her clitoris was somehow chained to her back teeth because her molars always began aching pleasurably when she got to this part.

Indifferent before, now she quickly became excited. Her fingers ringed faster around her sex, poking in and out of her vagina, pinching her clitoris. Involuntarily, her buttocks raised and she began to pump on her hand. She threw her head back and her mouth dropped slackly open. Images darted quickly in and out of her spinning mind, quicker even than her fingers lathered her clitoris. In another moment she would faint. Now! She had to do it now. If she did not do it now, it would be all over in an instant and she would have missed out.

From under the filthy rug she pulled a large hand mirror, the kind found on ladies' vanity tables. She settled her bottom onto the rug and then set the mirror between her feet, held it there, and then stared with rapt and grateful expression at the sight she loved most in the world: her own two stubby little fingers sunk deep in her cunt, getting off for all the world to see.

It was, as always, the best sex she ever had.

Stan felt as if he had the wind knocked out of him. His penis was rock-hard, but unlike the other men he refused to play with himself in front of Sirah. He turned on his heel and quickly left the bar. He worried that it would demean him in her eyes if he masturbated while she danced. He was afraid it would make him seem too much like the others. But in the sanctuary of the cab of his pickup, he couldn't help but succumb.

He had invited her to dinner after the show at a place called the Khartoum Kafe and she was two hours late. The owner had been glaring at him since midnight and the knot of other men and their dates waiting for tables by the door checked their watches every time he signaled for a waiter. He had already spent a fortune on beer and side dishes holding on to the table.

Finally, close to one-thirty, she showed up.

He pulled out a chair for her. "You're late, Sirah."

She heaved a petulant sigh and folded her arms across the baby breasts.

"You said one-thirty. It's one-thirty."

"I said eleven-thirty. I'm sure I said eleven-thirty."

When he saw she was getting angry, he backed off. "Maybe I said one-thirty. I probably said one-thirty."

What if she became so angry she jumped out of her chair and bolted? His heart tightened in his chest at the thought of it.

"Anyway," he said, a little desperate now to mollify her, "you must be hungry. Have something. Everything here comes from Bahrain. Eat, Sirah."

She patted her stomach uncertainly. "I don't know. When I eat my belly swells up, and I have another show at two-fifteen."

She maneuvered his wrist to read his watch. "I don't have much time."

Hurt, he said, "Can't you cancel, Sirah? You just got here—" He stopped abruptly when he saw she was angry again.

"You don't have to work, Sirah. I promised I'd support you. Look"—he pulled some money from his pocket, practically the last of his savings—"I have plenty of money. I'm only about a minute away from a strike."

Her eyes wandered around the room. "All of you—you're going to get rich. You're going to fly me around the world. You're going to give me furs and gold slippers."

"I will!"

"When, Stanley? I'm getting old waiting for you to fly me 'round the world. I have to earn a living. You tell me to eat, but I can't eat words."

She flicked her menu onto the table and put a hurt look on her face.

Stanley studied her, uncertain what to say next. He thought he should console her, but deep down he was thrilled that she was angry. Most women looked right through him when they took his money. But Sirah *reacted.* She pouted, she stormed, once she had even slapped him across the face. But she was never indifferent, the most painful sort of rejection. The nastier she became, the more he believed she truly cared. There was no behavior that he did not interpret through this equation.

A waiter came with a bowl of pickled carrots, and Sirah began to eat greedily. "I want a steak, Stanley," she said between mouthfuls.

"You'll get the best steak in the house!" As he signaled the waiter, he furtively fingered the money in his pocket through the fabric of his trousers, trying to get a count. Not much, and he'd had to spend a fortune on appetizers before she got here.

He checked his watch. Her next show was at two-fifteen. He didn't have much time. If he didn't speak now, he wouldn't see her again until the next time he came to town, at least a week. Filled with a mix of longing and dread, he decided to skate out on thin ice and said, "I mean it, Sirah. I don't want you to work after we're"—he screwed up his courage—"when we're married. When my ship comes in."

"When we're married you'll turn me into an old cow, Stanley."

Bingo! He felt such a rush of gratitude, such an expansion of joy that he thought he might order a celebratory steak himself. He hadn't eaten properly in weeks, hanging on to precious cash to satisfy Sirah's ravenous appetite, and would have loved a juicy piece of beef. Quickly, he put the thought by him; only money enough for one. It was a pleasure to give himself up for . . . his wife. Saying it in his mind ennobled his sacrifice. Anyway, maybe he wasn't so hungry after all. Sirah would marry him and all his big, strange appetites would be satisfied.

He settled his arm around her proprietorially, wanting the other men to see that she was his, but she shook it off.

"Have you talked to him yet?"

"Talked to who?"

"Who do you think?" She began combing through her huge mane of hair with her fingers. "To your friend Tarik, Stanley. I want you to get him to get that hideous White-Lyons to give me my passport back."

"But, honey, you won't need your passport when you're my wife. We'll have a passport together. We'll be a married couple."

She folded her arms over her baby breasts. "Who says?"

"But, Sirah, you said—"

"No, *you* said, Stanley. You said, 'when my ship comes in.' You said it! That could be months, years, and I'm supposed to sit in this rat hole all that time? That's not love." She narrowed her eyes at him. "You're just like him. You want to put me in prison like White-Lyons."

"No!"

"You want to chain me up and punish me for something I didn't do. Something you just *think* I did. I didn't do anything, Stanley, no matter what he says."

She slumped in her chair and the scooped neck of her dress dipped. He could just make out the narrow cleavage of her breasts. He leaned in closer so he might feel her sweet breath on his face. She carried on her skin the musky remnants of sweat, frankincense, and semen, although Stanley had not discerned that last pungent ingredient of her perfume.

"Do you want the passport so much, Sirah?"

"I do, Stanley," she said, slicing into the steak before the waiter had even removed his hand from the plate. "It will make an honest woman of me. And I won't let you marry me unless I'm an honest woman."

Het removed his compass from his uniform pocket and tried to read it by the quarter moon. When the thin light was not enough, he struck a match. He held the compass out so Clare could see too.

"East, Het? How did we get so far east?"

He shook his head miserably and tapped the compass face with his finger, willing the needle to move west miraculously.

She patted his arm. "Don't worry. We'll get straightened out at sunrise."

The Land-Rover had broken down only ten miles from Stanley's place and it had taken Het more than two hours to get it started again. By then the sun was well down and they were in total darkness. They had struggled on for a few miles, but Het was afraid the headlights would drain the battery and had pulled off the road and killed the engine.

The sun had taken all its warmth with it and Clare shivered bravely for a long time before Het worked up the courage to wrap her in his arms. They had been asleep like that for an hour when an engine sound woke them up.

In an instant Het was out of the Land-Rover, his hand wrapped around his machine gun. He made a motion for Clare to stay where she was and then he disappeared into the darkness. A moment later she heard him cry out in his own language.

She didn't bother calling his name. She grabbed Stan's pistol from under her seat and cocked it. With all the silent stealth she had used as a girl to stalk rattlers, she eased open the door of the Land-Rover. But before she could stretch one foot out to find the roadway, the door was yanked open and a rough arm grabbed her from behind in a hammerlock. With the breath squeezing out of her, she fired off one shot. Then the pressure increased, until blackness overtook her mind.

13

The tiny one-room home the army had commandeered from a bewildered widow and her daughter was built to house no more than two or three; fifteen men now stretched it to its limits.

Electricity snapped through the place as soldiers and advisers talking in loud voices clashed for the right to be heard above one another. Static noise blared; alone in a corner, a young soldier fiddled with the knobs on a large radio-telephone set, trying to reach an army column a few miles away. Other men poked their fingers around maps scattered on a rough table. An American army colonel, a military adviser, argued with a local commander. He was out of uniform, in khaki pants and plaid shirt. He chain-smoked, which allowed him to show off a West Point class ring the size of a small potato. Arthur Olson read a cable from Washington, jotted a response in the margin, and handed it back to a runner.

At the other end of the room Tarik maintained his isolation. There was in his manner an air of aloofness that bordered on contempt. His native coolness made the others' behavior seem outlandish by contrast.

He had not taken a chair since he arrived at the command post from the city that morning. He stood perfectly composed, his fingers knotted together behind his back. It was the behavior he instinctively offered, Nila's sly trick: inwardly raging, calm without. Yet his keen eyes missed nothing. They darted over the faces of the men, scanned reports, checked map locations, flew to the door when a new man entered. The men strained toward him, wanting to be next to him. He tolerated their questions, courtesy concealing his impatience. He had inherited his army and air force officers from Turkit and he thought most of them venal, stupid, and lazy. When the time came he planned to get rid of them and train new officers with men and techniques imported from the States.

For the time being, however, he had to ensure the loyalty of those he had. The base of his legitimacy still rested solely on his status as Malik's son. The army could go either way in a crisis.

When an unfamiliar officer entered with much saluting, the corners of Tarik's mouth curled in amusement and he detached himself from the core of men, feeling suddenly restless. He checked his watch and then walked to the window and stared out; as he did, several sets of eyes followed him. How did they see him? he wondered. As a sentimentalist probably. Would they take this as proof of some deeper human frailty?

The Yemenis wanted Duru. In exchange for getting it, they would return Clare to him. He knew without question that he would give it to them, and he understood with equal certainty that there were men in the room who would try to cut his throat for doing it.

Any day now some lucky prospector would bring up the sea of oil under that rocky plain and in one broad sweep problems extant since Abraham would be effaced. Overnight the wretched, fly-specked country becomes a power to be reckoned with, a verdant paradise. Children grow fat, with apple-red cheeks, old people die in their own familiar beds, the populace is educated, vaccinated, habitated. No more kicks in the teeth from the Europeans. Poverty, hunger, sickness—gone. Simply the best for everyone, and didn't they deserve it after all these years of shouldering the burden?

And he was going to give it all away. For a woman.

He frowned as he stared out the open window and watched two rutted-faced men, whippet-lean, hobble their horses and hunker down in the dirt to wait out a dust storm. He had brought just one regiment of troops with him—to show the Yemenis he meant business but not to pose such a threat that they would harm Clare. But also because if things went badly and the army turned on him, they would have only a limited number to do it with.

He glanced over his shoulder. He thought he'd heard White-Lyons come in the door. The old man had shown up uninvited and Tarik had sent him out to receive the Yemenis' terms, half hoping they would kill him. Suddenly it struck Tarik that the guerrillas might have actually done just that, killed White-Lyons, killed all of them, in fact, and for the first time he felt fear and lost himself in dreams of death. He could not go on if he did not have Clare.

Rather—of course he would go on. He was obligated to his mother and everything she had told him of Malik to go on, but it would be, he decided, as an alien to all who lived. This would be a strange arrangement he would make with the living, a condition of willed nonexistence. He made himself focus on an image of Clare, when they had first met, the night they were married. The last time they had been together.

He turned at a sound to find White-Lyons at his shoulder.

"How is she?" he asked without greeting. "Have they hurt her?"

"They roughed her up a little, but she's fine," White-Lyons reported. He was worn out, covered in dust, but thrilled all the same to be playing some role. "She put up a good fight. Got off a round and nicked one of them in the arm before they knocked her out."

"With Het's gun?"

"She told me that Stanley Cobb had given her a .22 pistol in Duru. And she used it."

Tarik repressed a smile.

White-Lyons slumped into a chair, looking tired past exhaustion. "My God, but these leftists are bloody bores. Forty-five minutes of Marxist-Leninist cant before you can even get the time of day. But yes, of course, there were no surprises: You give them Duru—with some sort of statement of apology for having held it in the first place—and they give you Clare. That's the deal they're offering."

"Good." Tarik turned and resumed staring out the window. The dust storm was nearly over and the two rutted-faced men were at the business of shaking sand out of their goods.

"In case you're thinking about volunteering your opinion, Colonel, don't bother. Most of the men here would rather I shoot myself in the head than hand Duru over. They figure I can always get another wife, but where else can I get the potential for nine hundred million barrels of oil a year?"

White-Lyons opened his mouth but Tarik stopped him. "It was a rhetorical question, Colonel. Doesn't require an answer. Anyway, I expect you more than any of them feels that way. Say, you didn't hire these Yemenis, did you? Hatch some scheme with Hadi to get rid of Clare and get me married to Topaz?"

When White-Lyons made indignant protest, Tarik put up his hand and smiled. "I was joking, Colonel. Relax."

"A joke in bad taste. How could you think . . . ?"

"I suspect you might be capable of anything. As for Hadi, well, nothing is beyond him."

"You know that if you give Duru to the Yemenis for Clare, you're finished."

"I don't know that at all. I give them Duru today, I take it back tomorrow. You have so little faith."

White-Lyons stared at him in frustration. Tarik's face remained expressionless. Those eyes were empty of emotion. White-Lyons would have understood if he had raged, wept, torn out his hair. But there was nothing but composed certainty, and that White-Lyons could not tolerate. He stooped to the lowest sort of blackmail: "I'm glad Malik is dead," he said. "I'm glad he's not here to see you behave so despicably. So selfish. Hadi will kill you. Take my word for it."

He had seen Azarak in town that morning and the madman had given him the death stare. When Hadi finds out that Tarik is trading Duru for Clare, he will make his move and then they will all be in hell together. White-Lyons felt irritated all over again. If it weren't for Clare, wouldn't they be on a smooth-sailing river of success? Wouldn't the two of them be pulling together down that river? This had been his dream for twenty-five years. Twenty-five years of a long, sweet dream life.

What a world of trouble this marriage had brought to all of them. What was love to the course of nationhood? In the quest for greatness? He wondered at this and then felt an immediate surge of remorse. The same consuming remorse that had punished his life once before; he had spent years suffering from its sadness.

Still, he felt a flush of pride at Tarik's boldness and at the quality of his character. No, to White-Lyons's way of thinking, the problem lay not with the trade, but with the item traded. Had this been Hadi's daughter Topaz, then the loss of the oil revenues would have been offset at least by the prospect of solid peace with the clans. Now there could be neither. He had some small regret that he had mentioned Malik, but he was a desperate man. In his heart he believed he needed only to find the one magic word that would turn Tarik around.

"Do as you wish," he said morosely. "I see I can't change your mind."

"I expect they want us to pull back," Tarik said.

"To Brater."

Tarik went out the door. Over his shoulder he said, "I want to be there when they release her."

"It might be safer if you—" But he was gone. White-Lyons brushed the dust off his visored cap. Memory should serve to instruct, not to punish, he decided bitterly as he followed him out the door. There ought to be a statute of limitations on remembrance.

* * *

The details of the exchange were simple. Five miles beyond the Duru town walls, the two opposing sides assembled, roughly a thousand yards apart. For an hour or so there was a great sense of arrival and departure; then, uneasy calm. The thirty-man security detail included twenty Americans from a crack service outfit that Olson had flown in from Cyprus the night before.

Tarik waited in an armored command car, Olson beside him, perspiring in the sweltering heat. He told Olson to drink more water and passed him his canteen.

"I forgot how awful it gets out here," Olson said weakly. "Last time I was on the plain in heat like this I was a kid. My body can't take it anymore."

He took a long pull of water and wiped his hand over his mouth. Immediately he felt a little better. "But it doesn't bother you, does it?" he asked with some resentment. His shirt was soaked with sweat and Tarik moved away when he felt the moisture on his arm. "Why is that, do you think? You're such a fine example of collective memory? Do you think genes can carry the ability to tolerate heat?"

Tarik turned and gave him the half-smile. "It doesn't bother me," he said, "because I don't let it."

When he turned back he saw activity across the no-man's-land that separated the two camps. He swung out of the vehicle and unbuckled the Colt Python on his hip, handed it to his driver, and walked out on the black gravel until he was a hundred yards from his bodyguard.

A Land-Rover was moving slowly toward him. At three hundred yards, it braked, and a short, stocky man with an old Webley revolver jumped out. Using the vehicle door as a shield, he scrutinized the bodyguard and glowered at Tarik. When he seemed to hesitate, the driver shouted something at him Tarik could not understand and abruptly the man reached into the backseat and yanked Clare out with such force that one of her knees hit the ground.

Instinctively, Tarik darted forward. The man jerked the revolver at him and then brought it around to Clare's temple and cocked it. Tarik backed up a step. Behind him he heard the toggle action of twenty M14's moving in unison. He stretched out his hands to the guerrilla in a supplicating gesture to show he was unarmed. The man hesitated and again the voice behind the wheel shouted.

The Yemeni jerked Clare to her feet and, using her as a shield, shuffled forward until they were within ten yards of Tarik. Suddenly, the driver accelerated, the Yemeni pushed Clare to the ground just as the Land-Rover roared past, and the guerrilla threw himself into it. The driver threw it into reverse, the vehicle shimmied wildly and tore its tires into the loose dirt before spinning around a hundred and eighty degrees and speeding away.

For a moment neither of them moved. She held her hand up, squinting against the sunlight and the cloud of dust kicked up by the Land-Rover. He could see they had been rough on her. Her mouth was swollen and an eye blackened. Her dress was ripped from hem to waist. But it was the uncertainty in her eyes that stopped him cold. He walked toward her through a halo of dust and sunlight, knowing he had never loved her more. He believed he could hear her heart beating out to him, pulling him to her like an anchor chain on a ship. When he reached her, he bent and brought her to her feet and together they walked back to where the others waited.

His driver handed him his Colt, the American colonel shaped up his troops, and within five minutes they were moving back to Duru in a long column.

Olson, who was in the front seat, turned around often to give Clare reassuring smiles, and a few of the American troops flashed her the thumbs-up sign. Ahead of them the red ball sun was settling into the horizon. Clare closed her eyes against its vivid rays, feeling the warmth penetrate down to her tired bones. After a while she turned to Tarik and asked if there had been word about Het. "The last time I saw him was yesterday morning," she told him. "They'd beaten him up pretty badly and he could hardly walk."

"They'll turn him loose once—" Tarik left it hanging. He wasn't sure how much she knew. "Once the troops are gone."

She turned her face away from him, looking out toward the plain, and said, "I know what the deal is. The Yemenis told me all about it."

He had barely heard her over the engine noise, so he leaned over and tried to get her to look at him. Olson turned around, thinking someone had spoken to him, and Tarik sat back in his seat. He did not want the others to be privy to their conversations. When they were alone, he would tell her that if they'd asked him, he would have given them the moon for her.

The column slowed when it reached Duru. The two trucks carrying the American soldiers went to the right. The truck carrying the native soldiers continued on through the gate, then pulled off in front of a decrepit-looking barracks. The convoy now consisted of Tarik's Land Rover and an escort of command cars front and rear, four soldiers in each.

They proceeded slowly through the narrow streets. With sunset only a few minutes away, the shopkeepers and homeowners had begun shuttering their doors and windows. Many of the people were already piling household goods in the street, preparing for the evacuation that would begin in the morning. Soldiers patrolled at every tiny intersection, directing traffic and explaining the pull-out to worried inhabitants. At one street crossing a large knot of people stopped them completely. The lead command car halted and an officer and three soldiers jumped out to clear the crowd. The officer waved Tarik's vehicle through, the rear command car slowing to avoid the pedestrians. When they reached the house that was their temporary headquarters, Tarik's party was separated entirely from any escort. Arthur Olson climbed out and turned to help Clare out of the backseat while the driver held open the door for Tarik.

It was Clare who spotted him first. Although he was tall and had the well-developed body of a grown man, Azarak possessed features unchanged since childhood, and everything in his face was stunted, atrophied, weird. His nose looked as if it had been amputated, and his mouth, which was slack and open, could not have been bigger than a fifty-cent piece. But it was his eyes that stopped Clare cold, tiny eyes wet with rage.

The action became hallucinatory. Azarak broke through the crowd; Clare took a moment to react, then turned to warn Tarik, who had already seen him. For a timeless moment Azarak's long arm wavered aloft, the metal of the knife in his hand reddened by the rays of the setting sun. Then the arm came down with force, once, twice, catching Tarik in a glancing blow across his chest. Tarik jerked the Colt from its holster and fired two shots. Azarak stepped back, lunged again, and caught two more bullets, both in the head. He straightened for a moment and looked down at his wounds, flicking at the cascading blood with a trembling finger. He stared at Tarik in disbelief, then back at his chest, then tipped slowly forward, and like a felled tree crashed straight into the dirt.

There was a long moment of stunned silence before women began screaming, the crowd scattered like startled birds, and soldiers ran up waving their guns around in panic. Panting heavily, Tarik stood with the gun in his hand until White-Lyons came and gently took it away.

* * *

Later, Dr. Van Damm sutured the knife wound under Tarik's ribs. Olson urged them to leave immediately for the capital for security reasons, but Tarik insisted that the main force not be split. If the Yemenis thought Duru was unprotected, they would come in early and catch the people in their beds. They would all spend the night in Duru and pull out together at dawn.

Hours passed before the little stone house was cleared and, with guards posted all around, Clare and Tarik could lie down in exhaustion. When the sun came up, she stepped outside to watch the chaos of the evacuation, but was driven back by White-Lyons, by the realization that it was all because of her.

She went back to lie down with Tarik. She was about to tell him they would never be separated again, when three of Hadi's men breached the security cordon. All were cut nearly in half by machine-gun fire; two died in their tracks and dropped in bloody pools to the ground. But the third man's brain was wired to Hadi's lunatic mission. He heard voices, he saw visions, he overcame his heart's longing to shut down. Blood pumping out of his carotid artery with the force of an engine, this third man lobbed the grenade through the open window of the stone house and brought an end to dreaming.

1964–1967

14

They had taken her to The Heights, to Lawrence Sayles, because his whole life, people had only ever done what Lawrence Sayles told them to do.

She went because she believed she had nowhere else to go.

"The Secretary sent along a gift, Clare—handmade table linens. Really quite lovely. One of my secretaries opened it by mistake and sends her apologies. She's used to opening all my packages, so I'll have to make a note to tell her not to do it anymore." Sayles could have been talking to himself as he prodded the big pine log with a fireplace poker until it flamed; Clare lay mutely under the bedcovers.

"He's asked us for dinner next week, by the way, but I begged off. I told him you're not really up and around yet."

He paused to assess the fire and, satisfied, continued. "You know, I realized coming home that you're going to have to have some warm clothing. I'll have Mrs. Esthershawl come around."

Sayles caught himself. Esthershawl had been Connie's dressmaker. He looked over for Clare's reaction, but never having heard of Marion Esthershawl, she simply gazed back at him. Relieved, he proceeded. "And you'll need a good warm coat, don't you think? A fur. No, not a fur; you're too young. A Burberry—a Burberry melton and an alpaca perhaps. And some sort of evening coat. That would do for this miserable winter." He set the poker down suddenly.

"Listen to me. I'm going on with all this nonsense. You'd think the world had stopped working except for this bizarre interest of mine in ladies' coats." His laughter was surprisingly robust, coming from that thin body.

For one of the few times in his life, Lawrence Sayles was prattling. There were other conversational avenues, of course, but

177

these might lead to certain unwelcome topics. Best for the time being to keep all their conversations superficial, even though this was against his nature. If anything, he had built his career on the frank presentation of issues—although it was also true that he had been a diplomat long enough to sense when a little meaningless chitchat went a long way in taking the edge off tensions. Besides, the notion that he might care for Clare right down to the minutiae of her wardrobe was so satisfying, it forestalled his usual reticence.

From the bed she watched him putter around the fire. It had not seemed strange to her when she realized at Hirth that it was Lawrence Sayles's private airplane she was boarding for the trip back to the States. As much as she could logic out anything, it struck her as having a kind of doomed inevitability, as though she had presumed too much in marrying for love. Nor did it seem odd that when Francis Riston met her at National Airport he was using Sayles's car and driver. They had brought her to The Heights and it all made sense. Where else would she have gone? Where else?

They were in a guest room on the third floor. Clare had not yet moved into his bedroom, and while he was too self-effacing to presume that she ever might, he longed for her to share his bed. That because of the arrangement of their marriage she might never was too disheartening for him to contemplate, much less reconcile himself.

He turned and looked at her on the bed, her back supported by pillows, legs swaddled in a comforter. Her left hand, broken in the blast, had come out of the cast that day, but her singed hair had been cut brutally short and would take months before it grew into something resembling the old Clare's. She was thin as a hummingbird and just as destructible, but it was her eyes that betokened her true condition—at the moment, unsettlingly flat and expressionless. As a condition of their marriage, she had insisted they compact to be honest with each other, but already they had slipped into the opacity of the old days. Sayles could not begin to puncture the skin of his reserve to ask her directly what she was feeling. Instead, he had made her eyes his touchstone.

He could convince himself of anything if he did not have to examine too deeply those eyes.

So he turned away, took up the poker again, and with its business end monkeyed with the fire. The fireplace was framed by two lovely William and Mary silver sconces, which the flames had colored bloody in the half-lit room. Flemish drapes were pulled tight across the window, but every so often a draft penetrated from outside, where it couldn't have been more than four or five degrees above zero, an uncharacteristically frigid winter. Feeling the cold on his skin, Sayles drew the drapes tighter.

The moment word had come that Clare's plane had left Hirth, Sayles had swung into action. He ordered the third-floor guest bedroom cleared of all furniture and then he and Preston had walked briskly through the house, expertly eyeing this piece and that. Sayles would stand back, press a finger to his lips, look over the lamp or chair, whatever it was, and then wave it away and move on or exclaim, "This one! Yes!" Preston had never seen him so animated, and his exhilaration became a contagion for the entire household staff.

When he came to the hodgepodge of collectibles Connie had scattered on tabletops on the first floor, Sayles stopped short, stared at them for a long moment that Preston believed was devoid of any poignancy or even nostalgia, and then ordered everything packed up for storage. For the butler it was a charged moment, however, full of exquisite pain and blinking sentiment. Preston's knees were raw from years spent kneeling at the shrine of Connie Sayles's exquisite taste. To his own thinking, even after years of service in some of the great houses of Europe and America, in breadth of imagination and scope of aesthetic, not even he could hold a candle to Connie's *goût raffiné*, a term he had once heard a Rothschild use to describe her.

Lovingly he wrapped the presentation portraits from three presidents, the celadon bowl from the president of Pakistan, the carved silver chest that was a gift from Nehru, in the society pages of the *Washington Post*, an obvious touch but one he thought Connie might enjoy anyway, wherever she was. The Russian dolls, the barometer from the emperor of Japan (man of science), the tiny silver dagger embedded with rubies and sapphires from King Saud, and on and on until there were more than a dozen carefully packed cartons and as many empty tabletops. Preston ran a chamois dustcloth over the places where the souvenirs had been as if he were wiping the fingerprints from a murder weapon.

If the resentments Preston had formed about Clare a year earlier already were not enough, they were joined now with petulance at this desecration of Connie Sayles's tabernacle to her celebrated marriage. Wrapping up a pair of gold-edged Venetian glasses she had bought in Battiston's, near Harry's Bar in Venice, Preston released one small, clear but well-meant teardrop for Connie, for his beautiful society swan.

Still, when Sayles asked him to drive out to Virginia for one of a pair of Louis XV armchairs he remembered and admired, Preston went without protest. He wasn't getting any younger, and gentlemen of the caliber of Lawrence Sayles didn't grow on trees. If not for Sayles, he might have to go to work for some other, less worthy person. Someone not in the Green Book. Someone without Secret Service clearance. Someone from an oil-producing nation. It was enough to chill his blood, and so he sped out to Middleburg for the chair.

When Sayles finally had made all his selections, Henry, his driver, Marguerite, the cook, and a gardener pressed into service hauled the valuable furniture up three flights of stairs. Sayles fussed over the placement of every piece, Henry and Marguerite dripping with perspiration from tugging the huge Chippendale four-poster around the room until Sayles finally decided it was perfect where it had been originally. Once everything was in place, Sophie, who tended to the upstairs housekeeping, dusted and polished until her fingertips burned from the effort. The gardener, breathless, bounded up the stairs with bunches and bunches of full-blown roses the color of lemons and swollen with scent, and stuffed them into every vase.

When they were finished they all stepped back and, a little agog, surveyed their work. Liberated from the constriction of its museumlike arrangement, the room swelled with life, color, luxury, hinting at what the rest of The Heights might become. A deep-caramel wool-covered sofa, a huge cashmere throw folded on its arm, Chinese rosewood tables at either end, sat along one wall. Across from these stood a desk made for Catherine, empress of Russia, in 1784, and alongside it the Louis XV armchair. Sayles had the largest private collection of rare books in the world, and he had hand-picked fifty he thought Clare might appreciate and placed them in the small Duncan Phyfe bookcase near the bed.

More astonishing than any of this was The Heights' captain himself. Freed from his habitual aloofness, his face heightened with color, Sayles seemed positively ready to jig. The staff made eyes at each other as he circled the room and exclaimed over each piece in turn, not quite certain what any of it meant but pleased and excited that this electric atmosphere signaled the beginning of a new regime.

He ordered the rest of the house be given a thorough polish and fires lit in every fireplace, and then sat back to wait for Clare.

When she arrived he could see right away that she was not the same woman who had once unstrung him. She had changed. Hurt and fear composed her emotions, and the set of her shoulders was more lax than he recalled. The confidence was out of her. Of course, he knew what she had suffered and what she had left behind, and he felt moved to compassion, but subtly he was pleased by her condition—oh, not in a malicious fashion, but he perceived her lack of spirit was to his advantage, the first he had ever had with her. She needed him and he intended to be a great deal of help.

Wisely he tempered his enthusiasm at seeing her. He was sedate, solicitous, an old friend. Preston had brought her a cup of tea, and Sayles had stepped into the solarium with Francis Riston, who briefed him on the details. After Riston left, Sayles had led Clare to the bedroom and settled her in. She had nothing to say; he didn't press her. For days she could scarcely eat; he dined alone. She wept in the dark of night; he heard, anguished, but did not go to her. He was a patient friend.

Two weeks after she arrived, she began experiencing nausea and he had thought she might be suffering the aftereffects of the grenade blast, but she was adamant that she was pregnant. He sent her to his internist, who quit taking her history and ordered a pregnancy test the minute he heard her symptoms—and of course she was.

Rather than being repulsed by this news, Sayles was delighted, because Clare's wish to protect Tarik's child at any cost was what finally enabled him to convince her they should marry. He made marriage to him sound like a service to Tarik, and that is exactly how she came to see it. She flew in his private plane to the Dominican Republic with a lawyer from the firm that represented him. A young Dominican lawyer met them at the airport and hustled her in and out of court in less than an hour. With her good hand, she signed a document in Spanish that she could not understand, and they were driven back to the airport. While she waited for the plane to be brought to the gate, she saw other North Americans, gloomy figures, wandering the fluorescent cavern of the terminal—matrimonial detritus, and, like her, in town for the quick one-two of Dominican justice. One woman, grandmotherly, openly wept into a cloth hankie. Clare stared at her for a long time, trying to force herself to compassion, until Barry Zwig, Sayles's pilot, brought the plane to the gate. Four hours later she was back in Washington. She hadn't even needed to change her money.

Two days later the rector of St. Paul's Episcopal Cathedral

came to The Heights and married them in the living room, under the rainbow glow of Connie's Waterford chandelier, the household staff their only witnesses.

Sayles had expected Clare to sleepwalk through the ceremony, but to his surprise she had concentrated fiercely, her marriage vows banking some fire within her that he could not imagine but still admired. When it came time to put the ring on his finger she had taken his hand with such determination that he was unnerved. He had no clear idea of what she was thinking, but the passion of her gesture alarmed him. Nervous, his jaw muscles twitched violently as he promised her his life. For all its thrilling heat, for Sayles, passion carried on its wings the threat of chaos and he feared nothing more than a loss of control. He had been relieved when, the ceremony over, the rector left and Clare, pleading exhaustion, excused herself and went to bed.

Later, he had turned the locks on all the doors and climbed to his second-floor library. He had settled himself into his favorite chair, and with a glass of cognac in one hand and a good cigar in the other he recomposed his nerves into their habitual calm. The house silent and sealed against despoilers, the cognac scalding winter out of his bones, he spent his wedding night dreaming over his future, thinking about Clare and her baby. He had always wanted children, of course, keep the family name alive and all that, but Connie had never been able to conceive.

He believed in himself, that was how he articulated his delusion. He believed in himself, and in time Clare would come to believe in their marriage. A month after the wedding she had barely stirred from the bedroom, but Sayles remained unperturbed. Like a rock resistant to a stream's persistent run, he promised himself he would outlast her grief.

The fire stained the room roseate. Sayles could feel his whole body relaxing. There had been a desperate weariness—he believed he had been born with it—and when he was with Clare it just disappeared. She was the only person in the world with whom he experienced this.

He walked across the room, and not presuming to actually sit on her bed, bent over and patted her hand. "Anyway, you look tired, Clare," he said. "We'll worry about clothes for you and for the baby another day. Sleep now and I'll see you in the morning. You must be tired." He looked into her eyes and decided they were clouded with worry. She's feeling hopeless, he thought. She's close to despair. Best to leave her be.

In fact, she felt nothing at all as she watched him go. She hadn't felt anything in weeks. Her heart was flint and she thanked God for it; not unreasonably she believed she would be undone if it were to soften. Besides, if numbness got her through the rest of her life, so be it. This state of suspended nonexistence was almost pleasurable. She felt ill equipped to face real life and all day, every day, the ache of longing.

Only the thought of Tarik's baby made her even consider coming to life again. She tucked her knees up to her chest and hugged them, rocking a little on the bed. She rubbed her sore left hand. The skin was scaly white where the cast had been. The hand still ached and she would have been happy to take aspirin or a painkiller if she hadn't been worried it would harm the baby. Anyway, the pain gave her something to focus on and kept her mind from clicking away in that awful way. If ever once she gave in, she would fall into despair and that would be the end of her, and the baby. Anything but despair. This is the part of Kath in my blood, she thought. Those miseries were incubating somewhere in her body, and if she let them hatch they would suck her down into desolation and then she would be Kath, fixed on might-have-beens and feeling cheated. Better to be numb.

Besides, nonexistence freed her for her real task, which was concentrating on the details of what had happened. She had fixed every word, pause, and gesture into photographic points of light and dark and then imprinted them on the backs of her eyes. She could close her eyes and replay the disaster anytime she wanted. The blast itself was nothing, unremembered, a phantom of heat and searing pain. Her hand wetted—Tarik's blood. Then, very clearly, waking to find White-Lyons beside her cot, a ribbon of perspiration along his hairline. The ice man sweats, that's a new one. His eyes wide and in them something close to panic. Also new. "It's time I told you the truth, Clare." He's dead. "No, not dead. Badly hurt, but not dead." And then he spoke the other truth.

A moment after she comprehended what he was telling her, she turned on him violently. He could have told her the day she arrived that Tarik had to marry Topaz.

"I would have left that day," she had told him.

"I doubt that very much," White-Lyons said.

She glared at him with large, contemptuous eyes. "Whatever was necessary. Whatever it took. I would have done it."

"The situation was . . ."

She watched his eyes shift. He was suffering, she could see

that, and it gave her a rush of satisfaction. She watched him searching for answers. The room was dark, she could barely see his face, so when he tried to turn away she flew across the floor and put her face in his.

"If you had told me what was at stake, I would have gone. Do you think I would have done anything to hurt him, to keep him from what he deserved? It's you who has hurt him, not I. If you'd told me, I would have gone. If you had told me the truth, he wouldn't have been hurt. You've done this."

She paced back and forth, shaking her broken hand to make it hurt more and feeling a little delirious. She would strip the bark off him with her rage. Strip him down and then cut him up. Slaughter the messenger. After a while she was so unstrung she couldn't concentrate on what she was saying and began to repeat herself. Furious rage was the object here, anything less and she would collapse. She couldn't get through this without the rocket fuel of outrage.

"I didn't believe he would let you go," White-Lyons said. There was no strength in him; she could sense that and moved in to wound him further.

"You didn't want to jeopardize your relationship with him!"

"That's not true, Clare. It's all well and good for you to say this now in hindsight, but even if you had wished it, he would not have let you go. He wouldn't let me tell you. He loves you."

"That's right!" she heard herself shouting. "That's how much he loves me! Not you, me."

As soon as she said it the anger died away into stupor. She sank onto the cot like lead. She tried to move her legs. Lead. Lead was in her mouth, her shoulders. She ran her splinted hand over her face. Nothing made sense anymore. She stared at White-Lyons as if she had never seen him before, and in this incarnation she hadn't. His razor-sharp crease was gone. His uniform was splotched with dust and perspiration and dried blood. His face was the color of beeswax.

"I want to see him before I go," she said after a long time, accepting finally that she would have to. "I want to see for myself that he's all right."

"It's just not possible, Clare. I'm sorry, I'm not being cruel, but we've had to move him to the capital; there's an American surgical team coming there from Frankfurt who can help him. Hadi knows by now that his assassins failed. It's only a matter of time before he tries again. It's imperative that you leave now. Hadi will never forgive Tarik for killing Azarak, but the marriage to Topaz will console him. When you go, the threat is ended. I'm sorry to be so brutal. I know you don't believe me but I am sorry."

She heard herself say, "Am I leaving soon?"

"Arthur Olson is handling the arrangements. You're leaving tonight from the air base at Hirth."

She sat there for a timeless moment, saying nothing. She'd been taken over by an edgy hyperawareness of things. Her senses were working overtime. She heard everything with a painful sharpness. Outside, a dog scavenged noisily and she turned in the direction of the sound. The smell of cardamom was in the air; somewhere someone stirred food over a cookfire. A truck's gears ground, a smithy clanged on molten iron. It occurred to her that this was another miserable truth—in the midst of her own desolation, others' lives proceed.

White-Lyons crossed the room and put his hand on her arm. It was a gesture of genuine consolation, but to Clare it held the menace of a snake's touch and she pulled away and stood up on her own.

"It seems to me I should be taking something with me." She looked around the room but there was nothing familiar here. "Am I in Duru?"

"No, this place is called Brater. Nal brought you in the Land-Rover, on a litter. Tarik went directly by helicopter to the capital. He was losing so much blood."

She turned and faced him.

"He's stabilized now," he said. "I wouldn't lie to you."

She gave him a melancholy smile. "Oh, yes, you would, White-Lyons," she said. "If you thought it would do him some good, you would lie about anything."

Sayles bought her a lipstick-red Jaguar XKE 3.8 liter roadster, front sub-frame, monocoque tub, independent suspensions all around.

Henry drove it gingerly home from the showroom and parked it on the street. As he wiped it down with a piece of chamois cloth, Sayles bounded outside to supervise.

"Some car, eh, Henry?"

"Yes sir," he answered, straightening up. Henry was an expansive man, full of good cheer for everyone except traffic cops and double-parked trucks. "This is some fine piece of machinery."

He was a black man, huge, over six feet two and tipping in at two hundred seventy pounds. He looked no more than fifty, but he was seventy-one and had served the Sayles family all his life.

Born on the Virginia property, he had been stable boy to Sayles's grandfather, houseman and driver to Sayles's father in Washington and London, and for nearly fifteen years Lawrence Sayles's driver, and like all men and women in service to the rich, there was no personal detail or eccentricity of the family that Henry was not privy to. He had made keeping family secrets to himself his bread and butter.

Sayles slipped behind the wheel and gunned the engine while Henry studied under the hood with an expert eye.

"She sounds good, doesn't she, Henry?" Sayles shouted above the motor's roar.

"Oh, yes indeed, sir. Finest-sounding thing I ever heard. Oh, my!" Then upon reflection, " 'Course, now, your dad had a Rolls-Royce that had the smoothest engine I ever heard. That car hummed! That's what they do, those Rolls motors, hum. Hand assembled, wood a hundred years old. Lord, but that car had style. And how I loved driving it! Drove it for twenty-five years. It's still out there in Virginia, you know, just sitting there in the garage, longing for somebody to come along and turn it loose."

"I know."

"Yes, sir. We oughta think about getting that Rolls out of mothballs. Lot better than that old piece-a junk." With his chin he indicated the Cadillac limousine across the street. "No good piece-a junk," he muttered, but not so low that Sayles couldn't hear him. The Cadillac with its power windows and vexatious motor was Henry's bane. He was forever wasting hours taking it in and out of the shop. "Junk," he snorted. It had no style, no *substance*, unlike the Rolls, which was stately as an ocean liner. Why, in that car he had driven Sayles's father up the curved driveways of the best homes on two continents, even through the gates of Buckingham Palace a time or two. "Detroit's no good and they car's no good. Got a brother-in-law from Detroit. Same thing. Junk."

Sayles thumbed through the Jaguar manual, used to Henry's tirades and only partly listening. "Now, Henry, you know we've got to drive American. Got to fly the colors every chance we get. Wouldn't look good for me to pull up at the White House in a foreign-built car, would it? It would look like I didn't have faith in my own country's products. On the other hand, I don't know why I think I have that responsibility," he went on absently, concentrating on the manual. "I ought to just leave it to the trade representative to worry about these things and do whatever I want. Anyway, now that I realize it, here I am with another British car.

Now we definitely can't drive the Rolls. I hadn't thought about that."

"Yes sir, that's right, sir," Henry said, which is what he always said when he wanted to convey the impression he agreed when of course he really didn't. He had been in service long enough to know that discretion was the better part of continued employment. He wanted the Rolls back in business. He was a big man. He deserved a big car, a car that wasn't a piece-a junk.

Sayles switched the radio on and off, moved the gearshift around, flipped the sun visors. The closest he ever got to any internal combustion engine was seated somewhere behind it. Nevertheless, the Jaguar delighted him so much that he was like a kid, out from behind the wheel now and peering under the hood, his thin, aristocratic nose inches from the fan belt, listening to Henry go on about fuel injection, pretending to understand, when Clare walked up.

She watched the two of them gazing interestedly at this very nice, highly desirable piece of machinery for a moment and then said, "You two planning to steal this car?"

Sayles bobbed up from under the hood.

"No, no." The sudden disarming smile split his patrician face, surprising her. "Can't steal your own car," he said.

She looked at the Jaguar, and then back at him with a what-are-you-talking-about? look on her face.

Henry slammed down the hood, then took a step back, grinning.

"It's yours, Clare," Sayles said finally, handing her the keys. "I bought it for you."

"You're kidding." Her eyes ran over it greedily.

"No, really, it's yours. Look," he said, reaching into the glove compartment, "your name's on the registration."

She stared stupidly at the little document, comprehended, then snatched the keys out of his hand so fast he laughed out loud. Squeezed behind the wheel, she shifted through the gears and flipped the dials around. It was the happiest he had seen her in the five months since she'd been back. He watched her from the sidewalk, feeling mightily pleased.

"Okay if I take it around the block?" she asked.

"Take it anywhere you like. Take it out to the country. It's yours to do with as you like."

She eased it away from the curb, then braked.

"Lawrence, thank you," she said, lowering the window on the passenger side.

"You're welcome, Clare. Enjoy it."

"Tell me, how did you know I wanted my own car?"

He laughed. "How could you think I wouldn't know?" And he waved her away.

He didn't even tell me to drive carefully, she realized appreciatively as she pulled out into the N Street traffic.

And she didn't drive particularly carefully that day, or any other, and the sight of Lawrence Sayles's very young, very pregnant wife, streaking through Rock Creek Park, out to the Middleburg estate, around the Beltway, past the monuments, through Dupont Circle, became the gossipy centerpiece of more than one Little Dinner. She would sometimes slow to see the flowering quince at Hains Point, or the redbud and dogwood on the residential streets, but mostly she drove on and on as fast as she could, thinking she could blur her life like the emerald lawns along the roadside. Through the greening countryside she steadied the Jag around curves and reminded herself that she was just as real as anyone else, although it was only in the car that she ever felt that for a moment. Sometimes, on the road to Virginia, she would feel content, making herself an extension of the Jaguar, and therefore competent, capable of amazing feats, but it was only the slenderest of notions and it quickly disappeared.

In June, when the weather warmed and the cherry blossoms broke their skins, she made Henry take the top off so she could feel the sun on her arms. By July, when the city began to swelter, Sayles thought she should let Henry drive her in the Cadillac, but she refused. She wanted to swelter and be sunburned. She wanted to be reminded of that other, more miserable heat.

These things she thought of as her work, her job. Sayles would rise before dawn for breakfast meetings or travel to Europe or New York. He was overseeing the sale of the family railway business and it took up much of his time. Sometimes it was noon before Clare got out of bed. She would eat the light breakfast Marguerite brought her, dress, and then without a word to any of them, gun the Jag and speed off.

Such behavior stiffened the spines of many of the political and social wives, who had worked lifetimes to blend into the wallpaper and still keep the weight off. Connie had attracted notice, yes, but for all the right reasons, and they could tick them off with a generosity they'd never shown her while she lived, their newfound charity toward her owing as much to the widower's taking a second wife as the sanctity bestowed by death. Death can work the most extraordinary changes in a person's reputation.

Besides, to be noticed is not to be mixed up with being conspicuous, or even worse exotic, which is what they decided Clare's crime was. This girl presumed to the hubris allowed in this town only to men. Only the men of these women were meant to have style, verve, wit—and if truth be told, almost none of them did—but never their wives. And only trollops had whiteblond hair and long legs and breasts with immoderate nipples.

But what drove them most wild was not that she was a rebel, which no Washington wife should ever be. Or that she was pretty and young (although this was certainly a large-caliber bullet to bite). Or that she was still sexy while voluminously pregnant and talked too long to other women's husbands—but that she had what they most lusted after—status. Her house, for it was hers now, was on the Georgetown House Tour. She had a full staff—cook, butler, housemaids, gardeners, chauffeur, a bodyguard when necessary, and a police escort if she telephoned for one, which she never did, and not one but two private airplanes. The administration bigshots and all the really great foreign dignitaries dined at her table. The White House tennis courts could be hers had she wanted them. She could sail into a party looking vague, whisper something in Sayles's ear, and he would turn on his heel and leave with her. Lawrence Sayles! A white rhino, on the run, bagged with a single shot from a small handgun at five hundred yards would not be a more impressive trophy than Lawrence Sayles at *your* party. A hostess could spend two weeks cajoling him into coming, and then he's whisked away by that damned blond wife. Clare Barrow of coal-camp-wherever Kentucky, with one bad (they presumed) marriage behind her, at age twenty-five had awarded herself one of the republic's few princes. And this great American statesman, this rich, and more important, stupefyingly powerful man loved her with all the obsessiveness of a filling station attendant from Utica, New York, for goddamned Jayne Mansfield.

Mulling all this over not unsympathetically, Sylvia O'Dowd decided it was incumbent upon her to befriend Clare and save her from herself.

She called for a lunch date.

"I never eat lunch, Sylvia. But thanks very much for asking."

"Well, then," Sylvia, who had never taken no for an answer in any lifetime she could remember, pressed, "let's get together for breakfast."

"Oh, never breakfast. Breakfast makes me feel full all day."

"Well, how about tea then? Late afternoon, stomach's nice and empty. How about tea?"

"No, I think tea isn't good for the baby. I don't go out much anyway."

"Now, dear, you've got to go out sometime."

"Not really."

"But we all see you speeding by in that little red car of yours."

"I like to be alone."

"Well then, dear," said Sylvia through a fastened jaw, "maybe after the baby is born. Maybe then we could have lunch."

"Maybe, Sylvia," Clare had said and rung off, not even bothering with good-bye.

She had made up her mind not to be the monkey on the chain for anyone. Deciding this filled her with discreet excitement, as if she had enlisted on some solitary mission that kept her in the world, but only just, like a nun, a Channel swimmer, an astronaut. People like Sylvia she saw as objects of study, worth only her disinterested scrutiny. The loss of Tarik had elected her, she believed, to a higher awareness. She considered herself tough, different from other women. She had shouldered the burden, she would go forward in spite of its grief. What they felt about how she managed the load was no concern of hers, even if at this point in her life she could not take the long view. Her eyes swam when she tried to telescope into the future and place herself there. The goals she set were modest. It was enough if she made it through the night.

The rebuff didn't thwart Sylvia in her pursuit, however. The night Sayles drew her as a dinner partner at the Soviet embassy she pressed her case. Sayles adored good gossip and no one dished loamier dirt than Sylvia. So after she had told him about the sports hero with political ambitions who'd gotten pissed on bourbon and relieved himself in a potted plant at a good home in McLean, Virginia, and the wife of the four-term senator from an industrial state who was having an affair with the boy who polished the hardwood floor on her handball court, it was time to zero in.

"You know, Lawrence," she said, turning away from her blinis, "you really are something. You surprise me! Here you have this young gorgeous wife that every other man would lock up at home for safekeeping, even if she is out-to-here pregnant, and you're letting her fly all over the countryside in that wild sports car, just asking those hot-eyed fellas to take a look at her. I think you have the confidence of ten men."

Sayles chuckled and sucked on his cigar. He had done a little homely fishing in his day. He knew a well-tied fly when he saw one.

"This is a good marriage you've made, Lawrence."

"You think so, do you, Sylvia?" He gave her a wolfish smile.

"Yes, I do, Lawrence. This is so much better than the other."

She narrowed her eyes at him, hoping he would ask her if she meant Clare's marriage to Tarik or his own to Connie, but of course he said nothing, just flicked a bit of cigar ash from his Johns & Peggs tuxedo with an élan that made her feel as if he were the Sun King and she was a girl singer with a Mexican band, which of course she had once been.

"You know," she said anyway, "your Clare is causing quite a stir."

"That so?" Cigar smoke.

"Oh, it is so, it is. Yes, kind of a racy stir for this tightass town. Speeding through Rock Creek Park like that. I heard she caused a horse to bolt and scared one of the Summit Club debs right out of her Hermès saddle. Broke her wrist."

"I don't believe it." Parabolas of smoke.

"Broke her hymen."

"Sylvia!"

"Well, come on, Lawrence, don't play hard to get with me."

He sucked contentedly on his cigar. He was enjoying himself, skittering away from Sylvia's hook, surprised that Clare's rebelliousness excited him so. He was normally such a careful man.

"Personally, I like it," she said, looking past him, a faraway look in her eyes. "She's just what we need. But I'm a little worried, Lawrence. Time will pass. Youth will fly—and don't I know it. What was thrilling at twenty-five can be deadly at forty. I don't want to see Clare friendless in an unfriendly town."

"What are you proposing?"

She gave him her best smile. "Lawrence, I'm pitching myself here. I'm pitching myself as friend, confidante, but more important, helmsman of experience, Lawrence. Someone to help her steer those rocky shoals. Someone to beat those sharks on the nose with a barge pole, Lawrence."

A man across the table from him with a loud and commanding Texas accent was demanding his attention and he turned his head away. The man had an interest in selling beef cattle to the Soviets and was curious to know what Sayles thought was the chance of that. Unfailingly courteous, Sayles offered an honest opinion to the striver, wished him all the best, "All the best to you," and conversationally moved on. The striver beamed, feeling as if he had been touched by the hand of God.

Other diners grinned inanely in Sayles's direction, and he bobbed his head here and there, dispensing the social graces and making all those in his presence believe that despite his vast wealth, despite that pedigree, he was actually one of them. It was a talent of his, a talent of his class. It kept those of lesser birth and wealth from rising up and cutting the throats of the Inheritors as they slept in their Chippendale beds.

In another minute, the Soviet chargé d'affaires was on his feet, offering incomprehensible toasts, and demanding one of Sayles's, former U. S. ambassador to the U.S.S.R.

Sayles pulled his reed-slim body from his chair, raised his glass, and with his usual charm and dignity made a witty toast in English and then translated it himself into Russian for his hosts.

He resumed his seat, pleased with the applause and with himself. After a moment he turned to Sylvia, and, leaning in to take her hands in his, said, "How can I say this, Sylvia? Clare is under my protection. I don't need to tell you of all people what that means. If Clare wants to wrap herself in wax paper and whistle 'Dixie' at the Lincoln Memorial, she can do it and the doors will still swing wide for her. She is all she'll ever need to be to never be vulnerable—my wife." Then he kissed her lightly on the cheek and sat back in his chair.

Sylvia dropped her head and absorbed this quietly. Her bosom was not quite what it once had been, and the cantilevered top of her strapless cocktail dress had journeyed south in the progress of the evening. Unsupported, her breasts sagged. When she was young, a hundred years ago, candlelight gave her skin the sheen of an orange sunset bobbling on a lake; now, at fifty, it looked dull as pig iron.

The humidity in the dining room had caused her makeup to leach into the creases in her face. The full, youthful mouth she had carefully painted in her bathroom mirror had worn off and her pale, thin lips had the irretrievably sad set of a middle-aged woman.

"Oh, well," she said, bringing her wineglass to her lips, "you can't say I didn't try. But mark my words, Lawrence, one of these days that girl's going to be in need of a friend."

Watching her toss back her wine and wave the waiter over for a refill, Sayles understood that it was, of course, Sylvia who was in need of friendship.

* * *

Other places may swelter in the summer heat more extravagantly than Washington, D.C.—places on the banks of the Amazon, or in central Africa—but this has yet to be demonstrated to anyone who has suffered through July and August in the shadow of the White House. So none but the poor, the unimportant, and the mentally deficient stay in town in the summer months. Those with money or connections escape the heat on Martha's Vineyard or in Rehoboth, Delaware. A few keep homes in Jamaica and pray some political or business crisis won't bring them back. All work stops. Congress is in recess, the President is out of town. The poor sweat it out. The rich, if they have any grace at all, count their blessings.

Sayles owned an oceangoing yacht, and when Connie was alive they would sail the Greek islands for two months, usually with a party of European statesmen, socialites, and businessmen, but the boat had been in drydock since she died. He would have been happy to spend the summer in Virginia, but with less than a month before her baby was due, Clare refused to leave The Heights and her doctors nearby. So they suffered in the city, staggered by heat not even air-conditioning could ameliorate.

It was on one of these blistering August days, so hot the beeswax polish on the furniture was melting, that Clare's baby chose to be born after a ten-hour, uncomplicated labor.

"What are you going to call him?" Sayles paced the bedroom of her three-room hospital suite, trying to appear indifferent.

She studied the tiny face for a long time and then said, "I thought I'd call him Alex."

He wanted to say *Alex Sayles, that has a ring to it,* but he stopped himself. His longing for her and the baby was anything but inchoate. It was specific and at that moment fairly raging, but his sensitivity to their situation had heightened all his sensations and he was almost supernaturally aware of her feelings.

So he said, "*Alex*, that's a fine, strong name, Clare. It's a name that will carry him through a good, long life." He wanted to reach under the yards of blanket and touch a little hand, to tell his son, because that's how he thought of him already, that his dad would never leave him, that he would want for nothing, but the sight of Clare's rapt face staring at her baby stopped him and made his heart cramp; if he didn't leave now, he might say something that would betray what was in it.

A little too demonstratively, he looked at his watch and feigned alarm. "Oh my. After seven. I've got to be at"—he named a famous television correspondent's home—"in less than ten minutes." But of course he had no real plans because he'd hoped she might ask him to stay to dinner. When she didn't protest, he headed for the door.

"Well, I'd better get a move on. Get some rest, Clare. I'll see you in the morning."

She wasn't even aware that he was gone, so intensely was she inventorying Alex. She laid the sleeping baby on the bed and undid the blanket and diaper so that he was naked. But he's so skinny, she thought, a little panicked. Nothing but bone. She put a finger in his palm and when he grabbed it fiercely, she instantly felt relieved. Strong little critter though, that's good. Ten fingers, ten toes, everything fine there. Then more worry. His face was beet-red and squished and there were tiny bruises along his chin from the struggle to be born. Her heart sagged. His hair was skimpy and wheat-colored, not thick and black as she had expected. His nose seemed flat and undistinguished. Was he tall? She could not remember how long babies were supposed to be. He didn't seem particularly tall. His ears, his fingers, the color of his skin—ghostly white, not a trace of color in them. Nothing, nothing at all.

She set her hand alongside her cheek and began to weep, the tears dripping one by one into her hair. Both hands came up over her eyes and her body shook with staggered sobs. The misery of nine months poured out of her, soaking the lace neckline of her nightie. She wanted to go back to the time when everything made sense. She wanted to lie with—she was terrified to even say his name in her mind. She wanted to lie with *him* in her little Georgetown apartment where they had first made love. On the massive Georgian bed in the palace, the heat like weights on their bodies. The smell of his hair had reminded her of mountain laurel, how could that be? She tried to cry the heart right out of her chest, and she might have if a tiny little hand hadn't jerked to life and scratched her with a ragged fingernail. Alex wiggled, kicked out his scrawny legs, and opened his mouth in a big wonderful toothless yawn, and as he did, he blinked once, twice, then fixed his eyes on Clare. Staring straight back into her own green eyes were two pale dove-gray ones, nearly transparent, and so intense that even unfocused as they were it seemed he could see right through flesh to bone. She screeched with glee and laughed so loud that the floor nurse came bolting through the door.

"Are you all right, Mrs. Sayles?"

"I'm fine."

The nurse bustled around the bedcovers, then noticed the naked baby. "Why is that baby all undone? Where's his diaper? He'll catch cold in this air-conditioning."

Clare folded the blanket edges over Alex and pulled him up to her breast. "No, he won't," she said, helping him find her nipple, taking his immediately greedy sucking as further sign of his natural self-confidence. "He can take it. He's used to dealing in extremes."

15

When Alex was three months old, Clare came to a decision.

She had been watching him sleep in the elaborate white cradle that had rocked generations of Sayles infants, thinking that if she had looked in and seen his head resting on a little purple pillow, she would not have been surprised. The handmade cradle was a huge affair, with elaborately carved rosettes and cherubs. The ornaments climbed to a delicately trellised canopy that supported what appeared to be a princely coronet, from which hung yards of swagged Alençon lace. The arrogance of the thing made Clare groan. *No wonder they grow up thinking they're royalty. The first thing they see when they open their eyes every day is a crown.*

The cradle was all the more ridiculous to her because its fat-bellied big-eyed cherubim had bits of gilt stuck to their wooden hair, and lips painted the palest mauve. What Sayles ancestor had commissioned this florid aberration in an otherwise soulless Protestant heritage? Clare teased Sayles that there was a flamenco dancer somewhere in the family tree, but he'd insisted straightfaced that Alex stay in the cradle until he grew out of it, which might be any day at the rate he was going.

She circled the thing, pausing to pick at a piece of paint that had come loose, feeling oddly content. After nearly a year of marriage she had decided finally that if Alex was going to have the kind of upbringing he deserved as Tarik's son, then she would have to be a wife to Lawrence Sayles in more than name. She would have to assume the responsibility of being his wife down to the last Little Dinner and charity ball, so that Alex could derive all the emotional security he would ever need from a warm, loving marriage between Mom and Dad. How she was going to accomplish this when she was still in love with another man was something she had decided to put out of her mind for the time being—forever, if she could manage it.

And if men deferred to Alex because he had a five-hundred-million-dollar trust fund, because his last name made doors open wide so fast there seemed to be no swing in them at all, then all the better. Whatever it took, she would do it for her son. Not that sharing a bed with Lawrence Sayles was such a sacrifice; it was not that long ago when she would have welcomed that particular arrangement. He was an excellent man. She had abandoned him to marry another and still he was loyal. In fact, he seemed to want her all the more. This time when she offered herself, he did not hesitate. He married her so fast it had made her head spin. That she was pregnant only seemed to double his enthusiasm. She knew now that he had always loved her. She knew also that since Tarik, she would never love him back with equal passion and that for some reason inexplicable to her, this was enough for him. Beyond this she didn't speculate.

She had decided this was enough for her—rather, for Alex. She and Sayles had entered into a dual deception, all the more compelling because neither of them ever articulated it, which was the first deception. The second deception they conspired to was to convince the world that she had willingly abandoned Tarik for him.

Unspoken, they had bartered an arrangement for living. In return for Lawrence delivering to Alex all the security and prestige of the great Sayles legacy, Clare would maintain the deception of the boy's paternity. After what had happened at Duru, she had decided that there were worse foundations for living.

But if she hadn't grasped how seriously Sayles embraced the deal from the passionate way he'd proposed marriage in January, she certainly couldn't fail to appreciate it on the day Alex came home from the hospital, and every day since. He was the proud papa right down to the Davidoff cigars he dispensed to all the famous names who came to pay their respects. He beamed, he boasted, he puffed out his chest. Clare had prepared herself for the gradual evolution of his paternal feelings, thinking it would take time for him to develop affection for another man's son. But his assumption of fatherhood arrived full-blown, on the spot, was stunning in its single-minded passion.

She pulled the blanket away from Alex's chin a little. He made a kind of whinnying sound as he slept, a baby snore, but he hardly moved and would wake up in the same position as when he went to sleep. He was just as composed when he was awake, looking at her with Tarik's eyes, crying little, taking things as they came. Familiar stuff.

Satisfied finally that he would sleep through the night, she turned off the light, walked through her own bedroom, which adjoined the nursery, and made her way down the dark hallway to the stairs. Descending to the second floor, she saw that Sayles's library door was open but that the room was dark. She continued past, then reached the place where the hallway forked. To the right were the back stairs used by the household staff. She bore left another twenty feet to Sayles's bedroom. The heavy door was shut, but, bending, she put her eye to the keyhole and saw his reading lamp was still on. Despite herself, she took a calming breath. Then she knocked softly and walked in.

The heart of the kingdom, and its geographic core, is the mountainous Sur region. It rises from a vast mud flat that collects rivulets and runoff into a treacherous bog. Few travelers unfamiliar with it can traverse this incrassated mix without becoming stuck fast in the mud. If lucky, a companion can rope the traveler out. If not, if a man is riding alone or in the company of a faithless friend, then life is over, starvation or the colorless sun will finish him off. The body, glued upright as a headstone in the mud, decomposes; the spinal column collapses, and the bones disappear slowly into the morass. Despite the many who die this way, however, many more attempt to cross the bog every year, lured by the fertile farmland and the people living on it in the mountain mists beyond.

These are the people of the Sur, geographical and cultural remnants of the great tenth-century-B.C. kingdom of Saba, the biblical Sheba, which dominated the elbow of land between the Red Sea and the Gulf of Aden, present-day Yemen. Lying at the crossroads of the Orient and Africa trade routes, Saba waxed fat and prosperous, plundering caravans and trading the precious goods of the ancient world—frankincense, ambergris, silk, gold, pearls, spices. But after ten centuries of success, a decline in the incense trade and invasions by the Himyarites and Persians pulled down the empire and the Sabaean people were assimilated or scattered. A handful retreated to the territory now comprising the kingdom and crossed the bog to a bastion of height and heat in the mountains of the Sur.

Haughty and warlike, the Sur people survived, peculiarly out of place, wholly original, passionately convinced of their ancient status as a great race. The most isolated of an isolated nation, separated and protected from the outside by the bog, they were a people whose fidelity to their ancient traditions was so strong it seemed impossible they would ever change. They had lost their position as great traders, but they discovered in the rich soil and cool mists of the highlands a talent for growing coffee and dealing it on world markets, while their lowland countrymen were left to swelter on the gravelly plain, scratching out a living from the parched earth or herding bony livestock.

And while the destruction of their empire created in the Sur a spiritual misery, it did nothing to diminish their pride in their own prowess and competence. Rather than becoming an anthropological curiosity, they cultivated their ancient values and traditions and thrived as the land across the bog was settled by the descendants of the soldiers of the great Islamic armies that swept through the region in the seventh century. The Sur treated these latecomers as if they were from the wrong side of the tracks, the lower orders, a weak, unhygienic, and unproductive lot who deserved whatever government they got. The lowlanders responded with a bitter resentment of their imperious, supercilious compatriots. Over the centuries, they and the Sur addressed their mutual loathing by having as little to do with each other as possible. The Sur were contemptuous of the monarchy and ruling families, forcibly resisted tax agents, and shrugged their shoulders when they were shut out of the kingdom's government. They watched with disdain from their mountain fortresses as the lowlanders hacked and slashed one another in power grabs below. But their total dependence on coffee revenues and a need for new technology brought them more and more under the suzerainty of the king, and when Turkit began arbitrating harvest dates, they were forced to deal with the sad deficiencies and problems of the government they had for so many centuries scorned. With manifest regret, in 1935 they crossed the bog in search of an alliance to overthrow the king. Because they refused to follow unless one of their own led, and because the lowlanders couldn't succeed against the Turkit-British combination without Sur money, a deal was struck to make civil war with an army generaled by a Sur named Malik. To seal the bargain of the revolution, Malik was married to Nila, the motherless daughter of Turkit's rebellious youngest brother.

If memory is eulogy, then Malik would require no further tribute. But he was a man so striking, both physically and in character, possessed of so many fine qualities, that it would be impossible to remember him without describing the path of heroism and suffering by which he attempted to help his people grope into the modern world. He was a good six inches over six feet, tall even for a Sur. He was powerfully built, with heavily muscled shoulders and a sharp hawk nose set over a full mouth. In the Sur tradition, he wore his curly black hair long, and in a land of bold black eyes, his were pale gray bordering on blue and wide set. From the cradle he had been raised with the unquestioning acceptance of having been born into a brilliant race, but it quickly became apparent that even in a distinctive society, he was unique.

He had a love of honor and a great longing to excel, and even in adolescence inspired the trust of much older men and the imitation of his mannerisms by young boys. It's probably apocryphal, but it was said that he was the tallest, strongest man in the country, with an explosive energy and a savage will to fight. What is certain is that he made enormous demands on himself and would break rather than bend to physical pain or danger. As he grew older, he became remote and aloof and his brilliance more barbed and subtle. He had such sexual magnetism that he could stand in the shadows of a room, his white teeth showing in a sardonic smile, and wordlessly bring all eyes around to him. No wonder, then, that wherever Malik led, Sur and lowlander were quick to follow.

He made mistakes in the three years of the insurrection, but from the moment he seized the opportunity to weld the two factions together and take them forward, he acted with vision and dispatch. Although he had no previous experience, he became a master of guerrilla warfare. He would emerge miragelike on the plain with a thousand men and demolish one of Turkit's battalions, disappear on the air and the next day issue forth suddenly to attack a mechanized column. He was a passing cloud of dust, a burst of rifle fire in the mountains. And wherever he went he left behind the bodies of Turkit's men pegged out to four stakes, their ragged decapitated heads nesting on their chests. It got so that Turkit's soldiers and their British commanders refused to leave their garrisons.

Desperate for a hero, the people of the kingdom sheltered him and his men and sacrificed their own pathetic provisions so that the rebel army could survive. In 1935 he burned the British munitions depot at Nizra. In 1936 he massacred seven hundred of the elite Household Guard at Im. In 1937, at Adam, he all but destroyed the air force, dynamiting the runways and blowing up four of Turkit's seven Mosquito fighters. But in late 1938 he was caught in his winter camp, lightly armed, with his cavalry dispersed, and was forced to turn and fight. Gathering his scattered horsemen together, he battled for three hours, tearing back and forth across the battlefield on his charger, his lank hair straightening out behind him, the only valorous man in the history of his country, until his center was broken by a special forces unit of the air force led by British officers. The cavalry scattered, the foot soldiers ran away, the rebel army was destroyed.

Gravely wounded by machine-gun fire, he was captured and taken to the palace in the capital, where after days of torture Turkit himself pounded out his brains with a two-foot length of rusted rain gutter. He then butchered his body and hand-fed it to his King Charles spaniels, cutting off Malik's head and fixing it to an arched wooden door in the capital city with a six-penny nail. Turkit then invited the Royal Air Force to make bombing runs over principal lowland villages and Sur mountain strongholds. But the ultimate revenge escaped him. No matter how hard he tried, he could not track down two-year-old Tarik, and unable to tolerate such frustration, he ordered the murder of all the country's male children three years of age and under. Passed along village to village, Tarik and Nila escaped that hellish, disordered brain to another environment, more kind, less brutal.

But while he was gone, Tarik was not forgotten by the people of the kingdom, who clung to his memory and the hope of his return as if it were the spar of a magnificent wrecked ship adrift on the ocean.

For as far as Tarik could see, coffee trees covered the Sur mountains. Six feet tall, with dense dark green leaves, the trees were arranged with gridlike precision on terraced hillsides, occupying the highlands with the compactness of tract homes. Each one perfectly shaped, perfectly ripe, and when coffee prices on the world market were high, perfect money trees. The air was full of their pungent scent and Tarik savored deep breaths of it. In the distance, workers carried heavy baskets loaded with coffee berries, laboring under their loads with ancient grace.

It was the same every day—workers out at sunrise full of chatter, back at sunset silenced by exhaustion. Reach, pick, stoop, reach, pick, stoop, their work was rhythmic as the ocean tides they had never seen, the arrangement of the bushes on the hillsides as ordered as a spider's web. Tarik never tired of looking at it.

He shifted his weight a little to his left leg; his right still ached, although less here than in the heat of the plain. This was emotional, he knew, because the damp of the highlands should have

made his leg ache and the broiling heat below balmed the pain.
The shrapnel from the grenade had destroyed cartilage in the knee
and made it flare almost every waking minute. Most nights he
couldn't get more than two or three hours of sleep before the pain
would wake him and he would rise, light his lantern, and work on
his papers. Or if the moon was full, saddle a horse and roam the
coffee fields and countryside.

When the left leg began to ache a little from carrying all the
weight, he leaned forward and clutched the balustrade of the little
balcony and put his weight on his hands and arms. Immediately,
he felt relief. He hadn't been able to walk for more than a month
after the explosion, although this was due as much to the abdom-
inal wounds as the leg injury. Almost three years later, pain was
still an ever-present part of his life.

He slackened the weight on his arms and put it back to his leg
in the continual process of trying to find comfort, rocking a little
from the swift return of misery. He closed his eyes against it, then
popped them open again. He had turned the endurance of pain
into a warrior exercise—get through it, put it by you, move on.
This kind of pain sweeps every other sensation before it the way
the prow of a huge tanker clears away seawater in a wall. Emotion, memory—everything is wiped out by pain. Which is why, as
staring for a long time at the reassuring orderliness of the coffee
trees emptied his brain of thought, he put all of his weight on his
two weak legs. *Orderliness and pain, I've narrowed it down to
the basics anyway,* he thought, and then of course he stopped
thinking because of the pain. He could appreciate the smoothness
with which the process worked.

The disappearing sunlight took the green coffee trees down to
purple-black. The evening mist had already begun shaping in the
valleys; by nightfall it would trail its damp fingers around every
hill and through the villages and the temperature would drop.
There was little firewood in the country. The Sur people cut peat
from the bog and burned it for cooking and for warmth, but even
this was in short supply and carefully husbanded. Het had per-
fected the art of building warm cookfires from small pieces of
peat and had one burning pleasantly in a room off the balcony that
was a combined kitchen and dining area. Feeling Tarik looking at
him, Het glanced up, then quickly lowered his eyes. It was a ritual
of discomfort they practiced daily.

Tarik knew that Het blamed himself for what had happened to
Clare outside Duru, and in every glance, no matter how friendly,
believed he saw reproach. Het's own self-reproach was such that

sometimes when he looked at Tarik his eyes would fill up, which would have been laughable because he was so massive and strong and in every other way such a menace, if it hadn't been so touching. It had occurred to Tarik lately that perhaps it was more than self-reproach that made Het so down at the mouth. Maybe he misses Clare. Maybe, like so few of the others, he understood the reasons why she left and feels compassion for him. Perhaps those watery eyes are meant for Tarik, and not for himself. But as Het never spoke, Tarik had no way of knowing for sure. He had given up reassuring him, just grew used to his steady, apologetic stare. He wanted Het with him, out of sentiment, to maintain the pain edge, because he was a good cook, for a dozen reasons he understood but couldn't name.

Other aspects of the past, or rather Malik's past, were happier to consider and had the effect of ameliorating the other hurts. Tarik came to the Sur because he knew that once he'd crossed the bog and made the long ascent by horse up to the towering, multilevel pink stone fortress that Malik had hung over a ravine, the visions that made his eyes swim would draw back and people and events could be viewed with clarity. The pain was less here, the physical pain, and the other. Chiefly, he came because this was where Malik could be felt, and if Malik wasn't what it was all about, then what did any of it mean?

His father's people had been the driving force of his teenage dreams, when he would skulk around the ships in the Embarcadero in San Francisco and try to shinny up the ropes that secured them to the docks. These tall, nervy people he could understand better than the sad, stunted lowlanders starving down below. These were his people. Cut from the same cloth, like-minded, same-blooded. They did not avert their eyes when they saw him. They assessed him coolly, with measuring stares that outsiders took as insult. He had had to prove himself to them. They'd checked him out, withheld judgment, put him to some crude tests, took the measure of his character and courage. Hadn't he taken the grenade in his gut and survived? Hadn't he taken back Duru from those filthy Yemenis even though he could hardly sit a horse? Hadn't he married Topaz, the daughter of Hadi, who was a Marib and thus a lowlander, to cement the alliance of the two peoples, just as Malik had married Nila? Hadn't he filled all of them with flickering expectation, and wasn't God sending them a message by returning Malik's son to them after all these years? They asked if they could shift the burdens of their problemed lives onto his shoulders, and of course he said they could and thanked them for it, and this was the ultimate test and indisputable evidence that he was Malik, returned to them.

After a little while Tarik began to grow into their expectations, and in his own mind the line between himself and Malik necessarily began to blur. He would lounge in the enormous audience room, usually on large damask cushions that had been thrown on the floor, the incensors burning frangipani and frankincense, beeswax candles giving off perfumed smoke and little light. The men would draw up to him as if he were a magnet, a few at first and then gradually more and more until the room was filled. They would explain the complicated threads of their history, of brutal kings who could take the skin off an enemy as if they were pulling off his nightshirt, of women with eyes so black a man could fall right into them and never see light again. And of course they always came back to Malik, because he had been the best of all of them.

Tarik would listen silently to their boasts and stories for hours, then stir a little in his seat, the signal to the senior man to give a little admonishing cough, and the others would fall into respectful silence.

Tarik would command the room with a glance, and then declare in a voice that made even the delivery of bad news easy to hear that the past was all well and good but it was the future they must deliver to their children. And because nothing was more important to the Sur than their children, they would nod their heads in unison and be eager to hear more. He told them about the schools he planned to build, the hospitals, the new farming techniques he intended to import, and ways of saving the coffee berries from parasites, which was a constant problem. That when the oil at Duru could be exploited, they would have everything they ever dreamed of, and that they all had to pull together until then.

The men sat back and pulled faces at the mention of the oil. Some of them had traveled and had met men in the oil-rich countries, men who wore gold chains and smoked English cigarettes and kept hookers on retainer in Monte Carlo. The Sur men wanted nothing to do with oil. Let the lowlanders below keep the oil and the whores. All they wanted was to grow the most fragrant coffee beans in the world. Better than the Brazilians, better than the Colombians. When the world has had enough of gold jewelry and whores, civilized men will still lay bare their hearts over a cup of strong coffee. Tarik listened to this with a grave face. He was tempted to tell them they would make a good ad for American

TV, but most of them hadn't yet heard a radio, much less seen TV, so he put his hand over his smile and kept quiet.

Instead, he swore that no matter what happened down below, no matter how many roads and high rises and hotels went up, how many oilmen came and went, he would never interfere with their culture and their laws. Because he was an honest man. Because he was Malik's son and one of them.

With the light draining out of the day and the highlands in deep shadow, Tarik turned from the balcony into the candlelit dining room. As he did, a soft rap at the door signaled the arrival of Topaz for their evening meal.

She was, as always, stalked by a sister. Tarik had no idea which sister this might be, as they all looked exactly alike; only their sheer number made them unique. He thought he had counted twenty sisters, although he also thought he might have counted some of them twice.

As always when she saw him, Topaz ran up and touched him lightly on the arm and he was struck again at what a genuinely warm person she was. She had black hair that when loosened from its many braids fell clear to the heels of her feet, and a small face with tiny features. Her eyes were a lively brown and Tarik had never seen her when she wasn't smiling. From the day Hadi had brought her to him in the capital, when he was heavily sedated and White-Lyons had not yet told him that Clare had left, Topaz had never been anything but kind and understanding. She clucked over his every need like a mother hen, was cautious of his health and diet, became teary-eyed when she saw him wince in pain.

Tiny as she was, she had the will of ten men—never shy, never less than assured that she had been born to cut his hair, berate his servants, hound Het about his cooking, do everything, in short, to make his life one easy slide to what she was positive would be greatness. She also had a rollicking sense of humor, which if too obscure for Tarik, was clearly shared by her bodyguard of sisters. Everywhere she went, they tagged along. If they had husbands and children, they came too, and servants. When he was young, Nila had taken him to the Ringling Bros. circus in the Cow Palace, just south of San Francisco, and the clowns had gotten on his nerves. They were noisy, rude, chaotic, and, to his way of thinking, not funny. Living with Topaz's sisters was those irritating clowns all over again, and he told his staff to keep them away from him or they'd have to answer for it. It seemed to him that

Hadi's children had struck a weird balance with nature—the men were all murderous and marginally insane, while the women were warm and lighthearted. Neither sex had a brain in their heads. Topaz believed she especially needed her sisters with her in the Sur, because she was a lowlander and the Sur people treated her (she thought) like dirt even though her marriage had elevated her to the highest station. So sisters shuttled in and out on a daily basis, tying up Tarik's Sur staff with endless requests for travel arrangements and exotic food for the legion of aunts and cousins. One of their own had hit the big time and they all planned to cash in. Their wants were pretty small, however. Most of the day they spent hiding their mouths with their little hands and howling with laughter.

Surrounded by the mob of Marib relations, isolated by the loss of Clare, Tarik had successfully detached himself emotionally in his new marriage. Still, Topaz was a tolerable mate. She was compassionate, thoughtful, hardworking, and utterly devoted to her husband. If only she hadn't had an intellectual capacity the size of a bottle cap, they might have made a real marriage. As it was, they had absolutely nothing to say to each other once he'd agreed with her that, yes, her sister Mira's daughter had a bad case of acne and he would certainly ask Dr. Van Damm to prescribe some good medication from the United States, and gone on to reassure her that her feet didn't seem to have grown but that her new slippers were probably just too small, they had plumbed the shallows of intellectual interchange. This was hardly Topaz's fault. Her culture had bred her to serve the man, not dazzle him with conversation. She was happy just to sit at Tarik's feet, drinking him in with her bright brown eyes, wholly satisfied.

In one area, however, satisfaction eluded Topaz, and as soon as Het had cleared away their dinner things, and the interchangeable sister had retired with a giggle, she let him know again that while the last time was all she had ever hoped for, it was *two* nights ago and how would she ever give him the son she knew he longed for if they did not do it again. Besides—and here she swept her eyelashes up and down in a parody of silent film vamp—she had a little itch.

She shuffled over to him on her knees and in quick and graceful movements unwound the gauze of indigo fabric around her bosom. She was rightly proud of her breasts, which were full, with nipples brown as her brown eyes. She cupped them in her hands and held them up to him with an expression of mild shock on her face when he did not immediately reach out to take the gift with his fingers.

Instead, he was fighting the impulse to run. He felt full of dread and dishonor, mindlessly selfish. His body responded; it always did. Even when his faith was in a state of suspension, his penis thought life was one long spin on the Tilt o'Wheel. Sensing this, Topaz began massaging it through his trousers. When she felt him stiffen, such a look of triumph came over her that he despised her, then immediately felt guilty. She was a good woman. She was determined to make the best of difficult circumstances.

But there was no time for assessments. Deftly she peeled off the rest of her clothes until she was naked. Fully aroused, she had a look of such terrifying single-mindedness on her face that he closed his eyes. Knowing that his legs pained him and that he couldn't get up on his knees, she straddled him, holding his penis in her tiny hand and angling it until it butted against her. Down deep, she was pleased about his bad legs. She'd come to prefer this method of penetration because she could exploit him for her own needs.

"Does this hurt?" she asked, trying to keep her weight off his thighs and knees.

He shook his head no.

When she was perfectly positioned, she began a slow, exquisite descent. By the time he was in her thoroughly, she was gasping. She paused, arched her back, and then commenced to screw him with an enginelike efficiency that he had come to dread. Her hips moved in a rhythmic, jerking motion. Her legs, which had been delicately splayed, shot out from her hips. Faster and faster she beat herself against him, groaning and biting her lip. After a few minutes of this, she slipped out of him for a better position, trying for a lowered center of gravity and greater friction. She planted her tiny feet alongside his thighs and brought her knees almost up to her chin. She no longer minded, which she had a moment ago, that he had not taken her nipples hungrily in his mouth, or fought her mouth open with his tongue. Such small needs had collapsed in the face of the greater, more terrifying responsibility—the quest for the heart-stopping, brain-numbing orgasm that she knew would be hers with just one more pump. One more pump, and another. Fifty more and still nothing. The worry that it might not happen sent snaking fingers of doubt into her brain, which she fought back with more pumping. She pulled out his penis, ascertained that it was stiff and slightly reddened and thus far from ready to release its baby-making liquid, and knew he would let her go on. She had to have an orgasm, many orgasms. That is what would make her a real woman. When she was a real woman she would get a baby. Mira had told her that and Mira should know: she was thirty and had six children.

She tightened herself around him and felt his penis jump and collide with her cervix. This so reassured her that she began to feel the slight, now-increasing pinching sensation around her clitoris that was a sure sign of impending orgasm. Too enraptured to raise her head from the sight of his penis dipping in and out of her, she examined her nipples with her fingers. Extended, hard. A sure sign she would come. Her toes curled and tickled. All of it so reassuring. He stirred under her, reaching his own climax.

She clamped her hands on his shoulders. He moaned a little, and jerked his hips. The heavens could not have presented her with a more propitious moment. She felt the semen racing into her. Another instant and he would be soft. She clenched her teeth and buried her face in the perfect V between his head and shoulder. She bucked, she spasmed, she screamed out loud. And then she reached her orgasm.

Or had she? After a moment of confidence she wasn't sure. They sat panting on the little couch, their hearts hammering together. His flaccid penis was still inside her and she thought—yes, she was sure, she still had the itch. She wanted to cry and beg him to do it again, but she suspected he had fallen asleep. She twisted off his lap and pulled their clothes up over them. Het's fire had extinguished. She was freezing, she was not a woman, she was wretched.

16

"What would you say if I told you that I'm considering resigning from the State Department?" wondered Arthur Olson.

They were walking through the hanging garden that clung to the rear wall of Malik's fortress. Spring-fed terraces of onions and garlic bordered the garden and the air was full of their musky scent. Every night when Olson was in the Sur, he and Tarik would walk off Het's cooking. They had reached a great gnarled tamarisk when Olson asked the question Tarik had known was coming for months.

"I would ask you not to do it," he told him. "I would tell you not to do it if for no other reason than that I need you here."

Olson carried his Scandinavian ancestry on every part of him. A moon face, slightly florid, a narrow nose that hung down in a point over his upper lip, and an emotional reserve that could be maddening if it hadn't been tempered by some Americanized exuberance. He had a passion for good cigars, wine, and good food. Many were the tables he had been unable to pry himself away from during a lifetime spent in the Middle East and Europe, and the feast had begun showing around his middle and at his nose, which was tattooed with spidery red lines, a tippler's nose.

"I'm flattered," Olson said, resuming their walk. "But don't be so quick to assume that I'm leaving the kingdom. Actually, I brought you out here to this gorgeous garden to advance a proposal. It's my intention not to end my usefulness to you, just my usefulness in my capacity at State. You've heard of OmniTech?"

"They're gearing up to handle the energy situation in Oman, among a dozen other things there, right? And something in Saudi Arabia, I forget what."

"That's right. It's headquartered in Sunnyvale, California, owned by"—he named a huge military defense contractor, which was owned in turn by a company that manufactured furnaces and air conditioners worldwide—"but it operates as a separate entity with a more varied program."

"Such as?"

"Legal, banking, water and energy services, transportation. And then, of course, security equipment, armaments, missile guidance systems."

Under his breath Tarik said, " 'A more varied program.' "

Olson laughed but quickly added, "And of course it has top-flight people in all categories. Most of them State veterans, of which I am soon to be one, Agency veterans. All of them are old hands in the region. The specific mission would be to consult on ways to improve the economy, but clearly there would be divergences from that. Defense, military, intelligence, as well as the civil services. The restructuring of the army, for instance, which you've planned already. And of course the bonus is with an all-American team you'd be out from under British influence forever, which I know you want."

"I take it you've been considering this for some time."

"They approached me several years ago, but I couldn't see the appeal. Now it's more apparent. I mean, you have to admit that within the resources and agencies of State we haven't been all that effective here, have we? No criticism intended, but what's the good in asking Washington to deliver systems when there's no infrastructure and never will be unless you simply impose one ready-made, which under current conditions you just can't.

"Far better to take the money from Washington, then hand it over to people who can do the job right now, no waiting. I've seen them work in other countries and you can't believe what's getting accomplished, and I say that with no disloyalty to Washington. And honestly, unless the Duru investment begins to pay off soon, I don't see how you can have any choice but to go with something like this—specifically this, if you don't mind my boosterism."

"Still, your play in it seems rather sudden, doesn't it, Arthur?"

"You remember I mentioned last year that they had come back to me."

"At the time I considered it speculative."

"At the time, it was."

"What changed your mind?"

"Time, advancing age, new mountains to climb."

They walked along in silence, following flagstones down a steep incline. Below them a small grove of frankincense trees released their aroma into the atmosphere. A man with a flat chisel chipped away at the gray bark on one of the trees until tears of milk-white resin appeared on the wound. In a few weeks he would have to return to make another cut, then another, before the milk hardened into solid golden globs that could be harvested. Olson watched him intently.

"Can you make any money off that?" he asked Tarik, indicating the trees with his thumb.

"Not enough of them, and we're competing with cheaper incense from India and elsewhere. It takes three cuts just to get the frankincense. A good harvest doesn't yield more than fifty pounds of the stuff. That man over there"—he pointed to the grizzled old man with a dirty rag wrapped around his head—"worked for my father, and now he works for me. Every night before sunset he lights an incensor and spreads frankincense smoke through my clothes, my bed, in every closet. I can't stand the stuff, but there's nothing I can do about it. It's the way it is. He makes me medicinal drinks of it and then hangs around to make sure I drink it all."

"What's it taste like?"

"It's terrible, but don't tell him."

"And does it work?"

"Well, it hasn't killed me, so from my point of view it works. It's supposed to be good for the gout, and for broken hearts."

Olson gave him a sidelong glance. Tarik hadn't so much as spoken Clare's name since the day Olson had told him she had married Lawrence Sayles and then several months later that she had had a baby. He had tried once or twice since to bring her up, thinking Tarik might want to confide in someone, but Tarik had given him that blank look and Olson had instantly backed off. *Don't ask me. Don't remind me. Don't talk about it.*

"Anyway, Arthur, you were saying?"

"I was saying that I think you ought to consider what I'm proposing. Certainly, Washington has no objection, in fact, they're enthusiastic, so I think it would be better all around if we began a gradual phasing in of the OmniTech arrangement."

Tarik considered this silently for so long that Olson thought he hadn't been listening. "And what do you get out of all this, Arthur?" he said finally. "The thanks of a grateful nation?"

Hearing the edge in his voice, Olson was immediately alert. He was an honest man, he had always dealt with Tarik in a straightforward fashion. He wasn't ashamed of his motivation. "I would be getting a fair percentage."

"Anything else?"

Olson looked at him blankly.

"No intangibles?"

"I honestly have no idea what you're talking about. Something in the abstract I would be taking from you? What?"

"Not abstract, Arthur. Philosophical."

Olson opened his eyes wide. "I don't know what you're talking about. Half the time, I don't know what the hell you're talking about."

Tarik looked off at the old man harvesting frankincense, who bowed deeply in his direction, then he threw an arm over Olson's shoulders and pumped them a little. "Half the time I don't know what I'm talking about either." But of course he did, he always knew. "Oh, come on, Arthur. You have a right to get rich, don't you?" he went on. "Take care of the kids in the future. All those years at State for pennies. You have the right. And I agree with you. We cannot get ahead the way we're operating now. I'd been thinking of coming to you with this kind of proposal anyway."

Olson turned and gave him an uncertain smile. Something he couldn't quite put his finger on, something of the old cynicism, was back in the younger man's smile and it always made him feel unsure of what was really passing between them.

They walked on until Olson happened to glance over his shoulder and then stopped abruptly. "You know, I have to tell you that I think you're making a big mistake, not having more of the bodyguard up here."

"Are you nervous?"

"For you, yes. Me? Well, no government would fall if I weren't around."

"I'm safe here in the Sur. I like not having the bodyguard around all the time. Even on good days they look panic-stricken."

"That's because they came so close to blowing it the last time. But, my friend, I disagree with you. You're never going to be safe. Not while Hadi is alive."

"Hadi has what he wants. He's not a threat as long as he has what he wants."

"And you're certain you know what that is?"

"Hadi's needs are biological, marginally political, but never philosophical—and not even financial. Every one of his sons is impotent. Can you imagine? Such a heavy reflection for such a mighty man. He wants a grandson, my grandson, Malik's grandson, that is. He believes it will make him immortal."

"And how are things on that score?"

"Nothing as yet." Not for want of Topaz's trying, he wanted to say, but didn't. His penis felt as if it had been through one of the debarking machines that Stan once ran at the Great Northern Paper Company, but he didn't plan on telling anyone that mild-mannered little Topaz was sexually insatiable.

"Anyway, Hadi isn't the only one after your skin," Olson said. "Oh, maybe not now, but in ten years the lines will be drawn more finely and you'll have to take better care of yourself. In ten years you will have earned your enemies."

When Tarik didn't respond, Olson stopped suddenly and put a finger close to his chest. "So that's how it is, is it? Going to take things as they come, are you? Tempt the gods and all that."

"I'm not tempting the gods. I'm simply saying that if I get it up here in the Sur, then something is sorely wrong with what I've been doing anyway."

Olson groaned out loud. "God, you haven't turned into a fatalist, have you? That would be the worst."

"You've been a cold warrior for too long, Arthur. What would be worse from your point of view—A, I believe my life is ruled by random events over which I have no control, so I don't bother trying—or B, I show up in Red Square dancing the mazurka and quoting Marx, or, even worse, Castro?"

"A, definitely A."

"Really? I'm surprised."

"B, you're a Communist and I'd know what to do with you— don't take it personally and forgive me for sounding like Elliott Tomlinson. But A, well, then you're a loose cannon, aren't you? Unpredictable at best. You might do something really silly, like stick your neck out, or get unfriendly on me. You'd have nothing to lose, a real menace."

They had reached a low wall, with bricks tumbling down out of it. Olson stepped over it, followed by Tarik, who lifted his legs with some effort. Inside was a graveyard.

"You didn't initiate this discussion with the plan to bring me here, did you?" Tarik asked him with a laugh. "Because if you did, your timing is beautiful."

Olson poked around the short marker stones, most of which had toppled over. Toward the back was a freshly dug grave. The earth heaped on it had been tamped down with boards, which gave it a checkerboard pattern and made it look ridiculously gay. A raven sat squarely on the pile screaming loudly at them until he flew off.

Olson reflected on the scene for a moment. "Think he died happy, Tarik?"

"Those are mutually exclusive terms."

Olson made a little snorting sound and pulled his shoulders up around his neck. "Oh, well," he said. He looked off into the distance at the neatly terraced coffee plantations. He could understand why Tarik loved the place. The people were warm, bright, and inventive, holding back nothing in their hospitality. The Sur was all outrageous aromas and cool vegetation. What a relief to feel the chill air after the inferno down on the plain. He took a deep breath.

"I could stay here forever," he said. "You know, we're really going to do something here. We're going to make a difference, I can feel it. Standing here with you, I can almost remember why I came to the kingdom all those years ago."

"Did you ever come to the Sur with my father?"

For a moment Olson's attention was taken by the flight of a hawk, now arcing a sharp turn in the ravine before turning in an easterly direction to the bog. "What's that? No, no. I never came here with Malik. I met him only once or twice. I always used a middleman for the arms shipments."

He sighed loudly and ducked his head. He could feel the beginnings of a headache collecting in the bones at the base of his skull. He needed to rest. He needed to think. "Well,"—he stuck out his hand and Tarik grasped it—"better get to bed. Long day tomorrow. Cairo, Paris, then Washington, to let them in on my plans. I wanted you to be the first to know."

"You'll submit some sort of job-by-job proposal so we can begin our new arrangement?"

"So you're willing?"

"I don't have a choice. Besides, I trust you, Arthur, to look after my interests. Where would I be, after all, if I didn't trust you?"

As soon as Olson was out of sight, Tarik turned back up the flagstone path. But when he reached the garden, instead of taking the long flight of stone stairs up to his apartments, he turned right until he reached a wall densely covered with ivy. Feeling around in the leaves, he touched a door latch, pushed hard against it, and after much moaning of antique metal, forced it open. He had discovered the door by accident, then hunted for others and eventually found more than a dozen, all of them leading to the same dank passageway that snaked underneath the building from the garden in the east to an overgrown path nearly six thousand feet away. From the passageway he could access nearly every floor in the building without being observed.

He climbed a flight of steps to the second floor and through a musty closet he entered the corridor and from there walked left to his apartments. To his surprise, Walter White-Lyons was sitting on a small settee outside his door.

"I saw you talking to Arthur Olson out there."

"Yes, that's right." Tarik attempted to brush by him, but White-Lyons put out his hand.

"He told you he was leaving?"

"Yes. How did you know?"

"He's not that difficult to read. He has something up his sleeve, I take it."

"He proposed OmniTech."

"What did you tell him?"

"I told him yes."

White-Lyons thought for a moment and then said, "Well, we'll see where it goes. Keep our eyes open, get what we can, and stay on guard. Can't do otherwise, can we?" He offered Tarik a smile, hoping to enlist him in some spirit of camaraderie, but Tarik refused to make eye contact and was about to push through the door when he remembered another piece of business.

"I need to speak to you about your friend Cobb."

"What about him?"

"He wants travel documents for that girl Sirah Thompkins. He wrote me again this week that she still hasn't got them and won't marry him until she does." White-Lyons snorted. "I told him no—now, in the future, forever. No."

Tarik forced himself to look White-Lyons in the eye. He could not bear to be in the man's presence. He blamed him directly for all that had happened with Clare and he never intended to let him forget how much he was hated.

"I'm going to tell you this once," he said. "I want Cobb to have anything he wants, and if he wants Sirah Thompkins, then he's going to have her."

White-Lyons smoothed his mustaches and straightened his shoulders. "Sirah Thompkins is an evil woman," he said firmly. "I don't know how much your friend Cobb knows." He cleared his throat. "Her father was English, a freebooter and no good at all. She murdered Harold Jenkins just as sure as if she'd put the gun to his head. Jenkins was my friend. We went to school together and started our service together in Aden. I got him his appointment on Turkit's general staff and, after Britain withdrew, the appointment to the finance office. Then he met this woman, this Sirah, and it was disaster. He looted the treasury for her. When Turkit found him out, his wife and children had to sell everything and go back to England like beggars. In the end, he shot himself. And I found his body. My friend."

He stiffened his spine. "Poor Harold couldn't bring himself to punish her, but I certainly can, and will. Does Cobb know that Sirah goes with the man with the deepest pockets? She's abandoned him a hundred times in the years since he's been in Duru. She'll never marry him. She's using his friendship with you to get herself a passport. That girl will rot here forever, and if you have any sense, you'll convince your friend to boot her out before she does the same to him. If you're any kind of friend."

"Stan's a grown man. He lives his own life." He did not want White-Lyons to know that Stanley was broke and that he had been sending him money on a regular basis for several years.

"Sirah Thompkins will never leave the kingdom. Stan Cobb may be your friend, but Harold Jenkins was mine and I don't intend to forget him."

With that, White-Lyons sat down in a chair and glared at Tarik so hard that finally Tarik had no choice but to turn and finally push through the door. The next morning he telephoned the capital and ordered a passport issued for Sirah Thompkins.

The wind always kicked up around sunset, throwing a stinging sheet of sand against Stanley Cobb's face. He covered his eyes with his hand and struggled on until habit told him he had reached the building that housed the controls of his drilling operation. Once inside, he took a moment to adjust his eyes to the dim light and then, frowning, crossed the tiny room.

"Wake up!" He shook the Algerian so hard the man fell out of his chair. "Wake up, you bum! You think I pay you to sleep on the job? Look at that—" Stanley stared at the panel of pressure regulators and battery indicators. "The pressure is up." He monkeyed with some dials before he felt satisfied enough to return to the little man, who, shocked out of sleep, sat stupidly for a moment, and then leapt to his feet with a cascade of apologies and explanations, which Stan was having none of.

"Get out!" He grabbed the man by the seat of his trousers and dragged him across the room. In one quick move Stan had him out the door and in a heap in the dirt outside. "Goddamn wogs!" He locked the door behind him. "Can't trust 'em for a minute."

The Algerian pounded on the door, then ran to the closed window to shout obscenities. Finally, he gave up and, still cursing, stalked away. Stan had fired one worker already that month, and two more had quit when he couldn't meet the payroll.

He walked over to the long panel with the dials and knobs that controlled the drills and slumped down into his chair, fed up.

He closed his eyes against the reproach of the unmoving dials and like magic, the image of Sirah appeared, easing all his worries. Unable to resist, he mentally stripped her, clamped his mouth on her breasts, and imagined he was coaxing her little nipples through their bonds of flesh, then moved his attention to the spot between her legs. He indulged himself in this way for a while, but was surprised when another, more sentimental fantasy intruded. Sirah in a wedding dress of white muslin, chaste enough to seem bridal, but yet so gauzy that it showed the outline of her legs through its long, filmy skirt. He had promised his heart to her and given her a little ring. Birds tweeted, posies bloomed.

Stan's eyes trembled behind their lids envisioning the moment when she would become his wife. Sure, her side of the Jenkins story sometimes leaked and broke from the weight of its discrepancies. Maybe she had been a bad girl once. He could imagine that might be so. Other men had told him tales about her that made him slap his hands over his ears and loudly hum the national anthem. They said that when she was gone from Duru she was at the air base at Hirth. That one night there she had gone with more than twenty men. But hadn't he once been a man for whom love was nothing more than a good screw at a bargain price? He had changed, so could Sirah; he knew it in his bones.

Deciding this eased his mind so much that he resumed his fantasy of what he would do to her breasts if she were there. Wondering where she might be at this moment, and with whom, raised a disquieting bubble of fear in his heart, and he had to concentrate hard on his fantasy to drive it away.

After a minute of imagining his lips had rounded the curve of her buttocks, Stanley felt his old friend stiffen obligingly. He opened his trousers and began to work in earnest. In his mind he flipped Sirah onto her knees, her backside waggling under his mouth. His head fell back and his mouth opened. He had never known such a thundering need to release—the whole ground seemed to be shaking under the pressure of his body's straining. His fingers found her little breasts at the same time that he entered her so forcefully that the act drove his chair across the floor. That woke him up.

He popped open unfocused eyes to find that every dial on the panel wiggled wildly in time with the pull of his hand on his cock. He had almost made up his mind to go outside and check things out, when his penis took another leap. Which is how it happened that the ocean of oil trapped since time began beneath the oasis of Duru had at last unloosed its bonds to shale and rock at the precise moment that Stan Cobb—not for the first nor the last time in his life—brought yet one more pornographic adventure to an orgasmic conclusion.

1969

17

Alex had been a long and beautiful baby, with pale hair and those cool dove-gray eyes. From the cradle he exhibited the aplomb of a world-weary thirty-year-old, a princely calm that Clare could only shake her head at. He hardly ever cried or complained, even when he teethed. Just sat in his little chair, taking in everything with those eyes. He especially loved Henry, who rode him around on his shoulders, and Marguerite, who fed him soft cookies and tarts, his favorite.

As for his paternity, well, it was never questioned. His nose could have been Sayles's, and his mouth and the cut of his chin. Babies at that age tend to look like whomever friends and family want them to look like. They gazed at Alex, then at Sayles, and pronounced the son the spitting image of the father. If there were doubts when Alex began to develop the square-jawed, broad-shouldered build of a boy entirely the opposite of Sayles, no one voiced them. Because there was that blond hair, after all, and those eyes. And because by then he was so thoroughly Lawrence Sayles's son that even nature seemed to conspire in the deception.

Sayles never contradicted this notion in private either, or ever referred to the circumstances of their marriage. Clare had come to believe that he had convinced himself that he actually was Alex's biological father.

He took to his new station as if it were the one mission in an illustrious career that he had long coveted but never before been granted. Even when Alex was a tiny baby he lugged him everywhere, to his K Street office, to Europe on the family Gulfstream—Alex had been to Geneva three times before he was even a year old—into the backseat of the Cadillac, Henry checking the rearview mirror to make sure father and son were firmly ensconced before stepping on the gas.

Sayles talked to Alex as if he were a valued assistant, pointing out things of interest on the roadside through the car window, explaining everything, his gray head bent low to pick up every bit of babble from the little boy. In return Alex adored him, rested melting eyes on him when he came into a room and wept bitterly when he said good-bye, which Clare was ashamed to admit made her a little jealous. Seeing them together lately, it had occurred to her that the unbounded devotion to Homer of her childhood might be the explanation for Kath's resentment.

Watching Alex grow was a time of unbearable, near-poisonous nostalgia for her, and the only way she could think to overcome it was to blot out the past in her mind and create a wholly different Clare from the one who had felt the colorless sun of the plain blistering the skin right off her arms. By 1968 she had made herself into a Washington Wife and taught herself the art of the Little Dinner. On one December evening alone she decanted ten bottles of Chateau Lafite-Rothschild 1945, an extravagant gesture that made Sayles blanch, even if the next morning he picked up the telephone and ordered five cases more from Sherry Lehmann in New York. And Petrossian caviar by the tub! If for no other reason, this alone would have made her reputation in Washington. Good caviar in quantities that allowed guests to graze like cattle was unheard of in the District. Cream cheese on celery sticks or a little crab dip was the high-end hors d'oeuvre served by most of the wives, even those nearly as wealthy as Sayles's.

Preston thought this profligate entertaining gauche and he curled his lip at Clare when she presented him with her shopping list and then clicked away on her high heels. Connie had had the lightest hand at mealtimes. Hors d'oeuvres—a few shrimp and maybe carpaccio of beef sliced so thin one could read a silver mark through it, and never more than two pieces per person. The menu was always clear broth, game bird—grouse or squab—sorbet, fruits, and cheeses. Perfect, although even he had to concede that if he'd shown up hungry after an eleven-hour workday and been offered such spare fare, then he too might have departed The Heights for McDonald's, as he'd once seen a White House counsel and his wife do.

And, if push came to shove, he had to admire Clare's nerve. Oysters flown in on the Gulfstream from Chincoteague Island off the coast of Virginia, Périgord truffles, Brie de Meaux wheels the size of radial tires. He had a grudging appreciation of the simple pattern she designed for her personalized Meissen china, Sayles's wedding gift to her, and the little paper doilies she had bought to slip between the plates so they wouldn't scratch each other when Marguerite put them back in the cupboards.

Clare, of course, hadn't known bone china from porcelain when she married Sayles, but once she'd set her foot on the path she was relentless. She read and listened and made a friend of the manager of the Georgetown Safeway who knew his beef and his Armagnacs. She was going to enjoy being rich. She would not be one of the old-moneys who were tighter than the bark on a tree, as Stan used to say. Let them cock their eyebrows at her extravagance; those who weren't carping were at her Little Dinners, getting fat and loving it.

She threw herself into charity fund-raising, a hobby practiced by society women with no talent to earn money in the real world. By the time Alex was two, Clare had co-chaired a dinner dance at the Smithsonian, twice offered a tour of The Heights as part of a fund-raising auction, become patron of a small theater group, hosted glittery parties for meaningful causes, including a half-dozen open houses at The Heights, and swept dance floors with her Balenciaga gowns at charity balls for children's aid societies, adoption services, diseases she could not pronounce, unlettered migrant workers, and homeless dogs and cats, all the while telling herself that this was useful and that she was making a difference in someone else's life.

She joined the most prestigious women's club in Washington, the Summit, over the protests of the white-gloved ancien régime governing board who resented her lack of pedigree. But she was Lawrence Sayles's wife and he was worth a fortune and was a god to them and had done everything noteworthy in this century but walk on the moon, and they not only had to take her, in the end they had to like her too. So they courted her with all the passion their desiccated sensibilities could permit, fawned over her smallest witticism, shared with her their cherished little economies—the little genius black seamstress with eleven children living in a tenement far from their own glamorous homes who could copy Chanel and Dior for pennies. And the second-hand store in Bethesda that paid top dollar for wedding and Christmas gifts they'd received but had no use for—Shreve goblets, lacquered picture frames, sterling silver cake plates, all of it good stuff. The frayed collars on old Thresher & Glenny shirts that could be turned around and stitched back on. The maids earning less than minimum wage and charged for every Coke they took from their mistress's refrigerator—they told her these things without an ounce of shame, and she thanked them politely and turned her head away so they wouldn't see her disgust.

She would never get over how tight with their money the truly rich were. Especially Lawrence. Like many who inherit their millions, cash transactions were the banal stuff of the masses and never sullied his days. From the cradle, others, usually paid employees, had lingered behind to settle his accounts—chauffeurs, secretaries, male assistants with incomes in the low five figures found themselves digging into their own pockets for hundreds of dollars a year without hope of reimbursement. The old rich invest their money, count their money, worship their money, but they do not spend their money. Which is why they have so much of it.

Clare despised this habit and had asked Sayles to carry cash and pay his restaurant checks himself. He had sent one of his secretaries to the bank for a big wad of bills, but Clare wasn't convinced that the money had ever crossed anyone's palm but his own because when she checked the bankroll after he emptied his pockets onto the dresser at night once in a while, it never seemed to grow lighter.

Unapologetically she considered herself nouveau riche and was shameless and unrepressed about what she spent, which was plenty even by the standards of the Sayles fortune. She made spending money a point of honor, which in another woman would have been the most transparent of rationalizations but for her was a way of measuring where she had been and how far she had come. And how they would never make her one of their own.

She left big tips, twenty percent where women of her class gave a miserly five. At Christmastime she handed her favorite salesladies little envelopes with twenty-dollar bills inside, and tipped the bag boys at the Safeway for carrying groceries out to her car all year. Clare knew the working class the way Sayles knew his way around post-Impressionist art. She wasn't opposed to money, just to most of the people who had it.

Two or three times a month, after she had run out of excuses, she lunched at the Summit Club with acutely thin, stiff-haired, pinched-lipped women. After two hours of nonstop chatter, her mouth, frozen in a smile, ached almost as much as her brain. She shopped where they shopped, wore their brand of sensible high heels, painted her nails with clear polish, battened down her breasts and never cinched her belt more than one or two notches so as not to call attention to her small hips and long legs. After four years of painful smiling in their direction, of dancing at their balls, clucking along in chorus over their biases, crossing her legs at her ankles, they finally told her in so many words that she was one of them, which she likened to being kissed on the lips by a Mafia button man. When she wasn't around, they compared her to Connie Sayles—and not unfavorably by this time. Because Connie was so complete in every facet that she didn't need them. Clare, they believed, was unformed, longing for instruction, willing to take their advice. So of course they were flattered and loved her.

This is not to say that her life was misery. On the contrary, she had what any woman in her right mind would kill for—a famous wealthy husband in whose eyes she could do no wrong, and a thriving son. She had The Heights, the Middleburg estate, a home in Hobe Sound, Florida, and another under construction in Lyford Cay in the Caribbean that would be finished in time for Christmas. In addition, Sayles had inherited from Connie's estate a stone cottage on seventy acres in the Bordeaux wine country of France; they had celebrated Alex's fourth birthday there last summer.

And there were the embassy parties, the White House state dinners, the very elegant private receptions in very elegant private homes, the lively gossip, the inside track on world events, the great food, the best wine, the U.S. Air Force Strolling Strings once or twice at Little Dinners at The Heights. And all the while she could feel Sayles's eyes on her, wondering what she was really thinking. She would have liked to tell him that she tried not to think too much. That she took her days as they came and that she cared for him more than she thought would be possible on the day they were married. But she didn't dare. She didn't want to raise his hopes. She had learned not to anticipate the future.

On an afternoon in March when Alex was with Sayles in Middleburg, Clare sat on a gold sofa in an antique-filled sitting room in the Summit Club, taking tea in a little Wedgwood china cup after a long luncheon of feigned interest in Lionel Tuttle's wife's description of her favorite charity. Clare was trying to remember, although she didn't really care, whether it was antivivisection or Venetian flood victims, when Sylvia O'Dowd strolled by, reeking of Arpège and Aqua Net and not a little bit of scotch. The other women reacted immediately—a concert of stiffened spines, clenched jaws, and hard, raking eyes. Sylvia didn't qualify to be a club member; she must have been someone's luncheon guest, or else she'd dashed past the doorman on a mission to annoy those who were.

The Chivas Regal fumes dividing the air before her, Sylvia broached them.

Even if there hadn't been the booze, the diamonds in daytime, the seamed black hose stuffed into fuck-me pumps a whole size too small, she would have been a pariah. As the wife of a columnist she was Political; they were old money and Green Book. They had arrived on this earth with money and they would leave with it, most of it the original issue. So even if Sylvia had been sober, or an acolyte to their pretenses—and she was definitely neither—they would have loathed her.

She approached on those tottering heels, slapped one hand on her hip, and tipped back her head in a posture that Clare had come to recognize as her fighting stance. "Vivien Tuttle, I haven't seen you since, why, since you tin-cupped for that Aztec corn god of yours!" she boomed.

Vivien's face collapsed into an expression that reminded Clare of molten iron. Over the years Vivien had embraced a group conceded by all save her to be undergifted, overinspired writers from underdeveloped countries who remained obscure and unread.

"Luis Ossio Estensorro," Vivien said, sounding every accent with Castilian precision. "A Guatemalan playwright, and a genius."

Sylvia clapped her palm against her forehead. "Good Christ, a playwright. How could I forget? Now, tell me, Vivien, what did he write exactly? The last thing I read, Archie asked Veronica to the prom. But honestly, he wore velour, that's what I remember about him. Crushed velour and this kind of shoal of jewels hanging down on his chest." She turned to Clare. "You should have seen it. It looked like an inner tube. Was it an old inner tube, Vivien? You remember when tires had inner tubes, don't you?"

Vivien worked her jaw so hard, Clare thought her fillings would pop.

"Not an inner tube, Sylvia. It was a replica of the ancient Mayan calendar. A grand lost civilization. A clock, you might say. You know what a clock is, don't you, Sylvia? It tells you when time has run out."

"Time has run out?" Sylvia pretended to ponder this, rocking back and forth on her heels. Clare wondered how she happened to be so drunk at two o'clock in the afternoon and why she was deliberately making an enemy of Vivien Tuttle, who was pompous and self-interested but hardly worth burning bridges for. Either Sylvia was incredibly foolish or she was very stupid, and Clare doubted that she was either. Drunk as she was, her eyes were

bright and snapping. All of a sudden Clare felt sorry for her, the way she pitied people in newspaper stories who committed suicide and left behind sad notes with which to punish their survivors. She tried to get her attention to give her a sign that held something of human warmth and comradeship, but already Sylvia had sent her jaundiced eye around the room and didn't notice.

"Look, Vivien," Sylvia whispered sotto voce, "isn't that Lillian Bates over there?" Without waiting for an answer, she leaned down and sent her barleyed breath against Vivien Tuttle's stony face with the news that Lillian had just the other day been released from the psychiatric ward of a local hospital.

"Look at her," Sylvia added, straightening, "she's had electroshock therapy, Vivien. Lights, camera, electricity, the whole nine yards. Fried her up like chicken wings. Look at her eyes. She looks like she's receiving messages from far, far away. Maybe from Colonel Sanders." She fell suddenly silent and stared, Clare thought, with some wistful envy at the blank-eyed Lillian, who by now was staring back, and then turned back to the group, no longer melancholy, and said, " 'Course you can't feel too sorry for old Lillian. She's got Astroturf for a heart. Kicked her own daughter out of the house for running off with a female track star from the University of Oregon."

Vivien was on her feet, red-faced and sputtering, her veins jumping up and down in her forehead. Clare thought it possible that she might start to bleed spontaneously from her ears and backed away a little.

"Christ, Vivien. That was *your* daughter!" Sylvia bellowed. "Heavens to Betsy, I'm sorry. Honestly, it was an honest mistake. How can I make it up to you, Vivien, honestly? The best of families, Vivien, absolutely the best can go wrong. Why, my brother Jack's son married a woman who was once the grandfather of six. Don't you go punishing yourself now. You did the right thing. Kick 'em out and keep 'em out!"

Vivien's mouth moved but no sound emitted. Her bony fingers worked the handle of her teacup so hard, Clare thought that at the very least she would fling its tepid contents into Sylvia's face. Even the muscles of her buttocks clenched; Clare watched the seat of her dark blue luncheon suit rippling. Yet after another moment, instinct, and that inflexible Anglican terror of pulling a scene in public, prevailed. Vivien set her mouth into a hard, thin line and she sat back down into her red satin chair, her quaking hands folded around the teacup. The most violent punishment she could muster was a harsh glare in Sylvia's direction.

They all sat there in electric silence for a moment, Sylvia wobbling over them with a look on her face that made Clare think she had just now realized what she had done, until Mary Aldrich gave a nervous little giggle and a cough. Vivien snapped her head and glared at poor Mary, who mouthed "sorry," and lowered her eyes. With Vivien's hot eyes burning into her, Sylvia said, "Well, people to see, places to go," waved in salute, and then made for the door, rather too quickly to be convincing, turning just before she left to burlesque a wink. There was a charged moment before anyone spoke, and then the long knives came out and Sylvia was butchered in less time than it took for Clare to say good-bye and get her coat. She didn't want to stick around for the bloodletting. Where she came from, menfolk gutted deer with more courtesy. The doorman, dressed in a black coat with *Summit* emblazoned in gold across the front, opened the door to her. Henry popped shut the door to the Cadillac and she was gone.

For a long time she had Henry just drive around the city while she made herself calm down. After a while she decided to stop at Garfinckel's to pick up a dress she'd ordered weeks before. When she came out, Henry had been chased away by the traffic cops. She walked to the corner of Connecticut Avenue to wait for him to come around the block, and it was there that she glanced into a garbage can next to a NO PARKING sign and saw a discarded *Wall Street Journal* with a front page story headlined: U.S. Said to Develop Kingdom As Major Ally, and under a photo of Tarik the caption, King of the Unexpected.

She pulled the paper out from under a soda bottle and a crumpled paper bag and read:

In the six years since a palace putsch led by a disgruntled former British Army officer brought to power the American-educated son of the country's only authentic hero, this strategically located and inaccessible kingdom has emerged as Washington's most staunch ally in the Persian Gulf area.

This is owed largely to the influence of more than a dozen American advisers to the country's energetic, absolute ruler, and to the further influence of the Sunnyvale, California–based OmniTech, Inc., which has installed through its own worldwide offices and considerable subcontractors, chiefly American, a smoothly functioning infrastructure on a country that traces its roots to the biblical Queen of Sheba.

Consequently, this virtually unknown nation has ironically

become a base for American intelligence, military implacements, and logistical preparations for any defense of the oil-producing nations of the Persian Gulf friendly to Washington. Although the thirty-two-year-old king declined a request for an interview, the country's chief foreign adviser, Arthur Olson, a former State Department assistant secretary, noted that the location of the kingdom, along with the king's predisposition to American interests, made it the ideal recipient for the massive amounts of American aid that has poured in since Tarik came to the throne suddenly in 1963.

That aid has diminished substantially since the discovery there of the world's third largest reserve of oil in 1967.

As the economic distress of the country is rapidly being overcome, the kingdom has taken its place among the oil-producing nations of the region and the results are dramatic.

The story jumped to the inside, and Clare thumbed quickly through the pages until she found it again.

The kingdom today is a nation yanked into the modern era. Propelled by almost two and a half million barrels of oil a day, it is a country involved in the act of self-creation. Hospitals, schools, office buildings, spring up daily. There are now over 200 miles of paved roadways, phenomenal for a place that six years ago had six miles of road, and those exclusively for the use of the curmudgeonly, sometimes murderous former ruler, Turkit, the present king's maternal uncle.

As for the king himself, he is described as extremely charming and confident, a man with a flair for the dramatic, unexpected gesture. Regarded by Washington as wholly pro-American, Tarik was raised in New York and San Francisco and educated at Stanford University and Georgetown University Law School. The king, initially somewhat uncertain in his role, today carefully cultivates the image of a traditional monarch. His photograph hangs in shops, offices, and most homes. He is the only son of this nation's revolutionary general, Malik, one of the Sur people, the remote and culturally distant tribe that occupies the coffee-rich area of the Sur highlands. In a nation that expects its kings to behave like kings, Tarik does not disappoint. Aloof and inaccessible after an assassination attempt in late 1963, he projects a subtle aura of wisdom and understanding, making him appear irresistibly larger than life. The king's politically satisfying marriage to the daughter of a local warlord

and the birth of a son, Karim, fulfilled dynastic requirements
and settled a regional political dispute.

Clare jerked the paper out of her hands as if bitten. Pedestrians
pushed by onto the crosswalk. Twice she heard Henry, who had
pulled up at the curb, say her name, but she stayed riveted to the
spot until he came around and opened the door for her.

In the backseat she gazed out the window, oppressed by the
passing scenery and feeling more alone than she had in a long
time. How do other people explain their lives? What visions did
Sylvia, for instance, close her eyes against when she lay her head
on her handsewn pillow slip at night? What had she convinced
herself of? Clare closed her eyes and felt the rhythm of her
breathing. She had thought of visions and her mind had begun to
work, and that would not do. She concentrated on her heartbeat,
worked to keep it contained within her. She crossed her arms over
the brass buttons of her little luncheon suit. It was difficult when
there were spasms and light, the sound of a voice, and the imagined sensation of touch. She squeezed her folded arms against her
breasts, against the wretched nostalgia. She knew the difference
between courage and martyrdom. She would not sacrifice herself
to remembrances. Homer hadn't raised her to play out her life in
inarticulate delusion. But her body was failing her and her mouth
was dust-dry and the rhythmic heartbeat had become scarily
ragged. She parted her lips so she could breathe through her
mouth, a little panicked. The backseat of the Cadillac had always
been a soporific, but now, as Henry wove the big car soundlessly
through traffic, it felt airless as the grave. She lowered the window, but instead of reviving her, the rush of air seemed to suck
the breath right out of her lungs and she began to gasp. She was
certain she was dying.

She banged on Henry's shoulder. "Stop the car! Henry, please
stop the car!"

"What's wrong, Mrs. Sayles?" In the rearview mirror his eyes
were round and terrified.

"Just stop!"

Henry braked the Cadillac against the curb. He leapt out
quicker than age and weight should have allowed, but Clare was
already gone and running. After a while, exhausted, she stopped
and leaned against an oak tree that was there. Her heart ham-
mered, her lungs ached, but they were full of breath again. She
was back among the living. Her face ran with sweat; she wiped
the sleeve of her suit jacket over it repeatedly. For the longest

time she just stayed there, bent over with her hands on her knees, panting. Some tourists walking by stared, but otherwise no one paid much notice. After a little while she lifted her head and looked around her. She shaded her eyes with her hand. Not far from this spot Stanley had eyed her suspiciously as he slid the car up to the curb. Stanley. God, how guilt-ridden he must have been for letting her go off with Het. Het. Whatever had become of her giant? She felt sick remembering how savagely the Yemenis had beaten him. When she saw him last, he was unconscious and blood covered his face. They had grabbed his hair and lifted his head so she could see the damage they'd done. One of them had gone to a polytechnic school in London. This is what will happen to you, he told her with a perfect working-class Londoner's accent. Poor Het. It felt good to say his name finally. Stanley, Het, one by one she said all their names in her mind—Nal, Hadi, Jule. With more reluctance, Topaz. Finally, Tarik. She hadn't said his name in years, hard to believe. As soon as she did, she could feel draining from her all the emotional numbness she had spent more than four years contriving. Empty places filled suddenly with aching memories, heart chambers pumped fluttery messages of longing. Against her will she made herself conjure up a picture of his face. He bent over her in a perfect photograph. She closed her eyes and felt his breath on her face—he was that real. It was all sensory, no words allowed. To give him speech would have made him a caricature.

She stood there for a long time, letting the memories break over her and after a while she began to feel oddly peaceful and determined. She could not imagine what the future held. It was enough that she finally presumed to examine the past.

When Henry staggered up to her, half dead from the exertion of running, she was smiling.

He gave her a scrutinizing look, assessing her, then held out his hand. He was a man of gentle probity. He had the grace not to ask questions of a woman who appeared to have lost her mind a little and just as quickly got it back.

He put a proprietary hand on her elbow and steered her lightly back to the car. She thought she might ask him not to tell her husband what had happened, but then decided that would be redundant. From the look on his face she knew that Henry would volunteer nothing. He reminded her of Het. She had had the good luck in her life to know one or two world-class men. When they have to be, she thought, some men can be acts of God.

She had him to drive her over to Arlington, to spend some time at Hillard's grave. Riding home later, she felt renewed and flaring with hope. The debilitating numbness had all dissolved and she recoiled from the memory of it. She could see things clearly, forward and back. She would close the door on her past. She was a mountain girl—enough said. Nothing would turn her around. She would fall in love with Lawrence Sayles—she loved him a little already. She hummed tunelessly and hunkered down in the seat, then bolted up again when she remembered Alex. How could she close the door when there was Alex? Her heart began racing again, but she calmed herself. This was to be expected. Old fears were not easily kept at bay. She would find a way to do it all.

She rummaged in her purse and found her little powder compact and a tissue. She used the tissue to mop her dripping face and plucked at her hair a little with her fingers. She was putting on lipstick when she caught the reflection of her eyes in the mirror and was brought up short. She peered closer, then abruptly snapped her compact shut and threw it into her purse. Behind her the skyline of Washington and its monuments fell away as they headed for Middleburg. She looked intently out the window at the passing cars. She had seen those eyes not an hour before, red-rimmed with booze and a little wild. Sylvia's eyes. Her eyes. Women with light eyes full of despair.

When Sylvia telephoned the next day to apologize for her behavior at the Summit Club, Clare asked her to lunch.

They went to Sans Souci on 17th Street, and for the longest time it was the usual business with Sylvia. The maître d' had seated them between a reporter from the *San Francisco Chronicle* and an undersecretary of the navy, neither of whom possessed nearly enough clout or status to satisfy Sylvia. She spent a good ten minutes trying to have their table changed, before surrendering to the hard stare of the maître d'. She had a hangover the size of a Buick and it had taken the fight out of her, so they stayed where they were, which was perfectly fine to begin with.

She stirred a restorative Bloody Mary with a long red fingernail.

"So why were you wasting your time with that hideous old Vivien Tuttle anyway?" she demanded before the waiter even handed them menus. "The beast. Everybody knows Lionel Tuttle spends so much time in New York because he can't stand her, and if he hadn't gotten so used to spending her money, he would have divorced her and married that Jewish nightclub singer he's been fucking for years." She blew a kiss to a late-arriving senator. "So why do you waste your time?"

Having no good answer, Clare shrugged. "Some things you just can't avoid," she said, knowing this sounded a little stupid.

Twenty minutes with Sylvia and already she was sorry she'd made the date. Sylvia hadn't stopped prattling and dishing since they sat down, craning her neck when the door opened, winking and nodding and blowing kisses and saying absolutely the worst things imaginable about everybody in town. By the time coffee arrived, Clare was feeling restive and absently began scratching her arm.

Dessert, and back to Vivien. "Poor Viv, her mind is blown. She sent her daughter to the Madeira School, brought her out at the Chevy Chase Club in a crushed pink taffeta dress, and now she's in the sheets with a girl with Dick Nixon's five o'clock shadow. Don't you think the rich have the most interesting vices? I mean, they're all either morphine addicts or have sex with their Thoroughbreds or murder their husbands and blame it on burglars—but as long as they do it on the lee side of Penobscot Bay in a sensible pair of boat shoes, nobody cares. Poor people wouldn't dream of trying to get away with any of this stuff."

Clare picked up her head. Finally, a topic she could warm to. Before the incident in the backseat of the Cadillac, she would have murmured meaningless agreement. But now, liberated from that numbness, she spoke her mind. "Interesting? I think it's all so predictable and boring. I'd have more respect for Vivien if she picked up some old Winchester rifle and put a load of lead where it would do some good. Instead, she'll just buy herself a tighter girdle and pretend it didn't happen. That's what I can't stand—all this grim grinning in the face of disaster. They have money but they don't have values, and they don't know what to do with themselves. You know, three weeks ago, after dinner at The Heights, I was in the pantry helping Preston find a bottle of port and through the doorway I saw one of the richest men in the Senate, one of the 'inheritors,' from a famous New England family, *Mayflower* every side, pocketing a little silver demitasse spoon. Can you imagine? I don't think their crimes are interesting. They are puny, so furtive. Anything that will fit into the pocket of a good double-breasted blue flannel blazer. At least the poor commit big crimes. Big messy murders. 'Unemployed gas meter reader blows up trailer park.' It has a certain commendable style to it."

Clare blushed and looked around, realizing she'd raised her

voice. She lowered her eyes and spooned sugar into her coffee, expecting Sylvia to pounce on her. But when she looked up, Sylvia was gazing at her as if she'd just discovered her long-lost twin.

"You mean"—she whispered the name of the rich, famous senator—"rips you off too? My God, I can't believe this guy. He's stolen so much good flatware from me he could open his own branch of Georg Jensen."

Clare shook her head. "He needs help."

"He needs to sign up at the bridal registry at Garfinckel's and get his silver the way the rest of us did. Anyway, he's sixty-five years old and beyond redemption. And by the way, don't lose sleep over this guy. He's a bastard to his secretaries, and he disowned his son, a really sweet guy, for marrying a Nigerian exchange student. His wife hasn't been out of her bedroom in years. Have you mentioned his bad habit to Lawrence, by the way?"

Clare looked around, hesitant to reveal a confidence, but she couldn't resist. "He told me Connie wouldn't let him in the house. But Lawrence . . . you know, he can't hold a grudge. And they've been friends, after a fashion, for years."

"I haven't mentioned anything yet to Charlie. I'm saving it."

"Would Charlie print something like this?"

"No, and he wouldn't repeat it either. But he'd know, and the senator would know, somehow, that he knew, and that would be enough for the two of them to transact some business. I'm saving it as a trade-off for something really juicy that I might need in the future."

"Like what?"

"Don't know yet." She sipped at her drink. "Of course, the senator is the least interesting character in these parts. You're the one we're all still trying to figure out."

"Me?" Clare asked, wary.

"Now, don't be coy with me. You married one of the richest, most eligible men in the country. This was a big fish you hooked. And look at you. Who are you anyway? Not that you aren't gorgeous and young, but everybody thought Lawrence would marry one of those power-mad Green Book types. Some broad with a million or two of her own, some Peabody Marblehead, or Marblehead Peabody. Somebody like, well, like Connie. And don't think those babes weren't sucking in their stomachs and plotting strategies. But he fooled them all. Tits and ass, a brain, and not a penny of your own. It almost drove them over the edge."

Clare sat in shocked silence.

After a beat Sylvia made an exaggerated sigh of relief. "Well, at least you didn't throw your drink in my face."

"I don't have a drink."

Sylvia signaled the waiter. "It's only fair you arm yourself, because I'm pressing on. Sayles never loved Connie. Does that surprise you? Everybody was so dazzled by her and her perfect teeth and place settings and small talk. They just assumed he was dazzled too. Nobody ever noticed that when Lawrence looked at Connie, he had this expression on his face like the Buddha in that bad Chinese restaurant on K Street, half amused, half resigned but totally void. He had done what his genes had driven him to do and married one of his class, and he would have again except that somewhere along the line he met you and you turned him into that most unlikely creature—the WASP as caveman. I don't believe there is another woman in the world who could have done it, and whatever you've got, you'd do me a favor if you'd let me in on it."

Sylvia raised her glass in salute and drained the remains of her old drink before reaching for the new one the waiter set in its place.

Clare pulled her own Bloody Mary toward her. "You're embarrassing me."

"If you didn't get embarrassed when someone paid you a compliment, then you wouldn't be any better than Connie. Or Vivien. You're all right, Clare. And as long as I'm telling you the truth, I'm not such a bad egg either. Maybe not as good as you, but I'm all right. Do you believe me?"

"Sylvia, as long as we're telling the truth, why should I? You drink too much, and you claim to hate all these people, yet you can't get enough of them. You could leave town, you know. You don't have to suffer the psychotic vagaries of the very rich. You can get a ticket out anytime."

"You mean and be a good person with a lot of integrity? Clare, I've misled you. Just because I'm no sycophant doesn't mean I hate these people. I don't hate this life. It feeds some deep, crazed pool of misery and self-loathing that bubbles around inside of me. I accept it, and it's fun."

"I don't believe that for a minute."

"Even so, it doesn't make me bad."

"It also doesn't make me wrong."

"Christ, a moralist. Tits and morality, a deadly combination. No wonder Sayles loves you the way he does. And as long as we're clearing the air here—and as long as I've had three drinks already—I've always wondered why you bought into it yourself. The first time I saw you, at one of Lawrence's dinner parties years ago, I said to myself, oh, boy, that girl is going to set us all on our ears. None of that Little Dinner, Summit Club shit for her. Then there was the mysterious marriage to that gorgeous man and Lawrence is ruined, absolutely ruined. I don't believe you can guess how smashed he really was. Then, here you are back again. In a puff of smoke, the gorgeous man is history, you're married, a mother, and Vivien Tuttle's best friend. Enough said."

As an afterthought she said, "Except for the Jag, I'll give you that. But I always wondered why you did it. And you didn't have to, you know. You could have gone in a gorilla suit to the White House and Sayles would have brought the bananas. I always wondered. Have you?"

Clare had the idea to dissemble a little, to talk about the charities and the theater group and all the good she was doing. But she'd seen herself in Sylvia's eyes at the Summit Club yesterday, and there she was again, swimming around with the vodka and the quiet desperation, so for a long time she didn't say anything. And then, out of nowhere, she said, "Well, if you must know, I have something, a project, I've been mulling over for a long time. Years, really. Have you ever heard of the A. W. Aylesworth Coal Company? Never mind. Nobody's ever heard of it. It's a dirty little bituminous coal operation on the Kentucky-Tennessee border. Only it's not so little anymore—and I'm going to buy it." She said it as if it had just occurred to her, which of course it had.

Sylvia's mouth dropped open. "You're buying a coal company?"

"Uh-huh. Only they don't know it yet. Nobody knows it, so I'd appreciate it if you wouldn't say anything to anyone."

"What are you going to do with a coal company?"

"I'm going to run it." She said it as much to herself as to Sylvia. "I'm going to run it as a mining cooperative. We're all going to make money taking coal out of Kentucky. Safely."

"How the hell are you going to do it? A coal company must cost millions."

"Uh-huh."

"My God. Lawrence Sayles is giving you millions so you can do it?"

"Maybe, maybe not. Maybe I'll come up with an option that doesn't require so much cash up front. Maybe I'll be able to raise it on my own. I've just started to sort out the details, to understand how it can be done. There's so much I don't know, so much

I have to know. It's going to take months. A year, maybe, but I'll do it. I'll do it if it kills me."

Sylvia shook the ice in her glass, then looked up, holding Clare with a look. "I wonder."

"What?"

"I wonder why you're doing it. You don't need the work, that's clear. Your husband is rich as Croesus. And you don't need to score points around here. It's enough in this life that you scored this marriage. So . . ."

"So?"

Sylvia was unused to the challenge of unfamiliar perceptions, conclusions qualifying suddenly as insight. She could feel Clare measuring her hesitation; the green eyes had narrowed in skepticism. She believes in herself, Sylvia realized all at once—and she hadn't met a woman who believed in herself in a hundred years. I did too, once upon a time, she decided. No, I never did. Not like this.

"So either you're dying to give up all of this"—she gestured around the room—"and go to work in some dirty backwater Kentucky hill town, or—and it's nothing to be ashamed of—you're exorcising some ghost. What does Lawrence think about all this?"

"Haven't told him yet, and I'm not going to until I have a plan. I'm starting cold, today. I know nothing about Aylesworth Coal. I haven't the faintest idea how to buy a company that might not even want to be bought. I haven't a clue how to find out about any of this. But I'll do it if it kills me."

Sylvia gave her a steady look. "No, not you. You'll get what you want. I have the feeling you always do."

The way in which Clare's features collapsed and she ducked her chin embarrassed Sylvia and told her she'd touched a nerve. But her natural instinct to move in for the kill at the first sign of vulnerability was absent. In fact, she felt a rush of protectiveness. Quickly, she signaled the waiter for the check and grabbed it when it arrived.

Clare rallied and said, "I asked you, remember?"

"No, it's my treat," Sylvia said. "Next time, you pay. We'll go out and spread some of Lawrence's old money around in some better bars. Or, better still, you can make it up to me by coming to the party Charlie is giving on Friday night in honor of some Italian babe he picked up in the bar of the Excelsior Hotel in Rome. He says she's descended from a Renaissance pope."

"Really?"

"The Whore of Babylon maybe, pope never. You think Lawrence would deign to mingle with the masses?"

"He'll come. He won't be able to resist meeting the pope's progeny."

They had said their good-byes on the sidewalk and begun walking in opposite directions when Clare suddenly called after her over the noise of the traffic, "How did you know he was gorgeous?"

"What?" Sylvia halted, mystified.

"My first husband. How did you know he was gorgeous?"

"I said that?"

"Uh-huh."

Sylvia pulled a cigarette from her jacket pocket and lit it. "I was in the bar, in the Willard. It was raining and I saw you through the window."

Clare looked off down the street.

"I was alone, Clare, I was drinking alone. I can't even remember now. I'll see you soon, okay?"

Clare turned back to her, her soul in her eyes. "Okay," she said. "Okay."

The party turned out to be as loud and noisy as Sayles warned her it would be, with famous politicians from dry Midwest states drunk all around her and their dull wives looking lost, loud rock music in the backyard patio, and a Swedish envoy playing a decent stride piano in the library. Periodically, Sylvia swooped down on them, trailing a chiffon scarf and blasting streams of cigarette smoke from the side of her mouth. Out by the potted azaleas, two oil lobbyists and an Anglican minister passed a joint back and forth. In the john off the kitchen, the heroin-addicted son of a Cabinet officer convinced the wife of a three-term senator to show him her breasts. In the stairwell a Hollywood actor famous for seducing other men's wives covertly stroked the penis of a waiter hired for the evening.

On the patio Clare danced to booming rock music, her eyes closed and her head back, feeling young for the first time in years and high on the music and three martinis. Even Sayles had fun. He drank four glasses of champagne and danced with half a dozen women.

At one in the morning, when Sayles was pulling Clare out the door, Sylvia grabbed her arm and furtively pushed a manila envelope into her hand, saying, "Here's a start, kid," and pushed her out onto the sidewalk.

* * *

"What do you think of her?" Lawrence asked Clare when they were finally home. He was sitting on the edge of the bed, already in his pajamas. He liked to watch Clare in the ritual of preparing for bed, taking off her watch and earrings and tucking them into her jewelry case, stepping out of her dress and walking with it to her closet. Precise as a Japanese tea ceremony, somehow every concentrated movement seemed erotic to him. From his position on the bed, he could see her reflection in the long closet mirror.

"Sylvia? I think she's all right," she said as much to herself as to him. "Better than I thought she would be."

He was watching her peel her panty hose down to her ankles. His body stirred when he saw she wasn't wearing panties. When she arched her back to unclasp her bra, his breath caught in his throat and suddenly he was aroused, his passion fueled as much by his fear that she would catch him peering at her as by her nakedness.

But Clare was unaware that he could see her in the mirror and continued to undress. She pulled off her lacy bra and stuck it into a drawer. He could see very clearly when her breasts bumped lightly against the brass pulls as she opened and shut more drawers. When she finally found the drawer she wanted, she rested her breasts lightly on its edge while she pulled out a long, flimsy nightgown.

With the nightie in her hand she said, "Anyway, Sylvia gives a great party. And I wouldn't mind if she invited us back. Would you go?"

"If you like."

They had spent a week in Hobe Sound the previous month and she was still tan—with no tan marks, he realized suddenly. Hadn't she worn a bathing suit? The pressure in his groin built pleasurably. Had she been naked by the pool? Had the pool man seen her? In his mind's eye Sayles pictured her in a lounge chair by the swimming pool, aqueous shadows flickering over her naked breasts, the pool man crouching in the bushes, his long pool filter abandoned at his feet, watching her.

Nervous and a little thrilled by this development, Sayles climbed quickly under the bedcovers. He had the idea of slipping out of his pajamas before she got into bed so he could feel the cool sheets on his skin. All his senses seemed heightened, but caution got the better of him. If she rejected him, being naked would make him feel even more vulnerable.

Clare turned out the closet light and crossed the room. In the lamplight he could see her legs and breasts silhouetted through the flimsy fabric.

She opened the door and turned her ear to the hallway, listening for sounds of Alex stirring. When she was satisfied that he slept soundly, she closed the door, pulled down the bedcovers on her side, and slipped under the blankets.

"Henry told Alex that he'd take him with him when he has the Cadillac serviced next week and Alex hasn't been the same since. He plans on staying in the car when the guys put it on the lift." Her voice was light, full of amusement.

Sayles hesitated, torn between his native courtesy and the heat that was rolling in waves through his body. But he was so inflamed that he couldn't stop himself, and once she had settled down, he reached over and took her by the shoulder and pulled her to him, his mouth blindly searching for hers. Surprised, she opened her mouth slightly. Shocked by his body's urgency, she stiffened a little, then made herself relax. She never wanted him to feel uncertain in their sexual relationship. She never wanted him to believe that she was anything less than responsive. She never wanted him to suspect that she was pretending he was someone else. His mouth worked at hers dizzily, and he propped himself up on one elbow so that he could kiss her more efficiently. His hands stroked her breasts and belly as his inward eye filled with a vision of her naked at the poolside, her legs parted slightly, the rucked flesh between her legs turned to the sun, the anonymous pool man watching, feeling the same tightness in his groin, the same panic to release.

He swung one leg over her, parted her legs, and then entered her. Her skin was dry and tight. The friction pinched his own tender skin but she seemed to tighten and pull him in deeper. He pumped slowly once or twice, then began moving much more quickly. He ached to finish it but was mindful of her own needs. He thought he felt her hands lightly stroking his back, and with what awareness he had left, he regretted not taking off his pajamas. How delicious to have her touching his skin while he was so deep within her. It was only a matter of seconds now. His jaw tightened. His head reared back. One more push and he felt himself emptying into her. For an instant he felt terrified, what he used to feel when he was a little boy on the beach at the family place at Dark Harbor and the surf ran back to the ocean and made the sand under his feet collapse. But then his mind cleared and there was only pride and deep satisfaction, familiar talismans to tell him everything was all right. He lifted his head slightly. In the dim light she looked like a vision to him. Now was the moment to tell her just how much he loved her. She deserved to know that he believed he couldn't go on without her, and Alex. But he hadn't the strength to make any sense, and he was so very very tired after dancing and champagne and a late night. His head fell onto the little nook between her shoulder and breast and in an instant he was asleep.

After a minute Clare slipped out from under him and stood up. She pushed the blankets around him gently and bent and lightly kissed his head, pulled on a cashmere robe, and then walked down the hallway to make a final check on Alex. Then she walked to the library, opened the clasp of the manila envelope Sylvia had handed her, and pulled out a single sheet of paper and two newspaper clippings. One of the clippings was yellowed and showed a man in a tuxedo shaking hands with the lieutenant governor of Maryland and with the other hand accepting some sort of plaque. Clare glanced at the photo, saw nothing that had anything to do with her, and then read the caption: Industrialist A. W. Aylesworth of Bethesda, recipient of the Governor's annual Award for Business Excellence. Aylesworth contributed close to fifty thousand dollars to the Republican gubernatorial campaign.

She squinted at the photo again. It was Muddy, all right. The owlish round glasses were the same, and the two long, protruding teeth, but the hair was new, a curly toupee that, fashionably long, swept his jacket collar.

The second clipping was more recent, a wedding announcement. Muddy's daughter, Melissa, had married a boy named McBride, a lawyer, whose father was a retired state supreme court judge and whose mother was headmistress of a private girls' school. The bride had considerably more of her own hair than her father, but she was not smiling. Her mouth was clamped shut in a little pout, probably, Clare supposed, to cover up the same rabbit teeth as her dad.

She returned to the piece of paper, on which Sylvia had written:

Clare, one of Charlie's secretaries has a brother at a brokerage house who got a profile on Aylesworth Coal Company, as follows: Aylesworth Coal Company, Inc., is a marketing-oriented eastern coal company with large, low sulfur, eastern steam coal reserves. Approximately 80% of its sales are under long-term contracts to utilities. Ownership breakdown: 100%–Arthur Wales Aylesworth II. Looking for strong 2Q 1969. Coal industry generally remains very strong in light of damage to TransArabian pipeline.

This is all I could get now, kid, but I'm sure there is lots more and I'm working on it.

S.

She reread the newspaper items and the note, set the papers on the desk, then glanced at her watch—close to four A.M. He would be up now. Pulling her soft robe around her, she walked into Sayles's office, picked up the telephone, and called her grandfather.

18

"Now what's this?" Homer pulled a face at the purplish food at the end of his fork.

"It's plums, Grandpa," Clare explained.

"Plums?! T'aint plums for dessert? And plums are hard. These are soft, and hot. I think the dessert got here first."

Preston, who was serving, gave Homer a sidelong look and offered the serving dish to Sayles.

Clare watched the butler's stony expression from the corner of her eye. "Marguerite, the cook, poaches the plums in hot water, Grandpa," she explained quietly, "then whips them with a little sugar and ginger. It's just something a little bit different and a sweet taste she thought you might like with your meal." She threw Sayles a helpless look.

"What would you like, Homer?" he asked. "Let me have Marguerite fix you something else."

"Well," said Homer, hunching over his plate, "I believe I have everything I need." He was embarrassed now that he'd made a fuss. He didn't want Clare or her husband to think him stupid. But he had never seen such a thing as hot whipped plums, and it had gotten the best of him. Every time he visited Washington something new came swimming his way and he was invariably disconcerted and left feeling a little bit of the rube. Not that he blamed Clare. But he was an old man with no ambition to change, and he missed his familiarities—his hogs, his rocking chair, the certainty that when the sun came up it would carry on its irradiant beams the haze of coal smoke, even if the smell of it did make his lungs ache and double him over coughing.

Still, he was not about to make a fuss. If they ate plums hot and whipped up north, he could adapt. So on a positive note, he said, "No thanks, Lawrence, I'm just fine. Now, this here is chicken, that's all right. An' this is potatoes something, butter, I guess, and milk, okay. This other—"

Sylvia, who had joined them for dinner, poked around his plate with her fork. "That's orange on the chicken, Homer."

"Oh," he said. "It's good. Wouldn't expect it, but it's good."

Preston set the serving dish on the sideboard and removed the cork from another bottle of white wine. He then began refilling the wineglasses on the table, but when he came to hers, to Sylvia's hostile eye, he seemed to linger over her empty goblet, to dispense the wine in one long, profound stream, to pour and pour until the wine was nearly at the lip of her glass, to draw, in other words, a giant arrow that pointed directly at her glass, a speaking arrow that shrieked, *She's having YET ANOTHER drink and we haven't even finished the main course!*

Sylvia pursed her lipsticked mouth and watched as the wine wobbled at the very rim of the glass, making it impossible to lift without spilling. Watched as Preston delicately caught an errant wine drop sliding down the bottle neck. Watched as he turned and left the room on mute soles. She caught Homer's eye and curled her lip. Homer curled his own lip in sympathy. Then, in a gesture that made up in gentlemanliness what it lacked in finesse, he stood and, bending over Sylvia's glass, put his mouth on the rim of the glass, sucked in enough of the wine to make it possible to be lifted, and handed it to Sylvia as if it were made of eggshell. The old miner then sat down, tucked his napkin under his chin, and said, "Some folks don't know their place."

As if that said it all, he cut into the chicken and changed the subject to his local church leader, the Reverend Ballard Nute, who had put the whole of Mills Bend into an uproar for allowing rattlesnake handling in the Advent Christian Church.

"You know Terrill Brookes?" he asked Clare.

"Is that Dewey Brookes's son?"

"That's right. Well, he's the sheriff now, and the district judge told Terrill that he had to keep old Ballard from passin' around those rattlers during the service."

Sayles's crystal wineglass braked in midair. "I don't understand," he said. "Why would there be rattlesnakes in church?" Although he'd come to expect the outrageous from his Appalachian in-law, this was a new one.

Homer puffed up a little, pleased that for once he could tell Sayles a thing or two.

"Mark 16, verses 17 and 18," he said imperiously. " 'In my name they shall cast out devils; they shall speak with new tongues; they shall take up serpents; and if they drink any deadly thing, it shall not hurt them.' That says—" Homer was distracted by Preston, who had returned to the dining room to offer second helpings.

"Anyway," Homer resumed, his eye on the butler, "Terrill comes a-walkin' up the church aisle in those big shoes and a pair of Dickie pants just as Reverend Nute is slidin' out four big rattlers and tells him it's against the law in this state to handle snakes and a-readin' him his rights and Reverend Nute's looking him in the eye and passing 'round the snakes and the next thing you know, Columbia Mullins shoves one about four feet long right into Terrill's hands and the snake clamps down on his forearm, Terrill falls down on the floor shaking and screaming and Ballard's standing over him waving his Bible, the whole congregation's carryin' on something awful. What a sight! Reverend Nute didn't even run for Doc Noor. Told Terrill God got him for the sin of pride, claiming that man's law is above the Lord's." Homer was shaking with laughter. "Sheriff from the county seat had to come over and put old Nute in jail. Snakes too."

"Have you ever been bitten, Grandpa?" Alex asked, his eyes big and round.

"Yes, I have."

"Does it hurt?"

"Oh, my, yes. It hurts about two hundred times worse than a bee sting."

"Were you touching rattlers in church?"

"Not me. Oh, no, son. Can't believe the Lord wants a man to get bit by a rattler, no matter what the Bible says. There's no faith in being a fool. No, I been bit out in the field the time old Isaac wandered over to the Collins property and I went to fetch him 'cause he was too scared to come back on his own." Isaac was his mule, long dead. "Never heard the rattles sing. Picked up a stick to poke him in the rump and got bit right here." He rolled up his shirt-sleeve and pointed to a dim scar just above his wrist bone. "Scared Isaac too, but he carried me all the way down to the coal camp so Doc Noor there could give me the antivenom. That was the day Bill Gwinn had a heart attack a-reachin' into a barrel of shotgun shells in the Dixie General Store. Now, Bill's great-grandfather worked on the Chesapeake & Ohio's Big Bend tunnel and—"

Later, when Clare put him to bed Alex would swear that he had heard it, and Sylvia, of course, vowed it had happened, but whatever the truth, somewhere between the moment when Homer was

telling how Bill Gwinn's great-grandfather blew rock on the C &
O tunnel and Preston bent to offer him more of the chicken à
l'orange, there was a sound in the room, something between air
let out of a tire and the snort of a pig. Homer halted in his speech,
removed his napkin from under his chin, and glared at Preston.

"Bud, you got a problem?"

Preston, helping Alex to another piece of chicken from the silver serving platter, said, "I don't know what you mean, sir."

"I mean, you got some problem with me tellin' about old Tim
Gwinn blowin' rock at the C & O?"

"I can't imagine that I would, sir."

"Now, you're a clever fella. Do you mean you don't have a
problem listenin' to it, or I got a problem tellin' it?"

"I mean, Mr. Barrow, that you are free to discuss anything you
like. It's immaterial to me. I'm going about my work, as always.
But if you like—"

"Homer, how about some more of that chicken? I know you
like it." Sayles wanted to forestall trouble before it started.

"Well, Lawrence, I wouldn't mind. But first I just feel I'd like
to know why this fella made that noise."

"I didn't make a noise, Mr. Barrow."

"I was sittin' right here."

"I may have sighed. It wasn't meant for you and the gentleman
from the . . . what was it, a bridge?"

"The C & O tunnel."

"I did not intentionally make a noise."

"Did so."

"Sir, I did not."

"Made a noise."

Homer set down his fork. He was thinner than ever and had
skinned back his white hair with water to be neat at the dinner table, making his whole head appear even more skull-like. He
turned his chair around so that he could see Preston more directly.
Clare could see his bony hands quaking beneath his dinner napkin.

Preston stood silent, willing himself to composure. Homer had
come north at Clare's insistence for pulmonary function tests. Six
months before, he'd begun a therapy of antitubercular drugs, used
in the treatment of complex pneumoconiosis, and the tests yesterday had shown that the drugs hadn't been effective; the shadow
on his lungs had grown larger. Clare had become emotional when
she found this out, full of self-recriminations. Preston could see
her now, giving him a look that said that if he knew what was

good for him, he'd apologize to her grandfather and get out. He and Homer had been at war since Homer arrived in Washington three days before. Homer had set up camp in the kitchen and from over the lip of his coffee cup had set his scalding eye on the contumelious butler, offering advice on the way the china was stacked, noting that the hall doorknob seemed loose, pointing out the oil stain in the driveway—a nonstop inventory of what, to Preston's way of thinking, were domestic shortcomings bordering on moral turpitude. And could the man talk! From dawn till dusk about the setting of timbers, mules versus man-trips, the canning of beets, and the rubbers on mason jars.

Preston stood in the dining room, all eyes on him. In his own mind's eye he saw himself breaking the wine bottle over the old hillbilly's head, saw himself doing some business on his eyeballs with the Phillips-head screwdriver that he kept in the pantry drawer. But he kept his voice flat and said, "Mr. Sayles, if I did anything to offend you, I apologize and I assure you it was not intentional."

"Not him—me," Homer barked. "But I accept the apology anyway. And now I think you ought to tell her you're sorry too."

"Tell whom?"

"This lady. Mrs. O'Dowd. A little while ago you treated her rudely. Filled her wineglass up to the rim so's she couldn't drink. Did it on purpose too."

"I assure you I didn't."

"Did too."

"Grandpa . . ."

"Clary, you got to take the stick hand with these fellas."

"Grandpa, can we talk about this—"

"All he has to do is say he's sorry to Sylvia here. I don't care about myself, but he owes her an apology."

It did not take Preston more than an instant to weigh the pros of confronting Homer Barrow the Irritating Hillbilly Coal Miner against the cons of going up against The Great Lawrence Sayles's Grandfather-in-Law. With the speed of a man with a lifetime of experience smooching the posteriors of the rich and famous, he rolled over the carpet in shoes buffed to a subtle glow and presenting himself to Sylvia O'Dowd, declared that he had in fact filled her wine goblet far too full, that he was very sorry and that he would never do it again.

"Thank you, toad," Sylvia said.

Then he busily removed the salt and pepper shakers from the table and, without a backward glance at any of them, exited the dining room. Clare released from her fingers the dinner napkin she had hopelessly crumpled in anxiety, Sayles sighed demonstrably, Sylvia raised her glass, and Homer spooned some of the whipped plums into his mouth. "You know," he said, ducking his head at Alex, "these t'aint half bad once you get over the shock."

The next morning, as a consolation, Sayles offered to take him around the Capitol building. Homer, who needed no consoling, accepted anyway.

They left around noon, with Sayles in the back, as usual, but Homer, making a political statement, riding shotgun with Henry, in whose life he expressed an inordinate interest.

"Black man never got a fair shake in this country," he told him as they entered the beltway. "Don't think I'm not sympathetic to that. White man in the mines not treated much better than a black man in a cotton field. We're all victims of the rich man. The haves and the have-nots. That's the wide river of division in this country."

"Yessir, that's right," Henry repeated many times, but with nervous eyes he checked the rearview mirror for Sayles's reaction.

At the Capitol, Sayles walked Homer through the corridors where history had been made, Homer nodding his head at everything he was told but saying almost nothing. He was wearing a pair of khaki pants, a white shirt with a black tie, and a navy blue jacket that Clare knew was part of the only suit he had ever owned, the suit he had worn as a bridegroom. She had nearly wept when he came downstairs buttoned up so properly. She knew that he was determined not to embarrass her in front of her husband, or embarrass himself in the hallowed halls of Congress. A few years earlier she had tried to buy him new clothes but he had looked at her appalled, as if she'd asked him to sell state secrets to the Russians.

Sayles was an unannounced visitor and senators and their aides hurried to pay homage to the unexpected hero in their midst. Self-possessed, aware of the figure that he cut, Sayles made his regal way through the corridors, his hand solicitously propelling Homer by the elbow. Although he was not an elected official, there was no facility, private or congressional, that was closed to him. All he had to do was show up and the seas parted.

He introduced Homer to everyone as his father-in-law, Homer Barrow of Mills Bend, Kentucky, and Homer pumped hands and grunted nice-to-meet-you noises, his eyes taking in everything. But when the Republican Party chairman tried to shake his hand, Homer ostentatiously shoved it into his pocket and showed the man his profile instead. Even for Clare's husband's sake, he refused to dirty his palm by pressing the flesh of the enemy.

He didn't have much to say when he got home, although Clare pressed him for details of his day. But she could tell that he had enjoyed himself because he allowed himself an extra whiskey after dinner.

"Are you tired, Grandpa?" she asked as they sat in front of the fire in the sitting room. Sayles was on the telephone in the library upstairs and so they were free to talk. "It was a long day, I know—and so soon after all those medical tests."

"Coulda told 'em not to bother. Knew they'd say the same thing as Doc Noor. Lung's gettin' worse. Not much point in going on with those TB pills." He took a long gulp of his drink. It was the best damned whiskey he had ever had, although he would die before he admitted this to Sayles.

"Not really. I don't consider it a debatable issue," Clare said firmly. "You'll go on with the medication until they tell you to stop."

Homer snorted. "Who says?"

"I say, that's who. Whatever it takes, you'll do it."

"You say . . . you say," he grumbled, but he was secretly pleased that she was so unequivocating. The more he insisted he would do what he wanted and the more she insisted he would do as she said, the more he felt loved and appreciated, which was why he kept it up. He set his glass on the arm of his chair and rubbed his hands before the fire. His bones were permanently chilled, no matter what the time of year, and this blazing fire on a fairly mild spring night seemed to Homer to be the supreme indulgence. He had an airtight wood stove, but he wished he also had a fireplace in that house of his in Mills Bend, but he didn't dare say so. Sayles would offer to build him a new house with a fireplace in every room, but he wanted no handouts from Lawrence Sayles, whose ancestors had made a fortune from railroads built on the broken backs of coolie labor. No, he'd get by with his old wood stove; he'd moved his bed into the kitchen so he could be close to it night and day. The whiskey was another story, however. If he had a steady supply of this fine whiskey every night to take the chill off, even deep winter wouldn't be quite so bad. He drained his glass.

Automatically, Clare retrieved the empty glass from his hand, walked to a liquor cabinet, and poured him another long drink.

"And you know, Grandpa, that black lung can just spontaneously stop. Not get worse. That could happen to you. You've got to have faith."

"We'll see . . . we'll see." He sipped his drink. "Well, t'aint you gonna ask me?" he wondered after she had settled herself into an armchair.

"Ask you what?"

"What do you think, Clary? You think I came all the way up north so some doctor could tell me what I already know? Hell, no. I came up here because it t'aint safe to use the phone back home." He looked around him. "Can't be too careful anywhere you are."

"What's the matter, Grandpa? What's wrong?"

"I done what you asked me."

"And?"

"Can't be too careful," he repeated. "Where's that fella?"

"He's in the kitchen, Grandpa. He doesn't know anything."

"You ought to get rid of him."

"He's difficult sometimes, but he's very good at his job. You just have to put up with him."

"*You* have to put up with him. I'm goin' home. So." He made a sound like he was clearing his throat and nodded his head at the open door.

"Oh, all right." Clare got up impatiently and closed the sitting room door. "Okay, now—what have you found out?"

"Well," Homer began, sipping at his whiskey, "you remember your cousin Noni Barrow? She works up in Ashland? No? Well, she got a friend—forget the name—works at a coal brokerage name of Columbia Brokers who sell coal to the power companies, mostly Carolina Electric Power. Now, this friend of Noni's been working at this brokerage place for almost five years, knows it inside and out, up and down, and it's always been kind of a mystery to her that she never in all those years met the owner of the outfit. Oh, there's some sort of manager all right, but the owner gets all his mail at a post office box in Richmond and has never showed his face anywhere near Ashland.

"Now, I wouldn't have thought a thing about it except that Noni had this meeting of her sewing cooperative, which brought her over near Warfield, and she told me, in passing, while I was standing around admiring her quilts, that this friend of hers had just happened to mention in passing one time that for the past three years or so this Columbia company's one and only client was—guess who?"

"Who?"

"Muddy. 'Course, this comes just a day or two after your phone call, and ordinarily I would have passed it off, but now it really starts my mind to workin'. So I ask old Noni if she wouldn't mind bringing her friend—Oda, that's her name!—up to the holler someday. I know by this time that Oda is the sister of Willa Blankenship, who is your second cousin, I believe, the one with all the children? So sure enough, good old Noni seven days later shows up on my porch with old Oda to set awhile. And I just naturally steer things around to Muddy and the low esteem in which he is held in these parts and she tells me that the land company that pays Harm West for his coal, the coal that Muddy mines, is named Tug River Land Lease Corp."

"But, Grandpa, the Tug River Corporation has all the leases for all the hollers for miles, including Mills Bend. Everybody knows that."

"Jes' hold on now. I started this from the beginning and if you stop me I'll lose my train. Now, this here Oda says that she had noticed that the Tug River Corporation pays Harm West—who is also a Barrow, by the way—one dollar and twenty-five cents a ton for his coal. Now, I don't say nothing to either of them because I don't want these women's mouths workin' up and down the holler and givin' away our game, but I know for a fact that Tug River pays Harm West just twenty-five cents a ton for his coal because I was there when he signed the original lease. And there ain't been no one-dollar increase. So how about that?"

He sat back in his chair and took a long, satisfied pull of whiskey.

"I'm not sure I understand, Grandpa."

He gave her an incredulous look. "You don't think it's odd that Oda works for a company with no boss whose only customer is Muddy Aylesworth? Or that Tug River Land Lease Corporation is lying about how much Muddy pays them for the coal? Now doesn't it stand to reason that Tug River and Muddy—excuse me, A. W. Aylesworth Coal Company—are all dealing out of one outfit in Richmond, are lying about the amounts paid for the coal, are livin' out of some postal box when every law-abiding, *law-abiding* company in this here country operates out of a real office. Now, girl, use your brain. There's something here, I can feel it.

"Now, Noni I can trust, so I asked her to snoop around some more. And in the meantime I asked your uncle Shelby to find out what Tug River's paying on some of the other leases in the holler and thereabouts. Shelby's not good for much, but he's fine at ferreting out what needs to be known. I promised him some of this whiskey of Lawrence's to make up for his trouble—he ain't had nothin' but 'shine for years—so you better give me a bottle or two for him before I go."

"Of course. Anything."

"And one for me. For my trouble."

They giggled for a minute, then fell silent.

Homer stared into the fire, watching the flames lick around a birch log. After a while he said, "I think this is a fine thing you're doin' for your dad, Clary. We haven't talked about it much all these years, but it's the right thing to do. I'm gonna have that Henry drive me out to Arlington Cemetery tomorrow so I can tell Hillard all about it. Paying Muddy back, settling with the miners. I don't know what your scheme is—I don't have a mind for these things. But I'm gettin' itchy just thinkin' about it. I can just feel your mind workin' away."

She gave him a sidelong look and smiled. "You always know what I'm thinking, don't you, Grandpa?"

"Most of the time. You've surprised me a time or two, though, and I've had to check the radar." Her marriages had stunned him; neither of them made much sense to him. He was still a little hurt that he hadn't met her first husband, the one they couldn't mention. He'd have liked to have been invited up for the wedding—but then, he hadn't raised her to be a slave to convention so he supposed it was all right in the end. Still, it was best not to bring this up. She got awfully prickly if he ever mentioned her marriages.

So he just sat there, warming his toes with flames and whiskey and sending her messages with his mind as he used to when she was little. Making recollections of her ambitions hang in fragments like a dream on the brain, releasing her conscience from automatic.

"Somebody—I don't know who—might make it rough for you down there," she told him. "Plenty of folks take Muddy's dollar and they might fear losing it. Right now there's only a few people who know what I'm up to, and I intend to keep it that way. What I need you to do is keep on a-doin' what you're doing now, picking up bits and pieces there and passing them on to me. Maybe Muddy's doing something bad, maybe he's not. But one thing's for sure, in the end I'm going to run Number 9 and all the rest of Muddy's mines the way the law says is right."

"The way the Lord says is right," Homer corrected her.

"That's right, Grandpa. That's right. Thank you for reminding me."

He felt a surge of pride hearing her say this. "Right," he added.

"So I thought you should be forewarned. I'm going to fight for Daddy, Grandpa. I always knew I would, I just didn't know how to go about it. Now, because of Lawrence, I can talk their language—money—that's the only thing they understand. I'm going to use my money to make them pay for what they did to Daddy."

He turned in his chair to face her, but she was looking off over his shoulder into the darkness of the room behind her, such a look of hard concentration on her face that Homer decided there was nothing he could say to her. But while her face was hard and set, her eyes were luminous, full of determination and melting certainty. He forced himself to look deeply into them and was thrilled. He hadn't seen that look in her for years and years, and it caught his breath in his throat a little and he had to turn his head away. He didn't want to frighten her. He didn't want her to see his own eyes, which glinted with tears and determination equal to her own. He had thought he had lost her to the richies, to those women who sigh to the money beat and drag through their days with bored, flat eyes. For five years she hadn't seemed to care for much beyond pretty dresses and strange, expensive food. He thought he'd lost her. But she was still his girl.

All of a sudden his blood pumped all over and he was warm. His bones relaxed and he could believe he'd never be cold again. He had the idea to tell her how much he loved her, how much he loved Hillard. It would do him some good to say it out loud. He collected himself and opened his mouth to speak, but he was a reticent man by nature, not given to spoken emotion, so all he could manage was a strangled "I can take whatever anybody dishes out." He wobbled to his feet, said, "You do right by your daddy, Clary, and let his old man take care of the rest," then he climbed up the stairs to his bed, but it was hours before he could stop his mind from racing and fall asleep.

On a Saturday morning the following month, Clare sat in the kitchen of the Middleburg house, eating a chocolate doughnut and staring out the window at a ruby-throated hummingbird, the notebook full of her research about Muddy in her lap. For days she had been trying to lure the birds to the sticky red liquid in the feeder. She had filled and refilled the bulbous feeder, watched the liquid evaporate, refilled it, waited some more, hoping the birds would find it. But it was only at that moment that one of the tiny fluttery creatures had finally caught the scent of the sweet liquid on the air and arrived for a taste. The male fluttered at right angles to the feeder, making a security check, sped away in a blur, then returned seconds later to dip his long needle-beak into the tiny opening and sip.

Feeling enormously satisfied, Clare took a bite of the doughnut and returned to her notebook. A moment later the female hummingbird arrived. Darkly iridescent, the male's partner had a dull gray throat in contrast to his vivid scarlet ribbon. But while he had taken only a drop before spinning away, she lingered for long seconds, drinking from every tiny opening, darting away and then quickly returning for more. To Clare this seemed to be justice— the trade-off of physical beauty for stamina, determination, and, ultimately, satisfaction.

"Look, Alex," she said as he sat down at the breakfast table and Marguerite put a big bowl of corn flakes and milk before him, "finally, a hummingbird!"

"How many?"

"Two now, but just wait. They'll tell all their friends and then I'll have a dozen."

Alex shook his head mournfully. "They're nasty, Mom. I hate it when they fight each other for the feeder. Henry has one outside his bedroom window and I watch them all the time. Why are they so mean?"

Clare had forgotten how ferocious the delicate birds could be and immediately felt deflated. Still, after all her hard work in luring them, she felt compelled to defend their behavior.

"Oh, I don't know, Alex. They each feel they're entitled. Grandpa told me that once he saw a huge bumblebee come up to a hummingbird feeder for a sip, and a hummingbird came by, checked out the bee, and then went *thwap* with his beak and sent the bee flying. I kind of like that. Hummingbirds look so fragile, like anything, even a bee, could squish them, but they're so tough!"

Alex pondered this. As he chewed his cereal a little milk dribbled down his chin. But when Clare reached over with her napkin to wipe it off, he pushed her hand away and wiped his own chin. He was a big boy now, almost five years old. He believed he had the right to mull over important issues and let milk dribble where it would in the necessary quest to perceive the true nature of the hummingbird.

"I suppose," he said finally. "But I still don't like them. And Dad said I don't have to understand everybody's point of view."

"He did? When did he say that?"

"He says it all the time." He spooned in more cereal. "He says that as long as *I* know what's what, that's good enough."

"Well, I hope he's not telling you you shouldn't be sympathetic to other people. I'm sure he couldn't mean that. You'll never get along with anybody if you don't understand what they're feeling. That's important, Alex. You've got to keep an open mind."

Alex's spoon splashed into his bowl. "Mom," he said, looking at her as if she had lost her mind, "I'm only talking about hummingbirds."

"Oh," she said, "right," and turned back to her work a little chagrined that she'd gotten so carried away.

They spent every weekend in Middleburg because Alex loved the country so. He said that living there was like being in a movie about animals and trees and all manner of wild things. Each Saturday and Sunday morning he and Henry set out for the piney woods behind the property with a huge pair of binoculars that had belonged to Sayles's father and a little notebook in which to jot down his record of all that he saw and heard. His diary was page after page of crude drawings of ducks, birds, insects, flowers. He considered the documenting of Virginia nature his job, and filled a notebook a week with observations.

A tiny stream ran through the woods, and beavers had built a dam there. At dawn and again at dusk Alex walked to where he could observe the beavers as they worked on their dam and on their lodge. He was telling Sayles, who had joined them at the breakfast table, all about it when Norman, the property's caretaker, came in the back door for a cup of Marguerite's coffee.

"Gonna have to take apart that dam, Mr. Sayles," Norman offered after listening for a minute.

Alex was appalled. "Don't do it, Dad!"

Norman gave Alex an impatient look. "Let 'em keep building, Mr. Sayles, and pretty soon the dam'll get so big it'll flood the road."

"We'll build another road, won't we, Dad?"

"Build another road, they'll build another dam," Norman persisted. He was not about to be overruled by a little boy.

"Then we'll build another one." Alex looked at his father for confirmation. They were allies in everything, particularly the preservation of any creature on the property.

"If we have to, I guess," Sayles said.

Frustrated, Norman twisted his battered cap in his hand and scraped his toe around the tile floor. "Stop that now, Norman," Marguerite scolded. If the kitchen floor got marked, Sophie, the housekeeper, would blame her and make her get down on her hands and knees and clean it. The two women were always bickering.

Norman ignored her. "Mr. Sayles, if you let the beavers take the trees down, pretty soon you won't have poplars, then the birch'll go. Pretty soon they'll all be gone and there won't be nothing to hold the soil. Dam'll get bigger, make a pond. Then you got mosquitoes. And don't forget the otter, Alex. Otters'll come around and eat the ducks and you hated it last year when the ducklings were taken by the otters."

Alex digested this for a moment. The business about the otters was true. They had eaten the merganser ducklings and he had been furious. He narrowed his eyes in concentration and rolled the options around in his mind. Life-and-death stuff; he saw it every day out in the countryside. He didn't want Norman to know it, but he hadn't dreamed the beavers could set in motion such dramatic events. Still, he couldn't bear to see them driven out of their home either, or watch as all their hard work was demolished. Then he remembered—there were kits in that beaver lodge; he'd seen them.

"There are babies in the lodge, Dad. You can't take the mother away from the kits or they'll die."

"Are there kits, Norman?" Sayles asked.

"Two or three."

"You can't do it, Dad. You just can't." Alex sat back in his chair, shaking his head.

"How long before the kits are weaned and on their own?"

"Say, three months, Mr. Sayles."

Sayles turned back to Alex. "What do you say, Alex? Let the beavers have their way and they upset the balance of the land. Or take them away and the kits die. You make the decision."

But Alex didn't have to think twice. "Keep the beavers," he said, folding his arms over his chest and looking defiantly at Norman.

So the beavers would stay, although later Sayles convinced Alex that once the kits were weaned in the fall, Norman might live-trap them and move them a few miles away to another pond, where their destructive busyness would have less effect on the estate. Norman accepted this with concealed resentment. He was the expert on wildlife, but Alex, well, he was Young Master Sayles, and birthright determined whose will prevailed every time. Actual explanations of this innate class order were never necessary. Sayles taught Alex by example, just as his father had taught him.

Sayles men sniff the air up on that higher ground and just follow their noses.

There were times when Sayles held meetings at Middleburg or The Heights with his diplomatic staff or with those who managed the many family investments, men whose word carried weight and who were quoted in the business pages of the world press. But if Alex ever stumbled into one of these meetings with some childish question or concern, about how a telescope worked or how spiders spin their webs, Sayles would stop cold, even if in the midst of discussing some earth-shaking matter, and pull him onto his knee and speak to him as if he had all the time in the world, while these men who were not of their class were left to cool their heels. The *cordon sanitaire* dropped between the two domains, business and family, and neither side had any doubt as to who could cross and who could not.

Raised in a pervasive atmosphere of exclusiveness and separated from "the others," Alex received the message loud and clear from the state: *You are a Sayles. You were born to reign. The world brakes for you, boy. You know it just as sure as sunrise—and they know it too.* All of it handled with the nonchalance that is the birthright of the born-rich.

Clare, witnessing the scene with Norman, wondered how she was ever going to convince her son that his father notwithstanding, the world would not dance to his tune.

She was swallowing the rest of her doughnut and pondering these matters, when Sayles asked her how the campaign to dislodge Muddy Aylesworth was going. "What did your uncle Shelby have to say on the phone yesterday?"

She gave a loud sigh. "Basically, he confirmed what Homer told me," she made herself say. "That Muddy has leases all over the hollow and that he's paying less than what the broker is paying him. Which once again brings up the interesting situation with the broker, whom no one can track down. I hired a private detective, by the way, to try to follow that angle. You weren't around and I had to make the decision on the spot."

He gave her an amazed look. "How on earth did you hire a private detective in Richmond, Virginia?"

"Sylvia."

"Oh, Lord."

"Really, she has the most incredible contacts. Always some fourth cousin of a lobbyist who owes her his life. There's this former congressman from Virginia, a state senate seat contender once upon a time who lost an election because of poll fraud and now wants to try a comeback in some rural district local election. Sylvia told him she might, just might, get Charlie to stay off his case in exchange for the private eye and total secrecy. But I have to pay the detective fifty dollars a day, plus expenses, to locate the real owner of the coal brokerage."

"Fifty a day? Usually these guys charge a hundred or two."

"Well, turns out the private eye owes the congressman." She cleared her throat. Wouldn't do to let him know that some of the details of her operation had begun to border on the seamy, thanks to Sylvia, but he was looking at her in a way that made her think he knew it already.

But he only said, "I think it's time to open a separate checking account, Clare. I'll give you some money to cover your expenses and you can deposit it. On second thought, that's no good. We'll use one of the corporate accounts in New York, something drawn on a brokerage house, turn it inside out until it's obscured. It's best at this point to keep your name confidential."

"You're afraid of being linked to all this?"

"Not at all. This is fun. No, you have to be careful to cover your tracks. If word gets back to Muddy, he'll move to protect himself. If he was clever enough to figure out this scheme, he'll be clever enough to trace a checking account."

She nodded her head.

"I'd like you to meet with Wendell Pell. He's a financial analyst who follows the coal industry and he should be familiar enough with Aylesworth Coal—even though it's a small operation—to give you a better picture of what kind of shape the company's in. Also, I think you ought to see an SEC counsel right away to find out what the legal guidelines are. Okay? I'll set it up for Monday and you can see them both then. What else do you need?"

She spoke slowly, looking directly into his eyes. She'd been rehearsing this speech for over a week. "I need to know you approve of what I'm doing. I haven't thought it all the way through yet, but if I get what I want, well, our lives are going to be turned upside down. I want to know that you understand that and approve. And I"—she hesitated—"I'm afraid this might cost you some money, Lawrence. I'm afraid it might cost you a lot of money, in fact."

Sayles allowed himself a moment of meditative silence. From the day she had told him she wanted to take over the Aylesworth—no, that was wrong. From the day when she had walked into his library and told him that she *intended* to take over the Aylesworth Coal Company, he had understood that there would be no turning her around, even though he could not conceive of how she would pull it off with anything less than fifty or sixty million dollars, which he would have to give her. But then the Barrow's Hollow jungle drums had begun the roll call of the mysterious land company leases, and the apparently hundreds of Barrow cousins and aunts and distant relations had checked in with their own bits and pieces, all of which had Muddy's grubby fingerprints on them, and so it seemed like she might have a chance to take the company from him in some way other than an outright purchase. The phone had been ringing off the hook for more than a month, all kinds of strange, muffled Appalachian voices threatening to finish Muddy with a knotted plow rope, knock the tar out of him, kill him dead. In any case, he was prepared to give her the money, if that's what it took. As usual, he was prepared to give her anything.

"I'm prepared to give you anything," he told her. "I'm prepared to commit as much money as it takes. Don't look so worried."

The little hummingbird had returned to the feeder, and Clare, distracted by its flurry, turned to watch it. Sayles followed her gaze. "Is that the female?"

"Yes," she answered, thinking about her earlier conversation with Alex. "The mean one."

"Look at her," he said. "She's drinking so fast because she's afraid the male will come along and drive her away."

Clare stared at the bird absently for a minute. "Maybe. Or maybe it's a payback," she said. "Maybe she's getting it all for herself so there won't be anything left for the male to drink."

He returned his gaze to her. "Really? Well, maybe I've underestimated you, Clare. Maybe you'll make a businessman after all. Anyway, what does Sylvia get out of all this?"

Clare pretended not to hear him.

"Clare? I know you heard me."

"You asked me something about Sylvia."

"What does she get out of all this?"

"Friendship."

"And?"

"That's all, friendship."

"For now."

"She's my friend."

He gave a little exasperated sigh and pushed himself away from the table. "She's going to have such a marker on you, Clare.

You're going to be going to every one of Charlie O'Dowd's
screwball house parties."

"Yeah, but that's the easy part. The hard part is I promised her
you'd come with me."

He gave her such a poisonous look as he walked out of the
kitchen that she laughed out loud.

19

"It's illegal. Oh, man, is it illegal."

The SEC Enforcement Division lawyer's name was Myers, and he rocked back and forth on his chair legs as he said it. "You can't pay one price to the guy from whom you're leasing the land the coal is mined on, and then take a higher price from the broker.

"Look at it this way: Say a man runs a coal company and has a land company off to the side with somebody fronting it. The land company holds the original leases from the landowners there in the mountains and subleases the property to the coal company at a higher number.

"So this man goes out and gets coal leases—or has people getting them for him, rather—but instead of putting them in his coal company, he puts them in a privately held or secret partnership land company, subleases it to the company at a higher price, and then skims the difference off the top of every ton of coal that's shipped. Now, that, as I said, is highly illegal."

"And could such a man also run the brokerage house?"

Myers giggled. "Only if the man were very, very larcenous."

He was young and flattered to have the young wife of Lawrence Sayles gazing at him as if he had the solution to all her problems.

"The broker arranges the contracts because, as you may know, the miner down in West Virginia or Tennessee doesn't get a contract directly from the power company or the steel company. The coal broker gets the sales contract.

"So, the sales contract calls for, let's say, fifty thousand tons a month, that's six hundred thousand tons a year. If the coal brings fifty dollars and the coal broker gets five percent, well, five percent of fifty dollars times six hundred thousand is real money. So if this theoretical bad guy owns, controls, has a piece of a coal

261

brokerage company off to the side, and all the coal the company has has to be sold through that broker, again he would be skimming off the top and making a fortune."

"And you would prosecute him if you found out?"

"Oh, yeah."

"And he would have to pay penalties?"

"Huge penalties, and the IRS would get him for millions on all that undeclared income."

"And—"

"Jail? For sure. The slammer for years and years."

Clare ducked her head to hide her glee.

"Well," she said, keeping a straight face as she gathered her papers together, "I really appreciate your taking this time, Mr. Myers. I hope I didn't wreck your schedule."

He opened his office door for her. "Not at all, Mrs. Sayles. My pleasure. You can find your way out?"

"Back and to the left. I remember."

"Don't hesitate to call me if you have more questions."

"Okay. Although I think I have all I need."

She started toward the elevators.

"You mind my asking why you need the information, Mrs. Sayles? Doing research for your husband or something?"

She gave him a blank look. "Yeah. Well, thanks again."

" 'Course, if you do uncover illegal practices in the coal industry," he called after her, "you're bound by law to report them, you know."

"Okay," she said over her shoulder. "I know."

"You're not going to, are you?"

"No!"

She was sitting with Sylvia in the bar of the Mayflower Hotel, their usual meeting place over the last two months.

"If I find out that all this stuff about Muddy is true, I'm not going to tell the SEC so they can put him in jail and put Aylesworth Coal into receivership, or sell it to somebody else instead of me.

"And listen to this—after I left the SEC I met for almost three hours with the coal industry analyst Lawrence recommended I see." She pulled out some papers from her purse and read from her notes. "He told me that Aylesworth Coal went public just a few months ago. I asked him if there were declarations of any land companies or brokerage firms associated with Aylesworth at the time it went public and he said none at all. So there's fraud right here."

She flipped pages till she found what she was looking for. "He also told me that coal prices have gone through the roof since a bulldozer accidentally broke the TransArabian Pipeline, the TAPline, earlier this year. That meant that oil that had been coming to the Mediterranean to be loaded and taken to refineries in North Africa and Spain suddenly had to be transported all around the continent of Africa. It put a strain on every available oil tanker, so the coal ships—they're called colliers—went over there from the U.S. to haul the oil and make tons of money, which meant that the ships that had been taking coal out of the United States for export suddenly disappeared because they went into the oil-hauling business.

"So while all the colliers were off carrying oil, none of the coal in this country could be moved, which caused a worldwide scarcity of coal at a time when there was a shortage of oil—so the price of coal has jumped from about three dollars and fifty cents a ton to fifteen dollars a ton. Lawrence had already mentioned this to me because it involved the railroad his family used to own. Anyway, the point of all this is that Muddy, along with every other coal company in the country, is suddenly making a fortune."

Sylvia grabbed a handful of peanuts, shook off the salt, and popped them into her mouth. "Is all of it this boring, Clare, or is this the good stuff?"

Clare ignored her and went on. "See, Muddy's got all kinds of money now, and greedy bastard that he is, he wants to make some more. That's why he decided to go public and put Aylesworth Coal on the New York Stock Exchange and sell shares."

Sylvia took a mirror from her purse and picked away at a piece of peanut stuck between her teeth. "Clare," she said, sighing and snapping the purse shut, "I'm lost."

"Look, Muddy plans to expand Aylesworth Coal by buying his own train facility so he can ship Aylesworth coal in Aylesworth train cars. And he wants to build a coal-washing plant because environmentalists are demanding clean air and restrictions on the burning of coal, which is a pollutant. Wash his own coal—Muddy avoids government restrictions and—"

"Makes more money."

"So he hopes to raise the three or four million dollars it will take to do all this by putting Aylesworth on the stock exchange and selling shares. Because the company is in such a good financial position thanks to the elevated price of coal, he won't have any trouble selling shares. And this, thank you, Muddy, is how I'm going to get him."

"Do you think I really need to know all this?"

"Yes! Because you're my friend."

"I am?"

"Of course. I wouldn't have gotten this far without you."

"I never know when to leave well enough alone."

"So, anyway—"

"Oh, God. You're going to tell me more." Sylvia wagged the empty peanut bowl at the waiter, who took it and walked away.

"So, anyway," Clare went on, "when he went public, Muddy was bound legally to make full disclosure to the Securities and Exchange Commission, which very clearly he hasn't, otherwise he would be in jail right now. So he's got a heavy secret about Columbia Brokers and the Tug River Land Lease Corporation that could send him away for years, and, most important, he's now selling stock in Aylesworth Coal, and guess who's going to buy some?"

"Huey Newton."

"Sylvia!"

"Okay, Clare Sayles is going to buy a lot of stock with Lawrence Sayles's money and then something happens, I don't know what, but I have a feeling I'm going to find out."

"Then I've got my foot in the door."

"Your foot in the door and Muddy's balls in the wringer." The waiter returned with more peanuts.

"Exactly."

"I know I'm going to regret asking this, but how does any of this get Muddy's private parts yanked?"

"I'm not going to tell you."

"There is a God."

"Not 'cause it bores you, Sylvia, but because I'm breaking the law, you know, if I don't tell the SEC this stuff. I'm not telling you so that you won't be a co-conspirator and only one of us will go to jail if it backfires. I've already told you too much. When I get ahold of Aylesworth Coal, I am the only one who'll know exactly how it was done."

"What about Lawrence?"

Clare checked her watch, made a face, and reached for her coat. "He's an American hero. He'd be duty-bound to try and stop me, and I don't blame him. So he's never going to know, and I'll wring your neck if you breathe a word to him—or anyone. This is a big secret now, Sylvia. You know how you love to dish the dirt."

Sylvia looked so hurt that Clare instantly tried to make it up to her. "Oh, what am I saying? You won't tell," she had countered so quickly that Sylvia brightened. "I'm just on edge because of all this. Forget I said it."

"Do you actually think I can even remember any of this? I know fag congressmen and drug-addicted debutante daughters. Give me a break from coal colliers and tap lines and land leases. I wouldn't know what to tell if I wanted to. Now, if some grimy young coal miner needs to be soaped down—"

"Nobody's getting soaped."

"All right, then. My lips are sealed."

"Right."

Sylvia fired up another cigarette and eyed her friend. "So what about you, Clare? You're about to break the law in a serious way. I'm scared for you. Aren't you scared?"

"Nope. Every time I start to develop a conscience, I think about Muddy coming up the hollow with a hundred-dollar bill in one hand and an eviction notice in the other. That takes care of my moral and legal scruples. Besides, unlike Lawrence, I'm no hero."

"And what happens if you find out old Muddy is clean?"

"He won't be. I'd stake my life on it."

And of course it turned out that way. Muddy, with his land leases and coal brokerage, was dirty as hell.

Clare woke before dawn, too nervous to sleep, showered, and then dressed in a conservative blue business suit, a white blouse, and black calfskin pumps. She smoothed her hair back with a barrette, and just to be annoying pinned a peace symbol on her lapel.

Sayles was waiting for her when she came downstairs. He took in the little protest button and smiled faintly. Last winter he had spent three months in Paris at the peace talks. "Have you had breakfast?" he asked.

"No, I'll get something later."

"You'll call me the minute you get out?"

"Yes."

He gave a little sigh. "Nervous?" he asked, monkeying with the knot in his necktie.

She shooed his hands away and straightened his tie herself. "Not nearly as nervous as you. Go on to your office, Lawrence. I'm going to be fine. Don't you be late for your meeting."

"Henry will drive you to the airport. And Barry will be on board the plane by the time you get there. They'll take you to the Marine Air Terminal, near LaGuardia Airport, okay? And there'll be a limousine right outside to take you to Fifty-seventh Street."

"I know, Lawrence. We went over it all last night."

"Now, if you decide to spend the night in New York, be sure to call my office and they'll contact Barry at the airport and let him know. Now, Fifty-seventh Street—"

"Lawrence, I'll be fine."

"You don't know New York all that well."

"The driver will." She brushed his cheek with her lips. "Now, go. I'll be fine."

Once he was gone, she had Marguerite bring her coffee, which she drank alone in the solarium. But she didn't review her notes. She had the facts down cold. Surrounded by the blooming magnolia bushes and dieffenbachia of the quiet sun-filled room, she closed her eyes and with her inward eye reconstructed that cold October day when her father, and Toby Stivers's father, went down and never came up. She could see her dad clear as day— grime blackened face, miner's helmet, tin dinner bucket, head bent, walking back up the holler every night as if he shouldered a ton of coal on his skinny shoulders.

She checked her watch, then stuffed the papers into her briefcase, snapped it shut, and was about to put it under her arm when she thought better of it. She pulled out the private detective's report, put it into her purse, then tossed the briefcase into a chair and walked out. The hell with it. She wanted both hands free just in case she decided to strangle him instead of simply ruining his life.

Preston held the door for her. His face was hard as ever but his eyes held some spark of human sympathy—a veritable dam-burst of emotion, considering the source.

"Good luck now, Mrs. Sayles," he said, and stepped out onto the gravel driveway as she went by. Preston was not privy to her business, but she suspected the household staff had picked up on the excitement in the house. Still, she was surprised at his interest and gave him an appreciative smile. "Why, thank you, Preston. I'll do my best."

"Are you nervous?"

"No, I'm fine."

Henry stood at the curb, holding open the car door. "Nervous, Mrs. Sayles?"

"No, I'm not nervous. Why is everybody so worried about my nerves?" she complained as she climbed in.

The entrance to the offices of the A. W. Aylesworth Coal Company, Inc., was tall and imposing—mahogany double doors with brass lettering, brass knobs, plates, and hinges. Clare had to put all her weight against them to get in.

Inside, a pretty, young, fresh-faced receptionist sat behind a slab of glass. The moment she saw Clare she was on her feet.

"Mrs. Sayles. Mr. Aylesworth and the others are waiting for you in the library."

Library! The last Clare knew, Muddy Aylesworth couldn't read the instruction on a stop sign.

"I'll take you," the young woman said.

The receptionist's smooth hair was pinned into a neat bun at the back of her head, and she wore a plain gray linen dress. Clare followed her down the hallway. The corridor was long and thickly carpeted and ran past several offices; little nameplates stuck on the wall beside each door announced the occupants. Most coal companies were bare-bones setups, painted floors and metal desks. Muddy's operation was deep-pile and hushed, like a branch office of IBM. Clearly, he had big plans for Aylesworth that didn't include dirty old bituminous coal.

They had arrived at the library. The receptionist gave a light knock, set her ear to the door, and smiled winsomely at the muffled "come in." She held the door open for Clare to enter, then closed it with a solid thud behind her.

It took Clare a moment to discern which of the three men springing to their feet was Muddy. He'd made himself over into a whole new edition of the grubby little varmint she'd known back in Kentucky. The eyeglasses had been replaced by contact lenses, and he was wearing a worsted suit high-styled as a Pierce Arrow; he could have flown to Santo Domingo on those lapels. His shirt was white, and when he stuck out his hand to shake hers, Clare saw that his initials were monogrammed white-on-white on its cuffs. He also wore a Balliol College tie, though Clare was sure the only Oxford Muddy Aylesworth knew was in Mississippi.

But it was the hair that made her mouth pop open. On the original owner, those locks must have been Byronic, but on its second go-round, the original property had been flayed and flattened into the kind of nasty-looking critter that's treed by hounds in the part of eastern Kentucky Muddy and Clare came from.

Feeling her eyes on it, he patted the roan-colored toupee self-consciously, cleared his throat to regain his composure, and pumped her hand. "Mrs. Sayles. It's an honor to meet you. Yessir, it sure is." He indicated the men at his side. "This is my lawyer,

Regis Wallace, and my son-in-law, also a lawyer, Newton McBride."

He held out a chair for her, then circled around his own desk and sat down. On a table at the side were a silver coffee service, delicate porcelain cups, and plates of pastries, but Clare refused everything, which seemed to disappoint him.

Still, he was upbeat when he began. "Mrs. Sayles—what an honor. I've certainly been looking forward to this meeting ever since Newt here brought your stock purchase to my attention. Twenty percent of the company—now, that made me sit up and take notice. I've been reading all about you in the newspapers for years and years and to have you here now—well, I'm a-mighty"—he braked for a colloquial one-eighty—"very thrilled, very, very thrilled."

He spread his hands open wide, palms down on the desk to show he meant it, and, beaming, nodded to Wallace, who added breathlessly, "That's exactly right. We want you to know, Mrs. Sayles, the high esteem in which we hold your husband, and, of course, yourself. Lawrence Sayles is one of the great men of this century, or any other, and we're very excited to think that he is associated—even by association—with, er, our corporation."

Clare frowned. "Thank you, but I should remind you that I'm the stockholder, not my husband." She crossed her legs at the knee and swung one leg back and forth impatiently.

Muddy shot Wallace a poisonous look and hastily added, "That's right, Mrs. Sayles, we understand that, and as I said, we're very honored."

"So you've said." Her tone was so frigid that the three men exchanged startled glances.

"So," Muddy pressed on, a little less certainty in his voice. "I asked you to come up here from Washington because I thought we ought to get to know each other in a friendly way, and to discuss issues that might possibly be of mutual benefit."

His look was so self-satisfied, he so clearly believed that he was reeling in the big fish, that Clare could hardly control herself. But she only said in a mild voice, "I don't understand."

"Well, ordinarily a stockholder is a stockholder." Muddy looked over at Regis and Newt, who nodded agreement. "But in your case, Mrs. Sayles, considering the vaunted esteem with which you are held, the depth of your understanding of topical issues, and, the fact—I must be honest here—that in this day and age, with women crying out for equal pay and equal rights, it would behoove the Aylesworth Company to go with the times—to have a girl such as you on its board of directors."

"You're offering me, a girl, a position on your board?"

Muddy leaned forward in his chair, his lips slipping so easily into the familiar weasel smile they could have been on ball bearings. "Normally, I would chit-chat a little bit, Mrs. Sayles, feel you out, so to speak, but, well,"—and he looked again with confidence at his comrades—"you come so well qualified, that—hell, I'm a businessman. Cut right to the heart of the matter. What's the point in dancin' 'round it?"

He pounded his hand on the table and hooted a little, but when Clare gave him a stony look, he mentally kicked himself for the gaffe. These damn richies. Twist yourself into bow-tie shapes to get it right and you're still screwed. And damn the old Muddy. He was always right under the new Muddy's skin, always poking out his bald head, honking like a hillbilly, making him look bad.

He sucked in his breath. He was more nervous than he'd anticipated, and his mind was spinning at such a rate of excitement that he could hardly contain himself.

And why not? Like a glittering prize, she was here for the taking—the wife of Lawrence Sayles (oh, the magic of that old New England name!), one of the richest, most famous men in the entire world, was not ten feet from him and by association, already he glittered too. He would mount a campaign to win her that was subtle as the fog creeping into a Kentucky holler at twilight. As Regis Wallace prattled on about the duties and responsibilities of board members, Muddy allowed his overheated imagination one delicious moment to spread his future out before him.

He would, naturally, start small, nothing too pushy or she would run scared. A small dinner in a good New York restaurant some night after the third or fourth monthly board meeting. Just a casual *How about a bite to eat, Clare.* After a few months it would become a habit. He would never pry, never ask questions. Just let her unfold herself for him quietly in intimate French restaurants. And then on one of these how-about-a-bite? nights she would mention that her husband was in New York on business. Would he mind if he joined them? Would he mind, in other words, if every day were the Fourth of July? The three of them in the backseat of a limousine, pleasantly undone from fine wine and great food, the warm good-byes and then the Famous Living Historical Monument squeezes his hand good-bye and says, *The*

*next time you're in Washington, A.W., give me a call. Clare will
give you my private number.*

And here the fantasy accelerated with the speed of a Japanese
bullet train: the shared confidences over snifters of good cognac,
business tips at the Metropolitan Club, juicy gossip after late-night
dinners in Georgetown, his arm slung around the shoulder of
some joking senior senator, and (Muddy's brain burned) the ultimate inside event—*the iron gates part slowly, the Secret Service
man checks the guest list, the long, slow drive up to the south por-
tico, "Ruffles and Flourishes," pleased to meet you, Mr. President* . . .

Ho! And this was only the beginning. He'd come a long way
from the holler; it made him shudder to think of himself in the old
days, slogging through the red dog, hating eyes all around him.
Well, he'd shown all of them—fooled them all. He'd outsmarted
all of those old hillbillies who had spat at him when his back was
turned. New house, new clothes, maybe even a new wife. Maybe
he'd swap that old hillbilly Adelle he'd left back on the Tug River
and marry someone younger, classier, kind of dewy. Kind of like
that fresh-faced piece he'd hired to sit behind the reception desk.
What a wonderful new life—all of it thanks to the little lady
seated across from him who had had the foresight, the genius, to
buy twenty percent of a coal mining company that, like its directors, was bound for glory. He could have vaulted his desk and
kissed her on the mouth in gratitude.

Only on second glance, she wasn't little at all. She was tall and
glaring at him with such contempt that his bowels all of a sudden
felt loose. Maybe he'd best wait a time or two to put his grand
plan into action. Maybe she was one of those ornery women who
needed a little greasing to come around. He stole a peek at his
watch. Twenty minutes had gone by since she'd sat down. Better
wrap it up while it still worked.

He cleared his throat. "Thanks for that, Regis. Well, what do
you think, Mrs. Sayles? Think a seat on the board of Aylesworth
Coal—we'll be dropping the 'Coal' soon, by the way, makin' it
'Industries'—might be up your alley? I'm not asking for an answer right this minute. A woman like you, with your schedule,
would need time to think it over."

He ruffled his desk calendar. "How about the twenty-fourth. I'll
call you that morning and you can give me your answer. In the
meantime"—he stood up—"feel free to call me, or Newt or Regis,
if you have any questions. We're here for you."

The three men stood together at the door, but Clare didn't

move. She recrossed her legs, pulled some papers from her purse, and then set the purse down next to her chair. The men exchanged nervous glances.

"I don't think so," she said. "I don't think I want to be called on the twenty-fourth. Let's not wait till then. Let's decide right now. The two of us." She looked directly at Muddy, who looked back at her as if she had lost her mind.

"You don't want them in the room?" He indicated the other men. "Is that it?"

"That's right. Just you and me."

He murmured something to the men and with his guts churning, closed the door and returned to his desk.

"Now, Mrs. Sayles. Is there a problem with our offer? Is there something about it that troubles you? Please tell me."

"Aylesworth—"

He held up his hand and with some effort shaped his lips into a big smile. "Let's not be so formal now. If we're going to work together, we ought to be on a friendlier basis. Everybody calls me A.W. Why don't you call me A.W. too?"

The library smelled of men's cologne and cigar smoke. And something sweet. Clare looked around, then saw the little table where the receptionist had so carefully set out the coffee and the pastries they had hoped to tempt her with. In the warmth of the room the pastries had released their cinnamon and sugar, and the aroma lay pleasantly on the air, so strong that Clare believed she could taste it. She passed her tongue over her lips and permitted herself a little smile. This is what they mean, she decided, about victory being sweet.

"Just call me A.W.," he repeated, giving her the weasel smile she'd known since girlhood.

"A.W.," she said in a weary voice, "I don't know. That doesn't sound quite right to my ear. Is that your nickname?"

"Yes, ma'am."

"But that's not a nickname. That's not a name other kids call you when you're playing softball or pounding through the woods hunting squirrel. A.W. is all they ever called you?"

"Uh-huh."

"Never anything else? Never had a name where you grew up?"

"Well, that was a long time ago."

"What did they call you then? I'm just curious. You can trust me. I won't tell anyone."

"It's not worth getting into."

"No, I'd like to know. We're going to work together, I'd like to find out a little bit about you. They called you something, all the other kids? Bud? Junior?"

"They did call me something, just about everyone. See, I grew up in a small town. My father was the most prominent man in town, you might say. Everyone tipped their hat to him when they passed him on the sidewalk."

"Sidewalk?!"

He gave her a quizzical look. "Yes, of course. Sidewalks everywhere in Chapel Hill, North Carolina."

"Chapel Hill, North Carolina?" She said it with such disbelief in her voice that he sat forward, patted his toupee, which hung stylishly over his ears, and pressed on. "That's right. Chapel Hill, North Carolina. And if you really must know, and you promise you'll never tell—my father was A. W. Aylesworth the first. I was A.W. the second, so in Chapel Hill, at the day school, at the country club, everyone called me Arthur the Deuce. Until I got to Choate, and then they just called me Deuce."

He sat back in his chair so demonstrably pleased with himself, so misted over with the fantasy of his blue-blooded youth, he hardly noticed that the incredulous expression on her face had become a smile, and that smile had turned into a high-pitched squeal that became so shrill and so loud that he looked uneasily at the door and then back to her, just as the smile evaporated.

She uncrossed her legs, leaned forward on his desk with both elbows, and in a voice that sent his heart to his throat looked him straight in the eye and said, "Well, A.W., you are so full of shit. You are so full of shit that your eyeballs are swimming and you can't even see. I've been sittin' here in front of you for half an hour thinkin' any minute now he is gonna jump up and recognize me, but you can't even see me, can you? Because you are so full of shit. You didn't even bother finding out who I was before I married Lawrence Sayles. You just got all puffed up thicker than the fur on a squirrel, didn't ya? You just think you are the sweetest thing ever come down the pike. Well, I wouldn't have you on a Christmas tree, you old murderer."

"Now, wait a minute!"

"You think you can put that hair hat on your head and just shuck the daylights out of me?"

"You from the union? Is that what this is? A shakedown from the union?"

"No. Better than that, A.W." Every time she said "A.W." it was like she'd brought up something bad from her stomach and had to get it out of her mouth in a hurry. It was getting on his nerves.

"Look here, Mrs. Sayles—"

"Take a good look." She held her arms out at her sides. She turned her face this way and that. "See anything you know? See anything that looks to you like bad timbers and short roof bolts? No ventilation, dog hole, dead miners?"

"You're Clary Barrow! I see it now that I say it. Hillard Barrow's girl. You're gonna try and make me feel bad all over again about that roof fall. Are you really married to Lawrence Sayles?"

"Yes, I am. You think you're the only one got past the mouth of the holler?"

"I'll be blowed. You got you right up there." He folded his arms on his chest and put the toughest look on his face he could muster. "So what you want, Clary? You all haired up about somethin', may's well lay your cards out, gal."

"A.W.—"

There it was again. "Listen here," he snarled, "if we're gonna do business, you gotta stop callin' me that that way, Clary. You make it sound like you got a mouthful of corn liquor and lye."

She sat back in her chair and threw him a big smile. "Now that we're old pals again, okay, I'll call you Muddy, Muddy. 'Cause you were full of shit then, and you're full of it now."

Outside, the air was clear and cool for midsummer. The limousine was gone from the curb, chased by a traffic cop; Clare saw its taillights swing right onto Sixth Avenue. She looked down to Fifth Avenue, to the clock over Tiffany's art deco front door. This late in the day it would take at least ten minutes for the driver to circle around to Fifth and return for her.

Jostled by pedestrians, she pulled back into the shadow of the building and clutched her purse to her chest. Couldn't let anything happen to that purse. Muddy had signed a lengthy document, witnessed by his lawyer, that put his shares of Aylesworth Coal in trust for the miners and released the company to her. She'd folded it into a square and put it into her purse, good as gold. He had kicked and screamed bloody murder, of course, but in the end, what was the point? She'd told him about Myers at the SEC, and the business about the slammer and the confiscation of all his ill-gained riches. *Give the company to me and the miners, and I'll let you keep all the cash in all your bank accounts, here and abroad.* He'd made her set the phone down on that one. He'd cussed her blue and gone wild, called her a fucking Barrow, and a fucking hillbilly, and a fucking fuck, but he'd signed in the end and that was all that mattered.

She took a deep breath and fought the impulse to scream at the top of her lungs. She walked east to Fifth Avenue, thinking to catch the car as it came around the block, but the limo was nowhere in sight. She wanted to celebrate. She wanted to dance in the street and buttonhole pedestrians and tell them how she'd just snagged a pesky snake that had been giving her trouble for years. She wished Lawrence were with her—and Homer, and Sylvia. This was a moment worth memorializing; it deserved something special. She checked the Tiffany clock again, then decided the hell with waiting. Let the car circle the block forever. She turned and walked north on Fifth to Fifty-eighth Street, cut through the cars parked alongside Bergdorf Goodman, and climbed the wide steps of the Plaza Hotel. She'd put herself to the test and passed, she could afford some unreasonable indulgence, some sort of reward. She took a seat in the Oak Room Bar. She deserved, at the very least, to kill an entire bottle of first-class champagne.

"I'm dying for a cigarette, Clary. Do you mind?"

Toby Stivers wanted a smoke in the worst way. It was sheer recklessness to smoke in the mines because of the risk of explosion, so he'd gone eight hours without a cigarette and then raced to meet Clare when his shift was ended. He'd showered and changed into clean clothes, but the grime clung to the skin around his hairline and, of course, under his fingernails.

"Smoke all you want, Toby. Mine owners claim all you miners have bad lungs from smoking cigarettes, not coal dust. Give them more ammunition. But don't let me make you feel foolish."

He shifted around uncomfortably in his chair and flashed her an impish smile. " 'Course, I could have a chew instead, Clary. Splat some Red Man juice all over your pretty shoes."

He bent down and looked under her desk. She was wearing jeans and work boots. "No pretty shoes. I thought you was rich."

"Shut up!"

He pulled out a cigarette, fired it up, and blew out a stream of smoke. "You always had a mouth on you, girl, but it's ten times worse since you moved up north. And runnin' this coal company ain't gonna make you any more charmin'. The men ain't gonna like it if you're always mouthin' off."

"Well, *I* think they're going to love me no matter what when they see this."

She pushed a pile of papers across the desk to him. It was five-thirty in the afternoon and they were alone in her office, the sun setting behind them through the windows and throwing slants of mellow light across the unpainted floor. The first thing she'd done was to take over the abandoned company store, an act of spite, and make it her headquarters. She'd hired a secretary, a local girl with a semester of secretarial school in Lexington, two male assistants, and assorted clerks. She had fired or retired virtually everybody in Muddy's organization, closed the New York office, and was in the process of luring top staff from competing companies with the guarantee of big money. Her assistants had been hired away from A. T. Massey Company for top dollar, knew everything there was to know about coal, and were on their way to figuring out a system for the disposal of waste rock in deep mines, so she figured they were worth it.

She watched Toby as he studied the papers she'd handed him. He had an easy, laconic way about him and didn't so much sit in a chair as envelop the thing with his long, lanky body. Everything about Toby was long—his narrow, tapered fingers, his nose, which was thin and improbably aristocratic, his eyelashes. He was handsome as ever, tall, hair black as when he was sixteen; it was wet now, with comb marks, and Clare believed she could detect the faint odor of musk aftershave. He'd spruced up for her. He wanted to look good to her. She was married, and a mother, but nothing had changed. Her cousin Willa Blankenship had told her that Toby hadn't married because he couldn't bear imagining some wife of his howling for him outside a mine mouth the way his mother had when they brought up his dad's body after the roof fall, but Clare wasn't convinced that was the reason.

He moved his lips slightly as he read and sucked on his cigarette.

"These deep cutting machines—any time the men see automated they're not going to like it."

"I have to go with the times, Toby, or go out of business. Better to have twenty men working than none at all. Besides, this machine produces less dust, so they've got to like that. And look"— she came around the desk to squat beside his chair and read aloud over his shoulder—"all this stuff—an automated roof bolter with its own roof support, shuttle cars with a swing-around cab, loading machines with their own joystick control, two-way voice communication. Nonunion mines never have stuff like this."

"Who's paying?"

"I am, of course. And I'm gettin' bank loans."

"For all your mines?"

"We'll start with Number 9, but eventually all of them, yeah." Toby tossed the papers back onto her desk. "The men will love you all right, Clary, but the other owners will skin you alive. You start installing all this new safety equipment in the mines and you're gonna screw it up for them. They're going to slash your tires. They'll break your legs."

"I don't care. I'm rich. I'll buy some more tires. I'll get new legs."

"Girl, there isn't enough money in the world to back up a coal operation that goes broke. Your old man's no fool. He's not going to blow his family fortune on a bunch of broken-down old mines down here in Kentucky."

"He won't have to. We're not going to go broke. We're going to make money."

"You've been gone too long, Clary. You've forgotten what it's like down here. You know how coal goes—one day up, the next day down and down. It's a roller-coaster ride. You've forgotten." He looped long fingers through his belt buckle, a bronzelike affair in the shape of a German short-hair hunting dog.

"Maybe that's not such a bad thing," she told him. "Maybe you ought to try to forget too." She threw her legs up on the desk and put a businesslike tone in her voice. "Actually, that's what I wanted to talk to you about."

Toby's chair scraped over the floor as he bolted to his feet. "I'm outta here."

"Come on, Toby."

"Clary, whatever it is you want, the answer is no." He walked over, opened the window, and flicked out his lighted cigarette.

"I want you to come work with me," she said in a soft, pleading voice.

"Come on."

"By next week I've got to decide about a new preparation plant. Now, what do I know about that? I've got to find designers who can do it right. I've got to understand feasibility studies. I've got to get familiar with our other operations and everything else. I've got a hundred and one things to do, all of which I know nothing about, and I've got about thirty seconds to do it in. Toby, I've spent the last five years deciding whether to serve the hors d'oeuvres hot or cold. I'm not up to this. You've got to help me."

"Please don't guilt-trip me. And anyway, I don't know any more about prep plants than you do. I'm a workingman, Clary. Never wanted to be a boss, and don't intend to start now."

"I need a man who knows miners to help me with the men. I need someone the men trust to act as a kind of ombudsman between me and them. Someone who understands their problems, who can help restructure a medical benefits and pension program. I want to make the Aylesworth mines meet par and then better par of any union mine in the country. This is a revolutionary thing we're doing here now, Toby. I need a revolutionary to help me do it. I need someone I can trust."

"You really believe you can change it all?"

"I have the will to change it, and, most important, I have the money, and that's how the world works. One thing I learned up north, with money you can do anything. I'm going to pour money into this operation because it's my only recourse at the moment, but I'm going to get very good at this, believe me, and I'm going to prove that coal can be mined safely and that an owner can do that, make money, and survive. If that's naïve, then so be it, but I can't believe that anyone in this town would oppose me on that. Especially you."

She was challenging him to think big, as she always had, and it didn't make him any more comfortable now than it had when they were kids. The problem with having a friend like Clare, Toby'd decided years ago, was that in their own way they always made you feel bad at the same time they were forcing you to be better than you were. She'd always supplied the drive in his life; when she went north, she'd stolen it from him and so he'd gone and gotten predictable, and bored and scared, just like every other miner.

A lot of the people in the town didn't like her despite what she had done for them. She had this I-don't-give-a-damn-what-anybody-thinks attitude, and that rubbed folks the wrong way, especially because it came from a woman. And even though they were her townfolk, and in the long skein of blood relationships in the hills many were her actual kinfolk, she didn't make any effort to get them to like her. She just gave her orders in an even voice, treated everybody pretty fairly, and went about her business as if emotion played no part in it. That wasn't the Clare he remembered.

"Clary, I blow coal. I don't know how to boss."

"It's not bossing. It's listening and explaining, that's all. It's doing for the miners what's fair and what's right. Don't tell me you don't want that too."

She sat down next to him on the windowsill and put a comforting tone in her voice. "I'll do anything to get what I want." She touched his hand and he raised his eyes to her. Maybe he did still love her a little bit. Maybe he did still think of her on those slow, cold nights. He probably should have married one of the local girls. But he hadn't, and now he felt past it, too old and set in his ways. Where was the shame in dreaming over the lost love of his youth as long as no one found out? He would die if he thought she guessed he still carried a torch for her.

"You can do it, Toby, you know you can. You're going to be the one who ensures their wages, who makes sure their kids have enough to eat, who arranges housing for them, who sees they're taken care of when they're injured or ill, or too old to take care of themselves. How can you say no? I'm going to help you get to heaven. They'll make you an angel."

"I'm a miner."

"Yeah, and I'm a miner's daughter," she said, a little irritated, "and if I'd done what I was supposed to do with my life, I'd be down here married to some dog-hole miner, living a corn-bread life, five kids, eating government cheese."

When he winced, she groaned and dropped her head, because, of course, if she'd stayed in Mills Bend, it would have been his scrawny kids, his desperation, their miserable marriage.

The truth lying there between them kept them both from speaking, so they sat together, silently staring out the window, breathing in time and feeling a little sad. The old town looked decrepit under the dappling sunbeams. There was a coat of coal film twenty years old on the IGA that no amount of scrubbing could dissolve. A mangy dog snuffled along the curb near a pickup, turned in a circle, then lifted his leg against a tire. When he was finished, he went on down the street, yipping at some boys who were kicking a 7-Up can against the side of the barbershop. Mr. Peters, the barber, rapped on his window to chase them away.

"The old place is looking pretty awful, isn't it?" she said. "I don't believe I've ever seen a town look so bad. Remember when we were kids, Toby, we used to dream about floating down strange rivers, facing down cannibals, seeing the world, eating something besides squirrel meat?"

"Flush toilets."

"Yeah, big-time stuff. Well, this is kind of it, this is our Amazon River, right here in Mills Bend. River came and found us."

He laughed at her melodrama, but he understood what she was saying. He didn't want to tell her that he'd lost his taste for adventure, that he felt diminished because she'd lived their every dream when he was nothing but a work beast. He didn't want her to know that he had less fear of the explosive charges he handled every day than he did of looking bad in her eyes. So in the end it was easier to tell her that he would work with her than to have to deal with what he would feel if he told her he couldn't. So after a long, hopeless wrestle with his conscience, he said without enthusiasm, "I guess I have to, don't I?"

She whooped. "Just like we dreamed when we were kids—dancing on old Muddy's grave."

"I'm probably not going to be any good at this," he added quickly. "You're probably gonna fire me the first week. Say"—he turned to her—"I'll always have a place in the mine, right? If things don't work out up here?"

"Your dog-hole days are over, Toby. Don't give it another thought. Now, let's go celebrate. Let's go on over to the tavern and get us a beer. Let's go honky-tonk."

"No way, not the knife and gun club."

She looped her arm through his and pulled him to his feet. "You'll take care of me. You always have. I want the men to see that I'm not stuck-up."

"They don't think you're stuck-up, Clary, they just think you're mean."

Hurt, she stopped to protest. "I'm not mean."

"You ain't friendly."

"I have my reasons."

"All right, and I can guess what they might be. You are the boss, not the pal. Backslapping would defeat what you're trying to do. But you ought to lighten up a little once in a while, Clary. You ought to try giving just a little smile."

"No, no smiling," she said. "Shopkeepers smile, whores smile. Smiling can get you into trouble. I'll pay the men good wages, I'll pay health benefits and retirement, I'll give them the best safety equipment money can buy, I'll go down into the hole for them if they get into trouble and breathe gas and suck up coal dust. But I won't smile at them, and that's that."

When they were kicking through the dry leaves in the street, Toby finally said, "All right, Clary, we'll do it your way, no smiles, nothing. But in return for my not trying to push you about it, promise me somethin', okay?"

"Okay."

"Promise me you won't be talkin' about Lawrence Sayles every minute."

"Huh?"

"Promise you won't make me feel like a jerk 'cause you married the richest guy in America."

"Lawrence isn't like that," she said. "You'll like him. He'll like you."

"Yeah. Sure."

The scruffy dog came over and nipped at Toby's pants leg. He gave him a little kick and the dog ran into the tavern when the door opened. "I can wait, Clary. I ain't in any hurry to meet the monument."

1973

20

A half-dozen illuminated derricks split the sky of the Duru oil field, their whirring probes sunk deep below the earth in search of even more deposits of liquid wealth. When exploration was completed in this spot, the rigs would be rolled to another, then another. In the end, more and more oil would flow every day toward the massive new port in the south, at the kingdom's narrow outlet to the sea. The five companies holding drilling rights to the Duru oil field last year had produced more than nine hundred million barrels, the kingdom taking eighty-two cents on each barrel.

What a shame, Tarik thought as he contemplated the derricks, that because of the oil embargo this year none of that oil would be going anywhere.

Reading his mind, Arthur Olson sighed in disgust. "A damn waste."

"Don't talk to me about it, Arthur. I warned you."

They had driven out that night from Brater to watch the sun go down, to talk things over. Het had set up a tent camp and made dinner—New Zealand lamb with mint and garlic, coarse bread, vegetables, nothing that couldn't be prepared over a cookfire and eaten off tin plates.

Later they sat casually in canvas campaign chairs, drinking strong Sur coffee.

They had known each other for ten years, and still Olson couldn't get over that peculiar sensation he always felt in Tarik's presence. His temperature must run a little hotter, his metabolism faster, it seemed to Olson, and this was altogether weird, a little abnormal. They mused about it back in Washington, trying to figure it out, and worried that if he had this intensity, this burn, he must know something they didn't. Stomachs churned back there because the kingdom's location dictated its strategic value as a potential military staging area for American operations in the area. It wouldn't do to have Tarik running on some weird afterburner, seeing himself as some kind of lone wolf.

Olson fingered the rim of his glass. Even here on the plain, not a soul stirring except for Het clearing the table of dinner remains, the bodyguard of twenty men a little apart quietly finishing their mess, he could feel Tarik's restlessness. Which didn't make what he had to say any easier.

"All that oil. All that money. What a waste." Olson looked over his shoulder at Het. "You don't suppose Het has any scotch in those saddlebags of his, do you? Just looking at this sun setting makes me thirsty. I keep thinking what it's going to be like out here in a couple of hours when it has the bad manners to come back up."

Tarik slung one leg over the other. His riding boots were scuffed and dusty. Most nights he was so tired he just fell down wherever he was and slept like a drunkard. Sometimes Het would pull off the boots, sometimes not. Het had his own agenda, one that Tarik could never predict, having to do with the preparation of food and long, solitary meditations. Tarik, naturally, said nothing about any of this. He had gone beyond such small concerns— not as a conscious decision, just part of the process that had begun years ago. If he struggled, it didn't show. If he sorrowed, nobody knew. Although anyone could come to him for succor, his needs, if they even existed, continued unspoken. He was consumed by work sunup to sundown, and it appeared to suit him.

Tarik rubbed the back of his neck with his hand. He had a headache. He'd been out in the sun all day and now his head pounded. Het had given him aspirin earlier, but it hadn't done much good. If Topaz were here, she would have massaged his neck and he would have felt better. He had gotten used to her ministrations, even come to welcome them in a way, as long as she didn't carry on too much. They'd worked out a system over the years. She'd learned to button her lip a little, and he'd forced himself to tolerate her prattle; somewhere between was relative peace. Still, he didn't want to spend much time with her, and to his great relief motherhood seemed to have doused those sexual fires of hers. He hadn't brought her with him to Duru, or anywhere else for that matter, in years, and truth be told, she wouldn't have wanted to come anyway. Since Karim had been born, she hadn't wanted to do much of anything but fuss with her son.

Tarik turned toward Olson, who looked somber and tired. Hollows were beginning to show under his eyes and his gut was expanding at a startling rate. His fine, rangy good looks had begun collapsing in the face of a lifetime of late nights and rich food.

"Het, bring Mr. Olson a scotch, will you?"

Relieved at the prospect of a drink, Olson cheered up. "So what did you bring me here to look at, the sunset or the derrick?" he asked.

"Do I have to say?"

"Yes, but don't make it another of those A or B choices of yours, okay?"

"You mean, sunset I'm a hopeless romantic, derrick and I'm a philistine?"

"Never mind. Doesn't matter anyway. They're both beautiful." Olson wanted only to sip his scotch.

In the failing light the plain lost even the little color it had in daytime. Only the sunset was electric, an orange disc melting away behind the derrick. To the southwest they could make out a dozen more derricks already pumping oil, their excess natural gas flaring fiery orange to match the sunset.

Tarik shifted around in his chair. "Arthur, when you start sounding hopeless, I know you're ready to pitch something."

Olson eyed him humorously. "I'm that transparent? Oh, God. All right. They've made me the messenger again." He lifted his glass and drank.

Tarik gave a little laugh. "I never understand why Washington doesn't get someone in the consular office to do it, Arthur. After all these years they always come back to you, and you don't even work for them anymore."

"Because I've ruined them for anybody else, like a good woman. Anyway," he went on sourly, "they've guilt-tripped me and I can never say no—also like a good woman. So the message is, when are you going to stop screwing around? Why are you doing this to them? Look at all they've done for you and now you've stabbed them in the back."

"Oh, Arthur. Come on."

"I'm only quoting. You're their boy. You're the one who's supposed to stay the course, toe the line forever and ever. They think you should be sending them your oil as if the embargo didn't exist. You screwed them, and now they're nervous that you might get the idea to do it again. They're nervous about all that military stuff up in Rahal and all those fighters and surface-to-air missiles. They've got a lot invested in you—and not just the material stuff. Your special relationship, that kind of thing. They're scared you might turn out like Diem, or, worse, Nasser. You're their guarantee around these parts, and now they're biting their nails, wondering if you're in or if you're out. Get my drift?"

"You mean, I show them how much I love them by cutting my own throat."

"Something like that. Actually, they don't care about your throat. You should bleed all over Duru for them, if that's what it takes. That's love."

Tarik signaled Het for more coffee. "Not where I come from, which happens to be where you come from, Arthur."

"Maybe, but my advice—completely self-serving, of course—is to get in and stay in." When Het came near, Olson held out his glass for more scotch.

"If you turn into some maverick out here," he went on once he'd gotten a refill, "well, they're not going to take it too kindly. They'll start muttering about the Red Menace and Hue and then the next thing you know, Elliott Tomlinson will be giving you one of his dead-meat looks. I'm warning you, that's all. Tapping that oil has changed everything. Their only hold over you now is a certain philosophical symmetry, a shared moral conviction."

When Tarik didn't respond, Olson sat up straight, looked at him incredulously, and said, "Christ, you haven't gone that far, have you?"

Tarik turned and gave him the smile, and his light eyes flared. His hair hadn't been cut in months and it curled, long and black, almost to his shoulders. His face, always handsome, was now lined and leathered by the sun. When he was relaxed, the smile softened the lines and made him seem even more attractive. But when he was tense, which he was now, the smile was nearly lupine.

"Of course not, Arthur," he said finally. "Don't be silly."

"Well, then stop being so cagey. Washington wants me to go back tomorrow morning and wire them that I have your assurance that the oil embargo is a one-time thing and that they're still the ones you love best."

Tarik shrugged. "Go ahead. Tell them it's still a marriage. Tell them I said it's important to take sides and that I still have the same beliefs. Tell them I looked you right in the eye and said so."

Olson raised his glass in salute. "I'll tell them that," he said. "Good. I'll tell them you still have your beliefs."

They sat in companionable silence for a long while, until Het came to tell them their cots had been made up in the tent. Olson sipped his drink and watched while Het pulled off Tarik's boots, then, distracted by the voices of the men outside, watched through the tent-flap opening at the bodyguard deploying itself around the area. Two soldiers with machine guns were posted at the tent entrance, two at each side, and two in the back. Another perimeter of guards had been set up ten feet from these, and another a hundred yards beyond that. Olson was pleased that on the plain at least, Tarik took precautions.

On his back on the cot he could see the evening star hung low over the horizon. He was surprised how good the hard cot felt under his body; probably the scotch softening up his old bones. The wind had come up a little bit and sand was beating lightly against the sides of the tent. If it had been a real breeze, he might have gotten up and walked outside to savor it. But he was not deceived. Not after all these years. There were no consoling breezes in this part of the world. Every wind was evil and carried on its wings the memory of some murderous moment that had happened millennia before, or was happening right now. He drank down the rest of his drink and looped his arm under his head for a pillow. He was just about to close his eyes, when in the darkness Tarik said, "Put it that way, Arthur. Say that I still have my beliefs."

"I will," Olson said, closing his eyes. "I will. Now get some sleep. I want to be out of here before sunrise. God, how I hate the sun."

The kingdom floated on an ocean of oil and the changes that oil money had brought were almost beyond comprehension. Change was everywhere, even on the gravelly plain, a quarter of which now was green and grassy. A huge water distillation plant that took seawater and made it potable had been built near the oil depot in the southern portion of the country. Tanker trucks sped over the new two-lane highway that criss-crossed the country, carrying water to slake thirsts and irrigate portions of the plain into farmland. In addition, a water strike near Im made by an oil exploration operation brought fresh water to the part of the country just east of Duru, with plans to build a water pipeline clear to the bog.

The capital city had spread beyond its ancient mud walls, and television antennas bristled on the rooftop of nearly every home. Office buildings, some of them fifteen stories high, had given the city a modern profile, and more were being built every year. Huge construction cranes made right angles of steel against the horizon.

The bazaars were full of Western appliances for the natives and ersatz Sur and Sheban geegaws for the tourists, an adventurous handful in the beginning but more and more were coming every day. Store shelves were stocked with food, and market stalls sold vegetables and lamb and, once in a while, good quality beef.

No one in the kingdom lacked a home, a job, an education, or medical services. Income was guaranteed. If a man's wages fell below an acceptable level, the state made up the difference, depending on family size and economic need. Education was compulsory to the age of sixteen, and a tiny but thriving university had been established on a campus just outside the city walls. The state paid all school tuitions, even for students who elected to go to universities abroad. The goal was to have the best-educated population of any nation in the region, and on that score Tarik was close to success. There was low-income government-built housing in the capital and in three locations in the countryside. Income tax did not exist. Public phones were free. If a man wanted a car or a television set or a telephone, these things were his virtually for the asking. The justice system allowed equal rights for everyone, trials were speedy, sentences just, religious preference determined by personal choice.

In the countryside, water flowed, sheep thrived, trees sprouted, and everything was a dream. The old people, who remembered Turkit, put their hands over their eyes and shook their heads in disbelief at their good luck, then went for a ride in their shiny new cars. Everybody got their fair share.

For the longest time Washington believed it had the sweetest deal imaginable. Tarik was the man, the chosen one. They'd made him, they believed they owned him, and if they told him to jump, they assumed he'd ask how high. Early in 1964 he had signed an agreement with Washington providing the United States with access to military installations in the kingdom in exchange for a guarantee of nearly half a billion dollars with which to modernize the country's three military bases—a most self-serving arrangement from Washington's point of view, as they planned to use those bases if American military were ever needed to protect American interests in the region.

What's more, the association with OmniTech, while theoretically independent from any formal foreign policy program, in reality guaranteed that Americans were placed in the most influential positions in the kingdom's government. Many of these OmniTech people were CIA or State Department alumni, like Olson, with shadowy ties to their old bosses. The U.S. had groomed the boy, greased the wheels, stacked the deck. It was a very sweet arrangement from their point of view.

But then Stan Cobb had found that elusive tap root at Duru, oil gushed in, and everything changed and—from the point of view of Washington—the worm turned.

Now the number of advisers and their influence on foreign affairs had begun to limit the participation of the kingdom's increasingly educated and skilled professionals. Young men and women returned from European universities and technical colleges to find that the good jobs were already held by Americans—and Tarik had no intention of turning out college graduates for nonexistent jobs, or establishing a well-funded welfare state with expensive and inefficient public enterprises that were make-work.

OmniTech had been responsible for speeding the development of the country, for overseeing the growth of communications, transportation, construction, public health, water, electricity and roads. OmniTech, under Olson's supervision, had developed the laws and the justice system and had created the bureaucracy that ran the country's infrastructure; it had also begged the question, Who really runs the place?

The more the company spread its fingers even to the most remote and sparsely populated area of the kingdom, the more Tarik resented it. He had turned over much of the civil authority in the country to OmniTech and its American advisers. Now he wanted that authority back. It wasn't that he wasn't grateful. It was just that somewhere between the time Clare left and he opted to join the OPEC oil embargo, he'd begun to think of himself as more native son and less Washington's golden boy. A horrifying transformation to Washington's way of thinking, like going to bed with Fay Wray and waking up with King Kong, which is how Arthur Olson put it to Francis Riston at the State Department during his latest trip back to Washington.

Tarik pondered all these things silently as the helicopter brought him back to the capital from Duru, Olson beside him. He loved and admired Olson and believed him to be the best possible of men, in fact, but it was this suffocating arrangement with OmniTech—and not the sun—that was giving him the headache.

They shook hands good-bye under the whirling rotor blades, both of them bent over and at a disadvantage. Olson piled into a sedan, while Tarik got behind the wheel of his Land-Rover.

He insisted on driving himself, usually with Het, his old Bren replaced by an Uzi submachine gun, tight by him in the front. Since Azarak's attack years before, a bodyguard of close to two hundred men, all of them fiercely loyal, had been assigned to his personal security. A portion of the bodyguard traveled with Tarik everywhere; the remainder stayed behind with Karim and Topaz.

Olson had tried to convince Tarik to let a trained man drive, but Tarik was too impatient for it and insisted on driving himself.

The Land-Rover's wheels ground over the fine gravel that blew in from the plain and covered the paved streets of the city. He drove fast, dodging old women balancing household treasures on their heads, and the occasional donkey. When he slowed to round a corner, a man selling sesame bread from a pushcart darted up to the Land-Rover to shove one of his skinny, warm loaves into Tarik's hands.

Taking bites on the soft bread, Tarik drove on, passing through the main gate from the new city to the old, edging the Land-Rover over cobblestoned narrow streets not much wider than the vehicle. He slowed to accommodate the jam of street merchants and some European tourists and caught sight of a troubadour playing a reedy tune on his flute, his eyes rolled up with pleasure at his own music. Every few feet or so another street seller squatted over a brazier, cooking the traditional thin pancakes spread with burnt sugar and hawking his sweet product in a grating voice. An open door revealed a grassy courtyard. Within, an old man sat on a three-legged stool, contentedly smoking a water pipe. The new wave of progress hadn't altered the familiar exotica.

A hundred feet from the palace, Tarik downshifted the Land-Rover and rammed to a stop. Het was out and at his side even before he had turned off the engine.

White-Lyons was on him the moment he was inside.

"Tomlinson is here to see you."

"I thought you were up at Hirth, White-Lyons. What are you doing here?"

"Karim telephoned to say he missed me, so I came back."

Tarik made no response.

"What's going on with Tomlinson?" White-Lyons persisted.

"I don't know. You tell me."

"He said it was personal. What could be personal between you and the CIA station chief?"

Annoyed, Tarik walked on. "I asked him to look into some business with Stanley Cobb."

"It's that woman, isn't it? Didn't I warn you?"

"A hundred times."

"Well, he's here."

"So you said. I'll see him."

They walked quickly up the corridor, White-Lyons a little breathless struggling to keep up. He was almost sixty-six years old, but his pale eyes were unblinking as ever. When he looked up at Tarik his face shone with the same admiration and interest that had been there a decade before, a small miracle considering that he had come to understand, finally, that Tarik meant to exclude him from the business of the state and that the adventure was not to be shared. So he had swallowed his grief, dug deep and found reasons for going on, for being almost useful, and every day summoned the will to pretend that black was white and that he could make a difference, the familiar tap-dance of the deluded. These things, however, he could consider only in the abstract, or, at the very most, in their minimal effect. That he had lived his life with the ambition of sharing its close with Tarik and that Tarik had almost from the beginning shown him nothing but contempt—well, some truths are too much for even the stiffest spine to bear. So White-Lyons swung his spindly legs over the edge of his bed every morning, scraped off his white whiskers without looking too deeply into his mirror, and convinced himself that everything was working out and that it was only a matter of time before Tarik saw the light.

In the meantime, he kept himself busy. He trained the bodyguard and the household guard, he devised and set up a small intelligence network—familiar work to the man who had operated Turkit's secret service—keeping tabs on the American advisers. Neither Tarik nor Elliott Tomlinson knew anything about this last activity, and White-Lyons intended to keep it that way. He rattled around the palace, operating much as he had for decades, almost supernaturally impervious to Tarik's intolerance, his own love unqualified and nonjudgmental. He understood better than any of them the essentials of survival. He understood even better than Tarik the risk of Olson and his crew. If only he could get a word in edgewise, he would tell Tarik and then the young man would view him differently. Might treat him with respect. Might forgive that long-ago crime.

"When you're done with Tomlinson, I'd like to see you," he said.

"No, the World Bank people are here."

"You don't need them."

"It's a courtesy call."

"Later, then. I've got something important to discuss with you."

"Later I'm going out to the countryside with Stanley and Karim, then up to the Sur."

"That's not on your schedule!"

"I've changed the schedule. The clear air will do Karim some good."

"Hadi wants to see you too."

"Hadi çan wait."

"No, he can't."

"He'll wait if you tell him to. Tell him to wait."

"He'll be furious."

"Tell him I'll see him when I get back."

"He'll be in the countryside."

"Dammit, White-Lyons. Figure it out with him yourself, then."
Abruptly he turned on his heel and stormed off, half running up
the stairs to the hallway that led to his office.

The walls of an anteroom off the corridor were covered with worn
damask silk in a pattern of the English countryside—riders and
hounds chased a fox over faded green hillocks. Trailing his finger
along the silk, Elliott Tomlinson followed the hunt scene over
fences and hills until, behind a mahogany writing table pushed
against a far wall, he came upon its gruesome conclusion. On a
foot-square patch near the woodwork, the hounds tore the fox
limb from limb.

Shocked, Tomlinson pulled back, made a face, and folded his
arms over his chest, a little indignant. Whatever else, he'd never
harmed an animal.

He turned his attention to the writing table, which he guessed
was either George II or George III. He'd learned a little something
about English antiques since he'd been in the kingdom. The country was loaded with furniture and silver pieces worth a fortune in
London and New York, and he'd made a little side business of ex-
porting them for sale. He ran his hand over the rectangular
desktop, some of the beeswax polish gathering under his fingernails, then opened all the drawers, which were empty. He
shrugged his shoulders and was about to check his watch again,
when he noticed the recessed paneled cupboard in the kneehole.
He stooped, tugged at the pull, which was stuck or locked, pulled
a penknife from his pocket, and was in the process of prizing it
open when Tarik walked in.

Flustered, he jerked to his feet.

"Ah, you can't have this one, Tomlinson," Tarik said in a teas-
ing tone. "It's George III, you know. Too good to sell."

"I don't want it. I dropped something. I was looking for it."

"A penknife?"

"Yeah."

"It's there in your hand."

The room, already small, seemed to shrink, and Tomlinson was aware, as he always was in Tarik's presence, of his own thin legs, his paltry hair, his pale, sunburned skin. He constantly felt dwarfed by the large, confident Tarik. He was waiting for the time in his life when he wouldn't care about his looks, especially in the presence of an attractive man. He was waiting for the day when the moral imperative of his philosophy would convey to his psyche the news that while he lacked physical stature, ethically he towered. But that day was not yet at hand. Not when with Tarik he just felt stumpy and ugly, and pissed off because of it. He tried to take the offensive. "I've been waiting almost an hour."

"Have you? I was with Arthur Olson in Duru. We were grounded by a dust storm for most of the morning. So, what have you found out?"

"Can we talk in there?" He indicated Tarik's office.

"Better here." Tarik had already taken the anteroom's only chair, his body language leaving no doubt who was superior, so Tomlinson had no choice but to stand while he stated his business. He tried to load some righteous indignation into his voice.

"This isn't my usual line of work, you know, checking up on stray wives like this."

"I'm sure."

"Not me."

"Okay."

"Only when it relates to national interest, that's what I mean. I don't like sneaking after errant wives if it doesn't serve any national purpose." His eyeglasses seemed to steam in the heat.

"Does it ever?"

"Does what?"

"Does it ever serve a national purpose to track down errant wives?"

"Sometimes."

"So you've done it before, then?"

Dry-throated, Tomlinson pulled a ball-point pen from his breast pocket and clicked it up and down while he mentally counted to ten.

He decided he would ignore the question and removed a small black notebook from his pants pocket and began reading in a monotone. "Sirah Thompkins Cobb—she's thirty-four by the way, not thirty. In the past twelve months, eight exit visas, all to London and Paris. She leases a flat in Grosvenor Square, five large rooms painted red as a whorehouse. She knows lots of guys in London, but chiefly there are two—one, a low-level cultural attaché at the French embassy, the other, an Englishman, a rare-pictures dealer with a gallery in Mayfair. It's pretty basic stuff—shopping, clubs, restaurants. The nighttime gets a little stickier. The Frenchman used to be posted to Algiers, so he has lots of creepy Third World connections hanging around, lots of drugs. Sex is Sirah's thing—so her drug tastes are pretty uneventful—a little coke, lots of hashish—but the Brit and the Frenchman don't mind popping their skin with hard stuff. Sexwise, the Frog takes it up the ass with anything or anyone who'll do it to him. We have photos of the three of them together in bed"—he started to pull the photos out of his pocket, but Tarik held up his hand—"No? Okay. Pretty hot stuff. Guys and guys, guys and gals. Your friend Cobb keeps her on a tight leash financially, but she has managed to build up a hefty bank account in London, which I'll bet he doesn't know about." He went back to his notebook. "Almost forty-five thousand pounds. Usually, she stays at the London apartment for a week or so, then packs up fifty or sixty suitcases full of expensive new clothes and moves on to Paris, where she spends some more money and then comes home.

" 'Course she's a busy little girl here too, though by necessity much more careful. When Cobb is in Duru she stays behind here in the city doing her usual thing. She's not too discriminating, I might add: Any old soldier or hod carrier will do. Get this, one night she did eighteen guys in a storeroom in the old city, a regular Messalina. We searched their home—hope you don't mind. She's got a suitcase full of cash in the back of a closet in her bedroom. You might want to mention that to Cobb, if you plan on mentioning any of this to him, that is."

He did a quick review of his notes. "That's about it. The usual suck and fuck. Looks like the husband is the last to know, as usual."

He flipped the little spiral notebook closed and returned it to his pocket, then cracked his knuckles in a gesture of self-satisfaction. " 'Course, I can't believe any of this comes as a surprise. She was a slut when he married her."

Tomlinson was pleased to note that when he said this, Tarik's eyelids briefly flickered, and like an archer who has found his range, he made a mental note to remember which barb had reached its mark.

"Of course, I won't bring it up with anyone," he added.

"Good." Tarik stood up and gave him his hand.

"You want me to follow up with this?"

"No, that's not necessary. I know all I need to."

"I'll call off the dogs," Tomlinson added as Tarik pushed open the door that led to his office and exited.

Tomlinson stood alone in the anteroom for a moment. He'd hit a soft spot all right with the bit about Sirah, and this had made him wonder suddenly about other vulnerabilities. He had always ceded the upper hand to Tarik as a natural act. Now it occurred to him that Tarik's family and friends might offer tempting, tender targets with which to prick him. He'd keep the surveillance going on Sirah, and maybe, just for the fun of it, go over everybody's background when he was back in Washington for meetings the following month. Maybe even drop a bug here and there around the city and in the Sur. Never know what might turn up.

Tomlinson bounced a little on his toes as he walked down the hallway, feeling better than he had in a long time, and thinking that, yardsticks to the contrary, he might be able to add an inch or two to his height. Anyway, he'd survived another meeting with Tarik with his balls intact, although he flicked his hands over them furtively, just to be sure.

Karim adored ice cream. He loved ice cream so much, in fact, that there was nothing he would rather have, although Stan never tired of trying to tempt him.

"Ice cream, or steering your father's Land-Rover?"

"Ice cream!"

"Okay." Stan racked his brain for another challenge. "Ice cream, or tickling Het's feet?" A desperate offer.

Karim looked shocked. Tickling Het's feet, or any other of his body parts, was the last thing he wanted to do. He didn't even deign to glance at Stan, just mouthed the words, "Ice cream."

Karim was a pale, thin little boy, sickly-looking almost, with none of his father's height or coloring, or his mother's either, for that matter. His hair was a shade of nicotine, his eyes amber moons, and at nearly six years of age he had the height and weight of a three-year-old. He resembled no one in Tarik's family, nor anyone in Topaz's. He could have been from the moon or from Mars for all his resemblance to any family member.

He seemed so puny and weak. He couldn't go up a flight of stairs without complaining, and he never won at games with other boys his age. Not that he cared about games or roughhousing anyway. He played at them only because everyone expected him to—and Karim was very shrewd at discerning what others wanted. If he had his way, he would read storybooks and cook on the big iron stove in the kitchen and chit-chat all day; those were the

things he did best. Besides, he knew better than anyone that his
frail appearance belied his true constitution. Except for the normal
childhood ailments, he hadn't been sick a day in his life. Karim,
whose skin was sheer as the skin of a pearl and who seemed every moment to be on the verge of coming down with some bug
that might carry him off to the shade world, was, in fact, healthy
as a horse. Let the world believe him weak as a willow, to
Karim's own way of thinking he was strong and tall and quite a
guy.

This truth almost none except White-Lyons could grasp. Although Tarik tried hard to see his son as the healthy boy he really
was, he stared at those bony legs and anemic complexion and lost
sleep worrying.

Poor Karim, under daily assault from Topaz's tribal/herbal rem-
edies, Stanley's wheat germ/whey health drinks, Het's buffalo
milk and exercise regimen in hopes of adding inches to his height
and roses to his cheeks. But he remained pale, wan, and, incongruously, full of life. Karim coughed but never caught cold; perspired profusely but was never febrile; slept little but never
seemed tired.

A bundle of contradictions physically, his personality was
equally tangled—one minute coy and charming, the next feisty,
with a wicked temper. And he had a decidedly unchildlike talent
for playing people as if they were violins. There were men in their
eighties who understood less about human nature than Karim
seemed to at five. He could spot vanity at ten feet and hypocrisy
at twenty. His red-rimmed eyes missed nothing in wordless assessments of character that came with the quickness of a kite tail
catching the wind.

The mystery was that everybody understood this about Karim,
could feel themselves being cunningly manipulated, and yet no
one objected or was even offended, because Karim's greatest skill
was to make each one in turn believe that he loved them best. To
make each feel that he was devoted to him and him alone and
grateful in the extreme to be loved in return.

Maybe his complicated personality resulted naturally from his
complicated birth.

For nine months Topaz carried "the heir" through alternating
loops of elated self-congratulation and skidding despair. Suppose
she delivered to Tarik—and to posterity—a child of the female order? Or a lifeless child? Or a dimwit, like her dead brother
Azarak, or all her brothers, for that matter?

Suppose fate collected all those scary, aberrant family genes over a hundred generations and wired them somehow to her baby, then compounded its abuse by making that baby female? Not that Topaz understood the nature of genes. Not that she considered that she might get a second crack at delivering a boy if the first child were a girl—or a third, or a fourth.

No, for Topaz there were but two outcomes of her pregnancy: either she is declared the mother of the nation, or she is cast out onto the plain to die alone and disgraced under the killing sun, shame of the country. In fact, Topaz's fears were not so outrageous. She was, after all, Hadi's daughter, and in her family household there were only life-or-death solutions to any problem.

So as the days came near when the mystery of her fate would be conveyed, Topaz became more and more agitated. She hid herself away to sob for hours, sometimes crouching on a cement bench in a small, tucked-away garden within the palace alongside a forgotten potting shed and greenhouse. Tarik found her there one evening a month before Karim was born.

"Why are you crying?" He sat down next to her on the bench and put his arm around her shoulder. He could not help but pity her; she was so pathetic. "Topaz, what's wrong? Has someone hurt you?"

She sobbed convulsively.

"Tell me," he demanded gently. She shook her head.

Genuinely concerned, he came down on one knee and hunted for her face within the enveloping folds of her gown. After a wrestle he managed to take her chin in his hand and raise it to his own face. Her features were so destroyed, her misery so apparent, he threw his arms around her and rocked her quietly for a long time.

Just when it seemed she might be calm enough to speak, there was another flood of tears. He coaxed her more, she hiccuped, blew her nose on his jacket, and declared, "I am a dead woman."

Shocked, he reared back. "No. Never."

"I am."

"Because of the pain? Is that it? You're afraid of childbirth?"

"No."

"You're sure?"

"No."

"You're afraid you'll die in childbirth, is that it?"

She chewed on her lip for a moment and then shook her head vigorously.

Tarik racked his brain. He meant to help her, but clues were in short supply.

"You're not afraid of the pain—?"

"Maybe a little."

"A little afraid of the pain. That's understandable. But not afraid you'll die?"

She shook her head side to side. Her tears had ceased and her face had brightened a little. She now seemed more interested in whether he could guess what caused her heartbreak than in revealing the heartbreak itself.

He pulled her to her feet and sat down with her on the little bench. It would have been helpful if she had told him what was making her so unhappy, but clearly she wanted him to discover it for himself. He thought she might be enjoying the attention and immediately felt sorry for her, and guilty.

"Please tell me why you're crying so. Let me help you. Has someone said something to you?" They were back where they started.

"No."

"It's something you're afraid someone will say?"

Her eyes sparkled. He was getting warm.

"Something about the baby? You're worried about when the baby is born?" More vigorous nodding. "About the baby itself?" Her head snapped like a flag caught in the breeze. "You're worried about the baby itself? You're worried it won't be healthy? You're worried"—he lowered his voice—"are you worried that it won't be a male?"

At that, she slid from the bench into a pile at his feet in what seemed to him at first to be a faint. She was so clearly relieved to unburden her fears after all these months that he let her alone for a moment to rest while he studied her with a great deal of pity. She'd been raised in a family where the patriarch exercised his whim in the worst kind of brutality, in a country where until just the other day homicide was considered the natural antidote to even the most trivial personal slight.

"Topaz, whatever happens with the baby—and nothing will, be sure of that—it won't be your fault. Haven't you eaten well? Haven't you followed every instruction Dr. Van Damm gave you? You've taken your vitamins. You've been examined every three weeks. You rest, you exercise. There's absolutely nothing you can reproach yourself for. The baby will be healthy, whatever its sex."

She squared her shoulders and a little testily said, "This is fine for you to say. You won't be the one driven out onto the plain if the child is female."

"That doesn't happen anymore. Things have changed."

"Not for the other they didn't."

"What other?"

She hesitated, wondering if she should speak what was in her heart. "The blond one," she said finally, between her teeth. "Your blond wife. She wasn't suitable, so she was sent away."

She had been wanting to say that for the longest time, but from his sharp intake of breath and the sudden flatness of his expression, she saw immediately she'd made a mistake. If only they could speak about the first wife. If she could be sure in her heart that he had put that marriage behind him, looked into his heart and realized that he loved the soon-to-be mother of his child, she would feel much better.

"That was different," he answered in a voice she couldn't read.

"But she wasn't suitable and she was sent away."

"Different."

"But how can—?"

"I don't want to discuss it. Anyway, we have a good marriage, don't we?"

"Yes."

"And I'm a good husband to you?"

"Yes . . ." She longed to tell him that sometimes when he slept he cried out gibberish in his sleep that she imagined was some strange American longing for the blond wife, but she didn't dare.

"And we're going to have a healthy child, boy or girl, whom we will love and cherish very much?"

"Yes."

"All right, then. You have nothing to fear. Besides, if anyone is driven anywhere, Topaz, it should be me. The male is the one who determines the sex of the child."

She stared at him empty-eyed.

"The male determines the sex," he repeated.

"No!"

"Yes. It's been scientifically proven. An element in the male's sperm determines the sex."

She digested this for some time, tempted to believe. It would be so much easier if Tarik was correct, but she'd never heard of such a thing. Everyone knew that a woman's body somehow decided whether a boy or girl baby would be born. Every woman knew at least one other woman whose disgruntled husband had divorced her—or worse—for giving him female children.

Her own sister Mira, who was her authority in all matters, had told her with conviction that the birth of a son could be guaranteed through secret spoken incantations and animal sacrifices—

very small animals in Topaz's case. Bugs, actually. She loved animals and couldn't bear thinking something small and helpless, like a bird or a baby rabbit, would die owing to her own body's failure. Topaz had pretended to take all of Mira's advice, but secretly she followed the regimen set down for her by Dr. Van Damm and then the American obstetrician Tarik had brought over from the States as her time came closer. He was a nice man, and she did what he told her, not especially out of belief or even trust, but because she loved Tarik and would rather die than seem backward in his eyes.

But here was more heretical thinking, more information contrary to everything Mira had ever told her, and it made her mind cloud over and her arms and legs weary.

"I don't believe you. You're so kind, you're trying to spare me the punishment if I fail."

"I'm not lying. It's true. I can prove it. Let's go ask the doctor. Let's do it right now. He'll get you the scientific literature."

She stuck out her bottom lip pathetically. "You know I can't read."

"I'll read it to you. The male determines the sex. That's all there is to it."

A week later, only after the obstetrician had a colleague in the U.S. express some material to him, which Tarik read to her with painstaking slowness followed by elaborate explanations, did she believe.

So, for a brief time the great burden floated away from Topaz's shoulders and she was free. But when Karim was born after a torturous thirty hours of labor four weeks later, she was right back where she started. Her son was frail and appeared sickly, as if he might not live through every new day, and for this, it can be said that Topaz, although blameless, was responsible. Until her marriage she had been half-starved like everyone else in the kingdom, and her malnourished body bore permanent damage that not even the ministrations of two physicians could reverse. Eventually, Karim added pounds—never many—grew teeth and hair, and walked at nine months, although his rickety legs were so shaky everyone ceased breathing when he took staggering steps.

He spoke in whole sentences at fourteen months, could read single-syllable words at two years, and storybooks at three and a half. He was intelligent and clever, but by the time he was four, no matter how much anyone tried to interest him in boyish pastimes, animals, or toys, or, later, trucks and games, the only things that ever intrigued Karim—and they occupied him obsessively—were other human beings.

He couldn't have cared less about nature. It was the two-legged variety of animal he was passionate for, male or female. How their brains worked, how their bodies worked. He asked the most detailed questions about bodily functions with all the detachment of a clinician. Why did one make water? Why do noses drip? Where are the ends of teeth going? How are babies born?

And you couldn't pull the wool over his eyes with drivel about storks or cabbage leaves or birds and bees; Karim was too smart for that. He wanted the nuts and bolts, anatomic descriptions, and after he was given them, he pulled down his drawers, inspected his own little penis with keen interest, and begged to see his mother's private parts, to her demonstrated horror. He made lengthy genealogical charts to understand family relationships, took oral biographies of anyone he could convince to give him the time. He listened to Cook pour out her troubles with her husband, one little leg crossed over the other, shaking his head gravely at each marital transgression. He watched Het with patient detachment, eyeing the giant up and down, the two of them on the same wavelength with no words involved.

He asked the most personal questions without flinching, was usually remonstrated harshly for the habit, then answered in intimate detail for hours and hours.

He seemed impervious to weather, to hunger, to anything but what was to him the fascinating ongoing saga of humans trying to make sense of their lives. Nothing else seemed to matter.

Tarik watched all this with no small amount of amusement, for the boy was completely lovable. Looking at his son, wondering on which moonbeam he had floated to earth, Tarik believed he was the most natural politician he had ever known, although he worried about the day when Karim's wants wouldn't be limited to ice cream. Once in a while he tried to instill in him a little instructive morality.

When Karim and Stan finished the ice cream game, Tarik pulled the little boy onto his knee. Karim, who loved to cuddle, wrapped Tarik's long arms around him and prepared to be loved.

"You know, son, you're a clever boy. I can tell when you make people give you what you want without their realizing it. You get them so turned around, they don't know quite what's going on."

Silence.

"You have to be careful not to make people feel you're using

them. The other day I heard you ask Het to give you the last bite
of his pie. And you know how much Het loves pie."

"But Het was happy. Het's always happy if I eat."

"That's true, but—"

"And there was more pie."

"No, that was the last piece."

"But there *will* be more pie. Het can ask Cook to bake him a
pie."

"If Cook has time."

"Everyone has time for Het. Everyone's scared of Het—but
me."

"You're not scared?"

"Nah, Het told me he liked me."

"Het told you he liked you? Het doesn't talk to anybody. He
doesn't even talk to me. Are you sure he told you he liked you?"

"Um, yes. He told me with his eyes. Het has very quiet eyes.
Noisy guns but quiet eyes, and I read a message there."

"Really?"

"I can read, you know."

"I know you can read books, but I didn't know you could read
eyes."

"Eyes and hands. The colonel told me a person's hands tell as
much about a person's heart as what comes out of their mouths.
So I can read what's in people's hearts that way. Except Mother.
Her hands are always moving, so I can't read the message fast
enough. Your hands are quiet. Like Het's eyes. Your hands are
big. Look"—he held up Tarik's hand and then measured his own
tiny one against it—"my hands are small but just 'cause they're
small doesn't mean they're not nice. It just means that what's
written in my heart is written in very tiny letters, but there's a lot
of writing."

Tarik cleared his throat. "But back to the pie, Karim. You
know, when you ask for something, people feel they have to give
it to you because you're my son. They're afraid they'll get into
trouble if they don't give you what you want."

Karim said nothing, so Tarik tickled his leg a little. "Did you
hear me?"

"Uh-huh."

"You'll remember when you ask for something again."

"I'll remember. But does this mean I can't ask for anything
ever again?"

"No, but you shouldn't ask for things that are difficult for people to give, or are a sacrifice for them to give you."

"But you do that all the time!"

"No."

"Yes, you do. Remember when we were in Switzerland? I heard you telling Mother that she couldn't have that diamond necklace she saw in the store window in the hotel because it wasn't right for her to walk around like the Queen of Sheba when so many other people have less. You told her she had to make a sacrifice."

"That was different."

"Oh."

"It was, and it's important for you to know the difference. Circumstances are what count here. You know what I mean."

Karim chewed his lip silently.

"You know what I mean, Karim, I know you do."

"Yes, I do. I know the difference. But trust me, Father." He jabbed the air with a thin finger and spoke emphatically, emphasizing every word: "Het—wanted—me—to—have—the—pie."

Tarik sighed, set the boy down, and stood up. "Probably he did, Karim. Knowing Het, probably he wanted you to have the pie. Anyway, I've got to go to work."

"We'll talk again soon, okay, Father?"

"Of course."

"But not about pie."

"No, no more about Het's pie."

It irritated Tarik that Karim loved White-Lyons and spent so much time with him. He had ostracized the man from his own personal life and he was jealous and resentful that his son found him so attractive. But then, Karim got along with everyone and had no enemies. To him the colonel was not old or obsolete, but an endless storybook of thrilling war stories and throbbing history lessons, full of bloodthirsty warriors and the worst kinds of murder. Like most young children, Karim loved grisly stories, the bloodier the better. White-Lyons didn't disappoint him, even treating him to tales of Turkit's most heinous crimes, some censorship applied in case of nightmares, of course. And if that weren't enough, he let Karim handle the guns. Het wouldn't let him so much as touch the muzzle of his Uzi with a fingernail, but White-Lyons let Karim break down the old Webley, clean it, pull the trigger if it was empty, and sometimes, not always, touch the cartridges. When Karim was a little older, White-Lyons promised, he would take him down a secret staircase to the very bottom of the palace, where no one could hear, and let him actually shoot the Webley. Karim trembled with anticipation at the prospect.

When they were together in public, White-Lyons insisted on proper military bearing, snapping off salutes, which he expected Karim to return briskly. But in private it was another matter. Karim never bothered to flirt with White-Lyons as he did with everyone else. Instinctively he understood that the man was immune to charm, so he learned quickly that he would do better to state his business plainly to get what he wanted. In his brown oxford shoes, Karim would walk—he never ran—down the corridor to the colonel's apartments, knock lightly on the door, and enter. A relaxed White-Lyons would be waiting for him in the big chintz-covered armchair in the bedroom, his army tunic folded neatly on the bed, the black suspenders anchored on his shoulders over a crisp white undershirt.

Karim would scramble into his lap and monkey with the suspenders while White-Lyons unspooled his fantastic tales. If the stories were particularly good or heart-thumping, Karim would wince and pinch White-Lyons's hands during the especially brutal parts, then kiss each finger one by one in gratitude when the tales came to their rousing ends. Afterward, he would ask White-Lyons to tell him about his boyhood in England, and about his mother, whose name was Ann, and his brother William, who died at age nine under the blades of a threshing machine. The thought of little William harvested along with the wheat always made Karim sob, and the colonel would have to hug him close to console him and explain that everything happened for a reason that only God might understand.

Tarik came upon them once like this and was so upset he turned on his heel and left—not because Karim was being so affectionate. He cuddled with everyone. But because the sight of a tender White-Lyons was too revolting for him to bear. In his mind he had dehumanized the man, and nothing, not even the sight of his little son in his arms, would be allowed to change that.

With his native intelligence Karim intuited the tension between his father and White-Lyons. He was too shrewd to ever question his father, but when Tarik pointedly excluded White-Lyons from family dinners or gatherings, Karim would give him a long, penetrating stare, then set off down the hallway to White-Lyons's rooms to let him know that he was loved, at least by a little boy in oxford shoes.

In White-Lyons's arms Karim allowed his brain to rebound with the Technicolor history of the kingdom, but no tale was more exciting or heart-swelling to him than that of Malik. Better still, the colonel had old black and white photos in a trunk under his bed—Malik on his charger, an Enfield rifle over his shoulder; Malik seated cross-legged outside his campaign tent, the eyes searing the camera lens; Malik and White-Lyons together, taken by a journalist from *The Times* of London. A small photo of Nila with Tarik in her arms. Four altogether, shuffled and reshuffled over the years until they slipped easily from the colonel's hands into Karim's and back again, shared and reverent nostalgia.

So while Topaz and the others twitched and jerked over his health, mussed his hair and pinched his cheeks, Karim, frail little boy that he was, made the Malik tale part of himself, decided he possessed the same heroic stature of his grandfather, and never, ever was ill.

21

For an instant, Stanley Cobb pondered putting on a light. Sitting in the dark for hours hadn't done anything for his spirits, nor had the half-bottle of Wild Turkey he'd consumed already. He reached out and made a feeble effort to flip on the light switch, but his arm fell back into his lap. What was the point? The sun itself couldn't lighten his mood. Better to sit in the dark. Better to get right down into it and just get curdled.

For at least the tenth time in five minutes he sighed loudly, the down-deep rattle of a ruined man. Finally, he slammed his empty glass down on the delicate tortoiseshell table beside him, grabbed the liquor bottle, roused his legs, and walked outside to the terrace, a patchwork of marble flagstones overshadowed by impeccable imported palms. In the center of the terrace was a marble reflecting pool, around which were marble dolphins with braided tails upholding marble fountains that ran water but could be made to flow champagne or colored bubbles, depending on the owner's whim.

But the elaborate terrace was incidental compared to the interior of the four-story home—no, villa—he had built in the new part of the capital city, just outside the old city walls, the most lavish, most expensive, most unrepentently gaudy in the country. The memory of Turkit's wives' quarters in the west wing of the palace had been burned into his brain. To Stan's way of thinking, those rooms were the apex of luxurious good taste. When he built his dream home, he ordered the exact same thing, with extras.

Every room shimmered with gold, every support column spiraled gold veins with golden *torchères* at their bases, a thousand gilded arabesques covered the ceilings. The place was an architectural tribute to Italian and French styles and its facade was colonnaded to a fare-thee-well. The furniture was of ivory, or mahogany and other precious woods, flamboyantly decorated with gold and brilliant colors. The walls of the salons were covered with silk, and lush brocades and shimmering satins covered the chairs, divans, and ottomans that lined every side of every room, sometimes two-deep, and all twenty-four rooms were heated with hot water pipes under the marble floors, a mindless extravagance in a country where the temperature rarely dropped below sixty degrees Fahrenheit, even on the coolest nights.

The beds were handmade in Syria, inlaid with mother-of-pearl and turquoise, the dinner service solid gold, the colossal chandeliers Bohemian crystal, the ceilings in the main salon elaborately painted, with lanceted windows. Every enameled porcelain vase was worth a fortune, every girandole that dripped from solid silver table lamps was cut Venetian crystal. Even the bottom of the swimming pool was veined in eighteen-karat gold, its cement walls painted to resemble marble. It was a place of sumptuous fantasy, of mind-boggling extravagance, of no holds barred, of doubtful taste and plenty of it. The home, in short, of a really big spender.

And why not? Hadn't Stanley Cobb, lately of Playland, the Great Highway, California, and a hundred other compass points—hadn't Stanley Cobb made a fortune, a *fucking* fortune, in the oil fields at Duru? Hadn't he held the biggest lease on the biggest oil hole in the whole kingdom? And hadn't that hole pumped liquid gold every day for years—*every day*? So, wasn't it Stanley Cobb's business if he wanted to sink a few million of his millions into chairs and chandeliers and solid silver toasters for his very own private one-man's castle? Of course it was.

The second part of the question: And if this same Stanley Cobb had a wife, a young, beautiful, mind-stoppingly sexy wife who spent his money as if it were water, who disappeared into European cities for weeks at a time, who *dated* (the cuckold's euphemism) other men, who flayed raw his nerves and self-esteem, well, if this man wanted to keep his wife no matter what the price—temporal or spiritual—was it anybody's business but his own? No, it wasn't.

He released another deep sigh as contentment mingled with intemperate self-righteousness, nagging doubt in hot pursuit.

Tarik was his friend. In his life Stanley had never known such loyalty, such love, shy as that thought made him. Were it not for Tarik, he would be a common job-holder, maybe digging ditches in some East Jesus place like Dar es Salaam, a loser once again instead of a man of wealth and power, which he was.

Tarik had taken him all the way up to the Sur to deliver the bad news because he knew that Stan loved it up there and hoped the breathtaking vistas and the hospitable Sur people would soften the blow. Thought that Karim, lively and full of talk, would show him some hope for living. That was friendship. That was a man who cared that another man was in a state of emotional and physical collapse.

If his best friend Tarik said that Sirah was double-dealing him, stealing his hard-earned money, putting drugs up her nose and letting any man who looked good to her put his—he couldn't finish the thought—then it had to be true. He would have been pissed off purple if it had come from anyone else, but from Tarik, well, he'd had to take it like a man.

Not that he hadn't always had his own doubts about her, but like all those in love with the faithless, self-delusion companioned love in easy accommodation. Years ago Stanley had rewritten his marital history. He'd elected to overlook the fact that the first time he'd seen his wife, an oil prospector old as Methuselah was fingering her private parts by the light of a Coleman lamp, under the noses of three dozen men. In Stan's revisionist version of his wife's history, she was less than a whore, more than a waitress. Kind of a massage parlor hostess.

He believed, then, that his love would save her, the way her love had rescued him, and turn her from mattress-back into wife and mother. Well, *face it, Cobb*, the makeover hadn't taken, and while he might deny his own suspicions, he could not ignore Elliott Tomlinson's hard evidence. Not even Stan Cobb, as Stan had told Tarik that morning, can fall into a pile of shit and call it roses.

Which didn't mean that he was out of hope for his marriage. This wasn't Stanley's Waterloo, or even Valley Forge. It was more like Munich. Because despite dire warnings and looming disaster, Stan had opted for accommodation.

Feeling his gut grinding, he poked three hairy fingers under his rib cage and winced. His stomach was on fire. The pain had been there for weeks, starting slowly but building up over the last couple of days till it felt like a hot poker had been stuck in his entrails. He gritted his teeth against the agony. No need to speculate about a sour gut any longer. He'd made a self-diagnosis—cancer. He'd caught "the cancer" from worrying over Sirah.

In the dark of the night, with only the glow of the eighteen-karat-gold trim of his fountains to enlighten his musings, Stanley threw his mind into the grim future. He saw himself sick, wasted, alone. Who would hold his hand while the disease ate him down to bone? Whose ear would catch his dying words? Not Sirah, who was always off somewhere else, who was never home to share a meal, a confidence, or even bicker with him before bedtime. Not Sirah.

His eyes brimmed with tears and he raised them to heaven so the tears wouldn't spill. After a minute he recomposed himself, rubbed his face, and located the comforting North Star. A shooting star skittered past and he made a wish, a prayer really. If it were true that his life was waning, please God let him live every moment now.

There were pear trees in the small park beyond the terrace, and even from a hundred yards he could smell their fragrant blossoms. He made a mental note to walk out there in the morning. He didn't care for pears especially, but he loved the pear tree blossoms and he didn't want to miss out on their fleeting beauty. Spread out there on the grass, they reminded him of a crocheted afghan that had covered his bed when he was a boy. His mother had made it for him by hand. His mother. She would have nursed him through the cancer he was now certain he had. She would have pressed her lips to his in a farewell kiss, put her ear to his lips to catch his dying words.

He put the bottle to his mouth and sucked down another consoling drink. A door thudded shut somewhere in the huge house and he pricked up his ears. He had given the staff the night off so that he could be alone with Sirah when she came home.

With the bottle still in his hand, he pushed aside the fluttering silk panels that divided the terrace from the main salon and walked cautiously, straining to hear any sound other than the clack of his own heels on the marble floors.

He turned out of the salon and crossed the colonnaded pavilion that formed the front room of the house. The huge crystal chandeliers had been dimmed, but in the thin light of a wall sconce he caught sight of Sirah's golden sandal turning the corner.

He bounded after her unsteadily, shouting, "Come here, Mrs. Cobb. I want to speak with you!"

But Sirah was fast and began to run up the main staircase, fourteen feet wide, to the second floor hallway that led to her private suite of rooms. She slammed the door shut behind her and threw herself, panting with fear, on one of the tiny divans in her sitting room. A second later she jumped up and ran to a bedside table, yanked open a drawer and pulled out a small chrome-plated gun.

Back on the divan, she tucked the gun into the billowing folds of her dress and pressed her feet tight to the floor.

After a lot of loud banging on the locked door, Stanley brought it down with a crash and reeled into the room.

She had never seen him drunk before. He always held his liquor without the slightest change in manner no matter how much he drank. With total contempt she watched him try to heave himself to his feet. *I should shoot him now. I could say that he was drunk and came after me and that I had to shoot him to defend myself.*

But she hesitated and in that moment of indecision Stanley lumbered over and seized her throat in his hands. Her hand felt around in the folds of her dress for the gun, but it had slipped down into the cushion of the divan. Terrified, she struggled against him. "Stanley," she gasped.

He mocked her drunkenly. *"Stanley!"*

"Stanley—" Her eyes rolled back in her head. She was more afraid than she had ever been in her life. He leaned over her, his face black and brutal. *God, but he's ugly. I'm being killed by a big hairy ape.*

He increased the pressure of his hands on her throat and her head fell back. The pain was unbearable and she tore furiously at his fingers. She was as angry as she was panicked, enraged to think that the ape would murder Sirah. Beautiful Sirah, the desired object of every natural man's lust. This reversal made no sense at all—men should kill for her. In the part of her brain that still worked, she decided she would not let the ape kill her without a price, and that she wouldn't die easily or quietly, for that matter. He could kill her, but he was going to remember for the rest of his life how much she hated him. With her final ounce of strength she rolled her eyes around and glared at him.

He had never seen such hating eyes. They bulged, and the whites seemed to go yellow while he watched, appalled.

The death rattle in her throat, she gasped, "Do it! Do it!"

At that, something was driven out of him and he slumped onto the floor beside her. He reached for the discarded whiskey bottle and drank slowly, watching her over the rim.

Sirah collapsed on the divan, panting for breath and trying to keep from trembling. With her long black hair hanging over her face, she fought to regain control of her body. She had a terrible urge to urinate, but she was back among the living now and remembered that she'd paid two thousand dollars for her gown in Paris and had no desire to ruin it. Minutes passed; it seemed like years. Her breath returned and she calmed her features. She lifted her head defiantly and threw her long mop of hair down her back.

Stanley sprawled on the floor, staring at her. But the instant she looked into his teary eyes, her nerves relaxed. She attempted to stand, but he threw himself so violently around her legs that they both tumbled back onto the little sofa.

"Sirah—"

"Get away from me!"

"Sirah, I'm sorry. I didn't mean it."

"Yes, you did. You tried to kill me, you bastard. Get out of my sight. I'm calling the police. You're out of your mind."

"No, Sirah, don't. Please . . ." Another sharp pain split his gut and he gulped air. He wiped his hand over his mouth, his eyes full of tears. He tried to imagine what Tarik would do if he were there. Kick her out, bag and baggage—but then, Tarik had always done the right thing, hadn't he? Right from the beginning? He'd bitten the bullet in a big way—he'd given up Clare. Stanley realized a shared strength remembering this and felt courageous for the first time.

He squared his shoulders. "I know everything," he said firmly.

Her quiet voice covered her alarm. "What did you say?"

"I know all the secrets you've been keeping."

She tried to sound casual and shook her leg slowly back and forth in a show of indifference. "I don't have any secrets."

"I know about those men in London, and the money." He snorted in disgust and drank again. "I know there's a suitcase in the closet. What did you think? That you could steal my money and run away with it?"

She stared at him for a very long time with her mouth slack and open, a look on her face that he could not read. Then it seemed to Stanley that she smiled for an instant before the scowl returned.

"I didn't plan on running away with *your* money—which, by the way, you always told me was *our* money. I was putting some away for my mother."

"You're a liar."

She stood and walked to her vanity table, picked up a hairbrush, and furiously began brushing her hair. "Believe what you want to believe. You hate my mother. I asked you to give my mother money and you refused, didn't you? Didn't you?"

He glared at her. "Your mother doesn't deserve my money."

"Except that you did say it was our money. And as far as the men in London are concerned, they're friends, nothing more."

"That's not true! I have the photos."

"Show them to me."

He dropped his head. He didn't have the photos. In fact, he hadn't even seen them. Tarik had said they existed and that was enough for him.

"I didn't want to see them. I didn't want to see my wife for the whore she is."

She crossed her arms over her chest and assessed him with narrowed eyes. After a moment she said, "Tarik is behind this, isn't he?"

"No."

"You can't fool me. Tarik and that miserable White-Lyons. I'm not good enough for their precious Stanley. They think a big rich guy like you needs another kind of wife. A nun, a saint. Some dried-up old woman, or a numskull like Topaz."

"They're my friends," he said weakly.

"Well, I'm your wife! You don't believe me, you don't trust me, why should I defend myself? I am what I am. Take it or leave it," she said, as if it were already finished between them.

"I love you."

"Trust is gone. When trust is gone, there's no love. There's no point in going on."

The compulsion to cry was almost more than he could bear, but he forced himself to look her in the face and he was astounded to see that she looked ugly to him. Her face shimmered with evil. It could have been anyone's face, just another face. Not the face of his Sirah, who even when buck naked, wagging her bare butt under the hot eyes of a hundred men, still seemed pure as the pear blossoms spread out on the lawn like his mother's afghan. He ought to turn on his heel and run away. Forget about her perfidy, forget about the money, start over with a good woman. But, oh, God, he was in love. Against all reason he wanted her, he loved her, and he needed her to help him die right.

Her eyes were full of challenge. He only felt tired. It was important to put his house in order. What kind of man would he be if he met his Maker with a whipped ass?

"I love you, Sirah. I trust you, but there're going to be some changes around here. There'll be no more trips to London, or anywhere else for that matter. I gave your passport to White-Lyons."

He was shocked when she didn't react violently to this news. He'd expected a firestorm, and when it didn't come, he went on, stronger.

"As far as money goes, you'll be on a regular allowance. You'll get the same amount every week and you'll have to account to me for every penny."

Now the hard part. He began to pace and chop the air with his hand like a man laying down the law. "And you'll stay in the house, except for certain hours when you can take a walk and do a little shopping, maybe. I'm hiring bodyguards for you, and make no mistake, Sirah, they'll be loyal to me. I'm going to pay them plenty to make sure of that. So there'll be no jaunts out on your own around town to warehouses, or whorehouses either." He toughened his voice to let her know he meant business and held up a remonstrating finger. "And unless you're crazy as a shithouse rat, miss, you'll do exactly as I tell you."

"I'm to be your prisoner?"

"Till you prove that you're loyal and worth my trust."

"I'll die."

"No, you won't." He gestured around the room. "Look, Sirah. Look at everything I've given you. You'll be a bird in a gilded cage."

He stepped closer and took the brush out of her hand. "I have to do it, Sirah," he said softly. "I love you and I know what's best for you. I always have." He ran the brush tenderly down her hair. "You'll see. It won't be so bad. We'll be together like we used to be."

He put his arm around her shoulder, tentatively at first, but when she didn't resist, when she almost seemed to welcome it, he pulled her against his chest.

"You love me, don't you, Sirah? You want to start again. I know you do." The pain stabbed. He rubbed his stomach. "I don't feel well, Sirah. I'm sick. I need you to help me now that I'm sick."

She looked up at him, losing his face in the glare of her own ambition. Her mind began flashing death signals, and her anger rolled along easily below the surface calm of her skin. She should have taken her mother's advice. She should have killed him quickly, cleanly. She'd wasted months funneling into his liquor bottles drops of the poisonous solvent the workmen used to clean the marble floors.

No, that was wrong. Her mother had given her stupid advice all her life. She'd made the right choice, taking her time with him. He'd been sick for weeks. If he fell over and died, everyone would see a certain inevitability to it. There'd be no autopsy; the widow's prerogative. Everyone liked him, so there'd be a big, impressive funeral. She could ride in a black Mercedes, perhaps with

Tarik. She'd wear black—no, she'd wear that fine dress of spun gold. She'd choke through her tears that Stanley wouldn't have wanted her in widow's weeds. Look to the future, and all that. After a decent interval she'd take his fortune out of the country and put it in a Swiss bank account, then leave this sun-baked rat hole forever.

She'd get rid of him, and no one would be surprised. She wasn't getting any younger. How long would she have to suffocate with the hairy ape while the pleasure world passed her by? She would be an old woman by the time he died a natural death and left her all his millions. It was only fair, and all her life, whatever Sirah wanted was the only fair thing.

So, with the pain from his ham hands still at her throat, she came to her decision: He goes—quick and fast.

Her stomach was empty and the rush she was getting thinking of the money and men that would be hers was giving her a woozy high.

She closed her hand around his hand and made herself a little bird in his arms. "You're not sick, Stanley," she purred. "I'll take care of you. You need only love to get better. I'll give you love. You'll see."

She batted her black butterfly lashes at him so convincingly that for a moment she almost believed it herself.

For weeks Sirah was as good as her word. She handled her allowance carefully—not that she had many places to spend money since the bodyguards kept her locked in her room for hours every day. Every Tuesday and Thursday they escorted her to shops in the new city, and twice a day she was allowed to walk around the grounds or swim in the pool, although even then she was circumspect, in a shapeless one-piece bathing suit with a bath towel wrapped around her until she slipped into the water. She was a model of rectitude, the very picture of the loyal wife, and although she had a huge staff to handle household chores, she scrubbed floors, dusted the elaborate furniture, wrapped a rag around her head to wash clothes, and performed every wifely duty short of taking the veil in her metamorphosis from Magdalene to Martha and Mary combined.

Completely convinced, Stan was thrilled to his bones by every new domestic wrinkle, especially when Sirah got it into her head to fix his meals right down to the dessert, cakes and pastries that she labored over for hours and that came out of the oven with the consistency of baked bricks. But he swallowed every bite cheerfully, a husband in love. Eventually, Sirah fired the cook, maintaining that a good wife cared for her husband singlehandedly. Except for a woman to shop and prepare the food for cooking and a scullion to clean up afterward, Sirah ran the kitchen herself.

She slapped Stan's hands away when he tried to snag samples from her bubbling pots. "No! You'll ruin your supper," she scolded as if he were a naughty boy, which he adored. Once when she was making a syrupy candy she let him lick the sweet sauce from her finger, very seductive, and that night allowed him to make love to her for the first time in months.

Cossetted by so much attention, Stan's health for a time seemed to improve. The roses bloomed in his cheeks, he gained weight, he lumbered jauntily in the familiar old way when he walked. Briefly, he was again the man who could wield a cant dog around a log boom the way lesser men handled toothpicks. He carried his simian body with the grace that comes to any large, ugly man who discovers to his astonishment that an attractive woman finds him attractive in return.

But then gradually he weakened and the burning in his innards returned—not as sharp, to be sure, but never gone. Yet while hope was exhausted, death now seemed a reasonable exchange for the love Sirah showed him. What might paradise be if this new joy was the price he must pay to achieve it?

Watching Stanley from the balcony off the family living quarters in the palace, Tarik found it impossible to share Stanley's cheery embrace of the Reaper and scoffed at Sirah's newly minted incarnation as submissive wife, doubting it could bear the weight of her true character for much longer. Still, he couldn't throw cold water on the big man's happiness by telling him so, especially since Stanley really did seem quite ill.

"Dyin' jumped-up Jesus, boy-o, I'm not going to go all the way to London so some quack can finish me off!" Stan boomed when Tarik begged him to fly to England to see a specialist. "I'd be a fool to turn myself over to them. Forget it. I'll stay with Dr. Prev"—a local man—"he's blacker'n Zip's ass, but he's a good man and he'll do me just fine."

Dr. Prev would do Stan just fine because Stan was afraid of needles and Doc Prev used no needles, or any other medical instruments for that matter. He'd come around to a patient's home, use a coffee spoon as a tongue depressor, and diagnose based on the state of the tonsils, which he considered the barometer of the body's total health. No needles. No surgery. No medical school degree. Tarik had given up trying.

Stan had brought Karim a coloring book when he came for dinner that evening, and now the two of them were stretched out full on the living room floor, Stan filling in the figures more earnestly than Karim, who was impatient and couldn't be bothered to finish one picture before moving on to the next.

Topaz was there, her sister Mira, and Mira's son, whose name escaped Tarik because Mira had five lookalike sons, all of whom had lost their hair by age seventeen, and her daughter, Iv. These four were playing some sort of complicated board game that Iv had bought in London, where she'd gone for a skin peel. Iv's bad complexion was the family tragedy, as even the best British and American doctors could not make her skin clear and bright like her aunts' and sisters' no matter how many expensive treatments. The girl was almost twenty, with no prospect of a husband in sight, which the family attributed to Iv's severe acne but which Tarik believed was more likely due to the fact that she was the stupidest person he had ever met in his life.

Every once in a while Topaz would look up from her game, squint at Tarik out on the balcony in the dark—her eyes were bad but she was too vain to wear glasses and too fearful for contact lenses—and wink at what she hoped was his eye and not the back of his head. She had been pressing him for another child and had announced just before dinner that she'd arrived at her most fertile time of the month, and in addition the moon was full, which Mira had told her nearly guaranteed fecundity. Although he had come to terms with his marriage, Tarik still winced at its sexual obligations; he would have preferred to be chaste. Miserable at the prospect of Topaz crawling all over him before Het had even cleared away the dinner dishes, Tarik hastily invited Stanley and as many of Topaz's family as were around to join them for dinner. He'd even told Karim to run down to White-Lyons's apartments and invite the colonel to dinner. Thrilled to be included in the family gathering, White-Lyons now sat in an easy chair, full of Het's good cooking and Tarik's fine wine, gazing pleasantly around at the faces in the room. He'd asked permission to smoke and had a partially lit pipe resting in his hand.

His family and friends backlit by warm lamplight, Tarik felt a measure of contentment. Even White-Lyons seemed tolerable to him. Yet every time he felt as if he might relax, some unnamed force made him resume his slow walk back and forth across the huge balcony. A stairway led down to a garden and periodically he walked to the top step, peered into the darkness for a moment, then clasped his hands behind his back and resumed his measured pace, limping slightly from the pain that still held on in his right leg. Half of him wanted to turn and walk inside, sit down among the ones who loved him, and partake of the convivial familial scene. But in the end it was always the other side of his nature that won out, pushing him to the margins of family life, dreading the moment when someone, usually Karim, took him by the hand and tugged him inside. Much as he loved them, some part of him resisted total emotional closeness. He'd lost his taste for that tender proximity; he never wanted it again. He intended to put himself beyond such things. He needed to be alone so that he could keep his secrets intact. At least that's what he would tell himself until Karim wiggled onto his lap and covered his face with kisses.

Some faint sound in the garden drew him back to the stairway. He cocked his ear in the direction of the noise, but there was nothing. He returned to the stone balustrade of the balcony and leaned against it.

The moon was full, and cloud wisps straggled past its surface like dense gray threads. He felt a surprising nostalgia for the old kerosene lamps. Then the stars would stand out against the sky in perfect relief, a billion of them. Now, with sodium vapor street-lights and incandescent lamps indoors, the radiance of the moon and stars had dissipated a little in the reflection of unnatural glare. Over to the east, near the bazaars, he heard the music of drums and a tinny horn. A party was in progress and he shuffled his feet a little in rhythm with the beat.

For the size of the city and the lateness of the hour, there were a surprising number of cars on the street. He watched three, driving close together, move around the traffic circle, pass the zoo, then drive around the circle twice more before pulling off to the south, toward him. He followed the bounce of their headlights for a minute or two as they passed through the gate into the old city, then lost interest when they disappeared in the maze of narrow streets.

The city exuded its own sweet perfume, cooking aromas—cardamom, cinnamon, burnt sugar—and blooming flowers, especially jasmine, which grew wild everywhere now that water was in good supply. It was impossible to think that any city in America could smell this good, and that notion was a comfort. He hadn't been back since arriving after Turkit was murdered, and he wondered sometimes what he would feel if he went. The thought that he might miss the States, even for a moment, was rejected as improbable weakness.

Het appeared and handed him a plate of fruit, which he ate slowly, taking pleasure in the cool pears and apples on a hot night. Unwillingly, he felt himself surrendering the tension of the day. He preferred keeping himself in a state of suspense in order to keep the heavy schedule going and certain memories at bay. He looked again at the moon, but its glare pained his eyes and he looked away. As he did, a rare breeze stirred his shirt and pulled it away from his chest, at the same time caressing his skin beneath. Shocked at this unexpected sensual touch, his breath caught in his throat. The breeze turned to play at his hair. He flicked his tongue over his lips, picking up the salty perspiration around his mouth. He closed his eyes. How long had it been since he felt even the slightest sexual pull? Years.

But the warm breeze carried a body heat on its wings, and it had found him out there in the darkness. His groin tightened pleasantly and desire flooded him so violently that he had to wrap his fingers around the balustrade to stay steady. His inward eye filled instantly with a vision of her breasts, her belly, her pink mouth opening like a bud. She was nude and her legs, which were long and nearly touched the floor, were thrown open and slung over the sides of an armchair. Even more than what his mind envisioned, it was what his skin remembered—the flutter of her nipples under the action of his tongue. The sting on his fingers when he touched the wet flesh between her legs. Her long hair lying over his mouth. God, was it possible that he could still smell her hair? He shook off the memory. No, that was the city's flowery perfume.

This wouldn't do. He straightened and looked around, guilty because his family was no more than ten feet away yet thrilled by the flooding memories. It was a lonely and dangerous business, out there on the balcony, tempting himself to remember.

Surely he didn't really still care for her, not in any material way. That was impossible. It had been ten years, after all, a lifetime. One couldn't still love someone he hadn't seen for a lifetime and he was scornful of the notion that this might be the case. The compulsion to believe in some kind of eternal redemptive love was universal, he could accept that. It explained the pleasurable retreat into memory. He was a man closer to forty than thirty, with an empty marriage and a lost love. It was potent nostalgia, he rationalized, that brought him back to Clare—a splendid body, a pink mouth sensually slack, that was all. All right, he had ceded the physical, he could also grant the intellectual—a shared will and the enthusiasm of youth. He'd hit upon a homely allegory: that years ago, after a long and solitary journey, he had found north.

But surely after all this time she was no longer flesh and blood for him, just some illusion of when times were good and life seemed simpler. Memory as metaphor. How could he still be fascinated after all these years? What he must do is to dig down to the taproot of his obsession, rip it out, and take it apart under the brutal glare of his intellect. That done, he could toss it away and go on with his life. The difficulty, of course, was that he had thought of her every day of every one of those ten years.

When he was young he was cool because he had no fear of annihilation. Now he was cool because he was too unconnected to anything to care about annihilation.

The moon illuminated the sky into something close to light. A knot of people had gathered on a side street, arguing. One man punched another man in the chest, and the man fell back against the pavement so hard that for a moment Tarik believed he had been stabbed. But then the man stirred, another man pulled him to his feet, and the argument resumed.

She had been beautiful, hadn't she? Hadn't her mouth been soft and fleshy—and her eyes, her hair? Great fires had roared in her heart and it made her a little crazy. In his own way he'd been just like her, the two of them banking those big fires, believing in everything, all of it all the more sweet because it was brief. She'd really been rather wonderful. He felt robbed suddenly, and moved to tears. A little sob caught in his throat and he groaned softly aloud.

"You're feeling ill?"

He wheeled to see that Hadi had climbed the steps from the garden and was walking toward him. He was too startled to open his mouth.

"You're ill? Let me get you something." Hadi darted toward the living room, but Tarik stepped into his path. "I don't need anything."

Hadi shrugged. He understood the gesture and backed off. No one had ever accused him of needing more than shadow plays to discern true meanings. In a land where treachery passed as politics, he'd survived. As a result, he'd always believed he could teach a thing or two to Western politicians, who mucked about the landscape with campaign slogans and public opinion polls. Hadi had developed a method all his own of polling his constituents, having to do with the long blade and the gun barrel. Everything else was a waste of time.

He gazed around the balcony as if bored, then inhaled deeply in mock rapture and slumped against the railing like a man in a swoon. "That odor! Do you smell it? Nowhere else in the world could a man find such a sweet scent. But then," he cackled, "I've never been anywhere else in the world, so I have to take it on the authority of others."

In a show of nonchalance Tarik poked around the fruit plate, picked up a slice of apple, and began to chew. "Don't bother to call ahead, Hadi, just come right over. You know, it occurs to me that I've never seen you in the sunlight. I'm told that you've been seen in remote, creepy places, at midnight, conferring with the devil. Do you go out only at night? Like a bat?"

Hadi giggled appreciatively. "You noticed! Yes, I'm a bat. I'm a vampire bat, like Bela Lugosi. Now, don't be surprised," he said, knowing full well Tarik would never dream of showing him surprise. "I've seen all the old movies. Now that we have television sets and waffle irons all over the country, I know everything about the modern world. I love Mary Astor. Do you know, is she dead? I'd love to write to her."

"You don't know how to write."

Hadi glared but ignored the remark, his lips curling up over dark teeth in a malevolent smile. He struck Tarik as so completely evil that he had to look away, a mistake when every conversation with Hadi was a fearful exercise and he could not afford to concede even the flick of an eyelash.

Hadi fluttered his hands around. "Now, where was I? I materialize on the air like a vampire bat at the most unexpected moment and scare the dickens out of everybody."

"I suppose this is considered some sort of talent. In the darker circles."

The evil one gave a modest bow. "You should have seen my father. Now, there was a man who could scare the hell out of anybody. He even scared the hell out of me, I must confess. He was the master at this business. You won't believe this, but my father could walk through walls. It's true! It had the most stunning effect. I tried it, of course, but I only bloodied my nose and looked very foolish. But I've always believed in the dramatic. It makes that which I have to say so much more effective."

"Do you have something to say?"

"Maybe."

"I'm waiting with bated breath." Tarik pulled a small piece of the apple's skin from between his teeth and flicked it away.

Hadi followed the motion. "I have three cars, you know," he offered. "None of that horseback riding for me anymore. I'm part of the new order. I've taken my share, you can believe that. Now we're all rich, aren't we? Thanks to you. I think I'll go to London and buy myself an expensive suit of clothes. Maybe I'll hire an expensive London tailor to come live under my roof and make me suits all day and all night. Look"—he pulled back his sleeve and stuck his arm under Tarik's nose—"I've got an expensive Swiss watch. It tells the phases of the moon, in case I forget what everything means. In case I get so rich I don't even have to examine the heavens ever again. Of course, now that you've stopped shipping oil, I might have to sell it and get my money back. We might be broke in another day or so."

The falcon's gaze was keen, and he stared into Tarik's eyes as if he could read his mind. But the tuberculosis that had been eating away at Hadi's body for decades had worn him down, and he suddenly seemed weak and rather bloodless. He halted periodically in mid-speech to choke or catch his breath.

When he broke off to cough again, Tarik took the opportunity to move into the moonlight a little.

"I'm bored, Hadi." He feigned a yawn. "It's bedtime. What do you want?"

Hadi struggled to speak after his coughing fit. Then he said, with pure malevolence, "You Surs. Such snobs. You think you can treat us any way you like and we'll take it. All right—I want to see my family. You keep them away from me and I miss them."

"You can see Topaz and your other daughters any time you want."

"Who's talking about those bags?" He shuddered exaggeratedly. "I don't know how you can stand that Topaz. I'd cut her head off if I were you." He paused to hack more, a deep coughing fit that brought tears to his eyes. He pulled out his handkerchief and spat into it, blood mixed with whitish material, the dead cells unleashed from the walls of his ravaged lungs. He took several deep breaths, a convulsive rattle in his throat, closed his eyes, and calmed his lungs. But when he spoke again, his voice was hard as a whore's heart.

"I want to see Karim."

"There he is." Tarik indicated the living room.

"You know what I mean. I want to *see* him, to be with him. I want to take him out to the countryside with me."

"No."

The hating eyes flickered briefly, then hardened so visibly that Tarik thought some magic might have been applied. He could feel Hadi's body slowly stiffen into stone. "No."

"For a week, for a day."

"It's out of the question."

"You think I'm so evil?"

"Yes."

"You think that in one day I could turn Karim into something of me?"

"No." Tarik laughed. "Karim is his own person. He was born his own person. No one could influence him to be something his nature was not originally. And believe me, Hadi, his nature is good. No, I don't want him to be with you because a little boy ought to have respectful memories of his grandfather. He ought to think that his grandfather was the best of men. I'm doing you a favor, you see. He'll never know you while you're alive, and when you're dead I'm going to mythologize you into something human. You ought to thank me."

Hadi pondered this for a moment. The moon had moved behind a cloud, and for the moment that its light was lost, Hadi pondered his options with a frown on his face that the darkness hid from Tarik. "That's a good plan," he said finally. "I like it."

"I'm glad you approve."

"The only snag is that I have no intention of dying."

"You seem quite ill to me. You seem practically on the brink." Tarik returned to the balcony railing and lounged over it, staring off into the night.

A little defensively, Hadi added, "I'm going to London to see a doctor and be cured. Tuberculosis is a disease of the old order, and we have embraced the new, haven't we? Thanks to you. Now that I think of it, I have you to thank for saving my life. What do you think about that?"

"I think you ought to have that expensive London suit made very soon, Hadi. I think they're going to lay you out in that suit and you'll look just fine."

Hadi's yellow eyes flickered. "I want to see my grandson. He looks sick. Everyone says it is he who might die any minute." He took a step closer. "I don't believe you understand what the boy means to me. He's my guarantee of the future. My vision. My genes."

"You have other grandsons."

"My other daughters' boys have mush for brains. I have hallucinators, madmen, assholes. There are things I must teach Karim. There are men that he must meet. Two hundred and fifty thousand Marib warriors, have you forgotten? I think you have. My seed unto the generations. My dynasty. I have the weird belief that I can impress myself upon the future, have I told you that? I had a dream when I was thirteen that a son of my youngest child would carry my vision into the future. It was something—I sat up straight in my bed and knew that I had seen the light. I made a bargain with White-Lyons. I have a right to the boy."

Tarik hadn't seen or felt him move, but Hadi was now very close to him, the buttons on his jacket pushing into Tarik's hands and his sour breath in his face.

"I know what the bargain was, Hadi," Tarik said mildly, maintaining his position. "You got your heir, that's all you get."

For an eternity Hadi poured his yellow cat-eyes into Tarik's, daring him to look away. In the moonswept darkness Tarik believed he actually saw the skin on Hadi's bones change color, silver to red to gray—some trick of magic or, more likely, sheer will. It occurred to him at that moment that this evil creature really was not much more than the malignant extreme of a string of men who had overarched his life since he was a teenager. Hadi as Francis Riston, Elliott Tomlinson, Arthur Olson, plus a few corpses and minus the collegiate old-boy polish. None of them really meant him any good—Olson, perhaps—but the rest had their own agendas. Thinking about Riston and Hadi as twins separated at birth amused him greatly, and he chuckled out loud.

Reading this as insult, Hadi opened his eyes wide, full of rage. He made a sudden feint toward the living room. Tarik raised his hand, palm outward, and there was such power in this simple gesture and in the blaze of his eyes that Hadi was halted automatically in his tracks.

"Karim is healthy as the horse you no longer care to sit on," Tarik hissed. "There's nothing wrong with him." He rolled up his eyes and examined the heavens. "It's time for you to leave now, Hadi. You don't want to make a scene in front of your family. Don't want Karim to see his grandfather for what he really is. Check your fancy Swiss watch, Hadi. I'm sure I'm right. Time for you to go."

Hadi longed to cough. He could feel his lungs frantically fighting for air. He closed his eyes against the temptation to open his mouth and gulp in air. It was difficult to be cool when what he wanted was to take out his gun, set its barrel against Tarik's eye, and pull the trigger. His intelligent face smoldered in the moonlight. His legs twitched with the effort to control himself. It was extremely unlikely that he would actually shoot Tarik here, but the thought of the bullet ripping through his eye and trailing his brains along the facade of the building was too pleasant a thought to surrender without effort.

He could feel his heart throbbing in his temple and he didn't care for its erratic beat. The need to cough was overwhelming him. At last he felt his lungs pump once, twice, reassuringly, and he relaxed and gave Tarik his most dreadful smile.

"Well"—he shrugged his shoulders—"in-law problems! The universal complaint." He rubbed his hands together and breathed deeply. His body uncoiled and he headed toward the stairs. "Give everyone my love," he said over his shoulder. "Be sure to tell them about my new suits." He was halfway gone when he turned with something else on his mind, another of his tricks.

"On another note—"

"Hadi, you really must learn to make a clean exit."

"I was just wondering . . . when I saw you standing in the moonlight—I wondered if you were thinking of your blond wife, the one you sent away. She was quite the looker, I remember. She had nice breasts. If I were married to you-know-who"—he jerked with his thumb at Topaz—"I'd think about the blonde."

"Well, I have you to thank for it, don't I?" Tarik's voice was harder than he intended, and he was furious with himself for taking Hadi's bait. But it was too late. Hadi instantly understood that he had probed a tender spot and flashed him a knowing smile.

"Ah . . ." he said impishly, "so you *were* thinking about the blonde. Well, that's a pity. She's long gone. Life is a well-worn path of woe, don't you think? A terrible tug-of-war. I've had my disappointments too, you know. I could tell *you* some stories." He shook his head in exaggerated sadness. "Not love exactly, but other things. Well—if we keep this up, we're both going to have to get out our handkerchiefs. Enough said—I just hope you don't hold the blonde against me."

He began descending the steps, then turned again to add, "But then, I'm sure you don't—any more than I hold it against you for the death of my son Azarak—he was my favorite, you know. Ah, well, everything evens out in the end. Checks and balances, even-steven. You believe me, don't you?" A giggle rattled in his throat.

Then the scrape of his shoes on the steps was gone and he was in the garden. In another minute Tarik heard car engines turn over, then followed the headlights of three cars out of the old city, around the traffic circle by the zoo, then north, toward the countryside.

Tarik whistled softly through his teeth.

"You don't have to tell me." White-Lyons stood in the doorway, lighting his pipe. "I know the bastard better than anyone."

"He's out of his mind."

"I wish. If he were out of his mind, he'd do something stupid and I'd have an excuse to shoot him. As it is he just gets more clever with age. I tell you, you have to be careful of him. He's capable of anything. Like sending another Azarak after you. He's still got a few dimwitted sons left, if I've counted correctly."

"Yes, but then that's the end of him. No grandsons from the male line."

White-Lyons clamped his hands behind his back and walked to the top of the stone steps to scrutinize the darkness and be sure Hadi had actually left. Satisfied, he relaxed, plucked an impatiens blossom from the flower box, and twirled it in his finger. "He came to see Karim?"

"He wants to get his hands on my boy," Tarik said. "He believes somehow that he can throw himself into the future through Karim. Some weird kind of immortality idea that Hadi's twisted brain has come up with and he thinks he needs to impress his message on the boy so that Karim can carry it forward into the future. Figure it out. Lunatic stuff about walking through walls, and bat flights, and homicidal hallucinations."

"They're not hallucinations."

"Anyway, I'd rather think I found Karim under a cabbage leaf than think he had any biological connection to that . . . thing. He wanted to take the boy back to the countryside with him. He thinks he doesn't look well."

White-Lyons set his battered little flower on the railing and toyed with it for a moment, sorry now that he had plucked it. In the past year he'd developed a love of flowers that he couldn't quite explain. Perhaps the Englishman's native love of gardening. More likely, a need to feel useful to someone, something, even these tiny blooms. He turned and gazed into the living room. Karim had long since tired of the coloring book and was on Stanley's lap to play the ice cream game. His skin appeared ochre-colored under the silk shade of the table lamp.

White-Lyons sucked on his pipe. Karim needed him; he felt useful there all right. Lovely petals and a bright little boy—he could live with that. "It's all image, isn't it? Image and reality.

I've never met a more loving child, or giving, than Karim. Or"—he smiled—"selfish, for that matter. Or a child with a stronger sense of who he is. But he doesn't look the way we want him to, does he? Doesn't have the big, broad shoulders, or the manly cast of features. Doesn't fulfill our need for him to look a certain way so that we can all feel safe and secure in our beds at night. The belief is that the mind must perfectly match the physicality. They're scared he won't be a leader in the heroic mold." Then he added, "As you are."

"And like my own father, I suppose," Tarik offered. "I doubt that anyone who saw Malik ever doubted that he was the one."

"No, there was never any doubt."

There was something in White-Lyons's voice that caused Tarik to turn and stare at him. But the colonel's face was a mask except for the two blue lights of his eyes, which showed the fatigue of some spiritual burden that made Tarik so uncomfortable he had to look away.

After an uneasy silence White-Lyons struck a match against his leg and restarted his pipe. "I've given a lot of thought to this business with OmniTech," he began, but Tarik did not respond. The notion of companioning White-Lyons on a sultry, lovely night, the moon in their eyes and the smell of blossoms all around, was repellent to him, and Tarik was sorry now that he'd engaged him in conversation, itchy to get away. He didn't want the old man's advice on OmniTech, on Karim, on any matter.

"It's going to be the devil to get rid of them. You're going to have to be very clever," the colonel pressed him.

"You think I should get rid of them, then?"

"I don't see that you have any choice. Unless, of course, you want some furnace manufacturer from Sunnyvale, California, running your country ten years from now."

Pricked, Tarik said briskly, "They're not going to be running the country, and it would be against their interests to seem to be doing so."

"Well, you can't have it both ways. You can't have them inside and outside at the same time. It's one thing to maintain the relationship with Washington, to let them use Rahal as a listening post and a staging area or storage facility, quite another to have the whole place crawling with American lawyers and bureaucrats and engineers besides. What are you going to do with all those educated boys and girls you're turning out if you have all these fellows from Iowa and Pennsylvania running around in golf shirts doing the work? I warned you about this from the beginning."

"It's not as if I haven't already thought about this, White-Lyons. I'm not operating a job market for these people. I'll make my decision."

"Well, you're going to have to make up your mind pretty damn quick. You can't be seen in this region as a surrogate for the United States or its corporations. You can be an independent nation allied with the West out of philosophy, or self-interest, not because you're their paladin—not in this part of the world. Believe me, you're not on the street as much as I am. The people are beginning to resent all these foreigners. A decade from now they're going to be more resentful—and there'll be more of them to let you know it. Turkit may have murdered your generation of men when he slaughtered those innocents, but the new generation is going to be trebled in size. They're going to give you trouble if you don't act now."

Tarik stretched and backed away a step, hoping to signal a natural close to the conversation. He wanted to be rid of the man. Wanted him to stop braying and telling him what he already knew. Chiefly, he wanted to get rid of the voice in his brain that was telling him that White-Lyons understood better than anyone what the political realities of his situation were. It made him miserable to think that the colonel might be the one man in the kingdom not operating out of self-interest and therefore the one man most truly his ally.

But White-Lyons had no wish to end their conversation. Rarely granted such access to Tarik, he wanted to make his points quickly before he was cut off.

"The more the people come to understand the real role of OmniTech in the day-to-day operations of the kingdom, the more resentment you're going to have. Especially when they find out how many of them have backgrounds in the CIA and the State Department. They did their bit for you, they made millions—billions probably—doing it, but it's time to phase them out, whether they like it or not. And don't think Washington is going to be pleased about this either. Be prepared to catch bloody hell. But do it anyway. Take a risk and you'll give any initiative real power and hold on to the people's imagination. Spend all your time holding on to the coalition and you'll lose the ability to move your constituency."

"When the time comes, I'll do what I have to do," Tarik snapped.

"And what is that?"

Tarik glared at him in the darkness. "I'll do whatever I want, and I won't check with you or anyone else about it first."

He turned to stare out over the old city. The moon was enormous, slung low against the horizon and changed from silver to hell-red. It seemed to be ensanguining, pulsating, and no longer benign, as if it were the dark partner of the daylight star, an evening sun that cast them all into shadow lives, where madmen transformed themselves into bats and old men with watery eyes had no fear or shame—and younger men were still not too weary for something that, especially on a dark and perfumed night, could be recognized as love.

His eyes returned to the city skyline. Then, almost as if it were a reflex over which he had no control, he turned to White-Lyons and heard himself in a low voice ask, "Do something for me?"

"Anything."

"Find out about Clare."

Taken aback, White-Lyons hesitated, then said, "Is that wise?"

Tarik gave him the smile. "No more wise, I suppose, than telling Arthur Olson that it's time to start packing."

White-Lyons sucked on his pipe and, finding it dead, tamped its contents down with a finger, added more tobacco, and set another match to the bulb, a lengthy ritual that gave him time to turn things over in his mind. "All right. If you want me to find out about her, I will."

"In total secrecy."

"Of course."

"Everything. I want to know what time she wakes up in the morning. What she buys at the supermarket. What kind of tires she puts on her car. Everything. And I want to—" he hesitated. He had never commented on Clare's child to a living soul. "I want to know about her son. He must be ten years old."

"Around that." If White-Lyons suspected what Tarik was driving at, he said nothing.

They stood silently for a moment, surveying the dark landscape.

"You know," White-Lyons said finally, "they're going to demand you go back to Washington to explain yourself once you tell Olson."

"I know."

"They might even take you to the highest level there. They're going to let you have it."

"Yes."

"Will you go?"

"Yes."

"They'll put the screws to you."

"If they can."

"But you're not afraid?"

"No. Nothing like a firm conviction, and nine hundred million barrels of oil, to give a man guts, is there, Colonel?"

At that, Tarik turned and left the balcony, passed through the living room, which was empty, and went to find Karim.

His son was already in bed, nearly asleep, Stanley temporarily tucked in alongside him for one last cuddle. Topaz puttered in the bathroom, examining the contents of the medicine cabinet, while Het folded clothes and arranged them neatly in the boy's bureau. When he finished there, he moved to the toy box and straightened out the cars and trucks that Karim had left in a jumble.

Tarik sat down on the foot of the bed and Karim immediately stirred.

"Guess what?" he said, his sleepy eyes little slits.

"What?"

"Guess?"

"You tell me."

"Stanley won tonight."

"Won what?"

"The ice cream game. He asked which I liked better—ice cream, or diving for pearls in the bottom of his swimming pool."

"And you picked—"

"Pearls! We're going to do it tomorrow, right, Stanley?"

"If your mother says it's okay."

Topaz flicked her tongue back and forth over her teeth. "Is the pool deep?"

"Mother, I can swim! Don't baby me. I'm practically six years old."

"I'll be right in the water with him," Stanley offered.

She looked at Tarik, who nodded his approval. "All right, I guess so. But I'm coming with you, and we'll have a life preserver, and a blanket. If you get a chill and a cold, Karim, who knows what can happen. I'll go with you and I'll take your bathrobe. Anything could happen in a swimming pool."

After a little more chatter, Karim's eyes closed tight. Tarik stroked his face with a finger for a moment, then kissed him lightly on the forehead. Surrounded by his parents, Het, and Stanley, Karim rushed to embrace sleep, where warriors with unpronounceable names thundered on chargers into battle, heads flew from bodies, brains flowed, blood poured, and all manner of other interesting things were dreamed.

But the problem was not with the swimming pool. Karim leapt and splashed and dove like the little boy he was for nearly an hour, was never winded, and allowed himself to be coaxed out only because he had to urinate so badly that his legs quivered.

No, the problem was not in the pool, but in the kitchen, or, rather, with the cake on a table in the kitchen, into which Sirah had poured all her ambition and lust. Except for sex, she had no art or imagination. Her method of dispensing death was as unoriginal as a dime-store novel, nothing subtle or inventive, just six ounces of pure, unadulterated curare poured down into a narrow gutter across the top of a chocolate layer cake and then camouflaged with an inch of chocolate frosting. It had been sitting there all day, a gooey beacon of disaster, waiting for Stanley alone, because Sirah, who had locked herself in her bedroom, had no way of knowing that a dripping-wet little boy whose mother had absolutely forbidden him to urinate in the swimming pool would spy it on the way to a bathroom off the housekeeper's bedroom. He'd begged and pleaded and finally thrown a righteous little temper tantrum, until they'd all sat down at the kitchen table. Stanley brought the plates from the pantry and with many flourishes cut three big pieces. They ate for an instant, and then all three collapsed, the blood-pink foam in their mouths and disappointment on their tongues. Topaz went first, in jerky, birdlike motions. Stanley, already primed from months of slow assault, hastened after her, his huge heart cramping one-two-three. The world would have been surprised to know that Karim was the last to go, his clever, agile brain to the very end pumping hope into his thin, incongruously sturdy little body.

It didn't take Hadi all that many days to find her. No one cared to shelter the woman who had murdered, however inadvertently, Tarik's wife and only child. Sirah was hiding in a sheepherder's shack outside a prospecting town called Lora. The wind was howling and beating dust against the sides of the place so she felt the blast of air when the door sprang open before she actually heard the noise of men's footsteps. She whimpered a little, but the sight of those animal eyes collapsed her will and with two of Mira's bald sons holding her arms straight out at her side, she gave up easily.

Hadi's dagger was curved, with a rhinoceros-horn handle, the gift of a Yemeni chieftain he had known when the British still ran the kingdom. He set the tip of the blade against the neckline of her dress and scraped it down until it had cut her dress into two neat halves. He stepped back and surveyed her naked body approvingly. He plucked at her babyish inverted nipples with his fingers and inched another finger into her vagina.

And up until the instant he drove the knife into her uterus, then ripped it up through her intestines, stomach, and diaphragm until it knocked into her sternum and could go no farther, Sirah, in the hell that was her heart, believed that Hadi of the four hundred thousand Marib, like every other man who had been bowed by the power of her sex, intended to make love to her.

1974

22

In other parts of eastern Kentucky there may have been talk of longwall/shortwall concepts, of Continuous Miners, narrow-head mining, simple-pivot arching and pantograph shields; of tripling output and productivity factors and improving face ventilation. But for years and years, in Mills Bend, in Number 9 and the ten other drift and strip mines in the Aylesworth operation, the mining of coal had been as it was: back-breaking, nerve-racking nonunion slave labor, pure and simple. Even after enactment of the Federal Coal Mine Health and Safety Act in 1969, in terms of an even break for miners around Mills Bend, not much had changed from the old pick and shovel days.

It's a rare seam in Appalachia where a deep miner can stand up straight; twenty-eight to thirty-one inches is about the norm. Put an average-size man in a space that size and that's a human body living at right angles to the ground.

Prone, supine, and hunkered down are the three ways a miner gets around in an eastern Kentucky drift mine. He goes in lying down in cars, even if it's a three-foot seam, which is considered very nice in that part of the world, and spends eight hours a day—twelve, not so very long ago—in about the same position. If he wants to sit, he has to dig himself a hole in the floor to set his feet into. Needs to go to the toilet, he crawls around the corner to the next abandoned tunnel, maybe digs out the roof a little bit, a little bit out of the floor, so he can squat.

His subterranean world is viewed through a scrim of coal dust. Even if his dinner bucket is sealed tight, by lunchtime his sandwich is full of sand—and not the kind found in clams or oysters in restaurants. This sand is thick, gritty coal dust that turns white bread gray and crunchy.

In the old days, Homer's era, the miners drilled into the coal, set charges, blew them, and hacked out their sixteen tons per man per shift for about two dollars a day. They were paid for the amount of coal they dug, not the time it took to dig it, so if there was an accident or some sort of delay, too bad; they had to make the quota or pay in the pocketbook. Or be told to pack up their equipment and get out. Every boss was a bastard, and men died because of it.

Mining coal is the most dangerous profession in the world, bar none. In 1971, two years after Clare told Muddy Aylesworth he could either hang on to his stock or just plain hang, there were one hundred thirty-two fatalities in mines in the United States and more than eleven thousand injuries. The death rate had dropped over the years, but the decline was probably due more to improved medical treatment of accident victims than to mandated mine safety laws, which the bosses usually ignored.

As for the United Mine Workers, there were those who believed that in the last two decades the union hadn't done all that much for the mining man, that it had become corrupt and insensitive. If a union man stuck out his neck to try to change things, his head might be taken off for the effort, as was that of Jock Yablonski, a union reformer who challenged the leadership and was assassinated in his bed in the dead of night, as were his wife and daughter, December 30, 1969. The union president, W. A. "Tony" Boyle, was indicted for complicity in the Yablonski murders and, in another case, for using union funds to help finance political campaigns, and he went to jail in 1973. In the meantime, after government intervention, the miners elected a new president, Arnold Miller, but the union was in chaos as the reformers took over from the corrupt old order and wasn't much good to anyone.

Mills Bend isn't a union stronghold anyway. The men had soured on the UMW long before, when they found out that its legendary president, John L. Lewis, a man who'd faced down even President Franklin Roosevelt, operated coal mines on the side. Lewis had had no qualms about cutting union membership to take pressure off mine operators when the economy went bad in 1958. The medical benefits system collapsed and the miners were condemned to dog holes, nonunion mines that paid half the wage for twice the work and danger, the kind of mine Muddy operated. The miners hated and feared the dog-hole mine, but if they were desperate for work, there was no choice but to go down.

In those days the union didn't stand behind the miner when it came to his health either. The union's protest was as feeble as an old woman's when the coal bosses claimed that black lung disease didn't exist, that miners smoked too many cigarettes and that explained pulmonary disorders. The bosses found doctors to swear that it wasn't pneumoconiosis but some sort of lung weakness that even an ordinary man on an ordinary job might contract. When some miners spoke up for reform at the union convention in 1964, goon squads from District 19 of southeastern Kentucky and eastern Tennessee clubbed them on the convention floor. The union, some miners muttered, had forgotten the everyday dreams and devotion of the workingman that had made it a powerful force in Congress and a voice in the White House.

But for the misery of what went on below, the sight of the gorgeous Appalachian Mountains, round-shouldered and hunkered down on the back of the earth, were a comfort. Unlike the jagged, towering Rockies, the Appalachians appear as weary as the mountain folk they shelter, close to worn out, still-proud but hardly boastful.

Clare was raised on the mutilated mantle of land southwest of Mingo County, West Virginia, and Pike County, Kentucky, the part of Appalachia where on every sensible man's bedside table rests a handgun, with a rifle or shotgun within easy reach. But then, people in this part of the world have always had an easy relationship with bloodshed. In 1882 Devil Anse Hatfield and his kinfolk avenged the murder of Ellison Hatfield by executing three McCoy brothers on Blackberry Creek, over the Tug Fork of the Big Sandy River, thereby setting off the legendary, sanguinary Hatfield-McCoy family feud.

Close by is Matewan, West Virginia, where Chief of Police Sid Hatfield led a pack of striking miners against detectives from the Baldwin-Felts Agency that left nine people dead in the street in 1920. The detectives had been in the employ of the mine owners, evicting striking miners' families from company houses at the Stone Mountain Mine.

Rifle fire was as everyday as the thud of picks on the coal face in those days. In the 1920s, miners fighting to unionize staged pitched battles with state police and sheriff's deputies—and even after the state troopers and detectives were gone, the tradition of violence and suspicion continued in the natural animosity between miners and mine owners, union and nonunion, and kept the coal counties of Appalachia in a state of constant warfare. The labor movement in this part of the world was nothing less than bloody civil war.

Mills Bend is just like a hundred other towns on the Kentucky–

West Virginia border—long and gray and set down in a narrow valley. It was founded by Edwin Mills, who'd gone to work in a coal field in Carbondale, Pennsylvania, in 1886 when he was six years old, immigrated to eastern Kentucky, and shipped the first coal from a mine he owned thirteen years later. By the time he was twenty-five he owned three more mines, a railroad to ship his coal around Kentucky, Tennessee, and Virginia, half of the buildings in Mills Bend, and most of the land all around. Mills was a millionaire, a claim not a single one of the men who mined his coal could match.

In the western part of the state there are soybean, corn, and tobacco fields; to the north, the famous green-bordered horse farms. But on the wide strip of land that spreads from eastern Kentucky nearly to the Atlantic Ocean is a thick black seam of fossil fuel, and when the money-men discovered its existence in the 1880s, they stormed Appalachia like an invading army. They bought land from the naive locals for twenty-five cents an acre, then turned around and leased it to mine operators for ten cents a ton royalty. By 1902, five million tons of coal poured annually from forty colliers, and three thousand beehive coke ovens pushed smoke and flame up into the atmosphere above towns owned outright by the coal companies. Every town had a coal camp, with identical wooden buildings side by side, the company store and its goods within easy reach of redeeming scrip. Not that a man had a choice on where to buy his necessities. If he didn't shop at the company store, he couldn't work in the company mine. The companies owned the camp, the towns and everybody who ran them, the caves, all the land, plus every soul living thereon.

The mine owners didn't live in the coal camps themselves, naturally. They built graceful stately mansions with the money they made. Muddy's father had come from Wales when he was five years old and gone right down into the mines. The little money he earned he invested in mules, which he then rented at a low rate to the mine owners for use in the mines. With those earnings he bought a parcel of land that he ultimately mined successfully. He kept up this incremental fortune-building, until a few million later he'd built himself a copper-roofed twenty-five-room beauty right off Main Street, the only street, in fact, in Mills Bend. Muddy's ex-wife, Adelle Aylesworth, who divorced him after the debacle with Clare, still lived there.

The coal camp was gone now; a trailer park and some prefab houses had taken its place. Just like most towns in Appalachia, Mills Bend had decayed in the coal price collapse that followed

World War II, when families drifted away to hillbilly ghettos in Chicago, Detroit, Cleveland, and Cincinnati. The depressed demand and the introduction of mechanized mining—the Wilcox and the Jeffrey continuous miners that could do the work of twenty men—between 1948 and 1970 increased productivity but obliterated two-thirds of all coal-mining jobs. A lengthy depression swept over the Kentucky coal country and Mills Bend went down for the count. Despite more than a decade of intensive federal assistance the coal counties of Appalachia had made little economic progress or developed other forms of livelihood. Shops were boarded up, cars rusted by the side of the road, abandoned houses fell down from lack of care. Just living was a desperate business, and the strength and pride of the mountain people was put to the test once again.

But coal is a cyclical business—boom, bust, boom—and when the OPEC oil embargo began in 1973, boom times were back. Overnight, coal, the fuel that everyone had forgotten, was in demand again; the embargo drove its price higher than it had ever been in history. Within a year, coal went from around seven dollars and fifty cents a ton to sixty dollars a ton, with no increase in the cost of making the coal in the first place. Companies that had been struggling suddenly found themselves awash in cash, including Aylesworth. Number 9 mined ten thousand tons a month and brought in roughly $3.6 million a year, and the other mines within the Aylesworth operation did nearly as well. Miners were on top again, thanks to the foreign oil-producing nations that had stopped shipping their oil.

It was amazing how quickly Clare and Toby had learned the coal business. Within a week of being hired, Toby had set up an office next to Clare's in the old store. She sent him to Richmond for two weeks to learn the basics of health-care planning, and within six months he had revamped the skimpy Aylesworth health benefits and pension plans. Sayles arranged for Wendell Pell, the financial analyst who followed the coal industry, to come down and spend a week with her, and she picked his brain on the phone almost every day after he went back to Washington.

She learned about preparation plants, improved her technical knowledge, studied flow charts, worked on the financial end. She traveled to each of the mines three times a week, hired new mine managers, found out everything about coal, its extraction, preparation, shipment, and sale that she could possibly comprehend. She put in eighteen-hour days and fell asleep in her jeans and boots, with books and reports blanketing her bed. She spent hours on the phone with Sayles, pumping him for his business acumen, taking his advice, allowing him to calm her down when she panicked.

When she first arrived she'd taken a small house in town for herself and Alex and tried to convince Homer to come live with them. But he'd bought a new sow and wouldn't leave her alone for a minute, so he stayed put in his own tiny house. Clare hired one of her cousins to come in and cook breakfast and dinner every day for him, and another cousin handled his housecleaning and laundry.

For a time Alex went to the Double Creek school, but when he turned eight, Sayles decided he would be better educated at St. Albans School, in Washington, D.C., and so his parents commuted to the capital to be with him, each of them alternating weeks depending on the pressure of work. They were all together every weekend and holiday, in Mills Bend, or Hobe Sound, Lyford Cay, or Europe, wherever work or whim took them. His parents had decided that when Alex turned fourteen, he would board at St. Albans, too, and come home on weekends. It had become Alex's life's goal to be the only boy in his exclusive prep school to have caught and skinned a rattler. Sayles had forbidden him to go anywhere near a snake hunt, but that didn't stop him from trailing along behind Dobbie Fields, the best rattler and copperhead catcher in the county, when Dobbie and Tommy Johnson went snaking in the hills up above the Mullens place.

It would be wrong to say that the townspeople welcomed Clare's return with open arms, or her announcement that she was now running Aylesworth Coal with anything but suspicion. That the company stocks were held in trust for the miners was too great and gratuitous a concept for them to grasp at first. The notion that they were, in effect, their own bosses took some getting used to, so for the first few months she was something of an outsider. Everyone remembered her as Hillard and Kath's daughter, of course, but in this incarnation, as the wife of one of the country's wealthiest men and the owner of Aylesworth Coal, she was the object of intense curiosity and skepticism. Mountain people are suspicious and aloof out of nature and necessity, and they gave her wide berth until she could prove that she'd come back to do them some good. Three years after she'd taken the company away from Muddy, the mines were running with new safety equipment installed or on the drawing board. The miners and their families had proof that they were going to participate in their own working lives in a way that was undreamed of before, and so they were less tentative with her. But she was always business. No smiles. It had been Nal's good advice years before, and it was good advice still.

Now, almost five years since she took over, all ten mines were operating smoothly, and people had gotten used to seeing her bouncing around in her Jeep, her omnipresent notebook in her hand. Thanks to the OPEC oil embargo, coal was selling at its highest price in history and everybody was feeling good about getting their fair share, not to mention owning a piece of the action. Homer finally grew tired of slogging through the red dog up and down the holler between his house and hers and moved into town with her. He built a pen in the backyard for the sow and spent hours out there, talking things over with her. Mysteriously, he refused to tell anyone what he had named the sow. "T'aint nobody's business but mine," he said when Clare asked him, which made her think that he might have lost a marble or two. "Okay, Grandpa," she said, backing off, "you don't have to tell. Just don't know why it's such a big deal."

"She knows and I know and that's all that needs to."

"All right, already. I won't ask you again."

Late at night, working under the light of a desk lamp in her second-floor bedroom, she could hear him in the pen in the backyard, cooing to his girl between lung wheezes. She crept up behind him once or twice when he went out to feed her, but she never could hear what he called her.

When it came to Lawrence Sayles, the citizens of Mills Bend looped between adoration and contempt. To one part of their thinking, he was hard to swallow. They were good egalitarian republicans, and he was of the princely class, bearer of the unspoken message that they must all keep quiet and accept their betters.

On the other hand, they could only dimly imagine what it must be like to possess *that much money*. To live the costless life. And so he was an immensely attractive prince and if they would only trust him and the others of his class, he would vouchsafe their nation's higher culture. This fact they could not articulate but instead sensed, the way a good birder lives to flush out partridge in tall grass; his instincts drive him to do it even if he doesn't know why.

Sayles, of course, was oblivious of the mad emotional scrambling that surged in his wake and never noticed how he was treated. He walked into Mills Bend like a *grand seigneur* come to survey his distant acres on horseback, yet managed at the same time to convey the impression that he was as plebeian as a farm-hand.

He studied the goods on the Agway shelves as if he actually knew what peat moss was. He dropped into the IGA store for a quart of milk and made small talk with the checker as though it were the natural thing to do, although Clare knew for a fact that he had never in his entire life made a single purchase in any grocery store. He behaved as if he had just dropped in from the Milky Way and Mills Bend, Kentucky, was the one place on the planet he'd ever wanted to visit.

He was big-eyed, he was kind and courteous, he turned an undefended ear to anyone with a word to say, and although he strode among them with all the hauteur of a Renaissance prince, he never made any of them feel that they were anything less than the most fascinating people he had ever met in his life. He had the sort of Olympian élan that engendered in everyone who met him the gloomy realization that they were mere mortals none too successfully mingling with a god. So naturally they came to love him and thought he put up with a whole lot being married to a woman like Clare Barrow, who pounded around the state with a handful of papers and a mouthful of productivity reports. Not that they didn't appreciate what she was doing; she'd gotten Muddy to give her the mines and put the stock shares in trust for them, after all. But Sayles—well, he was a god, and she was only a human being.

"I've always told you that when you go into business, things change," he said to her when she complained about it. "Nobody likes the boss, even if she is giving away the store. There's always some sort of complaint. Remember, you've got to rise above it, Clare. You've got to keep emotions out of it or you'll get into trouble."

"But, Lawrence, you don't—" She wanted to argue with him; it was a bad habit she had, fighting with him over details she thought she understood better than he. But he had complained about it and she was trying to learn to bite her tongue.

They were rocking on the porch after an early supper. A narrow finger of light was all that remained of the day, just above the horizon, and the air was fresh with the scent of new buds everywhere. The swallows finally had taken to their beds; earlier they had dive-bombed anyone who came close to their baby-filled nests and had driven Sayles off the porch. Watching him through the living room window, Clare had laughed out loud as he windmilled his arms to shoo them away.

Sayles was wearing a suit and necktie. Clare thought he'd been born with his umbilical cord tied in a Windsor knot. He wore silk pajamas to bed, and a suit, white shirt, and necktie everywhere else. He would have gone into the mine that way if Toby hadn't refused to go down until he slipped on overalls and a pair of borrowed boots. Sayles was a gentleman from the old, formal school. He wore the same suit to the NAPA store that he wore to the White House.

He lowered his tone and rocked. "I'm sure I don't have to tell you, Clare, that when emotions get in the way, terrible mistakes can be made. Lives, you know, can be jeopardized in a high-risk environment like a coal mine."

In the deepening twilight, the sound of the worshippers' hymn settled over the neighborhood from the Advent Christian Church across the street. The congregation turned to "Rock of Ages," a hymn he had grown particularly fond of since he began coming to Mills Bend. He croaked out a verse in his high-pitched voice. A home-going group of miners scuffed down the road toward Barrow's Hollow. They spoke in low, weary voices and he strained to overhear what they said. Another man of his rank might have averted his eyes when they looked in his direction; they'd carried the water for his class for generations.

But Sayles had worked hard for his country. He'd inherited a fortune, conserved and increased it for his heirs, and treated all men fairly along the way. Through the family philanthropy in New York, he'd given away millions to medical research, university scholarships, charitable foundations, the arts, environmental causes. The Sayles family business investments were above reproach; not one penny earned off the backs of South African gold miners or Guatemalan fruit pickers. Money gained came from honest investments—stocks, bonds, shopping malls, industrial parks, some high-end technology start-ups in California and Ireland.

He had nothing to reproach himself for. He smiled and gave a little wave to the miners, and they raised their chins at him in recognition.

From the corner of his eye he watched Clare chew her lip and fight to compose herself, an effort that always charmed him—perversely, he had to admit—because she suffered so in her struggles to seem calm and collected when she knew that all the time her nature was pushing her to fight back. He was rather in awe of this trait. Volatility had been bred out of the Sayles genes somewhere between the time his ancestors arrived from England on the

Mayflower and their descendants made the return trip, champagne flutes in hand, on the first-class decks of Cunard liners.

They rocked without speaking for a while more, listening to the churchgoers throw their hearts into the verses, before he liberated her from her misery by asking what she thought of the new conveyer system he'd overheard her assistants talking about.

The next morning, just as he did every morning when he was in Kentucky, Sayles strolled down to Number 9 to watch the men change shifts and talk things over with the mine manager. Later he convinced the train driver to let him ride with him a ways in the engine cab to the unloading site.

When Clare arrived close to noon, she surprised him as he struggled to climb down from the engine. He was winded and his face was pallid and perspired, and it struck her for the first time that he was getting old. He would be seventy on his next birthday.

She pretended she hadn't noticed and faked busying herself with some figures in her notebook so he could mop his face with his pocket handkerchief and catch his breath. She'd never thought of him as old, and when they sat down at lunch later that day, she narrowed her eyes and studied his looks for the first time in years. She'd only ever known him with silver hair, so there was no change there, except perhaps that the color had become more purely and intensely bright.

And the face was long and bony as always, but now the cords on his neck showed like a pair of thick parallel ropes, flesh draping loosely from them, the skin dried and wrinkled. But chiefly she noticed that he was so thin. Even in his exquisitely cut suits, he was old-man skinny. Skinny, she decided, as Homer. Noticing for the first time how clearly he had aged made her suddenly jittery, worried that he might be pushing himself too hard, that he had grown too frail to support his ambitions.

When she tried to suggest that he take it easier, he brushed her off. He told her he was going to hike up the holler and she was welcome to come if she wanted but not if she was going to fuss at him about his weight.

They walked up Barrow's Hollow, past the house she grew up in, firewood so old it was cut by Hillard and stacked under the run-down porch; past the caves where she hid when she was little; past the encircling pine that once sheltered her books and her fantasies.

Sayles stepped gingerly over the rocks that bridged a shallow section of the creek.

"I used to put a poke of salt over there for the deer." Clare indicated the pine. "I thought it would be fun to hang around reading James Fenimore Cooper and have some little doe there at the salt lick."

"Did the deer come by?" He brushed away the hand she offered to steady him over the last stepping-stone.

"No, deer and strip mining don't mix. No deer around here anymore. For years and years."

"I've always meant to ask you," he said, "why is there a *y* at the end of everybody's first name?"

"I don't know. In the mountains, that's what's done."

"Not Homer."

"Except for Homer. I can't imagine anyone being that familiar with him. He'd take their head off. Besides, it doesn't work with every name, does it?"

On the creek bank he stretched, stuck his hands on his hips, and said, "I love it up here, Clare. I could stay here forever."

"Not when it's cold and wet."

Inspired by the sight of the hump-backed, blue-tinged mountains, he said suddenly, "Let's build a house up here."

He turned in a circle excitedly. "Why didn't I think of it before? Let's build a beautiful house up here on the ridge, full of fireplaces and bedrooms and picture windows. Not too big or showy, something that's compatible with the environment. Something made of wood and stone and glass that would seem organic to the ridge. Alex could get up in the morning, slide open a glass door, and be right in the outdoors the way he loves."

"Oh, Lawrence, you'd die if you weren't in Washington."

"No, I wouldn't," he answered a little defensively.

"You'd die if you didn't know what was going on in the world every single minute."

"Never heard of the telephone? No television, but we'd definitely have a telephone. What do you say?"

She walked over to him, pine cones crackling under her heavy boots, and looped her arm through his. "You really want to?"

"Yes, yes, I do. I'm up here and I'm breathing the fresh air. I'm clearheaded and I think it's the smartest thing I've ever thought of. A magnificent house, right up here on the ridge, overlooking the hollow and the house where you and your father were born. God, but that appeals to me."

"Most of the land up above has been eroded by strip mining," she warned him, "so a lot of the trees are gone. There are no roots to hold the water when it rains. It all comes washing down through here."

He jammed his hands into his pockets. "Reforestation."

"That takes time."

"I've got time. I've got the means. I'll get somebody to figure it all out."

"You're going to have a time getting an earthmover up here and a backhoe to dig the foundation, not to mention lumber and fixtures, stringing electric and phone wire. It would cost a fortune. You'd have to work around the existing landscape or move a lot of the trees. Put in septics."

"Clare, if I didn't know you better, I'd think you're afraid of a challenge."

"Not me!"

"Anyway, it's my challenge. You run your company; I'll build this impossible house. We'll see who's in the black first."

"Is this a wager, then?"

"I believe it is."

"And the bet?"

He considered this for a moment. "I'll wager that I can hire more of your miners out of your mines to work on my house than you can keep working for you."

She opened her mouth in disbelief. "Lawrence Sayles, what a ratty bet!"

He snickered. "Yeah, it is kind of, now that you mention it." Then he smiled brightly. "I'm getting into the mood of the territory. I'm going to start thinking like one of those old-time union organizers standing up to the mine boss, which is you, by the way."

"You're turning into a snake."

"Thanks. A compliment."

She stood back a little to gauge him. "Are you serious?"

"I'm serious."

"This is eastern Kentucky, Lawrence. Look around you. Nobody here knows the Oval Office from Ovaltine. Can you really be satisfied living with miners and farmers and hill people?"

"I'm happy to be where you are, Clare. I want to be part of what you are, and what you are comes out of right here. I don't want you living a separate life from me anymore. I'll still be in Washington, and Virginia, and anywhere else in the world I have to be. But I have a wife on a coal ridge in Kentucky, and if that's where she is, then that's my home."

Within the contour of the mountain Clare imagined the house as Sayles described it. She advanced into the clearing a little and turned around slowly. It was an impressive sight—the ridge, the hollow falling away beneath it. Smoke from a stone chimney scalloped thinly into the sky. She would live in the shadow of the big pine. Her father would have liked that.

She crossed the clearing and kissed Sayles on the cheek.

"But I win either way, don't I?" she teased him. "I'm going to keep all my miners, plus get a beautiful new home right on the spot where I dreamed all my dreams."

"We'll see."

They stopped by at all the houses on their way back down the holler, Sayles admiring everyone's hand-sewn quilts and hand-raised hogs and chickens. Dobbie Fields invited him on a snake hunt, but Sayles said he didn't want any part of that. He'd known Joe Stalin, he declared, and that was snake enough to last a lifetime. (That just flew around town by the end of the day and because every right-thinking man and woman in Mills Bend hated the godless Communists, of course their eyes gleamed even brighter when he strolled among them.)

When he and Clare were nearly home, he complained that he was starving from all the fresh air.

"You're going to have to change the way you say things, Lawrence, now that you're going to be settling down here. You can't just say, 'I'm hungry.' That's so colorless, so bland, so like a northerner."

"What do I say?"

"You say, 'Why, I'm as hollow as an old burnt-out stump.' "

He repeated it in his stiff New England accent, and she hooted.

"I'll get it, Clary. You'll see, and I'm going to love it."

She bent a hickory twig and snapped it against his knees. "Maybe, maybe not. I don't know how much you're going to love it, Lawrence, when your neighbors start calling you Larry."

When he returned to Washington, everybody pestered her to know how soon he would be back—and by the way, how's business, Clary? She'd worked the miracle of wresting the mines from Muddy and changing all their lives, but Lawrence Sayles was the one who'd put them on the map.

Only Homer was not seduced. Although he'd accepted Sayles's hospitality in Washington and Virginia for a decade (especially that good whiskey!), he hadn't changed his mind much about the man and his ancestors in all those years. He and Sayles shared a tenuous civility when Lawrence was in Kentucky, but that was the extent of their rapport—none of it Sayles's doing.

Homer was downright rude. He stalked out of the room when Sayles entered, glowered at him when he spoke, brushed past him in the hallway on the way to the bathroom. Clare had hissed at him a few times, but Homer had gone all stony on her and finally she'd given up trying to mellow him. He had the worker's ancestral hatred of the privileged and was too old and too insatiable in his certainties to surrender it.

On a night when she was meeting a delegation of miners with Toby, soon-to-be-seventy-four-year-old Homer Barrow made dinner for his sixty-nine-year-old in-law. After fifteen minutes of mute chewing, he took his plate to the sink and scraped the remains of his dinner into a tin pail he'd put there.

Sayles pushed back from the table. "We've known each other quite a while now, Homer. Seems to me we ought to be on friendlier terms."

Homer turned on the hot water, started to rinse his plate, but said nothing.

Sayles persisted. "I think since Clare has this big burden to shoulder that the least we can do for her is to reach some sort of accord."

"You mean be friends?"

"Not if you'd rather not be."

"Good."

"Just a cessation of hostilities."

Homer's eyebrows rushed together in a frown, and Sayles quickly filled in. "Just a little more warmth. Do you hate me so much you can't even manage that?"

"Now, how you be knowin' what I feel?"

"I don't."

Homer glared around the room, his eye settling finally on the can opener screwed into the doorjamb. "I'm sure you're a good man, Lawrence, but here's what I think, and I don't intend to change my mind: It just ain't right for one man to have all the money in this world and the rest to have none. To have one man a slavey all his life with nothin' to show for it while the other man just has fortune handed to him on a platter, like meat."

"I'm not going to give it away, if that's what you're driving at, Homer," Sayles offered immediately. "There are hundreds of people dependent upon me, and I'm not about to change that now. But I've done the best I can my whole life. I've played fair with everyone who's ever worked for me, and I'll warrant I've done some good along the way. We're old men now, both of us. We ought to come to terms with this thing."

"Maybe." Homer held the plate under the hot running water and wiped it with his hand. When the plate was clean, he was careful to turn the faucet off tightly. Tap water indoors was a new development in an old life; he valued it in a way that someone born to handy water couldn't. "A man's got to stand by his convictions, especially when it gets close to the end," he said, turning around. "I'm not about to change my mind."

"I'm not asking you to change your mind about me. I'm just asking if you can't relax your vigilance to make Clare happy. I'm just asking you—for family peace—to fake it a little. I'm going to build a home here, you know, up on the ridge."

"Where?"

"By the big pine."

"Clary's pine?"

"Yes."

"Keepin' the tree?"

"Of course. I'm putting down roots. I'm making a commitment to Clare and her work here."

Homer dried his hands on a dishcloth, pondering this for such a maddeningly long time that Sayles finally sighed loudly.

"Well, I guess I could be more civil."

"Good."

"But don't you be goin' overboard."

"Not I."

"Good. Now, are you going to eat that?" He pointed at the ham hocks and white beans left untouched on Sayles's dinner plate.

"No."

"Don't like it?"

"No, it's very good."

"Not much a-one for ham hocks, are you?"

"I guess not."

"Oughta eat somethin'. You're nothin' but bone."

"Look who's talking."

"Can I have it, for her?" Homer jerked his thumb in the direction of the sow in the backyard.

"Sure."

"Thanks."

And that was the end of their discussion and, for a time, Homer's hostility.

23

The hat was the problem.

Sayles had arrived from Washington the Friday of the Columbus Day holiday with a six-sided box done up in stiff brown paper, tied with twine.

Homer was celebrating his birthday. That is, his family was celebrating Homer's birthday. The birthday boy himself had ducked out before dawn to hide somewhere up in the holler with the plan not to show up again until everyone had gone to bed. But at five-thirty that evening Clare caught him sneaking into the backyard to feed his sow and demanded he come inside to cut his cake. Right now!

After Homer had sullenly blown out the candles, Sayles sent Alex into the living room to fetch the mysterious box.

The instant he saw it, Homer turned mule-ornery, jammed his arms across his chest, and would have refused to even open the gift if Clare hadn't pushed down on his foot with her own so hard that his eyes watered in pain. He flashed her an evil look, pulled the box over to him, and unwrapped it without enthusiasm.

Clare chewed her knuckle all the while this was going on because Sayles and Alex were just beaming, thinking they had outfoxed the old man and come up with something he might actually enjoy. Neither of them had shared the surprise with her beforehand, so Clare hadn't been able to tell them not to bother with a gift, which is probably why they hadn't consulted with her in the first place.

After much sawing through with a buck knife and melodramatic wheezing from the exertion, Homer freed the twine and paper, and a businesslike cardboard hat box sat on the kitchen table.

He lifted the lid and from under a cloud of soft tissue paper pulled out a handsome dark brown felt hat. He turned it over in his hands as if it were a stick of dynamite.

"Try it on, Grandpa! Try it on," Alex urged him boyishly.

But Homer did no such-a thing.

Sayles made a stab. "It's from James Lock and Company, in London. I ordered it made for you the last time I was in London and they sent it to me in Washington. I took the measurement from your old miner's helmet. Look at the workmanship—sixteen weeks from rabbit skin to finished product." Sayles turned and flashed his smile at Clare. "The Duke of Edinburgh has his hats made at Lock." He'd yet to glean that Homer thought the hat's deep crown held every abuse ever perpetrated on the workingman.

"Isn't it a beauty? I thought you needed a new hat." His voice trailed off a little. Finally, he'd noticed that Homer's face had the look of a squall. "It's brown. Your favorite color," he added without spirit. He looked over at Clare, clearly disappointed. She shrugged her shoulders and rolled her eyes. She wanted to kiss him. She wanted to die.

Without a word Homer put the hat back into the box and folded the tissue over it.

"It's a great hat, Dad," Alex offered. "It's gonna look great on Grandpa. Right, Grandpa?"

Homer folded the brown paper in neat squares, made a small ball of the twine, and set both into the box, which he then covered squarely with the lid.

"Who's this duke fella?" he demanded.

"The Queen of England's husband," Sayles offered cautiously.

Homer snorted and stomped from the kitchen. The truce collapsed, and the hat, in its six-sided box, was shot unceremoniously to the back of his closet. He gave some thought of feeding it to his girl, but decided to hold off for a while, until Sayles went home. He paused long enough to take off his trousers, which were muddy, and change into a fresh pair. Then he clomped across the street to join the hymn singers at the Advent Christian Church, muttering under his breath until the verse of the hymn took hold and he tried to throw his voice into it before the effort doubled him over coughing.

The next morning Alex and Clare walked up the hollow to the Double Creek stream.

Alex was barefoot and wearing faded jeans. He still had his summer tan, and his hair was as white-blond as Clare's; it stood up in tufts all over his head when he wasn't wearing his International Harvester cap, a current favorite.

"You look like you were born here, Alex," Clare said, studying him. "You look like the real McCoy."

"Or the real Hatfield." He had immersed himself in the local lore. "Did they really massacre each other the way Grandpa says they did?"

"Oh, my, yes. And more. Maybe they still do, for all I know. Did he tell you about Sid Hatfield over in Matewan?"

"Uh-huh. That Sid was something," he said, balancing himself on a huge pine blow-down that hung out high over a stream polluted nearly scarlet by mining waste.

"Watch out, okay?" she warned. "That thing is really dangerous. If you fall in, you'll probably be radioactive when they pull you out."

She was sitting down in a small clear patch in a wide thicket of mountain laurel and was in the process of pulling off her boots and socks. Although many of the trees had already begun shedding their leaves, the East was sweltering under a muggy Indian summer. Clare and Alex had hiked high above the holler in search of a cool spot.

"I'm not going to touch a thing up here," she said to herself as much as to Alex while she looked around at the breathtaking view. "I'm going to leave it just as it is forever. That laurel smells wonderful."

"Can you clean up the stream?" Alex set one bare foot before the other, picking his way over the pine's dead limbs with care. He pointed. "Look how it's killed all the plant life on the banks. I bet it killed this tree."

"No, Alex—look at the big black scar on the underside. Lightning hit it and the tree died eventually. It's probably full of ants."

He scrambled down on all fours, pushed himself over the edge as far as he could, and checked out the two-foot gouge the lightning had made in the heart of the big pine. "Yeah, you're right." Then he was up on his feet, inching toward the top of the tree. "I think you should try with the stream, Mom. There's a solution to every problem." The voice of Lawrence Sayles.

Even in motion Alex moved in the distracted manner of those who from birth somehow possessed the certain knowledge that events and people would wait for them. He was preternaturally calm, and took in everything with a quiet equanimity, so the opposite of his mother. It was not the world that inspected Alex, it was Alex who could wait with the patience of a cat for the world to unfold itself for him and then unerringly choose that which he believed, preferred, espoused, whatever it was. Clare decided this sangfroid on the part of a ten-year-old was the result of an unclouded childhood; it was a less troubling explanation than paternity.

She turned her head away so she wouldn't have to watch him balance himself on the tip of the tree with all the confidence of a Wallenda. She didn't want to choke him with her own terrors. She wanted him to jump and run and climb and take chances the way she had when she was his age. Alex had to find out for himself what would hurt him and what wouldn't. That had been Homer's way, and that would be her way with her own kid. Thinking this didn't keep her stomach from flipping, however, as he dangled his body out over the stream, which although shallow, really did boil with noxious chemicals.

"I hope I can save the stream, but I'm not sure," she told him. "We've stopped the leaching of the chemicals, so it won't get worse, but I don't know if I can make it better. I'm going to try, you can be sure. Alex, come on, be careful."

She shook her fist at him after he waved her away, then fell back on the ground, looped her hands under her head, and closed her eyes against the hot sun. "Oh, God, Alex, there's so much to do. Maybe I'll just fall asleep here and forget about everything."

"Can't. You've got a meeting. And Barry's coming with the plane to take you back to Washington. I've got my eye on my watch."

"You won't need an appointments secretary when you get to the White House."

"Funny, Mom." With his arm outstretched for balance, he bounced up and down in an effort to rock the massive tree. He then shammed a few back dives and touched his toes in a pretend jackknife, hummed a tuneless song, and sat down to stare into the vermilion water.

"Let me stay a few extra days, okay? Dad'll bring me up on Tuesday. It's the last of the warm weather." He turned and gave her a baleful stare.

"I don't want you to miss any more school."

"Just two days. I'll make it up."

"I don't know . . ."

"Dad said I could."

"Oh, well, if Dad says," she mocked him.

"Grandpa's going to show me where he buried his mule, Isaac."

"I'd be more excited if he were going to tell you the name of his sow. Okay, you can stay. But this is the last long weekend till the Thanksgiving holiday, no matter what Daddy says, okay?"

"Thanks, Mom." He turned back to peer into the creek. "I'm gonna look for mutant fish."

On her back, Clare stretched her arms out from her sides. She'd stripped off her sweater and was in one of Alex's white cotton undershirts. It was a wonder, with its load of mining poisons, that the stream still flowed, but it made reassuring gurgling sounds as it passed over the rocks along its low banks; that was the only sound, except for the occasional crow cry and dry rustle as some critter moved through the underbrush.

Clare realized suddenly that a rattler could come slithering by and that she should sit up. But then a breeze kicked up to touch her face, the sun slipped behind a cloud, and the air lost some of its heat. The smell of the mountain laurel intensified lavishly, and she couldn't have moved if a family of rattlers curled up in her hair.

Don't fall asleep. She longed to go off under this piny canopy and sleep for days. She'd been up until well after midnight the previous night, reading schematics with a staff engineer and trying to translate concept into something like understanding in her brain. Hateful stuff.

She made herself open her eyes long enough to check on Alex. He was lying on his stomach and spitting as far as he could out into the water. The miracle was that he loved Kentucky, loved hiking up to the ridge, scuttering around the caves, getting dirty and grime-faced like the men. The keen observer of nature in Middleburg and Georgetown had transplanted happily to Appalachia. He spent whole days in the mountains, listening to the squirrels' shrill cries, teaching himself to track small game, hunting rattler with Dobbie Fields. He crawled up and down the blowdowns, inspected the caves—he'd staked one out as his hiding place—pulled off his clothes and swam in the swimming hole with the other kids. Sometimes he just lay flat on his back on the ground and stared at the sky, chewing gum and watching the hawks circle.

He'd made friends with Tommy Johnson, who kept his forge in a shallow cave near his farm. Tommy had taught Alex a little of the smithy and let him work the hand-cranked forge. Alex had helped him make a wagon brace, and for days it had been the talk of the house.

He'd gone down into Number 9 at least twice that Clare was

sure of, but she suspected there had been more adventures on the man-trip than she could bear to think about. Alex would hang out at the mine mouth during the shift changes, make those pale eyes glow as the men got ready to go down, and wangle a trip for himself to the coal face. Not that he hadn't already poked around every abandoned deep mine in the county. Behind her back, Homer stumbled around on hobbly legs with him to all the played-out shafts. The old man had lost a step or two, and his lungs seemed on the verge of collapse, but he could still regale Alex with a hundred years of the mountains' violent lore. He used a hickory stick nearly as tall and skinny as he was to keep him in step with his only grandchild.

"Now, up here," he'd wheeze, "is where a pretty good union organizer named Will Fentress was murdered. He wasn't a man to just get up and make a speech, collect dues, and then go home. Didn't say much at all, which is why the owners feared him, I suppose. They never could get a handle on what he was a-thinkin'.

"Over there"—he pointed with his stick to a ramshackle barn—"up there in the loft, hired men set up a machine gun, and when old Will come a-walkin' right past here"—he indicated a clump of wild rhododendron bushes—"they shot him. Maybe about a hundred times. Blood was a-runnin' all down this gully and down over those flat rocks there. Tore his body in half and left his brains all around this half-acre. Guess they figured if they killed old Will, they'd get rid-a the union. And they was right."

Homer had the mountain credo, and he'd put it into Alex: The free-spirited and independent man is the man at peace with his world; the forest is a living thing and has to be respected; nothing counts more than loyalty to the family because without family there is nothing; physical bravery is as important as self-respect; never forget where you come from, because in this nation no act of birth or accident of fortune can raise one man higher than another; never break in the face of misery or adversity, but—well, sometimes it don't matter what you do, life just kicks you in the teeth and that's that, so take a drink and forget about it.

Alex arrived in Kentucky the well-traveled, well-schooled heir to a grand New England heritage. In the five years since Clare had introduced him to Mills Bend, he'd become a boy who had a heart not just for the critters he loved, but for the mountain people who lived in harmony with them. Homer had imbued rich, worldly Alex with the characteristic rich, worldly Lawrence Sayles experienced only faintly—compassion. Even if she brought every miner in every dog hole in eastern Kentucky the security of a good, safe job at a decent wage, in her mind nothing counted as much as what the experience had done for Alex. He took in everything with his eyes, said little, but behind that placid expression she knew his mind was racing, clicking away as it formulated the values she hoped would guide him the rest of his life. She had established a certain fantasy of him as an adult: the rich, worldly, aristocrat with the sensibility of a Brahmin and the heart of a hill person. Thinking of him as a grown man caused her mind to fall into such a peaceful state that she drifted off to sleep.

She'd been dreaming for fifteen minutes when Alex roused her. Feeling pleasantly groggy, she picked her way back down the holler a step or two behind him. The smell of the laurel was still in her clothes and the serenity of the ridge clung to her spirit all the way to town. It was only when she reached Main Street that old truths crept into her reverie and tightened the muscles in her neck.

Truths half-hidden, a monumental deception—what would her son think of her if he knew the very nature of what he was was a lie? What would he think of himself? Pondering this, even fleetingly, made her head start to pound, and she spent the hours until Barry arrived to fly her up to Washington nursing a powerful headache.

The Sayles family jet was a Gulfstream II. Six of its deep-cushioned passenger seats faced each other, while the rest were arranged like banquettes along either side; all were covered in fine gray doeskin, velvet to the hand. The airplane was commodious enough to allow fifteen people to move around comfortably, and the mahogany cabinets aft were stocked with food, wine, liquor, and the latest newspapers and magazines. From her forward seat Clare could watch Barry Zwig, who had flown Lawrence Sayles around the globe in one plane or another for nearly twenty-five years, and his copilot, in the cockpit.

She stretched her long, tanned legs onto the seat opposite and relaxed. For a weary body and an addled brain, there is no soporific like going along at a tear, twenty-five thousand feet above the eastern seaboard in a luxury private jet.

She sipped again from the glass of white wine Barry had given her before takeoff, the Appalachian Mountains falling away behind her and the late-day sun glinting on the jet's wings. She was surprised at how good it was to be alone, that nothing was required of her but just to kick back and relax. She really was too busy for two days in Washington. She had little enough time to spend with Alex as it was and harbored some small resentment about her errand. But then, she'd never been good at turn-downs, even with Vivien Tuttle, who had cooked up some sort of award to give to her as a way of publicizing one of her obscure arts charities. Vivien had made many pathetic, supplicating phone calls to Mills Bend and had worn Clare down, then typically escalated her demands once Clare had accepted. Clare was expected to give press interviews, attend the reception, accept the Woman in Business Award, or some such thing, and make an acceptance speech. Clare cringed at the prospect, envisioning how stupid she would feel. The picture came to her mind of herself on the podium, a laminated wood plaque in her hand and contempt in her heart. She would have to come up with some anecdote to engage her audience, something about miners and mountain people that would touch their hearts and make her own skin crawl. She felt the old mechanism clicking in, the familiar loathing for what was now her own class, an unsentimental journey back to her previous lifetime. She had made an orthodoxy of her biases and recognized that she wasn't all that different from Homer in this regard.

Through the open cockpit door Barry told her there was heavy traffic over Washington and they would have to circle. She drained the last of the wine from her glass. Still, there would be a high point to the weekend. Sylvia would meet her at the reception and afterward they'd go to Lion d'Or for some exquisite food and too much drink, which Clare had a hankering for—and some juicy gossip, another plus. She roused herself at the thought of seeing Sylvia again.

Henry was there when the plane touched down at National Airport, nearly forty-five minutes late. He had pulled the Cadillac onto the tarmac at a section of the airport where private planes pull up and was in the process of dusting its front windshield in the failing light, when Barry lowered the jet stairs.

Traffic was heavy and they were behind schedule by the time Henry swung the Cadillac into The Heights' driveway. Clare would have to rush if she wanted to make her press interview in the Federal part of the District.

Preston popped open the kitchen door and stepped back as she blew into the house. He fussed over her suitcase, his sharp up-turned nose giving the impression that he disdained all of it.

"Mrs. Sayles—"

"Sorry, Preston," she said, rushing past him. "Do you think you could come up and find that black silk dinner dress in my closet and have Sophie press it?"

"Mrs. Sayles—" He dogged her up the stairs to the second floor. She was single-minded, on a mission, and didn't hear him, and by then she'd had second thoughts about the dress. "Maybe I'd better wear something cooler. Go into the storage closet on the third floor—do you mind?—and see if you can find that lime-green dress my husband gave me a thousand years ago. Ask Sophie to check if it's clean or needs ironing. Maybe you could have Marguerite bring me up some lemonade or something ice cold. And some crackers. I'm starving."

She pounded down the hallway, popping the snaps on her workshirt, Preston on her heels.

"Mrs. Sayles, Mrs. O'Dowd has telephoned at least a dozen times since noon. She wants you to know that she must speak with you."

Clare tossed her purse onto the bed and made a face. "She'd better not stand me up. I'm counting on her to get me through this thing. What did she say to you?"

"She said she had to speak with you urgently."

"That's all?"

"Very nearly. She said exactly, 'Tell Mrs. Sayles that I have to speak with her the instant she arrives, the instant. Got that, toad?'"

Clare bent and untied her boots so he wouldn't see her grinning, but she kept a casual tone in her voice and said, "What on earth can be urgent to Sylvia? Nothing is urgent to the woman for whom there are no surprises."

Oblivious to his appalled stare, she pulled off her workshirt to reveal a white undershirt. With a great deal of hauteur he looked down his nose at the garment.

Clare indicated the undershirt with pleasure. "It's Alex's," she told him as he looked away. She hadn't worn a dress or skirt for months. "Poor Alex, I've robbed him of all his underwear. Wearing his underpants too. Look—"

He rolled his eyes at her and walked over to the door.

"Try to reach Mrs. O'Dowd, will you, Preston?" she called after him. "I'm going to shower and wash my hair and then I'm out of here. And try to find that dress, okay?" She checked her watch. She was already ten minutes late.

By the time she finished showering, Sophie was there with the green dress and Marguerite was holding the glass of lemonade so Clare could drink while she combed her wet hair. Preston returned to say no one answered at Sylvia's.

Clare frowned into the mirror, worried that Sylvia was deserting her. Her hair was still wet, but already it frizzed and curled from the humidity, and her skin was dry from months of exposure to the sun. There was a fine web of lines around her eyes. She licked her lips and bent in close to the mirror.

"It's five till six, Mrs. Sayles." Preston walked to the door and opened it, but Clare stayed staring at herself. She ought to take the time to at least put on lipstick. With her hair kinking and the last of her summer tan, she was looking a little too wild, a few too many light-years from the Summit Club. Too much like she'd spent the summer in Samoa, in a sarong. She stepped back, turned sideways, and patted her stomach. The green dress, which had been tight ten years before, was now almost indecently so; her body had taken a different shape and these days her breasts were a little too round and her hips a tad too wide. She really should stop and change into the black silk.

"Better hurry, Mrs. Sayles."

She shimmied a little dance. The hell with it. They'd have to take her, tits and ass and all, and although she couldn't recognize it herself, of course, she looked terrific—sexy and a little out of control.

She jammed her feet into a pair of heels and ran down the stairs and out the door.

The interviews went smoothly. A quick stop at one of the television stations for a live bit during the six o'clock local news. Not even the reporter could pretend Vivien's event was of any import, except as a social note, but it was a slow news day, so they'd use it. And Lawrence Sayles's wife was someone to follow no matter how trivial her involvements, especially since she'd given up charity balls and moved to eastern Kentucky to run a coal company. The weirdness factor alone made it newsworthy. Clare had slipped in a self-serving commercial for coal, looking directly into the camera and saying as if it were the first thing on every viewer's mind that the country ought to get out from under dependence on foreign oil and back into coal. Afterward she gave a quick interview to the *Washington Post* style-page reporter, who met her at the TV studio.

Then she ran back to the car and Henry turned out from Connecticut Avenue in a peel of rubber, plunging into the traffic. Clare held her breath for the ten minutes it took to get there. The reception was on First Street, at the Library of Congress, an act of intellectual hubris on Vivien's part.

Henry braked the car at the curb. Clare bolted out and up the sidewalk, dashing past the Neptune fountain. Walking through a wall of heat and humidity that sucked out her breath and reddened her face, she took the steps of the library two at a time. From above, the busts of literary greats glowered down at her as she pushed through the door into the lobby, and a worried-looking young woman rushed to greet her. The girl flicked her eyes quickly around the curved body, shocked that Lawrence Sayles's wife had long, unruly hair and an ass that seemed to move even when the rest of her didn't. She'd expected someone with more of the pinched demeanor of the post-deb, someone more like herself—blond hair smoothed into a velvet bow in back, a blue linen suit and an Hermès scarf knotted over a white silk blouse. Someone not the least bit florid from the heat.

"Let's find Vivien, shall we?" she said in a caramelized Madeira School voice as she turned away.

They walked down rococo hallways, past reading rooms and long stretches of card catalogues. A heavy, musty odor rolled out of each room as they passed.

"I know what you're thinking," the girl said over her shoulder to Clare, who in fact was thinking nothing in particular. "The really valuable books are in vaults, safe and sound. This is only the third public event they've allowed in here. Vivien has a great deal of pull."

They rushed down another long hallway, made a jog to the left, and entered a large reception area crowded with guests, all of whom, it seemed to Clare, flipped narrowed, shocked eyes on her as she nearly fell into the room.

Vivien hustled over, her unpleasant, tight-featured faced screwed into the same starched smile as her assistant. She was shaking Clare's hand and bathing her in obsequious compliments before Clare could even utter a greeting. Always suspicious of Vivien, Clare received the flattery in silence. When a waiter passed by, she snagged a glass of champagne from his tray.

"We've got to be out of here by eight-fifteen," Vivien cautioned, watching her drink, "otherwise they'll turn the lights out on us. We're only the third public event ever allowed in here, you know."

"I know."

"By the way, Clare," she said in a stage whisper, "you're, uh, wet."

"I'm perspiring. It's warm and I've had to run."

"Well, it's all over your face. Christine"—she turned to the post-deb and said through her teeth—"find a tissue for Mrs. Sayles, will you? Discreetly, dear." Then back to Clare, "You mop

up, all right, darling? We'll get started. Not a bad turnout, huh?"
she gazed around the room with a satisfied look that made her
tiny eyes gleam.

With evident embarrassment Christine came back with some
tissue, which was actually toilet paper, and Clare wiped it around
her face. She passed it back to Christine, who reverently disposed
of it, at the same time fixing such a look of satisfaction on her
that Clare averted her eyes and made a show of gazing around the
room.

An enormous chandelier dangled above them, ablaze with light;
it was turned up to its maximum incandescence and put hard
edges around everyone. Vivien looked ghostly. Her gray hair was
pulled back from her face and caught up in her trademark short
ponytail so severely that it caused her eyes to slant. Clare was fascinated by their slant and wondered if the hairdo had a secondary
mission, to tighten Vivien's face without benefit of surgery. She
had been there when Sylvia reported to Vivien that exiled Queen
Frederika of Greece had gone in for eyelid surgery and died under
the anesthesia. Vivien had grilled Sylvia on the details. Probably
she was afraid of going out like the Greek queen, and the ponytail
was her jury-rigged solution. Clare dragged herself away from
speculation and back to the conversation.

"Tell me again about this award, Vivien."

"Well"—Vivien looped her arm through Clare's and began
walking her around the room—"it's a benefit for my writer's
group."

"People actually paid money to watch me get this award?"

Vivien assumed her most down-to-earth demeanor. "Truth is,
Clare, you're kind of the hook. I was rather hoping Lawrence
might come with you, but"—she shrugged her shoulders—"it was
enough to put his name at the head of the invitation. Be sure to
thank him again, will you? That got the foreign embassies and
two White House special assistants, and they brought more, of
course. The usual grazers, undersecretaries from various agencies,
but some pretty impressive names too, you can see. It all works
so smoothly once the right pieces are in place." Her eyes settled
on the middle distance behind Clare's shoulder and misted over,
and she began to speak as if her life were a photo shoot for *House
and Garden*. "You know," she said, "I like to think of every party,
of my life really, as a table setting. The perfect Georgian silver,
Meissen china, or Spode, bursting flowers, Pratesi table linens, a
Monet water lily somewhere around."

After another moment of rapt staring, she refocused her concentration on Clare and said, "Every element separate yet entire in its own right, and then it's all combined and transformed into a perfectly functioning single entity. Isn't it consoling to think of life this way?"

Clare bobbed her head up and down, torn between pity and contempt, decided on contempt, and immediately felt guilty. The champagne had turned on her, she decided, and had made her depressed. She set her glass on the tray when a waiter came past, brushed her hair away from her face, and vowed not to drink again until she was safely at Lion d'Or with Sylvia.

"Goodness," Vivien said, checking her watch, "we really must get the show on the road."

But she seemed in no particular hurry, and Clare thought she might be a little drunk or stoned as she whisked her over to a group of dark-skinned people, each of whom she introduced as a celebrated artist or writer in their native Latin American country. Clare towered over them all and had to stoop to pick up their accented English when she offered herself for conversation. When she responded to their questions, she found herself talking at the top of her voice over the din to make them hear her. Most of them seemed to have no understanding of who she was or what she was doing there, except that she was one of the richest people in America, which got their attention right off the bat. They bathed her with adoring glances and listened in respectful silence when she spoke, as if she were letting them in on the secrets of the cosmos. They bobbed their heads in agreement with everything she said. The men spent a good deal of the time staring at her breasts.

They seemed to be peasants, maybe Indians, not professional writers or artisans. "Right, right," she said whenever one of them began discussing their work. After a little while they were all worn out from trying to comprehend each other, and they turned their attention to someone who spoke Spanish and left Clare free to look around the room.

Many of the old crowd were there, the Summit set, the moneyed ones she had entertained at Little Dinners. She recognized an officer of the United Mine Workers, out of place in a lumpish wool suit, and couldn't imagine what he was doing there, but then, Vivien had traded high and hard on the Sayles name, so there should have been no surprises. The humidity had overcome the air-conditioning, and most of the men had given up and were standing around, roasting miserably in their suits, mopping their faces with their handkerchiefs. A hefty woman Clare did not know kept her Blackgama mink draped over her shoulders while steambath-size beads of perspiration rolled down her face.

Some of them were watching Clare hungrily from the corners of their eyes, or boldly trying to engage her with a smile, hoping she might acknowledge them and signal with a smile of her own that it was all right for them to approach her. Perhaps share a little chitchat—the heat, the traffic, oh-those-politicians, that kind of thing. The next time they saw her they'd remind her of it, maybe get an introduction to Lawrence Sayles. A base for casual friendship might be established. They could exit Vivien's little gathering and tell their friends they'd met Clare Sayles. Stock to be traded. It always amazed her how some people could dine out for years on even the most peripheral contact with a celebrity. Lawrence once told her that the reason he never used public rest rooms was that whenever he did, a parade of men trooped in behind him so they could boast later that they'd taken a leak alongside the great Lawrence Sayles. He could hold it forever when he was out, and she admired him for that.

Alone at the center of the party, she felt pleasantly alien. All her old friends were strangers again, a great relief. No matter what happened in Kentucky, she would never come back to Washington and lead the society life again. She'd rather spend the rest of her life in a dog hole. The woman in the mink was trying to catch her eye. Clare bent her lips into a faint smile but turned away on some feigned errand when the woman started for her. Across the room she saw Vivien furtively rub her front teeth with a finger to get rid of any lipstick. She no longer had need of them, and they perceived this, and it made her maddeningly desirable to them. She could have shown up tonight in her jeans and work boots and slopped Red Man juice on their good shoes and they still would have bathed her with the light of their luminous, fame-worshipping eyes.

The champagne was warm and the *petits chaussons au Roquefort* the waiters were passing had the consistency of sea sponges. Clare found herself wondering if Toby had gotten that new loading machine up and running. She wondered if Alex and Lawrence had gone up to the ridge with the surveyor to plan the new house, if Homer had found the power tool he wanted in the Gaines catalogue. Her eyes glazed over. Her brain became pleasantly soft. She felt her previous depression lifting and accepted another glass of champagne. She decided that if Sylvia really had stood her up, she'd get Barry to fly her back to Kentucky that night. And then suddenly, there was Sylvia walking toward her from the other side of the room.

Only it was not the usual Sylvia. There was no cynical smile, and she had a frazzled, frantic set to her features. Her hair was out of its chignon and half down her back, trailing hairpins. She gave Clare such an unsettling stare that Clare immediately stopped waving and began to walk toward her slowly.

Sylvia moved through the hot, crowded room as if in service to some fearsome mission, the idea of which panicked her. Once, she looked back over her shoulder, and when she turned back to Clare her eyes were full of uncharacteristic warning.

She was no more than three feet away, and Clare believed she could almost make out what she was saying when her gaze was taken by a shadow presenting itself in the doorway. Her eyes went past Sylvia's face to what seemed at first to be just a shape, a dark image only vaguely present. Irritated by the distraction, she returned to Sylvia. But now Sylvia, too, had turned to stare at the figure partially hidden by the door frame. Slowly, Clare followed her friend's eyes. Drawn by instinct, images of obscured memory flashing through her brain, she watched as the shape materialized into a man. An odd figure, tall and muscular in a black suit, towering over everyone else in the room and with the dust of the plain seemingly still clinging to him. Even at the margins of the party he dominated through his size and by that aura of cynical detachment that compelled even the most casual observer to attention. Several of those on the fringe of the crowd had turned to stare at him. It had been years and years, but in less than an instant Clare could compute the long body, the lanky hair, and finally the facial features in profile, softened by age and uncharacteristic self-indulgence. As always, his eyes swept the room restlessly, but then he turned slowly, deliberately, in her direction; her brain pitched and shock and sensation overcame her.

She must have wobbled, because Sylvia reached out to support her waist with an arm. She felt as if she were living underwater, where images floated with exaggerated, time-warped slowness. She heard Sylvia say her name, but when she turned back to acknowledge her, her eye was taken instead by Sylvia's earlobe, which was missing a tiny notch of flesh no more than an eighth of an inch long. Fixated suddenly on this absurd detail, Clare marveled that she had known Sylvia so many years and had never noticed the tender mutilation of her earlobe. Strange. Her hand went to her own ear distractedly. She felt weak. The very air seemed altered, and with her heightened senses the noise and heat of the room made her feel hectic. Her brain ran this way and that. There was now such a roar in her head and her heart knocked so violently against her ribs, she could not be sure of what she heard or saw. Against her will she went back to his face.

He stood in the doorway at a certain remove from himself, as if he were watching his own performance with wry amusement. Then his eyes found hers, their drowsiness liquefied, and like a dark and beautiful conjurer he began to send her messages with his skin, as he always had. He emptied his eyes into hers, then shifted his gaze and slowly began undressing her with his drowsy eyes, moving from her face to her breasts. When he reached her belly, his full mouth opened slightly and he gave her the long, slow smile of recognition.

Oh, that old, familiar look, and the long-forgotten sensation it provoked between her legs. She nearly jumped out of her skin when Vivien arrived to touch her arm and tug her up to the podium, the room furnace-hot and everyone unspeakably miserable.

Vivien made her presentation, and Clare stepped forward to take the award, which turned out to be a crystal bowl. She mumbled some words about hard work and determination, most of it uninteresting and nearly inaudible because she had ducked her head so close to her chest that she couldn't project a single word.

When it was over, Sylvia rushed her out the door. They went down the long hallway and through the exit. Outside, at the top of the stone steps, Clare saw Henry open the back door of the car and the light inside the Cadillac flicker on, a hopeful little beacon. She was very nearly to the sidewalk when he stepped out from behind the fountain.

Sylvia said her name and gave her a steadying look. Lights and sounds seemed incredibly sharp. Clare detected the scent of Sylvia's perfume, Emeraude. It seemed to float on a cloud all its own, enveloping her. The air seemed cooler. Had it rained? Or had her heart simply stopped pumping blood around her body?

Sylvia stepped over to her, kissed her on the cheek, took the crystal bowl from her hands, and climbed alone into the backseat of the Cadillac. In the darkness Clare could just make her out as she leaned forward to say something to Henry and then they rolled off through a pool of water into the traffic. It had rained, she realized, and now it was muggier than ever. She looked up at the sky; there were no stars, only a thick, humid mist. She hesitated on the sidewalk, looking back at the library, and then the old familiar pull exerted itself and she fell in step with Tarik, walking out into the dark street.

24

Without speaking, they went east on Independence Avenue, halting obediently at crosswalks for traffic lights to change. Once, when a police car went speeding past, they both turned automatically and followed it with their eyes, the wail of its siren hanging in the air between them after it disappeared. Another block, and a weary family of tourists trudged by single file, trailing two little girls wearing shorts and "I ♥ our Nation's Capital" T-shirts. The night air was sticky and Clare wiped her hand over her face, but even in a suit and tie he stayed maddeningly cool and composed.

For a long time they walked in silence, staring straight ahead, until she was taken by the sound of a car engine and turned to see that a massive black limousine was crawling along behind them next to the curb.

"Do you have bodyguards?" she asked.

"I shook them."

"Is that safe?"

"Things are different now. And anyway"—he turned and held her with a look for an instant before averting his eyes—"this is Washington, not Duru."

She wanted to ask him how he had found her, but when she opened her mouth to speak, the question seemed so inane she immediately stopped herself. Anything they might say to each other seemed meaningless, unless it could somehow stop time and put them back where they'd been before. She squeezed her eyes shut for a moment to clear her head. She felt stoned, blown away. She'd spent ten years thinking *What if? What if? What if he and I were strolling some city street on a sultry Indian summer evening?* And here they were, strolling the city street as if they had only ever done exactly that.

Then, reading her mind, he told her, "I was watching the news tonight and there you were. The reporter said the Library of Congress, so I went."

He laughed out loud when he saw that she winced.

"No, you were very good. I liked the advertisement for coal. Shameless but effective, and intriguing for a beautiful woman to be out there pitching a fossil fuel. You always did have a lot of imagination." He was pleased to see that she was blushing under her tan.

He listened for a moment to their footsteps on the pavement. His came loud—thundering, he thought—but hers seemed hardly to make any noise, and once he thought that she had dropped away somehow; he turned to make sure she hadn't. But he couldn't watch her for any length of time. He saw in her face and the way she held her body that she was trying to master herself. She wasn't even trying to be clever, and she seemed to him as hungry as she'd ever been. He watched her from the corner of his eye. Even in the dim light he could see her body moving around under the dress that was the exact color of her eyes. He would have taken her right there on the sidewalk, against a lamppost, if he hadn't been who he was. Well—if she hadn't been who *she* was. He realized that when it came to Clare, he was capable of anything.

He'd known for months that he would have to come back, that Riston and the others would be apoplectic until he returned in person to explain himself once he'd told Olson that he intended to "redesign"—his own euphemism—his deal with OmniTech. They were all pissed off—*to the highest level*, they'd warned him with knowing looks. The Man himself wanted to see him, wanted to straighten him out. He'd been at it all morning with all of them.

Straightening *them* out had been his first order of business, of course. First things first. But he had a secondary agenda all his own, a piece of business to wrap up, or start up, he could never decide which he meant. A bit of risky personal business that somebody with his wits about him would turn tail and run from; but he felt exhilarated, wanted to take hold of it, shake it, make it real.

He took his hands out of his pockets and swung them at his sides, a gesture of confidence. He hadn't felt this good in years, or this excited. It was a comfort to know that all this would be behind them both soon, something he would have felt much better about if he could have said it aloud to her. He certainly wanted to say it right there in the shadow of the Air and Space Museum, as good a place as any, but he checked himself. A great deal depended on his behavior. It was necessary to seem cool, detached—the exercise Nila had impressed upon him from the cradle. They would engage in some rational discourse, balm the old hurts with well-chosen words. He would have to tell her about Topaz and Karim, and Stanley, of course, and he wasn't sure he could make himself open that wound again, but ultimately he'd do it because it held the logic he intended to use to persuade her.

He had a well-rehearsed speech prepared, but in the end it would be a process of magic, then he would sit her down (lay her down, if she would let him) and tell her that he wasn't going to go back without her. What a thought.

If she hadn't just turned up in Washington like a miracle, he would have gone to Mills Bend to try to see her. Disguise himself as a miner, or a moonshiner, something—he hadn't thought that far ahead. Slip into town without making a stir. He had been thinking about it for months. He could play to fantasy, he could play to tradition, he knew the drill and he was good at it. He'd always been good at it, and he'd gotten even better; she would find that out.

He had expected that he would have to convince her of something. He had expected that he would be nervous, pent-up, giddy. What he had not prepared himself for was the sudden sorrow he felt at seeing her again, and he was a little disconcerted because of it. The sorrow, and on his part—and he was quite sure on hers as well—the sexual pull, which he was finding very difficult to control. He kept tasting her tongue in his mouth.

He rescued himself with some small talk. And he really needed to know what she was thinking.

"The city looks better than I thought it would," he said after another long silence. "I drove past my old place on Rhode Island Avenue yesterday. Drove around Georgetown. Everything looks good to me. I'd like to get out to San Francisco, but it won't work out."

"You don't have the time?"

"Well, I don't want to give the appearance of being on vacation. I had to come back so they could chastise me properly, put me in the corner and let me stand there for a while. It really gets on their nerves that I won't let them, but in the end, I don't want to rub their noses in it by flying around the country as if I didn't take this business seriously."

"You do take it seriously though, I know you do. I mean, you must. I'm out of touch down in Kentucky, but the papers have carried a little about it. I know you're right, but you're playing with fire. I don't have to tell you that."

He smiled agreement. "Maybe, maybe not. Maybe they're the ones playing with fire. When you've got nine hundred million barrels of oil every year, you get to call the shots. Anyway, I'm not going to change my mind," he said, stopping to look her full in the face for the first time. "So, I take it you still follow events. Do you"—he'd be damned if he'd mention Lawrence Sayles's name—"participate in any way?"

"No, I don't have the time now. And I got involved in another kind of life before that, for a number of years. It just sort of drifted away from me, but I keep my ears open." She didn't intend to bring up Lawrence either, the ghostly accompanist to their reunion.

"To tell you the truth, I knew already," he admitted. "I know all about what's happened to you over the years. I know about the society life and the theater projects. I know that your best friend is Sylvia O'Dowd, Charlie's wife. I met him in Rome, at the Excelsior, you know, last year. He was with twins from Ravenna who couldn't have been more than fourteen years old." He waited until she finished chuckling. "I know about Homer, and Toby Stivers. I know about Muddy Aylesworth and Aylesworth Coal. And I know a little something about the Tug River Land Lease Corporation, although I haven't figured out everything yet."

Her mouth dropped open.

"You're surprised? I have Walter White-Lyons on my payroll and I put him on the job. He was so thrilled at having something to do, he was relentless."

She ducked her head at the mention of her old nemesis. They were both uncomfortable now, thinking about White-Lyons and the role he'd played in their divorce.

"Anyway," Tarik went on finally, "you don't have to be full-time in the State Department to know that I'm not their golden boy anymore, in case you hadn't read that far."

He was so tall, he seemed so strong and certain. He wore his convictions like one of Lawrence's bespoke English suits, all crisp pleats and perfect tailoring. She felt again the peculiar sensation she'd always had in his presence. He was less a man, more a force of nature. Power radiated from him, even when he was completely still. Alex, she thought with a start. Alex is exactly like this.

"Your instincts have always been wonderful," she told him, "and absolutely correct." *Don't dare even think about Alex in his presence. What if he read your mind?* "But I'm worried about the price you might pay. I never trusted Arthur Olson."

"He's all right."

She folded her arms across her chest, pricked by the memory. "He always behaved toward me as if I were some horrible little schoolgirl he'd been saddled with on prom night. God, but he was hard on me. The simplest thing, the simplest little broken-down truck or bulldozer part, he'd look down that thin nose of his—"

"He's gotten quite fat, by the way."

"Has he?"

"Too much of the good life. He's gotten rich off OmniTech and it's filled him out."

She was silent for a moment, then in measured tones she said, "So . . . you still have White-Lyons?"

"After you left, he went up and lived in the Sur for a while, but he drifts back and forth. I feel I have to defend myself to you over this." He was tempted to tell her that Karim had loved White-Lyons for reasons which he never understood, but he decided to wait.

"You don't have to defend yourself to anybody." She said it more brusquely then she intended, her voice full of perceived betrayal.

"Look," he said, "what could I do? He was my only contact in the kingdom all the years my mother and I lived in the States. He killed Turkit. He knew my father. I feel a moral obligation not to turn my back on him entirely. He is an old soldier, from the old school. He thought he was doing the right thing. Duty, honor, country. Don't get me wrong, I loathe him personally, but I have to put up with him—my duty, my responsibility, that kind of thing."

She gave him a questioning look, but he turned his eyes away.

"He's old now," he said. "One of these days he'll drop dead and I'll put him in the ground, or ship him back to England, and I'll have him off my back, with nothing to reproach myself for. Besides, I don't have to kill him to punish him. He knows I have nothing but contempt for him, and it's killing him."

Loud music from the radio of a passing car distracted her, and she turned away from him a little to follow the sound.

Under the lamplight he studied her, his heart tightening. Her skin was clear. She smelled of flowers. She wore a green dress that showed off her lime-green eyes. She still had the unformed cheeks and eyes of a child that had disturbed his sleep on a thousand nights. Yet on inspection he could see that her jaw had a firmer set, and there was a tracery of fine lines at her eyes and mouth. Time had given her face a substance absent when he knew her last. But she still had that drumbeat of nervous energy and impatience that got him going. She was fidgeting her hands around, indignant about their shared history as if it were a current event. This flattered him and stoked his conviction that he hadn't come on a fool's errand. He felt his body kick into a state of pleasurable arousal, and he breathed in the night air.

Over his shoulder, a single light blazed high in the Capitol dome. Washington had laid the building's cornerstone in 1793. "He heads a short procession over naked fields," Daniel Webster had written of that day, "he crosses yonder stream on a fallen tree, he ascends to the top of his eminence where original oaks of the forest stood as thick around as if the spot had been devoted to Druidical worship, and here he performed the appointed duty of the day." Tarik had read that somewhere when he was in law school and committed it to memory. He savored the image of the solitary soldier going about his business with a religious purpose. It reminded him somehow of Malik.

"The one thing I really miss about the States," he mused softly, "is knowing that I could get in a car anywhere, anytime, and that somewhere along the road I would come up on an Esso station with an air pump and a Coke machine. I always appreciated the consolation of certainties. We don't have that in the kingdom. Or we didn't used to anyway. It's better now."

"They're called Exxon."

"What are?"

"Esso. They call it Exxon now. Exxon stations."

He gave an ironic laugh. "Actually, I know that. I was just being sentimental."

"But they still have Coke machines," she reassured him hastily. "You can still get a Coke anywhere. Not that much has changed. Not really, not like . . ." she hesitated. It was important to convey the proper message. She had to choose her words carefully. She'd slipped into old habits earlier. She was Lawrence Sayles's wife now, not his. "Not like where you come from."

He gave her a steady look, letting her know he could read between her lines, but said evenly, "But you know we've had tremendous changes. Did you know that Stan Cobb made the big oil strike, the first one?"

"You're kidding? Oh, I'd love to see Stanley with the fortune he'd chased after his entire life. I bet he bought a lot of gold jewelry. I bet he imported some really awesome hookers from the South of France. I bet you've got your hands full with Cobb as

Croesus. Did he come with you?" She wheeled and peered at the limousine. "He's not still driving you, is he? Not with all that money. Did he come with you? I'd love to see him."

She was laughing with pleasure and expected him to laugh with her, impart a few of Stanley's outrageous adventures complete with hand gestures and foul language the way he used to late at night, when they were in their own bed. But when they passed under lamplight, she saw that he wasn't smiling at all, that in the pale gray depth of his eyes there was a profound sadness that held her at bay. She had thought they might enter into a shared nostalgia at least, but she was wrong. She was shocked at how devastated this made her feel. She was afraid she couldn't read him anymore, and she had always been able to read him.

"Listen," he said suddenly, "I have someplace I want to show you. Will you come with me?"

"Where?"

"It's a surprise. Come with me and you'll see." Without waiting for an answer he turned and flagged the driver, who brought the big car up alongside them.

She hesitated on the curb, debating, then climbed into the backseat.

After ten minutes of driving through darkened streets, the driver stopped the car and jumped out to open the door for her, while Tarik came around the other side. She tried to stop him with a puzzled look when she recognized the address. He crossed the sidewalk and unlocked the front door of the Georgetown apartment building she had lived in years before. Inside, she followed him up the stairs, the wooden banister still familiar under her hand, and walked behind him to the apartment door. He found the key in his pocket, unlocked the door, and stood back to let her walk through.

She peered into the darkness for a moment, flushed with nervous excitement, then realized that the perfume filling the air so thickly that she could scarcely draw a breath was the scent of what had to be a thousand blossoms. He flipped on the light so she could see that on every inch of floor space, tabletop, propped into corners, and on the grillwork of the radiators was a room-filling rainbow of roses, gardenias, tulips, lilacs—every color and variety of flower, some of them in vases, but most just heaped in bundles all over. She laughed softly in excitement and turned around to take it all in.

"You did this?"

He grinned. "Pretty corny."

"No, I love it!"

"I'm a man of excess."

"No, you're not." She said it shyly, without looking at him.

"I've changed." This in a tone so full of the memory of shared intimacy that she walked over to fiddle nervously with a deep stack of white roses; she gathered some of them into her arms and brought them to her face. "And the people who live here?"

"No one lives in this apartment anymore."

She gave him a doubtful look.

"It's true, it's mine." He made a sweep with his arm. "All nine hundred square feet of it."

"You mean you rent it?"

"I mean I own it. I own the building, as a matter of fact. I bought it last year." He was enjoying himself. His light eyes were snapping.

She trailed her fingers across the most exquisite stalk of orchids she had ever seen. "Why?" she asked, a gratuitous question since she already knew the answer.

"I'm a romantic. I wanted a souvenir. I wanted you to know."

"What about the flowers? You only found out at six o'clock that I was in town."

"One of the people who travels with me has a talent for this kind of thing."

"Buying up flower stores for women?"

"Not for *women*, Clare. You're full of questions. I'd forgotten how querulous you are."

He lounged against the doorway and watched her. He had adopted his usual casual air, but his gaze was direct as he studied her every move, and while his voice was smooth as ever, it had taken on a vibrant tone that made her skin prickle.

She shouldn't be here. They shouldn't be alone together. With mounting nervousness she sidestepped the flowers to wander the tiny rooms, stalling for time and trying to compose herself. Her own body had begun to throb in company with his, and with its sudden arousal and her brain's whirl she felt frenzied. She rubbed her hand over her mouth several times, a gesture that he remembered and read again perfectly. The old obsession wrapped itself around her, sliding up her legs and breasts like ropes. She tried to distract herself with more small talk. "It's not the same furniture. This is definitely an upgrade since I lived here," she said vaguely, running her fingers over a chair back. "And the walls have been painted, I'm sure of that. I liked this place. My first home out of Kentucky."

"Our first home."

She stayed silent.

"Aren't you going to look in the bedroom?" He held his breath, waiting for her to step into his net.

"No," she answered. She flicked her eyes at him.

They stood in the tiny, flower-filled apartment in charged silence for long clock ticks that became time flow, until she could no longer resist the pull of his eyes and looked over at him. When she did, her eyes came to rest on his mouth. A mistake, because his lips parted slightly and she remembered vividly their hard, insistent strength, the way he could leave her weak and undone with just a kiss.

She lowered her eyes and watched him. *Get out now! Don't speak, don't think, just turn on your heel and run, or you'll regret this all your life. Run!* As soon as she thought it, she was on the move, but he was too quick for her and blocked her, bending over her before she could take a second step. He said her name. She put up her arm to push him away, but he covered her hand with his and bent it back hard against his shoulder. His face loomed over hers, his eyes unfocused, his mouth hunting for hers. She turned her head away, so he increased the pressure with his hand until the pressure became pain. She breathed his name, thinking this would stop him, but his breath was coming fast and he couldn't hear her over the heartbeat echoing in his ears. He put his other arm around her waist and in one motion jerked her hips tight against his. He put his full weight against her, pushing with his belly and thighs till her back was bent over.

With all her strength she tried to push him away, but then his tongue began working at hers and she no longer cared. His mouth unlocked the old door; beyond the door was the past she had never left. She wanted that past back. It felt so good, as if she'd gone her whole life without a drink of water and now here was water, raining down and making her moist and supple. His tongue took its time in her mouth, sending tremors all along her legs, evoking sensations she believed long forgotten. He worked a finger into the cleft of her buttocks and against her will she moaned. Her brain shaped uneasy declarations. She had a right to happiness. She was entitled to put herself an uncomfortable distance from the truth. Her arms flew up around his neck, her lips parted, found his, and then the weight of his body overwhelmed her and they fell to the floor.

He gasped when he moved his hand quickly up her bare legs and pulled off her panties. In one rough motion he shoved her dress up over her breasts, trailed his tongue down her belly and buried his mouth between her legs, taking all the pleasures she would allow him. Years, he had waited, years. His tongue caressed the warm, silken skin, probed deeper until she moved slightly and disturbed his reverie. Afraid she would run from him, he pushed her legs apart and thrust himself inside her, controlling for interminable minutes his compulsion to finish it. *How does she do this? How does her body take me into its damp grasp and then squeeze in such pleasant undulation that I feel as if the top of my head will fly away?* Her hands caught at his hair, then traced the old scars on his belly, Azarak's souvenir. Another moment and she arched her spine, threw back her head, and wailed. He surrendered himself to the shock of it and they finished together, on the floor, on the broken blossoms.

Quickly, he was hard again, and when she realized this, she rolled over and got up on all fours. Watching her do this made him more aggressive, and he went after her roughly from behind. But it was impossible to hurt her. He drove himself into her and she only opened up more to him, pushing her knees and palms into the floor, wanting to show him that she was just as strong and tough as he was. After he had come, when he started to withdraw, she squeezed herself around him so tight that he saw stars and would have fallen over if she hadn't pushed her backside against him with such force that he couldn't even move.

Later, in bed, he touched her along the curve of her hip with his fingers, the way one strokes a cat. When his hand came up and touched her mouth, she caught his fingers between her teeth and held them until finally she relaxed and fell asleep. He woke once in the night while they slept when her hand came to rest on his. For an instant he thought she was Karim.

Clare was completely happy when she woke just before dawn. She stretched out her arms and rubbed them with her hands. He was standing at the window, naked, with his back to her. The sun was not up yet, but its bright orange rays already split the dark sky; he stood silhouetted against them, his black hair unrelieved by any light. She followed the lines of his body with her eyes, the muscles of his back, committing every inch of him into her brain to make a photograph. Memorized every inch of his skin so that she could close her eyes and summon him up as he used to be. Instantly, her good mood evaporated. *Used to be.* She realized she had already begun to think of him in the past tense. She sank back into the bed pillows, too leaden even to cry.

She had only ever wanted this man. She had never wanted money, or fame, or any other man, for that matter. She had never cared about gaining the world; she could have accomplished that the first time with Lawrence, the night he gave her the green dress. Remembering the first Little Dinner she had hosted at The Heights made her wince. The dress was balled up on the living room floor; she could see it from the bed in the dim light and felt the first full stab of guilt.

Hearing her quick intake of breath, Tarik turned around, and she saw again how much he had not stood outside the reach of time. The mouth, always sensual, now had a vulnerable downcast, and the all-seeing light eyes, keen and bright, bore a shadow, caused by what, she couldn't guess; if anything, it made him even more attractive. She flattered herself to think that the years without her had taken their toll, but there was something else. Studying him, she was angry suddenly that she'd been cheated of companioning him even through his miseries. She sat up in bed with a purpose.

"Tell me something," she said.

He looked over at her expectantly, a smile playing around his mouth. But she felt uncomfortable trying to pry out his secrets and dropped her shoulders, holding her hands palms up in a gesture of helplessness. He watched her for a moment, measuring her hesitation, then began. "A lot has happened to me since, since we were together, Clare. For you as well, I know. I married Topaz, as I guess you knew I would. We had a child together, a boy."

"Yes."

He continued to hold her with his eyes. "Did you know what happened to them?"

"Something happened?"

As soon as he told her, she swung her legs over the edge of the bed and would have run across the room to him, but he held up his hand. "Just stay there, all right? I can't finish this any other way. Just let me get it out. Someday I'll tell you how they died; someday I'll tell you the whole story. Not now."

The *thwack* of a morning newspaper hitting a storm door distracted him, and he parted the window curtains to look out. How do children conceive of death? he wondered. Had he when he was a little boy? Had Karim, who licked his lips with glee over the most gruesome retelling of Turkit's atrocities? Surely this had been some abstract fantasy for that little boy because Karim was the most gentle human being Tarik had ever known.

Another newspaper found its mark against the glass of a door farther down the block. Tarik was disappointed to see that the deliverer was not some freckle-faced little schoolboy but a retarded man at least in his thirties who hobbled down the street with arms akimbo. The sight appalled him, and he let the curtain go and crossed the tiny room to sit down beside her on the bed. The sheet had fallen into her lap and he stared at her breasts for a very long time, as if he had never seen such things before. With a finger he lightly touched one nipple, then the other. At his age he could still look at her breasts and believe all problems could be solved if only his mouth might envelop that perfect point.

With a resigned sigh he pulled the sheet up to her chin. "Something else, Clare." He told her that Stan Cobb was dead too. After she'd calmed down, he propped the pillows up behind her and pushed her back against them firmly. Then he began to tell her in poignant, nostalgic detail about Karim.

She listened without comment, indulging in her nervous habit of chewing on her finger. She felt lonely suddenly, and impotent because she believed she could never console him. But the longer he spoke, the more it became fear that composed her emotions most completely. Because if he was so utterly devastated by the death of his son, and he clearly was, was it not her choice now to console him, console them both, in fact, for all they had lost and sacrificed over the last ten years, by revealing to him that he had another son, in character and disposition so completely like him that he could only be his son? A tall, handsome, clever boy who handled himself in every situation, who was never flummoxed or ill at ease. Sound familiar? A boy to dream over after he had finished grieving for Karim.

Her mouth moved from her knuckle and began to gnaw on a ragged fingernail, because by then the longing to tell him was all-consuming, and if she took the bitten finger out of her mouth it would come rushing out of her. Alex of the pale, fathomless, all-seeing gray eyes could be the balm for all his sorrows, the discovery and blessing of a lifetime. Hope. Again.

So she kept the finger in her mouth, kept her eyes lowered and anguished out the dilemma in her mind while he spoke anecdotes, sad little tales of brown oxford shoes and a love of sweets, thin fingers and transparent skin. She hid behind her hair while her mind raced. There had always been an unbreakable bond between them, even after all these years of sharing beds and lives with others who loved them.

The tone of his voice shifted to one of contempt. He was speaking of Sirah. Lost in her own thoughts, Clare hadn't picked up all the details. Something about Hadi. Something about disembowelment, familiar stuff from the kingdom. He glanced over at the window, giving her a chance to raise her eyes and look at him directly. His expression was sad and bright at the same time, as if he needed to elaborate on his problem in vivid detail before amazing her with its dramatic solution.

She sunk her teeth into her thumb. She loved him as much as she did the day she married him. How could that be, when she knew that she also loved Lawrence Sayles? Oh, not in the same way, but ten years of marriage had mellowed her past the misery of her wedding day to real devotion. But she still loved Tarik. She was a reasonable woman; she was prepared to entertain explanations for this. But none presented itself, and so it seemed to her the thing couldn't bear analysis, and she was ashamed from trying after all these years.

She had borne a child with the man now tangled up in bedsheets with her, and this event united her to him in a way that nothing on earth could alter.

It occurred to her that the last time they were together, in the little stone house in Duru, she had promised him that nothing would ever separate them again, not Hadi, not Azarak, and that he had come all these miles, and brought her here to this familiar little apartment so that he could collect on that old promise.

She was beginning to feel unreal. Her chest had tightened so painfully that she wondered if there was something wrong with her heart. She took several deep breaths, but her heart was there all right, jumping, skittering. Her breath came more sharply. She closed her eyes, and in her inner eye saw a pit opening up at her feet. Her feet began to slide on the slippery sides of the pit, and she began to fall. He stopped talking and stared at her. Then he opened his mouth to speak, and of course she knew exactly what he was going to say.

"It's miserable to think about, isn't it? That we get our second chance because Topaz died? I think about that and I don't sleep at night. But just because I feel terrible about it doesn't change it, Clare. These years that are lost, we can't bring them back. Can't bring Karim back, or Topaz, or Stanley. But we can bring ourselves back. We can do it again. Start again."

He was up and moving around the room, the old confidence in him and that tone of assurance in his voice that in the past had always made her feel as if even the most impossible problem needed only his brief attention to be solved. Except that on this steaming Indian summer dawn the problem couldn't be solved. Not her problem anyway, and because of that not his.

"It doesn't matter anymore what Hadi does or doesn't want, you understand. What secret handshakes White-Lyons made or hasn't made. That's all been over for a long time. Only I decide what obtains now, you see. I make all the choices. I say what I want." He exhaled, his face suffused by the light of certain knowledge. "And I want you. Just as I always have. Nothing has altered that. I'm not ashamed to admit that all these years I've only ever wanted you. Even when Topaz was alive. I feel sorry now that that was the case, but I'm not ashamed."

His eyes were wide, unmasked. She was terrified that he would stop talking, turn those eyes on her, and she'd have to tell him. As long as he kept talking, maybe a miracle would save her.

"I had thought at first that I could persuade you to come back with me right now, but I realize now that would be foolish, so I won't pressure you by asking. I know you well enough to understand that you couldn't do that to Sayles. It will take time to make the break."

He took her hand in his and gave her a look that swept right through her eyes to her heart. And when he could see, finally, that what was in her heart was not relief but actual fear, he sat back and drew a sharp, surprised breath. He squeezed her hand tighter, and took another tack. But he was nervous now, talking faster.

"I know that Alex is mine, Clare."

"Tarik . . ."

"I know he's mine. We got him that morning in Duru. You married Sayles because you were pregnant with Alex and you didn't have anywhere to turn." He relaxed his grip on her hand and kissed the palm. "It's all right. No one has to know, not yet anyway. We'll pick a time to tell him. Believe me, it won't be as bad as you think—"

"Alex is Lawrence's son, Tarik."

He dropped her hand and stared at her for a long time. Then he said, "Alex is *my* son. I'm not stupid. I know this is upsetting to you, but I know it's true. I have a right to him."

"I married Sayles because I had nowhere else to go, you're right. But not because I was pregnant with your child. Because I thought my life was over. Because it was a chance to save my grandfather. I wanted to die. But Lawrence was there, pushing me. I didn't have time to debate it. I'm sorry."

He stared at her for the longest time, trying to decide if she was telling him the truth. Then he stood and walked back to the window. This time he kept his back to it, afraid he might have to look at the retarded paperboy again. She watched as he collected himself.

He stayed there for a long time, not speaking. Finally, he said, in a barely audible voice, "I just assumed. I . . . wanted Alex to be mine."

"I'm sorry."

"But I still have you. I would never want to interfere with your son's relationship with his father. I wouldn't attempt to replace the boy in his father's affection—" His voice gave out, and he couldn't finish.

When he spoke again, a little of the vigor was back in his voice. "I know that I've just come waltzing in here after all this time, asking you to give up everything you've built over the years, but we deserve this, don't we? I mean, we deserve it."

"I wish it were that easy."

"We could have stayed together these last ten years if it had been easy. It won't be."

Already she could feel them parting. Every word he spoke, she saw herself saying good-bye to him. What hellish God had created this dilemma for her? To bring him back after all this time of longing for him just so she could send him away again. She didn't have the strength even to weep. She analyzed the injustice of it with the eye of the jaundiced observer.

There was such a pain in her throat she could hardly speak. "I cannot leave Lawrence."

He came and sat down next to her on the bed and put his ear close to her lips. He whispered, "Yes, you can."

"I can't leave Lawrence. Not after all this time, not after what he's done for me. You don't know him. He would die, Tarik. He would just lie down and die. To take Alex away from him—Alex is his world, his whole world." In a softer voice she added, "And I'm his world."

The drowsy aloofness was gone from his face. For the first time, she saw that his fear matched her own. The fever of revelation was actually making him tremble. She felt more afraid for him than for herself. How much losing Karim must have destroyed him. How swiftly she could save him if she told him about his other son. But if she told him about Alex, he would walk all the way to Kentucky to claim him. He would never leave if he knew about Alex, and that would destroy Lawrence, and perhaps Alex. Her head felt as if it would crack in two. She dug her fingertips into the roots of her hair and pressed down hard, trying to stop the pounding in her brain. But what was the point? She would kill for Tarik, die for him, but she would not tell him the truth about Alex.

"I can't do it. I owe Lawrence."

"Owe him what?"

She looked away.

He took her roughly by the chin and turned her face to himself. "What could you possibly owe Lawrence Sayles?"

"That's not fair. He married me. I was sick and lost, and he married me even though he knew I was still in love with you."

He gave a short, sneering laugh. "This is tragedy? Such a sacrifice on the part of old Lawrence to marry the girl he'd letched after since she was a teenager? Who had her picked up in the kingdom and tucked up in his bed before she even knew where she was?"

"It didn't happen like that."

"Well, if it didn't, it wasn't for want of his wishing it would. So he sacrifices himself by marrying the beautiful young girl, gets a great wife and a kid in the bargain. Forgive me, Clare, but the last time I looked, this wasn't Medal of Honor stuff."

"You don't understand."

He persisted. "Now, if you want to tell me that you feel loyalty toward him, that I understand. He's the father of your son. He's taken good care of you, probably loves you to death. You owe him respect and honor and all that. You owe him an easy letdown and a slow transition. But after that, I'm sorry, I'm in the dark. I love you, Clare, all these years. How do you think I've kept going? I've come all the way back here, at no inconsiderable risk, to ask you to marry me again. My wife is dead, my son is dead, but I believe that I still have it in me to try again because of you. Because it's only ever been you, only with you, corny as that sounds. I'll do anything to get you to say you'll come back with me. I'll wait months, years, whatever it takes. I'll twist myself in knots. Look, I'm down on my knees. I'm here to say that I still love you and want you to marry me. No one is sorrier than I am about what happened in Duru. I blame myself for all of it. I should have cut off Hadi's head with my own hands rather than let you get away from me, but I was arrogant and I thought I could handle everything. But it's true—I had to let you go—and I knew that you knew you had to go. You knew it, I knew it. I made the big sacrifice. Just the way poor old Sayles did when he wedded and bedded you, or do I have the order of events wrong?"

"Please, don't do this."

"You're killing me, you know that?" He took a deep breath to try to calm down. When he spoke again his voice was low. "I want to make love to you again. I want you to divorce Lawrence Sayles and marry me. I want to know your son. I want to have a child with you."

She put her hands over her ears. "Please stop."

A tiny vein in his temple had begun to pulse with blood, and his face had a high color she'd never seen in him before. But it was his agitation that was terrifying. She had never seen him anything but utterly composed, and the sight of him distraught, pacing the floor, his face contorted, undid her. Where had she seen such a look before? She squeezed her brain, trying to remember.

He said, "All these years, I thought . . . I assumed you felt the way I did. I thought that Alex was mine. Maybe I should have communicated with you. Written a letter or sent some sort of message. But I believed that we didn't need words. That no matter what happened, there was this . . . this"—he made a helpless gesture—"connection."

He squared his shoulders. "It's been a long time, ten years. Feelings change. You've led a wonderful life with Sayles. You have a son together. You're rich and famous. It would be a great jeopardy to abandon these things at this late stage—and I could never promise you anything other than jeopardy."

He took a deep, aching breath. "You love him."

He looked directly at her, hoping she would deny it, the anger out of him and replaced by a kind of listlessness. "After ten years of marriage, you've fallen in love with your husband." His eyes challenged her to say it wasn't so.

Clare felt the earth move under her. The pit yawned wider and the ground collapsed. She clawed at the dirt, but there was nothing to wrap her fingers around. She felt her body surrendering and she allowed herself to slip down, down. With the last of her vision she looked up and saw the pit close over her head. Not a pit, she realized—a grave. She was a dead woman. It was only left for her to speak her last words.

She rolled her eyes up to his, and looking clearly into them said with the last of her strength, "You're right. I love Lawrence Sayles. I've always loved him and I won't leave him, not even for you."

And then she remembered where she had seen that look before—on Homer's face, when the mine siren rang, when Hillard died in the roof fall.

1975

25

In a land where rain never fell, the sudden downpour on a late afternoon was as astounding to the people of the kingdom as would have been the appearance of a unicorn, a mermaid, a dragon. Recalled by ancient ones as the watershed event of youth, disbelieved by children and the unimaginative, the afternoon shower in a place where rain fell on average once every thirty-five years was the ephemeral event of a lifetime.

So when an inky cloud floated over the face of the sun, the wind picked up and the air chilled down and the sky rolled twice with thunder, the people threw aside their tools and schoolbooks and coffee cups and dashed outside. In concert they tipped back their heads and extended their tongues to receive the droplets of water from heaven—for one incongruous moment Christian communicants.

Only Arthur Olson was oblivious of the miracle. He walked fast down the capital's main street past citizens still turning over the moisture on their fingertips as if it were faceted diamonds, turned left on Allenby Street, and approached the palace.

Inside an air-conditioned guardpost, a lone sergeant sat behind a computer terminal, twisting back and forth in a swivel chair, bored. In Turkit's day, before electricity, before telephones—before food, as a matter of fact—two lions had been posted in cages on either side of the palace gate, squads of garishly uniformed dragoon guards beside them. Turkit had designed their purple and red outfits in the late 1930s after Swiss Guard uniforms he'd seen at the Vatican, but the peacock-feather headdresses, a nod to the kingdom's Sheban heritage, had been his own invention. Olson remembered the uniforms because he always had to stick a pencil or a finger in his mouth to keep from giggling when he saw them.

Less amusing was the guards' reputation for viciousness. Once, in 1938, he had arrived at the palace and was inflating his titles and offices to the guard in order to gain entry, when out of the corner of his eye he noticed a circle of dragoons yelping with laughter at something on the ground. He hunkered down to see that a man had been buried up to his neck in dirt and that an enormous land crab was covering the man's face, feeding on it. That the man was still alive, conscious and feeling, was not as interesting to the soldiers as how, in a country surrounded by mountains with just one narrow outlet to the sea one hundred miles away, the crab had inched its way to the city. It shamed Olson that years later when he remembered the incident, he too speculated more about the crab and less about the man.

Back in the days when he was playing both sides against the middle, back in the good old days (which turned out not to be so dissimilar from current times, Olson had recently decided) he would come twice a year to the capital to make obeisances to Turkit and try to sell him on the high points of making time with Americans instead of Brits and by necessity be swept up in the insanity that passed for national culture. He would wait in some fly-specked village on the Yemen border for months, waiting for Turkit to let him in, make the brutal cross of the plain in a Land-Rover with a hostile escort, usually Nal, and show up at the gate of the palace with a bad sunburn and terror building in his bowels.

Court life then was one part ceremony, nine parts auto-da-fé. One never knew from one moment to the next on whom the royal glower and call to temper might fall—who burned, who eviscerated, cast out, made fingerless, cockless, sightless? Now the palace was as benign and smooth-functioning as Houston Control, but back then, in the late 1930s and early 1940s when Olson was a young Foreign Service officer, so low on the career ladder that even a posting to the kingdom was a step up, the country was in the full swing of absolute depraved monarchy unmatched in the twentieth century, maybe even any century.

Life revolved totally around the whim of Turkit. It was understood that every man at court was there to serve a purpose. The trick was knowing which task one was supposed to perform without being told—actually, it was more a survival tactic than a skill, because Turkit believed he had the power to send messages around the room from his brain to the brains of others. If one could not read the message directed at oneself, then one had faulty antennae in need of a little tinkering with a hot penny nail or the point of a knife. Or worse: not being able to divine the Di-

vine One made one a doubter of the gifts of the Elect of God.
Made the Second Sun out to have a faulty transmitter, a bent
mind—cause for the death stare, perhaps followed swiftly by
death itself.

So one learned to read intentions and desires in the curl of
Turkit's lip, in the cast of his feral eye, in the condition and coloration of his fecal matter for truly desperate augurers, and in the
panicked, nonstop gossip that dinned in every back room and corridor regarding the wishes and whims of the Unsullied One that
occupied courtiers' every waking moment.

The lucky ones were those whom Turkit told outright what was
expected; it was less fun for him, but it got things done. One such
courtier was his human timepiece. His job was to dip slightly at
the waist every quarter hour and bob and weave every thirty seconds in imitation of a clock part. Another had the task of wiping
off the urine of the royal dogs when they irrigated the shoes of
court attendees. Another fanned away the royal farts with a censer
once part of Cesare Borgia's Holy Mass service. Turkit would say,
"Ah, Noren"—or Zoren, or whatever the man's name was—"the
King of Kings has just passed some gas. Sweeten it a little, wilt
thou, with that bad pope's pretty vessel. Although hardly fetid,
nothing deficits from the scent of frankincense, now, does it?"
Much clanking of censer chains. "Lord, you are too right!" The
man would have bathed in royal farts, and gladly, rather than un-
dergo the radar test. No job was too demeaning, too excremental,
too humiliating as long as its ultimate gain was to ensure the
monarch's contentment and maintain heads atop shoulders, where
nature intended them to be.

It was an exhausting job to dance attendance on the Stainless
One, with no vacations, no sabbaticals, sometimes not even sleep
if Turkit was on amphetamines, which he very often was after
1938, after Tarik and Nila escaped. But consider the alternative in-
flicted on the masses forbidden to come to the capital city, much
less to the palace: poverty, starvation, death by disease or thirst, or
disembowelment at the hand of rural warlords. There were worse
fates than fanning farts or swabbing dog piss.

All of this bizarre behavior occurred amid the most fabulous
diamondite mist of opulence Olson had ever seen, had ever believed could have existed. Atop solid gold thrones dimpled with
rubies and emeralds the size of a baby's fist. In the glare of a
thousand cut-crystal chandeliers. With dirt-blackened feet ensconced in slippers made of spun gold so tissue-thin they could be
worn just once. Upon carpets so downy, with a pile so deep and

perfectly woven, that they could carry even the most ponderous weight and still emit no sound, not even when His Most Perspicacious Majesty's favorite Rolls-Royce Silver Shadow was driven over them into the main court room, which it once was.

In the mid-1930s there was young Olson hunkered at the back door trying to ace out the Brits, while at the same time smuggling arms to Malik through Yemen because everybody swore on their grandmother's eyes that Turkit had too many bats in his belfry to make it one more day and that Malik was the man to put an end to the insanity. But instead, Turkit had put an end to Malik.

In the 1940s, when the world was tearing itself apart and murder was wholesale and in some places institutionalized and *the way we live* itself seemed in the balance, Turkit sucked the marrow from the bones of the grouse the British shipped him in the gear wells of Mosquito fighters and whined that he had run out of his favorite Hazel Bishop lipstick because of wartime blockades. He was in the catbird seat and could afford to pout because the British desperately needed oil to win the war and were convinced it was only a matter of hours before Duru would yield its crop. The hours became twenty-five years.

Ah, the food, the gems, the mayhem, the bare-assed dancing girls, the hallucinatory, halcyon days of youth. Olson would daydream more than once forty years later during those board meetings in the OmniTech headquarters conference room in soulless Sunnyvale, California.

The Exalted One had some charm, some weird panache. He strangled his finance minister after the national debt reached seven figures, then appointed his best friend, a King Charles spaniel, to the post because, he said, the dog had twice as much sense and smelled only half as bad as his late minister. The dog, Turkit declared, had come up with a money-making scheme for turning sea-gull guano into pressboard housing material that could be sold throughout the region. As the kingdom has no coastline to speak of, and thus no gulls and no gull shit, one hundred thousand tons of the stuff were imported from Chile. The guano sat in warehouses at Izz for more than two years, stinking up the countryside, before the whole mess was towed out into the Gulf of Aden one day when the Yemenis weren't looking.

Later, Turkit decided the dog hadn't said guano but guava. He thought this gaffe hilarious and poked fun at himself for weeks, although his functionaries were wise enough not to laugh along too loudly or Turkit might have the last laugh. So he howled and they chewed their lips, waiting for him to give them a sign, waiting for him to wire a message to their brains.

The sergeant behind the desk flashed Olson a broad smile and noted his name in the daily log book. In the bad old days, people were forbidden to show their teeth in a smile because it was considered the worst kind of bad manners. Besides, their teeth were terrible. Now, since Tarik, they were encouraged to smile, even laugh out loud, and show off their bright new understanding of sociability and dental hygiene.

The lions once caged on this spot were thin and mangy, with the flat eyes of blooded killers. Deliberately kept half starved, they would have eaten concrete had it been offered. Turkit was a prankster, addicted to practical jokes—whoopee cushions, hand buzzers, that kind of thing. But his favorite prank was to once or twice a year, near sundown, creep down to the lions' cages, poke them with pointed sticks to rile them up, and then unshackle the beasts and let them take to the streets. How those peacock feathers would fly as guards shinnied up poles or climbed smooth stone walls as if they were ladders!

On quick, starved paws, the lions would undulate their bony backsides down the narrow streets, stalking dinner. And within seconds there would be such a stampede of people right and left, such screams of panic and roaring lions that it drowned out everything but Turkit's shrill giggle. The beasts would cut out from the human herd the blind, the halt, children, old people. Olson had arrived at court one night a few minutes after Turkit's grenadiers dragged in some poor beggar after a lion had snagged him by the backside before being beaten off with sticks. The man's buttocks were gone, just a dripping gruel of blood, flesh, and muscle. Man of Science, Turkit tried to set the screaming victim to rights with the applications of cauterizing hot pokers and a sewing needle and thread. He pronounced the surgery a success, although the patient was a bad sport and died. Like Dr. Mengele, God's Favorite was in the unique position of dispensing both the misery and its cure.

Olson released a melancholy sigh, which caused the sergeant to look at him quizzically. Really, it was obscene to feel nostalgic about Turkit and the bad old days. He was filled with self-disgust to think he'd rather be scrambling over bodies in Turkit's courtyard than facing down these horrible demons that were ruining his sleep and his life.

The sergeant telephoned another desk somewhere in the command center of the building, gave an affirmative answer, and replaced the phone in its cradle. An instant later Olson heard the gate click, another soldier held the heavy door for him, and he passed through.

He walked with his head down, his fists balled up and shoved deep into the pockets of a rumpled suit jacket. He was very careful usually about his appearance, but today he had his excuses. Normally, he'd take a roundabout route from Washington to the kingdom. A flight to Paris, where he'd check into the Ritz—his favorite hotel in the world—and spend a day or two eating and drinking his way through the Sixteenth Arrondissement. He remembered particularly that last time, in an out-of-the-way place on Île St. Louis, he discovered a bottle of cabernet sauvignon from an obscure little vineyard that had rolled around on his tongue like velvet. He'd planned to find the restaurant again, have another bottle or two of the wine, but when the plane landed in Paris, he was too depressed to move, so he sulked in his seat for three hours while the airplane was cleaned and refueled.

And he hadn't gotten off in Riyadh either, where he had friends and knew a woman who made couscous with the softest lamb on earth and who sometimes, if he was lucky and if his brain wasn't too plagued by thoughts of his wife at home in suburban Maryland, he could convince to take him to bed.

But he stayed onboard at Riyadh too, thinking disconsolately of the woman and the couscous and inhaling with dull envy the mint and garlic that clung to the skin of the Saudis who boarded there.

He was the Executioner of Dreams, and the Executioner did not deserve to eat or rest or feel anything soft and yielding moving between his legs. So he kept his seat belt cinched around his belly the whole eighteen hours in the air and six on the ground and brooded.

The first-class section of the airplane was full of businessmen, most of them American, lawyers, oil company managers, a few oil-field workers whose companies perqued them to maintain goodwill. In the tourist section were more of the same, along with some of the kingdom's new middle class who'd boarded in Paris with shopping bags from Galeries Lafayette. It was an upscale passenger list, none of those churning masses yearning to breathe free that Olson remembered from flights on Air Niger, or even Alitalia. This mass of people didn't yearn for anything beyond better airline scheduling and extended credit lines on their Visa cards. The kingdom had the highest per capita income in the region; people were fighting to get in.

When they passed over the coastline, the slant of the new day's sun had showed under Olson's window and he'd popped up the shade and stared out miserably. The sight of the dawn's pink sky and plump, hopeful clouds oppressed him. He was not deceived by their soporific perfection, for down there, where he could follow the shadow of the big plane on the surface of desert, mountain, and farm field, were men and women with broken hearts, with half-starved babies, empty heads, tiresome ambitions, murder on their minds. With sleep-starved, red eyes he stared out the window of the plane, thinking that nothing looked very good in the world at all, not even from a distance of thirty-five thousand feet. The steward was pouring cups of hot Sur coffee. Olson watched impassively while one of the passengers complained that his cup should have been warmed first. In the unreal confines of the first-class section of a Boeing 747 jetliner, warmed coffee cups counted for something. Olson stared at the complaining passenger with stolid disgust. Very soon there would be such a weeping and gnashing of teeth that the world—his world, at least, and Tarik's—would never be the same.

They came in low over the Sur mountains in preparation for landing. In the distance, through the mists, Olson could just make out the pearlized towers of Malik's pink fortress. Another ten minutes and they were over the capital, the runways pin-straight just ahead. Then it was flaps down, wheels down. The Executioner had landed.

A car was waiting for him at the airport, as was customary. He was a frequent and most honored guest here and accorded every amenity. An official of OmniTech came onto the airplane to escort him off even before anyone else deplaned. There was no customs, none of the necessary border inconveniences imposed on conventional travelers. He walked quickly down the plane steps, across a short stretch of tarmac blistered by heat, into the air-conditioned comfort of a Lincoln Town Car.

He caught a glimpse of himself in the rearview mirror, grimaced, and turned away. When he was a young man, he'd been proud of his appearance, vain really. He thought he remembered that Hemingway had said that twenty-seven was a man's best age. A man should be twenty-seven forever. On reflection, Olson decided he had been stupendous at twenty-seven. On to bigger and better career moves, not yet married, and so unbowed. Six feet two inches, trim and wiry with none of his father's pudding-faced Norwegian looks. To his own way of thinking, he appeared more a tenth-generation New Englander than a Nordesman—that bowsprit jaw, that birthright set of shoulder, that face attractively

roughed from vacations at the helm of the family Islander, out of
Marblehead. Through twenty-foot seas, no compass, on guts and
world-class genes alone.

In fact, Olson had never sailed in his life, would have drowned
in ten seconds in a cresting wave of any size. He was a concrete
sailor, born and raised in New York City. He'd put himself
through Columbia University working for a company that sold
frankfurter buns to Nathan's Famous Hot Dogs in Times Square,
then went to the Georgetown School of Foreign Service on a par-
tial scholarship. The rest of the tuition he made by caddying at
Burning Tree and baby-sitting the children of White House support personnel. He had the same coloring as his dad, that generic
north-European look—hay-colored hair and skin the same
shade—but when he was young, he believed, anyway, he might
have been mistaken for a Boston Brahmin, for someone, say, like
Lawrence Sayles.

Only Brahmins are not devoted to rich red wine and heavy food
and Havana cigars personally clipped and set aflame by the Castro
brothers. They do not spend long hours alone, hunkered over
strange local wines in Eastern Europe and in those parts of the
Middle East where a man can still buy decent bootleg liquor.
They age themselves honestly from years of tracking the interest
rates on multimillion-dollar trust funds across the financial pages
of the *Boston Globe*, not staring down the neck of a wine bottle,
looking for answers. So now he had to admit that the decades of
red meat, red wine, and scotch had finally showed on him and he
no longer looked so much like Henry Cabot Lodge as he did
Sebastian Cabot. Life was full of bitter truths, and this was one of
them.

Olson walked down one palace corridor, encountered another sentry and another snappy salute, which he waved away, and continued down yet another long, familiar corridor. On either side of the
hallway was Turkit's exquisite collection of Ming porcelain, ac-
quired at auction at Sotheby's in 1946 by his London agent. In the
tyrant's day, the priceless porcelain had been set loosely on three-
cornered tables, vulnerable to the whim of the monarch and the
wide sweep of the gowns of his wives. Olson recalled the time
Turkit had snatched one of the priceless platters from a hallway
table and set on it the freshly severed head of one of his tribal ri-
vals. He then fed the thing to one of his spaniels, which had left
the brain in the skull to eat last. Olson had watched this impassively, the way one observes another man knot his necktie. It

struck him all these years later how oblivious he had been then of those gruesome events, how he'd dined out on these tales with the boys back at State when he was home.

He wondered now if there hadn't been something terribly wrong with him all along, some physical disorder he should have checked out when he got back to the States. Or was he looking in the wrong discipline—some expensive psychoanalyst? Something down deep vacant where his moral sensibilities should have shaped up in boyhood? Yet if he were so morally vacant, why was he suffering so now? Or maybe he was tearing his guts out for nothing. Maybe what was wrong with him was as simple as the elements that composed the case of then versus now. Perhaps it was the difference between blood and shit. Blood he could tolerate. Blood could be thrilling, an opera of life and death, heroic, desperate. But shit, well, shitty was a moment that did not last long, that was played out in the mud by ordinary men leading unheroic lives. Blood came and went with heraldic trumpets, the grind of tank treads, the assassin's swift escape. But shit was here to stay. And this was definitely a shitty assignment he'd taken on himself.

Thinking this, he came to the end of the long, imposing, red-carpeted hallway feeling rather better. He pulled his hands from his pockets and vaguely passed them over the lapels of his sweat-soaked seersucker suit. He wished now that he'd worn a necktie.

The young lieutenant behind the desk came swiftly to attention. This was Arthur Olson of OmniTech, after all, probably the number-two man in all the country. Looking pretty seedy at the moment, but still the number two.

"Sir! Good morning, sir!"

The instant the officer flashed him that wide, insincere smile, Olson's misery returned. He hadn't met the man before, but he knew the type; they were all over the kingdom. Four years at West Point, a stint in Vietnam with the First Cav for some battle seasoning. A command-post position back in the capital city. A rotation at the receptionist's desk because there were just too many of these educated, seasoned, talented young officers around. Young, ambitious guys with nothing to do but keep appointment books are usually plagued by ambitious fantasies—about power trips, goon squads, coups d'état. There it was again—the difference between blood and shit. Olson decided it was the theme for the day, maybe the rest of his life. Another time he would have made a mental note to bring it up with Tarik. Guys like this eager young lieutenant, whom Olson decided he now despised, could be trouble in the future. Time to find them meaningful work, hustle them out of the country to European postings, where they could discover for themselves cabernet sauvignons from little vineyards and be ruined.

But he wouldn't warn Tarik today, or any other day. He doubted he would ever speak to Tarik again, and certainly not to warn him about jumped-up lieutenants with ambitions of glory. The Executioner does not converse with the victim. He merely drops his ax and moves on.

"Morning," Olson replied brusquely.

"He's right down the hallway, in the little office," the lieutenant said in perfect unaccented English. "He had a ten-thirty, but it's the Algerian delegation, so of course he won't be long." He gave Olson a look of satisfaction. His eyes were knowing, smug.

"I'm after the old man this morning."

"The colonel?" The officer stuck out his lip and opened his eyes wide to convey surprise. No one ever asked for the colonel.

"I don't even know if he's in the city."

"He's here. I spoke with him from Washington the other day and he said he'd see me here. He said I might find him in his arboretum."

"He calls it an arboretum, does he?" the young officer marveled with complete insincerity. "Let's look for him there."

He moved out briskly from behind his desk, unhooked a huge wad of keys from his Sam Browne, and handed them to his assistant, along with some sort of code book, and then pushed off briskly down the hallway, his gleaming boots clicking smartly over the travertine marble floor.

Watching those slim hips, the crisp uniform shaped over perfect, tight buttocks depressed Olson even further. Not so much because the young man was physically perfect, pretty-faced, and with a muscular body, but because he carried so much hope in the way he marched around corners, as if he actually were on his way to something and eager to get there. Some memory in Olson clicked in at the sight, and faded images of his own tall, lanky self in a fresh new seersucker suit flitted through his inward eye. Years in the desert, gun-running, uppity Brits. Malik. Ghosts, himself. The photos fluttered away. He struggled to keep pace with the young officer, who tried to engage him once or twice in conversation. Olson pretended to listen, trying to read something in the dazzling white teeth, the easy grin, the ability to walk forward briskly while looking in the opposite direction.

Social designations no longer strictly applied in the kingdom.

This young lieutenant might have been from the lower castes. Certainly, those dark brown eyes with their lightish-yellow whites put him in the category of a lowlander born to the worst kind of conditions on the plain. It was a genetic characteristic indicative of early starvation and base behavior, a death sentence years ago but able to be corrected through education, improved diet, and exercised ambition in the new order. He might be a small landowner now, Olson speculated, years in the military, a few bucks in his pocket, maybe he'd gone back and bought the land his father, and his father's father all the way back to the Flood, had serfed on for the local warlord. He could be a man on a mission, with a slick and easy grin, a big brain. He might be ambitious. He might be vicious. All things were possible in the new order.

"I hear the old man loves violets," the officer said with a faint smirk, letting Olson know that he was inside the loop. Like everybody else, he understood that the colonel was out of the power loop and just a doddering relic of the bad old days. "Talks to himself, I understand."

Olson raised his chin at him to convey comprehension, at the same time following with his eyes the pistol that bobbed along on his hip.

Finally, after they had walked down a succession of narrow hallways and passed through a dozen doorways, they came to a tiny cedarwood-paneled room bare of furniture. Off the room was a tiny atrium with a stone bench. The officer extended his arm and Olson followed the point of his finger. In a wall of granite stones overhung by a cypress tree was a low wood-framed doorway, barely the height of a man. Looking up, Olson saw that the roof of the building was glass windows set at thirty-degree angles to allow long slants of sunlight to pass through the windows to the space below.

"He's probably in there. If not, I don't know. Maybe sitting in his room in the dark, cleaning one of his old Webleys. He's a nasty guy. Won't talk to anybody but his violets." He gave Olson a conspiratorial look, which Olson returned with a glare. Best not to let these punks think they can grease you with cheap talk.

The young officer tried to read the look, decided it meant nothing, but backed off just to be on the safe side. "Still, a harmless kind of guy," he quickly added. "Prerogatives of age, fair enough. Would you like me to wait, Mr. Olson?"

Olson decided not to acknowledge him by making eye contact. "No," he said, and showed him his back. He walked abruptly away toward the open doorway. He felt the officer's hesitation, perceived a shrug, then heard footsteps clicking away back down the marble corridor.

For a long moment Olson paused in the open air of the tiny garden, beside a low stone bench, and let the sun beat down on him. He thought suddenly of Chesapeake Bay, where his sister had a summer place. He'd visited her there once and had caught a fish, a big Bay salmon. He'd been ashamed to admit then how thrilling this fish catch had been for him. His arms had ached and he'd nearly fainted from the exertion, but he hadn't had an on-top moment like that in years. *When this is over, maybe I'll go back to Chesapeake Bay and buy a place for myself, year-round. Fish all day and then cook it up at night. Make friends and have them over. People ask me what I do for a living, 'Retired,' I'll say.* A pleasant scenario began to develop within his brain. He was a rich man now. He could take his pension from OmniTech, almost three quarters of a million dollars a year—keep his stock, of course— but chuck all the rest. Settle some money on his wife and leave her there in suburban Maryland to fuss with the grandkids, which is all she wanted to do anyway. Let those Chesapeake Bay waters wash away his sins and restore him to what he'd once been. Maybe he'd finally learn to sail. Make himself into a sailor after all, with a slow southern smile. Wash off all the shit.

The sound of White-Lyons's voice drifted out to the garden to him. The man had spent forty-five years in the kingdom and he still sounded as if he'd just stepped off a White Star liner from Southampton. Olson walked slowly to the doorway, shaking his head.

Within, White-Lyons bent to the task of transplanting a small house-variety violet from a larger pot to a smaller one. Without looking up he said, "Always makes me sad to admit defeat, Olson. Look at this." He squeezed one of the leaf stems and brought a tiny bug on the tip of his finger under Olson's nose for inspection.

"Parasites. Bloody things are everywhere. I've lost nearly half my little violets in a month. The pity is, I can't figure out how the hell they got here. I'm scrupulous about insects. I never import any plants— everything here is homegrown. This is pretty much a sterile environment as far as plants are concerned. And look— deadly invaders. Coming over the ramparts. To the left and right of me. Fighting them off every day, and back they come in another wave. Don't know what I'm going to do."

Involved suddenly, Olson felt sympathy for an old man's last great battle. He lowered his voice empathetically. "Maybe you ought to bring in a specialist, a horticulturist. I could look one up for you. Fly him in. I'm sure it's a problem that could be solved. Or you could start again. We could arrange to have a whole new crop of violets brought in. It wouldn't be hard. You know we get machine parts here almost overnight. Could do the same for these plants. My wife has a gardener in Silver Spring. I might ask her to ask him to help. What do you think?"

White-Lyons looked at him as if he'd lost his mind. In a voice dripping with commingled contempt and mockery, he hissed, "Christ, they're only bleeding houseplants, Olson. Don't go over the top. I'm not bloody Gordon at Khartoum."

Olson went red and unexpectedly sneezed twice. White-Lyons stared at him balefully while he wiped his nose with a handkerchief, then moved a step away to minister to another limp violet. "But I appreciate the concern."

He picked up a small bag of white fertilizer pellets and began to mix them with the soil of the violet, adding a little water now and then. He worked in silence for so long that Olson thought for a moment he'd forgotten he was there. Tactfully, he cleared his throat.

"I haven't forgotten about you, Olson," the old man said. "Just got to concentrate. It's harder when you get older. You don't know that yet, but you will. Got to bear down on just one thing at a time."

After he'd finished, he put his hands at the small of his back and straightened up with difficulty. His bones made a popping sound. He cracked his knuckles, then reached back and pulled from under his military tunic a dog-eared catalogue with colored pictures of flowers and flowering plants.

"Tulips are going to be my new thing. I've given up on these violets." He read from the copy: " 'Tulip bulbs by the dozen. All colors. We'll help you grow them even under the most adverse conditions. No charge for shipping.' What do you think, Olson? Tulips everywhere. I'm going to expand on this little shed and make it a proper arboretum."

He looked off into the distance, his mind filling, Olson imagined, with the vision of a suburban Rotterdam tulip field. "I'll make it beautiful and people will come from all over the kingdom to see my beautiful tulips and be amazed. I'll let 'em line up and smell the things and it will all be free. Everybody in this country is just too turned around by money. Have you noticed that, Olson? Everybody shopping and trading stocks, watching television night and day, even the kiddies. What can it all mean? They ought to stop once in a while—I can't believe I'm actually going to say this, Olson—but they ought to stop once in a while and smell the flowers."

He read another sentence from the brochure to himself, shook his head, then folded the booklet in half and stuck it back in his pocket.

His hands, his clothes, and his face were coated with the rich dark potting soil that spilled from broken bags scattered around the room. Olson noticed that his feet were bare and also black with soil, a shocking breach of decorum. The old man must really be slipping to be out of his boots.

Shards of broken clay pots were scattered all around the little shed, and small spades and other gardening tools were tossed here and there in chaotic disarray. The place had a musty, earthy odor, pleasant to Olson's senses, but the disorder evinced a mind not functioning smoothly and that made Olson anxious and his task all the more odious.

Off in one section were the dead, dried-up remains of the violets that had succumbed to the parasites. The old man had made a big, unsentimental heap of them. Most of the pots were smashed, as if in a fit of temper he'd thrown them against the wall. Despair over their death? Had the ancient plant doctor killed all of the plants and none of the bugs in his addle-brained state?

"I need to get a money order to get started, Olson, on this tulip project. Do you know, I've never had a bank account in my life—no, and I never wanted one either. Never wanted some bank inspector mucking about with my private income. 'Course, Turkit didn't allow private bank accounts anyway, so it didn't matter. Not even for me."

"The army didn't handle things for you?"

"When I was still with 'em, yes. But after Turkit kicked us out, I stayed behind, you know that, so I was on my own. Stayed behind to try to run the show for the bastard. Tried to bring a little sanity to the show. Voice of reason, don't you know."

"You weren't very successful."

"No, but I finally saw the light and put things to right. You'd think they would have made me a national hero, wouldn't you, Olson? Instead of what I am."

"And what are you?"

"Darling"—he turned, looking at Olson with blue eyes full of old trouble, and said, "I am the ghost of assassins past." Then he poured some water from an old Campbell's soup can into the repotted violet and pushed the plant away.

"You know, White-Lyons, I hope you don't mind my asking, but I've always wondered. How did you come up with the idea to hide the bomb in the charlotte russe? I've always wondered about the details. It was rather inspired. No one could get near Turkit. He was pathological on the subject of his own security."

Flattered, White-Lyons immediately stopped working. It wasn't often he had a chance to recount the glory of that particular day. Since Karim died, it wasn't often he was allowed to recount anything at all. His soul cried out to make himself heard by someone, anyone. "Well, it wasn't as if I didn't have years to think it through, you know," he began. "Years and years. Every time I would come up with something to outfox the old bastard, he'd go and do another thing to confound me. I think he knew I was trying to get him. He gave me the death stare more than once, but I kept my wits about me. And at the end there wasn't a moment when he wasn't surrounded by bodyguards. Men that couldn't be bought or bribed because every one of them had a father somewhere or a mother in hostage to Turkit, or some deep, hideous secret they couldn't let out, and Turkit knew every last secret of every last person in the country."

"Even you?"

White-Lyons turned his large white head, assessed Olson for a long, penetrating moment, then continued. "He had eyes in the back of his head. But into the Valley of Death rode the ten thousand—and for want of a nail a battle was lost. For me it was a wire whisk."

"A wire—?"

"A wire whisk, man, a whisk!" He made a circular beating motion with his hands. "Whisk up egg whites, whisk up cake frostings." Olson gave him a blank look. "Whisk! Whisk!" White-Lyons shouted in exasperation. "Good Christ, Olson, you're fat as a pig. You may not have held a wire whisk in your hand, but you've certainly incorporated its efforts into that body!"

Olson blushed beet-red. "Like for egg whites, meringue?" he asked softly.

"Yes," White-Lyons hissed, and rolled his eyes exaggeratedly. "Anyway. It was a whisk that did in the madman. Remember Turkit's pastry chef, Dinh-Hoa?"

"No."

"I thought you would have. Anyway, Dinh-Hoa made the most marvelous confections. The most towering cakes and delicacies this side of the Sacher Café. Turkit nearly lost his mind—that's redundant, isn't it?—over these things. But it was the charlotte

russe that he loved best. Only, Dinh-Hoa—half mad himself—
refused to make it until he had the absolutely right wire whisk for
the beating of egg whites. The two of them would bicker and
fuss; it was the most remarkable thing. Dinh-Hoa could get away
with anything because Turkit loved his pastries so much.

"So it occurred to me that the charlotte russe was the key to the
thing. That Turkit would never let the food tasters tear it apart or
adulterate it. But where on earth was I going to get a wire whisk?
It took me a year to convince old Bunny Brewster, who sold
Turkit the Silver Shadow, to send me one from home. You remember Bunny?"

"He must have been after my time."

"Well, he had a devil of a time getting it, because they certainly
didn't have them in Britain in those days. Didn't need a whisk to
mix up Bovril. Didn't need a whisk to coddle eggs. He got it from
the bloody Frogs, I believe. And then I got it, and the rest, as they
say—and in this case it's certainly true—is history. You look terrible, by the way."

"I've been flying all night."

"On your own, or in an airplane?"

Olson picked up one of the small clay pots and in a distracted
way began very slowly to rub away some green mold that was
covering it.

White-Lyons snatched it out of his hands. "I don't have many
visitors, Olson. No one burrows back here to see me. No one
knows if I come or go. So I was a little surprised by your telephone call the other day. Things must be pretty desperate if you're
paying a visit to the pariah."

"That's right."

"Something about the trip to Washington, I fancy. You didn't
like the outcome?"

"Not particularly."

White-Lyons sighed. "That's the trouble with you boys. You
start the game, you make up the rules as you go along, and then
you're all irate and dumbfounded when the new team comes on
and changes them. Huffing and puffing, it can kill men your age.
The real problem, I think, is lack of imagination. That's what I
suspect it is. That, and greed."

"That's what it is, you think?"

"Yes, I do."

"You know, your boy has caused a lot of trouble."

"I know. He's got lots of guts. He's not afraid of you. He's not
afraid to make the big gesture. You know, he arrived with

power—about him, physically, I mean. Some leaders evolve, but I tell you, he was born that way. And with a total ideological scheme in mind for himself from the very beginning."

"So we discovered."

"Well, that's what I meant about imagination, Olson. You should have guessed."

Olson set the pot down on the workbench. "Do you have a chair around here, Walter? I'd like to sit down. I'm tired. You wouldn't happen to have a drink, would you?"

White-Lyons scraped a three-legged stool across the cement floor to him. "Need a drink, do you?"

"Very much."

"Well, I don't have any for you. Never touch the stuff, not since I realized that the older I get the more forgetful I become. The liquor accelerates that. I believe it does."

"So you're losing your memory?"

"Every day. What happened yesterday or this morning. I've even forgotten what we were talking about five seconds ago. Why, I can't even remember why you're here, Olson, do you?"

"But the long-ago memories, they're still intact, are they, Walter?"

"My, yes, but I remember everything. I can remember exactly our first telephone, two rings. Our number was three-four, and my mother was so tiny she had to stand on a stool to speak into the mouthpiece. I remember the coronation of George V. We came all the way into London to see it. My father waved the most perfectly white linen handkerchief. I remember every detail—and I was only three years old!"

"And what else?"

"Well ... I missed the war, you know, the Big One. A bitter time for me, Olson, shut up here away from the action. I would have given my right arm to be in the thick of it, but ... I did what I was told. I was very disappointed. So no memories there."

"But earlier, White-Lyons, you had some exciting times in the thirties. You saw some action, out there on the plain. I know you did."

"The plain?" White-Lyons raised his eyes and gave Olson an empty look.

"Yes, weren't you on the plain?"

"Well, yes, of course. One can't be in the kingdom and not venture out onto the plain. And of course, I've been living here a lifetime. I had hoped to be posted to Jerusalem originally. Did I tell you that? I really thought Palestine more to my taste."

"But you were quite regularly on the plain in the thirties."

"I was posted to the military base at Nizra."

"But surely you went occasionally to the plain? I remember seeing you there."

"Yes, I saw you once or twice in those years, but at court, wasn't it? I actually remember you quite well. You were tall and thin and exceedingly young. You were a nervous boy-o, Olson, but you had a presence. Too bad you got fat and lost it all." White-Lyons turned and gave him a weak smile. "Do you think you'll ever be your former self again, Olson? You'll have to leave the food alone, and the scotch. Can you do it?"

But Olson would not be baited and guessed correctly that the old man knew he was on the scent and was trying to throw him off.

"It was on the plain that I saw you, Walter, not at court. I saw you with Malik. Why won't you admit it? It was no crime to be helping Malik when you worked for the British army and for Turkit. You knew the Brits were doubledealing the old bastard; we all were. So what were you doing on the plain, selling arms to Malik?"

"That was your job."

"That's right. But you were with Malik more than I. How did you do it? I'm curious. You were with him in the winter, when he went after the outpost at Im. What's the harm in admitting it all these years later. Still afraid you'll seem disloyal?"

White-Lyons shrugged. "Well, there's no harm, is there? Not now. Yes, I was with him. Helped him plan his strategy if you must know. Oh, not a lot. Just an idea here and there—as long as it was native troops he was after and none of my own countrymen. I was very, very careful. I operated strictly on my own because I was no fool. There was no such thing as loyalty, not among the courtiers, and certainly not among my fellow officers. You have never seen such toadying in your life, Olson. God, but it was something to witness. How we thought we needed Turkit back in those days. Couldn't get by without him. But look, he's gone, we're still here and we're doing just fine. Or I think we're doing fine, anyway. Never read newspapers anymore. Can you imagine what he would have done to me if he'd found out I was helping Malik? All those years, he never even guessed. It was an exciting time in my life, I'll tell you."

"You loved Malik."

White-Lyons rolled his eyes. "I wouldn't call it love. They're not exactly lovable, those types. Oh, they fire up the people. They have the vision and people need the vision. And he was heroic all right—tall in the saddle, reckless, brave. Best damned looking man I've ever seen before or since. Handsome like a movie star. But I wouldn't call him lovable, not on a personal level anyway. Those people never are. They can't love on an individual basis. They can love only in the abstract. So they love 'the people,' 'the cause,' 'freedom,' that sort of thing. But no, they're not personally lovable."

Abruptly, he stopped speaking and a look of concentration flickered briefly over his features. He hesitated for a moment, then shook the soil off the roots of another little violet. But he had passed his tongue over his dry lips and through that gesture Olson knew he had him.

"You're wondering how I knew you spent time in the winter camp."

"No."

"Come on."

"I guess you had your sources."

"But you still wonder."

"No, it's none of my business. They're all dead now anyway, ghosts—like me."

Olson shook his head in mock surprise. "None of your business that through tremendous skill and daring you found a way to aid Malik not just philosophically but materially and outsmart Turkit in the process? It must have been monumentally difficult meeting him, reaching him. You must have been extraordinarily clever, Walter."

"I was very clever."

"You must have been completely devoted to him."

"I was very clever."

"But you didn't spend the whole winter with him, did you?"

"Of course not. I couldn't be gone from Nizra for more than a day or two without drawing suspicion."

"Four or five days, more likely."

"I don't remember."

"Two days with Malik, then three days elsewhere, is that how it went?"

"It was nearly forty years ago. I don't remember."

"Where did you go when you left Malik?"

"I traveled back to Nizra."

"Across the plain?"

"I guess so."

"In the heat?"

"Olson, this is tiresome. I can't remember all these details."

"You went to Im."

"If you say so."

"You went to Im to be with Nila."

This time White-Lyons visibly started. "No," he said. Then more firmly, "I most certainly did not. Nila was . . . How do I remember where Nila was?"

"You went to Im to be with Nila because Nila was your lover. You convinced Malik to winter on the plain so you would be able to go to Im once a week or so, to be with Nila, without arousing suspicion. That whole winter you traveled back and forth between the two of them."

White-Lyons threw down the plant in its little pot. "This is nonsense." He turned and started to walk to the door.

The smell of the rich potting soil, a moment ago so warm and bespeaking of all things good and clean and earthy, had now begun to oppress Olson. He believed it had seeped through his nose into his brain and that he was suffocating from it. The dense rich soil was in his mouth, choking his breath. He was tired past exhaustion. He would finish this business and then he would sleep for days, weeks. Sleep would obliterate memory; it would have to, because he wanted to go on living after this was over.

"Malik wintered on the plain in February and March 1936," he went on in a weary voice. "Nila was at Im. Malik returned to Im in early April 1936. Tarik was born in October 1936."

White-Lyons stopped in his tracks and wheeled around. His face was set in such rage that Olson immediately came to his feet.

"You call that proof of anything?" he snorted. "Proof of what? What are you getting at? You think Nila and I were lovers."

"Yes."

"Then prove it."

Olson stood stonily silent.

White-Lyons gave him a sneering smile. "Come to the bar of justice without any proof, haven't you? Just a bag of hot wind."

"Not really."

"Well, you can't prove a thing."

"Not so."

White-Lyons hesitated. Behind his narrowed eyes his brain was picking its way through the conversation as if it were a mine field. He tried to distract Olson with more scorn. "I think you've lost your mind. I think I should go back to my little violets and that you should go home and get some sleep." He snatched at a white violet and began fussing with it.

But Olson was undeterred. "You and Nila were lovers for more than a year. In 1935, while Malik was campaigning in the countryside, you found ways to be with her."

"No."

"You were lovers, and you had a child together."

"Preposterous. You count these months up on your fingers and you think you've come up with something? This is a pathetic gesture, Olson, and one I'm going to be sure your superiors hear about. He kicked your ass and now you're so desperate to come up with something to pull him in that you try even this dime-store-novel trick. It's disgusting. You're the worst kind of barbarian, Olson. Worse even than Turkit. The barbarian with a briefcase. Well, it won't work. I'm not playing the numbers game with you. Tarik is Malik's son. He has his rightful position in the world because of it. So I'll thank you to get out of my sight and never come back." The tiny violet he held disintegrated in the fist action of his hand. Embarrassed, he smoothed his hand on his pant leg and crossed the room to another workbench and sat down.

Feeling as if he were moving in strobe-light time, Olson with his left hand pulled open the jacket of his suit and with his right reached into his breast pocket and removed a blue airmail-weight envelope. He walked across the floor and offered it to White-Lyons, who stared at it mutely.

"She couldn't read or write, you know," Olson said. "She spoke eloquently, but she couldn't read or write."

White-Lyons's face slackened. Olson believed that in that instant the flesh had somehow fallen away from his bones, because he seemed nothing but a skeleton. A skeleton figure in an army uniform and dirty bare feet. Olson was only slightly younger than White-Lyons, but the colonel appeared ancient, desiccated. Olson's own father had become very thin as an old man. The more he ate, the less he seemed to weigh. But White-Lyons never appeared to even think of food. Olson couldn't remember the last time he had seen him take a bite. Perhaps he was starving himself to death. Perhaps he had put the last ounce of his energy into the potting of violets.

"She was very frightened of childbirth," Olson continued. "She believed that she had sinned and that God would punish her by taking away her life and deprive her forever of the sight of her child. She was quite primitive. Like Topaz. They're all that way here. Used to be, anyway."

White-Lyons stared at the envelope as if Olson had ripped his heart from his chest and offered it to him in his hand. For a moment he seemed to be mounting an offensive, but then his mouth fell open slightly, the energy ran out of him, his bones seemed to disconnect from each other, and he visibly sagged. He was too old. He no longer had the wit or will to deny it.

He said, "She was very wise. Very wise."

"I remember. She had a difficult labor. Malik was nowhere around, not surprising. You were right about him, you know. A warm heart for the cause, but as cold a heart as I have ever met. But she was lovely, warm. I can understand why you loved her."

White-Lyons nodded his large white head up and down. His pale blue eyes clouded over with memory, and he seemed on the verge of tears.

Olson lowered his voice to a whisper. "I was at Im when her labor came on. I hadn't planned it that way, but a dust storm blew up and I had to pull up. She liked me, I think, and trusted me. I amused her with stories of the carryings-on at court. We were together for days, in a little stone hut. She had a lot of pain and the baby took forever to be born. She was desperate. She asked me to write things down for her. A final letter to you because she believed she was going to die. It's all in here. She loved you very much. She was pleased to be having your child. But afraid at the same time. Afraid Malik would find out. I promised I would never tell."

"And your word was your bond, is that it, Arthur?"

Olson looked away. "It was you who got them out of the country."

"In one of the old bombers."

"And got them to the States."

"Yes, I didn't want them to go to Britain. Turkit had the resources to harm them there. He had nothing in the States. And . . . I was looking for a new world for them."

"And you're the one who wrote Tarik about the Soviet fighters back in sixty-three? Did they really exist?"

"No." White-Lyons almost laughed when he said it.

"I thought not. And then you killed Turkit to bring Tarik over."

"Turkit was an evil man. He deserved to die."

"And you wanted Tarik with you."

"With me, yes. But he was a great man. I knew it from the letters he wrote me when he was growing up. I still have them. I have nothing left of her but him."

Olson shook his head. "Oh, Walter, it's a bad thing you've done here. Hearts are going to be broken. Blood will flow."

They stood in silence for a long time, neither of them thinking anything in particular, the ache in their hearts too great to support thought.

Then Olson roused himself and in a hard voice said, "So, Walter, let's keep it simple. You can tell him, or I can, whichever you choose. But in the end, to save himself, he'll have to return to the previous course. The old way, the way it was agreed upon all those years ago. None of this lone-wolf stuff. No one will ever know but the three of us. It will never be mentioned again. When I leave the kingdom tomorrow I'll never come back. I'm leaving OmniTech. I'm going away. I'm going to buy a place on Chesapeake Bay. I'm going to fish."

He released an enormous sigh. In some perverse way he was glad to have this out in the open, his guilty secret of thirty-nine years. But he couldn't escape certain ironic speculations. If Turkit hadn't lasted so long, if White-Lyons hadn't been so determined, if Tarik hadn't been the man he was, why, who would have cared about the love affair between a native girl and a bachelor who'd finally discovered he had a heart to give? Why hadn't he given the letter to White-Lyons back then? He could no more explain that than tell why he was giving over the letter now, except that he'd always been able to recognize a due bill when he saw it. It was the difference between shit and blood, and he was, he decided, shit.

"Would you like the letter?"

"Please."

White-Lyons extended his blue-veined old-man hand and took the weightless envelope, which crackled pleasantly at the touch of his fingertips. He held it at a distance for a moment, as if it were a small bird that might take flight at any start. Then with an awe that seemed to Olson to be rapture, he slowly brought the letter to his colorless lips and kissed it as one would a lover.

At the sight of this, Olson gasped, then ran from the glassed-in room as fast as his bulk would allow, back down the marble corridor, left, right, taking corners fast.

He was perspiring heavily from the exertion. Or was that wetness tears? He touched his face. These might be tears. Yes, he thought they must be. He was aware of the sound of his footsteps, the sound falling away on the cold marble behind him, all the time saying over and over to himself—

The thing of it is, all the time you're alive you think that life is out there, shaking its fist at you. It's going to eat me, life's going to eat me, and you're afraid. But—and this is the joke—you get

*old and worn from watching out that life doesn't eat you, and in
the end life doesn't eat you. You are made to eat life. I have this
on good authority. I'm the Executioner and there are some things
that I know better than anyone.*

Olson slowed to a walk, breathing so hard he had to undo the
top two buttons of his shirt, pleased now that he hadn't worn the
necktie. He turned the last corner. The receptionist's desk was in
sight. He could almost make out the oily young lieutenant with
the shark-white teeth sitting there.

He was counting the steps to the front door, when from behind
him, flying with the force of a locomotive and seeming to suck up
the air around it as it moved, came a sound. A sound from back
there, in the potting shed, that stopped him in his tracks.

He began to run again, his big American shoes pounding down
Italian marble floors worth a fortune. The force of the noise
pushed him along, out the door. A scream, no, a howl. The howl
of an old man in the act of eating life.

Elliott Tomlinson, reclining on a couch in his office, inspected an
eighteenth-century Meissen figure of an egg seller and wondered
if it was one of a pair.

He'd been making a quick reckoning of what the figurine might
fetch at Christie's in London, when the old man's howl shocked
him out of his calculations. Later he would remember that he
moved as if on the bottom of the ocean, wrapping the figure carefully in newspaper, locking it into a desk drawer, moving it to the
long library table where he stacked his electronics equipment—all
of it seemed to take hours. His stomach tensed in excitement as
he squinted to find the rewind button in the dim light.

On the table were reel-to-reel tape recorders, boxes of cata-
logued tapes, earphones, speakers, cables everywhere, the harvest
of the dozen or so bugs he'd kept stashed around the palace offices and living quarters for years.

He removed his glasses and clamped them between his front
teeth, then hunkered down to read the tape player's digital
counter. He hit the rewind button, the tape squealed, then played
back at normal speed. He adjusted the volume.

For a long time he stayed there on the floor, on the Aubusson
carpet he had lifted from Turkit's favorite nephew's old bedroom,
playing and replaying the conversation.

After a while, after his excitement had abated and his mind
cleared and he became the involved observer, he made himself
more comfortable, settling behind his desk, his feet up, the tape

volume up, listening over and over to the scene played out between White-Lyons and Olson in the loamy ambience of the potting shed.

Then he threaded a new tape onto an adjacent recorder, made a dub, walked the original over to his floor safe, and locked it up. He spooled the duplicate onto a smaller reel, discarded the leftover, and put the tape into his jacket pocket. Then he locked his office door behind him, walked through a series of short corridors, down two flights of stairs, and stepped outside into the sunlight.

His office was located in the new civic center complex, a neatly laid-out grid of ten-story office buildings housing government offices, international banks, high-tech importers, OmniTech headquarters, and a host of smaller business concerns. The buildings faced a broad, tree-lined avenue, on either side of which were restaurants, stores of international reputation, beauty parlors, all the real estate of a modern, up-to-date society.

Still walking, within ten minutes he had left that world behind and was passing through the gates into the old city. Here the air was full of clove and cinnamon and Tomlinson sucked it in gratefully, savoring it as if for the first time. He pushed past two women haggling over a huge basket of sardines, and ordinarily would have stopped to buy a bag of almonds or fresh fruit, but he wasn't hungry in the slightest. He felt full up, satisfied, complete. He carried on his bony shoulders the feather weight of the most complete joy he had ever known. He swung his arms uncharacteristically. If he'd known how to whistle, he would have.

He had no idea where he was going. He walked aimlessly, turning left and right at whim. He didn't particularly care. He only knew that no matter where he set his foot that morning, he was on the path to glory. He who had never heeded birdsong now marveled at the noise of the bulbuls, the whoosh of the breeze in the cypress trees, the aromas of burnt sugar and frankincense that wafted over it all. The shake of a street singer's tambourine, the sullen pout of a young boy with a fresh haircut. All of it so damned interesting, why had he never noticed before?

Retrieving the hidden tape machine from the potting shed had been an afterthought. He had left the voice-activated device there years before, when Tarik and Topaz used to sit on the little stone bench in the garden and anguish over the sex of her coming baby. Boring stuff. He'd forgotten about the machine; it was a wonder it still worked. And it would have stayed there overlooked forever if that cheesy young lieutenant from the reception desk hadn't showed up in his office yesterday with the news that something had gone on between White-Lyons and Olson in the potting shed. That the Number Two had run out of the palace like a man who'd just met his own ghost. News that the lieutenant figured was worth mentioning to the station chief.

Tomlinson turned east, the just-risen sun bright in his eyes. Through an open door he watched a man weaving at a loom; some still practiced the ancient art and had no use for the fabric manufactured in the big textile plant outside town.

What a fascinating place, he decided with his newfound awareness. Why hadn't he noticed earlier the riot of color, the heady blend of seductive aromas, the bright-eyed men and women crowding narrow sidewalks? What a remarkable place. He ran his fingers through his thin hair.

But after a very little while, he was tired of walking, and the teeming pedestrians and their smelly dray animals had begun to get on his nerves, and so he sat down at an outdoor café and ordered a Tab. He slung one leg over the other, sipped his soda, and began turning things over in his mind.

Olson intended not to share the secret with anyone at OmniTech or in Washington; he thought he could drop the bomb and then manage damage control by himself. *I have the field all to myself,* Tomlinson realized. The tape was a career-maker all right, the break he'd been waiting for. Now, what he ought to do is get on the next plane out, get to the States fast as he could and let the big boys know that their problem was solved—that is, Elliott Tomlinson had solved their problem. He stared at the café wall as if his life's future were unspooling on a screen there. They would pound him on the back and spill their celebratory drinks on him and say Oops! sorry, excitement had gotten the best of them. After the excitement died down, he'd be able to write his own ticket, get out of this burg and onto something more critical, Cairo maybe, Riyadh at the very least.

Silver hoops dangling from her earlobes, a young girl sauntered past, gave Tomlinson a sidelong glance, and walked on. He followed her with his eyes, wondering if she was a prostitute, until she passed through a green-painted door and was gone. He wouldn't have to pay for it from now on, he realized. He had the power, and when you had the power, you had the women. He wondered what kind of a pay raise he would be getting, or would they just settle a sum of money on him and let him use it at his discretion?

He signaled the waiter for another Tab and settled back in his chair.

On the other hand, what if they didn't give him a cent? What if after the backslapping and drink-slopping were over, some Agency accountant told him there was nothing in it for him? He was paid to do his job, he'd done it, that was all the reward he deserved. What if they told him a job well done should be his reward? It didn't seem reasonable, or fair, but they could say that. They could say anything.

And further, what if they took credit for the problem solved themselves. What if they took the tape out of his hands, patted him on his almond-shaped head, and said thanks a lot and goodbye. They could do that too. He wasn't a player. He was outside the power loop. They could shaft him good and then he'd be back here and Tarik would be on his ass, and Olson, and White-Lyons. They'd find a way to fix him, knock him over with one of those big Land-Rovers, call it an accident.

He sipped his soda through a plastic straw for over an hour, turning his options this way and that. No matter what he came up with, the result was the same—Tarik might be ruined, but Elliott Tomlinson would be fucked. Shit.

He paid for the soft drinks, stood, and began walking back in the direction he'd come, faster now, oblivious of the donkeys, the street singers, the kohl-eyed girls in hot-pink and blue dresses. He jammed his hands into his pockets, chin chucked down to his chest. No way was he not going to come out of this a winner. No way was he going to let them outfox him, screw him over, or anything else.

He passed beyond the old city walls, picking up his step until he was trotting. In the parking lot behind his office building was his light-blue Ford. He turned over the engine, gunned it, waited a moment, then flipped on the air-conditioning. He checked the fuel gauge, then counted the money in his pocket. There was a roadmap in the glove compartment and he checked route numbers for a minute. But there wasn't much point. There was really only one road in the whole place. All he had to do was follow it straight out to where the Marib lived. To the man who would cherish the message, and the messenger. To Hadi.

Tomlinson put the car in gear, pulled carefully into traffic, and set out on the three-hour trip across the plain.

26

Homer Barrow's airway wasn't obstructed like poor old Zeke Cardell's. And he hadn't developed the heart problems that pneumoconiosis can bring, like the Reverend Nute's brother Morton, who was bedridden. And although he breathed imperfectly, he wasn't on a respirator like that fella he'd seen over in Pikeville two weeks ago. Willa Blankenship had driven him over for some respiratory therapy and he'd seen a lot of old miners there hacking and coughing and bringing up stuff from their lungs that looked like the devil's business. That one fella had a hole in his throat, with a nasty plastic tube trailing out of it hooked up to a ventilator that whooshed like a bellows. The man was glassy-eyed and worn out from the struggle for breath. It looked to Homer like he didn't have too much farther to paddle.

So he was grateful, he really was. He just had a hard time showing it.

It was Saturday morning and Sayles was at the kitchen table, staring absently at a pile of papers, when Homer threw open the back door, letting in a draft of chill, damp air. Tears standing in his eyes, gasping for breath, he hurried through the kitchen without speaking.

Sayles cocked his ear to the staircase, heard Homer stagger into his bedroom upstairs, heard him thump around, kick away a chair, slam a drawer, finally settle down in the rocking chair. When there was total silence finally, Sayles knew he was up there inhaling oxygen from the tank he kept near his bed, trying to calm his lungs.

Sayles got up from his own chair to close the back door Homer had left standing open. He was taken suddenly at the sight of his hands on the doorknob. They were bony, and heavy bluish cords stood out on their backs. He brought them to the level of his eyes.

Why, they were transparent as an X ray. He could see every purple vein clearly, make out muscle and bone. Daylight could pass through those hands as surely as it beamed through the clear glass of the kitchen door's panes.

He shoved them into his pockets, shut the door with a shove of his elbow, walked back to the kitchen table, and resumed examining his papers.

He had made a multimillion-dollar endowment to Berea College and the school had invited him to join its board of governors. He felt some obligation but was already on so many boards and committees and trusts that he couldn't imagine how he could find the time. After scratching out a note in his own hand saying he could accept some honorary position and volunteering his name for fund-raising but board membership and active participation were out of the question, he pushed back his chair and went to the percolator on the stove for more coffee. He did things for himself these days. Except for Clare's cousins who cooked and cleaned, they were all on their own in Mills Bend.

Construction on the ridge house had been going on for a year, as difficult a project as Clare had predicted it would be, and he was torn constantly between his obligations to Alex, at St. Albans, in Washington, and to the work in Kentucky. Much of the management of the family businesses had been turned over to the assistants Sayles had been grooming for years, and the Sayles philanthropic foundation was well served by a large staff in New York. The empire could run without him, until Alex came of age.

Still, three additional phone lines had to be installed to handle the volume of incoming calls when he was in Kentucky, and although he maintained the fully-staffed office on K Street in the capital, he still needed Clare's secretary to handle correspondence when he was down there. A major New York publisher wanted him to write his memoirs, and he was toying with the idea. Even though he kept up a brutal schedule, commuting, consulting, house-building, in Washington and Mills Bend, he considered himself retired.

He'd adjusted to life on a coal seam. He looked good—tall, lanky, a brush of rose in his cheeks. He wore flannel shirts, usually dark plaid patterns, neatly pressed khaki pants, and work boots he kept the local cobbler busy maintaining. He still put on a necktie every morning, but they were knitted now, not silk. Callers from Washington and New York addressed him familiarly as "Ambassador," the locals called him "Mr. Sayles," and no one, despite Clare's dire warning, ever presumed to call him Larry.

He was seventy years old. Sometimes he forgot the details of what he had done the day before. Sometimes, walking down Main Street, he would forget where he was going, and have to circle back to his front door in order to jog his memory. His body no longer metabolized food the way it once had. He was losing weight and eating twice as much in a futile attempt to gain some back. Sometimes his heart did funny little flips and he would become anxious and make himself take deep calming breaths. He thought a lot about his mother and father. He could relive vividly his first year at St. Paul's, but for the life of him he could not remember what he had had for lunch yesterday. Chiefly, he drank in his days and nights, loved Clare and Alex, and marveled with his lifelong native smoothness at the incongruities that had come his way this late in his life.

He was out of sight, but not out of touch. The current regime in the White House had tried to enlist him in various international issues, but the old enthusiasm just wasn't there. He'd spent six days in Moscow at the invitation of the Russians the previous spring. His alma mater, Harvard, had given him an honorary degree that June. He'd conducted a seminar at the Hoover Institution at Stanford in September, attended testimonials at the Smithsonian and the Harkness (he'd taken Sylvia to that one), but he wasn't much seen in the capital these days. He spoke on the phone with Francis Riston at the State Department, just to stay current, but when his old friends asked him what he was up to, he described himself as a rusticant.

Actually, he was busy every minute with the house, and with concerns more in line with his new life. The federal government had failed to solve the problems of Appalachia, despite the Appalachian Regional Development Act Lyndon Johnson had signed in 1965. After ten years the region was as economically depressed as ever; the suicide rate was twice the national average and welfare payments nearly half as great as those in the rest of the country.

Worse yet, mine employment was down again. The oil embargo had ended but the country had gone right back to the massive consumption of foreign oil. The coal industry was caught again in the eternal downward spiral, and it was only going to get worse with federal clean air regulations and the shift of steel production to foreign plants, particularly Japan. Mechanized mining put more and more men out of work, and the demand for certain types of coal was in decline, the coal Clare took out of Number 9 and the rest of her mines. Some mines had closed down permanently.

So after a brief boom time the people of Appalachia faced

again the hundred-year-old problems of money, jobs, housing, education, and health care. It seemed a long time ago indeed since Jack Kennedy, campaigning for president in West Virginia, got his first hard look at Appalachian poverty and was stunned by what he saw.

Mills Bend wasn't on the ropes yet but anybody could predict where the place—and where coal—would be in another decade. Lawrence Sayles didn't presume to be around when it happened, but he knew it would come and he had the idea that the last great mission of his life would be to do something about it.

His first thought had been to import more coal-dependent industry to the area—processing plants, coal cleaning operations, and the like. But he was too sanguine to linger long on that notion. No, the only solution was to break out of the vicious economic cycle, to end, or at least diminish, the town's dependence on such an unstable industry as coal. For the first time in his life he had begun thinking about, to actually *feel*, the worries of the common man. These people had no incentive to change their lives. They were permanently broke, broken down, or on the dole. The past was one long misery, and the future, well, the future was as dim as the coal face at the end of a two-mile deep-mine.

And because they had been in the misery system so long, they had no imagination for solving the problem themselves—Lawrence Sayles's stock-in-trade. He was of the class of men who felt the responsibility to lift them up above the flood waters of their broken-back ambitions. He could save them from themselves and accomplish what the federal government couldn't—teach them new skills and different kinds of economies.

Lately he had been thinking that cattle farming might be the ticket, and one that would dovetail neatly with the hill people's love of their animals. He had been consulting over the telephone with livestock managers around the country and was scheduled to fly one in from Virginia sometime next week. He had also been debating within his own mind whether to strike out on his own, make things happen with his wealth and his will, or organize some sort of blue-ribbon committee and hope to turn it into more of a national imperative. But he'd overturned that idea. If the mighty apparatus of the Great Society hadn't done much for the betterment of the Appalachian man and woman, how could some puny committee?

As he sipped his coffee and pondered these choices, Homer came back into the kitchen. "You weren't long enough on the oxygen to do you any good, Homer."

No comment.

"Your lungs have taken a terrible beating. You need to help them out. Do what the doctor told you."

"Mind your own lungs."

"I do. I take good care of myself."

"Gonna live forever, are ya? The devil be a-knockin' at your door one day soon. And he ain't gon' take no check or cash."

"Never give up on that business, do you?"

"Not while I got breath."

"Well, you hardly have any breath left, Homer. Maybe you ought to save it."

Clomp to the cupboard for a mug, a slosh of coffee from the percolator, heading for the door.

"I'm going to walk over to Clare's office, Homer. You want anything from town?"

"Nope."

"By the way, they're going to start setting the stone fireplaces and chimneys up at the ridge house today. You know a lot about that kind of work. Like to come up and supervise?"

"Maybe."

"Well, let me know."

"Maybe not."

Stomp out the door, door slam, important business with his sow in the backyard.

Sayles downed the last of his coffee and set his rinsed cup on the drainboard. He picked up his hat and coat in the living room and shut the front door behind him. He stopped to check the mailbox at the end of the front walk, lowering the little red flag and sorting quickly through the more than a dozen letters with official-looking return addresses that were for him, one for Clare from Sylvia, and a seed catalogue for Homer.

He jammed the envelopes into the pocket of his goosedown jacket and turned his collar up against the chill. The damp air felt full of coming snow. It was the time of year when normally they would go down to Hobe Sound for the sun, but because of the pressure of Clare's work they would all be sticking it out in Kentucky.

Satisfied by the ritual of collecting the mail, he began strolling in the direction of town. When the sidewalk ran out, he stepped into the roadway, careful to keep to the sandy shoulder. He was relieved that the coal trucks kept out of town. They'd nearly blown him off the roadway once when he was walking by himself up on the two-lane highway above town.

Many of the houses had American flags clipped to their clapboard shingles, advertising their national devotion, but many more had rusted cars, busted snowmobiles, twisted engines, and lawn mowers sitting on their front lawns or in driveways. Sayles wondered disinterestedly why rural America turned old engine parts into lawn ornaments.

Most of the houses in Mills Bend were of the prefab postwar type, laid out in tight, depressing grids along the town's few streets. There was a small trailer park near the truck garage and a half-dozen two-family homes. Several of the houses were literally falling down, abandoned when families moved north during the great exodus of miners in the forties and fifties. The coal camp of Homer's day was decaying and deserted. The only building that relieved the monotony of misery was the old Aylesworth mansion. Sayles always looked forward to coming upon the place, set back from the street in a small grove of hickory and willow trees, when he walked to town. Muddy's ex-wife, Adelle, was watching him now from the window. She waved timidly from behind a Victorian lace curtain, and he touched his hat brim in gentlemanly acknowledgment as he walked past.

The town was laid out in a horseshoe shape around a bend of the Tug River. To the north, the river itself; to the south, the railroad tracks. He picked his way over those tracks gingerly. There were huge hunks of coal lost from train cars spread carpetlike over the ties, and they could trip up old-man legs if he tried to cross too quickly.

Several businesses had closed down in the past twelve months, and the Hub Store and the Witness Drug Company buildings, abandoned for decades, were on the verge of tumbling down. The movie theater was shuttered but the tavern and the launderette were going great guns. The squat brutality of the run-down buildings signaled the surrender of the coal business and the people who worked at it, and Sayles felt depressed just being in the midst of it all.

He reached Clare's office building and climbed the flight of stairs to the second floor, not the least bit winded from the effort. He had been feeling good for days, and this made him confident and happy.

Clare's secretary flashed him a broad smile as he entered and indicated a manila folder of letters he should sign when he had time.

He nodded at the assistants sitting at their metal desks and threaded his way through file cabinets back to Clare's office.

Through the glass of the office partition he could see her at her desk, long legs folded under her in the chair, talking to Toby, who looked inconsolable. He caught her eye and took a chair to wait outside. After less than a minute Toby came out with his head down and walked past without noticing him.

Sayles went into her office. "I've brought you a letter from Sylvia, and a card from Alex."

She examined them briefly. "Thanks."

"I thought you might like some lunch."

She shuffled through the heap of papers piled on her desk. "I just don't have the time, Lawrence. I'm not hungry anyway."

"You better eat something. You're losing weight."

"You're a fine one to talk."

"I'm old. I'm not supposed to work perfectly."

"Don't say that."

"Why not? It's true."

She twisted in her chair and pulled her legs out from under her. "I just think I should stay on and work."

"Come have something with me."

He said this in such a soft, urgent voice that Clare raised her eyes to his. His felt hat was tipped back on his head, and in his country clothes he almost had the rough-hewn, hardscrabble look of a retired miner. But Clare was not deceived. The patrician soul of Lawrence Sayles was still discernible under that Woolrich shirt, the easy burden of generations of inherited wealth and the air of superiority that conveyed. He looked a little like Lord Mountbatten impersonating Tom Joad in *The Grapes of Wrath*. It was a credible performance but no one would ever mistake it for anything other than acting.

"Come on," he said again.

She smiled, unable to resist him, and then called to her secretary that they would be at Shirley's Chicken Shack in case she was needed.

They took a table near the window. The place was empty except for two retired miners hunkered down over their piled-high plates of food. The men ate with their hats on and their teeth out.

Shirley's was a perfect barometer of the times. Beat-up chairs and tables were jammed every which way. The jukebox sat mute, its cord out of the wall plug and snaking uselessly across the torn-up linoleum floor, a film of grease and steam over it all.

In the kitchen out back, Shirley settled chicken parts and french fries into fry baskets and then plunged them into boiling oil. Customers never inquired after the menu. At the Chicken Shack, chicken was it.

In a little while Shirley came out of the kitchen to drop their lunches down in front of them on the mismatched plates. Clare pulled a paper napkin from the holder on the table. Lawrence contemplated the chicken for a very long time and then began to probe a leg with a knife and fork.

"What was on Toby's mind?" he asked her, sawing with his knife.

"Black Hat mine voted last night. I didn't know it was coming."

"Union?"

"Uh-huh."

He speared a piece of meat with his fork, shook salt and pepper over it, and then set it cautiously into his mouth. He didn't want to press her for details. He didn't want to add his concern to her misery. He intended to present himself as a calm force of reasoned thinking. Tentatively, he chewed and swallowed the chicken.

"Are you going to go down there and talk to them?"

"What's the point, Lawrence? What can I say? 'Stick with me, and we'll get back on our feet again'? I don't believe it myself. We're a cooperative coal company. Wages are commensurate with profit. We're not making any money, so there are pay cuts. I guess they figure with bad times coming, they're better off with the union." She tugged a piece of meat off a thigh bone disconsolately.

"What about Number 9?"

"It's only a matter of time."

"What does Toby think?"

She wiped the paper napkin over her mouth and sat back in her chair to look at him levelly for the first time since they'd come in. "I think he believes it's inevitable. I think in some way he wants it. He's worn out from the problems. I think if I ask him directly, he would say that we are fighting a losing battle. I think he's worried that I'll get stubborn and resist and knowing how things escalate around here that it could get nasty. He has no faith in coal and he never has had. Why should he? Why should any of us?"

"And you can't meet the union package yourself?"

"Not with the market price at this level. And if Wendell Pell is right, things are only going to get worse. The Japanese are making all the steel, and only so many American coal companies can provide the power industry with what it needs. I'm small. I can't take business away from Peabody or the other big guys. What we have is what the men get."

She glanced around the restaurant. The slide of Aylesworth Coal from boom to bottom was the hot topic of conversation in town. The two old miners stared at her with unabashed interest, trying to read her lips. Sullenly she dragged her eyes back to Lawrence's face. "I thought they would hang in a little longer. I'm disappointed and a little angry, if you want to know."

"I'm so sorry." He pushed his plate away. No amount of worry about his weight could get him to eat Shirley's chicken.

"Thanks," she said. "The layoffs at Black Hat were the final blow, but having to cut back on the health benefits . . . You know the union—that's where they offer big."

They sat in silence, Clare pushing the chicken around her plate, her chin nearly on her chest. Another retired miner came in, halloed Shirley at her fry baskets in back, and took a seat. Clare recognized him as Matty Thomas from Beckley's Hollow and lifted her chin at him in acknowledgement.

"I understand it—and yet I don't, Lawrence. If they'd stick with me and the cooperative, at least they'd have a chance to earn more than they ever could with a union mine. I'm not running dog holes here, after all. These are some of the most safely operated mines in the country, in the world. Even with the union, the big coal companies lie constantly about the dust levels. The men know this. They were here for the good times. I think at least they should stick around for the bad."

"Except you know how things go in this business, Clare. Five good years and fifteen bad. They read the papers, they know the writing is on the wall. It's not as if there are no precedents for downward spirals. Things are likely to get much worse before they get better, and they're scared for their families. You can appreciate that better than anyone."

"You think it's a lost cause."

"I'm saying that you've never been afraid to face facts. You may have to operate union mines and abandon the idea of the cooperative. They know you've done the best you can, but you can't make the steel business come back to this country. You can't get the federal government to change the clean-air acts. They feel more secure with the union. Hard times are coming."

For a long time she just sat there, her eyes finding some consoling element in the scratched Formica of the table. "I didn't sign on for this," she said finally in a firm, sad voice. "I signed on for the cooperative. It was never my plan to run just some ordinary old coal mines. I never wanted to be that kind of businesswoman. I don't care that much about this thing if we can't work the way we started out."

He covered her hand with his. "I think you shouldn't make choices now you might regret later. I think you ought to give it a chance. You have a good thing going here."

"I just wanted to do something interesting, something useful," she said with emotion, her voice rising. "Something that would make a difference. The thought of running union mines—I can just feel the enthusiasm draining out of me."

"Well, consider this," he offered, "I can help. I can arrange a loan from our family capital. Let me finish—you could then match the union package, pump up the health and pension plans. Another idea: You could go public. Muddy had some pretty good notions when it came to that. Or, we might develop new markets."

"Where?"

"Here, abroad. We'll figure it out."

"Lawrence, you know as well as I there are no new markets for coal. I mean, I appreciate your suggestions, but you know better than anyone that it's a dead end."

Shirley materialized at their table. She was a short, beefy woman who smelled, unsurprisingly, of grease and chicken fat. On the pretense that she was interested in them equally, she asked, "You folks want something else?" But she refused to even so much as glance at Clare and flipped huge, melting eyes over Sayles.

"Afternoon, Mr. Sayles," she trilled.

Sayles came to his feet slightly and dipped his head. "Shirley, it's good to see you."

"We have ice cream, Mr. Sayles. With chocolate sauce."

"Too rich for my blood." He laughed her off with a wave of his bony hand. "Your chicken is already enough."

"Oh, Mr. Sayles, ice cream wouldn't do you a bit of harm." But he protested more, and after bathing him in another long, adoring glance that caused him to finally clear his throat in embarrassment, she turned hard eyes on Clare.

"Missus?" she asked in a dead voice.

"Sweet of you to ask, Shirley, but no thanks."

The woman gave her a poisoned look, gathered up the dirty plates and glasses, and walked away, her fat rump bouncing around inside a pair of skintight acid-washed blue jeans.

Clare watched her go. "She hates me. They all hate me already, Lawrence. I can feel it. If they think I'm getting in their way, I'll wake up some night with the barrel of a Winchester down my throat."

"Oh, come on."

"You don't know these people. If the miners want union, they'll kill to get it. Go out and commune with the spirit of old Sid Hatfield if you don't believe me."

She scraped her chair across the linoleum and stood up. "I'd better get back."

"We still have a lot of talking to do."

"We'll talk some more tonight. Are you going up to the ridge house now?"

"They're setting the chimneys. I thought I'd take a look. I asked Homer to come up and supervise, but he wouldn't say yes or no."

They were out on the street, heading in opposite directions. She started to walk away, a picture of dejection with her head down. He watched her go, then ran to catch up for a moment, settling his arm on her shoulder.

"We'll work it out, Clare. No matter what happens here, we'll work something out. We have the house to look forward to." She kissed him lightly on the cheek, then pulled away.

Sayles caught the phone on the seventh ring, settling quickly into the armchair in the living room to take the call.

Francis Riston was in the habit of telephoning for general discussion. He liked to detail new developments, get Sayles's advice, gossip, bitch and moan about goings-on at State. Sayles had never asked Riston explicitly to brief him on Clare's former husband, but over the years Riston had come to understand that Sayles welcomed details of a personal nature, revelations Clare could know nothing about. So he knew, for instance, when Arthur Olson convinced Tarik to sign on with OmniTech. He knew almost as quickly as Washington that Topaz and Karim had died. He knew, in fact, that when Tarik was in Washington the year before, Clare had spent the night with him. And after he hung up with Riston this time, he once again knew what she did not, that Tarik was not Malik's son, and, further, that Tomlinson had gone renegade, that everybody now knew about the conversation between Olson and White-Lyons in the potting shed, that Tarik had gone up to the Sur mountains with all his enemies arrayed against him, that he was isolated, alone. That the very foundation of his belief in his legitimacy was rocked and they could not imagine what would happen with him.

So that night, when Sayles became suddenly withdrawn, Clare had no way of knowing it was because of the conversation with Riston. She thought he was being considerate of her own debilitating problems. She felt only quiet appreciation that he cared so much for her weeks of misery and made no comment when for days he would excuse himself from the dinner table immediately after they had finished eating on the pretext of needing fresh air. Or when she awoke in the middle of the night and found him staring silently out into the dark from the edge of their bed. She pressed his hand tight, told him she would be all right, and blessed herself for having a husband who cared so much.

And on the following Saturday, with Alex in Mills Bend as usual, she had no way of knowing that the prince of the republic, the nation's unfailing political inspiration, had been altered fundamentally in his nature. Whether it was age, or fate, or the sure recognition of a moment past which he would never be the same, in the silence of his solitary walks and the wrestle with his conscience, Lawrence Sayles had discovered there was an unfinished place in his life and that he could not go on until he had filled it.

He woke Alex at nine that morning. They chatted about school over toast and eggs Sayles fixed, then pulled on their coats and headed out the door. They opted to walk up the hollow to the ridge house rather than drive the rough road cut the previous year to handle trucks carrying workmen and supplies.

Tommy Johnson was tending to the woodpile alongside his place as they slogged through the red dog up the forest slope. The roof sagged in the middle and its clapboards were bleached white from age and weather. "Mornin', Alex."

"Hey!"

"How's school?"

"Boring."

Johnson brought his ax down hard on a piece of green pine. "Didn't get past the third grade myself. Never saw the need for it."

"Gonna work at the forge today, Tommy? Can I help?"

"Well"—whack with the ax—"I had a mind to go off with Dobbie today and get us a sack of copperheads. Old man Mullins says there were three of the critters right under his porch swing yesterday and you know how much he needs that swing. Dobbie and me gonna go over and catch the things. Think you might want to—"

Alex opened his eyes wide at him in warning. Sayles would

throw a fit if he thought Alex was anywhere around the deadly snakes.

"Yeah, I guess I'll be around the forge today, get it fired up. You might wanna come by. Say, did I tell you I found the bee tree?"

"Yeah? Are there bees there?"

"No, it's too cold now, but in a few weeks, warm up, they'll be back. So, Alex, you stop in on the way back down, okay? We'll work the forge, or whatever." He threw him a subtle wink, then rested on his ax handle and bending in the direction of Sayles said, " 'Day, sir."

Lawrence touched his hat brim in response and he and Alex moved on up the hollow, past run-down houses with little brothers and sisters playing in the yards and scattering the chickens. Up a little farther, they came upon Tutie Blankenship gathering poke and other wild greens. She shyly offered some to Sayles, who promised he'd pick them up on the way back down.

After several hundred yards of nearly vertical climbing, they reached a clearing close to the top of the mountain. The morning fog had lifted, and there were views for three hundred sixty degrees over the blue-green, worn-smooth Appalachian Mountains. Sayles settled down on a huge rock, his hands resting on his knees, panting.

Alex surveyed the state of the hilltop. "Another month or so and we'll have redbuds," he volunteered. "They make such a pretty glow." He turned and stared at Sayles. "You okay?"

"Catch my breath."

Alex kicked around through the heavy undergrowth. "Dug the wells yet?"

"Augured five wells and not one of them will be any good. All the ground water is polluted. Your mother was right when she said we'd have problems." He took a white handkerchief from his pocket, unfolded it, and blotted it around his face. Absently, he continued rubbing his forehead. Alex watched him for a moment, then stepped over a rhododendron bush to sit down alongside him on the rock.

"What about the lumber?"

"It's all up here except for the finish wood. The men spent a week sticking it and covering it with tarps, but it's all up."

"Wish I could take the rest of the school year off and work with you on the house, Dad. Think about how much I'd learn. I'm being cheated out of a whole wonderful experience. What if I ever have to make my living as a contractor, or carpenter?"

"Don't start, Alex."

"What if I were lost in the woods and had to learn to survive? I'd need those skills. Or they might drop the bomb and I'd have only my own resources to fall back on."

"No, no. You'll graduate from St. Albans, trust me on that."

"Please."

"Please, yourself. You'll go back to school Sunday night and that's that."

Alex stamped his toe into the little rhododendron bush in frustration. "You're making a mistake, Dad. You can't tell what's going to happen. Life is full of surprises."

The irony of the remark took Sayles aback so suddenly that the breath seemed to rush out of him and he visibly sagged.

Instantly anxious, Alex touched his sleeve with one finger. "You all right, Dad?"

"Alex . . ."

"Don't you feel well?"

"I'm fine. Son, there's something we need to talk over. Something you need to know."

Sayles composed his thoughts. On this clear morning, from their vantage high above Barrow's Hollow, Sayles could see the river bending gently, the town folding around the contour of its banks. The land gouged by strip mining lay above them another quarter-mile or so, hidden from their view by tall pines and deciduous trees. Since the layoffs, Saturday was no longer a workday in Number 9, so there was no coal smoke, no thundering trucks. In their place, he heard the chatter of an irritable squirrel, and somewhere perhaps, he imagined, a buck nosed his quiet way around green ground cover untouched by frozen earth.

"We have a good life, don't we Alex?" he said with pride. "We have had a wonderful family life."

Wary, Alex stared straight ahead.

His sad eyes on the river below, Sayles went on. "I love you more than I have ever loved any human being in my life. Before you, I was . . ." Unused to forming sentences of such true emotion, he stammered. "I was . . . all alone. I had made my life into something . . . into public service, and that was good, very good. But I met your mother and, well, you know what I'm trying to say."

"I guess so." Alex wiped his hands on his pants legs nervously. Such demonstrated emotion from his father was too unsettling for his stomach to tolerate, and it was tightening unpleasantly.

Sayles bent down to fuss with the little rhododendron, rubbing one of the verdant leaves between his fingertips. "I'm not one of those people who believes that it's necessary to tell the absolute truth all the time, Alex. I think that's some kind of emotional incontinence that's peculiar to Americans. There have been times in my life, in my career, that the greater good was served by withholding the absolute truth. Not lying, mind you, but not disclosing every detail. That's the way it's done in the diplomatic world. That's the way it's done in the real world, and it works.

He brought the plant leaf to his nose and held it there, thinking he could detect the fragrance of the dormant flower. "But circumstances change. You have to rethink old ideas. Sometimes you're better off facing down the truth." He turned and faced Alex. "This is one of those times, Alex." He paused. "I've lied to you. Your mother and I have been lying to you."

Alex jumped to his feet. "Maybe we should go see Mom," he protested. "Maybe we should go home and talk about this."

"I lied to you. I lied to you about the most important thing in your life, and now I'm going to tell you the truth."

Alex sat back down heavily. The irate squirrel ceased complaining, the sound of the wind disappeared on the air. Silence. Stunned, absolute silence coupled with real fear for the first time in his life.

"I want to begin, Alex, by telling you that I love you more than my ability to describe." Sayles took Alex's chin in his hand and turned up his face. "When you remember this day, and you always will, I want you to remember most of all that you are the most loved boy that ever was. Everything was done because we love you."

"You're scaring me, Dad."

"Don't be afraid, son. The truth hurts, but it can't destroy—that's one of the most important things you can ever know. I'm going to tell you this and you're going to be able to handle it. I guarantee you will handle it, Alex."

"It's this—I'm the father who loved and raised you, but I am not your biological father."

"What do you mean, you're not my biological father?"

"I mean precisely that—that even though I am your true father because I raised you from the day you were born, I am not the man who made you with your mother."

"That's—not—true!"

"Yes, it is. Your mother was married to another man before she married me and that man is your father."

Alex felt as if he were swimming. His arms and legs were

thick, heavy, impossible to move. And his head! It seemed to be filling with water and ready to explode. He sat for so long in terrified silence that finally Sayles prodded him.

"Did you hear me, Alex?"

"Yes."

"You understand what I've said to you?"

"Yes."

"You want to just sit with it for a minute?"

"Yes."

He stayed quiet for a long moment, then asked softly, "Who is my . . . biological father?"

"Your biological father lives far from here, in another country. He doesn't know you exist. Mom never told him."

"Why didn't they stay married?"

"They wanted to stay married, but they weren't allowed to for reasons that are complicated and will take a long time to explain. There were people around them who didn't want them to be married and they attacked your father, and your mother too, and in the end your mother had to leave him and come back to the United States. That was eleven years ago."

"Were you married to Mom when I was born?"

"Yes, I married her almost as soon as she came back to this country. She divorced her first husband and married me right away. So that you would have someone to take care of you. I knew her before she married and I loved her very much, but she loved your biological father more."

"You could have told me from the beginning. You didn't have to trick me all these years!"

"I did what I thought was best. I guess maybe I was wrong. But from the day you were born I . . . I guess I pretended you really were mine. And after a while I began to believe that you were. If I had told you the truth, then I would have had to face the truth myself and I didn't want to do that."

"Why did you tell me now?" Alex demanded, angry now.

"When we get home I'll show you some papers I had sent down from Washington about him. Maybe you've even heard his name before. He's a very unhappy man at the moment. A desperate man because somebody didn't tell him the truth. Because somebody deceived him and now it's taken away everything he's ever believed in. That's why I decided to tell you the truth now, Alex. Because I realized that what has happened to him could happen to you. He had been lied to all his life about his father by the people who said they loved him the most and now someone has used the truth against him and he's in trouble. I never want that to happen to you. I've thought hard about this and I've decided that as much as it hurts us—Alex, I couldn't let it happen to you."

At that, Alex began to weep, angry tears at first that after a while softened into hurt and confusion.

They spent nearly an hour at the clearing, Alex's emotions looping wildly between rage and despair. Once in a while hope flared that he had misunderstood what had been said and he would shake his head back and forth violently to get rid of the words. But in the end he gave in to his own exhaustion and Sayles's calm, unrelenting recounting of Tarik and his strange, remarkable history.

Finally came the moment when he accepted. He took a deep breath and squared his shoulders as if he heard some inner trumpet. He wiped his hands over his face, narrowed his eyes for an instant, and shouldered the burden. The awesome gulf that had grown so suddenly between him and the world just as suddenly receded. He turned his eyes on Sayles and the look he gave him was all Sayles needed to know of happiness. Then, in an act of infinite tenderness and compassion, he fit his boy's hand into that of his father and squeezed. Together they resumed the walk up the holler to the ridge house.

Wordlessly they approached the half-built house on the ridge that was intended to embody their family life, an irony too exquisite for either of them to give voice to.

The cellar had been dug the previous October, but weather and the difficulty of the terrain had made progress slow. The concrete block foundation was in place. Floor joists supported lumber girders and Alex balanced himself on one of them.

In some strange way he felt relieved, high almost, and liberated. His father—could he still call him Dad?—had been right. Uncrushed by the truth, the truth had made him stronger. He would not realize it for a very long time, but he had come to some arrangement with the world. Watching him walking the narrow boards with considerable élan, Sayles believed him the most composed creature he had ever seen. *I have done the right thing. Really, I've done the right thing.*

"You did what?"

"I told Alex the truth. I told him that Tarik is his biological father."

Clare glared at him from their bed, too stunned to do anything but work her jaw in rage. "You didn't think you might have discussed it with me first? You just hauled off and told him?"

Sayles went on unbuttoning his flannel shirt. "I thought about it for a long time, Clare. It didn't just come blurting out. I decided that there was a distinct possibility that he could be more grievously injured by not knowing the truth than by hearing it from me."

"Why couldn't you at least have told me first? We could have told him together. I had the right to have some say in this."

"You would have tried to stop me."

She sat up in the bed, angrily rearranging the blankets. "If I'd known any of this, I could have come home from work. You picked a day when you knew I'd be over at Black Hat till after nine. You could have had him wait up for me, or telephoned."

"He was exhausted. We talked all day and he couldn't keep his eyes open." Wearily, he pulled off the shirt and draped it neatly over a straightback chair; then he went to work on his trousers.

"You can talk to him in the morning. I didn't want to have a long-drawn-out discussion over this," he countered in a weary voice. "I knew what I had to do."

She was having trouble controlling her temper. In eleven years they had never had anything even remotely resembling an argument. Hadn't even ever raised their voices. Had never, in fact, either one of them, said to each other what was honestly in their hearts. Now here he was suddenly dismantling the very foundation of their arrangement, and she was rocked.

"You had no right to tell him," she muttered again.

His somber gaze went past her. In his eyes was the look of a man who knew everything there was to know and for whom there were now no surprises.

Seeing this, Clare shivered and dug deeper down under the covers of the bed.

His eyes came back to her, full of newfound self-awareness. The timbre of his voice was livelier. "I liked it."

"What?"

"I enjoyed telling the absolute truth. I enjoyed the unburdening of it."

"Well, that's wonderful for you, Lawrence. But what about Alex? What about me?"

"Alex will deal with it. He's already begun. He'll be angry for a time. Who wouldn't be? But he'll get over it, and when he does he'll appreciate that I stood up for him. You'll deal with it too. You'll see, we'll all be the better for it."

"What did you tell him about Tarik?"

"I put him on the phone with Francis Riston."

"You talk to Francis Riston?"

"Once a month or so, sometimes twice. He just likes to keep me filled in."

"Filled in about what?"

"Goings-on at State, gossip."

"How come you never told me?"

"It wasn't a secret. I speak to a lot of people on the telephone."

"But—Francis?" She was shocked by what she saw as subterfuge. "And Tarik just came up."

"That's right."

"Has he ever come up before?"

"Once or twice."

Sayles sank into a chair and pulled his pants off over his shoes, a habit of undressing that Clare normally thought was amusing but that now seemed the height of stupidity.

"Why not let Francis fill him in?" he said to her. "He knows more than I do. He can give him all the details. Alex can meet him in Washington and talk to him in person if he wants to. He can handle anything that comes his way. He's a fabulous boy."

His voice was cool but she could discern the emotion ripping through the words. After all these years he had breached the wall of reserve that had allowed them to live emotionally separated for more than a decade. The separation gave notice of the danger in the uncharted territory that lay on the other side.

She tried to keep a neutral tone in her voice and asked him, "Why now, Lawrence? What did Francis say to you about Tarik that made you tell Alex?"

"He told me that Arthur Olson had done a very bad thing. Or a good thing, depending on your point of view. He told Tarik that Malik wasn't his father."

"Not his father?"

"He telephoned a week or so ago."

"He thought you'd be that interested?"

"Well, it's pretty damn interesting, don't you think?"

"Did he tell you who Tarik's real father is?"

"He said it was that British army colonel, White-Lyons."

This time she couldn't keep the interest out of her voice. Her mouth flew open. "What?"

"That old army colonel. Walter White-Lyons."

She was too stunned to speak. She wanted more details, but he had walked over to the clothes closet. She could hear him carefully hanging up his clothes, setting his shoes under their bed. The house was cold at night and he was wearing long underwear and, incongruously, an ancient Sulka silk dressing gown that had belonged to his father. The bedsprings hardly moved as he lay his skinny body down on the mattress.

"Were you in the habit of discussing Tarik with Francis Riston?"

"I wouldn't exactly call it habit." He folded the top of the sheet neatly over the blanket hem and plumped his pillow. "It just came up in conversation."

"What else came up in conversation?"

"I don't know, bits and pieces. Get some sleep, Clare. Alex'll probably have a million questions for you in the morning. Or perhaps he won't have any. That's the beauty of the boy."

He turned off the light and they were instantly enveloped in darkness and night sounds.

He knows. Oh, God, he knows. Clare buried her face in the blankets. *Riston has been telephoning him with every move Tarik's made for all these years. He knows I went to bed with him last year. He knows.*

She froze in the bed, terrified. *Surely he must hear the thudding of my heart. Surely any second he will rise up and accuse me.* But there was no sound other than his breathing. She bent her body nearly double and gathered the blankets around her face.

For a timeless moment she waited for her life to end. She willed her heart to stop so she could die and never have to face him. She braced herself for the coming storm.

But there was nothing. No hunting eyes, no enraged bewilderment, no reproaches. Nothing but the chill air collecting around her hands.

As soon as she realized there would be no angry outburst, she was swamped by her own guilt. He was the best man she had ever known. She loved him, and she had betrayed him. She shifted around in the bed, fighting a compulsion to confess. She decided that was what he was waiting for. She would confess and he would forgive her, but he would never forget. He would stand silent before her and she would debase herself with apologies. This was more in keeping with his nature. He would wince but he would never raise his voice. He would understand, and that would kill her all the more.

She twisted the sheets in her hands. She would tell him how

sorry she was—no, he would see through her transparency. The extent of her ruin became clear to her. *He is lying there waiting for me to tell him the truth.*

But Lawrence Sayles was thinking no such thing. With every ounce of his strength, he was trying to recall what his first wife, Connie, had looked like—he'd been trying all day. He was shocked that he could not for the life of him recall her face. They had been married all those years. They'd sat down together at all those Little Dinners. He'd watched her swim all those laps in the Middleburg pool as she chipped away at nonexistent body fat. All that beeswax furniture polish.

It came as a profound shock to him that he could not remember the face of a woman who had had the patience to stand immobile for hours while some couturier dressmaker pinned fabric on her emaciated body.

How had she done it? He slipped his arm out from under the covers and held it straight up from his shoulder for as long as he could stand it. After a few minutes he gave up, and his arm fell back on the bed. Then he began chuckling softly. All that torture, for a Little Dinner dress.

The following Friday, the workmen at the ridge house finally augured a water supply that was unpolluted. The last chimney had been set, the pine framing had begun going up on the east side of the house, and the power company set the first pole that would eventually carry electricity all the way up to the ridge and light the house. The contractor had declared that if the weather held and the spring was not too wet, the exterior would be finished by late May.

Sayles loved this time of day, after the workmen had left but with enough light still in the day to examine their progress alone, without distraction. He paced the distance between the foyer and the living room, and as he did, his heart gave another of those disquieting little flips. He decided he was probably tired and settled himself down for a rest on the rough sill where the huge picture window that would form almost the entire western side of the house would go. Below him the Tug River ribboned the gap between the town and the forest to the south. From where he sat he could see nothing but untouched nature. The gouged-out hillsides, the gasping smoke, the coal washer, the coal cars, the train tracks through the craft of the architect were hidden from his view. What he saw was the natural evidence of the peace that life might bring—the smooth water, the flowering trees that when the sun drew closer would resume their buds, the pines that sheltered the valley.

Working with the interior designer, Sayles had begun to choose the materials that would go inside. He could see it picture-perfect in his mind's eye. This was to be a house like no other he had ever owned. There would be no Federal or Empire furniture. No Louis XVI chairs or Queen Anne tables. This was a house carved out of a Kentucky ridge; its interior would be as culturally compatible with its surroundings as its exterior was with the environment.

Etta Wales Wilson had given him a sample square of the quilt she was making for one of the pine log beds that would go into the ridge house bedrooms. He had commissioned her and her friends to make as many quilts as their quick fingers could manage. The square was a bright splash of red. Over its scarlet lawn, yellow and black daisies danced in a flowery necklace. She would stitch a hundred more squares to the quilt before she was finished.

He had instructed the designer to locate authentic Appalachian antiques and newly made chairs and tables from the hill people who supported themselves making furniture for sale in northern galleries. He had never lived in a home not organized around the effete tastes and affectations of some lofty devotee of style, and he was enjoying himself.

He didn't precisely care to have a house where men would put their feet up on the furniture, but he had the idea of creating a showplace for regional crafts and at the same time aid in the economic support of the locals. Public service, the higher ideal; it had ever been thus for Lawrence Sayles.

Never in his life had he owned anything so vulgar as fire-engine red. He peered deeply at the square, believing suddenly that he could draw up through the gay cotton fabric some of the spirit of the woman who had made it and of the hills that inspired its design. The strength of the mountain people, on familiar terms with despair and somehow full of undiminished faith in their own grit, was there in his hands.

A revolutionary idea occurred to him, a notion that would have eluded his father: Perhaps they were not all that different from one another, the Boston Brahmin and these craggy hill people. Hard workers all—satisfaction without sensuality or sensationalism.

The notion made him chuckle. Well, maybe he had stretched the parallel too far, but it still appealed to him and he decided he would reflect more completely on it over time. That he and his class had the power to literally crush these people was an irony too vulgar to speak.

After another hour or so of contemplative sitting, he watched as the sun began dissolving behind the pencil-line horizon. Crickets sent up a storm of noise. He should head back down the holler. In a matter of moments it would be dark. He reached for the Coleman lamp, hesitated—just another moment for the sun to sink. He had never seen such bloody beauty. The starch was out of his body for once and he stretched his arms pleasantly, appreciating the suppleness of flesh and spirit he still possessed. He had Clare to thank for this release. Whatever she felt about Tarik, she had not disappointed him. He had Clare to thank for . . . *for everything*. That realization curved his thin lips into an appreciative smile.

The smile was still on his lips when the search party that had struggled up the holler in total darkness found him hours later, still poised on the rough sill. The men caught the smile in the light of the lamps on their miner's tin hats.

Silently, Tutie Blankenship tucked a bunch of wild greens into his lifeless hand. Wordlessly, Tommy Johnson pulled him off the sill. The body had settled somewhat into its mortal rigor, and they had had to twist and turn him to get him onto the litter that would carry him down the holler and home.

Most of the miners had had a hand in moving bodies before, up from under roof falls to the mine mouth and into the arms of their families. But this body required a more considerate touch. They manipulated the rigid arms and legs with infinite tenderness. Homage must be paid. A prince of the republic, after all, deserves all due respect.

27

Tarik walked quickly through the overhanging garden, around the knot of old Sur men, who stirred expectantly as he went by and fell to disappointed murmuring when he continued without speaking. From the outer perimeter of the garden he could look over the distant frankincense trees and almost make out the bog. He stared out at the view for long minutes, then turned and went back the way he came.

He returned the salute of the security detail and mounted the narrow stone steps into the faded pink fortress that had been Malik's stronghold. The twilight air was full of mist and the heavy scent of coffee beans. In another hour the mist would fill the valleys and everyone would quit their business for the day, stoke their peat fires, and settle down around iron stoves to consume their dinners. And to shake their heads over the sad, sorry state of the one they loved the best.

At the top of the stairs he turned left and walked the long veranda that wrapped around every part of the fortress except that section which anchored the whole to the mountainside. Laurel trees draped enormous skirts of green leaves from the baskets that hung all along the veranda. The air, as always, swirled with the odors of peat smoke, coffee, and herbs. The aromatic brew had once consoled him. But on this evening the air felt too rich, too full of life, too much a painful remnant of what had been lost.

A guard popped a salute as he passed through a cypress-wood door into a series of small reception rooms. He walked through one room, then another. The rooms were trimmed with Lebanon cypress carved into whorls and twists but were virtually bare of furniture. The spareness of the rooms was deliberate, the traditional Sur antidote to the opulence of the lowlanders and their kings and clan chiefs.

After he had gone down another long hallway, he paused before a closed door, hesitated, then went in.

The room was nearly dark and stank from the remains of peat fires left too long in an uncleaned fireplace. Soundlessly he crossed the room, pulled apart the heavy curtains, and opened the windows to let in the air. With the last light of the day he could see clearly the objects all around him.

This had been Malik's bedroom.

Tarik hadn't come here for years, since well before Elliott Tomlinson sent him the tape-recorded conversation between Olson and White-Lyons in the potting shed. Tarik had never slept here, in fact, out of respect, and out of affection had long ago decided that the room should be preserved exactly as it had been when Malik last did.

He crossed the worn carpet to a damask-silk-covered chair so worn it looked as if it had been shredded by cats. He pushed the chair against the window so that in the fading light he might see every aspect of the room.

The bedroom was spartan—a bureau, a large bed covered with damask identical to the chair covering, a simple wooden desk. The old kerosene lamps, their chimneys still blackened by smoke, were scattered around on tabletops. Although Malik's fortress had electricity now, Tarik's insistence on the preservation of this room intact had extended even to its illumination, or lack of it. The Sur despised ornamentation. In their dress and furnishings the object was complete simplicity. The cultural ethic conveyed was that a man should present what he is, straight, without disguise, and that only a deceiver would choose to conceal his true nature with decoration.

The irony of this principle as it now applied to himself seemed particularly cruel and ironic to Tarik. For was there a more deceived and thus deceiving man, in the very essence of his form, than himself? It was difficult to keep despair at bay. If he examined these things with too much clarity, he would be tempted to close his eyes and never wake up.

He sat in Malik's bedroom for a very long time. Outside, the night sounds collected into a soft din of crickets, rustling trees, men calling out to each other on garden paths. There had been nights, sitting in this room years earlier, when he believed he could discern the soft thud of coffee berries as they fell, overripened, from their trees. Beyond the door he could hear the pleasant scrape of the censer chains as the servants went around purifying rooms. He heard them pause outside the door and then go on, leaving him in the mud, at rock bottom. At least he could locate himself in geography.

Still, the thing about the mud was that he didn't love it enough to want to linger. He wasn't one of those in love with disgrace. Malik had been the foundation of his life and calling. The legitimacy of all his claims in the kingdom rested on that single fact; without that authenticity he was irrevocably damaged.

But not destroyed. Nearly twelve years—and how many billions of barrels of oil?—had changed the people's perception of what constitutes legitimacy and what doesn't. He could live with that. Hadi had tried to paint him as the tool of the Americans, the perpetrator of a great hoax that stretched back for decades. Some had swallowed this, some had not. Tarik had pointed out that it was he who had joined the oil embargo and kicked out OmniTech and who in every way had demonstrated loyalty only to his own kind.

Some of the people had believed, some had not. Even as he sat in Malik's old room, elements of the armed forces and popular support wavered between loyalty to the reality of the last eleven years, and outrage at the dark forces of conspiracy Hadi declared were arrayed against them. Hadi had announced that his personal mission, his last great crusade before tuberculosis claimed him, was to save the nation from the evil ones. He had assembled an army at the edge of the bog and declared that Tarik had to go back where he'd come from all those years ago or have his head stuck on a tent pole out in the plain. Knowing Hadi as they did, everyone understood which he would prefer. He had made a convincing argument. He pronounced himself ready to fight to the death. He said that no power in heaven or on earth would keep him from his mission. Publicly he asked God to stand behind him on the battlefield, but privately he sent word that he was willing to make a deal.

Malik's room was nearly dark. Without light, the bed, bureau, and desk lost their definition. In a very clear way, this was how Tarik saw his connection to Malik: once illuminated as a beacon to take him through the adventure, now virtually extinguished. To get out of the room he would have to feel his way in the darkness. This struck him as a suitable metaphor for the rest of his life.

His mother, Nila, had loved White-Lyons. How could this have been? Of all the demons that Tarik had wrestled with in the past ten days, this one proved the most ferocious. He believed White-Lyons to be a bad person. Not just manipulative, but bad. Yet the ones that he loved best—Nila and Karim—had loved White-

Lyons. Could he have missed some essential quality in the man that they had recognized? What had they perceived that he hadn't? Some people are experts at concealing the malevolent parts of their natures. They teach Sunday school to kiddies in the morning and then go home and beat their wives.

Tarik had just made up his mind that White-Lyons was exactly this kind of deceiver, when his conscience wheeled him to the truth: He hated White-Lyons because he had driven Clare away. It made Tarik physically ill to admit that White-Lyons was his father. He had been robbed of the great romantic Malik—soul-crushing enough!—but to be handed in his stead the desiccated martinet, the despoiler of all his happiness? He was furious, although he chose with difficulty not to examine that anger too much. He needed to preserve the memory of Nila to stay intact. He couldn't tamper with Nila and still feel fit to go on.

It made him sick to acknowledge White-Lyons. It made him sick to appreciate that White-Lyons had done everything for his success. In ancient musty bedrooms, he resisted creepy revelations. If Clare had not been forced to leave and Hadi had moved against him, in all likelihood he would have destroyed Hadi and been able to keep Clare. Ah, but then there would have been no Karim. It was easier not to attempt sleep. Every time he closed his eyes, his mind swam with recriminations.

After a while he stood up and in total darkness began to feel his way out of the room. Picking through his conscience was a luxury he couldn't afford, not with Hadi at the bog and threatening civil war.

He felt around for the door handle. Nal would be hunting for him, ready to take his answer back to Hadi. He looked down the long hallway and when he didn't see Nal, he signaled for an escort of bodyguard, rewalked the corridors, and returned to the garden anyway. Hadi could wait. Hadi had a warped sense of time. Hadi also had no imagination. His deal had a grim quality of déjà vu: Hadi's dreams of dynasty hadn't cooled. He would leave the kingdom in peace if Tarik would designate one of Mira's sons, a creature by the name of Balan, as his heir.

Tarik tried hard to remember which of Mira's bald boys this was, but all he could see in his mind was Iv's bad complexion.

The garden was cool. On another evening he would have felt his muscles unwinding. But relaxation, like soul-searching, was yet another luxury he couldn't indulge. He intended to stall Hadi; he needed time to think. In the past, he would have turned to Arthur Olson. But now, well . . . he didn't care to finish the thought.

One thing he would have to decide, however—what was he going to do about White-Lyons? He couldn't go on in this torment. No one had seen the old man for days; Tarik rather hoped he'd gone off like Judas and hanged himself.

After she had calmed down, Clare had the idea that she might bury Lawrence up on the ridge. But she surrendered the notion even before the deluge of phone calls from Washington and Boston. Lawrence Sayles, no matter how content he might have grown on the banks of the Tug River, would never molder at ease where grime-faced men slogged through red dog on their way to broken-back labor. He would go, of course, to the family plot in Mt. Auburn Cemetery in Cambridge, Massachusetts.

The funeral cortege was small. The ceremony would be private. That was the way it was done. No noisy public show, just the closest of relations and closest of friends. Months from now there would be a memorial service at the National Cathedral in Washington, where the highest elected officials in the land, the top rung of the diplomatic corps, and the patrician New England brethren who, like Sayles, had also dedicated their lives to the higher culture and the public good, would gather to render honor to the best of their own class.

But here at the graveside it was all very quiet and understated. The pastor of Trinity Church would say some words over the casket. The White House had sent a heartfelt handwritten message. Telegrams and tributes poured in from around the globe to all the residences and offices. The *New York Times* carried the obituary on the front page—above the fold, the highest tribute. The *Boston Globe* set two full columns in a black box under a banner headline.

Because on that day there were no wars, no mass murders, no plane crashes, the death of Lawrence Sayles became the lead story on the evening news of all three television networks. Those who knew him personally paused to recall his human qualities. Those who did not learned again from the media the facts of his magnificent accomplishments.

But for Clare and Alex and the ones who loved him best the loss was much more personal than the passing of a national monument entombed in his accomplishments decades before.

They stood at the edge of the grave in the freezing March air. No bouquets covered the casket; the brass of its handles was dulled, as if they had never been polished. Nothing beyond burnished wood signaled that within lay the remains of one of the country's wealthiest men.

No flowers or buds had survived the winter or gave notice of coming spring. The ground was rock-hard from the cold and inlaid with an icy cover variegated as lace. Ironically, only palpable human grief brought the scene to life.

Surrounding the Sayles family plot were the graves of others of his class. Their headstones were ornately whorled and gigged, like most of the tombstones in the garden cemetery, granite pretending to be fluid as water. But in life and death the Sayles family stood apart. Lawrence Sayles would be buried, like his mother and father and ancestors all the way up the family tree, under a plain granite headstone.

There was no eulogy. The minister read from St. Paul and kept his eyes from Clare's face, which was pinched with the effort of staving off tears.

Once or twice Clare turned to look at Alex, his reddened eyes nearly puffed shut from a long night of tears. If only she could cry. She had maintained this frozen composure from the time they brought him down off the ridge to the house, to the flight on the Gulfstream to Boston, to Mt. Auburn. She wasn't sure anymore that she actually could cry.

The minister snapped shut his prayer book and offered an improvised blessing that was pious and rather inspiring. The mourners stood mutely in a circle around the grave, rocking back and forth to ward off the cold. Clare's eyes took in their faces— Sayles's surviving sister, whom she had met only a dozen times; several cousins and two nephews, all of them older than she; famous faces from government service; Henry, Marguerite, Sophie, and Preston; Sylvia.

And bobbing around behind them, fidgeting madly with something she couldn't see, was Homer. He was itchy, ill at ease, monkeying with the buttons on his coat, waging some sort of moral arm-wrestle in his brain. Curious, Clare watched him speculatively, saw him squeeze his eyes shut tight, pinch his nose with his left hand, and then in a gesture as quick as it was deliberate, up swooped his right hand to pop onto his head a hat, an elegant dark brown hat. The bespoke hat Sayles had given him on his last birthday.

Homer steadied the fedora, his fingers attracted against their will by the soft felt. He ran one tentative finger around the brim to make sure it was smooth and straight, and then squared his shoulders. The act was more than the simple victory of courtesy over relentless orthodoxy. The hat planted on his head, he surrendered to a sudden, unnatural calm, as if in finally accepting the gift he also accepted its giver. Clare watched him working it out in his mind, his features softening into composure, then into sadness. Regret was all over his face.

When he realized Clare was staring at him, he rolled his eyes just enough to let her comprehend the gesture and the respect for Sayles contained within it.

When the service was over and the others had begun departing with muted condolences and farewells, she was unable to move away.

"Mom, I guess we have to go." The coffin was on a portable catafalque with black bunting around its base. Alex stared at the bunting, imagining the grave it concealed. "Mom, we have to go."

Four workmen, gravediggers, lingered at a respectful distance. When the family and mourners departed, they would move in to lower the casket and push the earth over it. Clare saw that they had parked a small backhoe off behind a cluster of Douglas firs.

"I want to stay a minute, Alex. I don't want them to put Daddy in the ground with none of us here to watch over him. You get in the car with Grandpa."

"I can stay with you." He said this in a voice full of uncertainty. He did not want to be there when they lowered the casket into the frozen earth. He did not want to watch them bury the one he loved best in the world. His dad would be dead for sure then, irrevocably dead, and he could not bear that. So he barely protested when Clare insisted he walk to the waiting limousine.

Uncertain as to what to do with the widow still on the scene, the workmen conferred among themselves, decided to smoke more cigarettes, and stamped their feet to keep from freezing.

Clare felt some obligation to let them do their job, but she could not make her own feet go. She didn't want to abandon him in the cold. And she did not want to leave him alone in this unfamiliar place. She couldn't imagine walking away without him. They had done everything together for so long.

Dry-throated, she watched heavy ridges of clouds form over the cemetery, clouds that looked as if they might come rolling right down to the ground, swallow her up, carry her away. What a relief that would be. Her chest felt spongy from grief, and guilt.

She could not get the memory of that night out of her head— lying beside him in bed in a state of agonized suspense while he laughed softly. What did it mean? Was he laughing at her, at their situation, at himself?

She tried to blank her mind, but memories marched past her like ghosts, occupying her brain one by one. Mostly it was trace sensations—the smoothness of the satin of the lime-green dress, the smudgy aftertaste of good red wine in the dining room of The Heights, her panic after Alex was born. Lovemaking in the Chippendale bed in their bedroom. Her eyes wandered over to the marker on Connie's grave, just as plain as Sayles's would soon be. No garish angels, no serifed lettering. The aloof reserve that marked their class in life certified them in death. Connie's headstone had the unbroken, elegant lines of one of her Mainbocher evening gowns.

Realizing this distracted Clare from her misery, and once it was gone she found it impossible to resume. She had loved him, what could she reproach herself with? She had loved him, and if she lived their life together on her terms, well, he must have intended this or he would have married one of his own. She didn't have the nature to bow to his cultural ethic, and while she couldn't claim that he reveled in her difference, he seemed content. What was she saying? He *was* content. He did revel. He loved her. He loved Alex. They were a family. She had nothing to reproach herself with. Nothing.

The bright glare of sunlight streaming through the trees caught her by surprise, and she interpreted its sudden arrival as a signal that she was thinking along the right lines. He was a magnificent man. He was amusing and had an attractive vitality that was impossible to resist. She was lucky to have known him. She was honored to have been his wife.

She would feel better once she cried. That's what was missing, the sure relief of tears. All this upper-class ritual had made her forget who she was. She might take comfort in a little drink of whiskey. That was it—she would go back to her sister-in-law's with Homer and they would sit down in front of the fire and drink whiskey and she'd fall asleep in a chair. Alex too. They'd toast Sayles and maybe they'd toast Hillard.

She glanced over at the gravediggers. She could see their warm breath combine with plumes of cigarette smoke in the frigid air, wreathing their faces in translucent white billows. They quit talking when they saw her glancing their way and sent back expectant looks. They were cold. The sun hadn't warmed a thing. Best to let them get on with it. She couldn't stay here forever.

Behind her, the long black limousine purred, its windows frosty, the exhaust pouring out of it collected in a huge balloon of white vapor. She would have to get into the car. She could not postpone the moment any longer.

Reluctantly, she turned back for a final time to stare at the coffin. Stepping forward, she ran her fingers over its glowing wood. Hillard's coffin had been draped with an American flag. It occurred to her that at the very least, Lawrence Sayles's coffin should have been covered with the flag. She walked around the thing, fingering the brass handles, turning everything into a photograph for her memory. The activity seemed to warm her—no, this was more than blood-circulating exercise. She stopped and placed both hands upon the coffin. Definitely the wood warmed her, she was sure of it.

If she laid her cheek upon it, her whole body would grow warm—and so she did. And she did grow warm. Warmed so much that finally her body could release the tears that had been frozen in her heart for days. She wept soundlessly, no deep dramatic sobs. She would not disgrace him with demonstrated emotion. The tears slipped down the burnished wood and went to ice on the frozen ground.

After a few minutes she straightened, wiped her gloved hand over the wetted wood, and said good-bye.

She was about to turn and look directly at the gravediggers to convey to them a subtle signal that they could commence their gloomy work, when a blurry outline took her attention away. A form taking shape at the edge of the ragged square the workmen had formed by the trees. The figure of a man walking slowly toward her.

From that distance he could have been anyone. A king, a pauper, the specter of Death itself. Uncertain, she began stepping backward slowly in the direction of the limousine. But in his deliberate march, the unsound set of his body, the dreadful figure compelled her to stay. Had he been there all along? Hadn't she noticed him earlier, when the minister was quoting St. Paul? A shadow only dimly outlined on a gray day against the viridian trees?

Of course—some mourner unknown to her and only now finding the courage to approach. But as soon as she decided this, she knew instantly she was wrong, because there was something so defeated in the slope of his shoulders, something utterly punished in his gait that it couldn't have been an ordinary man.

She could see him more clearly. His overcoat was new, ill-fitting, and unsuited to his body; it hung on his frame like a hair shirt. The hat was also new and just as uncomfortably pulled down over his forehead, obscuring his face. He looked like a man who'd never known the cold, who'd shopped on a tear for warm winter clothing. Everything he wore seemed to belong to somebody else. He was nearly to the edge of the grave.

"Mom, let's go!"

She turned toward the limousine. Alex had opened the window a crack. "Coming, Alex." In the time it took to turn back, he was before her. As soon as she stared into those pale blue eyes that did not blink, she knew, of course, who he was and her heart froze.

Walter White-Lyons pulled the too-big hat from his head and turned it over uncertainly in his hands.

Eyes swimming with history, they stared at each other for an eternity over Lawrence Sayles's casket.

"It's bad timing," he offered finally.

She was too stunned to speak.

"I waited over there." He pointed to the stand of trees. He was nervous, shifting from one leg to the other. "I saw you were upset. I wasn't even sure I would come over, but you started for the car and I wouldn't know where to find you if you drove away."

He shivered and gave her a bland smile. "I'm not used to the cold," he said. "It's been so many years since I've experienced winter."

He was looking over his shoulder at the limousine. "Your family?" he asked, indicating the car with his chin.

"Yes."

His eyes returned to her face.

"I have to go." She turned in the direction of the car.

"Please, not yet."

"I'm leaving."

"There are very bad things loose in the world."

She turned and gave him a withering look. *"Please."*

"Bad things," he repeated, shaking his head. Had he even heard her?

She took a step forward and snarled, "You're not wanted here."

She believed it was necessary to drive him away now, before he drew her into whatever misery he was plotting. She impugned the worst kinds of motives to him. It was of no help that he looked like a whipped dog.

"Please leave."

But he only turned and looked wistfully in the direction of Sayles's coffin. "He was a great man."

She wondered if he had been drinking. He seemed stoned, babbling to ghosts on the air.

"You were lucky to have married him. I guess you know that."

Her silence deepened.

"So many strange things happen over a lifetime, it's hard to fathom."

"White-Lyons, I'm cold. My husband is dead. I want to leave. I'm not interested in anything you have to say."

For the first time, his eyes met hers and she was shocked at the desperation there. Hunting eyes trying to see into her soul. "Ah, but how you hate me, more than anyone in your life," he whispered.

"You give yourself too much credit."

"I had hoped the wound would be balmed."

Her pain was transparent. Embarrassed, she turned away, grieved that it was still there for him to see. In a moment he would move in to pierce her further. But he remained staring at the coffin.

"My family is waiting."

"You have to come back with me."

Taken aback, she laughed softly. "What?"

"You have to come back with me."

"I—"

"You have to bring Alex and come back."

She studied him for a moment, then said, "You old bastard. You're hatching some poison and you need me to make it work. You did this to him, you're to blame, and now you're here to get me to put it together again. You're trading me for something. I'm bait. You did it before."

"I never made you bait, Clare."

"He loved me."

"He was naive."

"He trusted you and you sold him out."

She waited for the muzzle flash of his anger. He had always been a better marksman than she. But there was nothing. In the silence that followed her words, she saw that he was crushed, beaten, hardly the same man who had so blithely plotted against her all those years ago. The sag in his shoulders was such that she knew instantly that no amount of cruelty from her could match the castigation he'd already heaped on himself.

He stood silent before her. He appeared to be undefended, holding on to the hat as if it were his last friend in the world. In a tone so soft she had to bend to hear him, he said, "I am the devil. You are right."

Then, in a disembodied voice, he went on. "I wish you had

known Karim. He was such a strange, sweet little boy. Not like anyone at all. A dragonfly. Like a breeze. He made me feel"—he held his hand upright, as if he could find the word he sought on the frigid air—"not heavy. Karim. He's dead now, you know. All three of them, dead."

His head was bent by the weight of his sorrow. He drifted back and forth in time, and Clare had trouble following his thinking.

"You can't make me feel sorry for you," she told him. "You can't have my pity. You're the one who perpetuated this whole Malik thing in his mind. You are the most totally dishonest person I have ever known. You have given him all his hurt. His father."

"Ah, so you know, then. Who told you? Olson? Francis Riston? Never mind, doesn't matter. You can't understand what it was like back then. You can't know the brutality. The suffering of the people was so that my heart broke and the parts flew off in so many directions that I couldn't follow them all. I was in love with the idea, don't you see? Malik was such a good idea, such a bad man.

"I wanted to claim the boy. I wanted to say that he was mine. But Malik died and the myth was just *there* and it was too late for me to change it. I went along, don't you see? Circumstance intervened and I just went along because he surely would have died too. It was the only way to save the two of them, to get them out of the country to safety. What would anyone have cared for some old army man's son? Turkit was murdering all the babies. Don't you think he would have murdered this baby too? My baby? Everyone believed he was Malik's son and so they saved him. Once it was started, it couldn't be changed. And in the end, I guess, I made myself believe it, just like the people. I wanted to make it up to them. I blame myself. If I hadn't loved her so, perhaps I would have given Malik better advice."

"Are you saying that you did something deliberate to hurt Malik?"

"No, never! But I wasn't . . ." Again he sought answers on the air. "I wasn't enough . . . *aware*. I had never been in love, you see." His voice caught in his throat and he ducked his head.

She was shocked that he had moved her, the two of them shaking with cold. Shocked that he had made her feel something for him. "You're freezing, White-Lyons. Why don't you get into the car with me. We'll go back to the house and I'll give you some whiskey to drink. There's no point in going on like this out here."

His blue eyes were wide and unmasked and his lower lip trembled as if he might cry.

"How long has it been since you've eaten something?" she asked him. "You don't look well." In fact, he looked as if he might collapse at her feet any moment, his sorrow was that profound.

Bewildered, he shook his head back and forth.

"Let's get into the car, Colonel," she urged him. "You'll feel better when we get into the warm car."

She put her arm across his back and felt the bones jabbing through the fabric of his new overcoat. She tried to guide him to the limousine, and for a moment it seemed that he had put the weight of his life on her capable arm, drawing into the crook of her elbow as if it were a harbor and he a storm-tossed ship. But then he jerked away.

"There isn't time. I'm ashamed that I came here. I was on my way to Washington or Kentucky to find you, and then I saw in the newspaper that Mr. Sayles had died. I regret disturbing you here. But I can't stand on ceremony. If you had driven away, there's no telling where you'd go and how long it would take me to find you."

He was speaking forcefully now and seemed to have rediscovered some of the old military spine. The words came out in a torrent. "That old bastard Hadi is at the bog. He says he'll kill everyone. He says that Tarik has to go now that he's no longer Malik's son. He says he will tear the country apart—in fact, he's already started."

"I can't help you anymore. I gave Hadi what he wanted, and it wasn't enough."

"No." He measured his words. "There is one more thing you have."

She gave him a baffled look. "I have nothing that Hadi would want."

"You have something that Tarik would want and that would finish Hadi." His eyes went past her to the limousine.

She followed his eyes. "Alex? You're here for Alex?"

His color was high. The fight was back in him—just like that. The death pallor had disappeared and the vigor in his voice was astounding for such a feeble old man.

"Alex is Tarik's son." He said it in a voice of total certainty. She started to deny it but stopped herself. She needed to hear what was coming.

"Tarik has an heir and that will satisfy the people."

"Why are you so certain that Alex is his?"

"I *know* he's Tarik's son. I've seen his photograph. A long time ago Tarik asked me to find out everything about you. I have dozens of photographs of Alex."

"And you think he's Tarik's son from looking at photographs? He doesn't look anything like Tarik."

"Not Tarik. My brother William. He looks just like my brother William."

"William?"

"He was a little blond boy, like your Alex. He died a long time ago."

"You never showed the photographs to Tarik?"

"I showed him a few. They weren't very good and he couldn't make out the boy clearly. I told him the private detective was worried about getting too close, drawing attention. I didn't want him to see that blond hair. I didn't want to start him thinking. I couldn't win either way. I didn't want him wondering why Alex had such fair coloring if he was his own son, if he was Malik's grandson. But then, I didn't want to break his heart by showing him the photographs and letting him draw the conclusion that Alex really belonged to Lawrence Sayles. He wanted Alex to be his, especially after Karim died. We were all ruined when Karim died."

"And now you want me to tell him Alex is his."

"Alex *is* his. You lied, but you can tell the truth now. Tell me the truth about Alex."

"I have an obligation to Lawrence Sayles."

"Lawrence Sayles is dead."

"The obligation isn't."

"You have an obligation to Tarik."

"Why would they accept Alex when they're not certain if they'll keep Tarik?"

"Because in their heart of hearts they're longing to embrace him again. Because Hadi's grandson belongs to the old order, and they're not going to go back. They'll settle for Alex. They understand that the name of the father matters less than the character of the son."

She gave him a wan smile. "Are you talking about Alex—or Tarik?"

"Come back with me tonight."

"I can't."

"You can do anything you want to do. I took him away from you once, and now I'm giving him back."

She stammered, "I don't see how—"

"You don't love him?"

"I didn't say that. But, Lawrence—"

"You have to decide now, Clare." He wrapped his hands around hers. "I wish I could have come a year from now, after you'd buried your dead. But it's now or never. You know Hadi, and Hadi won't wait for a widow to form a resolution."

As if he had said it all, he took a step backward and jammed the hat back on his head. "Well, I've done my best. I'm leaving tonight. He's up in the Sur; I'll go back there. You can reach me through Nal, like always. If you're not there in a day or two, I'll know you're not coming."

He turned to go, then wheeled with one more insight. "You've lost a lot, Clare. But he's lost more. Stanley, Topaz, Karim. Now Malik. It's more than one man should bear."

He turned and began walking off in the direction of the trees while she struggled frantically to sort things out in her mind. If she had learned anything in the last week, it was not to anticipate the future.

She thought she would faint. She put her arms out to steady herself. "Wait!" she called after him.

He wasn't sure he'd heard her. He turned, the icy ground crunching under his feet. She noticed for the first time that he was wearing his old army boots under his trousers.

"Tell him that Alex is his son. Tell him that I lied. Alex is his."

He accepted this quietly. "If you don't come, I won't tell him about Alex," he told her. "No need to torture the man further."

She backed away to the limousine, opened the door, and was nearly inside when she heard him say her name.

"Didn't you ever wonder about that blond hair, Clare?" he called out to her through the bitter cold air. "Didn't Lawrence Sayles *ever* wonder?"

The big jet inched to a halt on the boiling-hot tarmac. A ground crew pushed tall steps out to the door while a steward inside wrestled open the latch. Clare watched from the window as three Land-Rovers pulled up and soldiers in battle helmets and camou-flage fatigues jumped out to deploy themselves at the bottom of the stairs.

When the plane door opened, a furnace blast of heat rushed in, carrying with it every one of the memories she had kept of the place.

They hadn't brought much with them. Alex had only a back-pack, and wore jeans, a T-shirt, and a blue blazer with a dull square over the breast pocket where his St. Albans school emblem had been. He'd picked at it on the long flight over and had finally gotten the thing off just before they landed.

Clare had changed into a cotton shirtwaist dress in the airplane lavatory, taking off woolen pants and jacket and stuffing them into a bag. When they gathered up their belongings from the airplane overheads, she left behind the bag of winter clothes.

They followed the other passengers to the door of the airplane, past stewards who smelled of Aqua Velva and spoke flawless English. Past the pilot, who fingered the metal wings pinned to his blue uniform jacket while he smiled good-bye.

At the door Alex paused. "Don't be nervous, Alex," she told him, thinking he needed reassurance. But when he looked at her, his eyes were flat-calm.

"I'm not nervous. I'm making my mind blank so that from here on in I can remember every single thing. You're more nervous than I am, Mom."

He had stopped at the top of the plane steps, holding up the other passengers, who glared as they pushed past. He stared out at the flat horizon to the east, making an arc with his eyes across the skyline of the capital city to the distant, purplish silhouette of the Sur mountains.

"That's where he is, right?" He pointed to the peaks in the distance.

Clare shielded her eyes with her hand. "Yes. About halfway up."

"They look close."

"No, they're farther away than they look. The light is tricky here."

"Doesn't look much like the Appalachians."

"Nope."

"Well, at least it's mountains."

Satisfied that for the moment he had seen all there was to see, Alex took Clare's arm and together they began walking down the plane steps. They were nearly halfway down when he stopped dead in his tracks.

Looming at the bottom of the steps, nearly blotting out the sun with his size, stood the giant Het. His Uzi was threaded between fingers the size of artillery shells. The curlicued hair that hung over his shoulders was still black as the mouth of a cave, but his long beard was speckled with gray. He wore a Colt semiautomatic pistol on each hip, and a fierce-looking bone-handled knife with a curved blade was jammed into a Sam Browne belt that encircled a waist almost as wide around as he was tall.

He was awesome. He bristled with armament. He looked like a man who broke tree trunks over his knee for firewood. Like a man who ate prep-school boys for breakfast.

Het put one booted foot on the plane steps. Alex backed up one step. Het advanced. Alex retreated, up the plane steps until he was nearly back to the door.

Het saluted Clare, then Alex, his eyes moving back and forth between the two of them. Then, as if Atlas had suddenly laid down his burden, he released the misery of eleven years of short gains and fatal losses and began to weep. Weep in proportion to his fantastical size, huge, loud racking sobs that boomed like cannon fire. He turned his face up to the heavens and tears poured out of him, coursed down his face, and wetted his khaki uniform shirt.

The scene continued that way for at least two minutes, Het pausing every once in a while to stare at Clare in disbelief that she was finally his again, then new cascades of tears that of course she was. Struck dumb by the bizarre scene, Alex stared incredulously.

Clare advanced one of her fingers tentatively to stroke one of Het's massive ones as if it were the breast of an injured hummingbird. Almost immediately he quieted down.

He shook his head from side to side vigorously to clear his mind, then pulled a handkerchief the size of a ship's sail from his back pocket and swabbed it around his face. He honked loudly into it, shook his head again as if he could not believe God had given him this second chance at happiness, then raised his chin at her to let her know that he was now all right.

Together they walked down the plane steps and over to the Land-Rovers. The soldiers stood around, staring at Het wide-eyed, not believing what they'd just witnessed, but Het was oblivious.

He settled Alex into the backseat of his vehicle, Clare beside him in the front; the soldiers piled into theirs. Once he had satisfied himself that all was in order, he signaled the lead vehicle to move out and eased the Land-Rover into gear. The other command car fell in behind them.

They had driven nearly a hundred miles when the sun became just a flat angle of orange light and the darkness began gathering at the horizon. The caravan turned off the roadway and drove over hardened gravel to a barren stretch of land that Clare recognized as somewhere near Ior.

Quickly, the soldiers raised a small sleeping tent for Clare and Alex, a cookfire was lit, and food, blankets, cots, and other supplies pulled from four large metal lockers. Two small camp chairs were set up close to the fire. Tired, Clare immediately slumped into one of them and patted the other for Alex to sit down. But he looked at her as if she were crazy to think that he'd sit with his *mother* while all around men checked their weapons and arranged themselves into sentry positions, did soldiers' work, threw down their gear, and set themselves up for the night.

When the campfire flared, Het shooed away the protesting soldier-cook and set about making the meal himself.

Clare extended her long legs, folded her arms behind her head, and almost against her will felt the old enslavement to the land and heat begin anew.

The sun was completely gone, the last of its rays reddening the ground. In a matter of minutes that blistering heat would go out of the day and dew would stain their clothes. The sky would blacken, then in another moment blaze with the silence of stars. They would lie on their backs and stare up at the overarching heaven, feeling impotent, without strength, and yet somehow full of hope. She felt her body relax. She felt as if she had come home.

Het was slicing lamb into big chunks, tossing the meat with oil, then throwing it into a sizzling frying pan. He minced garlic on a small rock with his curved knife and with a finger scraped the garlic from the blade onto the lamb and shook the frying pan violently. Satisfied, he turned to a small cotton sack and pulled out sprigs of fresh mint, scattered them over the seared meat and covered the whole thing with a pot lid. The aroma of the cooking meat drifted to her on the air. She closed her eyes sleepily.

Her arm dangled to the ground and idly she gathered up some of the dry earth. The stuff was grittier, more conventionally desertlike in this part of the kingdom, a wide swath of quartz gravel and fine sand. When the wind kicked up, the lashing sand could cut skin like a razor blade, the way it had enveloped her and Nal and Dr. Van Damm that day near Hirth and made her dizzy in the head.

She was not a complicated person. Easily drawn parallels were the ones that suited her best. Coming back here had an orderliness that made her feel at ease. She had not thought things through completely. She had not resolved in her mind what she would do with Aylesworth Coal. She was content, in the meantime, to let Toby take the mines union; that was what the men wanted—and as bitter a recognition as that was for her, she would give them what they wanted. Maybe Toby should run the mines; maybe she should take them public, or sell them outright. A.T. Massey had already expressed an interest.

There was time to decide about coal; no time at all left for Tarik. The sight of the soldiers reminded her that Hadi could not be all that far away. There had been no signs of fighting along the roadway, no smoking cars or ruined villages. Things seemed to continue with the same ancient grace as before. Perhaps White-Lyons had exaggerated to bring her here. The famous manipulator was not above intrigue, she believed, even in his ruined state.

Across the silence of her thoughts, a rustling sound. As if he read her mind, Het knelt beside her chair with a tin cup of hot Sur coffee in his hand. He held out the cup and with his soft eyes urged her to drink. He waited while she took several swallows, watching her all the time.

"So much to remember, Het," she said, looking down into his eyes. "Not all of it good."

His head nodded as if caught in a gentle breeze.

"The road to Duru is in which direction?"

He put up a remonstrating finger and wagged it near her lips.

"You don't want me to talk about it?"

Het made a chopping motion with his hands, an it's-finished, over gesture.

"I won't talk about it then."

"Good," he said in perfectly accented English.

She didn't protest when he took away her cup, refilled it with more steaming coffee, and pushed it back into her hand. Then he resumed his tender treatment of the dinner meal.

What resides in that strange, dark mind? Clare wondered as she watched him. The ease with which he dropped one form and assumed another? The warrior, the soft and considerate provider. What bizarre contradictions reside in that intimidating body? How much he was like Stanley Cobb.

Nothing in this place made any sense anyway. Not three hundred yards from where she sat was a green thicket of asla wood and tall grass, a verdant, juicy garden existing somehow in this arid stretch. Chaos companioned composure, heat the cold, sand the fertile ground, none of it predictable, all of it following some mad, disordered natural scheme.

Alex had engaged two soldiers in hand-sign conversation. He had convinced one of them to let him hold his M-16 rifle and was sighting along the barrel. The other men settled down as the light disappeared entirely from the sky. The soldiers had their mess and were huddling around the campfire, criticizing the

When dinner was finished they assumed guard positions at four points of the camp and doused their torches and lanterns.

The pungent lamb still staining their lips, Alex and Clare tipped back their heads to stare at the canopy of stars. Alex had sworn he was going to keep guard duty with the soldiers, but after a minute of star-gazing his head was bobbing on his chest and Clare had to shake him awake.

Het walked them to the tent, settled them down with blankets and pillows, and extinguished their lantern. Too exhausted to speak, they were asleep in an instant.

She dreamed she was on the plain. Ahead lay a hovel with a small boy playing outside. She stopped to ask him directions and followed the point of his finger for many miles until the ground became spongy under her feet and suddenly she was in the bog. She couldn't move her legs. She struggled, but the harder she worked the more fixed she became. All around her men were stuck, dead or half dead, with staring eyes. The men changed, became transformed into old men—Homer, Lawrence, White-Lyons—one blending into the other and back again. All of them sinking into the mud, calling out to her.

Tarik appeared at the edge of the bog. He motioned to her to stay where she was. She felt an immediate sense of relief, a rush of sensation—how much she loved him. How magnificent he was. He walked toward her, one step, then another, and he, too, began to sink.

Her heart thundering, she jerked awake. After a moment she sat up and helped herself to some water from the canteen Het had left tucked in her blankets. Her mouth was dry; the water revived her. She checked that Alex was sleeping soundly, lay down again, determined to fall asleep right away.

But the images of the dream lay on her brain, making her nerves surge. How much of her life had been determined by the whim of old men. Homer, Lawrence, White-Lyons—a trinity of old bones and prevailing ambitions and predatory motives. They had used and shaped her. She had wanted their wisdom, their worldliness, was willing to fight their battles or battle them. Her rewards had been as sweeping as her troubles.

Through a gap in the tent flap she could make out Het, prowling around in the darkness.

The tent had a slightly fetid smell, as if it had been packed away for a very long time in a damp room. She sat up and pushed the flap aside for some air. Het gave her a sign with his hand that she should lie down, sleep more, and continued his chores. She tossed for a few more minutes, then sat up again.

The sky in the east had begun to gain color. In another hour he would rouse the camp and they would move on to the Sur.

She was the author of her dream. If Tarik had slipped, it was the dreamer who had made him falter. Is that how she saw him? Had she lost her faith in his ability to save her? Or was it merely a reflection of what White-Lyons had said, that he had skidded into ruin, lacked faith to save even himself, much less her?

That she was free for the first time in years to speculate about him filled her with a profound excitement. Time fractured. They had never been apart. She could see him as clearly as she could now see Het lighting a cookfire on the open ground. The image of him chased away the malignant fragment of the dream, and she was suddenly madly happy, wildly elated. Bring on the sunrise, bring on the day when they would be together again. She was so alive, so sure of what she was doing. He needn't save her; she would save him.

And then just as quickly she felt ashamed. She should mourn better for Lawrence. She ought to struggle in her widow's weeds for years. She owed him that. She was wrong to feel so happy. She shut her eyes and summoned up a vivid remembrance of his face. He was not trapped in the bog. He was not Homer, not White-Lyons. Lawrence Sayles was clear-eyed, utterly self-confident. His eyes were the cool penetrating blue of a man with certain recognition of a destiny embraced fully, its fulfillment achieved with that wonderful, courteous equanimity.

She focused on this image for a very long time. He had helped to define her. More than that, he had known her better than she knew herself. Most important, he had loved Alex.

She experienced an odd sensation, a mix of ecstasy and true fear. Things were moving very fast. She was torn between guilt and elation that she would finally have what she had only ever wanted. She rubbed her hand over her forehead. It was making her as dizzy as a dust storm at Hirth.

"You okay, Mom?" Alex was staring at her from his cot. "You were rubbing your head."

She shrugged.

"It's weird to be here," he said, rubbing his hand around his face.

"Yes, it is."

"But exciting."

"It's always exciting here."

He hesitated. "Are you nervous about seeing him again?"

She gave him a grudging smile. "How about you?"

"A little. Well, not really. I can't wait. But it's still weird."

He sat up on one elbow, a look of concentration on his face.

"I know what you're thinking, Mom. You're thinking about Dad."

She looked off through the tent opening to the cookfire. Het had set a coffeepot on the flames, and steam was rising from it.

"I'm thinking about Dad too. I'm thinking about what he would say. I think he knew."

"What do you think he knew?"

"I think he knew he was going to die and he didn't want to die without telling me the truth. I think he knew that if he died, we would come here, and he wanted to set things up for us."

She turned around in her blankets to face him.

"What do you mean, set things up?"

"Well, I think Dad knew he was going to die and by telling me the truth he was sending us a signal that it was okay to come here and live with my father. That we had his approval."

"No, Alex. I think he was afraid you would find out from someone else that you had been lied to and that you would be devastated."

"Yeah," he admitted slowly, "but I think that's part of it. I don't know who would have told me. Only you and Dad knew the truth. If he didn't tell, and you didn't tell, who's left? See, that's why I think he wanted us to know that when he wasn't here anymore to take care of us that it was okay for us to go to my real father to have him take care of us. I think that's the hidden message in everything that happened."

The instant he said it she was released. She gazed over at him with such an expression of relief in her eyes that he smiled at her.

"It makes me feel better to think of it this way too," he said with a big smile. "It makes sense. Besides, Dad would have enjoyed himself here, don't you think? He would have been out there checking with the soldiers. And he would have liked Het."

"He would have, wouldn't he?" She smiled at the thought. "He would have been out there right now supervising the breakfast."

She reached across the blankets and squeezed Alex's hand.

"We're going to be all right," he said. "You'll see. It's going to be an adventure."

Everything was going to be fine. She was liberated. She lay back down and in and out of dreams of Tarik slept for an hour before Het shook her awake.

* * *

After they had eaten, they broke camp and resumed the journey. Alex insisted on sitting with Het in the front seat. He was quiet, taking in every inch of landscape with all-seeing eyes and slyly scrutinizing the giant out of the corner of his eye. Het's monosyllabic loquaciousness of the night before had given way to his usual stoic silence; Alex was too sanguine to try to make small talk.

The day became hotter and hotter as the sun drew close with no cloud cover to intervene. As morning passed into afternoon, the outline of the mountains grew steadily more defined, closer. They were only fifty miles from the point where they would pick up a larger escort, protection against the Marib, and Het became more tense, alert.

The Land-Rovers passed over a dry watershed, down into a striated stretch of volcanic rock the color of Georgia clay. After a half-mile, the rock became a gorge of coarse-faced stone, not especially towering but filled with grumbling boulders and brittle-looking shelves.

The lead vehicle slowed, downshifted. A huge boulder sat in the roadway. Het gunned his engine, urging the other driver forward fast. He pulled the Uzi from between his knees. Steering and shifting with his left hand, he released the safety of the Uzi with his right hand and grasped it hard. The vehicles accelerated, circled the boulder in a choke of dust, shifted up when they were clear and there were no further roadblocks.

They turned off the roadway, crossed several water channels that had not held moisture for millennia, and entered an area of granite shards that forced them to stop.

Piling out of the Land-Rovers, they walked perhaps a mile over low hill-bubbles till they reached a narrow zigzag path that ran between some stunted thorn trees. They were now far off the roadway, in a part of the country Clare had never seen, and the continuous appearance of first one, then another variety of sharp rock and prickling bush, the steep incline of the path, filled her with apprehension.

Finally, after they had climbed this way for another fifteen minutes, the ground suddenly flattened out, grass sprouted everywhere, weeds bloomed purple and yellow flowers, and her anxiety evaporated. About three hundred yards away she could make out soldiers resting on the ground, propped up against trees. Behind an outcropping of rock she believed she saw helicopter blades wobbling. The chopper would take them up over the bog and the Marib to the fortress.

She had expected the soldiers to rise at their approach, but they were asleep in the hot sun and made no move. Het would give them hell in another minute. He was just ahead of her, laboring from the effort of walking such a narrow path for such a distance.

She glanced behind her at Alex, who was perspiring under his blazer. When they reached the soldiers they would fall on the ground, drink water, and refresh themselves before setting off in the helicopter. She might have a chance to clean her face. Her hands felt in her pocket for the comb and lipstick she'd tucked in earlier in the day.

Reassured, she lowered her head and put her legs into the last yards. On the other side of the ridge was the bog. Or she thought the bog would be there. She was utterly turned around and had lost her sense of direction. She didn't have much of an idea where they were at all.

Her heart, beating from the exertion of the march, was now joined by another, more pleasant flutter when she realized how close they were to Tarik. After all this time, it was only a matter of minutes.

Het was the first to realize that the soldiers on the ground were unnaturally still, even for sleepers. He growled deep in his throat, saw shadows crouching behind the rocks. Someone shouted. A sudden burst of rifle fire. Instinctively, Clare turned to Alex, wrapped her arm around his neck, and drove him into the ground. Just as quickly the huge bulk of Het was on top of them both. He had one knee on the ground, the other into Clare's back, squatting in a firing position. His body twisted wildly back and forth with the sweep of his Uzi fire. Clare thought her chest would crack from the weight of him.

Dirt kicked up around them as the bullets skipped the ground. Most of the shots seemed to be over her head. The first time she realized Het had been hit was the drip of his blood onto her wrist.

28

"Jeez, Clare. I didn't think he'd tie you up."

Elliott Tomlinson hunkered down alongside her on the ground, his face full of apparent concern.

"He murdered his own father, Elliott. Somehow I think tying us up doesn't strike Hadi as the crime of the century." She shook her head in disgust, trying to get rid of him. The conversation was taking too much out of her.

They were in a palm grove, at least out of the direct sunlight. Her hands were roped behind her back and scraped raw from the rough skin of the palm tree. Her legs were stretched out in front of her, tied at the ankles. Her feet were bare; they'd taken away her shoes.

"How was I supposed to know you would show up here?" Tomlinson demanded. His voice was full of crabbed irritation.

"Am I supposed to feel sorry for you, Elliott?"

Tomlinson stood and jammed his hands into his pockets. If he'd thought the thing through a little bit more, he wouldn't be in this mess. Wouldn't be caught here with Hadi of the fogged brain and shivering eyeballs. Wouldn't be caught here with Clare black and blue around both eyes and *very* pissed off. Tarik would probably cut all their balls off when he saw the damage Hadi had already done to her.

He had to stay steady. He had to appear to know what he was doing. If only he could sit for half an hour in a hot bath, he would be able to sort things out and make smart choices. He had been out here, on the plain or at the bog, far too long for his taste and he was sticky, itchy.

"Hey, don't worry about me, Clare," he said, putting the right amount of toughness in his voice. "I can take care of myself." Then, trying to sound conciliatory, as if he were actually on her side, he looked around conspiratorially and whispered, "Listen, everything's going to turn out okay. We'll get this business with Hadi sorted out and then you and your boy can get on with your own stuff."

He thought of winking to let her know there was some sort of secret business he couldn't let her in on, but the presence of a particularly fierce-looking Marib made him think better of it. So he backed up a few steps, grinned at Alex, and drifted away slowly. He had never been much of a sportsman. Definitely not the type who was any good at straddling two horses at the same time. Best to retreat into the bushes and mull over his options. Get into his blue Ford, drive back to the city, and try to figure out how to turn this shit into gold.

Hadi walked in ever-tightening circles, declaiming on the vagaries of individual fortunes.

"Take, for instance, my father!" he said abruptly, as if this example had just occurred to him; in fact, it was the mainstay of his repertoire.

"Now, if he had had another kind of son, it might be he, here in the catbird seat. He with the power within reach. But"—he shrugged his shoulders elaborately and smiled—"fate delivered him a certain kind of son—I mean me, of course—and eventually it became clear to me that I could succeed only if my father failed. In turn, fate required me to—" He burlesqued a knife being drawn across his throat.

"What do you think about that, little boy?" He squatted and jammed a finger into Alex's ribs.

Alex glared up at him from his trussed-up position on the ground. Three of the soldiers from the escort were also lying on the ground, blindfolded and tied. The bodies of those killed in the ambush had been left behind in the underbrush.

Het had bled profusely from a scalp wound, but now the blood was dried to muddy patches over half his face and down the front of his uniform shirt. Like the others, he was propped up against a palm, but he alone was hog-tied. Every movement caused the rope that looped between his neck and ankles to slice into his skin, making his face scarlet and the veins in his head pop. But in the hours since their capture, he'd been able to twist himself around so that he had a good view of Clare and Alex and was taking in everything with dark, furious eyes.

Hadi never looked in Het's direction but had focused his obsequious attention on Clare.

The usual leaven of insincerity was much in abundance and Hadi was even more than usual twisting his brain into puns and parodies. He was forever studying Clare and her son out of the corner of his sly, bland eye.

Clare kept her own eyes averted, afraid that if she met his she would somehow quicken his madness. It seemed smart not to try to talk him out of anything. But now here he was, hunkered down on the ground next to her, affecting to regard himself as her best, most warmhearted friend. The dizzying speed with which he switched gears exhausted her.

"So, here you are, after all this time," he said, shaking his head at the wonder of it. "Who would have thought? You know, the last time I saw you was in Duru. Remember?"

She attempted not to answer, but he kept moving his head around until he found her eyes, and she thought she'd better say something.

"I don't remember."

"You don't remember Duru, or you don't remember seeing me?"

"The latter."

"The latter." He mimicked an American accent and his men laughed.

"You know my son Azarak was killed that day at Duru. Your husband shot him twice in the chest and twice in the head. He was hard to kill."

Her heart was thundering but she offered mildly, "Yes, I remember."

"Well, I would hope so," he said, rearing back with indignation. "You had his blood all over you."

"He tried to kill my husband."

"Which husband?"

She'd made a mistake trying to converse with him. She refused to answer and stared straight ahead.

"Touched a nerve, did I?" He giggled. "Of course, your husband—the first one—did me a favor. Azarak probably would have done to me what I did to my father. So he got me off the hook."

He started to laugh, and that triggered a coughing fit. He doubled over in obvious pain, hacking and gasping for breath. Finally, he brought up viscous white fluid into a handkerchief, examined it with disgust, and then replaced the handkerchief in his pocket.

"Anyway," he resumed, panting a little as he spoke, "I never thought to see you again, Mrs. Sayles. I don't think anybody did.

We all thought you had left this place for good. Of course, everything has changed here, you know. You've missed out on some good things. But—who am I kidding? You've led a pretty interesting life yourself."

He leaned back on both elbows, his legs out in front of him, and studied the cloudless sky with those flat yellow eyes as if he had all the time in the world. He had gotten thinner, more hollow-chested than Clare remembered, and his breath was shallow.

"Did you see the capital city?"

She exhaled through her teeth in impatience.

"Something, eh? I go there myself every chance I get. I used to visit my grandson Karim there. Tarik let me come all the time, big family dinners, card parties, that sort of thing. We were all very close." He sighed. Then he fell silent.

They were very near the bog. The land around was spongy and the air sticky. There was a heavy coating of humidity on Clare's skin, making her feel as if she were suffocating. There were about twenty men milling around, staring at them, fooling with rifles and fighting over tobacco and food. Hadi had promised her that there were ten thousand men on the other side of the palm grove, at the bog road, but she couldn't see or hear anything other than the occasional hawk cry, and it seemed to her improbable that so many thousands would make so little noise. Could it be possible that these few ragtag were all that he had? She made a furtive assessment of their weapons, which were not the old Enfields she remembered but smart American-made assault rifles. It may have been wishful thinking but she began to pray devoutly that Hadi, after all these years and the arrival of the new order, had lost his sway over the Marib.

He was working overtime on his amiable-fellow affectation. The longer it went on, the more anxious and desperate she became. They had been there almost six hours, and it seemed to her exhausted brain that Hadi had been talking for every one of them.

But it appeared he had fallen into a sudden sleep. His hooded eyes were blank and staring, and the twitching lids drooped. Twisted behind her back, her arms ached beyond description and sweat flooded her eyes. When she turned her head around, she had a clear view of Alex, directly behind her. She tried to load her gaze with warning, but he wasn't having any of that; he went on glaring at Hadi with hating eyes.

After a silent communication with her son, she turned her own eyes back to Hadi. He seemed to be asleep still, but was it her imagination or had he come closer? She could feel the heat coming off his body on her bare arms. The more she stared at him, the more it seemed to her that he was moving somehow—inert and yet on the move, creeping closer. She shook her head to clear her brain, and then of course he was awake, removing an orange from his pocket and peeling it with deliberate, maddening care. As he pulled apart the sections, its spray prickled the air, perfuming her misery. They had not been offered any food or water since they were captured.

Alert suddenly, he began anew. "So here we are, out here in the countryside. Clean air—you don't have that where you come from. Plenty to eat and drink."

"Not for us, apparently."

"I don't want to waste good food and water on people who might be dead any minute."

"You're going to kill us, Hadi?"

"I don't know." He popped a slice of orange into his mouth. "Maybe if conversation runs thin."

"What would you like to talk about?"

He chewed the orange and spat out the pulp. "Well, we could talk about my son, Azarak."

"I thought we had."

"That's true. We can talk about your son."

"I'd rather not."

"We could talk about sons in general."

He looked at her evenly, unsmiling. "You know, you're still a very attractive woman. I can see why he was never able to get you out of his mind. He didn't love her, you know, my daughter. She was stupid, short, like a midget. You should be nice to me. I have all the gossip. I know everything he's done for all these years. I could fill you in."

"I'll wait to get it from him."

He nodded pleasantly. "All right. Well . . . we'll see. You know, I had thought that when they found out all this business about Malik, the people would just hand him over to me. I was shocked to my teeth when it turned out that most of them loved him. Can you imagine? He went up there to that pink fortress and nobody will even hand him over to me. Of course, I think it's just those Sur people acting stuck-up again. If the king of Spain came along and asked for him, they'd probably hand him over, but not for me. Not for a lowlander."

He seemed genuinely peeved, digging a hole in the ground with the toe of his boot.

"And can you beat it? That old goat White-Lyons? I never

guessed. Did you ever guess?" He pulled a sullen expression. "Well, I didn't. He put over a great joke on all of us. Fathers and sons." He sighed melodramatically. "I only ever wanted my son to carry my vision into the future. All this deception, two generations. One of Mira's boys can read—see, we're not all in the ozone—and he read *Giant* to me just last week. I love Edna Ferber. I think she could have really made something out of this.

"And, look—" Fresh inspiration! "Tarik killed my son—and even though Azarak was out of his mind, he still had a right to get ahead in this world. If Turkit could last forty years on the throne, Azarak would have lasted eighty! Tarik killed my son"— and here he turned to face her and hissed with real malevolence— "and now I'm going to kill your son.

"Oh, don't think I don't get very nervous thinking about doing this. I mean, what if I kill your son and Tarik catches me? He would rip my head off. He would tear my guts out and trail them in front of my eyes. He would"—he checked Alex—"I don't want the boy to hear. He would cut my balls off and stick them down my throat—and despite what you've heard about me, I would not like that at all." He made a face, as if he'd tasted something sour.

"In fact"—he glanced at the enormous gold watch on his wrist—"I'm sure Tarik must know by now. It's been hours. Maybe he's not coming. I never thought of that. It's been hours since I sent that Nal back with a message."

He came up to his feet suddenly, as if the thought of missing out on murdering Tarik was too much for him. He resumed pacing while his men stared at him with big eyes. He walked over to where water jugs had been set up and took a long drink. The anxiety that success might not be so securely in his grasp filled him suddenly with inexplicable quiet.

He had said that he would kill Alex. She twisted so that she could see her son. His face was covered with perspiration and dust. The little shiny spot on his blazer where his school emblem had been was a sweet, sad souvenir of their life. Had it been only forty-eight hours since they were in Boston, in good clothes, sitting on the fine leather seats of a very expensive car? She shifted around, grimacing in pain as her knuckles scraped the bark of the palm. Het opened his eyes wide at her and went back to staring at Hadi, who had resumed pacing in frantic circles.

In a little while the sun would begin to drop into the horizon. It would cool off—too much, probably, to sleep. She settled herself against the tree. Over the hammering of her heart she turned her ears into radar. She made herself sort through the rustle of the wind as it moved through the date palms, the hawk cry that echoed in the ravines deep in the Sur. She sought his heartbeat pulsing down to her from the mountain passes and tried to discern the rumor of their salvation on the air. When the sun went down, she gave a backward glance at Alex and fell into exhausted sleep.

Slumped in a chair, White-Lyons also slept, his old Webley revolver in his lap. The day before yesterday Clare had telephoned Nal to say that she and Alex were coming, and so he had sent Het to the city to get her and now they were hours overdue; Tarik had four squads of soldiers out hunting them and everybody was nervous, blaming each other. White-Lyons himself was full of self-recrimination. He should have sent a helicopter to the airport and flown them right up to the Sur. But Clare said she wanted to bring Alex by road; she wanted him to get a feel for the people and the countryside. Mostly, she wanted to demonstrate to Het that she still had faith in his ability to protect her, despite what had happened on the road from Duru. White-Lyons blamed himself; he should have overruled her.

His sleep deepened. He shifted position in his chair and the Webley slipped from his lap onto the floor.

He hadn't expected Tarik to throw an arm around his shoulders when he told him that he'd gone to Boston to see Clare; not even courtesy was reserved for him, and he knew that. But he had expected at least some sign of appreciation when he offered him the secret of Alex. He'd thought this gift might temper the hatred, but he was wrong. Tarik received the miracle with typical composure—that White-Lyons could have predicted. But to look in those light eyes and see not even a flicker of human compassion was too much for White-Lyons, and he'd run away to his room. He'd thrown himself into the chair. Then he'd taken the Webley, checked that it had a full load, and with no deliberation at all put the barrel of the revolver in his mouth. He kept it there for some time, until suddenly he felt demeaned. Despite everything, he still believed in himself.

He'd lowered the Webley into his lap, closed his eyes, resumed the rhythm of his breathing, and fallen into old-man sleep.

In the drift of sleep, he dreamed a familiar dream.

He and his brother William were in a field of tall, unmowed hay. At one side of the field was a stone fence. Behind the fence a massive bull surveyed them with red eyes. The hay was high and deep. It was difficult to walk, but the brothers made progress. He turned to say something to William, but the setting sun had settled behind William's head and Walter was blinded by the glare. No matter how William turned his head, the sun followed him. It seemed to Walter that William's head was just a golden jewel. His eyes watered from the effort of looking at him.

Beyond the fence, the bull made a ferocious sound that drew White-Lyons's attention away. When he turned back, William was walking ahead, making the hay move like the waves on the ocean. Then the hay seemed to swallow William, and Walter was alone in the field with the red-eyed bull glowering at him. He was terrified, abandoned. He began to scream his brother's name.

In fact, it was while they were harvesting hay in the fall of 1920, that William, minding the yoke in the back, fell into the reaper blades. White-Lyons, driving the horse that pulled the reaper, never heard his younger brother cry out. William was nine; Walter, twelve.

White-Lyons stirred in his sleep. He loved seeing William again. He willed himself to this dream at least once a week.

He could also will himself to dream about Karim, and with no effort he shifted his unconscious from his brother to Karim.

He and Karim were together on the plain. On the road they met a little girl who was crying because her dog had fallen down a well. Then they were somehow at the well, and Karim, who was slim as a worm, decided he could wriggle down the well to save the dog. Before White-Lyons could stop him, Karim was in the well, his tinny little voice sending up bulletins of his progress. He went down and down until nothing could be heard, and White-Lyons was overcome with grief and beating his head against the ground. Then, like a miracle, Karim was alongside him, the little dog in his arms. But the dog had become Nila . . . and there was William and they were all together drinking from the well.

White-Lyons stirred in his sleep and smiled. He loved seeing everyone together. They were a family.

A rough voice jerked him awake. The room was full of orange light from the sunrise. From the open doorway Tarik was calling to him.

Still fogged by the dreams, White-Lyons shook his head and rubbed his hand over his eyes. Tarik was wearing riding boots and he hadn't seen that in years. "Nal says that Hadi has Alex and Clare. I'm going down over the bog now to get them back. I thought you might like to come with me," he said.

White-Lyons scrambled for the Webley he'd earlier intended to use to end his life. He grabbed his jacket and cap and raced on stiff legs out the door, down the long hallways, shaking off the dreamed nostalgia as he ran.

Clare was awake the instant the first light hit the sky. Something—a moan, no, a breath held for an interminable moment then released in a resigned sigh—had penetrated her sleeping brain and shot her eyes open.

Hidden by the canopy of palm leaves, they remained in dark shadow while the sun turned the ground not a hundred feet away a golden red. Eerily untouched by daylight, they were suspended in some time warp that struck Clare as completely ominous. As if nature itself conspired with Hadi to hide his crime.

She was in terrible pain because of the ropes. She tried to relax her muscles but she couldn't move around enough to do it. She'd never known such physical pain and thought she'd go crazy if she wasn't untied soon.

Alex also stirred and groaned a little from pain. She opened her eyes wide to warn him and mouthed *Don't talk!* Hadi appeared to be still asleep. Anyway, he was curled up on the ground in the fetal position that passed for sleep. She stared over at Het, who blinked his eyes at her. Het appeared not to have slept at all. There was nothing in the air but the sleep sounds of men.

After another moment of tense listening, she discerned something else—something malicious transported on vapors. She decided that if they all kept quiet, it might sniff at them, size them up, float on.

But it was too late. Hadi rolled over on his back, spread his arms out directly from his sides, and in a gesture that made Clare disbelieve her eyes, in one fluid motion seemed to propel himself to his feet magically. He stood, adjusted his clothing, and whirled abruptly to look her right in the eye.

If it had been night, she might have had the advantage of not having to look into those eyes. But the sun was nearly up and she could see everything too clearly.

He shrugged his shoulders, checked his expensive watch, and gave her a look like a man who just realized he was late for an appointment. He slicked his movements with the grease of sheer malevolence, and it conferred a power on his body that altered time and defied gravity.

Without seeming to have moved, he was suddenly right in front of her. In his eyes she saw the evidence that he had dreamed the ending of the adventure and that the dream had stopped his breath

and shattered his sleep. It was Hadi who had released the sigh that
had awakened her.

He stood there for a little while, just looking at her. Then he
settled the fingertips of his left hand onto the wrist of his right and
felt for his pulse. She watched him as he mentally counted, and,
satisfied, gave her the slow, relieved smile that the living bestowed upon the dead.

Or so it seemed. He had reached some conclusion within himself. Some message had come to him from the shade world in his
sleep, and before the sun was up completely, he'd decided
he would kill them all and not wait for Tarik.

She said Alex's name aloud. If they were going to go, she
wanted her son to have time to compose himself, although she
was terrified and her mind raced in a thousand conflicting circles.
Alex was glaring at Hadi with a nerve that made her proud. Het
was somehow up on one elbow; she watched him fighting with
the ropes.

Hadi looked her up and down. The last time he'd split a woman
stem to stern she'd looked at him as if he were about to make
love to her. He'd stuck a dirty finger up her and diddled around,
just to tease her. He wouldn't try a stunt like that with the blonde
here. She had tough eyes, hating eyes, eyes that brooked no com-
promise. She might have teeth where her sex was. If he put his
finger in, he might not get it out again.

In a gesture distorted to painful slowness from her terror and
his trickery, he parted the fold of his coat and ran his hand over
the bone hilt of his carving knife, the same knife he'd used to split
Sirah.

His eyes pouring into hers, he pulled the knife out an inch at
a time. At this point he expected her to cry, and it irritated him
that she just kept staring at him with those mean eyes; if he told
the truth, he felt his bowels tightening a little because of it. But,
he was not the kind of man to let a woman call his bluff, especially a woman trussed up in ten feet of good hemp.

Deliberately, he slid the knife all the way out of his coat and
admired it indecently in the ruby sun rays. Then he elevated it,
chalicelike, over her breast. The Marib were all awake now and
watching him. The realization that he was about to kill the one
person in the world to whom Tarik owed total devotion struck
them suddenly as pretty risky business. It began to occur to them
that these eleven years with Tarik hadn't been so bad. They had
food now, water, German cars, California wines, if they wanted
these things. Hadi's eyes swam with visions, his ears discerned

voices; they were satisfied if the color on their television sets was balanced. Dynastic fantasies belonged to Hadi, not to them. In the new order they had discovered new loyalties.

The knife glinted in the sunlight. The heat was coming back into the day. Life could go on as usual. They exchanged worried glances and began melting away. Hadi was too enthralled to notice.

The impulse to surrender was enormous, but Clare kept her eyes marble-hard and put contempt in her face. If she was going, and clearly she was, she had the means in her character to go with pennants flying. *Daddy must have felt like this on the other side of that roof fall,* she decided. *He must have looked at that ton of coal and known he would never get away.* The instant she pictured her father that way, she was strong. Nothing could turn her around. Her mind stopped racing, her pulse smoothed, and her life became a consolation to her. She was thirty-five years old. She'd done her best. She'd been married to two remarkable men. She'd been rich and she'd been poor. She understood the limits of her endeavors and she had been at home in the world. She'd staked out territories since girlhood—temporal, spiritual, emotional—kingdoms all, and just as real to her as this place. She'd taken her licks, and she could take this one. She'd raised a son as remarkable as his father, whatever name that father went by.

Alex! It was one thing to consign her own life to memory, quite another to know that her only child was about to be slaughtered. She had to save Alex somehow.

"You don't need to kill my son, Hadi. He's nothing to you. And he's only a little boy. Even you don't kill little boys."

"Turkit killed little boys, babies."

"Turkit was insane."

"That's true. But he was smart too. He knew what happens when little boys grow up. They surprise you in the night and cut your throat. Look what happened—Turkit didn't kill Tarik and Tarik came back and killed him. This boy will come back and bash my brains in."

"Alex will go right back to America. I promise you."

"You'll be dead."

"On my soul I promise you—everyone can hear me say it— Alex will turn right around and go home. Won't you, Alex?"

Hadi chewed his lip. "I don't know . . ."

"Nal will take him back. You trust Nal."

"No, I don't. I don't trust anyone. Everybody hates me."

"Elliott Tomlinson. Look at what he's done for you. Tomlinson will take him back."

"I think he left already."

"Hadi! Send someone to bring him back."

"I don't know . . . The same movie keeps looping around in my brain. Here you are, trying to save your son, and there was White-Lyons, trying to save his son all those years ago. And then my son . . . and now your son. You see what I mean? It just keeps turning around and around, like an apple in the hand."

"You had a son, Hadi—Azarak. You had a boy that you loved." She heard Homer, pleading with Muddy Aylesworth for Hillard's life. "Didn't you have a boy of your own?"

"I had a dozen sons, and not one of them was worth spit."

"I'm begging you, Hadi. Kill me, don't kill my boy!"

Hadi made a *tsk* sound. "The problem with memories"—he shook his head theatrically—"is that once you start with them you can't stop. It's all well and good to remind me of my son, but then you remind me also of how he died. You called out to Tarik when you saw Azarak, I heard you; I was there. If you hadn't cried out, Azarak might have killed Tarik instead of the other way around. Really, the more I think of it, the more I understand what has to be done here."

He crossed over to Alex and jerked him up to his feet. Bound with ropes, the boy could hardly stand and wobbled back and forth. His eyes were huge. He was terrified. Hadi drew his arm back. The blade reflected in the red sun.

She had brought her boy to this, some gritty palm grove in a hell he hadn't made. She could have left him in his little St. Alban's School blazer at The Heights in Georgetown. He would have led a long and happy life as Lawrence Sayles's heir. She had killed her son just as surely as Sirah had murdered Karim, just as surely as Turkit had murdered the babies. She was tied up from her feet to her neck. She couldn't move a fingertip. With the blade positioned at Alex's throat, she knew she had to do something, anything, to save her boy. She threw her head back and from her outraged soul sent up a scream of such violence that Hadi was startled out of his work. His knife slipped from the thin groove he had already cut in Alex's flesh. "Be quiet," he spat out at her.

His hand returned to its task. He set the blade in the groove. She saw him lean his body into the effort. Time halted. Her eyes began to shiver in denial at what they witnessed. Her heart ceased to pump. She willed herself to death. And then she heard what must have been a bird cry. Or a monkey scream. Or a rifle shot.

She snapped her head up. Definitely a rifle shot; she'd known that sound since childhood. There was the sound of more shooting off beyond the palm trees, in the direction of the bog. She could make out the pleasant thrash of rotor blades; helicopters were coming closer.

She looked back at Hadi. He hadn't moved. His hand still held the big knife. His yellow eyes remained fastened on Alex's neck. No movement. Tick. Tick. What moved, finally, was the trickle of blood from the hole in his right temporal lobe. It was taking its time coming out of the bullet hole in his skull. She stared, fascinated, as the blood pooled in the collar of his shirt.

Then he turned, and the hand with the knife dropped to his side. He gazed at her for a maddening moment before the hating eyes revolved up into his head and he fell, directly backward, into the ground.

She heard a noise. Behind her, Tarik, the rifle in his hand, was cutting Het loose.

Hours later she stood on the veranda of the pink palace and stared out at the orchard of frankincense trees. She could feel her heart beating down to her fingertips. The half-lit landscape gradually surrendered to the shadow of the setting sun. The day had become pleasantly opaque. She didn't feel sorrow or physical pain, just a consoling numbness. Like peace of mind.

Behind her Alex sat quietly next to Het, the two of them staring at Tarik, who once in a while came over and said something to his son. White-Lyons hovered tentatively at the edge of this familial tableau, going about the business of fussing with his pipe, filling it, tamping it. One of the servants handed her a plate of food, which she set aside without touching.

She was determined to maintain the moment. They were all a little in shock. She had had it in her mind to come out here and assess her life and try to reach some understanding of all that had happened to her. But in the end she'd decided this was trivial. Instead, she sipped her wine and speculated on the harvest of the frankincense.

When the sun was almost gone, she heard Tarik come up behind her. She turned, gave him her best smile, and returned to her study of the view below.

He stood alongside her. He stared out over the valley. The sight of the coffee trees, in their orderly grids, had always acted as a soporific for him. Sometime in the future he would examine more closely everything that he felt. It was enough at the moment to feel this calm. He deserved to sleep.

The hills turned purple, then inky black as the light went out of the day. Finally, tired past caring, they went inside.